Also by Arthur C. Clarke

FICTION

Against the Fall of Night
Childhood Ends
Childhood's End
The City and The Stars
The Deep Range
Dolphin Island
Earthlight
A Fall of Moondust
The Fountains of Paradise
The Ghost from the Grand Banks
Glide Path
The Hammer of God
Imperial Earth
Islands in the Sky
The Lion of Comarre
The Lost Worlds of 2001
A Meeting with Medusa
Prelude to Space
Reach for Tomorrow
Rendezvous with Rama
The Sands of Mars
The Songs of Distant Earth
2001: A Space Odyssey
2010: Odyssey Two
2061: Odyssey Three
3001: The Final Odyssey

With Gentry Lee:
Cradle
Rama
The Garden of Rama
Rama Revealed

With Mike McQuay
Richter 10

With Mike Kube-McDowell:
The Trigger

With Stephen Baxter
The Light of Other Days

SHORT FICTION

Across the Sea of Stars
An Arthur C. Clarke Omnibus
An Arthur C. Clarke 2nd Omnibus
The Best of Arthur C. Clarke
The Collected Stories
Expedition to Earth
From the Oceans, From the Stars
More Than One Universe
The Nine Billion Names of God
The Other Side of the Sky
Prelude to Mars
The Sentinel
Tales from Planet Earth
Tales from the White Hart
Tales of Ten Worlds
The Wind From the Sun

NON-FICTION

Ascent to Orbit
Astounding Days
By Space Possessed
The Challenge of the Sea
The Challenge of the Spaceship
The Coast of Coral
The Exploration of the Moon
The Exploration of Space
Going into Space
Greetings, Carbon Based Bipeds!
How the World was One
Interplanetary Flight
The Making of a Moon
Profiles of the Future
The Promise of Space
The Reefs of Taprobane
Report on Planet Three
The Snows of Olympus
The View from Serendip
Voice Across the Sea
Voices From the Sky
The Young Traveller in Space
1984: Spring

With the Astronauts:
First on the Moon

With Mike Wilson:
Boy Beneath the Sea
The First Five Fathoms
Indian Ocean Adventure
Indian Ocean Treasure
The Treasure of the Great Reef

With Peter Hyams:
The Odyssey File

With the Editors of Life:
Man and Space

With Robet Silverberg:
Into Space

With Chesley Bonestell:
Beyond Jupiter

With Simon Welfare and John Fairley:
Arthur C. Clarke's Mysterious World
Arthur C. Clarke's World of Strange Powers
Arthur C. Clarke's Chronicles of the Strange & Mysterious
Arthur C. Clarke's A-Z

AS EDITOR
(*Fiction*)
Science Fiction Hall of Fame III
Three for Tomorrow
Time Probe
Arthur C. Clarke's Venus Prime 1-VI
(Non-Fiction)
The Coming of the Space Age
Arthur C. Clarke's July 20, 2019
Project Solar Sail

Edited by Keith Daniels:
Arthur C. Clarke & Lord Dunsany – A Correspondence
Arthur C. Clarke & C. S. Lewis – A Correspondence

The Space Trilogy

ARTHUR C. CLARKE

This edition published in Great Britain in 2001 by

Gollancz
An imprint of the Orion Publishing Group
Orion House, 5 Upper St Martin's Lane, London WC2H 9EA

A CIP catalogue record for this book is available
from the British Library

ISBN 1 85798 780 2

Printed in Great Britain by
Clays Ltd, St Ives plc

Contents

Foreword   xi

ISLANDS IN THE SKY   1

THE SANDS OF MARS   133

EARTHLIGHT   345

Foreword

It is now hard to realise that, as late as the 1950s, to most people the concept of travel beyond the Earth seemed total fantasy. The attitude in those days was well summed up by a statement which Britain's Astronomer Royal was never able to live down: 'Space travel is utter bilge!' The very next year – 1957 – the Space Age opened with the launch of Sputnik I.

The three novels in this volume were all written well before that event, when I was an active member of the tiny British Interplanetary Society – now, I am happy to say, a large and respected organisation. So these early works were, it must be confessed, partly propaganda, aimed to convince the sceptical public that we premature Space Cadets really knew what we were talking about.

They were preceded by an earlier novel, *Prelude to Space* (1951) – long out of print, and now of no more than historic interest (if that!). *Prelude* was written soon after World War II, when the advent of atomic energy made space travel seem both imminent and practical. Fired by enthusiasm which turned out to be misplaced, I was optimistic enough to imagine that Britain could go it alone, using the newly established Australian launch-site at Woomera. Yet the date I suggested – 1978! – was pessimistic; who would have dreamed that men would fly round the Moon exactly a decade earlier?

Islands in the Sky (1952) was written for what is sometimes disparagingly referred to as the 'juvenile' market, but I hope this is indicated only by the age of the main character. It may well have been one of the first novels which described the use of satellites for communication, as well as many other concepts which are now taken for granted – but which were totally unfamiliar to most readers half a century ago, and so had to be carefully explained.

Earthlight (1955) was one of my earliest attempts to describe conditions on the Moon, and today I am slightly ashamed of the space battle sequences; there have now been far too many *Star Wars* on screens of all sizes. (Why, alas, do explosions have such a universal and elemental appeal?)

I cannot claim that this was the first story in which unprotected humans were able to survive in a vacuum; I stole the idea, as well as much else, from the brilliant and sadly short-lived Stanley Weinbaum (1902–35). To the millions who have seen David Bowman's confrontation with HAL, I am happy to say that the space medics now confirm that a minute (or even two) in space need not be particularly injurious to one's health.

In my wildest dreams, I would never have imagined that, less than two decades after this book was written, I would receive a beautiful three-dimensional map of the *Mare Imbrium*, showing the track of the Lunar Rover skirting a crater labelled 'Earthlight' – and bearing the inscription '*To Arthur Clarke with best personal regards from the crew of Apollo 15 and many thanks for your visions in space.*'

> *(Signed) Dave Scott, Al Worden and Jim Irwin.*

The Sands of Mars – though it goes much further afield than the other two novels – was published earlier, in 1951. At that time almost everything we 'knew' about Mars was completely wrong, yet even in the 50s, we were beginning to suspect that it was a much more barren and inhospitable place than had been imagined by legions of writers, notably Edgar Rice Burroughs and my good friend Ray Bradbury. Now, thanks to a series of brilliantly successful space probes, we have a much clearer idea of conditions there, and even know exactly what small portions of Mars look like. NASA's Jet Propulsion Laboratory kindly sent me a beautiful twenty foot-wide panorama, created from the images beamed back by Sojourner. When I wear 3D glasses, I feel that I can reach out and pick up individual pebbles . . .

But Mars demands a Foreword of its own.

Please turn to page 135 . . .

Arthur C. Clarke
Colombo, 21 January 2001

ISLANDS IN THE SKY

One
JACKPOT TO SPACE

It was Uncle Jim who'd said, 'Whatever happens, Roy, don't *worry* about it. Just relax and enjoy yourself.' I remembered those words as I followed the other competitors into the big studio, and I don't think I felt particularly nervous. After all, it was only a game ... however badly I wanted the prize.

The audience was already in its place, talking and fidgeting and waiting for the programme to begin. It gave a little cheer as we walked up on to the stage and took our seats. I had a quick look at the five other competitors, and was a bit disappointed. Every one of them looked quite sure that *he* was going to win.

There was another cheer from the audience as Elmer Schmitz, the Quiz-master, came into the studio. I'd met him before, of course, in the semi-finals and I expect you've seen him often enough on TV. He gave us some last-minute instructions, moved to his place under the spot-lights, and signalled to the cameras. There was a sudden hush as the red light came on: from where I was sitting, I could see Elmer adjusting his smile.

'Good evening, folks! This is Elmer Schmitz, presenting you the finalists in our Aviation Quiz Programme, brought to you by arrangement with World Airways, Incorporated. The six young men we have here tonight ...'

But I guess it wouldn't be very modest to repeat the things he said about us. It all added up to the fact that we knew a lot about everything that flew – in the air and outside it – and had beaten about five thousand other members of the Junior Rocket Club in a series of nationwide contests. Tonight would be the final elimination test to find the winner.

It started easily enough, on the lines of earlier rounds. Elmer fired off a question at each of us in turn, and we had twenty seconds in which to answer, Mine was pretty easy – he wanted to know the altitude record for a pure jet. Everyone else got their answer right too. I think those first questions were just to give us confidence.

Then it got tougher. We couldn't see our scores, which were being flashed up on a screen facing the audience, but you could tell when you'd given the right answer by the noise they made. I forgot to say that you *lost* a point when you gave the wrong reply. That was to stop guessing: if you didn't know, it was best to say nothing at all.

As far as I could tell, I'd only made one mistake, but there was a kid from New Washington who hadn't made any – though I couldn't be sure of this, because it was difficult to keep track of the others while you were wondering what Elmer had coming up for you. I was feeling rather gloomy when suddenly the lights dimmed and a hidden movie projector went into action.

'Now,' said Elmer, 'the last round! You'll each see some kind of aircraft or rocket for *one second*, and in that time you've got to identify it. Ready?'

A second sounds awfully short, but it isn't really. You can see a lot in that time – enough to recognize anything you know really well. But some of the machines they showed us went back over a hundred years – yes, one or two even had propellers! This was lucky for me: I'd always been interested in the history of flying, and knew some of these antiques. That's where the boy from New Washington fell down badly. They gave him a picture of the original Wright biplane, which you can see in the Smithsonian any day – and he didn't know it. He was only interested in rockets, he said afterwards, and it wasn't a fair test. But I thought it served him right.

They gave me the Dornier DO-X and a B.52, and I knew them both. So I wasn't really surprised when Elmer called out my name as soon as the lights went up. Still, it was a proud moment as I walked over to him, with the cameras following me and the audience clapping in the background.

'Congratulations, Roy!' said Elmer heartily, shaking my hand. 'Almost a perfect score – you only missed on one question. I have great pleasure in announcing you the winner of this World Airways contest. As you know, the prize is a trip, all expenses paid, to any place in the world. We're all interested to hear your choice. What's it going to be? You've anywhere you like between the North and South Poles!'

My lips went kind of dry. Though I'd made all my plans weeks ago, it was different now that the time had actually come. I felt awfully lonely in that huge studio, with everyone so quiet all round me, waiting for what I was going to say. My voice sounded a long way off when I answered.

'I want to go to the Inner Station.'

Elmer looked puzzled, surprised and annoyed all at once. There was a sort of rustle from the audience and I heard someone give a little laugh. Perhaps that made Elmer decide to be funny too.

'Ha, ha! very amusing, Roy! But the prize is anywhere on *Earth*. You must stick to the rules, you know!'

I could tell he was laughing at me, and that made me mad. So I came back with: 'I've read the rules very carefully. And they *don't* say "on Earth". They say "to any part of the Earth". There's a big difference.'

Elmer was smart. He knew there was trouble brewing, for his grin faded out at once and he looked anxiously at the TV cameras.

'Go on,' he said. I cleared my throat.

'In 2054,' I continued, 'the United States, like all the other members of the Atlantic Federation, signed the Tycho Convention. That decided how far into space any planet's legal rights extended. Under that Convention, the Inner Station is part of Earth, because it's inside the thousand-kilometre limit.'

Elmer gave me a most peculiar look. Then he relaxed a little and said: 'Tell me, Roy, is your dad an attorney?'

I shook my head.

'No, he isn't.'

Of course, I might have added: 'But my Uncle Jim is.' I decided not to: there was going to be enough trouble anyway.

Elmer made a few attempts to make me change my mind, but there was nothing doing. Time was running out, and the audience was on my side. Finally he gave up and said with a laugh:

'Well, you're a very determined young man. You've won the prize, anyway – it looks as if the legal eagles take over from here. I hope there's something left for you when they've finished wrangling!'

I rather hoped so, too . . .

Of course, Elmer was right in thinking I'd not worked all this out by myself. Uncle Jim – who's counsellor for a big atomic energy combine – had spotted the opportunity, soon after I'd entered for the contest. He'd told me what to say and had promised that World Airways couldn't wriggle out of it. Even if they could, so many people had seen me on the air that it would be very bad publicity for them if they tried. 'Just stick to your guns, Roy,' he'd said, 'and don't agree to anything until you've talked it over with me.'

Mom and Pop were pretty mad about the whole business. They'd been watching, and as soon as I started bargaining they knew what had happened. Pop rang up Uncle Jim at once and gave him a piece of his mind (I heard about it afterwards). But it was too late for them to stop me.

You see, I'd been mad to get out into space for as long as I can remember. I was sixteen when all this happened, and rather big for my age. I'd read everything I could get hold of about aviation and astronautics, seen all the movies and telecasts from space, and made up my mind that some day I was going to look back and watch Earth shrinking behind me. I'd made models of famous spaceships, and put rocket units in some of them until the neighbours raised a fuss. In my room I'd got hundreds of photographs – not only most of the ships you care to name but all the important places on the planets as well.

Mom and Pop didn't mind, but they thought it was something I'd grow out of. 'Look at Joe Donovan,' they'd say (Joe's the chap who runs the 'copter repair depot in our district). '*He* was going to be a Martian colonist when he was your age. Earth wasn't good enough for him! Well, he's never been as far as the Moon, and I don't suppose he ever will. He's quite happy here . . .' But I wasn't so sure. I've seen Joe looking up at the sky as the outgoing rockets draw their white vapour trails though the stratosphere, and sometimes I think he'd give everything he owns to go with them.

Uncle Jim (that's Pop's brother) was the one who really understood how I felt about things. He'd been to Mars two or three times, to Venus once, and to the Moon so often he couldn't remember. He had the kind of job where people actually *paid* him to do these things. I'm afraid he was regarded round our house as a very disturbing influence.

It was about a week after winning the contest that I heard from World Airways. They were very polite, in an icy sort of way, and said that they'd agreed that the terms of the competition allowed me to go to the Inner Station. (They couldn't help adding their disappointment that I hadn't chosen to go on one of their luxury flights *inside* the atmosphere. Uncle Jim said what really upset them was the fact that my choice would cost them at least ten times as much as they'd bargained for.) There were, however, two conditions. First, I had to get my parents' consent. Second, I would have to pass the standard medical tests for space-crew.

I'll say this about Mom and Pop – though they were still pretty mad, they wouldn't stand in my way. After all, space-travel was safe enough, and I was only going a few hundred miles up – scarcely any distance! So after a little argument they signed the forms and sent them off. I'm pretty sure that World Airways had hoped they'd refuse to let me go.

That left the second obstacle – the medical exam. I didn't think it was fair having to take that: from all accounts it was pretty tough, and if I failed no one would be more pleased than World Airways.

The nearest place where I could take the tests was the Department of Space Medicine at Johns Hopkins, which meant an hour's flying in the Kansas–Washington jet and a couple of short 'copter trips at either end. Though I'd made dozens of longer journeys I was so excited that it almost seemed a new experience. In a way, of course, it was, because if everything went properly it would open up a new chapter in my life.

I'd got everything ready the night before, even though I was only going to be away from home for a few hours. It was a fine evening, so I carried my little telescope out of doors to have a look at the stars. It's not much of an instrument – just a couple of lenses in a wooden tube – but I'd made it myself and was quite proud of it. When the Moon was half-full it would show all the bigger lunar mountains, as well as Saturn's rings and the moons of Jupiter.

But tonight I was after something else – something not so easy to find. I knew its approximate orbit, because our local astronomers' club had worked out the figures for me. So I set up the telescope as carefully as I could and slowly began to sweep across the stars to the south-west, checking against the map I'd already prepared.

The search took me about fifteen minutes. In the field of the telescope was a handful of stars – and something that was not a star. I could just make out a tiny oval shape, far too small to show any details. It shone brilliantly up there in the blazing sunlight outside the shadow of the Earth, and it was moving even as I watched. An astronomer of a century before would have been sorely puzzled by it, for it was something new in the sky. It was Met. Station Two, six thousand miles up and circling the Earth four times a day. The Inner Station was too far to the south for it to be visible from my latitude: you had to live near the Equator to see it shining in the sky, the brightest and most swiftly moving of all the stars.

I tried to imagine what it was like up there in that floating bubble, with the emptiness of space all around. At this very moment, the scientists aboard must be looking down at me just as I was looking up at them. I wondered what kind of life they led – and remembered that with any luck I'd soon know for myself.

The bright, tiny disc I had been watching suddenly turned orange, then red, and began to fade from sight like a dying ember. In a few seconds it had vanished completely, though the stars were still shining as brightly as ever in the field of the telescope. Met. Station Two had raced into the shadow of the Earth and would remain eclipsed until it emerged again, about an hour later, in the southeast. It was 'night' aboard the space-station, just as it was down here on Earth. I packed up the telescope and went to bed.

East of Kansas City – where I went aboard the Washington jet – the land is flat for five hundred miles until you reach the Appalachians. A century earlier I should have been flying over millions of acres of farm land, but that had all vanished when agriculture had moved out to sea at the end of the twentieth century. Now the ancient prairies were coming back, and with them the great buffalo herds that had roamed this land when the Indians were its only masters. The main industrial cities and mining centres hadn't changed much, but the smaller towns had vanished and in a few more years there would be no sign that they had ever existed.

I think I was a lot more nervous when I went up the wide marble steps of the Department of Space Medicine than when I entered the final round of the World Airways contest. If I'd failed that, I might have had another chance later – but if the doctors said 'No' then I'd never be able to go out into space.

There were two kinds of tests – the physical and the psychological. I had to do all sorts of silly things, like running on a treadmill while holding my breath, trying to hear very faint sounds in a noise-proof room, and identifying dim, coloured lights. At one point they amplified my heart-beat thousands of times: it was an eerie sound and gave me the creeps, but the doctors said it was O.K.

They seemed a very friendly crowd, and after a while I got the definite impression that they were on my side and doing their darndest to get me through. Of course that helped a lot and I began to think it was all good fun – almost a game, in fact.

I changed my mind after a test in which they sat me inside a box and spun it round in every possible direction. When I came out I was horribly sick and couldn't stand upright. That was the worst moment I had, because I was sure I'd failed. But it was really all right: if I *hadn't* been sick there would have been something wrong with me!

After all this they let me rest for an hour before the psychological tests. I wasn't much worried about those, as I'd met them before. There were some simple jigsaw puzzles, a few sheets of questions to be answered ('Four of the following five words have something in common. Underline them' . . .) and some tests for quickness of the eye and hand. Finally they attached a lot of wires to my head and took me into a narrow, darkened corridor with a closed door ahead of me.

'Now listen carefully, Roy,' said the psychologist who'd been doing the tests. 'I'm going to leave you now and the lights will go out. Stand there until you receive further instructions, and then do exactly what you're told. Don't worry about these wires – they'll follow you when you move. O.K.?'

'Yes,' I said, wondering what was going to happen next.

The light dimmed, and for a minute I was in complete darkness. Then a very faint rectangle of red light appeared, and I knew that the door ahead of me was opening, though I couldn't hear a sound. I tried to see what was beyond the door, but the light was far too dim.

The wires that had been attached to my head were, I knew,

recording my brain-impulses. So whatever happened, I should try to keep calm and collected.

A voice came out of the darkness from a hidden loudspeaker.

'Walk through the door you see ahead of you, and stop as soon as you have passed it.'

I obeyed the order, though it wasn't easy to walk straight in that faint light, with a tangle of wires trailing behind me.

I never heard the door shutting, but I knew, somehow, that it had closed, and when I reached back with my hand I found I was standing in front of a smooth sheet of plastic. It was completely dark now – even the dim red light had gone.

It seemed a long time before anything happened. I must have been standing there in the darkness for almost ten minutes, waiting for the next order. Once or twice I whistled softly, to see if there was any echo so that I could judge the size of the room. Though I couldn't be sure, I got the impression that it was quite a large place.

And then, without any warning, the lights came on – not in a sudden flash, which would have blinded me, but in a very quick build-up that took only two or three seconds. I was able to see my surroundings perfectly – and I'm not ashamed to say that I yelled.

Yet it was, apart from one thing, a perfectly normal room. There was a table with some papers lying on it, three armchairs, bookcases against one wall, a small desk, an ordinary TV set. The sun seemed to be shining through the window, and some curtains were waving slightly in the breeze. At the moment the lights came on, the door opened and a man walked in. He picked up a paper from the table, and flopped down in one of the chairs. He was just beginning to read when he looked up and saw me. And when I say 'up', I mean it. For that's what was wrong with the room. I wasn't standing on the floor, down there with the chairs and bookcases. I was fifteen feet up in the air, scared out of my wits and flattened against the *ceiling* – with no means of support and nothing within reach to catch hold of. I clawed at the smooth surface behind me, but it was as flat as glass. There was no way to stop myself falling – and the floor looked very hard and a long way down.

Two
GOODBYE TO GRAVITY

The fall never came, and my moment of panic passed swiftly. The whole thing was an illusion of some kind, for the floor felt firm beneath my feet whatever my eyes told me. I stopped clutching at the door through which I had entered – the door which my eyes kept trying to convince me was really part of the ceiling.

Of course – it was absurdly simple! The room I seemed to be looking *down* at was really seen reflected in a large mirror immediately in front of me – a mirror set at an angle of forty-five degrees to the vertical. I was actually standing in the upper part of a tall room that was 'bent' horizontally through a right angle, but because of the mirror there was no way of telling this.

I went down on my hands and knees and cautiously edged my way forward. It took a lot of will-power to do this, as my eyes still told me that I was crawling head-first down the side of a vertical wall. After a few feet, I came to a sudden drop and peered over the edge. There below me – *really* below me this time! – was the room into which I had been looking. The man in the armchair was grinning up at me as if to say, 'We gave you quite a shock, didn't we?' I could see him equally well, of course, by looking at his reflection in the mirror straight ahead of me.

The door behind me opened and the psychologist came in. He was carrying a long strip of paper in his hand and he chuckled as he waved it at me.

'We've got all your reactions on the tape, Roy,' he said. 'Do you know what this test was for?'

'I think I can guess,' I said a little ruefully. 'Is it to discover how I behave when gravity is wrong?'

'That's the idea. It's what we call an orientation test. In space you won't have any gravity at all, and some people are never able to get used to it. The test eliminates most of them.'

I hoped it wouldn't eliminate me, and I spent a very uncomfortable half-hour waiting for the doctors to make up their minds. But I needn't have worried. As I said before, they were on my side and were just as determined to get me through as I was myself...

The New Guinea mountains, just south of the Equator and rising in places more than three miles above sea level, must once have been about the wildest and most inaccessible spots on Earth. Although the helicopter had made them as easy to reach as anywhere else, it was not until the twenty-first century that they became important as the world's main springboard to space.

There are three good reasons for this. First of all, the fact that they are so near the Equator means that, because of the Earth's spin, they're moving from west to east at a thousand miles an hour. That's quite a useful start for a ship on its way out to space. Their height means that all the denser layers of the atmosphere are below them, so that air resistance is reduced and the rockets can work more efficiently. And – perhaps most important of all – there's ten thousand miles of open Pacific stretching away from them to the east. You can't launch spaceships from inhabited areas: apart from the danger if anything goes wrong, the unbelievable noise of an ascending ship would deafen everyone for miles around.

Port Goddard is on a great plateau, levelled by atomic blasting, almost two and a half miles up. There is no way to reach it by land – everything comes in by air. It is the meeting place for ships of the atmosphere and ships of space.

When I first saw it from our approaching jet, it looked a tiny white rectangle among the mountains. Great valleys packed with tropical forests stretched as far as one could see. In some of those valleys, I was told, there are still savage tribes that no one has ever contacted. I wonder what they think of the monsters that fly above their heads and fill the sky with their roaring...

The small amount of luggage I had been allowed to take had been sent on ahead of me, and I wouldn't see it again until I reached the Inner Station. When I stepped out of the jet into the cold, clear air of Port Goddard I already felt so far above sea level that I automatically looked up into the sky to see if I could find my destination. But I wasn't allowed time for the search: the reporters were waiting for me and I had to go in front of the cameras again.

I haven't any idea what I said, and fortunately one of the Port officials soon rescued me. There were the inevitable forms to be filled up, I was weighed very carefully and given some pills to swallow (they made sure that I did, too) and then we climbed aboard a little truck that would take us out to the launching site. I was the only passenger on this trip, as the rocket on which I was travelling was really a freighter.

Most spaceships, naturally enough, have astronomical names. I was flying in the 'Sirius', and though she was one of the smaller ships, she looked impressive enough as we came up to her. She had already been raised in her supporting cradle so that her prow pointed vertically at the sky, and she seemed to be balanced on the great triangles of her wings. These would only come into action when she glided back into the atmosphere on her return to Earth: at the moment they served merely as supports for the four huge fuel tanks, like giant bombs, which would be jettisoned as soon as the motors had drained them dry. These streamlined tanks were nearly as large as the ship's hull itself.

The servicing gantry was still in position, and as I stepped into the elevator I realized for the first time that I had now cut myself off from Earth. A motor began to whine, and the metal walls of the 'Sirius' slid swiftly past. My view of Port Goddard widened: now I could see all the administrative buildings clustering at the edge of the plateau, the great fuel storage tanks, the strange machinery of the liquid ozone plant, the airfield with its everyday jets and helicopters. And beyond all these, quite unchanged by everything that man had done, the eternal mountains and forests.

The elevator came gently to a halt, and the gates opened on to a short gangway leading into the 'Sirius'. I walked across it, through the open seals of the airlock, and the brilliant tropical sunlight gave way to the cold electric glare of the ship's control room.

The pilot was already in his seat, going through the routine checks. He swivelled round as I entered and gave me a cheerful grin.

'So you're the famous Roy Malcolm, are you? I'll try and get you to the Station in one piece. Have you flown in a rocket before?'

'No,' I replied.

'Then don't worry. It's not as bad as some people pretend. Make yourself comfortable in that seat, fasten the straps, and just relax. We've still got twenty minutes before take-off.'

I climbed into the pneumatic couch, but it wasn't easy to relax. I don't think I was frightened, but I was certainly excited. After all these years of dreaming, I was really aboard a spaceship at last! In a few minutes, more than a hundred million horsepower would be hurtling me into the sky.

I let my eyes roam around the control cabin. Most of its contents were quite familiar from photographs and films, and I knew what all the instruments were supposed to do. The control panel of the spaceship is not really very complicated, because so much is done automatically.

The pilot was talking to the Port Control Tower over the radio, as they went through the pre-take-off routine together. Every so often a time-check broke through the conversation: 'Minus Fifteen Minutes . . . Minus Ten Minutes . . . Minus Five Minutes.' Though I'd heard this sort of thing so often before, it never failed to give me a thrill. And this time I wasn't watching it on TV – I was in the middle of it myself.

At last the pilot said, 'Over to Automatic,' and threw a large red switch. He gave a sigh of relief, stretched his arms, and leaned back in his seat.

'That's always a nice feeling,' he said. 'No more work for the next hour!'

He didn't *really* mean that, of course. Although the robot controls would handle the ship from now on, he still had to see that everything was going according to plan. In an emergency, or if the robot pilot made an error, he would have to take over again.

The ship began to vibrate as the fuel pumps started to spin. A complicated pattern of intersecting lines had appeared on the TV screen – something to do, I supposed, with the course the rocket was to follow. A row of tiny lights changed, one after another, from red to green. As the last light turned colour, the pilot called to me swiftly: 'Make sure you're lying quite flat.'

I snuggled down into the couch – and then, without any warning, felt as if someone had jumped on top of me. There was a tremendous roaring in my ears, and I seemed to weigh a ton. It required a definite effort to breathe – that was no longer something you could leave to your lungs and forget all about.

The feeling of discomfort lasted only a few seconds: then I grew accustomed to it. The ship's own motors had not yet started: we were climbing under the thrust of the booster rockets, which would burn out and drop away after thirty seconds, when we were already many miles above the Earth.

I could tell when this moment came by the sudden slackening of weight. It lasted only a moment: then there was a subtly changed roaring as our rockets started to fire. They would keep up their thunder for another five minutes. At the end of that time, we would be moving so swiftly that the Earth could never drag us back.

The thrust of the rockets was now giving me more than three times my normal weight. As long as I stayed still, there was no real discomfort. As an experiment, I tried to see if I could raise my arm. It was very tiring, but not too difficult. Still, I was glad to let it drop back again. If necessary, I think I could have sat upright: but standing would have been quite impossible.

On the TV screen, the pattern of bright lines seemed unaltered. Now, however, there was a tiny spot creeping slowly upwards – representing, I supposed, the ascending ship. I watched it intently, wondering if the motors would cut out when the spot reached the top of the screen.

Long before that happened, there came a series of short explosions and the ship shuddered slightly. For one anxious moment, I thought that something had gone wrong. Then I realized what had happened: our drop-tanks had been emptied, and the bolts holding them on had been severed. They were falling back behind us, and presently would plunge into the Pacific, somewhere in the great empty wastes between Tahiti and South America.

At last the thunder of the rockets began to lose its power, and the feeling of enormous weight ebbed away. The ship was easing itself into its final orbit, five hundred miles above the Equator. The motors had done their work, and were now merely making the last adjustments to our course.

Silence returned as the rockets cut out completely. I could still feel the faint vibration of the fuel pumps as they idled to rest, but there was no sound whatsoever in the little cabin. I had been partially deafened by the roar of the rockets, and it took some minutes before I could hear properly again.

The pilot finished checking his instruments, and then released himself from his seat. I watched him, fascinated, as he floated across to me.

'It will take you some time to get used to this,' he said, as he unbuckled my safety strap. 'The thing to remember is – always move gently. And never let go of one handhold until you've decided on the next.'

Gingerly, I stood up. I grabbed the couch just in time to stop myself zooming to the ceiling. Only, of course, it wasn't really the ceiling any more. 'Up' and 'down' had vanished completely. Weight had ceased to exist: I had only to give myself a gentle push and I could move any way I wished.

It's a strange thing, but even now there are people who don't understand this business of 'weightlessness'. They seem to think it's something to do with being 'outside the pull of gravity'. That's nonsense, of course: in a space-station or a coasting rocket five hundred miles up gravity is nearly as powerful as it is down on the Earth. The reason why you feel weightless is not because you're outside gravity, but because you're no longer resisting its pull. You could feel weightless, even down on Earth, inside a freely falling elevator – as long as the fall lasted. An orbiting space-station or rocket is in a kind of permanent fall – a 'fall' that can last for ever because it isn't towards the Earth but *around* it.

'Careful, now!' warned the pilot. 'I don't want you cracking your head against my instrument panel! If you want to have a look out of the window, hang on to this strap.' I obeyed him, and peered through the little porthole whose thick plastic was all that lay between me and nothingness.

Yes, I know that there have been so many films and photographs that everyone knows just what Earth looks like from space. So I won't waste much time describing it. And to tell the truth, there wasn't a great deal to see, as my field of view was almost entirely filled by the Pacific Ocean. Beneath me it was a surprisingly deep azure, which softened into a misty blue at the limits of vision. I asked the pilot how far away the horizon was.

'About two thousand miles,' he replied. 'You can see most of the way down to New Zealand and up to Hawaii. Quite a view, isn't it?'

Now that I had grown accustomed to the scale of things, I was able to pick out some of the Pacific islands, many showing their coral reefs quite clearly. A long way towards what I imagined was the west the colour of the ocean changed quite abruptly from blue to a vivid green. I realized I was looking at the enormous sea-farms that fed the continent of Asia, and which now covered a substantial part of all the oceans in the tropics.

The coast of South America was coming into sight when the pilot began to prepare for the landing on the Inner Station. (I know the word 'landing' sounds peculiar, but it's the expression that's used. Out in space, a lot of ordinary words have quite different meanings.) I was still staring out of the little porthole when I got the order to go back to my seat, so that I wouldn't fall around the cabin during the final manoeuvres.

The TV screen was now a black rectangle, with a tiny double star shining near its centre. We were about a hundred miles away from the Station, slowly overhauling it. The two stars grew brighter and further apart: additional faint satellites appeared sprinkled around them. I was seeing, I knew, the ships that were 'in dock' at the moment, being refuelled or overhauled.

Suddenly one of those faint stars burst into blazing light. A hundred miles ahead of us, one of the ships in that little fleet had started its motors and was pulling away from Earth. I questioned the pilot.

'That would be the "Alpha Centauri", bound for Venus,' he replied. 'She's a wonderful old wreck – it's really time they pensioned her off. Now let me get on with my navigating. This is one job the robots can't do.'

The Inner Station was only a few miles away when we started to put on the brakes. There was a high-pitched whistling from the steering jets in the nose, and for a moment a feeble sensation of weight returned. It lasted only a few seconds: then we had matched speeds and had joined the Station's other floating satellites.

Being careful to ask the pilot's permission, I got out of my couch and went to the window again. The Earth was now on the other side of the ship, and I was looking out at the stars – and the space-station. It was such a staggering sight that I had to stare for a minute before it made any sense at all. I understood, now, the purpose of that orientation test the doctors had given me . . .

My first impression of the Inner Station was one of complete chaos. Floating there in space about a mile away from our ship was a great open lattice-work of spidery girders, in the shape of a flat disc. Here and there on its surface were spherical buildings of varying sizes, connected to each other by tubes wide enough for men to travel through. In the centre of the disc was the largest sphere of all, dotted with tiny eyes of portholes and with dozens of radio antennae jutting from it in all directions.

Several spaceships – some almost completely dismantled – were attached to the great disc at various points. They looked, I thought, very much like flies caught in a spider-web. Men in space-suits were working on them, and sometimes the glare of a welding torch would dazzle my eyes.

Other ships were floating freely, arranged in no particular system that I could discover, in the space around the Station. Some of them were streamlined, winged vessels like the one that had brought me up from Earth. Others were the true ships of space – assembled here outside the atmosphere and designed to ferry loads from world to world without ever landing on any planet. They were weird, flimsy constructions, usually with a pressurized spherical chamber for the crew and passengers, and larger tanks for the fuel. There was no streamlining, of course: the cabins, fuel tanks and motors were simply linked together by thin struts. As I looked at these ships I couldn't help thinking of some very old magazines I'd once seen which showed our grandfathers' ideas of spaceships. They were all sleek, finned projectiles looking rather like bombs. The artists who drew those pictures would have been shocked by the reality: in fact, they would probably not have recognized these queer objects as spaceships at all . . .

I was wondering how we were going to get aboard the Station when something came sweeping into my field of vision. It was a tiny cylinder, just big enough to hold a man – and it *did* hold a man, for I could see his head through the plastic panels covering one end of the device. Long, jointed arms projected from the machine's body and it was trailing a thin cable behind it. I could just make out the faint misty jet of the tiny rocket motor which propelled this miniature spaceship.

The operator must have seen me staring out at him, for he grinned back as he flashed by. A minute later there came an alarming 'clang' from the hull of our ship. The pilot laughed at my obvious fright.

'That's only the towing cable being coupled – it's magnetic, you know. We'll start to move in a minute.'

There was the feeblest of tugs, and our ship slowly rotated until it was parallel to the great disc of the Station. The cable had been attached amidships, and the Station was hauling us in like an angler landing a fish. The pilot pressed a button on the control panel, and there was the whining of motors as our undercarriage lowered itself. *That* was not something you'd expect to see used in space, but the idea was sensible enough. The shock-absorbers were just the thing to take up the gentle impact on making contact with the Station.

We were wound in so slowly that it took almost ten minutes to make the short journey. Then there was a slight jar as we 'touched down', and the journey was over.

'Well,' grinned the pilot. 'I hope you enjoyed the trip. Or would you have liked some excitement?'

I looked at him cautiously, wondering if he was pulling my leg.

'It was quite exciting enough, thank you. What other sort of excitement could you supply?'

'Well, what about a few meteors, an attack by pirates, an invasion from outer space, or all the other things you read about in the fiction magazines?'

'I only read the serious books, like Richardson's *Introduction to Astronautics* or Maxwell's *Modern Spaceships* – not magazine stories.'

'I don't believe you,' he replied promptly. 'I read 'em, anyway, and I'm sure you do. You can't fool me.'

He was right, of course. It was one of the first lessons I learned on the Station. All the people out there have been hand-picked for intelligence as well as technical knowledge. If you weren't on the level, they'd spot it right away.

I was wondering how we were going to get out of the ship when there was a series of bangings and scrapings from the air-lock, followed a moment later by an alarming hiss of air. It slowly died away, and presently, with a soft sucking noise, the inner door of the lock swung open.

'Remember what I told you about moving slowly,' said the pilot, gathering up his log book. 'The best thing is for you to hitch on to my belt and I'll tow you. Ready?'

It wasn't a very dignified entry into the Station, I couldn't help thinking. But it was safest to take no risks, so that was the way I travelled through the flexible, pressurized coupling that had been clamped on to the side of our ship. The pilot launched himself with a powerful kick, and I trailed along behind him. It was rather like learning to swim underwater – so much like it, in fact, that at first I had the panicky feeling that I'd drown if I tried to breathe.

Presently we emerged into a wide, metal tunnel – one of the Station's main passageways, I guessed. Cables and pipes ran along the walls, and at intervals we passed through great double doors with red EMERGENCY notices painted on them. I didn't think this was at all reassuring. We met only two people on our journey: they flashed by us with an effortless ease that filled me with envy – and made me determined to be just as skilful before I left the Station.

'I'm taking you to Commander Doyle,' the pilot explained to me. 'He's in charge of training here and will be keeping an eye on you.'

'What sort of man is he?' I asked anxiously.

'Don't you worry – you'll find out soon enough. Here we are.'

We drifted to a halt in front of a circular door carrying the notice 'Cdr R. Doyle, i/c Training. Knock and Enter.' The pilot knocked and entered, still towing me behind him like a sack of potatoes. I heard him say:

'Captain Jones reporting, Mr Doyle – with passenger.' Then he shoved me in front of him and I saw the man he had been addressing.

He was sitting at a perfectly ordinary office desk – which was rather surprising in this place where nothing else seemed normal. And he looked like a prize-fighter: I think he was the most powerfully-built man I'd ever seen. Two huge arms covered most of the desk in front of him, and I wondered where he found clothes to fit – his shoulders must have been over four feet across.

At first I didn't see his face clearly, for he was bending over some papers. Then he looked up, and I found myself staring at a huge red beard and two enormous eyebrows. It was some time before I really took in the rest of the face: it's so unusual to see a real beard nowadays that I couldn't help staring at it. Then I realized that

Commander Doyle must have had some kind of accident, for there was a faint scar running diagonally right across his forehead. Considering how skilled our plastic surgeons are nowadays, the fact that anything was still visible meant that it must originally have been very bad indeed.

Altogether, as you'll probably have gathered, Commander Doyle wasn't a very handsome man. But he was certainly a striking one – and my biggest surprise was still to come.

'So you're young Malcolm, eh?' he said, in a pleasant, quiet voice that wasn't half as fearsome as his appearance. 'We've heard a lot about you. O.K., Captain Jones – I'll take charge of him now.'

The pilot saluted and glided away. For the next ten minutes Commander Doyle questioned me closely, building up a picture of my life and interest. I told him how I'd been born in New Zealand and had lived for a few years in China, South Africa, Brazil and Switzerland, as my father – who's a journalist – moved from one job to another. We'd just gone to Missouri because Mom was fed up with mountains and wanted a change. As families go these days, we hadn't travelled a great deal, and I'd never visited half the places all our neighbours seemed to know. Perhaps that was one reason why I wanted to go out into space – though I'd never thought of it that way before.

When he had finished writing all this down – and adding a lot of notes I'd have given a good deal to read – Commander Doyle laid aside the old-fashioned fountain-pen he was using and stared at me for a minute as if I were some peculiar animal. He drummed thoughtfully on the desk with his huge fingers, which looked as if they could tear their way through the material without much trouble. I was feeling a bit scared, and to make matters worse I'd drifted away from the floor and was floating helplessly in mid-air again. There was no way I could move anywhere unless I made myself ridiculous by trying to swim – which might or might not work. Then the Commander gave a chuckle and his face crinkled up into a vast grin.

'I think this may be quite amusing,' he said. While I was still wondering if I dared to ask why, he continued, after glancing at some charts on the wall behind him: 'Afternoon classes have just stopped – I'll take you to meet the boys.' Then he grabbed a long metal tube, that must have been slung underneath the desk, and launched himself out of his chair with a single jerk of his huge left arm.

He moved so quickly that it took me completely by surprise. A moment later I just managed to stifle a gasp of amazement. For as he moved clear of the desk, I saw that Commander Doyle had no legs.

When you go to a new school, or move into a strange district, there's always a confusing period so full of new experiences that you can never recall it clearly. My first day on the space-station was like that. So much had never happened to me before in such a short time. It was not merely that I was meeting a lot of new people. I had to learn how to live all over again.

At first I felt as helpless as a baby. I couldn't judge the effort needed to make any movement. Although weight had vanished, momentum remained. It required force to start something moving, and more force to stop it again. That was where the broomsticks came in.

Commander Doyle had invented them, and the name, of course, came from the old idea that once upon a time witches used to ride on broomsticks. We certainly rode around the Station on ours. They consisted of one hollow tube sliding inside another. The two were connected by a powerful spring, and one tube ended in a hook, the other in a wide rubber pad. That was all there was to it. If you wanted to move, you put the pad against the nearest wall and shoved. The recoil launched you into space, and when you arrived at your destination you let the spring absorb your velocity and so bring you to rest. Trying to stop yourself with your bare hands was liable to result in sprained wrists.

It wasn't quite as easy as it sounds, though, for if you weren't careful you could bounce right back the way you'd come . . .

It was a long time before I discovered what had happened to the Commander. The scar he'd picked up in an ordinary motor crash when he was a young man – but the more serious accident was a different story, and had occurred when he was on the first expedition to Mercury. He'd been quite an athlete, it seemed, so the loss of his legs must have been an even bigger blow to him than to most men. It was obvious why he had come to the Station – it was the only place where he wouldn't be a cripple. Indeed, thanks to his powerfully developed arms, he was probably the most agile man in the Station. He had lived here for the last ten years and would never return to Earth, where he would be helpless again. He wouldn't even go over to any of the other space-stations where they had gravity, and no one was ever tactless or foolish enough to suggest such a trip to him.

There were about a hundred people on board the Inner Station, ten of them apprentices a few years older than myself. At first they were a bit fed up at having me around, but after I'd had my fight with Ronnie Jordan everything was O.K. and they accepted me as one of the family. I'll tell you about that later.

The senior apprentice was a tall, quiet Canadian named Tim Benton. He never said much, but when he did speak everyone took notice. It was Tim who really taught me my way around the Inner Station, after Commander Doyle had handed me over to him with a few words of explanation.

'I suppose you know what we *do* up here?' he said doubtfully when the Commander had left us.

'You refuel spaceships on their way out from Earth, and carry out repairs and overhauls.'

'Yes, that's our main job. The other stations – those further out – do a lot else as well, but we needn't bother about that now. There's one important point I'd better make clear right away. This Inner Station of ours is really in two parts, with a couple of miles between them. Come and have a look.'

He pulled me over to a port and I stared out into space. Hanging there against the stars – so close that it seemed I could reach out and touch it – was what seemed to be a giant flywheel. It was slowly turning on its axis, and as it revolved I could see the glitter of sunlight on its observation ports. I could not help comparing its smooth compactness with the flimsy, open girder work of the station in which I was standing – or, rather, floating. The great wheel had an axle, for jutting from its centre was a long, narrow cylinder which ended in a curious structure I couldn't understand. A spaceship was slowly manoeuvring near it.

'That's the Residential Station,' said Benton disapprovingly. 'It's nothing but an hotel. You've noticed that it's spinning – because of that, it's got normal Earth gravity at the rim, owing to centrifugal force. We hardly ever go over there: once you've got used to weightlessness, gravity's a nuisance. But all incoming passengers from Mars and the Moon are transhipped there. It wouldn't be safe for them to go straight to Earth after living in a much lower gravity field. In the Residential Station they can get acclimatized, as it were. They go in at the centre, where there's no gravity, and work slowly out to the rim, where it's Earth normal.'

'How do they get aboard if the thing's spinning?' I asked.

'See that ship moving into position? If you look carefully, you'll see that the axle of the station *isn't* spinning – it's being driven by a motor against the station's spin so that it actually stands still in space. The ship can couple up to it and transfer passengers. The coupling's free to rotate, and once the axle revs up to match speed with the station, the passengers can go aboard. Sounds complicated, but it works well. And see if you can think of a better way!'

'Will I have a chance of going over there?' I asked.

'I expect it could be arranged – though I don't see much point in it. You might just as well be down on Earth – that's the idea of the place, in fact.'

I didn't press the point, and it wasn't until the very end of my visit that I was able to get over to the Residential Station, floating there only a couple of miles away . . .

It must have been quite a bother showing me round the Station, because I had to be pushed or pulled most of the way until I'd found my 'space-legs'. Once or twice Tim only just managed to rescue me in time when I'd launched myself too vigorously and was about to plunge headlong into an obstacle. But he was very patient, and finally I got the knack of things and was able to move around fairly confidently.

It was several days before I really knew my way around the great maze of interconnecting corridors and pressure chambers that was the Inner Station. In that first trip I merely had a quick survey of its workshops, radio equipment, power plant, air-conditioning gear, dormitories, storage tanks and observatory. Sometimes it was hard to believe that all this had been carried up into space and assembled here five hundred miles above the Earth. I didn't know, until Tim mentioned it casually, that most of the material in the Station had actually come from the Moon. The Moon's low gravity made it much more economical to ship equipment from there instead of from the Earth – despite the fact that Earth was so much closer.

My first tour of inspection ended inside one of the airlocks. We stood in front of the great circular door, resting snugly on its rubber gaskets, that led into the outer emptiness. Clamped to the walls around us were the space-suits, and I looked at them longingly. It had always been one of my ambitions to wear one and to become a tiny, self-contained world of my own.

'Do you think I'll have a chance of trying one on while I'm here?' I asked.

Tim looked thoughtful: then he glanced at his watch.

'I'm not on duty for half an hour, and I want to collect something I've left out at the rim. We'll go outside.'

'But ...' I gulped, my enthusiasm suddenly waning. 'Will it be safe? Doesn't it take a lot of training to use one of these?'

He looked at me calmly.

'Not *frightened*, are you?'

'Of course not.'

'Well, let's get started.'

Tim answered my question while he was showing me how to get into the suit.

'It's quite true that it takes a lot of training before you can operate one of these. I'm not going to let you try – you sit tight inside and tag along with me. You'll be as safe there as you are now, as long as you don't meddle with the controls. Just to make sure of that, I'll lock them first.'

I rather resented this, but didn't say anything. After all, he was the boss.

To most people, the word 'space-suit' conjures up a picture of something like a diving dress, in which a man can walk and use his arms. Such suits are, of course, used on places like the Moon. But on a space-station, where there's no gravity, your legs aren't much use anyway – outside, you have to blow yourself round with tiny rocket units.

For this reason, the lower part of the suit was simply a rigid cylinder. When I climbed inside it, I found that I could only use my feet to work some control pedals, which I was careful not to touch. There was a little seat, and a transparent dome covering the top of the cylinder gave me good visibility. I *could* use my hands and arms. Just below my chin there was a neat little control panel with a tiny keyboard and a few meters. If I wanted to handle anything outside, there were flexible sleeves inside which I could push my arms. They ended in gloves which, although they seemed clumsy, enabled one to carry out quite delicate operations.

Tim threw some of the switches on my suit and clamped the transparent dome over my head. I felt rather like being inside a coffin with a view. Then he chose a suit for himself and attached it to mine by a thin nylon cord.

The inner door of the air-lock thudded shut behind us and I could hear the vibration of the pumps as the air was sucked back into the station. The sleeves of my suit began to stiffen slightly. Tim called across at me, his voice distorted after passing through our helmets.

'I won't switch on the radio yet. You should still be able to hear me. Listen to this.' Then he went over to the familiar radio engineer's routine: 'Testing, One, Two, Three, Four, Five . . .'

Around 'Five' his voice began to fade. When he'd reached 'Nine' I couldn't hear a thing, though his lips were still moving. There was no longer enough air around us to carry sound. The silence was quite uncanny, and I was relieved when the loudspeaker in my suit started to talk.

'I'm opening the outer door now. Don't make any movements – I'll do all that's necessary.'

In that eerie silence, the great door slowly opened inwards. I was floating freely now, and I felt a faint 'tug' as the last traces of air puffed out into space. A circle of stars was ahead of me, and I could just glimpse the misty rim of Earth to one side.

'Ready?' asked Tim.

'O.K.,' I said, hoping that the microphone wouldn't betray my nervousness. The towing line gave a tug as Tim switched on his jets, and we drifted out of the air-lock. It was a terrifying sensation, yet one I would not have missed for anything. Although, of course, the words 'up' and 'down' had no meaning here, it seemed to me as if I were floating out through a hole in a great metal wall, with the Earth at an immense distance below. My reason told me that I was perfectly safe – but all my instincts shouted, 'You've a five hundred mile fall straight down beneath you!'

Indeed, when the Earth filled half the sky, it was hard not to think of it as 'down'. We were in sunlight at the moment, passing across Africa, and I could see Lake Victoria and the great forests of the Congo. What would Livingstone and Stanley have thought, I wondered, if they had known that one day men would flash across the Dark Continent at 18,000 miles an hour? And the day of those great explorers was only two hundred years behind us. It had been a crowded couple of centuries . . .

Though it was fascinating to look at Earth, I found it was making me giddy, and so I swivelled round in my suit to concentrate on the Station. Tim had now towed us well clear of it, and we were almost out among the halo of floating ships. I tried to forget about the Earth, and now that I could no longer see it, it seemed natural enough to think of 'down' as towards the Station.

This is a knack everyone has to learn in space. You're liable to get awfully confused unless you pretend that *somewhere* is down. The important thing is to choose the most convenient direction, according to whatever you happen to be doing at the moment.

Tim had given us enough speed to make our little trip in a reasonable time, so he cut the jets and pointed out the sights as we drifted along. This bird's-eye view of the Station completed the picture I'd already got from my tour inside, and I began to feel that I was really learning my way about.

The outer rim of the Station was simply a flat network of girders trailing off into space. Here and there were large cylinders – pressurized workshops big enough to hold two or three men, and intended for any jobs that couldn't be handled in vacuum.

A spaceship with most of its plating stripped off was floating near the edge of the Station, secured from drifting away by a couple of cords that would hardly have supported a man on Earth. Several mechanics wearing suits like our own were working on the hull. I wished I could overhear their conversation and find out what they were doing, but we were on a different wavelength.

'I'm going to leave you here a minute,' said Tim, unfastening the towing cord, and clipping it to the nearest girder. 'Don't do anything until I get back.'

I felt rather foolish, floating round like a captive balloon, and was glad that no one took any notice of me. While waiting, I experimented with the fingers of my suit and tried, unsuccessfully, to tie a simple knot in my towing cable. I found later that one *could* do this sort of thing, but it took practice. Certainly the men on the spaceship seemed to be handling their tools without any awkwardness, despite their gloves.

Suddenly it began to grow dark. Until this moment, the Station and the ships floating beside it had been bathed in brilliant light from a sun so fierce that I had not dared to look anywhere near it. But now the Sun was passing behind the Earth as we hurtled across the night side of the planet. I turned my head – and there was a sight so splendid that it completely took away my breath. Earth was now a huge, black disc eclipsing the stars, but all along one edge was a glorious crescent of golden light, shrinking even as I watched. I was looking back upon the line of the sunset, stretching for a thousand miles across Africa. At its centre was a great halo of dazzling gold where a thin sliver of sun was still visible. It dwindled and vanished: the crimson afterglow of the sunset contracted swiftly along the horizon until it too disappeared. The whole thing lasted not more than two minutes, and the men working around me took not the slightest notice of it. After all, in time one gets used even to the most wonderful sights, and the Station circled the Earth so swiftly that sunset occurred every hundred minutes...

It was not completely dark, for the Moon was half full, looking no brighter or closer than it did from Earth. And the sky was so crowded with millions of stars, all shining quite steadily without a trace of twinkling, that I wondered how anyone could ever have spoken of the 'blackness' of space.

I was so busy looking for the other planets (and failing to find them) that I never noticed Tim's return until my tow-rope began to tug. Slowly we moved back towards the centre of the Station, in such utter silence that it hardly seemed real. I closed my eyes for a minute – but the scene hadn't changed when I opened them. There was the great black shield of Earth – no, not quite black, for I could see the oceans glimmering in the moonlight. The same light made the slim girders around me gleam like the threads of a ghostly spider's web, a web sprinkled with myriads of stars.

This was the moment when I really knew that I had reached space at last, and that nothing else could ever be the same again.

Three
'THE MORNING STAR'

'Now on Station Four, do you know what our biggest trouble used to be?' asked Norman Powell.

'No,' I replied, which was what I was supposed to say.

'*Mice*,' he exclaimed solemnly. 'Believe it or not! Some of them got loose from the biology lab, and before you knew where you were, they were all over the place.'

'I don't believe a word of it,' interrupted Ronnie Jordan.

'They were so small they could get into all the air shafts,' continued Norman, unabashed. 'You could hear them scuttling around happily whenever you put your ear to the walls. There was no need for them to make mouse-holes – every room had half a dozen already provided, and you can guess what they did to the ventilation. But we got them in the end, and do you know how we did it?'

'You borrowed a couple of cats.'

Norman gave Ronnie a superior look.

'That *was* tried, but cats don't like zero gravity. They were no good at all – the mice used to laugh at them. No: we used *owls*. You should have seen them fly! Their wings worked just as well as ever, of course, and they used to do the most fantastic things. It only took them a few months to get rid of the mice.'

He sighed.

'The problem *then*, was to get rid of the owls. We did this–'

I never learned what happened next, for the rest of the gang decided they'd had enough of Norman's tall stories and everyone launched themselves at him simultaneously. He disappeared in the middle of a slowly revolving sphere of bodies, that drifted noisily round the cabin. Only Tim Benton, who never got mixed up in these vulgar brawls, remained quietly studying, which was what everybody else was supposed to be doing.

Every day all the apprentices met in the classroom to hear a lecture from Commander Doyle or one of the Station's technical officers. The Commander had suggested that I should attend these talks – and a suggestion from him was not very different from an order. He thought I might pick up some useful knowledge, which was true enough. I could understand about a quarter of what was said, and spent the rest of the time reading something from the Station's library of ultra-light-weight books.

After the classes there was a thirty-minute study period, and from time to time some studying *was* actually done. These intervals were much more useful to me than the lessons themselves, for the boys were always talking about their jobs and the things they had seen in space. Some of them had been out here for two years, with only a few short trips down to Earth.

Of course, a lot of the tales they told me were, shall I say, slightly exaggerated. Norman Powell, our prize humorist, was always trying to pull my leg. At first I fell for some of his yarns, but now I'd learned to be cautious . . .

There were also, I'd discovered, some interesting tricks and practical jokes that could be played in space. One of the best involved nothing more complicated than an ordinary match. We were in the classroom one afternoon when Norman suddenly turned to me and said: 'Do you know how to test the air to see if it's breathable?'

'If it wasn't, I suppose you'd soon know,' I replied.

'Not at all – you might be knocked out too quickly to do anything about it. But there's a simple test which has been used on Earth for ages, in mines and caves. You just carry a flame ahead of you, and if it goes out – well, you go out too, as quickly as you can!'

He fumbled in his pocket and extracted a box of matches. I was mildly surprised to see something so old-fashioned aboard the Station.

'In here, of course,' Norman continued, 'a flame will burn properly. But if the air were bad it would go out at once.'

He absent-mindedly stroked the match on the box and it burst into light. A flame formed around the head – and I leaned forward to look at it closely. It was a very odd flame, not long and pointed but quite spherical. Even as I watched it dwindled and died.

It's funny how the mind works, for up to that moment I'd been breathing perfectly comfortably, yet now I seemed to be suffocating. I looked at Norman, and said nervously: 'Try it again – there must be something wrong with the match.'

Obediently he struck another, which expired as quickly as the first.

'Let's get out of here,' I gasped. 'The air-purifier must have packed up.' Then I saw that the others were grinning at me.

'Don't panic, Roy,' said Tim. 'There's a simple answer.' He grabbed the match-box from Norman.

'The air's perfectly O.K. but if you think about it, you'll see that it's impossible for a flame to burn out here. Since there's no gravity and everything stays put, the smoke doesn't rise and the flame just chokes itself. The only way it will keep burning is if you do this.'

He struck another match, but instead of holding it still, kept it moving slowly through the air. It left a trail of smoke behind it, and kept on burning until only the stump was left.

'It was entering fresh air all the time, so it didn't choke itself with burnt gases. And if you think this is just an amusing trick of no practical importance, you're wrong. It means we've got to keep the air in the Station on the move, otherwise *we'd* soon go the same way as that flame. Norman, will you switch on the ventilators again, now that you've had your little joke?'

Joke or not, it was a very effective lesson. But it made me all the more determined that one of these days I was going to get my own back on Norman. Not that I disliked him, but I *was* getting a little tired of his sense of humour.

Someone gave a shout from the other side of the room. 'The "Canopus" is leaving!'

We all rushed to the small circular windows and looked out into space. It was some time before I could manage to see anything, but presently I wormed my way to the front and pressed my face against the thick transparent plastic.

The 'Canopus' was the largest liner on the Mars run, and she had been here for some weeks having her routine overhaul. During the last two days fuel and passengers had been going aboard, and she had now drifted away from the Station until we were separated by a space of several miles. Like the Residential Station, the 'Canopus' slowly revolved to give the passengers a sense of gravity. She was shaped rather like a giant doughnut, the cabins and living quarters forming a ring around the power plant and drive units. During the voyage the ship's spin would be gradually reduced, so that by the time her passengers reached Mars they would already be accustomed to the right gravity. On the homeward journey, just the reverse would happen.

The departure of a spaceship from an orbit is nothing like as spectacular as a take-off from Earth. It all happens in utter silence, of course, and it also happens very slowly. Nor is there any flame and smoke: all that I could see was a faint pencil of mist jetting from the drive units. The great radiator fins began to glow cherry red, then white hot, as the waste heat from the power plant flooded away into space. The liner's thousands of tons of mass were gradually picking up speed, though it would be many hours before she gained enough velocity to escape from Earth. The rocket that had carried me up to the Station had travelled at a hundred times the acceleration of the 'Canopus': but the great liner could keep her drive units thrusting gently for weeks on end, to build up a final speed of almost half a million miles an hour.

After five minutes she was several miles away and moving at an appreciable velocity – pulling out away from our own orbit into the path that led to Mars. I stared hungrily after her, wondering when I, too, would travel on such a journey. Norman must have seen my expression, for he chuckled and said:

'Thinking of stowing away on the next ship? Well, forget it. It can't be done. Oh, I know it's a favourite dodge in fiction, but it's never happened in practice – there are too many safeguards. And do you know what they'd do to a stowaway if they found one?'

'No,' I said, trying not to show too much interest – for to tell the truth I had been thinking rather along these lines.

Norman rubbed his hands ghoulishly.

'Well, an extra person on board would mean that much less food and oxygen for everyone else – and it would upset the fuel calculations too. So he'd simply be pushed overboard.'

'Then it's just as well that no one ever has stowed away.'

'It certainly is – but of course a stowaway wouldn't have a chance. He'd be spotted before the voyage began. There just isn't room to hide in a space-ship.'

I filed this information away for future reference. It might come in handy some day.

Space Station One was a big place, but the apprentices didn't spend all their time aboard it, as I quickly found out. They had a club-room which must have been unique, and it was some time before I was allowed to visit it.

Not far from the Station was a veritable Museum of Astronautics, a floating graveyard of ships that had seen their day and had been withdrawn from service. Most of them had been stripped of their instruments and were no more than skeletons. On Earth, of course, they would have rusted away long ago, but here in vacuum they would remain bright and untarnished for ever.

Among these derelicts were some of the great pioneers – the first ship to land on Venus, the first to reach the satellites of Jupiter, the first to circle Saturn. At the end of their long voyages, they had entered the five-hundred mile orbit round Earth and the ferry-rockets had come up to take off their crews. They were still here where they had been abandoned, never to be used again.

All, that is, except the 'Morning Star'. As everyone knows, she made the first circumnavigation of Venus, back in '85. But very few people know that she was still in an excellent state of repair, for the apprentices had adopted her, made her their private headquarters, and, for their own amusement, had got her into working condition again. Indeed, they believed she was at least as good as new and were always trying to 'borrow' enough rocket fuel to make a short trip. They were very hurt because no one would let them have any.

Commander Doyle, of course, knew all about this and quite approved of it – after all, it was good training. Sometimes he came over to the 'Morning Star' to see how things were getting on, but it was generally understood that the ship was private property. You had to have an invitation before you were allowed aboard. Not until I'd been around for some days, and had become more or less accepted as one of the gang, did I have a chance of making the trip over to the 'Morning Star'.

It was the longest journey I had made outside the Station, for the 'Graveyard' was about five miles away, moving in the same orbit as the Station but a little ahead of it. I don't quite know how to describe the curious vehicle in which we made the trip. It had been constructed out of junk salvaged from other ships, and was really nothing more than a pressurized cylinder, large enough to hold a dozen people. A low-powered rocket unit had been bolted to one end, there were a few auxiliary jets for steering, a simple air-lock, a radio to keep in touch with the Station – and that was all. This peculiar vessel could make the hop across to the 'Morning Star' in about ten minutes, being capable of achieving a top speed of about thirty miles an hour. She had been christened 'The Skylark of Space' – a name apparently taken from a famous old science-fiction story.

The 'Skylark' was usually kept parked at the outer rim of the Station where she wouldn't get in anybody's way. When she was needed, a couple of the apprentices would go out in space-suits, loosen her mooring lines, and tow her to the nearest air-lock. Then she would be coupled up and you could go aboard through the connecting tube – just as if you were entering a real space-liner.

My first trip in the 'Skylark' was a very different experience from the climb up from Earth. She looked so ramshackle that I expected her to fall to pieces at any moment, though in fact she had a perfectly adequate margin of safety. With ten of us aboard, her little cabin was distinctly crowded, and when the rocket motor started up the gentle acceleration made us all drift slowly towards the rear of the ship. The thrust was so feeble that it only made me weigh about a pound – quite a contrast to the take-off from Earth, where I could have sworn I weighed a ton! After a minute or so of this leisurely progress we shut off the drive and drifted freely for another ten minutes, by which time a further brief burst of power brought us neatly to rest at our destination.

There was plenty of room inside the 'Morning Star': after all, she had been the home of five men for almost two years. Their names were still there, scratched on the paintwork in the control cabin, and the sight of those signatures took my imagination back almost a hundred years, to the great pioneering days of space-flight, when even the Moon was a new world and no one had yet reached any of the planets.

Despite the ship's age, everything inside the control room still seemed bright and new. The instrument board, as far as I could tell, might have belonged to a ship of my own time. Tim Benton stroked the panel gently. 'As good as new!' he said, with obvious pride in his voice. 'I'd guarantee to take you to Venus any day!'

I got to know the 'Morning Star' controls pretty well. It was quite safe to play with them, of course, since the fuel tanks were empty and all that happened when one pressed the 'Main Drive – Fire!' button was that a red light lit up. Still, it was exciting to sit in the pilot's seat and to daydream with my hands on the controls . . .

A little workshop had been fitted up just aft of the main fuel tanks, and a lot of model-making went on here – as well as a good deal of serious engineering. Several of the apprentices had designed gadgets they wanted to try out, and were seeing if they worked in practice before they took them any further. Karl Hasse, our mathematical genius, was trying to build some new form of navigational device – but as he always hid it as soon as anybody came along, no one knew just what it was supposed to do.

I learned more about spaceships while I was crawling round inside the 'Morning Star' than I ever did from books or lectures. It was true that she was nearly a century old, but although the details have altered, the main principles of spaceship design have changed less than one might expect. You still have to have pumps, fuel tanks, air-purifiers, temperature regulators, and so on. The gadgets may change, but the jobs they must do remain the same.

The information I absorbed aboard the 'Morning Star' was not merely technical, by any means. I finished my training in weightless-ness here: and I also learned to fight in free-fall. Which brings me to Ronnie Jordan.

Ronnie was the youngest of the apprentices, about two years older than myself. He was a boisterous, fair-haired Australian – at least, he'd been born in Sydney, but had spent most of his time in Europe. As a result, he spoke three or four languages, sometimes accidentally slipping from one to the other.

He was good-natured and light-hearted, and gave the impression that he'd never quite got used to zero gravity but still regarded it as a great joke. At any rate, he was always trying out new tricks, such as making a pair of wings and seeing how well he could fly with them. (The answer was – not very well. But perhaps the wings weren't properly designed.) Because of his high spirits, he was always getting into good-humoured fights with the other boys – and a fight under free-fall conditions is fascinating to watch.

The first problem, of course, is to catch your opponent, which isn't at all easy if he refuses to cooperate – he can shoot off in so many directions. But even if he decides to play, there are further difficulties. Any kind of boxing is almost impossible: the first blow would send you flying apart. So the only practicable form of combat is wrestling. It usually starts with the two fighters floating in mid-air, as far as possible from any solid object. They grasp wrists, with their arms fully extended – and after that it's difficult to see exactly what happens. The air is full of flying limbs and slowly rotating bodies. By the rules of the game, you've won if you can keep your opponent against any wall for a count of five. This is much more difficult than it sounds, for he only has to give a good heave to send both of you flying out into the room again. Remember that as there's no gravity, you can't just sit on your victim until your weight tires him out.

My first fight with Ronnie arose out of a political argument. Perhaps it seems funny that, out in space, Earth's politics matter at all. In a way they don't – at least, no one worries whether you're a citizen of the Atlantic Federation, the Panasiatic Union or the Pacific Confederacy. But there were plenty of arguments about which country was the best to live in, and as most of us had travelled a good deal everyone had different ideas.

When I told Ronnie that he was talking nonsense he said, 'Them's fightin' words,' and before I knew what had happened I was pinned in a corner while Norman Powell lazily counted up to ten – to give me a chance. I couldn't escape, because Ronnie had his feet braced firmly against the other two walls forming the corner of the cabin.

The next time I did slightly better, but Ronnie still won easily. Not only was he stronger than I was, but I didn't have the technique.

In the end, however, I did succeed in winning – just once. It took a lot of careful planning, and maybe Ron had got over-confident as well.

I realized that if I let him get me in a corner I was done for – he could use his favourite 'star-fish' trick and pin me down, by bracing himself against the walls where they came together. On the other hand, if I stayed out in the open his superior strength and skill would soon force me into an unfavourable position. It was necessary, therefore, to think of some way of neutralizing his advantages.

I thought about the problem a lot before discovering the answer – and then I put in a good deal of practice when nobody else was around, for it needed very careful timing.

At last I was ready. We were seated round the little table bolted to one end of the 'Morning Star's' cabin – the end which was usually regarded as the floor. Ron was opposite me, and we'd been arguing in a good-humoured manner for some time. It was obvious that a fight was going to start at any minute. When Ron began to unbuckle his seat straps I knew it was time to take-off ...

He'd just unfastened himself when I shouted, 'Come and get me!' and launched myself straight at the 'ceiling', fifteen feet away. This was the bit that had to be timed carefully. Ron kicked himself off a fraction of a second after me, once he'd judged the course I was taking.

Now in free orbit, of course, once you've launched yourself on a definite path you can't stop until you bump into something again. Ron expected to meet me on the 'ceiling': what he *didn't* expect was that I'd only get half-way there. For my foot was tucked in a loop of cord that I'd thoughtfully fastened to the floor. I'd only gone a couple of yards when I jerked to a stop and dragged myself back the way I'd come. Ron, of course, couldn't do anything but sail right on. He was so surprised at seeing me jerk back that he rolled over as he was ascending, to watch what had happened, and hit the ceiling with quite a thud. He hadn't recovered from this when I launched myself again – and this time I *didn't* hang on to the cord. Ron was still off-balance as I came up like a meteor. He couldn't get out of the way in time and so I knocked all the wind out of him. It was easy to hold him down for the count of five: in fact Norman got to ten before Ron showed any signs of life. I was beginning to get a bit worried when he finally started to stir ...

Perhaps it wasn't a very famous victory, and a number of people thought I'd cheated. Still, there was nothing against this sort of thing in the rules.

It wasn't a trick I could use twice, and Ron got his own back next time. But, after all, he *was* older than me ...

Some of our other games weren't quite so rough. We played a lot of chess (with magnetic men), but as I'm no good at this it wasn't much fun for me. About the only game at which I could always win was 'swimming' – not swimming in water, of course, but swimming in air.

This was so exhausting we didn't do it very often. You wanted a fairly large room, and the competitors had to start floating in a line, well away from the nearest wall. The idea was to reach the winning-post by clawing your way through the air. It was much like swimming through water, but a lot harder – and a lot slower. For some reason I was better at it than the others, which is rather odd because I'm not much good at ordinary swimming.

Still, I mustn't give the impression that all our time was spent in the 'Morning Star'. There is plenty of work for everyone on a space-station, and perhaps because of this the staff made the most of their time off. And – this is a curious point that isn't very well known – we had more opportunities for amusement than you might think, because we needed very little sleep. That's one of the effects of zero gravity. All the time I was in space, I don't think I ever had more than four hours of continuous sleep.

I was careful never to miss one of Commander Doyle's lectures, even when there were other things I wanted to do. Tim had advised me, tactfully, that it would make a good impression if I were always there – and the Commander was a good speaker, anyway. Certainly I'm never likely to forget the talk on meteors which he gave to us.

Looking back on it, that's rather funny, because I thought the lecture was going to be pretty dull. The opening was interesting enough, but it soon bogged down in statistics and tables. You know, of course, what meteors are – tiny particles of matter which whirl through space and burn up through friction when they hit the Earth's atmosphere. The huge majority are much smaller than sand grains, but sometimes quite large ones – weighing many pounds – come tumbling down into the atmosphere. And on very rare occasions hundred- or even thousand-ton giants come crashing to Earth and do considerable local damage.

In the early days of space-flight many people were nervous of meteors: they didn't realize just how big space was, and thought that leaving the protective blanket of the atmosphere would be rather like entering a machine-gun barrage. Today we know better: yet though meteors are not a serious danger, small ones occasionally puncture stations or ships and it's necessary to do something about them.

My attention had strayed while Commander Doyle talked about meteor streams and covered the blackboard with calculations showing how little solid matter there really was in the space between the planets. I became rather more interested when he began to say what would happen if a meteor ever did hit us.

'You've got to remember,' he said, 'that because of its speed a meteor doesn't behave like a slow-moving object such as a rifle bullet, which moves at a mere mile a second. If a small meteor hits a solid object – even a piece of paper – it turns into a cloud of incandescent vapour. That's one reason why this Station has got a double hull: the outer shell provides almost complete protection against any meteors we're ever likely to meet.

'But there's a still a faint possibility that a big one might go through both walls and make a fairly large hole. Even that needn't be serious. The air would start rushing out, of course, but every room that has a wall towards space is fitted with one of these.'

He held up a circular disc, looking very much like a saucepan-cover with a rubber flange around it. I'd often seen these discs, painted a bright yellow, clipped to the walls of the Station, but hadn't given them much thought.

'This will deal with leaks up to six inches in diameter. All you have to do is to place it against the wall near the hole and *slide it along* until it covers the leak. Don't try and clamp the disc straight over the hole. Once it's in place, the air pressure will keep it there until a permanent repair can be made.'

He tossed the disc down into the class.

'Have a look at it and pass it round. Any questions?'

I wanted to ask what would happen if the hole were *more* than six inches across, but was afraid this might be regarded as a facetious question. Glancing around the class to see if anyone else looked like breaking the silence, I noticed that Tim Benton wasn't there. It was unusual for him to be absent and I wondered what had happened to him. Perhaps he was helping someone on an urgent job elsewhere in the Station.

I had no further chance of puzzling over Tim's whereabouts. For at that precise moment there was a sudden, sharp explosion, quite deafening in this confined space. And it was followed instantly by the terrifying, high-pitched scream of escaping air – air rushing through a hole that had suddenly appeared in the wall of the classroom.

Three
A PLAGUE OF PIRATES

For a moment, as the out-rushing air tore at our clothes and tugged us towards the wall, we were far too surprised to do anything except stare at the ragged puncture scarring the white paint. Everything had happened too quickly for me to be frightened: *that* came later. Our paralysis lasted for a couple of seconds: then we all moved at once. The sealing plate had been lying on Norman Powell's desk, and everyone made towards it. There was a moment of confused pushing, then Norman shouted above the shriek of air, 'Out of my way!' He launched himself across the room, and the air current caught him like a straw in a mill-race, slamming him into the wall. I watched in helpless fascination as he fought to prevent himself being sucked against the hole. Then, as suddenly as it had begun, the whistling roar ceased. Norman had managed to slide the seal into place.

For the first time, I turned to see what Commander Doyle had been doing during the crisis. To my astonishment he was still sitting quietly at his desk. What was more, there was a smile on his face – and a stop-watch in his hand. A dreadful suspicion began to creep into my mind – a suspicion that became a certainty in the next few moments. The others were also staring at him, and there was a long, icy silence. Then Norman coughed, and very ostentatiously rubbed his elbow where he had bruised it against the wall. If he could have managed a limp under zero gravity, I'm sure he'd have done so as he went back to his desk. When he had got there, he relieved his feelings by grabbing the elastic band that held his writing pad in place, pulling it away, and letting it go with a 'Thwack!' The Commander only kept on grinning.

'Sorry if you've hurt yourself, Norman,' he remarked. 'I really must congratulate you on the speed with which you acted. It only took you five seconds to get to the wall, which was very good when one allows for the fact that everybody else was getting in the way.'

'Thank you, sir,' replied Norman, with quite unnecessary emphasis on the 'sir'. I could see he still didn't like the idea of having a practical joke played on him, for a change. 'But wasn't it rather a dangerous – er – trick to play?'

'Not at all. If you want the technical details, there's a three-inch pipe around that hole, with a stop-cock at the end of it. Tim is sitting out there in a space-suit, and if we hadn't sealed the leak inside ten seconds, he'd have closed the tap and cut off the flow.'

'How was the hole made?' someone asked.

'Just a small explosive charge – a very small one,' replied the Commander. His grin had vanished and he had become quite serious again.

'I didn't do this just for fun. One day you may run into a real leak, and this test may make all the difference – you'll know what to do. As you've seen, a puncture this size can make quite a draught and could empty a room in half a minute. But it's easy enough to deal with if you act quickly and don't panic.'

He turned to Karl Haase, who, like the good student he was, always sat in the front row.

'Karl, I noticed you were the only one who never moved. May we know why?'

Karl answered without any hesitation in his dry precise voice.

'It was simple deduction. The chance of being hit by a large meteor at all is, as you had explained, inconceivably rare. The chance of being hit by one just when you'd finished talking about them was – well, so rare that it's nearly impossible. So I knew there was no danger, and that it must be some sort of test. That's why I just sat and waited to see what would happen.'

We all looked at Karl, feeling a little sheepish. I suppose he was right: he always was. It didn't help to make him any more popular.

One of the biggest excitements of life in a space-station is the arrival of the mail rocket from Earth. The great interplanetary liners can come and go, but they're nothing like so important as the tiny, bright yellow ships that keep the crews of the stations in touch with home. Radio messages are all very well, but they can't compare with letters and – above all – parcels from Earth.

The Station mail department was a cubby-hole near one of the air-locks, and a small crowd usually gathered here even before the rocket had coupled up. As soon as the mail bags came aboard, they would be ripped open and some high-speed sorting would take place. Then the crowd would disperse, everyone hugging his correspondence – or else saying, 'Oh, well, I wasn't expecting anything this time . . .'

The lucky man who got a parcel couldn't keep it to himself for long. Space mail is expensive, and a parcel usually meant one of those little luxuries you couldn't normally obtain on the Station.

I was very surprised to find that I had quite a pile of letters, most of them from perfect strangers, waiting for me after the first rocket arrived. The great majority were from boys of my own age who'd heard about me – or maybe had seen my TV appearances – and wanted to know all about life on the Station. If I'd answered every one, there'd have been no time for anything else at all. What was worse, I couldn't possibly *afford* to acknowledge them, even if I had the time. The postage would have taken all my spare cash.

I asked Tim what I'd better do about it. He looked at some of the letters and replied:

'Maybe I'm being cynical, but I think most of them are after space-mail stamps. If you feel you *ought* to acknowledge them, wait until you get back to Earth. It'll be much cheaper . . .'

And that was what I did, though I'm afraid a lot of people were very disappointed.

There was also a parcel from home, containing a good assortment of candy and a letter from Mom telling me to be quite sure and wrap up tight against the cold. I didn't say anything about the letter, but the rest of the parcel made me very popular for a couple of days.

There cannot be many people on Earth who have never seen the TV serial 'Dan Drummond, Space Detective'. Most of you, at some time or another, must have watched Dan tracking down interplanetary smugglers and assorted crooks, or have followed his never-ending battle with Black Jervis, most diabolical of space pirates.

When I came to the Station, one of my minor surprises was discovering how popular Dan Drummond was among the staff. If they were off duty – and often when they weren't – they never missed an instalment of his adventures. Of course they all pretended that they tuned in for the laughs, but that wasn't quite true. For one thing, 'Dan Drummond' isn't half as ridiculous as many of the other TV serials: in fact, on the technical side it's pretty well done and the producers obviously get expert advice, even if they don't always use it. There's more than a suspicion that someone aboard the Station helps with the script, but nobody has ever been able to prove this. Even Commander Doyle has come under suspicion, though it's most unlikely that anyone will ever accuse him outright...

We were all particularly interested in the current episode, as it concerned a space-station supposed to be orbiting Venus. Blackie's marauding cruiser, 'The Queen of Night', was running short of fuel, so the pirates were planning to raid the station and replenish their tanks. If they could make off with some loot and hostages at the same time, so much the better. When the last instalment of the serial had ended, the pirate cruiser, painted jet black, was creeping up on the unsuspecting station, and we were all wondering what was going to happen next.

Now of course there's never been such a thing as piracy in space, and as no one except a multi-million combine can afford to build ships and supply them with fuel it's difficult to see how Black Jervis could hope to make a living. This didn't spoil our enjoyment of the serial, but it sometimes caused fierce arguments about the prospects for spatial crime. Peter van Holberg, who spent a lot of his time reading lurid magazines and watching the serials, was sure that *something* could be done if one were really determined. He amused himself by inventing all sorts of ingenious crimes and asking us what was to stop one getting away with them. We rather felt that he had missed his true vocation.

Black Jervis's latest exploit made Peter unusually thoughtful, and for a day or so he went around working out just how valuable the contents of the Station would be to an interplanetary desperado. It made an impressive figure, especially when one included the freight charges. If Peter's mind hadn't already been working along these lines, he would never have noticed the peculiar behaviour of the 'Cygnus'.

Besides the spaceships on the regular, scheduled runs, about two or three times a month ships on special missions touched at the

Station. Usually they were engaged on scientific research, occasionally something really exciting like an expedition to the outer planets. Whatever it was they were doing, everyone aboard the Station always knew all about it.

But no one knew much about the 'Cygnus', except that she was down in Lloyd's Register as a medium freighter, and was about due to be withdrawn from service since she had been in operation for almost five years without a major overhaul. It attracted little surprise when she came up to the Station and anchored (yes, that's the expression still used) about ten miles away. This distance was larger than usual, but that might only mean that she had an ultra-cautious pilot. And there she stayed. All attempts to discover what she was doing failed completely. She had a crew of two – we knew that because they jetted over in their suits and reported on Control. They gave no clearance date and refused to state their business, which was unheard of but not illegal.

Naturally this started many theories circulating. One was that the ship had been chartered secretly by Prince Edward, who as everybody knew had been trying to get out into space for years. It seems the British Parliament wouldn't let him go, the heir to the throne being considered too valuable to risk on such dangerous amusements as space-flight. However, the Prince is such a determined young man that no one will be surprised if he turns up on Mars one day, having disguised himself and signed on with the crew. If he ever tries anything like this, he'll find plenty of people ready to help him.

But Peter, of course, had a much more sinister theory. The arrival of a mysterious and untalkative spaceship fitted in perfectly with his ideas on inter-planetary crime. If you wanted to rob a space-station, he argued, how else would you set about it?

We laughed at him, pointing out that the 'Cygnus' had done her best to arouse suspicion rather than allay it. Besides, she was a small ship and couldn't carry a very large crew. The two men who'd come across to the Station were probably all she had aboard.

By this time, however, Peter was so wrapped up in his theories that he wouldn't listen to reason, and because it amused us we let him carry on, and even encouraged him. But, of course, we didn't take him seriously.

The two men from the 'Cygnus' would come aboard the Station at least once a day to collect any mail from Earth and to read the papers and magazines in the rest room. That was natural enough, if they had nothing else to do, but Peter thought it highly suspicious. It proved, according to him, that they were reconnoitring the Station and getting to know their way around. 'To lead the way, I suppose,' said someone sarcastically, 'for a boarding-party with cutlasses.'

Then, unexpectedly, Peter turned up fresh evidence that made us take him a little more seriously. He discovered from the Signal Section that our mysterious guests were continually receiving messages from Earth, using their own radio on a waveband not allocated for official or commercial services. There was nothing illegal about that – they were operating in one of the 'free ether' bands – but once again it was distinctly unusual. *And they were using code.* That, of course, was very unusual, to say the least. Peter was naturally very excited at all this. 'It proves that there's something funny going on,' he said belligerently. 'No one engaged on honest business would behave like this. I won't say that they're going in for something as – well, old-fashioned – as piracy. But what about drug smuggling?'

'I should hardly think,' put in Tim Benton mildly, 'that the number of drug addicts in the Martian and Venusian colonies would make this very profitable.'

'I wasn't thinking of smuggling in *that* direction,' retorted Peter scornfully. 'Suppose someone's discovered a drug on one of the planets and is smuggling it back to Earth?'

'You got *that* idea from the last Dan Drummond adventure but two,' said somebody. 'You know, the one they had on last year – all about the Venus lowlands.'

'There's only one way of finding out,' continued Peter stubbornly. 'I'm going over to have a look. Who'll come with me?'

There were no volunteers. I'd have offered to go, but I knew he wouldn't accept me.

'What, all afraid?' Peter taunted.

'Just not interested,' replied Norman. 'I've got better ways of wasting my time.'

Then, to our surprise, Karl Haase came forward.

'I'll go,' he said. 'I'm getting fed up with the whole affair, and it's the only way we can stop Peter harping on it.'

It was against safety regulations for Peter to make a trip of this distance by himself, so unless Karl had volunteered he would have had to have dropped the idea.

'When are you going?' asked Tim.

'They come over for their mail every afternoon, and when they're both aboard the Station we'll wait for the next eclipse period and slip out.' That was the fifty minutes when the Station was passing through Earth's shadow: it was very difficult to see small objects at any distance then, so they had little chance of detection. They would also have some difficulty in finding the 'Cygnus', since she would reflect very little starlight and would probably be invisible from more than a mile away. Tim Benton pointed this out.

'I'll borrow a Beeper from Stores,' replied Peter. 'Joe Evans will let me sign for one.'

A Beeper, I should explain, is a tiny radar set, not much bigger than a hand-torch, which is used to locate objects that have drifted away from the Station. It's got a range of a few miles on anything as large as a space-suit, and could pick up a ship a lot farther away. You wave it around in space and when its beam hits anything you hear a series of 'Beeps'. The closer you get to the reflecting object, the faster the beeps come, and with a little practice you can judge distances pretty accurately.

Tim Benton finally gave his grudging consent for this adventure, on condition that Peter kept in radio touch all the time and told him exactly what was happening. So I heard the whole thing over the loudspeaker in one of the workshops. It was easy to imagine that I was out there with Peter and Karl, in that star-studded darkness, with the great shadowy Earth below me, and the Station slowly receding behind.

They had taken a careful sight of the 'Cygnus' while she was still visible by reflected sunlight, and had waited for five minutes after we'd gone into eclipse before launching themselves in the right direction. Their course was so accurate that they had no need to use the Beeper: the 'Cygnus' came looming up at them at just about the calculated moment, and they slowed to a halt.

46

'All clear,' reported Peter, and I could sense the excitement in his voice. 'There's no sign of life.'

'Can you see through the ports?' asked Tim. There was silence for a while, apart from heavy breathing and an occasional metallic click from the space-suit's controls. Then we heard a 'bump' and an exclamation from Peter.

'That was pretty careless,' came Karl's voice. 'If there's anyone else inside, they'll think they've run into an asteroid.'

'I couldn't help it,' protested Peter. 'My foot slipped on the jet control.' Then we heard some scrabbling noises as he made his way over the hull.

'I can't see into the cabin,' he reported. 'It's too dark. But there's certainly no one around. I'll go aboard. Is everything O.K.?'

'Yes: our two suspects are playing chess in the recreation room. Norman's looked at the board and says they'll be a long time yet.' Tim chuckled: I could see he was enjoying himself and taking the whole affair as a great joke. I was beginning to find it quite exciting.

'Beware of booby-traps,' Tim continued. 'I'm sure no experienced pirates would walk out of their ship and leave it unguarded. Maybe there's a robot waiting in the air-lock with a ray-gun!'

Even Peter thought this unlikely, and said so in no uncertain tones. We heard more subdued bumpings as he moved round the hull to the air-lock, and then there was a long pause while he examined the controls. They're standard on every ship, and there's no way of locking them from outside, so he did not expect much difficulty here.

'It's opening,' he announced tersely. 'I'm going aboard.'

There was another anxious interval. When Peter spoke again, he was much fainter owing to the shielding effect of the ship's hull, but we could still hear him when we turned the volume up.

'The control room looks perfectly normal,' he reported, more than a trace of disappointment in his voice. 'We're going to have a look at the cargo.'

'It's a little late to mention this,' said Tim, 'but do you realize that *you're* committing piracy, or something very much like it? I suppose the lawyers would call it "unauthorized entry of a spaceship without the knowledge and consent of the owners". Anyone know what the penalty is?'

Nobody did, though there were several alarming suggestions. Then Peter called to us again.

'This is a nuisance. The hatch to the stores is locked. I'm afraid we'll have to give up – they'll have taken the keys with them.'

'Not necessarily,' we heard Karl reply. 'You know how often people leave a spare set in case they lose the one they're carrying. They always hide it in what they imagine is a safe place, but you can usually deduce where it is.'

'Then go ahead, Sherlock. Is it still all clear at your end?'

'Yes: the game's nowhere near finished. They seem to have settled down for the afternoon.'

To everyone's extreme surprise, Karl found the keys in less than ten minutes. They had been tucked into a little recess under the instrument panel.

'Here we go!' shouted Peter gleefully.

'For goodness' sake don't interfere with anything,' cautioned Tim, now wishing he'd never allowed the exploit. 'Just have a look round and come straight home.'

There was no reply: Peter was too busy with the door. We heard the muffled 'clank' as he finally got it open and there were scrapings as he slid through the entrance. He was still wearing his space-suit, so that he could keep in touch with us over the radio. A moment later we heard him shriek: 'Karl! Look at this!'

'What's the fuss?' replied Karl, still as calm as ever. 'You nearly blew in my ear drums.'

We didn't help matters by shouting our own queries, and it was some time before Tim restored order.

'Stop yelling, everybody! Now, Peter, tell us exactly what you've found.'

I could hear Peter give a sort of gulp as he collected his breath.

'This ship is full of *guns*!' he gasped. 'Honest – I'm not fooling! I can see about twenty of them, clipped to the walls. And they're not like any guns I've ever seen before. They've got funny nozzles and there are red and green cylinders fixed beneath them. I can't imagine what they're supposed—'

'Karl!' Tim ordered. 'Is Peter pulling our legs?'

'No,' came the reply. 'It's perfectly true. I don't like to say this, but if there *are* such things as ray-guns, we're looking at them now.'

'What shall we do?' wailed Peter. He didn't seem at all happy at finding this support for his theories.

'Don't touch anything!' ordered Tim. 'Give us a detailed description of everything you can see, and then come straight back.'

But before Peter could obey, we all had a second and much worse shock. For suddenly we heard Karl gasp: 'What's that?' There was silence for a moment: then a voice I could hardly recognize as Peter's whispered: 'There's a ship outside. It's connecting up. What shall we do?'

'Make a run for it,' whispered Tim urgently – as if whispering made any difference. 'Shoot out of the lock as quickly as you can and come back to the Station by different routes. It's dark for another ten minutes – they probably won't see you.'

'Too late,' said Karl, still hanging on to the last shreds of his composure. 'They're already coming aboard. There goes the outer door now.'

Five
STAR TURN

For a moment no one could think of anything to say. Then Tim, still whispering, breathed into the microphone: 'Keep calm ! If you tell them that you're in radio contact with us, they won't dare touch you.'

This, I couldn't help thinking, was being rather optimistic. Still, it might be good for our companions' morale, which was probably at a pretty low ebb.

'I'm going to grab one of those guns,' Peter called. 'I don't know how they work, but it may scare them. Karl, you take one as well.'

'For heaven's sake be careful!' warned Tim, now looking very worried. He turned to Ronnie.

'Ron, call the Commander and tell him what's happening – quickly ! And get a telescope on the "Cygnus" to see what ship's over there.'

We should have thought of this before, of course, but it had been forgotten in the general excitement.

'They're in the control room now,' reported Peter. 'I can see them. They're not wearing space-suits, and they aren't carrying guns. That gives us quite an advantage.'

I suspected that Peter was beginning to feel a little happier, wondering if he might yet be a hero.

'I'm going out to meet them,' he announced suddenly. 'It's better than waiting in here, where they're bound to find us. Come on, Karl.'

We waited breathlessly. I don't know what we expected – anything, I imagine, from a salvo of shots to the hissing or crackling of whatever mysterious weapons our friends were carrying. The one thing we didn't anticipate was what actually happened.

We heard Peter say (and I give him full credit for sounding quite calm): 'What are you doing here, and who are you?'

There was silence for what seemed an age. I could picture the scene as clearly as if I'd been present – Peter and Karl standing at bay behind their weapons, the men they had challenged wondering whether to surrender or to make a fight for it.

Then, unbelievably, someone laughed. There were a few words we couldn't catch, in what seemed to be English, but they were swept away by a roar of merriment. It sounded as if three or four people were all laughing simultaneously, at the tops of their voices.

We could do nothing but wait and wonder until the tumult had finished. Then a new voice, sounding amused and quite friendly, came from the speaker.

'O.K., boys – you might as well put those gadgets down. You couldn't kill a mouse with them unless you swatted it over the head. I guess you're from the Station. If you want to know who we are, this is Twenty-First Century Films, at your service. I'm Lee Thomson, assistant producer. And those ferocious weapons you've got are the ones that Props made for our new interstellar epic. I'm glad to know they've convinced *somebody* – they always looked quite phoney to me.'

No doubt the reaction had something to do with it, for we all dissolved in laughter then. When the Commander arrived, it was quite a while before anyone could tell him just what had happened.

The funny thing was that, though Peter and Karl had made such fools of themselves, they really had the last laugh. The film people made quite a fuss of them and took them over to their ship, where they had a good deal to eat and drink that wasn't on the Station's normal menu.

When we got to the bottom of it, the whole mystery had an absurdly simple explanation. Twenty-First Century were going all out to make a real epic – the first *interstellar* and not merely interplanetary film. And it was going to be the first feature film to be shot entirely in space, without any studio faking.

All this explained the secrecy. As soon as the other companies knew what was going on, they'd all be climbing aboard the bandwagon. Twenty-First Century wanted to get as big a start as possible. They'd shipped up one load of props to await the arrival of the main unit with its cameras and equipment. Besides the 'ray-guns' that Peter and Karl had encountered, the crates in the hold contained some weird four-legged space-suits for the beings who were supposed to live on the planets of Alpha Centauri. Twenty-First Century were doing the thing in style, and we gathered that they had another unit at work on the Moon.

The actual shooting was not going to start for another two days, when the actors would be coming up in a third ship. There was much excitement at the news that the star was none other than Linda Lorelli – though we wondered how much of her glamour would be able to get through a space-suit. Playing opposite her in one of his usual tough, he-man roles would be Tex Duncan. This was great news to Norman Powell, who had a vast admiration for Tex and had a photograph of him stuck on his locker.

All these preparations next door to us were rather distracting, and whenever they were off-duty the Station staff would jump into suits and go across to see how the film technicians were getting on. They had unloaded their cameras, which were fixed to little rocket units so that they could move slowly around. The second spaceship was now being elaborately disguised by the addition of blisters, turrets and fake gun-housings to make it look (so Twenty-First Century hoped) like a battleship from another Solar System. It was really quite impressive.

We were at one of Commander Doyle's lectures when the stars came aboard. The first we knew of their arrival was when the door opened and a small procession drifted in. The Station Commander came first, then his deputy – and then Linda Lorelli. She was wearing a rather worried smile and it was quite obvious that she found the absence of gravity very confusing. Remembering my own early struggles, I sympathized with her. She was escorted by an elderly woman who seemed to be quite at home under zero 'g' and gave Linda a helpful push when she showed signs of being stuck.

Tex Duncan followed closely behind: he was trying to manage without an escort, and not succeeding very well. He was a good deal older than I'd guessed from his films – probably at least thirty-five. And you could see through his hair in any direction you cared to look. I glanced at Norman, wondering how he'd reacted to the appearance of his hero. He looked just a shade disappointed.

It seemed that everyone had heard about Peter and Karl's adventure, for Miss Lorelli was introduced to them and they all shook hands very politely. She asked several quite sensible questions about their work, shuddered at the equations Commander Doyle had written on the blackboard, and invited us all across to the Company's largest ship, the 'Orson Welles', for tea. I thought she was very nice – much better than Tex, who looked bored stiff with the whole business.

After this, I'm afraid, 'The Morning Star' was quite deserted – particularly when we found that we could make some money giving a hand on the sets. The fact that we were all used to weightlessness made us very useful, for though most of the film technicians had been into space before they were not very happy under zero 'g' and so moved slowly and cautiously. We could manage things much more efficiently, once we had been told what to do.

A good deal of the film was being shot on sets inside the 'Orson Welles', which had been fitted up as a sort of flying studio. All the scenes which were supposed to take place inside a spaceship were being shot here against suitable backgrounds of machinery, control boards, and so on. The really interesting sequences, however, were those which had to be filmed out in space.

There was one episode, we gathered, in which Tex Duncan would have to save Miss Lorelli from falling helplessly through space into the path of an approaching planet. As it was one of Twenty-First Century's proudest boasts that Tex *never* used stand-ins but actually carried out even the most dangerous feats himself, we were all looking forward to this. We thought it might be worth seeing, and as it turned out we were quite right . . .

I had now been on the Station a fortnight, and considered myself an old hand. It seemed perfectly natural to have no weight, and I had almost forgotten the meaning of the words 'up' and 'down'. Such matters as sucking liquids through tubes instead of drinking them from cups or glasses were no longer novelties but part of everyday life.

I think there was only one thing I really missed on the Station. It was impossible to have a bath, the way you could on Earth. I'm very fond of lying in a hot tub until someone comes banging on the door to make certain I haven't fallen asleep. On the Station you could only have a shower, and even this meant standing inside a fabric cylinder and lacing it tight round your neck to prevent the spray escaping. Any large volume of water simply formed a big globe which would float around until it hit a wall. When that happened, some of it would break up into smaller drops which would go on wandering off on their own – but most of it would spread all over the surface it had touched, making a horrid mess.

Over in the Residential Station, where there was gravity, they had baths and even a small swimming-pool. Everyone thought that this last idea was simply showing off.

The rest of the staff, as well as the apprentices, had come to take me for granted and sometimes I was able to help in odd jobs. I'd learned as much as I could, without bothering people by asking too many questions, and had filled four thick notebooks with information and sketches. When I got back to Earth, I'd be able to write a book about the Station if I wanted to.

As long as I kept in touch with Tim Benton or the Commander, I was now allowed to go more or less anywhere I liked. The place that fascinated me most was the observatory, where they had a small but powerful telescope that I could play with when one else was using it.

I never grew tired of looking at the Earth as it waxed and waned below. Usually the countries beneath us were clear of cloud, and I could get wonderfully distinct views of the lands over which we were hurtling. Because of our speed, the ground beneath was rolling back five miles every second. But as we were five hundred miles up, if the telescope was kept tracking correctly you could keep an object in the field of view for quite a long time, before it got lost in the mists near the horizon. There was a neat automatic gadget on the telescope mounting that took care of this: once you'd set the instrument on anything, it kept swinging at just the right speed.

As we swept round the world, I could survey in each hundred minutes a belt stretching as far north as Japan, the Gulf of Mexico and the Red Sea. To the south I could see as far as Rio de Janeiro, Madagascar and Australia. It was a wonderful way of learning geography, though because of the Earth's curvature the more distant countries were very much distorted and it was hard to recognize them from ordinary maps.

Lying as it did above the Equator, the orbit of the Station passed directly above two of the world's greatest rivers – the Congo and the Amazon. With my telescope I could see right into the jungles and had no difficulty at all in picking out individual trees and the larger animals. The great African Reservation was a wonderful place to watch, because if I hunted around I could find almost any animal I cared to name.

I also spent a lot of time looking outwards, away from Earth. Although I was, for all practical purposes, no nearer the Moon and planets than I had been down at home, now that I was outside the atmosphere I could get infinitely clearer views. The great lunar mountains seemed so close that I wanted to reach out and run my finger along their ragged crests. Where it was night on the Moon I could see some of the lunar colonies shining away like stars in the darkness. But the most wonderful sight of all was the take-off of a space-ship. When I had a chance, I'd listen to the radio and make a note of departure times. Then I'd go to the telescope, aim it at the right part of the Moon, and wait.

All I'd see at first would be a circle of darkness. Suddenly there'd be a tiny spark that would grow brighter and brighter. At the same time it would begin to expand as the rocket rose higher and the glare of its exhausts lit up more and more of the lunar landscape. In that brilliant blue-white illumination I could see the mountains and plains of the Moon, shining as brightly as they ever did in daylight. As the rocket climbed, the circle of light would grow wider and fainter, until presently it was too dim to reveal any more details of the land beneath. The ascending spaceship would become a brilliant, tiny star moving swiftly across the Moon's dark face. A few minutes later, the star would wink out of existence almost as suddenly as it had been born. The ship had escaped from the Moon, and was safely launched on its journey. In thirty or forty hours, it would be sweeping into the orbit of the Station and I would be watching its crew come aboard as unconcernedly as if they'd just taken a 'copter-ride to the next town.

I think I wrote more letters while I was on the Station than I did in a year at home. They were all very short, and they all ended: 'P.S.

Please send this cover back to me for my collection.' That was one way of making sure I'd have a set of Space-mail stamps that would be the envy of everyone in our district. I only stopped when I ran out of money, and a lot of distant aunts and uncles were probably surprised to hear from me.

I also did one TV interview – a two-way affair with my questioner down on Earth. It seems there'd been a good deal of interest roused by my trip up to the Station and everyone wanted to know how I was getting on. I told them I was having a fine time and didn't want to come back – for a while, at any rate. There were still plenty of things to do and see – and the Twenty-First Century film unit was now getting into its stride.

While the technicians were making their final preparations Tex Duncan had been learning how to use a space-suit. One of the engineers had got the job of teaching him, and we learned that he didn't think much of his pupil. Mr Duncan was too sure that he knew all the answers, and because he could fly a jet he thought handling a suit would be easy.

I got a ringside seat the day they started the free-space shots. The unit was operating about fifty miles away from the Station and we'd gone over in the 'Skylark' – our private yacht, as we sometimes called her.

Twenty-First Century had had to make this move for a rather amusing reason. One would have thought that now they had, at great trouble and expense, got their actors and cameras out into space they would have only had to go ahead and start shooting. But they found that it didn't work out that way. For one thing, the lighting was all wrong . . .

Above the atmosphere, when you're in direct sunshine, it's as if you had a single, intense spotlight playing on you. The sunward side of any object is brilliantly illuminated, the dark side utterly black. As a result, when you look at an object in space you can see only part of it: you may have to wait until it's revolved and been fully illuminated before you can get a picture of it as a whole.

One gets used to this sort of thing in time, but Twenty-First Century decided that it would upset audiences down on Earth. So they decided to get some additional lighting to fill in the shadows. For a while they even considered dragging out extra floodlights and floating them in space around the actors, but the power needed to compete with the Sun was so tremendous that they gave up the idea. Then someone said: 'Why not use mirrors?' That idea would probably have fallen through as well – if somebody else hadn't remembered that the biggest mirror ever built was floating in space only a few miles away.

The old solar power station had been out of use for over thirty years, but its giant reflector was still as good as new. It had been built in the early days of astronautics to tap the flood of energy pouring from the Sun, and to convert it into useful electric power. The main reflector was a great bowl almost three hundred feet across, shaped just like a searchlight mirror. Sunlight falling upon it was concentrated on to heating coils at the focus, where it flashed water into steam and so drove turbines and generators.

The mirror itself was a very flimsy structure of curved girders, supporting incredibly thin sheets of metallic sodium. Sodium had been used because it was light, and formed a good reflector. All these thousands of facets collected the sunlight and beamed it at one spot, where the heating coils had been when the station was operating. However, the generating gear had been removed long ago, and only the great mirror was left, floating aimlessly in space. No one minded Twenty-First Century using it for their own purpose if they wanted to. They asked permission, nicely, were charged a nominal rent and told to go ahead.

What happened then was one of those things that seems very obvious afterwards, but which nobody thinks of beforehand. When we arrived on the scene the camera crews were in place about five hundred feet from the great mirror, some distance off the line between it and the Sun. Anything on this line was now illuminated on both sides – from one direction by direct sunlight, from the other by light which had fallen on the mirror, been brought to a focus, and spread out again. I'm sorry if this all sounds a bit complicated, but it's important that you understand the set-up.

The 'Orson Welles' was floating behind the cameramen, who were playing round with a dummy to get the right angles when we arrived. When everything was perfect, the dummy would be hauled in and Tex Duncan would take its place. Everyone would have to work quickly, because they wanted the crescent Earth in the

57

background. Unfortunately, because of our swift orbital movement, Earth waxed and waned so quickly that only ten minutes in every hour were suitable for filming.

While these preparations were being made, we went into the power station control room. This was a large pressurized cylinder on the rim of the great mirror, with windows giving a good view in all directions. It had been made habitable and the air-conditioning brought into service again by one of our technicians – for a suitable fee, of course. They had also had the job of swinging the mirror round until it faced the Sun once more. This had been done by fixing some rocket units to the rim and letting them fire for a few seconds at the calculated times. Quite a tricky business, and one that could only be done by experts.

We were rather surprised to find Commander Doyle in the sparsely furnished control room. For his part, he seemed a little embarrassed to meet us. I wondered why he was interested in earning some extra money, since he never went down to Earth to spend it.

While we were waiting for something to happen, he explained how the station had operated, and why the development of cheap and simple atomic generators had made it obsolete. From time to time I glanced out of the window to see how the cameramen were getting on. We had a radio tuned in to their circuit, and the Director's instructions came over it in a never-ending stream. I'm sure he wished he were back in a studio down on Earth, and was cursing whoever had thought of this crazy idea of shooting a film in space.

The great concave mirror was a really impressive sight from here on its rim. A few of the facets were missing and I could see the stars shining through, but apart from this it was quite intact – and, of course, completely untarnished. I felt like a fly crawling on the edge of a metal saucer. Strangely enough, although the entire bowl of the mirror was being flooded with sunlight, it seemed quite dark from where we were stationed. All the light it was collecting was going to a point about two hundred feet out in space. There were still some supporting girders reaching out to the focus point, where the heating coils had been – but now they simply ended in nothingness.

The great moment arrived at last. We saw the air-lock of the

'Orson Welles' swing open, and Tex Duncan emerged. He had learned to handle his space-suit reasonably well – though I'm sure I could have done better if I'd had as much chance of practising.

The dummy was pulled away, the Director started giving his instructions, and the cameras began to follow Tex. There was extremely little for him to do in this scene except to make a few simple manoeuvres with his suit. He was, I gathered, supposed to be adrift in space after the destruction of his ship, and was trying to locate any other survivors. Needless to say Miss Lorelli would be among them, but she hadn't yet appeared on the scene. Tex had the stage – if you could call it that – all to himself.

The cameras continued shooting until the Earth was half full and some of the continents had become recognizable. There was no point in continuing then, for this would give the game away. The action was supposed to be taking place off one of the planets of Alpha Centauri, and it would never do if the audiences recognized New Guinea, India or the Gulf of Mexico. That would destroy the illusion with a bang.

There was nothing to do but wait for thirty minutes until Earth became a crescent again, and its tell-tale geography was hidden by mist or cloud. We heard the Director tell the camera crews to stop shooting and everyone relaxed. Tex announced over the radio, 'I'm lighting a cigarette – I've always wanted to smoke in a space-suit.' Somebody behind me muttered: 'Showing off again – serve him right if it makes him space-sick!'

There were a few more instructions to the camera crews, and then we heard Tex again.

'Another twenty minutes, did you say? Darned if I'll hang round all that time. I'm going over to look at that glorified shaving mirror.'

'That means us,' remarked Tim Benton in deep disgust.

'O.K.,' replied the Director, who probably knew better than to argue with Tex. 'But mind you're back in time.'

I was watching through the observation port and saw the faint mist from Tex's jets as he started towards us.

'He's going pretty fast,' someone remarked. 'I hope he can stop in time – we don't want any more holes in our nice mirror.'

Then everything seemed to happen at once. I heard Commander

Doyle shouting: 'Tell that fool to stop! Tell him to brake for all he's worth! He's heading for the focus – it'll burn him to a cinder!'

It was several seconds before I understood what he meant. Then I remembered that all the light and heat collected by our great mirror was being poured into that tiny volume of space towards which Tex was blissfully floating. It was equal to the heat, someone had told me, of ten thousand electric fires – and it was concentrated into a beam only a few feet wide. Yet there was absolutely nothing visible to the eye, no way in which one could sense the danger until it was too late. Beyond the focus the beam spread out again, soon to become harmless. But where the heating coils had been, in that gap between the girders, it could melt any metal in seconds. And Tex had aimed himself straight at the gap. If he reached it, he would last about as long as a moth in an oxy-acetylene flame . . .

Six
HOSPITAL IN SPACE

Someone was shouting over the radio, trying to send a warning to Tex. Even if it reached him in time, I wondered if he'd have sense enough to act correctly. It was just as likely that he'd panic and start spinning out of control, without altering his course at all.

The Commander must have realized this, for suddenly he shouted:

'Hold tight, everybody ! I'm going to tip the mirror!'

I grabbed the nearest hand-hold. Commander Doyle, with a single jerk of those massive forearms, launched himself across to the temporary control panel that had been installed near the observation window. He glanced up at the approaching figure and did some rapid mental calculations. Then his fingers flashed out and played across the switches of the rocket firing panel.

Three hundred feet away, on the far side of the great mirror, I saw the first jets of flame stabbing against the stars. A shudder ran through the framework all round us: it was never meant to be swung so quickly as this. Even so, it seemed to turn very slowly. Then I saw that the Sun was moving off to one side – we were no longer aimed directly towards it, and the invisible cone of fire converging from our mirror was now opening out harmlessly into space. How near it passed to Tex we never knew, but he said later that there was one brief, blinding explosion of light that swept past him and left him blinded for minutes.

The controlling rockets burned themselves out, and with a gasp of relief I let go my hand-hold. Although the acceleration had been slight – there was not enough power in these small units to produce any really violent effects – it was more than the mirror had ever been designed to withstand, and some of the reflecting surfaces had torn adrift and were slowly spinning in space. So, for that matter, was the whole power station: it would take a long period of careful juggling with the jets to iron out the spin that Commander Doyle had given it. Sun, Earth and stars were slowly turning all about us and I had to close my eyes before I could get any sense of orientation.

When I opened them again, the Commander was busily talking to the 'Orson Welles', explaining just what had happened and saying exactly what he thought of Mr Duncan. That was the end of shooting for the day – and it was quite a while before anyone saw Tex again.

Soon after this episode, our visitors packed their things and went farther out into space – much to our disappointment. The fact that we were in darkness for half the time, while passing through the shadow of the Earth, was too big a handicap for efficient filming. Apparently they had never thought of this, and when we heard of them again they were ten thousand miles out, in a slightly tilted orbit that kept them in perpetual sunlight.

We were sorry to see them go, because they had provided much entertainment – and we'd been anxious to see the famous ray-guns in action. To everyone's surprise, the entire unit eventually got back to Earth safely. But we're still waiting for the film to appear . . .

It was the end, too, of Norman's hero-worship. The photo of Tex vanished from his locker and was never seen again.

In my prowling around, I'd now visited almost every part of the Station that wasn't strictly 'Out of Bounds'. The forbidden territory included the power-plant – which was radioactive anyway, so that nobody could go into it – the Stores Section, guarded by a fierce quartermaster, and the Main Control Room. This was one place I'd badly wanted to go to: it was the 'brain' of the Station, from which radio contact was maintained with all the ships in this section of space, and, of course, with Earth itself. Until everyone knew that I could be trusted not to make a nuisance of myself, there was little chance of me being allowed in *here*. But I was determined to manage it some day, and at last I got the opportunity.

One of the tasks of the junior apprentices was to take coffee and light refreshments to the Duty Officer in the middle of his watch. This always occurred when the Station was crossing the Greenwich Meridian: since it took exactly a hundred minutes for us to make one trip around the Earth, everything was based on this interval and our clocks were adjusted to give a local 'hour' of this length. After a while one got used to being able to judge the time simply by glancing at the Earth and seeing which continent was beneath.

The coffee, like all drinks, was carried in closed containers (nicknamed 'milk bottles') and had to be drunk by sucking through a plastic tube – since of course it wouldn't pour in the absence of gravity. The refreshments were taken up to the Control Room in a light frame with little holes for the various containers, and their arrival was always much appreciated by the staff on duty – except when they were dealing with some emergency and were too busy for anything else.

It took a lot of persuading before I got Tim Benton to put me down for this job. I pointed out that it relieved the other boys for more important work – to which he retorted that it was one of the few jobs they *liked* doing. But at last he gave in.

I'd been carefully briefed, and just as the Station was passing over the Gulf of Guinea I stood outside the Control Room and tinkled my little bell. (There were a lot of quaint customs like this aboard the Station.) The Duty Officer shouted 'Come in!' I steered my tray through the door, and then handed out the food and drinks. The last milk bottle reached its customer just as we were passing over the African coast.

They must have known I was coming, because no one seemed in the least surprised to see me. As I had to stay and collect the empties, there was plenty of opportunity of looking round the Control Room. It was spotlessly clean and tidy, dome-shaped, and with a wide glass panel running right round it. Besides the Duty Officer and his assistant, there were several radio operators at their instruments, and other men working on equipment I couldn't recognize. Dials and TV screens were everywhere, lights were flashing on and off – yet the whole place was quite silent. The men sitting at their little desks were wearing headphones and throat microphones so that two people could talk without disturbing the others. It was fascinating to watch these experts working swiftly at their tasks – directing ships thousands of miles away, talking to the other space-stations or to the Moon, checking the myriads of instruments on which our lives depended.

The Duty Officer sat at a huge glass-topped desk on which glowed a complicated pattern of coloured lights. It showed the Earth, the orbits of the other Stations and the courses of all the ships in our part of space. From time to time he would say something quietly, his lips scarcely moving, and I knew that some order was winging its way out to an approaching ship – telling it to hold off a little longer, or to prepare for contact.

I dared not hang around once I'd finished my job, but the next day I had a second chance and, because things were rather slack, one of the assistants was kind enough to show me round. He let me overhear some of the radio conversations, and explained the workings of the great display panel. The thing that impressed me most of all, however, was the shining metal cylinder, covered with controls and winking lights, which occupied the centre of the room.

'This,' said my guide proudly, 'is HAVOC.'

'What?' I asked.

'Short for Automatic Voyage Orbit Computer.'

I thought this over for a moment.

'What does the *H* stand for?'

'Everyone asks that. It doesn't stand for anything.' He turned to the operator.

'What's she set up for now?'

The man gave an answer that consisted chiefly of mathematics, but I did catch the word 'Venus'.

'Right: let's suppose we wanted to leave for Venus in – oh, four hours from now.' His hands flicked across a keyboard like that of an overgrown typewriter.

I expected HAVOC to whirr and click, but all that happened was that a few lights changed colour. Then, after about ten seconds, a buzzer sounded twice and a piece of tape slid out of a narrow slot. It was covered with closely printed figures.

'There you are – everything you want to know. Direction of firing, elements of orbit, time of flight, when to start braking. All you need now is a spaceship!'

I wondered just how many hundreds of calculations the electronic brain had carried out in those few seconds. Space-travel was certainly a complicated affair – so complicated that it sometimes depressed me. Then I remembered that these men didn't seem any *cleverer* than I was: they were highly trained, that was all. If one worked hard enough, one could master anything.

My time on the Inner Station was now drawing to an end – though not in the way anyone had expected. I had slipped into the uneventful routine of life: it had been explained to me that nothing exciting ever happened up here and if I'd wanted thrills I should have stayed back on Earth. That was a little disappointing, and I'd hoped that something out-of-the-ordinary would take place while I was here – though I couldn't imagine what. As it turned out, my wish was soon to be fulfilled.

But before I come on to that, I see I'll have to say something about the other space-stations, which I've neglected so far.

Ours, only five hundred miles up, was the nearest to the Earth, but there were others doing equally important jobs at much greater distances. The farther out they were, the longer, of course, they took to make a complete revolution. Our 'day' was only a hundred minutes, but the outermost stations of all took twenty-four hours to complete their orbit – with curious results which I'll mention later.

The purpose of the Inner Station, as I've explained, was to act as a refuelling, repair and transfer point for spaceships, both outgoing and incoming. For this job, it was necessary to be as close to the Earth as possible. Much lower than five hundred miles would not have been safe – the last faint traces of air would have robbed the station of its speed and eventually brought it crashing down.

The Meteorological Stations, on the other hand, had to be a fair distance out so that they could 'see' as much of the Earth as possible. There were two of them, six thousand miles up, circling the world every six and a half hours. Like our Inner Station, they moved over the Equator. This meant that though they could see much farther north and south than we could, the polar regions were still out of sight or badly distorted. Hence the existence of the Polar Met. Station, which – unlike all the others – had an orbit passing over the Poles. Together, the three stations could get a practically continuous picture of the weather over the whole planet.

A good deal of astronomical work was also carried on in these stations, and some very large telescopes had been constructed here, floating in free orbit where their weight wouldn't matter.

Beyond the Met. Stations, fifteen thousand miles up, circled the biology labs and the famous Space Hospital. Here was carried out a great deal of research into zero-gravity conditions, and many diseases which were incurable on Earth could be treated. For example, the heart no longer had to work so hard to pump blood round the body, and so could be rested in a manner impossible on Earth.

Finally, twenty-two thousand miles out, were the three great Relay Stations. They took exactly a day to make one revolution – and therefore they appeared to be fixed for ever over the same spots on the Earth. Linked to each other by tight radio beams, they provided TV coverage over the whole planet. And not only TV, but all the long-distance radio and phone services passed through the Relay Chain, the building of which, at the close of the twentieth century, had completely revolutionized world communications.

One station, serving the Americas, was in Latitude 90 West. A second, in 30 East, covered Europe and Africa. The third, in 150 East, served the entire Pacific area. There was no spot on Earth where you could not pick up one or other of the Stations. And once you had trained your receiving equipment in the right direction, there was never any need to move it again. The Sun, Moon and planets might rise and set – but the three Relay Stations never moved from their fixed positions in the sky.

The different orbits were connected by a shuttle-service of small rockets which made trips at infrequent intervals. On the whole, there was little traffic between the various Stations – most of their business was done directly with Earth. At first I had hoped to visit some of our neighbours, but a few inquiries had made it quite obvious that I hadn't a chance. I was due to return home inside a week, and there was no spare passenger space available during that time. Even if there had been, it was pointed out to me, there were many more useful loads that could be carried . . .

I was in the 'Morning Star' watching Ronnie Jordan put the finishing touches to a beautiful model spaceship, when the radio called. It was Tim Benton, on duty back at the Station. He sounded very excited.

'Is that Ron? Anyone else there – what, only Roy? Well, never mind – listen to this, it's very important.'

'Go ahead,' replied Ron. We were both considerably surprised, for we'd never heard Tim really excited before.

'We want to use the "Morning Star". I've promised the Commander that she'll be ready in three hours.'

'*What!*' gasped Ronnie. 'I don't believe it!'

'There's no time to argue – I'll explain later. The others are coming over right away – they'll have to use space-suits, as you've got the "Skylark" with you. Now then, make a list of these points, and start checking . . .'

For the next twenty minutes we were busy testing the controls – those, that is, which would operate at all. We couldn't imagine what had happened, but were too fully occupied to do much speculating. Fortunately I'd got to know my way around the 'Morning Star' so thoroughly that I was able to give Ron quite a bit of help, calling meter readings to him, and so on.

Presently there was a bumping and banging from the airlock and three of our colleagues came aboard, towing batteries and power tools. They had made the trip on one of the rocket tractors used for moving ships and stores around the Station, and they'd brought two drums of fuel across with them – enough to fill the auxiliary tanks. From them we discovered what all the fuss was about.

It was a medical emergency. One of the passengers from a Mars–Earth liner which had just docked at the Residential Station had been taken seriously ill and had to have an operation within ten hours. The only chance of saving his life was to get him out to the Space Hospital – but unfortunately there were no ships available to make the journey. All the ships at the Inner Station were being serviced and would take at least a day to get space-worthy.

It was Tim who'd talked the Commander into giving us this chance. The 'Morning Star', he pointed out, had been very carefully looked after, and the requirements for a trip to the Space Hospital were really very trivial. Only a small amount of fuel would be needed, and it wouldn't even be necessary to use the main motors. The whole journey could be made on the auxiliary rockets.

Since he could think of no alternative, Commander Doyle had reluctantly agreed – on a number of conditions. We had to get the 'Morning Star' over to the Station under her own power so that she could be fuelled up – and *he* would do the piloting.

67

During the next hour, I did my best to be useful and to become accepted as one of the crew. My chief job was going over the ship and securing loose objects, which might start crashing round when power was applied. Perhaps 'crashing' is too strong a word, as we weren't going to use much of an acceleration. But anything adrift might be a nuisance, and could even be dangerous if it got into the wrong place.

It was a great moment when Norman Powell started the motors. He gave a short burst of power at very low thrust, while everyone watched the meters for signs of danger. We were all wearing our space-suits as a safety precaution. If one of the motors exploded, it would probably not harm us up here in the control-room – but it might easily spring a leak in the hull.

But everything went according to plan. The mild acceleration made us all drift towards what had suddenly become the floor. Then the feeling of weight ceased again, and everything was normal once more.

There was much comparing of meter readings, and at last Norman said: 'The motors seem O.K. Let's get started.'

And so the 'Morning Star' began her first voyage for almost a hundred years. It was not much of a journey, compared with her great trip to Venus. In fact, it was only about five miles from the 'graveyard' over to the Inner Station. Yet to all of us it was a real adventure – and, indeed, quite a heart-warming experience, for we were all very fond of the wonderful old ship.

We reached the Inner Station after about five minutes, and Norman brought the ship to rest several hundred yards away – he was taking no risks with his first command. The tractors were already fussing around, and before long the tow ropes had been attached and the 'Morning Star' was hauled in.

It was at this point that I decided I'd better keep out of the way. Rear of the workshop (which had once been the 'Morning Star's' hold) were several smaller chambers, usually occupied by stores. Most of the loose equipment aboard the ship had now been stuffed into these and lashed securely in place. However, there was still plenty of room left.

I want to make one thing quite clear. Although the word 'stowaway' has been used, I don't consider it at all accurate. No one had actually told me to leave the ship, and I wasn't hiding. If anybody had come through the workshop and rummaged around in the store room, they would have seen me. But nobody did, so whose fault was that?

Time seemed to go very slowly while I waited. I could hear distant, muffled shouts and orders, and after a while there came the unmistakable pulsing of the pumps as fuel came surging into the tanks. Then there was another long interval. Commander Doyle must be waiting, I knew, until the ship had reached the right point in her orbit around the Earth before he turned on the motors. I had no idea when this would be, and the suspense was considerable.

But at last the rockets roared into life. Weight returned: I slid down the walls and found myself really standing on a solid floor again. I took a few steps to see what it felt like – and didn't enjoy the experience. In the last fortnight I had grown so accustomed to the lack of gravity that its temporary return was a nuisance.

The thunder of the motors lasted for three or four minutes, and by the end of that time I was almost deafened by the noise, though I had pushed my fingers into my ears. Passengers weren't supposed to travel so near the rockets, and I was very glad when at last there was a sudden slackening in thrust and the roar that was surrounding me began to fade. Soon it ebbed into silence, though my head was still ringing and it would be quite a while before I could hear properly again. But I didn't mind that: all that really mattered was that the journey had begun – and no one could send me back.

I decided to wait for a while before going up to the Control Room. Commander Doyle would still be busy checking his course, and I didn't want to bother him while he was occupied. Besides, I had to think of a good story.

Everyone was quite surprised to see me. There was a complete silence when I drifted through the door and said: 'Hello! I think someone might have warned me that we were going to take off.'

Commander Doyle simply stared at me: for a moment I couldn't decide whether he was going to be angry or not. Then he said: 'What are *you* doing aboard?'

'I was lashing down the gear in the Store Room.'

He turned to Norman, who looked a little unhappy.

'Is that correct?'

'Yessir – I told him to do it. But I thought he'd finished.'

The Commander considered this for a moment. Then he said to me: 'Well, we've no time to go into this now. You're here and we'll have to put up with you.'

This was not very flattering: but it might have been much worse. And the expression on Norman's face was worth going a long way to see.

The remainder of the 'Morning Star's' crew consisted of Tim Benton, who was looking at me with a quizzical smile, and Ronnie Jordan, who avoided my gaze altogether. We had two passengers. The sick man was strapped to a stretcher which had been fixed against one wall, and must have been drugged for he remained unconscious for the whole journey. With him was a young doctor who did nothing but look anxiously at his watch and give his patient an injection from time to time. I don't think he said more than a dozen words during the whole trip.

Tim explained to me later that the sick man was suffering from an acute, and fortunately very rare, type of stomach trouble caused by the return of high gravity. It was very lucky for him that he had managed to reach the Earth's orbit: if he had been taken ill on the two months' voyage, the medical resources of the liner could not have saved him.

There was nothing for any of us to do while the 'Morning Star' swept outwards on the long curve that would bring her, after some three and a half hours, to the Space Hospital. Very slowly, Earth was receding behind us. It was no longer so close that it filled almost half the sky. Already we could see far more of its surface than was possible from the Inner Station, skimming low above the Equator. Northwards, the Mediterranean crept into view: then Japan and New Zealand appeared almost simultaneously over opposite horizons.

And still the Earth dwindled behind us. Now it was a sphere at last, hanging out there in space, small enough for the eye to take in the whole of it at one glance. I could see so far to the South that the great Antarctic ice cap was just visible, a gleaming white fringe beyond the tip of Patagonia.

We were fifteen thousand miles above the Earth, swimming into the path of the Space Hospital. In a moment we would have to use the rockets again to match orbits: this time, however, I should have a more comfortable ride, here in the sound-proof cabin.

Once again weight returned with the roaring rockets. There was one prolonged burst of power, then a series of short corrections. When it was all over, Commander Doyle unstrapped himself from the pilot's seat and drifted over to the observation port. His instruments told him where he was far more accurately than his eyes could ever do – but he wanted the satisfaction of seeing for himself. I also made for a port that no one else was using.

Floating there in space beside us was what seemed to be a great crystal flower, its face turned full towards the Sun. At first there was no way in which I could judge its true scale or guess how far away it was. Then, through the transparent walls, I could see little figures moving around, and could catch the gleam of sunlight on complex machines and equipment. The station must have been at least five hundred feet in diameter, and the cost of lifting all that material fifteen thousand miles from the Earth must have been staggering. Then I recalled that very little of it *had* come from Earth, anyway. Like the other stations, the Space Hospital had been constructed almost entirely from components manufactured on the Moon.

As we slowly drifted closer, I could see people gathering in the observation decks and glass-roofed wards to watch our arrival. For the first time, it occurred to me that this flight of the 'Morning Star' really was something of an event – all the radio and TV networks would be covering it. As a news-story, it had everything – a race for life, and a gallant effort by a long-retired ship. When we reached the Hospital, we would have to run the gauntlet.

The rocket-tractors came fussing up to us and the tow ropes started to haul us in. A few minutes later the airlocks clamped together and we were able to go through the connecting tube into the Hospital. We waited for the doctor and his still unconscious patient to go first, then went reluctantly forward to meet the crowd waiting to welcome us.

Well, I wouldn't have missed it for anything – and I'm sure the Commander enjoyed it as much as any of us. They made a huge fuss and treated us like heroes. Although I hadn't done a thing, and really had no right to be there at all (there were some rather awkward questions about that), I was treated just like the others. We were, in fact, given the run of the place.

It seemed that we would have to wait here for two days before we could go back to the Inner Station – there was no Earth-bound ship until then. Of course, we could have made the return trip in the 'Morning Star', but Commander Doyle vetoed this.

'I don't mind tempting Providence once,' he said, 'but I'm not going to do it again. Before the old lady makes another trip, she's going to be overhauled and the motors tested. I don't know if you noticed it, but the combustion chamber temperature was starting to rise unpleasantly while we were doing our final approach. And there were about six other things that weren't all they should have been. I'm not going to be a hero twice in one week: the second time might be the last.'

It was, I suppose, a reasonable attitude: but we were a little disappointed. Because of this caution the 'Morning Star' didn't get back to her usual parking place for almost a month, to the great annoyance of her patrons.

Hospitals are, I think, usually slightly depressing places – but this one was different. Few of the patients here were seriously ill, though down on Earth most of them would have been dead or completely disabled owing to the effect of gravity on their weakened hearts. Many were eventually able to return to Earth, others could only live safely on the Moon or Mars, and the severest cases had to remain permanently on the station. It was a kind of exile, but they seemed cheerful enough. The Hospital was a huge place, ablaze with sunshine, and almost everything that could be found on Earth was available here – everything, that is, that did not depend on gravity.

Only about half of the station was taken up by the Hospital: the remainder was devoted to research of various kinds. We were given some interesting conducted tours of the gleaming, spotless labs. And on one of these tours – well, this is what happened.

The Commander was away on some business in the Technical Section, but we had been invited to visit the Biology Department, which we were promised would be highly interesting. As it turned out, this was quite an understatement.

We'd been told to meet a Dr Hawkins on Corridor Nine, Biology Two. Now it's very easy to get lost in a space-station: since all the local inhabitants know their way around perfectly, no one bothers with signposts. We found our way to what we thought was Corridor Nine, but couldn't see any door labelled 'Biology Two'. However, there was a 'Biophysics Two', and after some discussion we decided that would be near enough. There would certainly be someone inside who could redirect us.

Tim Benton was in front, and opened the door cautiously.

'Can't see a thing,' he grumbled. 'Phew – it smells like a fishmonger's on a hot day!'

I peered over his shoulder. The light was very dim indeed, and I could only make out a few vague shapes. It was also very warm and moist sprays were hissing continuously on all sides. There was a peculiar odour that I couldn't identify at all – a cross between a zoo and a hothouse.

'This place is no good,' said Ronnie Jordan in disgust. 'Let's try somewhere else.'

'Just a minute,' exclaimed Norman, whose eyes must have become accustomed to the gloom more quickly than mine. 'What do you think! They've got a *tree* in here. At least, it looks like it – though it's a mighty queer one.'

He moved forward, and we drifted after him, drawn by the same curiosity. I realized that my companions probably hadn't seen a tree, or even a blade of grass, for many months. It would be quite a novelty to them.

I could see better now. We were in a very large room, with jars and glass-fronted cages all around us. The air was full of mist from countless sprays, and I felt as if we were in some tropical jungle. There were clusters of lamps all round, but they were turned off and we couldn't see the switches.

About forty feet away was the tree that Norman had noticed. It was certainly an unusual object. A slender, straight trunk rose out of a metal box to which were attached various tubes and pumps. There were no leaves, only a dozen thin, tapering branches drooping straight down, giving it a slightly disconsolate air. It looked like a weeping willow that had been stripped of all its foliage. A continual stream of water played over it from clusters of jets, and added to the general moistness of the air. I was beginning to find it quite difficult to breathe.

'It can't be from Earth,' said Tim, 'and I've never heard of anything like it on Mars or Venus.'

We had now drifted to within a few feet of the object – and the closer we got, the less I liked it. I said so, but Norman only laughed.

His laugh turned to a yell of pure fright. For suddenly that slender trunk leaned towards us, and the long branches shot out like whips. One curled around my ankle, another grasped my waist. I was too scared even to yell: I realized, too late, that this wasn't a tree at all – and its 'branches' were tentacles.

Seven
WORLD OF MONSTERS

My reaction was instinctive and violent. Though I was floating in mid-air and so unable to get hold of anything solid, I could still thrash around pretty effectively. The others were doing the same, and presently I came into contact with the floor so that I was able to give a mighty kick. The thin tentacles released their grip as I shot towards the ceiling. I just managed to grasp one of the light fittings in time to stop myself from crashing into the roof, and then looked down to see what had happened to the others.

They had all got clear, and now that my fright was subsiding I realized how feeble those clutching tentacles had really been. If we had been on solid ground with gravity to help us, we could have disengaged ourselves without any trouble. Even here, none of us had been hurt – but we were all badly scared.

'What the devil is it?' gasped Tim when he had recovered his breath and untangled himself from some rubber tubing draped along the wall. Everyone else was too shaken to answer. We were making our ways unsteadily to the door when there was a sudden flood of light, and someone called out: 'What's all the noise?' A door opened, and a white-smocked man came drifting in. He stared at us for a moment and said:

'I hope you haven't been teasing Cuthbert.'

'Teasing!' spluttered Norman. 'I've never had such a fright in my life. We were looking for Dr Hawkins and ran into this – this monster from Mars, or whatever it is.'

The other chuckled. He launched himself away from the door and floated towards the now motionless cluster of tentacles.

'Look out!' cried Tim.

We watched in fascinated horror. As soon as the man was within range, the slim tendrils struck out again and whipped round his body. He merely put up an arm to protect his face, but made no other movement to save himself.

'I'm afraid Cuthbert isn't very bright,' he said. 'He assumes that anything that comes near him is food, and grabs for it. But we're not very digestible, so he soon lets go – like this.'

The tentacles were already relaxing. With a gesture exactly like disdain, they thrust away their captive, who burst out laughing at our startled faces.

'He's not very strong, either. It would be quite easy to get away from him, even if he wanted to keep you.'

'I still don't think it's safe,' said Norman with dignity, 'to leave a beast like that around. What is it, anyway? Which planet does it come from?'

'You'd be surprised – but I'll leave Dr Hawkins to explain that. He sent me to look for you when you didn't turn up. And I'm sorry that Cuthbert gave you such a fright. That door should have been locked, but someone's been careless again.'

And that was all the consolation we got. I'm afraid our mishap had left us in the wrong mood for conducted tours and scientific explanations, but despite this bad start we found the Biology Labs quite interesting. Dr Hawkins, who was in charge of research here, told us about the work that was going on, and some of the exciting prospects that low gravity had opened up in the way of lengthening the span of life.

'Down on Earth,' he said, 'our hearts have to fight gravity from the moment we're born. Blood is being continually pumped round the body, from head to foot and back again. Only when we're lying down does the heart really get a good rest – and even for the laziest people that's only about a third of their lives. But here, the heart's got *no* work at all to do against gravity.'

'Then why doesn't it race, like an engine that's got no load?' asked Tim.

'That's a good question. The answer is – Nature's provided a wonderful automatic regulator. And there's still quite a bit of work to be done against friction, in the veins and arteries. We don't know yet just what difference zero gravity's going to make, because we haven't been in space long enough. But we think that the expectation of life out here ought to be well over a hundred years. It may even be as much as that on the Moon. If we can prove this, it may start all the old folk rushing away from the Earth!

'Still, all this is guesswork. Now I'm going to show you something which I think is just as exciting.'

He led us into a room with walls consisting almost entirely of glass cages, full of creatures which at first sight I could not identify. Then I gave a gasp of astonishment.

'They're flies! But – where did they come from?'

They were flies, all right. Only one thing was wrong – these flies were a foot or more in wing-span.

Dr Hawkins chuckled.

'Lack of gravity, again, plus a few special hormones. Down on Earth, you know, an animal's weight has a major effect on controlling its size. A fly this size couldn't possibly lift itself into the air. It's odd to watch these flying – you can see the wing-beats quite easily.'

'What kind of flies are they?' asked Tim.

'*Drosophila* – fruit flies. They breed rapidly, and have been studied on Earth for about a century and a half. I can trace this fellow's family tree back to around 1920!'

Personally, I could think of much more exciting occupations, but presumably the biologists knew what they were doing. Certainly the final result was highly impressive – and unpleasant. Flies aren't pretty creatures, even when normal size . . .

'Now there's a bit of a contrast,' said Dr Hawkins, making some adjustments to a large projection microscope. 'You can just about see this chap with the naked eye – in the ordinary way, that is.'

He flicked a switch, and a circle of light flashed on the screen. We were looking into a tiny drop of water, with strange blobs of jelly and minute living creatures drifting through the field of vision. And there in the centre of the picture, waving its tentacles lazily, was –

'Why,' exclaimed Ron, 'that's the creature that caught us!'

'You're quite right,' replied Dr Hawkins. 'It's called a hydra, and a big one is only about a tenth of an inch long. So you see Cuthbert didn't come from Mars or Venus – but from Earth. He's our most ambitious experiment yet.'

'But what's the idea?' asked Tim.

'Well, you can study these creatures much more easily when they're this size. Our knowledge of living matter has increased enormously since we've been able to do this sort of thing. I must admit, though, that we rather overdid it with Cuthbert. It takes a lot of effort to keep him alive, and we're not likely to try and beat this record.'

After that, we were taken to see Cuthbert again. The lights were switched on this time – it seemed that we'd stumbled into the lab during one of the short periods of artificial 'night'. Though we knew that the creature was safe, we wouldn't go very close. Tim Benton, however, was persuaded to offer a piece of raw meat, which was grabbed by a slim tentacle and tucked into the top of the long, slender 'trunk'.

'I should have explained,' said Dr Hawkins, 'that hydras normally paralyse their victims by stinging them. There are poison buds all along those tentacles – but we've been able to neutralize them. Otherwise Cuthbert would be as dangerous as a cageful of cobras.'

I felt like saying I didn't really think much of their taste in pets – but I remembered in time that we were, after all, guests here . . .

Another highlight of our stay at the Hospital was the visit to the Gravity Section. I've already mentioned that some of the space-stations produce a kind of artificial gravity by spinning slowly on their axes. Inside the Hospital they had a huge drum – a centrifuge – that did the same thing. We were given a ride in it, partly for fun and partly as a serious test of our reactions to having weight again.

The gravity chamber was a cylinder about fifty feet in diameter, supported on pivots at either end and driven by electric motors. We entered through a hatch in the side, and found ourselves in a small room that would have seemed perfectly normal down on Earth. There were pictures hanging from the walls, and even an electric light fitting suspended from the 'ceiling'. Everything had been done to create an impression, as far as the eye was concerned, that 'up' and 'down' existed again.

We sat in comfortable chairs and waited. Presently there was a gentle vibration and a sense of movement: the chamber was beginning to turn. Very slowly, a feeling of heaviness began to steal over me. My legs and arms required an effort to move them: I was a slave of gravity again, no longer able to glide through the air as freely as a bird . . .

A concealed loudspeaker gave us our instructions.

'We'll hold the speed constant now. Get up and walk around – but be careful.'

I rose from my seat – and almost fell back again with the effort. 'Gosh!' I exclaimed. 'How much weight have they given us? I feel as if I'm on Jupiter!'

My words must have been picked up by the operator, because the loudspeaker gave a chuckle.

'You're just half the weight you were back on Earth. But it seems a lot, doesn't it, after you've had none at all for a couple of weeks!'

It was a thought that made me feel rather unhappy. When I got down to Earth again, I'd weigh twice as much as this! Our instructor must have guessed my thoughts.

'No need to worry – you got used to it quickly enough on the way out, and it will be the same on the way back. You'll just have to take things easily for a few days when you get down to Earth, and try and remember that you can't jump out of top floor windows and float gently to the ground.'

Put that way, it sounded silly – but this was just the sort of thing I'd grown accustomed to doing here. I wondered how many spacemen had broken their necks when they got back to Earth . . .

In the centrifuge, we tried out all the tricks that were impossible under zero gravity. It was funny to watch liquids pour in a thin stream, and remain quietly at the bottom of a glass. I kept on making little jumps, just for the novel experience of coming down quickly again in the same place.

Finally we were ordered back to our seats, the brakes put on, and the spin of the chamber was stopped. We were weightless again – back to normal!

I wish we could have stayed in the Hospital Station for a week or so, in order to explore the place thoroughly. It had everything that the Inner Station lacked and my companions, who hadn't been to Earth for months, appreciated the luxury even more than I did. It was strange seeing shops and gardens – and even going to the theatre. *That* was quite an unforgettable experience. Thanks to the absence of gravity, one could pack a large audience into a small space and everyone could get a good view. But it created a very difficult problem for the producer, as he had to give an illusion of gravity somehow. It wouldn't do, in a Shakespeare play, for all the characters to be floating around in mid-air. So the actors had to use magnetic shoes – a favourite dodge of the old science-fiction writers, though this was the only time I ever found them used in reality.

The play we saw was 'Macbeth'. Personally, I don't care for Shakespeare and I only went along because we'd been invited and it would have been rude to stay away. But I was glad I went, if only because it was quite a tonic to see how the patients were enjoying themselves. And not many people can claim that they've seen Lady Macbeth, in the sleep-walking scene, coming down the stairs with magnetic shoes . . .

Another reason why I was in no great hurry to return to the Inner Station was simply this – in three days' time I'd have to go aboard the freighter scheduled to take me home. Although I'd been mighty lucky to get out here to the Space Hospital, there were still a lot of things I hadn't seen. There were the Met. Stations – the great observatories with their huge, floating telescopes – and the Relay Stations, another seven thousand miles farther out into space. Well, they would simply have to wait for another time.

Before the ferry rocket arrived to take us home, we had the satisfaction of knowing that our mission had been successful. The patient was off the danger list, and had a good chance of making a complete recovery. But – and this certainly gave the whole thing an ironic twist – it wouldn't be safe for him to go down to Earth. He'd come all those scores of millions of miles for nothing. The best he could do would be to look down on Earth through observation telescopes, watching the green fields on which he could never walk again. When his convalescence was over, he'd have to go back to Mars and its lower gravity.

The ferry rocket that came up to fetch us home had been diverted from its normal run between the Observatory Stations. When we were aboard, Tim Benton was still arguing with the Commander. No – arguing wasn't the right word: no one did *that* with Commander Doyle. But he was saying very wistfully, that it really was a great pity that we couldn't go back in the 'Morning Star'. The Commander only grinned and said: 'Wait until you see the report of her overhaul – then you may change your mind. I bet she needs new tube-linings, at the very least. I'll feel a bit happier in a ship that's a hundred years younger!'

Still, as things turned out, I'm pretty sure the Commander wished he'd listened to us...

It was the first time I'd been aboard one of the low-powered inter-orbit ferries – unless one includes our home-built 'Skylark of Space' in this category. The control cabin was much like that of any other spaceship, but from the outside the vessel looked very peculiar indeed. It had been built here in space and, of course, had no streamlining or fins. The cabin was roughly egg-shaped, and connected by three open girders to the fuel tanks and rocket motors. Most of the freight was not taken inside the ship but was simply lashed to what were rather appropriately called the 'luggage racks' – a series of wire-mesh nets supported on struts. For stores that had to be kept under normal pressure, there was a small hold with a second air-lock just behind the control cabin. The whole ship had certainly been built for efficiency rather than beauty.

The pilot was waiting for us when we went aboard, and Commander Doyle spent some time discussing our course with him. 'That's not his job,' Norman whispered in my ear, 'but the old boy's so glad to be out in space again that he can't help it.' I was going to say that I thought the Commander spent *all* his time in space: then I realized that, from some points of view, his office aboard the Inner Station wasn't so very different from an office down on Earth...

We had nearly an hour before take-off – ample time for all checks and last-minute adjustments that would be needed. I got into the nearest bunk to the observation port, so that I could look back at the Hospital as we dropped away from its orbit and fell down towards Earth. It was hard to believe that this great blossom of glass and plastic, floating here in space with the sun pouring into its wards, laboratories and observation decks, was really spinning round the world at eight thousand miles an hour. As I waited for the voyage to begin, I remembered the attempts I'd made to explain the space-stations to Mom. Like a lot of people, she could never really understand why they 'didn't fall down'.

'Look, Mom,' I'd said, 'they're moving mighty fast, going around the Earth in a big circle. And when anything moves like this, you get centrifugal force. It's just the same when you whirl a stone at the end of a string.'

'I don't whirl stones on the end of strings,' said Mom, 'and I hope you won't either – at least not indoors.'

'I was only giving an example,' I said impatiently. 'It's the one they always use at school. Just as the stone can't fly away because of the pull of the string, so a space-station has to stay there because of the pull of gravity. Once it's given the right speed, it'll stay there for ever without using any power. It can't *lose* speed, because there's no air-resistance. Of course, the speed's got to be calculated carefully. Near the Earth, where gravity's mighty powerful, a station has to move fast to stay up. It's like tying your stone on to a short piece of string – you have to whirl it quickly. But a long way out, where gravity's weaker, the stations can move slowly.'

'Yes,' said Mom. 'I knew it was something like that. But what worries me is this – suppose one of the stations *did* lose a bit of speed. Wouldn't it come falling down? The whole thing looks dangerous to me. It seems a sort of balancing act. If anything goes wrong –'

I hadn't known the answer then, so I'd only been able to say: 'Well, the *Moon* doesn't fall down, and it stays up just the same way.' It wasn't until I got to the Inner Station that I learned the answer, though I should have been able to work it out for myself. If the velocity of a space-station *did* drop a bit, it would simply move into a closer orbit. You'd have to carve off quite a lot of its speed before it came dangerously close to Earth – and it would take a vast amount of rocket braking to do this. It couldn't possibly happen by accident.

I looked at the clock. Another thirty minutes to go. Funny – why do I feel so sleepy now? – I had a good rest last night. Perhaps the excitement's been a bit too much. Well, let's just relax and take things easy – there's nothing to do until we reach the Inner Station in four hours' time. Or is it four days'? I really can't remember, but anyway it isn't important. Nothing is important any more – not even the fact that everything around me is half-hidden in a pink mist –

And then I heard Commander Doyle shouting. He sounded miles away, and though I had an idea that the words he was calling should mean something, I didn't know what it was. They were still ringing vainly in my ears when I blacked out completely: 'Emergency Oxygen!'

Eight
INTO THE ABYSS

It was one of those peculiar dreams when you know you're dreaming and can't do anything about it. Everything that had happened to me in the last few weeks was all muddled up together – as well as flashbacks from earlier experiences. Sometimes things were quite the wrong way round. I was down on Earth, but weightless, floating like a cloud over valleys and hills. Or else I was up in the Inner Station – but had to struggle against gravity with every movement I made.

The dream ended in nightmare. I was taking a shortcut through the Inner Station, using an illegal but widely practised method that Norman Powell had shown me. Linking the central part of the Station with its outlying pressurized chambers are ventilating ducts, wide enough to take a man. The air moves through them at quite a speed, and there are places where one can enter and get a free ride. It's an exciting experience, and you have to know just what you're doing or you may miss the exit and have to buck the airstream to find a way back. Well, in this dream I was riding the airstream, and had lost my way. There ahead of me I could see the great blades of the ventilating fan, sucking me down towards them. *And the protecting grill was gone* – in a few seconds I'll be sliced like a side of bacon . . .

'He's all right,' I heard someone say. 'He was only out for a minute. Give him another sniff.'

A jet of cold gas played over my face, and I tried to jerk my head out of the way. Then I opened my eyes and realized where I was.

'What happened?' I asked, still feeling rather dazed.

Tim Benton was sitting beside me, an oxygen cylinder in his hand. He didn't look in the least upset.

'We're not quite sure,' he said. 'But it's O.K. now. A change-over valve must have jammed in the oxygen supply when one of the tanks got empty. You were the only one who passed out, and we've managed to clear the trouble by bashing the oxygen distributor with a hammer. Crude, but it usually works. Of course it will have to be stripped down when we get back – someone will have to find out why the alarm didn't work.'

I still felt rather muzzy, and a little ashamed of myself for fainting – though that wasn't the kind of thing anyone could help. And, after all, I *had* acted as a sort of human guinea-pig to warn the others. Or perhaps a better analogy would be one of the canaries the old-time miners took with them to test the air underground.

'Does this sort of thing happen very often?' I asked.

'Hardly ever,' replied Norman Powell. For once he looked serious. 'But there are so many gadgets in a space-ship that you've always got to keep on your toes. In a hundred years we haven't got all the bugs out of space-flight. If it isn't one thing, it's another.'

'Don't be so glum, Norman,' said Tim. 'We've had our share of trouble for this trip. It'll be plain sailing now.'

As it turned out, that remark was about the most unfortunate that Tim ever made. I'm sure the others never gave him a chance to forget it.

We were now several miles from the Hospital – far enough away to avoid our jets doing any damage to it. The pilot had set his controls and was waiting for the calculated moment to start firing. Everyone else was lying down in their bunks: the acceleration would be too weak to be anything of a strain, but we were supposed to keep out of the pilot's way at blast-off and there was simply nowhere else to go.

The motors roared for nearly two minutes: at the end of that time the Hospital was a tiny, brilliant toy twenty or thirty miles away. If the pilot had done his job properly, we were now dropping down on a long curve that would take us back to the Inner Station. We had nothing to do but sit and wait for the next three and a half hours, while the Earth grew bigger and bigger until it once more filled almost half the sky.

On the way out, because of our patient, we hadn't been able to talk, but there was nothing to stop us now. There was a curious kind of elation, even light-headedness, about our little party. If I'd stopped to think about it, I should have realized that there was something odd in the way we were all laughing and joking – but at the time it seemed natural enough.

Even the Commander unbent more than I'd ever known him to before – not that he was ever really formidable once you'd got used to him. But he never talked about himself; and back at the Inner Station no one would have dreamed of asking him to tell the story of his part in the first expedition to Mercury. And if they had, he certainly wouldn't have done so – yet he did now. He grumbled for a while, but not very effectively. Then he began to talk.

'Where shall I start?' he mused. 'Well, there's not much to say about the voyage itself – it was just like any other trip. No one else had ever been so near the Sun before, but the mirror-plating of our ship worked perfectly and stopped us getting too hot by bouncing eighty per cent of the Sun's rays straight off again.

'Our instructions were not to attempt a landing unless we were quite sure it would be safe. So we get into an orbit a thousand miles up and began to do a careful survey.

'You know, of course, that Mercury always keeps one face towards the Sun, so that it hasn't days or nights as we have on Earth. One side is in perpetual darkness – the other in blazing light. However, there's a narrow 'twilight' zone between the two hemisphere where the temperature isn't too extreme. We planned to come down somewhere in this region, if we could find a good landing place.

'We had our first surprise when we looked at the day side of the planet. Somehow everyone had always imagined that it would be very much like the Moon – covered with jagged craters and mountain ranges. But it wasn't. There are no mountains at all on the part of Mercury directly facing the Sun – only a few low hills and great, cracked plains. When we thought about it, the reason was obvious. The temperature down there in that perpetual sunlight is over seven hundred degrees F. That's much too low to melt rock – but it can soften it, and gravity had done the rest. Over millions of years, any mountains that might have existed on the day side of Mercury had slowly collapsed, just as a block of pitch flows on a hot day. Only round the rim of the night land, where the temperature was far lower, were there any real mountains.

'Our second surprise was to discover that there were lakes down there in that blazing inferno. Of course, they weren't lakes of water, but of molten metal. Since no one's been able to reach them yet we don't know what metals they are – probably lead and tin, with other things mixed up with them. Lakes of solder, in fact! They may be pretty valuable one day, if we can discover how to tap them.

'As you'll guess from this, we weren't anxious to land anywhere in the middle of the day side. So when we'd completed a photographic map we had a look at the Night Land.

The only way we could do that was to illuminate it with flares. We went as close as we dared – less than hundred miles up – and shot off billion-candle-power markers one after another, taking photographs as we did so. The flares, of course, shared our speed and travelled along with us until they burned out.

'It was a strange experience, knowing that we were shedding light on a land that had never seen the Sun – a land where the only light for maybe millions of years had been that of the stars. If there was any life down there – which seemed about as unlikely as anything could be – it must be having quite a surprise ! At least, that was my first thought as I watched our flares blasting that hidden land with their brilliance. Then I decided that any creatures of the Night Land would probably be completely blind, like the fish of our own ocean depths. Still, all this was fantasy: *nothing* could possibly live down there in that perpetual darkness, at a temperature of almost four hundred degrees below freezing point. We know better now, of course . . .

'It was nearly a week before we risked a landing, and by that time we'd mapped the surface of the planet pretty thoroughly. The Night Land, and much of the Twilight Zone, is fairly mountainous, but there were plenty of flat regions that looked promising. We finally chose a large shallow bowl on the edge of the Day Side.

'There's a trace of atmosphere on Mercury, but not enough for wings or parachutes to be of any use. So we had to land by rocket braking, just as you do on the Moon. However often you do it, a rocket touch-down is always a bit unnerving – especially on a new world where you can't be perfectly sure that what *looks* like rock is anything of the sort.

'Well, it *was* rock, not one of those treacherous dust-drifts they have on the Moon. The landing gear took up the impact so thoroughly that we hardly noticed it in the cabin. Then the motors cut out automatically and we were down – the first men to land on Mercury. The first living creatures, probably, ever to touch the planet.

'I said that we'd come down at the frontiers of the Day Side. That meant that the Sun was a great, blinding disc right on the horizon. It was strange, seeing it almost fixed there, never rising or setting – though because Mercury's got a very eccentric orbit, the Sun does wobble to and fro through a considerable arc in the sky. Still, it never *dropped* below the horizon, and I always had the feeling that it was late afternoon and that night would fall shortly. It was hard to realize that "night" and "day" didn't mean anything here . . .

'Exploring a new world sounds exciting, and so it is, I suppose. But it's also darned hard work – and dangerous, especially on a planet like Mercury. Our first job was to see that the ship couldn't get overheated: we'd brought along some protective awnings for this purpose. Our 'sunshades', as we called them. They looked peculiar – but they did the job properly. We even had portable ones, like flimsy tents, to protect us if we stayed out in the open for any length of time. They were made of white nylon and reflected most of the sunlight, though they let through enough to provide all the warmth and light we wanted.

'We spent several weeks reconnoitring the Day Side, travelling up to twenty miles from the ship. That may not sound very far, but it's quite a distance when you've got to wear a space-suit and carry all your supplies. We collected hundreds of mineral specimens and took thousands of readings with our instruments, sending back all the results we could by tight-beam radio to Earth. It was impossible to go far enough into the Day Side to reach the lakes we'd seen – the nearest was over eight hundred miles away, and we couldn't afford the rocket fuel to go hopping around the planet. In any case it would have been far too dangerous to go into that blazing furnace with our present, untried equipment.'

The Commander paused, staring thoughtfully into space as if he could see beyond our cramped little cabin to the burning deserts of that distant world.

'Yes,' he continued at last, 'Mercury's *quite* a challenge. We can deal with cold easily enough, but heat's another problem. Yet I suppose I shouldn't say that, because it was the cold that got me, not the heat . . .

'The one thing we never expected to find on Mercury was life, though the Moon should have taught us a lesson. No one had expected to find it *there*, either. And if anyone had said to me, "Assuming that there is life on Mercury, where would you hope to find it?" I'd have replied, "Why, in the Twilight Zone, of course." I'd have been wrong again . . .

'Though no one was very keen on the idea, we decided we ought to have at least one good look at the Night Land. We had to move the ship about a hundred miles to get clear of the Twilight one, and we landed on a low, flat hill a few miles from an interesting-looking range of mountains. We spent an anxious twenty-four hours before we were sure that it was safe to stay. The rock on which the ship was standing had a temperature of minus three hundred and fifty degrees, but our heaters could handle the situation. Even without them on, the temperature in the ship dropped very slowly, because of course there was a near vacuum round us and our silvered walls reflected back most of the heat we'd lose by radiation. We were living, in fact, inside a large Thermos flask – and our bodies were also generating quite a bit of heat.

'Still, we couldn't learn much merely by sitting inside the ship: we had to put on our space-suits and go out into the open. The suits we were using had been tested pretty thoroughly on the Moon during the lunar night, which is almost as cold as it is on Mercury. But no test is ever quite like the real thing. That was why three of us went out. If one man got into trouble, the other two could get him back to the ship we hoped.

'I was in that first party: we walked slowly round for about thirty minutes, taking things easily and reporting to the ship by radio. It wasn't as dark as we'd expected, thanks to Venus. She was hanging up there against the stars, incredibly brilliant, and casting easily visible shadows. Indeed, she was too bright to look at directly for more than a few seconds: using a filter to cut down the glare, one could easily see the tiny disc of the planet.

'The Earth and Moon were also visible, forming a beautiful double star just above the horizon. They also gave quite a lot of light so we were never in complete darkness. But, of course, neither Venus nor Earth gave the slightest heat to this frozen land.

'We couldn't lose the ship, because it was the most prominent object for miles around and we'd also fixed a powerful beacon on its nose. With some difficulty we broke off a few small specimens of rock and carried them back with us. As soon as we took them into the air-lock, an extraordinary thing happened. They became instantly covered with frost, and drops of liquid began to form on them, dripping off to the floor and evaporating again. It was the air in the ship condensing on the bitterly cold fragments of stone. We had to wait half an hour before they had become sufficiently warm to handle.

'Once we were sure that our suits could withstand the conditions in the Night Land, we made longer trips, though we were never away from the ship for more than a couple of hours. We hadn't reached the mountains yet – they were just out of range. I used to spend a good deal of time examining them through the electronic telescope in the ship – there was enough light to make this possible.

'And one day, I saw something moving. I was so astonished that for a moment I sat frozen at the telescope, goggling foolishly through the eye-piece. Then I regained enough presence of mind to switch on the camera.

'You must have seen the film. It's not very good, of course, because the light was so weak. But it shows the mountain wall with a sort of landslide in the foreground – and there's something large and white scrabbling round among the rocks. When I saw it first it looked like a ghost and I don't mind saying that it scared me. Then the thrill of discovery banished every other feeling and I concentrated on observing as much as I could.

'It wasn't a great deal, but I got the general impression of a roughly spherical body with at least four legs. Then it vanished, and though I waited for half an hour it never reappeared.

'Of course we dropped everything else and had a council of war. It was lucky for me that I'd taken the film, as otherwise everyone would have accused me of dreaming. We all agreed we must try and get near the creature: the only question was whether it was dangerous.

'We had no weapons of any kind, but the ship carried a flare pistol which was intended for signalling. If it did nothing else, this should frighten any beast that attacked us. I carried the pistol, and my two companions – Borrell, the navigator, and Glynne, the radio operator – had a couple of stout bars. We also carried cameras and lighting equipment in the hope of getting some really good pictures. We felt that three was about the right number for the expedition: fewer might not be safe and – well, if the thing was *really* dangerous, sending the whole crew would only make matters worse.

'It was five miles to the mountains, and it took us about an hour to reach them. The ship checked our course over the radio and we had an observer at the telescope, keeping a search in the neighbourhood so that we'd have some warning if the creature turned up. I don't think we felt in any danger: we were all much too excited for that. And it was difficult to see what harm any animal could do to us inside the armour of our space-suits – as long as the helmets didn't get cracked. The low gravity, and the extra strength that it gave us, added to our confidence.

'At last we reached the rock slide – and made a peculiar discovery. Something had been collecting stones and smashing them up: there were piles of broken fragments lying around. It was difficult to see what this meant, unless the creature we were seeking actually found its food among the rocks.

'I collected a few samples for analysis while Glynne photographed our discovery and reported to the ship. Then we started to hunt around, keeping close together in case of trouble. The rock slide was about a mile across: it seemed that the whole face of the mountain had crumbled and slid downwards. We wondered what could have caused this, in the absence of any weather. Since there was no erosion, we couldn't guess how long ago the slip had occurred. It might have been a million years old – or a billion.

'Imagine us, then, scrambling across that jumble of broken rocks, with Earth and Venus hanging overhead like brilliant beacons, and the lights of our ship burning reassuringly down on the horizon. By now I had practically decided that our quarry must be some kind of rock-eater, if only because there seemed no other kind of food on this desolate planet. I wished I knew enough about minerals to determine what substance this was.

'Then Glynne's excited shout rang in my earphones.

'"There it is!" he yelled. "By that cliff over there!"

'We just stood and stared, and I had my first good look at a Mercurian. It was more like a giant spider than anything else – or perhaps one of those crabs with long, spindly legs. Its body was a sphere about a yard across, and was a silvery white. At first we thought it had four legs, but later we discovered that there were actually eight – a reserve set being carried tucked up close to the body. They were brought into action when the incredible cold of the rocks began to creep too far up the thick layers of insulating horn which formed its feet or hooves. When the Mercurian got cold feet, it switched to another pair!

'It also had two handling limbs, which at the moment were busily engaged in searching among the rocks. They ended in elaborate, horny claws or pinchers which looked as if they could be dangerous in a fight. There was no real head, but only a tiny bulge on the top of the spherical body. Later we discovered that this housed two large eyes, for use in the dim starlight of the Night Land, and two small ones for excursions into the more brilliantly illuminated Twilight Zone – the sensitive large eyes then being kept tightly shut.

'We watched, quite fascinated, while the ungainly creature scuttled among the rocks, pausing now and again to seize a specimen and smash it to powder with those efficient-looking claws. Then something that might have been a tongue would flash out, too swiftly for the eye to follow, and the powder would be gobbled up.

'"What do you think it's after?" asked Borrell. "That rock seems pretty soft. I wonder if it's some kind of chalk?"

'"Hardly," I replied. "It's the wrong colour – and chalk's only formed at the bottom of seas, anyway. There's never been free water on Mercury."

'"Shall we see how close we can get?" said Glynne. "I can't take a good photo from here. It's an ugly-looking beast, but I don't think it can do us any harm. It'll probably run a mile as soon as it sees us."

'I gripped the flare pistol more firmly and said: "O.K. – let's go. But move slowly, and stop as soon as it spots us."

'We were within a hundred feet before the creature showed any signs of interest in us. Then it pivoted on its stalk-like legs and I could see its great eyes looking at us in the faint moon-glow of

Venus. Glynne said, "Shall I use the flash? I can't take a good picture in this light."

'I hesitated, then told him to go ahead. The creature gave a start as the brief explosion of light splashed over the landscape, and I heard Glynne's sigh of relief. "That's *one* picture in the bag, anyway! Wonder if I can get a close-up ?"

"'No," I ordered, "that would certainly scare it – or annoy it, which might be worse. I don't like the look of those claws. Let's try and prove that we're friends. You stay here and I'll go forward. Then it won't think we're ganging up on it."

'Well, I still think the idea was good – but I didn't know much about the habits of Mercurians in those days. As I walked slowly forward the creature seemed to stiffen, like a dog over a bone – and for the same reason, I guessed. It stretched itself up to its full height, which was nearly eight feet, and then began to sway back and forth slightly, looking very much like a captive balloon in a breeze.

"'I should come back!" advised Borrell. "It's annoyed. Better not take any chances."

"'I don't intend to," I replied. "It's not easy to walk backwards in a space-suit, but I'm going to try it now."

'I'd retreated a few yards when, without moving from its position, the creature suddenly whipped out one of its arms and grabbed a stone. The motion was so human that I knew what was coming and instinctively covered my visor with my arm. A moment later something struck the lower part of my suit with a terrific crash. It didn't hurt me, but the whole carapace vibrated for a moment like a gong. For an anxious few seconds I held my breath, waiting for the fatal hiss of air. But the suit held, though I could see a deep dent on the left thigh. The next time I might not be so lucky, so I decided to use my "weapon" as a distraction.

'The brilliant white flare floated slowly up towards the stars, flooding the landscape with harsh light and putting distant Venus to shame. And then something happened that we weren't to understand until much later. I'd noticed a pair of bulges on either side of the Mercurian's body, and as we watched they opened up like the wing-cases of a beetle. Two wide, black wings unfurled – *wings*, on this almost airless world! I was so astonished that for a moment I was too surprised to continue my retreat. Then the flare slowly burned itself out, and as it guttered to extinction the velvet wings folded themselves and were tucked back into their cases.

'The creature made no attempt to follow, and we met no others on this occasion. As you can guess, we were sorely puzzled, and our colleagues back in the ship could hardly credit their ears when we told them what had happened. Now that we know the answer, of course, it seems simple enough. It always does . . .

'Those weren't really wings that we'd watch unfold, though ages ago, when Mercury had an atmosphere, they had been. The creature I'd discovered was one of the most marvellous examples of adaptation known in the Solar System. Its normal home is the Twilight Zone, but because the minerals it feeds on have been exhausted there it has to go foraging far into the Night Land. Its whole body has evolved to resist that incredible cold: that's the reason why it's silvery white, because this colour radiates the least amount of heat. Even so, it can't stay in the Night Land indefinitely: it has to return to the Twilight Zone at intervals, just as on our own world, a whale has to come up for air. When it sees the Sun again, it spreads those black wings, which are really heat absorbers. I suppose my flare must have triggered off this reaction – or maybe even the small amount of heat given off by it was worth grabbing.

'The search for food must be desperate for Nature to have taken such drastic steps. The Mercurians aren't really vicious beasts, but they have to fight among themselves for survival. Since the hard casing of the body is almost invulnerable, they go for the legs. A crippled Night-Lander is doomed, because he can't reach the Twilight Zone again before his stores of heat are exhausted. So they've learned to throw stones at each other's legs with great accuracy. My space-suit must have puzzled the specimen I met – but it did its best to cripple me. As I soon discovered, it succeeded rather too well.

'We still don't know much about these creatures, despite the efforts that have been made to study them. And I've got a theory I'd like to see investigated. It seems to me that, just as some of the Mercurians have evolved so that they can forage into the cold of the Night Land, there may be another variety that's gone into the burning Day Side. I wonder what *they'll* be like?'

The Commander stopped talking: I got the impression that he

didn't really want to continue. But our waiting silence was too much for him, and he carried on.

'We were walking back slowly to the ship, still arguing about the creature we'd met, when suddenly I realized that something had gone wrong. My feet were getting cold – very cold. The heat was ebbing out of my space-suit, sucked away by the frozen rocks beneath me.

'I knew at once what had happened. The blow my suit had received had broken the leg heater circuits – and there was nothing that could be done about it until I got back to the ship. And I had four miles still ahead of me . . .

'I told the others what had happened and we put on all the speed we could. Every time my feet touched the ground I could feel the appalling chill striking deeper. After a while all sensation was lost: that at least was something to be thankful for. My legs were just wooden stumps with no feeling at all, and I was still two miles from the ship when I couldn't move them any more. The joints of the suit were freezing solid . . .

'After that my companions had to carry me, and I must have lost consciousness for a while. I revived once while we were still some way from the end of that journey, and for a moment I thought I must be delirious. For the land all around me was ablaze with light: brilliant-coloured streamers were flickering across the sky: overhead, waves of crimson fire were marching beneath the stars. In my dazed state, it was some time before I realized what had happened. The Aurora, which is far more brilliant on Mercury than on Earth, had suddenly decided to switch on one of its displays. It was ironic, though at the time I could scarcely appreciate it. For although the land all around me seemed to be burning, I was swiftly freezing to death.

'Well, we made it somehow, though I don't remember ever entering the ship. When I came back to consciousness, we were on the way back to Earth. But my legs were still on Mercury.'

No one said anything for a long time. Then the pilot glanced at his chronometer and exclaimed: 'Wow! I should have made my course check ten minutes ago!' That broke the suspense, and our imaginations came rushing back from Mercury.

For the next few minutes the pilot was busy with the ship's

position-finding gear. The first space-navigators only had the stars to guide them, but now there were all sorts of radio and radar aids. One only bothered about the rather tedious astronomical methods when one was a long way from home, out of range of the Earth stations.

I was watching the pilot's fingers flying across the calculator keyboard, envying his effortless skill, when suddenly he froze over his desk. Then, very carefully, he pecked at the keys and set up his calculations again. An answer came up on the register – and I knew that something was horribly wrong. For a moment the pilot stared at his figures as if unable to believe them. Then he loosened himself from the straps holding him to his seat, and moved swiftly over to the nearest observation port.

I was the only one who noticed: the others were now quietly reading in their bunks or trying to snatch some sleep. There was a port only a few feet away from me and I headed for it. Out there in space was the Earth, nearly full – the planet towards which we were slowly falling.

Then an icy hand seemed to grip my chest: for a moment I completely stopped breathing. By this time, I knew, Earth should already be appreciably larger as we dropped in from the orbit of the Hospital. Yet unless my eyes deceived me, it was *smaller* than when I had last seen it. I looked again at the pilot, and his face confirmed my fears.

We were heading out into space.

Nine
THE SHOT FROM THE MOON

'Commander Doyle,' said the pilot, in a very thin voice. 'Will you come here a minute?'

The Commander stirred in his bunk.

'Confound it – I was nearly asleep!'

'I'm sorry, but – well, there's been an accident. We're – we're in an escape orbit.'

'What!'

The roar woke up everyone else. With a mighty heave the Commander left his bunk and headed for the control desk. There was a rapid conference with the unhappy pilot; then the Commander said: 'Get me the nearest Relay Station. I'm taking over.'

'What's happened?' I whispered to Tim Benton.

'I think I know,' said Tim, 'but wait a minute before we jump to conclusions.'

It was almost a quarter of an hour before anyone bothered to explain things to me – a quarter of an hour of furious activity, radio calls, and lightning calculations. Then Norman Powell, who like me had nothing to do but watch, took pity on my ignorance.

'This ship's got a curse on it,' he said in disgust. 'The pilot's made the one navigation error you'd think was impossible. He should have cut our speed by point nine miles a second. Instead, he applied power in exactly the wrong direction – we've *gained* speed by that amount. So instead of falling Earthwards, we're heading out into space.'

Even to me, it seemed hard to imagine that anyone could make such an extraordinary mistake. Later, I discovered that it was one of those things – like landing an aircraft with wheels up – that isn't as difficult to do as it sounds. Aboard a spaceship in free orbit, there's no way of telling in what direction and at what speed you're moving. Everything has to be done by instruments and calculations – and if at a certain stage a minus sign is taken for a plus, then it's easy to point the ship in exactly the wrong direction before applying power.

Of course, one is supposed to make other checks to prevent such mistakes. Somehow they hadn't worked this time, or the pilot hadn't applied them. It wasn't until a long time later that we found the full reason. The jammed oxygen valve, not the unhappy pilot, was the real culprit. I'd been the only one who had actually fainted, but the others had all been suffering from oxygen starvation. It's a very dangerous complaint, because you don't realize that there's anything wrong with you. In fact, it's rather like being drunk: you can be making all sorts of stupid mistakes, yet feel that you're right on top of your job.

But it was not much use finding why the accident had happened. The problem now was – what should we do next?

The extra speed we'd been given was just enough to put us into an escape orbit. In other words, we were travelling so fast that the Earth could never pull us back. We were heading out into space, somewhere beyond the orbit of the Moon – we wouldn't know our exact path until we got HAVOC to work it out for us. Commander Doyle had radioed our position and velocity, and now we had to wait for further instructions.

The situation was serious, but not hopeless. We still had a considerable amount of fuel – the reserve intended for the approach to the Inner Station. If we used it now, we could at least prevent ourselves flying away from Earth, but we should then be travelling in a new orbit that might take us nowhere near any of the space-stations. Whatever happened, we *had* to get fresh fuel from somewhere – and as quickly as possible. The short-range ship in which we were travelling wasn't designed for long excursions into space, and carried only a limited oxygen supply. We had enough for about a hundred hours: if help couldn't reach us by that time, it would be just too bad . . .

It's a funny thing, but though I was now in real danger for the first time, I didn't feel half as frightened as I did when we were caught by Cuthbert, or when the 'meteor' holed the classroom. Somehow, this seemed different. We had several days' breathing-space – literally! –

before the crisis would be upon us. And we all had such confidence in Commander Doyle that we were sure he could get us out of this mess.

Though we couldn't really appreciate it at the time, there was certainly something ironic about the fact that we'd have been quite safe if we'd stuck to the 'Morning Star' and not ultra-cautiously decided to go home on another ship . . .

We had to wait for nearly fifteen minutes before the computing staff on the Inner Station worked out our new orbit and radioed it back to us. Commander Doyle plotted our path and we all craned over his shoulder to see what course the ship was going to follow.

'We're heading for the Moon,' he said, tracing out the dotted line with his finger. 'We'll pass its orbit in about forty hours, near enough for its gravitational field to have quite an effect. If we like to use some rocket braking, we can let it capture us.'

'Wouldn't that be a good idea? At least it would stop us heading out into space.'

The Commander rubbed his chin thoughtfully.

'I don't know,' he said. 'It depends if there are any ships on the Moon that can come up to us.'

'Can't we land on the Moon ourselves, near one of the settlements?' asked Norman.

'No – we've not enough fuel for the descent. The motors aren't powerful enough, anyway – you ought to know that.'

Norman subsided, and the cabin was filled with a long, thoughtful silence that began to get on my nerves. I wished I could help with some bright ideas, but it wasn't likely they'd be any better than Norman's.

'The trouble is,' said the Commander at last, 'that there are so many factors involved. There are several *possible* solutions to our problem. What we want to find is the *most economical* one. It's going to cost a fortune if we have to call up a ship from the Moon, just to match our speed and transfer a few tons of fuel. That's the obvious, brute-force answer.'

It was a relief to know that there *was* an answer. That was really all that I wanted to hear. Someone else would have to worry about the bill.

Suddenly the pilot's face lit up. He had been sunk in gloom until now and hadn't contributed a word to the conversation.

'I've got it!' he said. 'We should have thought of it before! What's wrong with using the launcher down in Hipparchus? That should be able to shoot us up some fuel without any trouble – as far as one can tell from this chart.'

The conversation then grew very animated and very technical, and I was rapidly left behind. Ten minutes later the general gloom in the cabin began to disperse, so I guessed that some satisfactory conclusion had been reached. When the discussion had died away, and all the radio calls had been made, I got Tim into a corner and threatened to keep bothering him until he explained exactly what was going on.

'Surely, Roy,' he said, 'you know about the Hipparchus launcher?'

'Isn't it that magnetic thing that shoots fuel tanks up to rockets orbiting the Moon?'

'Of course: it's an electro-magnetic track about five miles long, running east and west across the crater Hipparchus. They chose that spot because it's near the centre of the Moon's disc, and the fuel refineries aren't far away. Ships waiting to be refuelled get into an orbit round the Moon, and at the right time they shoot up the containers into the same orbit. The ship's got to do a bit of manoeuvring by rocket power to "home" on the tank, but it's much cheaper than doing the whole job by rockets.'

'What happens to the empty tanks?'

'That depends on the launching speed. Sometimes they crash back on the Moon – after all, there's plenty of room for them to come down without doing any harm! But usually they're given lunar escape velocity, so they just get lost in space. There's even more room out *there*...'

'I see – we're going near enough to the Moon for a fuel tank to be shot out to us.'

'Yes: they're doing the calculations now. Our orbit will pass behind the Moon, about five thousand miles above the surface. They'll match our speed as accurately as they can with the launcher, and we'll have to do the rest under our own power: it'll mean using some of our fuel, of course – but the investment will be worth it!'

'And when will all this happen?'

'In about forty hours: we're waiting for the exact figures now.'

I was probably the only one who felt really pleased with the prospect, now that I knew we were reasonably safe. To the others, this was a tedious waste of time – but it was going to give me an opportunity of seeing the Moon at close quarters. This was certainly far more than I could have dared hope when I left Earth: the Inner Station already seemed a long way behind me . . .

Hour by hour Earth dwindled and the Moon grew larger in the sky ahead. There was very little to do, apart from routine checks of the instruments and regular radio calls to the various space-stations and the lunar base. Most of the time was spent sleeping and playing cards, but once I was given a chance of speaking to Mom and Pop, way back on Earth. They sounded a bit worried, and for the first time I realized that we were probably making headlines. However, I think I made it clear that I was enjoying myself and there was no real need for any alarm.

All the necessary arrangements had been made, and there was nothing to do but wait until we swept past the Moon and made our appointment with the fuel container. Though I had often watched the Moon through telescopes, both from Earth and from the Inner Station, it was a very different matter to see the great plains and mountains with my own unaided eyes. We were now so close that all the larger craters were easily visible, along the band dividing night from day. The line of sunrise had just passed the centre of the disc, and it was early dawn down there in Hipparchus, where they were preparing for our rescue. I asked permission to borrow the ship's telescope, and peered down into the great crater.

It seemed that I was hanging in space only fifty miles above the Moon. Hipparchus completely filled the field of vision – it was impossible to take it all in at one glance. The sunlight was slanting over the ruined walls of the crater, casting mile-long pools of inky shadow. Here and there upthrust peaks caught the first light of the dawn, and blazed like beacons in the darkness all around them.

And there were other lights in the crater shadows – lights arranged in tiny, geometric patterns. I was looking down on one of the lunar settlements: hidden from me in the darkness were the great chemical plants, the pressurized domes, the space-ports and the power stations that drove the launching track. In a few hours they would be clearly visible as the Sun rose above the mountains – but by then we should have passed behind the Moon and the Earthward side would be hidden from us.

And then I saw it – a thin bar of light stretching in a dead straight line across the darkened plain. I was looking at the floodlights of the launching track, ranged like the lamps along an arterial road. By their illumination, space-suited engineers would be checking the great electromagnets and seeing that the cradle ran freely in its guides. The fuel tank would be waiting at the head of the track, already loaded and ready to be placed on the cradle when the time arrived. If it had been daylight down there, perhaps I could have seen the actual launch. There would have been a tiny speck racing along the track, moving more and more swiftly as the generators poured their power into the magnets. It would leave the end of the launcher at a speed of over five thousand miles an hour – too fast for the Moon ever to pull it back. As it travelled almost horizontally, the surface of the Moon would curve away beneath it and it would swoop out into space – to meet us, if all went well, three hours later.

I think the most impressive moment of all my adventures came when the ship passed behind the Moon, and I saw with my own eyes the land that had remained hidden from human sight until the coming of the rocket. It was true that I had seen many films and photographs of the Moon's other side – and it was also true that it was very much the same as the visible face. Yet somehow the thrill remained. I thought of all the astronomers who had spent their lives charting the Moon, and had never seen the land over which I was now passing. What would they have given for the opportunity that had now come to me – and come quite by chance, without any real effort on my part!

I had almost forgotten Earth when Tim Benton drew my attention to it again. It was sinking swiftly towards the lunar horizon: the Moon was rising up to eclipse it as we swept along in our great arc. A blinding blue-green crescent – the South Polar cap – almost too brilliant to look upon, the reflection of the sun forming a pool of fire in the Pacific Ocean – that was my home, now a quarter of a million miles away. I watched it drop behind the cruel lower peaks until only the faint, misty rim was visible: then even this disappeared. The Sun was still with us – but Earth had gone. Until this moment it had always been with us in the sky, part of the background of things. Now I had only Sun, Moon and stars.

The fuel container was already on its way up to meet us. It had been launched an hour ago, and we had been told by radio that it was proceeding on the correct orbit. The Moon's gravitational field would curve its path and we would pass within a few hundred miles of it. Our job then was to match speeds by careful use of our remaining fuel and, when we had coupled our ship up to the tank, pump across its contents. Then we could turn for home and the empty container would coast on out into space, to join the rest of the debris circulating in the Solar System.

'But just suppose,' I said anxiously to Norman Powell, 'that they score a direct hit on us! After all, the whole thing's rather like shooting a gun at a target. And *we're* the target.'

Norman laughed.

'It'll be moving very slowly when it comes up to us, and we'll spot it in our radar when it's a long way off. So there's no danger of a collision. By the time it is really close, we'll have matched speeds and if we bump it'll be about as violent as two snowflakes meeting head-on.'

That was reassuring, though I still didn't really like the idea of this projectile from the Moon tearing up at us through space . . .

We picked up the signals from the fuel container when it was still a thousand miles away – not with our radar, but thanks to the tiny radio beacon that all these missiles carried to aid their detection. After this I kept out of the way while Commander Doyle and the pilot made our rendezvous in space. It was a delicate operation, this jockeying of a ship until it matched the course of the still-invisible projectile. Our fuel reserves were too slim to permit of many more mistakes, and everyone breathed a great sigh of relief when the stubby, shining cylinder was hanging beside us.

The transfer took only about ten minutes, and when our pumps had finished their work the Earth had emerged from behind the Moon's shield. It seemed a good omen: we were once more masters of the situation – and in sight of home again.

I was watching the radar screen – because no one else wanted to use it – when we turned on the motors again. The empty fuel container, which had now been uncoupled, seemed to fall slowly astern. Actually, of course, it was *we* who were falling back – checking our speed to return Earthwards. The fuel capsule would go shooting on out into space, thrown away now that its task was completed.

The extreme range of our radar was about five hundred miles, and I watched a bright spot representing the fuel container drift slowly towards the edge of the screen. It was the only object near enough to produce an echo. The volume of space which our beams were sweeping probably contained quite a number of meteors, but they were far too small to produce a visible signal. Yet there was something fascinating about watching even this almost empty screen – empty, that is, apart from an occasional sparkle of light caused by electrical interference. It made me visualize the thousand-mile-diameter globe at whose centre we were travelling. Nothing of any size could enter that globe without our invisible radio fingers detecting it and giving the alarm.

We were now safely back on course, no longer racing out into space. Commander Doyle had decided not to return directly to the Inner Station, because our oxygen reserve was getting low. Instead, we would home on one of the three Relay Stations, twenty-two thousand miles above the Earth. The ship could be reprovisioned there before we continued the last lap of our journey.

I was just about to switch off the radar screen when I saw a faint spark of light at extreme range. It vanished a second later as our beam moved into another sector of space, and I waited until it had swept through the complete cycle, wondering if I'd been mistaken. Were there any other spaceships around here? It was quite possible, of course.

There was no doubt about it – the spark appeared again, in the same position. I knew how to work the scanner controls, and stopped the beam sweeping, so that it locked on to the distant echo. It was just under five hundred miles away, moving very slowly with respect to us. I looked at it thoughtfully for a few seconds, and then called Tim. It was probably not important enough to bother the Commander. However, there was just the chance that it was a really large meteor, and they were always worth investigating. One that gave an echo this size would be much too big to bring home, but we might be able to chip bits off it for souvenirs – if we matched speed with it, of course.

Tim started the scanner going as soon as I handed over the controls. He thought I'd picked up our discarded fuel container again – which annoyed me since it showed little faith in my commonsense. But he soon saw that it was in a completely different part of the sky and his scepticism vanished.

'It must be a space-ship,' he said, 'though it doesn't seem a large enough echo for that. We'll soon find out – if it's a ship, it'll be carrying a radio beacon.'

He tuned our receiver to the beacon frequency, but without result. There were a few ships at great distances in other parts of the sky, but nothing as close as this.

Norman had now joined us and was looking over Tim's shoulder.

'If it's a meteor,' he said, 'let's hope it's a nice lump of platinum or something equally valuable. Then we can retire for life.'

'Hey!' I exclaimed, '*I* found it!'

'I don't think that counts. You're not on the crew and shouldn't be here anyway.'

'Don't worry,' said Tim, 'no one's ever found anything except iron in meteors – in any quantity, that is. The most you can expect to run across out here is a chunk of nickel-steel, probably so tough that you won't even be able to saw off a piece as a souvenir.'

By now we had worked out the course of the object, and discovered that it would pass within twenty miles of us. If we wished to make contact, we'd have to change our velocity by about two hundred miles an hour – not much, but it would waste some of our hard-won fuel and the Commander certainly wouldn't allow it, if it was merely a question of satisfying our curiosity.

'How big would it have to be,' I asked, 'to produce an echo this bright?'

'You can't tell,' said Tim. 'It depends what it's made of – and the way it's pointing. A space-ship could produce a signal as small as that, if we were only seeing it end-on.'

'I think I've found it,' said Norman suddenly. 'And it *isn't* a meteor. You have a look.'

He had been searching with the ship's telescope, and I took his place at the eyepiece, getting there just ahead of Tim. Against a background of faint stars a roughly cylindrical object, brilliantly lit by the sunlight, was very slowly revolving in space. Even at first glance I could see it was artificial. When I had watched it turn through a complete revolution, I could see that it was streamlined and had a pointed nose. It looked much more like an old-time artillery shell than a modern rocket. The fact that it was streamlined meant that it couldn't be an empty fuel container from the launcher in Hipparchus: the tanks it shot up were plain, stubby cylinders, since streamlining was no use on the airless Moon.

Commander Doyle stared through the telescope for a long time when we called him over. Finally, to my joy, he remarked: 'Whatever it is, we'd better have a look at it and make a report. We can spare the fuel and it will only take a few minutes.'

Our ship spun round in space as we began to make the course-correction. The rockets fired for a few seconds, our new path was rechecked, and the rockets operated again. After several shorter bursts, we had come to within a mile of the mysterious object and began to edge towards it under the gentle impulse of the steering jets alone. Through all these manoeuvres it was impossible to use the telescope, so when I next saw my discovery it was only a hundred yards beyond our port, very gently approaching us.

It was artificial all right, and a rocket of some kind. What it was doing out here near the Moon we could only guess, and several theories were put forward. Since it was only about ten feet long, it might be one of the automatic reconnaissance missiles sent out in the early days of space-flight. Commander Doyle didn't think this likely: as far as he knew, they'd all been accounted for. Besides, it seemed to have none of the radio and TV equipment such missiles would carry.

It was painted a very bright red – an odd colour, I thought, for anything in space. There was some lettering on the side – apparently in English, though I couldn't make out the words at this distance. As the projectile slowly revolved, a black pattern on a white background came into view, but went out of sight before I could interpret it. I waited until it came into view again: by this time the little rocket had drifted considerably closer, and was now only fifty feet away.

'I don't like the look of the thing,' Tim Benton said, half to himself. 'That colour, for instance – red's the sign of danger.'

'Don't be an old woman,' scoffed Norman. 'If it was a bomb or something like that, it certainly wouldn't advertise the fact.'

Then the pattern I'd glimpsed before swam back into view. Even on the first sight, there had been something uncomfortably familiar about it. Now there was no longer any doubt.

Clearly painted on the side of the slowly approaching missile was the symbol of Death – the skull and crossbones.

Ten
RADIO SATELLITE

Commander Doyle must have seen that ominous warning as quickly as we did, for an instant later our rockets thundered briefly. The crimson missile veered slowly aside and started to recede once more into space. At the moment of closest approach, I was able to read the words painted below the skull and crossbones – and I understood. The notice read:

WARNING!
RADIOACTIVE WASTE!
ATOMIC ENERGY COMMISSION

'I wish we'd got a Geiger counter on board,' said the Commander thoughtfully. 'Still, by this time it can't be very dangerous and I don't expect we've had much of a dose. But we'll all have to have a blood-count when we get back to base.'

'How long do you think it's been up here, Sir?' asked Norman.

'Let's think – I believe they started getting rid of dangerous waste this way back in the 1970s. They didn't do it for long – the Space Corporations soon put a stop to it! Nowadays, of course, we know how to deal with all the by-products of the atomic piles, but back in the early days there were a lot of radio-isotopes they couldn't handle. Rather a drastic way of getting rid of them – and a short-sighted solution, too !'

'I've heard about these waste-containers,' said Tim, 'but I thought they'd all been collected and the stuff in them buried somewhere on the Moon.'

'Not this one, apparently. But it soon will be when we report it. Good work, Malcolm ! You've done your bit to make space safer !'

I was pleased at the compliment, though still a little worried lest we'd received a dangerous dose of radiation from the decaying isotopes in the celestial coffin. Luckily my fears turned out to be groundless – we had left the neighbourhood too quickly to come to any harm.

We also discovered, a good while later, the history of this stray missile. The Atomic Energy Commission is still a bit ashamed of this episode in its history, and it was some time before it gave the whole story. Finally it admitted the despatch of a waste-container in 1981 that had been intended to crash on the Moon but had never done so. The astronomers had a lot of fun working out how the thing had got into the orbit where we found it – it was a complicated story involving the gravities of the Earth, Sun and Moon.

Our detour had not lost us a great deal of time, and we were only a few minutes behind schedule when we came sweeping into the orbit of Relay Station Two – the one that sits above Latitude 30 East, over the middle of Africa. I was now used to seeing peculiar objects in space, so the first sight of the Station didn't surprise me in the least. It consisted of a flat rectangular lattice-work, with one side facing the Earth. Covering this face were hundreds of small, concave reflectors – the focusing systems that beamed the radio signals to the planet beneath, or collected them on the way up.

We approached cautiously, making contact with the back of the Station. A pilot who let his ship pass in front of it was very unpopular – as he might cause a temporary failure on thousands of circuits, as he blocked the radio beams. For the whole of the planet's long-distance services, and most of the radio and TV networks, were routed through the Relay Stations. As I looked more closely, I saw that there were two other sets of radio reflector systems, aimed not at Earth but in the two directions sixty degrees away from it. These were handling the beams to the other two stations, so that altogether the three formed a vast triangle, slowly rotating with the turning Earth.

We spent only twelve hours at the Relay Station, while our ship was overhauled and reprovisioned. I never saw the pilot again, though I heard later that he had been partly exonerated from blame. When we continued our interrupted journey, it was with a fresh captain who showed no willingness to talk about his colleague's fate. Space pilots seem to form a very select and exclusive club: they never let each other down or discuss each other's mistakes – at least, not with people outside their trade union. I suppose you can hardly blame them, since theirs is one of the most responsible jobs that exist.

The living arrangements aboard the Relay Station were much the same as on the Inner Station, so I won't spend any time describing them. In any case, we weren't there long enough to see much of the place, and everyone was too busy to waste time showing us around. The TV people did ask us to make one appearance to describe our adventures since leaving the Hospital. The interview took place in a makeshift studio so tiny that it wouldn't hold us all, and we had to slip in quietly one by one when a signal was given. It seemed funny to find no better arrangements here at the very heart of the world's TV network. Still, it was reasonable enough – a 'live' broadcast from the Relay Station was a very rare event indeed.

We also had a brief glimpse of the main switch-room, though I'm afraid it didn't mean a great deal to us. There were acres of dials and coloured lights, with men sitting here and there looking at screens and turning knobs. Loudspeakers were talking softly in every language: as we went from one operator to another we saw football games, string quartets, air races, ice-hockey, art displays, puppet shows, grand opera – a cross-section of the world's entertainment. And it now all depended on these three tiny metal rafts, twenty-two thousand miles up in the sky. As I looked at *some* of the programmes that were going out, I wondered if it was really worth it . . .

Not all the Relay Station's business was concerned with Earth, by any means. The interplanetary circuits passed through here: if Mars wished to call Venus, it was sometimes convenient to route messages through the Earth Relays. We listened to some of these messages – nearly all high-speed telegraphy, so they didn't mean anything to us. Because it takes several minutes for radio waves to bridge the gulf between even the nearest planets, you can't have conversation with someone on another world. (Except the Moon – and even there you have to put up with an annoying time-lag of nearly three seconds before you can get any answer.) The only speech that was coming over the Martian circuit was a talk beamed to Earth for rebroadcasting by a radio commentator. He was discussing local politics and the last season's crop. It all sounded rather dull . . .

Though I was only there such a short time, one thing about the Relay Station did impress me very strongly. Everywhere else I'd been, one could look 'down' at the Earth and watch it turning on its axis, bringing new continents into view with the passing hours. But here, there was no such change. The Earth kept the same face turned forever towards the Station. It was true that night and day passed across the planet beneath – but with every dawn and sunset, the Station was still in exactly the same place. It was poised eternally above a spot in Uganda, two hundred miles from Lake Victoria. Because of this, it was hard to believe that the Station was moving at all – though actually it was travelling round the Earth at over six thousand miles an hour. But, of course, because it took exactly one day to make the circuit, it would remain hanging over Africa for ever – just as the other two stations hung over the opposite coasts of the Pacific.

This was only one of the ways in which the whole atmosphere aboard the Relay seemed quite different from that down on the Inner Station. The men here were doing a job that kept them in touch with everything happening on Earth – often before Earth knew it itself. Yet they were also on the frontiers of real space – for there was nothing else between them and the orbit of the Moon. It was a strange situation, and I wished I could have stayed here longer.

But unless there were any more accidents, my holiday in space was coming to an end. I'd already missed the ship that was supposed to take me home, but this didn't help me as much as I'd hoped. The plan now, I gathered, was to send me over to the Residential Station and put me aboard the regular ferry, so that I'd be going down to Earth with the passengers homeward-bound from Mars or Venus.

Our trip back to the Inner Station was quite uneventful, and rather tedious. We couldn't persuade Commander Doyle to tell any more stories, and I think he was a bit ashamed of himself for being so talkative at the start of the return journey from the Hospital Station. This time, too, he was taking no chances with the pilot . . .

It seemed like coming home when the familiar chaos of the Inner Station swam into view. Nothing much had changed – some ships had gone and others taken their place, that was all. The other apprentices were waiting for us in the air-lock – an informal reception committee. They gave the Commander a cheer as he came aboard – though afterwards there was a lot of good-natured leg-pulling about our various adventures. In particular, the fact that the 'Morning Star' was still out at the Hospital caused numerous complaints, and we never succeeded in getting Commander Doyle to take all the blame for this.

I spent most of my last day aboard the Station collecting autographs and souvenirs. The best memento of my stay was something quite unexpected – a beautiful little model of the Station, made out of plastic and presented to me by the other boys. It pleased me so much that I was tongue-tied and didn't know how to thank them – but I guess they realized the way I felt.

At last everything was packed, and I could only hope it was inside the weight limit. There was only one good-bye left to make.

Commander Doyle was sitting at his desk, just as I'd seen him at our first meeting. But he wasn't so terrifying now, for I'd grown to know and admire him. I hoped that I'd not been too much of a nuisance, and tried to say so. The Commander grinned.

'It might have been worse,' he said. 'On the whole you kept out of the way pretty well – though you managed to get into some – ah – unexpected places. I'm wondering whether to send World Airways a bill for the extra fuel you used in our little voyage. It must come to a sizeable amount.'

I thought it best to remain silent here, and presently he continued, after ruffling through the papers on his desk.

'I suppose you realize, Roy, that quite a lot of youngsters apply for jobs here, and not many get 'em – the qualifications are too steep. Well, I've had a good eye on you in the last few weeks and have noticed how you've been shaping up. If, when you're old enough – that will be in a couple of years, won't it? – you want to put your name down, I'll be glad to make a recommendation.'

'Why – thank you, Sir!'

'Of course, there'll be a tremendous amount of study to be done. You've seen most of the fun and games – not the hard work. And you've not had to sit up here for months waiting for your leave to come along and wondering why you ever left Earth.'

There was nothing I could say to this: it was a problem that must hit the Commander harder than anyone else in the Station.

He propelled himself out of his seat with his left hand, stretching out the right one towards me. As we shook hands, I again recalled our first meeting. How long ago that now seemed! And I suddenly realized that, though I'd seen him every day, I'd almost forgotten that Commander Doyle was legless – he was so perfectly adapted to his surroundings that the rest of us seemed freaks. It was an object lesson in what willpower and determination could do.

I had a surprise when I reached the air-lock. Though I hadn't really given it any thought, I'd assumed that one of the normal ferry rockets was going to take me over to the Residential Station for my rendezvous with the ship for Earth. Instead, there was the ramshackle 'Skylark of Space', her mooring lines drifting slackly. I wondered what our exclusive neighbours would think when this peculiar object arrived at their doorstep, and guessed that it had probably been arranged especially to annoy them.

Tim Benton and Ronnie Jordan made up the crew and helped me to get my luggage through the air-lock. They looked doubtfully at the number of parcels I was carrying, and asked me darkly if I knew what interplanetary freight charges were. Luckily, the homeward run is by far the cheapest, and though I had some awkward moments, I got everything through.

The great revolving drum of the Residential Station slowly expanded ahead of us: the untidy collection of domes and pressure-corridors that had been my home for so long dwindled astern. Very cautiously, Tim brought the 'Skylark' up to the axis of the Station. I couldn't see exactly what happened then, but big, jointed arms came out to meet us and drew us slowly in until the air-locks clamped together.

'Well, so long,' said Ron. 'I guess we'll be seeing you again.'

'I hope so,' I said, wondering if I should mention Commander Doyle's offer. 'Come and see me when you're down on Earth.'

'Thanks – I'll do my best. Hope you have a good ride down.'

I shook hands with them both, feeling pretty miserable as I did so. Then the doors folded back, and I went through into the flying hotel that had been my neighbour for so many days, but which I'd never visited before.

The air-lock ended in a wide circular corridor, and waiting for me was a uniformed steward. That at once set the tone of the place: after having to do things for myself, I felt rather a fool as I handed over my luggage. And I wasn't used to being called 'Sir' . . .

I watched with interest as the steward carefully placed my property against the wall of the corridor, and told me to take my place beside it. Then there was a faint vibration, and I remembered the ride in the centrifuge I'd had back at the Hospital. The same thing was happening here: the corridor was starting to rotate, matching the spin of the Station, and centrifugal force was giving me weight again. Not until the two rates of spin were equal would I be able to go through into the rest of the Station.

Presently a buzzer sounded, and I knew that our speeds had been matched. The force gluing me to the curved wall was very small, but it would increase as I got farther from the centre of the Station, until at the very rim it was equal to full Earth gravity. I was in no hurry to experience that again, after my days of complete weightlessness.

The corridor ended in a doorway which led, much to my surprise, into an elevator cage. There was a short ride in which curious things seemed to happen to the vertical direction, and then the door opened to reveal a large hall. I could hardly believe that I was not on Earth: this might be the foyer of any luxury hotel. There was the reception desk with the residents making their enquiries and complaints: uniformed staff were hurrying to and fro: from time to time someone was being paged over the speaker system. Only the long, graceful bounds with which people walked revealed that this wasn't Earth. And above the reception desk was a large notice:

GRAVITY ON THIS FLOOR = 1/3RD EARTH.

That, I realized, would make it just about right for the returning Martian colonists: probably all the people around me had come from the Red Planet – or were preparing to go there.

When I had been checked in I was given a tiny room, just large enough to hold a bed, a chair and a wash-basin. It was so strange to see freely flowing water again that the first thing I did was to turn on the tap and watch a pool of liquid form at the bottom of the basin. Then I suddenly realized that there must be baths here as well, so with a whoop of joy I set off in search of one. I had grown very tired of showers, and all the bother that went with them . . .

So that's how I spent most of my first evening at the Residential Station. All around me were travellers who had come back from far worlds with stories of strange adventures. But they could wait until tomorrow. For the present I was going to enjoy one of the experiences that gravity *did* make possible – lying in a mass of water which didn't try to turn itself into a giant, drifting raindrop . . .

Eleven
STARLIGHT HOTEL

It was late in the 'evening' when I arrived aboard the Residential Station. Time here had been geared to the cycle of nights and days that existed down on Earth. Every twenty-four hours the lights dimmed, a hushed silence descended and the residents went to bed. Outside the walls of the Station the sun might be shining, or it might be in eclipse behind the Earth – it made no difference here in this world of wide, curving corridors, thick carpets, soft lights and quietly whispering voices. We had our own time and no one took any notice of the Sun.

I didn't sleep very well on my first night under gravity, even though I had only a third of the weight to which I'd been accustomed all my life. Breathing was difficult – and I had unpleasant dreams. Again and again I seemed to be climbing a steep hill, with a great load on my back. My legs were aching, my lungs panting and the hill stretched endlessly ahead. However long I toiled, I never reached the top . . . At last, however, I managed to doze off, and remembered nothing until a steward woke me with breakfast, which I ate from a little tray fixed over my bed. Though I was anxious to see the Station, I took my time over this meal – it was a novel experience which I wanted to savour to the full. Breakfast in bed was rare enough – but to have it aboard a space-station as well was really something !

When I had dressed, I started to explore my new surroundings. The first thing I had to get used to was the fact that the floors were all curved. (Of course, I also had to get used to the idea that there *were* floors anyway, after doing without 'up' and 'down' for so long.) The reason for this was simple enough. I was now living on the inside of a giant cylinder, that slowly turned on its axis. Centrifugal force – the same force that held the Station in the sky – was acting once again, gluing me to the side of the revolving drum. If you walked straight ahead you could go right round the circumference of the Station and come back where you started. At any point 'up' would be towards the central axis of the cylinder – which meant that someone standing a few yards away, farther round the curve of the Station, would appear to be tilted towards you. Yet to them, everything would be perfectly normal and *you* would be the one who was tilted ! It was confusing at first, but like everything else you got used to it after a while. The designers of the Station had gone in for some clever tricks of decoration to hide what was happening, and in the smaller rooms the curve of the floor was too slight to be noticed.

The Station wasn't merely a single cylinder, but three – one inside the other. As you moved out from the centre, so the sense of weight increased. The innermost cylinder was the 'One-Third Earth Gravity' floor, and because it was nearest to the air-locks on the Station's axis it was mainly devoted to handling the passengers and their luggage. There was a saying that if you sat opposite the Reception Desk for long enough, you'd see everyone of importance on the four planets . . .

Surrounding this central cylinder was the more spacious 'Two-Thirds Earth Gravity' floor. You passed from one floor to the other either by elevators or by curiously curved stairways. It was an odd experience, going down one of those stairs – and at first I found it took quite a bit of will-power, for I was not yet accustomed even to a third of my Earth weight. As I walked slowly down the steps (gripping the hand rail very firmly) I seemed to grow steadily heavier. When I reached the floor, my movements were so slow and leaden that I imagined that everyone was looking at me. However, I soon grew used to the feeling. I *had* to, if I was ever going to return to Earth!

Most of the passengers were on this 'Two-Thirds Gravity' floor. Almost all of them were homeward bound from Mars, and though they had been experiencing normal Earth weight for the last weeks of their voyage – thanks to the spin of their liner – they obviously didn't like it yet. They walked very gingerly, and were always finding excuses to go 'up' to the top floor, where gravity had the same value as on Mars.

I had never met any Martian colonists before, and they fascinated me. Their clothes, their accents – everything about them – had an air of strangeness, though often it was hard to say just wherein the peculiarity lay. They all seemed to know each other by their first names: perhaps that wasn't surprising after their long voyage, but later I discovered it was just the same on Mars. The settlements there were still small enough for everyone to know everybody else. They would find things very different when they got to Earth ...

I felt a little lonely among all these strangers, and it was some time before I made any acquaintances. There were some small shops on the 'Two-Thirds Gravity' deck, where one could buy toilet goods and souvenirs, and I was exploring these when a bunch of three young colonists came strolling in. The oldest was a boy who looked about my age, and he was accompanied by two girls who were obviously his sisters.

'Hello,' he said. 'You weren't on the ship.'

'No,' I answered. 'I've just come over from the other half of the Station.'

'What's your name?'

So blunt a request might have seemed rude, or at least ill-mannered, down on Earth, but by now I had learned that the colonists were like that. They were direct and forthright, and never wasted words. I decided to behave in the same way.

'I'm Roy Malcolm. Who are you?'

'Oh!' said one of the girls. 'We read about you in the ship's newspaper.' 'You've been flying round the Moon, and all sorts of things.'

I was quite flattered to find that they'd heard of me, but merely shrugged my shoulders as if it wasn't anything of importance. In any case, I didn't want to risk showing off, as they'd travelled a lot farther than I had ...

'I'm John Moore,' announced the boy, 'and these are my sisters, Ruby and May. This is the first time we've been to Earth.'

'You mean you were born on Mars?'

'That's right. We're coming home to go to college.'

It sounded strange to hear that phrase 'coming home' from someone who's never set foot on Earth. I nearly asked, 'Can't you get a good education on Mars, then?' but luckily stopped myself in time. The colonists were very sensitive to criticism of their planet, even when it wasn't intended. They also hated the word 'colonist', and you had to avoid using it when they were around. But you couldn't very well call them 'Martians', for that word had to be saved for the original inhabitants of the planet.

'We're looking for some souvenirs to take home,' said Ruby. 'Don't you think that plastic star-map is beautiful?'

'I liked that carved meteor best,' I said. 'But it's an awful price.'

'How much have you got?' said John.

I turned out my pockets and did a quick calculation. To my astonishment, John immediately replied, 'I can lend you the rest. You can let me have it back when we reach Earth.'

This was my first contact with the quick-hearted generosity which everyone took for granted on Mars. I couldn't accept the offer, yet didn't want to hurt John's feelings. Luckily I had a good excuse.

'That's fine of you,' I said, 'but I've just remembered that I've used up my weight allowance. So that settles it – I can't take home anything else.'

I waited anxiously for a minute in case one of the Moores was willing to lend me cargo space as well, but fortunately they must all have used up their allowances too.

After this, it was inevitable that they took me to meet Mr and Mrs Moore. We found them in the main lounge, puzzling their way through the newspapers from Earth. As soon as she saw me, Mrs Moore exclaimed: 'What *has* happened to your clothes!' and for the first time I realized that life on the Inner Station had made quite a mess of my suit. Before I knew what had happened, I'd been pushed into a brightly coloured suit of John's. It was a good fit, but the design was startling – at least by Earth standards, though it certainly wasn't noticeable here.

We all had so much to talk about that the hours spent waiting for the ferry passed extremely quickly. Life on Mars was as novel to me as life on Earth was to the Moores. John had a fine collection of photographs which he'd taken, showing what it was like in the great pressure-domed cities and out on the coloured deserts. He'd done quite a bit of travelling and had some wonderful pictures of Martian scenery and life. They were so good that I suggested he should sell them to the illustrated magazines. He answered, in a slightly hurt voice: 'I already have.'

The photograph that fascinated me most was a view over one of the great vegetation areas – the Syrtis Major, John told me. It had been taken from a considerable height, looking down the slope of a wide valley. Millions of years ago the short-lived Martian seas had rolled above this land, and the bones of strange marine creatures were still embedded in its rocks. Now new life was returning to the planet: down in the valley, great machines were turning up the brick-red soil to make way for the colonists from Earth. In the distance I could see acres of the so-called 'Airweed', freshly planted in neat rows. As it grew, this strange plant would break down the minerals in the ground and release free oxygen, so that one day men would be able to live on the planet without breathing masks.

Mr Moore was standing in the foreground, with a small Martian on either side of him. The little creatures were grasping his fingers with tiny, claw-like hands, and staring at the camera with their huge, pale eyes. There was something rather touching about the scene: it seemed to dramatize the friendly contact of the two races in a way that nothing else could do.

'Why!' I exclaimed suddenly, 'your dad isn't wearing a breathing mask!'

John laughed.

'I was wondering when you'd notice that. It'll be a long time before there's enough free oxygen in the atmosphere for us to breathe it, but some of us can manage without a mask for a couple of minutes – as long as we're not doing anything very energetic, that is.'

'How do you get on with the Martians?' I asked. 'Do you think they had a civilization once?'

'I don't know about that,' said John. 'Every so often you hear rumours of ruined cities out in the deserts, but they always turn out to be hoaxes or practical jokes. There's no evidence at all that the Martians were ever any different from what they are today. They're not exactly friendly, except when they're young – but they never give any trouble. The adults just ignore you unless you get in their way. They've got very little curiosity.'

'I've read somewhere,' I said, 'that they behave more like intelligent horses than any other animal we've got on Earth.'

'I wouldn't know,' said John. 'I've never met a horse.'

That brought me up with a jerk. Then I realized that there couldn't be many animals that John *had* met. Earth would have a great many surprises for him.

'Exactly what are you going to do when you get to Earth?' I asked John. 'Apart from going to college, that is.'

'Oh, we'll travel round first and have a look at the sights. We've seen a lot of films, you know, so we've a good idea what it's like.'

I did my best to avoid a smile. Though I'd lived in several countries, I hadn't really seen much of Earth in my whole life, and I wondered if the Moores really realized just how big the planet was. Their scales of values must be quite different from mine. Mars is a small planet, and there are only limited regions where life is possible. If you put all the vegetation areas together, they wouldn't add up to much more than a medium-sized country down on Earth. And, of course, the areas covered by the pressure-domes of the few cities are very much smaller still.

I decided to find out what my new friends really did know about Earth. 'Surely,' I said, 'there are some places you particularly want to visit.'

'Oh yes!' replied Ruby. 'I want to see some forests. Those great trees you have – we've nothing like them on Mars. It must be wonderful walking beneath their branches, and seeing the birds flying around.'

'We've no birds, either, you see,' put in May rather wistfully. 'The air's too thin for them.'

'I want to see the ocean,' said John. 'I'd like to go sailing and fishing. It's true, isn't it, that you can get so far out to sea that you can't tell where the land is?'

'It certainly is,' I replied.

Ruby gave a little shudder.

'All that water! It would scare me. I should be afraid of being lost – and I've read that being on a boat makes you horribly sick.'

'Oh,' I replied airily, 'you get used to it. Of course there aren't many boats now, except for pleasure. A few hundred years ago most of the world's trade went by sea, until air transport took over. You can hire boats at the coast resorts, though – and people who'll run them for you.'

'But is it *safe*?' insisted Ruby. 'I've read that your seas are full of horrible monsters that might come up and swallow you.'

This time I couldn't help smiling.

'I shouldn't worry,' I replied. 'It hardly ever happens these days.'

'What about the land animals?' said May. 'Some of those are quite big, aren't they? I've read about tigers and lions, and I *know* they're dangerous. I'm scared of meeting one of those.'

Well, I thought, I hope I know a bit more about Mars than you do about Earth! I was just going to explain that man-eating tigers weren't generally found in our cities when I caught Ruby grinning at John – and realized that they'd been pulling my leg all the time.

After that we all went to lunch together, in a great dining-room where I felt rather ill at ease. I made matters worse by forgetting we were under gravity again and spilling a glass of water on the floor. However, everyone laughed so good humouredly at this that I didn't really mind – the only person who was annoyed was the steward who had to mop it up.

For the rest of my short stay in the Residential Station I spent almost all my time with the Moores. And it was here, surprisingly enough, that I at last saw something I'd missed on my other trips. Though I'd visited several space-stations, I'd never actually watched one being built. We were now able to get a grandstand view of this operation – and without bothering to wear space-suits. The Residential Station was being extended, and from the windows at the end of the 'Two-Thirds Gravity' floor we were able to see the whole fascinating process. Here was something that I could explain to my new friends: I didn't tell them that the spectacle would have been equally strange to me only two weeks ago.

The fact that we were making one complete revolution every ten seconds was highly confusing at first, and the girls turned rather green when they saw the stars orbiting outside the windows. However, the complete absence of vibration made it easy to pretend – just as one does on Earth – that *we* were stationary and it was really the stars that were revolving.

The Station extension was still a mass of open girders, only partly covered by metal sheets. It had not yet been set spinning, for that would have made its construction impossibly difficult. At the moment it floated about half a mile away from us, with a couple of freight rockets alongside. When it was completed, it would be brought gently up to the Station, and set rotating on its axis by small rocket motors. As soon as the spins had been matched exactly, the two units would be bolted together – and the Residential Station would have doubled its length. The whole operation would be rather like engaging a gigantic clutch.

As we watched, a construction gang was easing a large girder from the hold of a ferry rocket. The girder was about forty feet long, and though of course it weighed nothing out here, its mass or inertia was unchanged. It took a considerable effort to start it moving – and an equal effort to stop it again. The men of the construction crew were working in what were really tiny spaceships – little cylinders about ten feet long, fitted with low-powered rockets and steering jets. They manoeuvred these with fascinating skill, darting forward or sideways and coming to rest with inches to spare. Ingenious handling mechanisms and pointed metal arms enabled them to carry out all assembling tasks almost as easily as if they were working with their own hands.

The team was under the radio control of a foreman – or, to give him his more dignified name, a Controller – in a little pressure-hut fixed to the girders of the partly constructed station. As they moved to and fro or up and down under his direction, keeping in perfect unison, they reminded me of a flock of goldfish in a pool. Indeed, with the sunlight glinting on their armour, they did look very much like underwater creatures.

The girder was now floating free of the ship that had brought it here from the Moon, and two of the men attached their grapples and towed it slowly towards the Station. Much too late, it seemed to me, they began to use their braking units. But there was still a good six inches between the girder and the skeleton framework when they had finished. Then one of the men went back to help his colleagues with the unloading, while the other eased the girder across the remaining gap until it made contact with the rest of the structure. It was not lying in exactly the correct line, so he had to slew it through a slight angle as well. Then he slipped in the bolts and began to tighten them up. It all looked so effortless – but I realized that immense skill and practice must lie behind this deceptive simplicity.

Before you could go down to Earth, you were supposed to spend a twelve-hour quarantine period on the 'Full Earth Gravity' floor – the outermost of the Station's three decks. So once again I went down one of those curving stairways, my weight increasing with every step. When I had reached the bottom, my legs felt very weak and wobbly. I could hardly believe that *this* was the normal force of gravity under which I had passed my whole life.

The Moores had come with me, and they felt the strain even more than I did. This was three times the gravity of their native Mars, and twice I had to stop John falling as he tottered unsteadily about. The third time I failed, and we both went down together. We looked so miserable that after a minute each started laughing at the other's expression, and our spirits quickly revived. For a while we sat on the thick rubber flooring (the designers of the Station had known where it would be needed!) and got up our strength for another attempt. This time, we didn't fall down. Much to John's annoyance, the remainder of his family managed a good deal better than he did.

We couldn't leave the Residential Station without seeing one of its prize exhibits. The 'Full Earth Gravity' floor had a swimming-pool – a small one, but its fame had spread throughout the Solar System.

It was famous because it wasn't flat. As I've explained, since the Station's 'gravity' was caused by its spin, the vertical at any spot pointed towards the central axis. Any free water, therefore, had a concave surface, taking in fact the shape of a hollow cylinder.

We couldn't resist entering the pool – and not merely because once we were floating gravity would be less of a strain. Though I'd become used to many strange things in space, it was a weird feeling to stand with my head just above the surface of the pool, and to look along the water. In one direction – parallel to the axis of the Station, that is – the surface was quite flat. But in the other it was curved upwards on either side of me. At the edge of the pool, in fact, the water level was higher than my head. I seemed to be floating in the trough of a great frozen wave ... At any moment I expected the water to come flooding down as the surface flattened itself out. But, of course, it didn't – because it was 'flat' already in this strange gravity field. (When I got back to Earth I made quite a mess trying to demonstrate this effect by whirling a bucket of water round my head at the end of a string. If you try the same experiment, do make sure you're out of doors...)

We could not play round in that peculiar pool as long as I would have liked, for presently the loudspeakers began to call softly and I knew that my time was running out. All the passengers were asked to check that their luggage was packed, and to assemble in the main hall of the Station. The colonists, I knew, were planning some kind of farewell, and though it didn't really concern me I felt sufficiently interested to go along. After talking to the Moores I'd begun to like them and to understand their point of view a good deal better.

It was a subdued little gathering that we joined few minutes later. These weren't tough, confident pioneers any more: they knew that soon they'd be separated and in a strange world, among millions of other human beings with totally different modes of life. All their talk about 'going home' seemed to have evaporated: it was Mars, not Earth, they were homesick for now.

As I listened to their farewells and little speeches, I felt suddenly very sorry for them. And I felt sorry for myself, because in a few hours I, too, would be saying goodbye to space.

Twelve
THE LONG FALL HOME

I had come up from Earth by myself – but I was going home in plenty of company. There were nearly fifty passengers crowded into the 'One-Third Gravity' floor waiting to disembark. That was the complement for the first rocket: the rest of the colonists would be going down on later flights.

Before we left the Station, we were all handed a bundle of leaflets full of instructions, warnings and advice about conditions on Earth. I felt that it was hardly necessary for me to read through all this, but was quite glad to have another souvenir of my visit. It was certainly a good idea giving these leaflets out at this stage in the homeward journey – for it kept most of the passengers so busily reading that they didn't have time to worry about anything else until we'd landed.

The air-lock was only large enough to hold about a dozen people at a time, so it took quite a while to shepherd us all through. As each batch left the Station, the lock had to be set revolving to counteract its normal spin, then it had to be coupled to the waiting spaceship, uncoupled again when the occupants had gone through, and the whole sequence restarted. I wondered what would happen if something jammed while the spinning Station was connected to the stationary ship. Probably the ship would come off worse – next, that is, to the unfortunate people in the air-lock! However, I discovered later that there was an additional movable coupling to take care of just such an emergency.

The Earth ferry was the biggest spaceship I had ever been inside. There was one large cabin for the passengers, with rows of seats in which we were supposed to remain strapped during the trip. Since I was lucky enough to be one of the first to go aboard, I was able to get a seat near a window. Most of the passengers had nothing to look at but each other – and the handful of leaflets they'd been given to read.

We waited for nearly an hour before everyone was aboard and the luggage had been stowed away. Then the loud-speakers told us to stand-by for take-off in five minutes. The ship had now been completely uncoupled from the Station and had drifted several hundred feet away from it.

I had always thought that the return to Earth would be rather an anticlimax after the excitement of a take-off.

There was a different sort of feeling, it was true – but it was still quite an experience. Until now we had been, if not beyond the power of gravity, at least travelling so swiftly in our orbit that Earth could never pull us down. But now we were going to throw away the speed that gave us safety. We would descend until we had re-entered the atmosphere and were forced to spiral back to the surface. If we came in too steeply, our ship might blaze across the sky like a meteor and come to the same fiery end.

I looked at the tense faces around me. Perhaps the Martian colonists were thinking the same thoughts: perhaps they were wondering what they were going to meet and do down on the planet which so few of them had ever before seen. I hoped that none of them would be disappointed.

Three sharp notes from the loud-speaker gave us the last warning. Five seconds later the motors opened up gently, quickly increasing power to full thrust. I saw the Residential Station fall swiftly astern, its great spinning drum dwindling against the stars. Then, with a lump in my throat, I watched the untidy maze of girders and pressure chambers that housed so many of my friends go swimming by. Useless though the gesture was, I couldn't help giving them a wave. After all, they knew I was aboard this ship, and might catch a glimpse of me through the window . . .

Now the two component parts of the Inner Station were receding rapidly behind us, and soon had passed out of sight under the great wing of the ferry. It was hard to realize that, in reality, *we* were losing speed while the Station continued on its unvarying way. And as we lost speed, so we would start falling down to Earth on a long curve that would take us to the other side of the planet before we entered the atmosphere.

After a surprisingly short period, the motors cut out again. We had shed all the speed that was necessary and gravity would do the rest. Most of the passengers had settled down to read, but I decided to have my last look at the stars, undimmed by atmosphere. This was also my last chance of experiencing weightlessness, but it was wasted because I couldn't leave my seat. I did try, and got shooed back by the steward.

The ship was now pointing *against* the direction of its orbital motion, and had to be swung round so that it entered the atmosphere nose-first. There was plenty of time to carry out this manoeuvre, and the pilot did it in a leisurely fashion with the low-powered steering jets at the wing-tips. From where I was sitting I could see the short columns of mist stabbing from the nozzles, and very slowly the stars swung around us. It was a full ten minutes before we came to rest again, with the nose of the ship now pointing due east.

We were still almost five hundred miles above the Equator, moving at nearly eighteen thousand miles an hour. But we were now slowly dropping Earthwards: in thirty minutes we would make our first contact with the atmosphere.

John was sitting next to me, and so I had a chance of airing my knowledge of geography.

'That's the Pacific Ocean down there,' I said. And something prompted me to add, not very tactfully: 'You could drop Mars in it without going near either of the coastlines.'

However, John was too fascinated by the great expanse of water to take any offence. It must have been an overwhelming sight for anyone who had lived on sea-less Mars. There were not even any permanent lakes on that planet – only a few shallow pools that form round the melting ice-caps in the summer. And now John was looking down upon water that stretched as far as he could see in every direction, with a few specks of land dotted upon it here and there.

'Look!' I said, 'there, straight ahead! You can see the coastline of South America. We can't be more than two hundred miles up now.'

Still in utter silence the ship dropped Earthwards and the ocean rolled back beneath us. No one was reading now if they had a chance of seeing from one of the windows. I felt very sorry for the passengers in the middle of the cabin, who weren't able to watch the approaching landscape beneath.

The coast of South America flashed by in seconds, and ahead lay the great jungles of the Amazon. *Here* was life on a scale that Mars could not match, not even, perhaps, in the days of its youth. Thousands of square miles of crowded forests, countless streams and rivers – they were unfolding beneath us so swiftly that as soon as one feature had been grasped, it was already out of sight.

And now the great river was widening as we shot above its course. We were approaching the Atlantic, which should have been visible by this time, but which seemed to be hidden by mists. As we passed above the mouth of the Amazon, I saw that a great storm was raging below. From time to time brilliant flashes of lightning played across the clouds: it was uncanny to see all this happening in utter silence as we raced high overhead.

'A tropical storm,' I said to John. 'Do you ever have anything like that on Mars?'

'Not with rain, of course,' he said. 'But sometimes we get pretty bad sandstorms over the deserts. And I've seen lightning once – or perhaps twice.'

'What, without rainclouds?' I asked.

'Oh yes – the sand gets electrified. Not very often, but it *does* happen.'

The storm was now far behind us, and the Atlantic lay smooth in the evening sun. We could not see it much longer, however – for darkness lay ahead. We were nearing the night side of the planet, and on the horizon I could see a band of shadow swiftly approaching as we hurtled into twilight. There was something terrifying about plunging headlong into that curtain of darkness. In mid-Atlantic, we lost the sun: and at almost the same moment we heard the first whisper of air along the hull.

It was an eerie sound, and it made the hair rise at the back of my neck. After the silence of space any noise seemed altogether wrong. But it grew steadily, as the minutes passed, from a faint, distant wail to a high-pitched scream. We were still more than fifty miles up, but at the speed we were travelling even the incredibly thin atmosphere of these heights was protesting as we tore through it.

More than that – it was tearing at the ship, slowing it down. There was a faint but steadily increasing tug from our straps: the deceleration was trying to force us out of our seats. It was like sitting in a car when the brakes are being slowly applied. But in this case, the braking was going to last for two hours, and we would go once more round the world before we slowed to a halt . . .

We were no longer in a spaceship, but an aeroplane. In almost complete darkness – there was no Moon – we passed above Africa and the Indian Ocean. The fact that we were speeding through the night, travelling above the invisible Earth at many thousands of miles an hour, made it all the more impressive. The thin shriek of the upper atmosphere had become a steady background to our flight: it grew neither louder nor fainter as the minutes passed.

I was looking out into the darkness when I saw a faint red glow beneath me. At first, because there was no sense of perspective or distance, it seemed at an immense depth below the ship, and I could not imagine what it might be.

A great forest fire, perhaps – but we were now, surely, over the ocean again. Then I realized, with a shock that nearly jolted me out of my seat, that this ominous red glow came from our wing . . . The heat of our passage through the atmosphere was turning it cherry red.

I stared at that disturbing sight for several seconds before I decided that everything was really quite in order. All our tremendous energy of motion was being converted into heat – though I had never realized just how *much* heat would be produced. For the glow was increasing even as I watched: when I flattened my face against the window, I could see part of the leading edge, and it was a bright yellow in places. I wondered if the other passengers had noticed it – or perhaps the little leaflets, which I hadn't bothered to read, had already told them not to worry.

I was glad when we emerged into daylight once more, greeting the dawn above the Pacific. The glow from the wings was no longer visible, and so ceased to worry me. Besides, the sheer splendour of the sunrise, which we were approaching at nearly ten thousand miles an hour, took away all other sensations. From the Inner Station, I had watched many dawns and sunsets pass across the Earth. But up there, I had been detached, not part of the scene itself. Now I was once more inside the atmosphere and these wonderful colours were all around me.

We had now made one complete circuit of the Earth, and had shed more than half our speed. It was much longer, this time, before the Brazilian jungles came into view, and they passed more slowly now. Above the mouth of the Amazon the storm was still raging, only a little way beneath us, as we started out on our last crossing of the South Atlantic.

Then night came once more, and there again was the redly glowing wing in the darkness around the ship. It seemed even hotter now, but perhaps I had grown used to it for the sight no longer worried me. We were nearly home – on the last lap of the journey. By now we must have lost so much speed that we were probably travelling no faster than many normal aircraft.

A cluster of lights along the coast of East Africa told us that we were heading out over the Indian Ocean again. I wished I could be up there in the control cabin, watching the preparations for the final approach to the space-port. By now, the pilot would have picked up the guiding radio beacons, and would be coming down the beam, still at a great speed but according to a carefully prearranged programme. When we reached New Guinea, our velocity would be almost completely spent. Our ship would be nothing more than a great glider, flying through the night sky on the last dregs of its momentum.

The loud-speaker broke into my thoughts.

'Pilot to passengers. We shall be landing in twenty minutes.'

Even without this warning, I could tell that the flight was nearing its end. The scream of the wind outside our hull had dropped in pitch, and there had been a just perceptible change of direction as the ship slanted downwards. And, most striking sign of all, the red glow outside the window was rapidly fading. Presently there were only a few dull patches left, near the leading edge of the wing. A few minutes later, even these had gone.

It was still night as we passed over Sumatra and Borneo. From time to time the lights of ships and cities winked into view and went astern – very slowly now, it seemed, after the headlong rush of our first circuit. At frequent intervals the loud-speaker called out our speed and position. We were travelling at less than a thousand miles an hour when we passed over the deeper darkness that was the New Guinea coastline.

'There it is!' I whispered to John. The ship had banked slightly, and beneath the wing was a great constellation of lights. A signal flare rose up in a slow, graceful arc and exploded into crimson fire. In the momentary glare, I caught a glimpse of the white mountain peaks surrounding the space-port, and I wondered just how much margin of height we had. It would be very ironic to meet with disaster in the last few miles after travelling all this distance.

I never knew the actual moment when we touched down, the landing was so perfect. At one instant we were still airborne, at the next the lights of the runway were rolling past as the ship slowly came to rest. I sat quite still in my seat, trying to realize that I was back on Earth again. Then I looked at John. Judging from his expression, he could hardly believe it either.

The steward came round helping people release their seat straps and giving last-minute advice. As I looked at the slightly harassed visitors, I could not help a mild feeling of superiority. *I* knew my way about on Earth, but all this must be very strange to them. They must be realizing, also, that they were now in the full grip of Earth's gravity – and there was nothing they could do about it until they were out in space again.

As we had been the first to enter the ship, we were the last to leave it. I helped John with some of his personal luggage, as he was obviously not very happy and wanted at least one hand free to grab any convenient support.

'Cheer up!' I said. 'You'll soon be jumping around just as much as you did on Mars!'

'I hope you're right,' he answered gloomily. 'At the moment I feel like a cripple who's lost his crutch.'

Mr and Mrs Moore, I noticed, had expressions of grim determination on their faces as they walked cautiously to the air-lock. But if they wished they were back on Mars, they kept their feelings to themselves. So did the girls, who for some reason seemed less worried by gravity than any of us.

We emerged under the shadow of the great wing, the thin mountain air blowing against our faces. It was quite warm – surprisingly so, in fact, for night at such a high altitude. Then I realized that the wing above us was still hot – probably too hot to touch, even though it was no longer visibly glowing.

We moved slowly away from the ship, towards the waiting transport vehicles. Before I stepped into the bus that would take us across to the Port buildings, I looked up once more at the starlit sky which had been my home for a little while – and which, I was resolved, would be my home again. Up there in the shadow of the Earth, speeding the traffic that moved from world to world, were Commander Doyle, Tim Benton, Ronnie Jordan, Norman Powell, and all the other friends I'd made on my visit to the Inner Station. I remembered Commander Doyle's promise, and wondered how soon I would remind him of it . . .

John Moore was waiting patiently behind me, clutching the door-handle of the bus. He saw me looking up into the sky and followed my gaze.

'You won't be able to see the Station,' I said. 'It's in eclipse.'

John didn't answer, and then I saw that he was staring into the east, where the first hint of dawn glowed along the horizon. High against these unfamiliar southern stars was something that I did recognize – a brilliant ruby beacon, the brightest object in the sky.

'My home,' said John, in a faint, sad voice.

I started into that beckoning light, and remembered the pictures John had shown me and the stories he had told. Up there were the great coloured deserts, the old seabeds that man was bringing once more to life, the little Martians who might, or might not, belong to a race that was more ancient than ours.

And I knew that, after all, I was going to disappoint Commander Doyle. The space-stations were too near home to satisfy me now – my imagination had been captured by that little red world, glowing bravely against the stars. When I went into space again, the Inner Station would only be the first milestone on my outward road from Earth.

THE SANDS
OF MARS

Arthur C. Clarke's introduction to
THE SANDS OF MARS

In 2001 – where have I seen that date before? – it will be exactly half a century since this novel was published. Or to put it in perhaps better perspective: it is already more than half way back in time, dear reader, between you and the Wright Brothers' first flight . . .

Though I have not opened it for decades, I have a special fondness for *Sands*, as it was my first full-length novel. When I wrote it, we knew practically nothing about Mars – and what we did 'know' was completely wrong. The mirage of Percival Lowell's canals was beginning to fade, though it would not vanish completely until our space probes began arriving in the late seventies. It was still generally believed that Mars had a thin but useful atmosphere, and that vegetation flourished – at least in the equatorial regions where the temperature often rose above freezing point. And where there was vegetation, of course, there might be more interesting forms of life – though nothing remotely human. Edgar Rice Burroughs' Martian princesses have joined the canals in mythology.

When I tapped out 'The End' on my Remington Noiseless (ha!) Portable in 1951 I could never have imagined that exactly twenty years later I should be sitting on a panel with Ray Bradbury and Carl Sagan at the Jet Propulsion Laboratory, waiting for the first real Mars to arrive from the Mariner space probes. (See *Mars and the Mind of Man*, Harper & Row, 1973). But that was only the first trickle of a flood of information: during the next two decades, the Vikings were to give stunning images of the gigantic Mariner Valley and, most awe-inspiring of all, Olympus Mons – an extinct volcano more than twice the height of Everest. (Pause for embarrassed cough. Somewhere herein you'll find 'There are no mountains on Mars!' Well, that's what even the best observers, straining their eyes to make sense of the tiny disk dancing in the field of their telescope, believed in the 1950s.

Soon after maps of the real Mars became available, I received a generous gift from computer genius John Hinkley of his Vistapro image processing system. This prompted me to do some desk-top terraforming (a word, incidentally, invented by science fiction's Grandest of Grand Masters, Jack Williamson). I must confess that in *The Snows of Olympus: a Garden on Mars* (Gollancz, 1994) I frequently allowed artistic considerations to override scientific ones. Thus I couldn't resist putting a lake in the caldera of Mount Olympus, unlikely though it is that the most strenuous efforts of future colonists will produce an atmosphere dense enough to permit liquid water at such an altitude.

My next encounter with Mars involved a most ambitious but, alas, unsuccessful space project – the Russian MARS 96 mission. Besides all its scientific equipment, the payload carried a CD/Rom disk full of sounds and images, including the whole of the famous Orsen Welles *War of the Worlds* broadcast. (I have a recording of the only encounter between H.G. and Orson, made soon after this historic demonstration of the power of the new medium. Listening to the friendly banter between two of the greatest magicians of our age is like stepping into a time machine.)

It was intended that all these 'Visions of Mars' would, some day in the 21st century, serve as greetings to the pioneers of the next New World. I was privileged to send a video recording, made in the garden of my Colombo home: here is what I said:

MESSAGE TO MARS

My name is Arthur C. Clarke, and I am speaking to you from the island of Sri Lanka, once known as Ceylon, in the Indian Ocean, Planet Earth. It is early spring in the year 1993 but this message is intended for the future.

I am addressing men and woman – perhaps some of you already born – who will listen to these words when they are living on Mars.

As we approach the new millennium, there is a great interest in the planet which may be the first real home for mankind beyond the mother world. During my lifetime, I have been lucky enough to see our knowledge of Mars advance from almost complete ignorance – worse than that, misleading fantasy – to a real understanding of its geography and climate. Certainly we are still very ignorant in many areas, and lack knowledge which you take for granted. But now we have accurate maps of your wonderful world, and can imagine how it might be modified – terraformed – to make it nearer to the heart's desire. Perhaps you are already engaged upon that centuries-long process.

There is a link between Mars and my present home, which I used in what will probably be my last novel, *The Hammer of God*. At the beginning of this century, an amateur astronomer named Percy Molesworth was living here in Ceylon. He spent much time observing Mars, and now there is a huge crater, 175 kilometres wide, named after him in your southern hemisphere.

In my book I've imagined how a New Martian astronomer might one day look at his ancestral world, to try and see the little island from which Molesworth – and I – often gazed up at your planet.

There was a time, soon after the first landing on the moon in 1969, when we were optimistic enough to imagine that we might have reached Mars by the 1990s. In another of my stories, I described a survivor of the first ill-fated expedition, watching the earth in transit across the face of the sun on May 11 – 1984!

Well, there was no one on Mars then to watch the event – but it will happen again on November 10, 2084. By that time I hope that many eyes will be looking back towards the earth as it slowly crosses the solar disk, looking like a tiny, perfectly circular sunspot. And I've suggested that we should signal to you then with powerful lasers, so that you will see a star beaming a message to you from the very face of the sun.

I too salute to you across the gulfs of space – as I send my greetings and good wishes from the closing decade of the century in which mankind first became a space faring species, and set forth on a journey that can never end, so long as the universe endures.

Alas, owing to a failure of the launch vehicle, MARS 96 ended up at the bottom of the Pacific. But I hope – and fully expect – that one day our descendants on the red planet will be chuckling over this CD/Rom – which is a delightful combination of science, art and fantasy. (It is still available from the Planetary Society, 65, N. Catalina Ave., Pasadena, Ca, 91106,USA.)

On 4 July 1997, with a little help from the World Wide Web, Mars was news again. Pathfinder had made a bumpy landing in the Ares Vallis region and disgorged the tiny but sophisticated rover, Sojourner, whose cautious exploration of a distant place in the sky became a real world.

Shortly afterwards, to my surprised delight, the engineer who had run the program sent me her autobiography *Managing Martians* (Broadway Books, 1998) with a dedication 'To Arthur Clarke, who inspired my summer vacation on Mars'. Reading further, I was even more pleased to see that it opened with a quotation from *The Sands of Mars* . . . But let Donna Shirley tell you the story in her words . . .

Foreword

I was about 12 years old when I first read *The Sands of Mars*. I read it feverishly, completely entranced by the concept of a group of people actually living and working on Mars. I had already decided to be an aeronautical engineer and build aeroplanes when I grew up, but now the idea of building spaceships to go to Mars began to nibble at the edges of my mind.

Forty-five years later, on July 4, 1997, I achieved my dream of landing on Mars – at least virtually – when Pathfinder delivered the microwave oven-sized Sojourner Rover to the surface of the red planet. From 1992 to 1994 I had been the manager of the team that built the rover and in 1997 I was managing the United States' entire robotic Mars Exploration Program.

A year later I published an autobiography, *Managing Martians*, in which the Pathfinder project figured largely. I could think of nothing more appropriate than to include quotes from my first inspiration, *The Sands of Mars*, in my book. In fact, I found an appropriate quote for every chapter (although the publisher only chose to use one at the beginning and end). Sir Arthur Clarke graciously allowed me to use the quotes.

Rereading *Sands* as I wrote my book brought back the sense of wonder and adventure that it inspired in my childhood. I found it astounding how fresh and relevant the story remains. The characters are much like the people I worked with at the Jet Propulsion Laboratory for 32 years – brilliant and hard-working, but also funny and human. The way that humans would live on Mars (for example, domes and pressurised rovers) are still the concepts being used by NASA planners. Some of the details of the Mars environment unfortunately turned out to be optimistic. The little Martian 'Squeak' and the plants he fed on could not survive on the bleach-sterilised surface that we first discovered with the Viking landers. Some primitive life might have existed on Mars sometime in the past, or may even be surviving deep underground, but the butterscotch-coloured surface is dead.

And humans will not reach Mars for a few more years. Sadly, humanity's progress has lagged Arthur Clarke's vision of exploring Mars – no commercial liners yet ply the interplanetary space lanes. But commercial space ventures are beginning. People are making money from communication satellites and are paying to be flown to the Russian Mir Space Station. Private launch vehicle companies are springing up. And an international fleet of robotic spacecraft continue the exploration of the skies and sands of Mars.

There is a growing interest in Mars exploration, with organisations like the Planetary Society and the Mars Society providing a focus for the personal dreams of private citizens. An international educational project called the Mars Millennium Project, for which I was the official spokesperson in 1999–2000, used a vision of a human colony of 100 people on Mars in the year 2030 (see www.mars2030.net) to inspire children to think about how communities work and prosper. Hundreds of thousands of children designed colonies which often looked very much like the colony portrayed in *The Sands of Mars*. I hope its republication will inspire this same generation of children to keep the dream of human exploration of Mars alive.

Donna Shirley
Assistant Dean of Engineering
University of Oklahoma

One

'So this is the first time you've been upstairs?' said the pilot, leaning back idly in his seat so that it rocked to and fro in the gimbals. He clasped his hands behind his neck in a nonchalant manner that did nothing to reassure his passenger.

'Yes,' said Martin Gibson, never taking his eyes from the chronometer as it ticked away the seconds.

'I thought so. You never got it quite right in your stories – all that nonsense about fainting under the acceleration. Why must people write such stuff? It's bad for business.'

'I'm sorry,' Gibson replied. 'But I think you must be referring to my earlier stories. Space-travel hadn't got started then, and I had to use my imagination.'

'Maybe,' said the pilot grudgingly. (He wasn't paying the slightest attention to the instruments, and take-off was only two minutes away.) 'It must be funny, I suppose, for this to be happening to you, after writing about it so often.'

The adjective, thought Gibson, was hardly the one he would have used himself, but he saw the other's point of view. Dozens of his heroes – and villains – had gazed hypnotized at remorseless second-hands, waiting for the rockets to hurl them into infinity. And now – as it always did if one waited long enough – the reality had caught up with the fiction. The same moment lay only ninety seconds in his own future. Yes, it *was* funny, a beautiful case of poetic justice.

The pilot glanced at him, read his feelings, and grinned cheerfully.

'Don't let your own stories scare you. Why, I once took-off standing up, just for a bet, though it was a damn silly thing to do.'

'I'm not scared,' Gibson replied with unnecessary emphasis.

'Hmmm,' said the pilot, condescending to glance at the clock. The second-hand had one more circuit to go. 'Then I shouldn't hold on to the seat like that. It's only beryl-manganese: you might bend it.'

Sheepishly, Gibson relaxed. He knew that he was building up synthetic responses to the situation, but they seemed none the less real for all that.

'Of course,' said the pilot, still at ease but now, Gibson noticed, keeping his eyes fixed on the instrument panel, 'it wouldn't be very comfortable if it lasted more than a few minutes – ah, there go the fuel pumps. Don't worry when the vertical starts doing funny things, but let the seat swing where it likes. Shut your eyes if that helps at all. (Hear the igniter jets start then?) We take about ten seconds to build up to full thrust – there's really nothing to it, apart from the noise. You just have to put up with that. I SAID, YOU JUST HAVE TO PUT UP WITH THAT!'

But Martin Gibson was doing nothing of the sort. He had already slipped gracefully into unconsciousness at an acceleration that had not yet exceeded that of a high-speed elevator.

He revived a few minutes and a thousand kilometres later, feeling quite ashamed of himself. A beam of sunlight was shining full on his face, and he realized that the protective shutter on the outer hull must have slid aside. Although brilliant, the light was not as intolerably fierce as he would have expected: then he saw that only a fraction of the full intensity was filtering through the deeply tinted glass.

He looked at the pilot, hunched over his instrument board and busily writing up the log. Everything was very quiet, but from time to time there would come curiously muffled reports – almost miniature explosions – that Gibson found disconcerting. He coughed gently to announce his return to consciousness, and asked the pilot what they were.

'Thermal contraction in the motors,' he replied briefly. 'They've been running round five thousand degrees and cool mighty fast. You feeling all right now?'

'I'm fine,' Gibson answered, and meant it. 'Shall I get up?'

Psychologically, he had hit the bottom and bounced back. It was a very unstable position, though he did not realize it.

'If you like,' said the pilot doubtfully. 'But be careful – hang on to something solid.'

Gibson felt a wonderful sense of exhilaration. The moment he had waited for all his life had come. He was in space! It was too bad that he'd missed the take-off, but he'd gloss that part over when he wrote it up.

From a thousand kilometres away, Earth was still very large – and something of a disappointment. The reason was quickly obvious. He had seen so many hundreds of rocket photographs and films that the surprise had been spoilt: he knew exactly what to expect. There were the inevitable moving bands of cloud on their slow march round the world. At the centre of the disc, the divisions between land and sea were sharply defined, and an infinite amount of minute detail was visible, but towards the horizon everything was lost in the thickening haze. Even in the cone of clear vision vertically beneath him, most of the features were unrecognizable and therefore meaningless. No doubt a meteorologist would have gone into transports of delight at the animated weather-map displayed below – but most of the meteorologists were up in the space-stations, anyway, where they had an even better view. Gibson soon grew tired of searching for cities and other works of man. It was chastening to think that all the thousands of years of human civilization had produced no appreciable change in the panorama below.

Then Gibson began to look for the stars, and met his second disappointment. They were there, hundreds of them, but pale and wan, mere ghosts of the blinding myriads he had expected to find. The dark glass of the port was to blame: in subduing the Sun, it had robbed the stars of all their glory.

Gibson felt a vague annoyance. Only one thing had turned out quite as expected. The sensation of floating in mid-air, of being able to propel oneself from wall to wall at the touch of a finger, was just as delightful as he had hoped – though the quarters were too cramped for any ambitious experiments. Weightlessness was an enchanting, a fairy-like state, now that there were drugs to immobilize the balance organs and space-sickness was a thing of the past. He was glad of that. How his heroes had suffered! (His heroines too, presumably, but one never mentioned that.) He remembered Robin Blake's first flight, in the original version of *Martian Dust*. When he'd written that, he had been heavily under the influence of

D. H. Lawrence. (It would be interesting, one day, to make a list of the authors who *hadn't* influenced him at one time or another.)

There was no doubt that Lawrence was magnificent at describing physical sensations, and quite deliberately Gibson had set out to defeat him on his own ground. He had devoted a whole chapter to space-sickness, describing every symptom from the queasy premonitions that could sometimes be willed aside, the subterranean upheavals that even the most optimistic could no longer ignore, the volcanic cataclysms of the final stages, and the ultimate, merciful exhaustion.

The chapter had been a masterpiece of stark realism. It was too bad that his publishers, with an eye on a squeamish 'Book of the Month Club', had insisted on removing it. He had put a lot of work into that chapter: while he was writing it, he had really *lived* those sensations. Even now—

'It's very puzzling,' said the MO thoughtfully as the now quiescent author was propelled through the airlock. 'He's passed his medical tests OK, and of course he'll have had the usual injections before leaving Earth. It must be psychosomatic.'

'I don't care what it is,' complained the pilot bitterly, as he followed the cortège into the heart of Space Station One. 'All I want to know is – who's going to clean up my ship?'

No one seemed inclined to answer this heart-felt question, least of all Martin Gibson, who was only vaguely conscious of white walls drifting by his field of vision. Then, slowly, there was a sensation of increasing weight, and a warm, caressing glow began to steal through his limbs. Presently he became fully aware of his surroundings. He was in a hospital ward, and a battery of infra-red lamps was bathing him with a glorious enervating warmth, that sank through his flesh to the very bones.

'Well?' said the doctor, presently.

Gibson grinned feebly.

'I'm sorry about this. Is it going to happen again?'

'I don't know how it happened the first time. It's very unusual: the drugs we have now are supposed to be infallible.'

'I think it was my own fault,' said Gibson apologetically. 'You see, I've got a rather powerful imagination, and I started thinking about the symptoms of space-sickness – in quite an objective sort of way, of course – but before I knew what had happened—'

'Well, just stop it!' ordered the doctor sharply. 'Or we'll have to send you right back to Earth. You can't do this sort of thing if you're going to Mars. There wouldn't be much left of you after three months.'

A shudder passed through Gibson's tortured frame. But he was rapidly recovering, and already the nightmare of the last hour was fading into the past.

'I'll be OK,' he said. 'Let me out of this muffle-furnace before I cook.'

A little unsteadily, he got to his feet. It seemed strange, here in space, to have normal weight again. Then he remembered that Station One was spinning on its axis, and the living quarters were built around the outer walls so that centrifugal force could give the illusion of gravity.

The great adventure, he thought ruefully, hadn't started at all well. But he was determined not to be sent home in disgrace. It was not merely a question of his own pride: the effect on his public and his reputation would be deplorable. He winced as he visualized the headlines: 'GIBSON GROUNDED! SPACE-SICKNESS ROUTS AUTHOR-ASTRONAUT'. Even the staid literary weeklies would pull his leg, and as for *Time* – no it was unthinkable!

'It's lucky,' said the MO, 'that we've got twelve hours before the ship leaves. I'll take you into the zero-gravity section and see how you manage there, before I give you a clean bill of health.'

Gibson also thought that was a good idea. He had always regarded himself as fairly fit, and until now it had never seriously occurred to him that this journey might not be merely uncomfortable but actually dangerous. You could laugh at space-sickness – when you'd never experienced it yourself. Afterwards, it seemed a very different matter.

The Inner Station – 'Space Station One', as it was usually called – was just over two thousand kilometres from Earth, circling the planet every two hours. It had been Man's first stepping-stone to the stars, and though it was no longer technically necessary for spaceflight, its presence had a profound effect on the economics of interplanetary travel. All journeys to the Moon or the planets started from here: the unwieldy atomic ships floated alongside this outpost of Earth while the cargoes from the parent world were loaded into their holds. A ferry service of chemically fuelled rockets linked the Station to the planet beneath, for by law no atomic drive-unit was allowed to operate within a thousand kilometres of the Earth's surface. Even this safety margin was felt by many to be inadequate, for the radioactive blast of a nuclear propulsion unit could cover that distance in less than a minute.

Space Station One had grown with the passing years, by a process of accretion, until its original designers would never have recognized it. Around the central spherical core had accumulated observatories, communications labs with fantastic aerial systems, and mazes of scientific equipment which only a specialist could identify. But despite all these additions, the main function of the artificial moon was still that of refuelling the little ships with which Man was challenging the immense loneliness of the Solar System.

'Quite sure you're feeling OK now?' asked the doctor as Gibson experimented with his feet.

'I think so,' he replied, unwilling to commit himself.

'Then come along to the reception room and we'll get you a drink – a nice hot drink,' he added, to prevent any misunderstanding. 'You can sit there and read the paper for half an hour before we decide what to do with you.'

It seemed to Gibson that anticlimax was being piled on anticlimax. He was two thousand kilometres from Earth, with the stars all around him: yet here he was forced to sit sipping sweet tea – tea! – in what might have been an ordinary dentist's waiting-room. There were no windows, presumably because the sight of the rapidly revolving heavens might have undone the good work of the medical staff. The only way of passing the time was to skim through piles of magazines which he'd already seen, and which were difficult to handle as they were ultralightweight editions apparently printed on cigarette paper. Fortunately he found a very old copy of *Argosy* containing a story he had written so long ago that he had completely forgotten the ending, and this kept him happy until the doctor returned.

'Your pulse seems normal,' said the MO grudgingly. 'We'll take you along to the zero-gravity chamber. Just follow me and don't be surprised at anything that happens.'

With this cryptic remark he led Gibson out into a wide, brightly lit corridor that seemed to curve upwards in both directions away from the point at which he was standing. Gibson had no time to examine this phenomenon, for the doctor slid open a side door and started up a flight of metal stairs. Gibson followed automatically for a few paces, then realized just what lay ahead of him and stopped with an involuntary cry of amazement.

Immediately beneath his feet, the slope of the stairway was a reasonable forty-five degrees, but it rapidly became steeper until only a dozen metres ahead the steps were rising vertically. Thereafter – and it was a sight that might have unnerved anyone coming across it for the first time – the increase of gradient continued remorselessly until the steps began to overhang and at last passed out of sight above and *behind* him.

Hearing his exclamation, the doctor looked back and gave a reassuring laugh.

'You mustn't always believe your eyes,' he said. 'Come along and see how easy it is.'

Reluctantly Gibson followed, and as he did so he became aware that two very peculiar things were happening. In the first place, he was gradually becoming lighter: in the second, despite the obvious steepening of the stairway, the slope beneath his feet remained at a constant forty-five degrees. The vertical direction itself, in fact, was slowly tilting as he moved forward, so that despite its increasing curvature the gradient of the stairway never altered.

It did not take Gibson long to arrive at the explanation. All the apparent gravity was due to the centrifugal force produced as the station spun slowly on its axis, and as he approached the centre the force was diminishing to zero. The stairway itself was winding in towards the axis along some sort of spiral – once he'd have known its mathematical name – so that despite the radial gravity field the slope underfoot remained constant. It was the sort of thing that people who lived in space-stations must get accustomed to quickly enough: presumably when they returned to Earth the sight of a normal stairway would be equally unsettling.

At the end of the stairs there was no longer any real sense of 'up' or 'down'. They were in a long cylindrical room, crisscrossed with ropes but otherwise empty, and at its far end a shaft of sunlight came blasting through an observation port. As Gibson watched, the beam moved steadily across the metal walls like a questing searchlight, was momentarily eclipsed, then blazed out again from another window. It was the first indication Gibson's senses had given him of the fact that the station was really spinning on its axis, and he timed the rotation roughly by noting how long the sunlight took to return to its original position. The 'day' of this little artificial world was less than ten seconds: that was sufficient to give a sensation of normal gravity at its outer walls.

Gibson felt rather like a spider in its web as he followed the doctor hand-over-hand along the guide ropes, towing himself effortlessly through the air until they came to the observation post. They were, he saw, at the end of a sort of chimney jutting out along the axis of the station, so that they were well clear of its equipment and apparatus and had an almost unrestricted view of the stars.

'I'll leave you here for a while,' said the doctor. 'There's plenty to look at, and you should be quite happy. If not – well, remember there's normal gravity at the bottom of those stairs!'

Yes, thought Gibson; *and* a return trip to Earth by the next rocket as well. But he was determined to pass the test and to get a clean bill of health.

It was quite impossible to realize that the space-station itself was rotating, and not the framework of sun and stars: to believe otherwise required an act of faith, a conscious effort of will. The stars were moving so quickly that only the brighter ones were clearly visible and the Sun, when Gibson allowed himself to glance at it out of the corner of his eye, was a golden comet that crossed the sky every five seconds. With this fantastic speeding up of the natural order of events, it was easy to see how ancient man had refused to believe that his own solid earth was rotating, and had attributed all movement to the turning celestial sphere.

Partly occulted by the bulk of the station, the Earth was a great crescent spanning half the sky. It was slowly waxing as the station raced along on its globe-encircling orbit: in some forty minutes it would be full, and an hour after that would be totally invisible, a black shield eclipsing the Sun while the station passed through its cone of shadow. The Earth would go through all its phases – from new to full and back again – in just two hours. The sense of time became distorted as one thought of these things: the familiar divisions of day and night, of months and seasons, had no meaning here.

About a kilometre from the station, moving with it in its orbit but not at the moment connected to it in any way, were the three spaceships that happened to be 'in dock' at the moment. One was the tiny arrowhead of the rocket that had brought him, at such expense and such discomfort, up from Earth an hour ago. The second was a lunar-bound freighter of, he guessed, about a thousand tons gross. And the third, of course, was the *Ares*, almost dazzling in the splendour of her new aluminium paint.

Gibson had never become reconciled to the loss of the sleek, streamlined spaceships which had been the dream of the early twentieth century. The glittering dumb-bell hanging against the stars was not *his* idea of a space-liner: though the world had accepted it, he had not. Of course, he knew the familiar arguments – there was no need for streamlining in a ship that never entered an atmosphere, and therefore the design was dictated purely by structural and power-plant considerations. Since the violently radioactive drive-unit had to be as far away from the crew quarters as possible, the double-sphere and long connecting tube was the simplest solution.

It was also, Gibson thought, the ugliest; but that hardly mattered since the *Ares* would spend practically all her life in deep space where the only spectators were the stars. Presumably she was already fuelled and merely waiting for the precisely calculated moment when her motors would burst into life, and she would pull away out of the orbit in which she was circling and had hitherto spent all her existence, to swing into the long hyperbola that led to Mars.

When that happened, he would be aboard, launched at last upon the adventure he had never really believed would come to him.

Two

The Captain's office aboard the *Ares* was not designed to hold more than three men when gravity was acting, but there was plenty of room for six while the ship was in a free orbit and one could stand on walls or ceiling according to taste. All except one of the group clustered at surrealist angles around Captain Norden had been in space before, and knew what was expected of him, but this was no ordinary briefing. The maiden flight of a new spaceship is always an occasion and the *Ares* was the first of her line – the first, indeed, of all spaceships ever to be built primarily for passengers and not for freight. When she was fully commissioned, she would carry a crew of thirty and a hundred and fifty passengers in somewhat spartan comfort. On her first voyage, however, the proportions were almost reversed and at the moment her crew of six were waiting for the single passenger to come aboard.

'I'm still not quite clear,' said Owen Bradley, the electronics officer, 'what we are supposed to do with the fellow when we've got him. Whose bright idea was this, anyway?'

'I was coming to that,' said Captain Norden, running his hands through where his magnificent blond hair had been only a few days before. (Spaceships seldom carry professional barbers, and though there are always plenty of eager amateurs one prefers to put off the evil day as long as possible.) 'You all know of Mr Gibson, of course.'

This remark produced a chorus of replies, not all of them respectful.

'I think his stories stink,' said Dr Scott. 'The later ones, anyway. *Martian Dust* wasn't bad, but of course it's completely dated now.'

'Nonsense!' snorted astrogator Mackay. 'The last stories are much the best, now that Gibson's got interested in fundamentals and has cut out the blood and thunder.'

This outburst from the mild little Scot was most uncharacteristic. Before anyone else could join in, Captain Norden interrupted.

'We're not here to discuss literary criticism, if you don't mind. There'll be plenty of time for that later. But there are one or two points the Corporation wants me to make clear before we begin. Mr Gibson is a very important man – a distinguished guest – and he's been invited to come on this trip so that he can write a book about it later. It's not just a publicity stunt.' ('Of course not!' interjected Bradley, with heavy sarcasm.) 'But naturally the Corporation hopes that future clients won't be – er discouraged by what they read. Apart from that, we *are* making history: our maiden voyage ought to be recorded properly. So try and behave like gentlemen for a while: Gibson's book will probably sell half a million copies, and your future reputations may depend on your behaviour these next three months!'

'That sounds dangerously like blackmail to me,' said Bradley.

'Take it that way if you please,' continued Norden cheerfully. 'Of course, I'll explain to Gibson that he can't expect the service that will be provided later when we've got stewards and cooks and Lord knows what. He'll understand that, and won't expect breakfast in bed every morning.'

'Will he help with the washing-up?' asked someone with a practical turn of mind.

Before Norden could deal with this problem in social etiquette a sudden buzzing came from the communications panel, and a voice began to call from the speaker grille.

'Station One calling *Ares* – your passenger's coming over.'

Norden flipped a switch and replied, 'OK – we're ready.' Then he turned to the crew.

'With all these hair-cuts around, the poor chap will think it's graduation day at Alcatraz. Go and meet him, Jimmy, and help him through the airlock when the tender couples up.'

Martin Gibson was still feeling somewhat exhilarated at having surmounted his first major obstacle – the MO at Space Station One. The loss of gravity on leaving the station and crossing to the *Ares* in the tiny, compressed-air driven tender had scarcely bothered him at all, but the sight that met his eyes when he entered Captain Norden's cabin caused him a momentary relapse. Even when there was no gravity, one liked to pretend that *some* direction was 'down', and it seemed natural to assume that the surface on which chairs and table were bolted was the floor. Unfortunately the majority decision seemed otherwise, for two members of the crew were hanging like stalactites from the 'ceiling', while two more were relaxed at quite arbitrary angles in mid-air. Only the Captain was, according to Gibson's ideas, the right way up. To make matters worse, their shaven heads gave these normally quite presentable men a faintly sinister appearance, so that the whole tableau looked like a family reunion at Castle Dracula.

There was a brief pause while the crew analysed Gibson. They all recognized the novelist at once: his face had been familiar to the public ever since his first best-seller, *Thunder in the Dawn*, had appeared nearly twenty years ago. He was a chubby yet sharp-featured little man, still on the right side of forty-five, and when he spoke his voice was surprisingly deep and resonant.

'This,' said Captain Norden, working round the cabin from left to right, 'is my engineer, Lieutenant Hilton. This is Dr Mackay, our navigator – only a PhD, not a *real* doctor, like Dr Scott here. Lieutenant Bradley is Electronics Officer, and Jimmy Spencer, who met you at the airlock, is our supernumerary and hopes to be Captain when he grows up.'

Gibson looked round the little group with some surprise. There were so few of them – five men and a boy! His face must have revealed his thoughts, for Captain Norden laughed and continued.

'Not many of us, are there? But you must remember that this ship is almost automatic – and besides, nothing ever happens in space. When we start the regular passenger run, there'll be a crew of thirty. On this trip, we're making up the weight in cargo, so we're really travelling as a fast freighter.'

Gibson looked carefully at the men who would be his only companions for the next three months. His first reaction (he always distrusted first reactions, but was at pains to note them) was one of astonishment that they seemed so ordinary – when one made allowance for such superficial matters as their odd attitudes and temporary baldness. There was no way of guessing that they belonged to a profession more romantic than any that the world had known since the last cowboys traded in their broncos for helicopters.

At a signal which Gibson did not intercept, the others took their leave by launching themselves with fascinatingly effortless precision through the open doorway. Captain Norden settled down in his seat again and offered Gibson a cigarette. The author accepted it doubtfully.

'You don't mind smoking?' he asked. 'Doesn't it waste oxygen?'

'There'd be a mutiny,' laughed Norden, 'if I had to ban smoking for three months. In any case, the oxygen consumption's negligible. Back in the old days we had to be more careful. One tobacco firm once put out a special astronaut's brand, impregnated with some oxygen-carrier so that it didn't use air. It wasn't popular – and one day a batch got an overdose of oxygen. When you lit them, they went off like squibs; and that was the end of *that* idea.'

Captain Norden, thought Gibson a little ruefully, was not fitting at all well into the expected pattern. The skipper of a space-liner, according to the best – or at least the most popular – literary tradition, should be a grizzled, keen-eyed veteran who had spent half his life in the ether and could navigate across the Solar System by the seat of his pants, thanks to his uncanny knowledge of the spaceways. He must also be a martinet; when he gave orders, his officers must jump to attention (not an easy thing under zero gravity), salute smartly, and depart at the double.

Instead, the captain of the *Ares* was certainly less than forty, and might have been taken for a successful business executive. As for being a martinet – so far Gibson had detected no signs of discipline whatsoever. This impression, he realized later, was not strictly accurate. The only discipline aboard the *Ares* was entirely self-imposed: that was the only form possible among the type of men who composed her crew.

'So you've never been in space before?' said Norden, looking thoughtfully at his passenger.

'I'm afraid not. I made several attempts to get on the lunar run, but it's absolutely impossible unless you're on official business. It's a pity that space-travel's still so infernally expensive.'

Norden smiled.

'We hope the *Ares* will do something to change that. I must say,' he added, 'that you seem to have managed to write quite a lot about the subject with ah – the minimum of practical experience.'

'Oh, that!' said Gibson airily, with what he hoped was a light laugh. 'It's a common delusion that authors must have experienced everything they describe in their books. I read all I could about space-travel when I was younger and did my best to get local colour right. Don't forget that all my interplanetary novels were written in the early days – I've hardly touched the subject in the last few years. It's rather surprising that people still associate my name with it.'

Norden wondered how much of this modesty was assumed. Gibson must know perfectly well that it was his space-travel novels that had made him famous – and had prompted the Corporation to invite him on this trip. The whole situation, Norden realized, had some highly entertaining possibilities. But they would have to wait: in the meantime he must explain to this landlubber the routine of life aboard the private world of the *Ares*.

'We keep normal Earth-time – Greenwich Meridian – aboard the ship and everything shuts down at "night". There are no watches, as there used to be in the old days: the instruments can take over when we're sleeping, so we aren't on continuous duty. That's one reason why we can manage with such a small crew. On this trip, as there's plenty of space, we've all got separate cabins. Yours is a regular passenger stateroom: the only one that's fitted up, as it happens. I think you'll find it comfortable. Is all your cargo aboard? How much did they let you take?'

'A hundred kilos. It's in the airlock.'

'A hundred kilos!' Norden managed to repress his amazement. The fellow must be emigrating – taking all his family heirlooms with him. Norden had the true astronaut's horror of surplus mass, and did not doubt that Gibson was carrying a lot of unnecessary rubbish. However, if the Corporation had OK'd it, and the authorized load wasn't exceeded, he had nothing to complain about.

'I'll get Jimmy to take you to your room. He's our odd-job man for this trip, working his passage and learning something about spaceflight. Most of us start that way, signing up for the lunar run during college vacations. Jimmy's quite a bright lad – he's already got his Bachelor's degree.'

By now Gibson was beginning to take it quite for granted that the cabin-boy would be a college graduate. He followed Jimmy – who seemed somewhat overawed by his presence – to the passengers' quarters. They glided like ghosts along the brightly lit corridors, which were fitted with a simple device that had done a good deal to make life aboard gravitationless spaceships more comfortable. Close to each wall, an endless belt with hand-holds at regular intervals was continually moving along at several kilometres an hour. One had only to reach out a hand to strap-hang from one end of the ship to the other without the slightest effort, though a certain amount of skill was required at intersections to change from one belt to another.

The stateroom was small, but beautifully planned and designed in excellent taste. Ingenious lighting and mirror-faced walls made it seem much larger than it really was, and the pivoted bed could be reversed during the 'day' to act as a table. There were very few reminders of the absence of gravity: everything had been done to make the traveller feel at home.

For the next hour Gibson sorted out his belongings and experimented with the room's gadgets and controls. The device that pleased him most was a shaving mirror which, when a button was pressed, transformed itself into a porthole looking out on the stars. He wondered just how it was done.

At last everything was stowed away where he could find it: there was absolutely nothing else for him to do. He lay down on the bed and buckled the elastic belts around his chest and thighs. The illusion of weight was not very convincing, but it was better than nothing and did give some sense of a vertical direction.

Lying at peace in the bright little room that would be his world for the next hundred days, he could forget the disappointments and petty annoyances that had marred his departure from Earth. There was nothing to worry about now: for the first time in almost as long as he could remember, he had given his future entirely into the keeping of others. Engagements, lecture appointments, deadlines – all these things he had left behind on Earth. The sense of blissful relaxation was too good to last, but he would let his mind savour it while he could.

A series of apologetic knocks on the cabin door roused Gibson from sleep an indeterminate time later. For a moment he did not realize where he was: then full consciousness came back, he unclipped the retaining straps and thrust himself off the bed. As his movements were still poorly coordinated he had to make a cannon off the nominal ceiling before reaching the door.

Jimmy Spencer stood there, slightly out of breath.

'Captain's compliments, sir, and would you like to come and see the take-off?'

'I certainly would,' said Gibson. 'Wait until I get my camera.'

He reappeared a moment later carrying a brand-new Leica XXA, at which Jimmy stared with undisguised envy, and festooned with auxiliary lenses and exposure meters. Despite these handicaps, they quickly reached the observation gallery, which ran like a circular belt around the body of the *Ares*.

For the first time Gibson saw the stars in their full glory, no longer dimmed either by atmosphere or by darkened glass, for he was on the night-side of the ship and the sun-filters had been drawn aside. The *Ares*, unlike the space-station, was not turning on her axis but was held in the rigid reference system of her gyroscopes so that the stars were fixed and motionless in her skies.

As he gazed on the glory he had so often, and so vainly, tried to describe in his books, Gibson found it very hard to analyse his emotions – and he hated to waste an emotion that might profitably be employed in print. Oddly enough neither the brightness nor the sheer number of the stars made the greatest impression on his mind. He had seen skies little inferior to this from the tops of mountains on Earth, or from the observation decks of stratoliners; but never had he felt so vividly the sense that the stars were all around him, down to the horizon he no longer possessed, and even below, under his very feet.

Space Station One was a complicated, brightly polished toy floating in nothingness a few metres beyond the port. There was no way in which its distance or size could be judged, for there was nothing familiar about its shape, and the sense of perspective seemed to have failed. Earth and Sun were both invisible, hidden behind the body of the ship.

Startlingly close, a disembodied voice came suddenly from a hidden speaker.

'One hundred seconds to firing. Please take your positions.'

Gibson automatically tensed himself and turned to Jimmy for advice. Before he could frame any questions, his guide said hastily, 'I must get back on duty,' and disappeared in a graceful power-dive, leaving Gibson alone with his thoughts.

The next minute and a half passed with remarkable slowness, punctuated though it was with frequent time-checks from the speakers. Gibson wondered who the announcer was: it did not sound like Norden's voice, and probably it was merely a recording, operated by the automatic circuit which must now have taken over control of the ship.

'Twenty seconds to go. Thrust will take about ten seconds to build up.'

'Ten seconds to go.'

'Five seconds, four, three, two, one . . .'

Very gently, something took hold of Gibson and slid him down the curving side of the porthole-studded wall on to what had suddenly become the floor. It was hard to realize that up and down had returned once more, harder still to connect their re-appearance with that distant, attenuated thunder that had broken in upon the silence of the ship. Far away in the second sphere that was the other half of the *Ares*, in that mysterious, forbidden world of dying atoms and automatic machines which no man could ever enter and live, the forces that powered the stars themselves were being unleashed. Yet there was none of that sense of mounting, pitiless acceleration that always accompanies the take-off of a chemically propelled rocket. The *Ares* had unlimited space in which to manoeuvre: she could take as long as she pleased to break free from her present orbit and crawl slowly out into the transfer hyperbola that would lead her to Mars. In any case, the utmost power of the atomic drive could move her two-thousand-ton mass with an acceleration of only a tenth of a gravity: at the moment it was throttled back to less than half of this small value. Atomic propulsion units operated at such enormous temperatures that they could be used only at low power ratings, which was one reason why their employment for direct planetary take-offs was impossible. But unlike the short-duty chemical rockets, they could maintain their thrust for hours at a time.

It did not take Gibson long to re-orientate himself. The ship's acceleration was so low – it gave him, he calculated, an effective weight of less than four kilogrammes – yet his movements were still practically unrestricted. Space Station One had not moved from its apparent position, and he had to wait almost a minute before he could detect that the *Ares* was, in fact, slowly drawing away from it. Then he belatedly remembered his camera, and began to record the departure. When he had finally settled (he hoped) the tricky problem of the right exposure to give a small, brilliantly lit object against a jet-black background, the station was already appreciably more distant. In less than ten minutes, it had dwindled to a distant point of light that was hard to distinguish from the stars.

When Space Station One had vanished completely, Gibson went round to the day side of the ship to take some photographs of the receding Earth. It was a huge, thin crescent when he first saw it, far too large for the eye to take in at a single glance. As he watched, he could see that it was slowly waxing, for the *Ares* must make at least one more circuit before she could break away and spiral out towards Mars. It would be a good hour before the Earth was appreciably smaller and in that time it would pass again from new to full.

Well, this is it, thought Gibson. Down there is all my past life, and the lives of all my ancestors back to the first blob of jelly in the first primeval sea. No colonist or explorer setting sail from his native land ever left so much behind as I am leaving now. Down beneath those clouds lies the whole of human history: soon I shall be able to eclipse with my little finger what was, until a lifetime ago, all of Man's dominion and everything that his art had saved from time.

This inexorable drawing away from the known into the unknown had almost the finality of death. Thus must the naked soul, leaving all its treasures behind it, go out at last into the darkness and the night.

Gibson was still watching at the observation post when, more than an hour later, the *Ares* finally reached escape velocity and was free from Earth. There was no way of telling that this moment had come and passed, for Earth still dominated the sky and the motors still maintained their muffled, distant thunder. Another ten hours of continuous operation would be needed before they had completed their task and could be closed down for the rest of the voyage.

Gibson was sleeping when that moment came. The sudden silence, the complete loss of even the slight gravity the ship had enjoyed these last few hours, brought him back to a twilight sense of awareness. He looked dreamily around the darkened room until his eye found the little pattern of stars framed in the porthole. They were, of course, utterly motionless. It was impossible to believe that the *Ares* was now racing out from the Earth's orbit at a speed so great that even the Sun could never hold her back.

Sleepily, he tightened the fastenings of his bedclothes to prevent himself drifting out into the room. It would be nearly a hundred days before he had any sense of weight again.

Three

The same pattern of stars filled the porthole when a series of bell-like notes tolling from the ship's public address system woke Gibson from a comparatively dreamless sleep. He dressed in some haste and hurried out to the observation deck, wondering what had happened to Earth overnight.

It was very disconcerting, at least to an inhabitant of Earth, to see two moons in the sky at once. But there they were, side by side, both in their first quarter, and one about twice as large as the other. It was several seconds before Gibson realized that he was looking at Moon and Earth together – and several seconds more before he finally grasped the fact that the smaller and more distant crescent was his own world.

The *Ares* was not, unfortunately, passing very close to the Moon, but even so it was more than ten times as large as Gibson had ever seen it from the Earth. The interlocking chains of crater-rings were clearly visible along the ragged line separating day from night, and the still unilluminated disc could be faintly seen by the reflected earth-light falling upon it. And surely – Gibson bent suddenly forward, wondering if his eyes had tricked him. Yet there was no doubt of it: down in the midst of that cold and faintly gleaming land, waiting for the dawn that was still many days away, minute sparks of light were burning like fireflies in the dusk. They had not been there fifty years ago: they were the lights of the first lunar cities, telling the stars that life had come at last to the Moon after a billion years of waiting.

A discreet cough from nowhere in particular interrupted Gibson's reverie. Then a slightly over-amplified voice remarked in a conversational tone:

'If Mr Gibson will kindly come to the mess-room, he will find some tepid coffee and a few flakes of cereal still left on the table.'

He glanced hurriedly at his watch. He had completely forgotten about breakfast – an unprecedented phenomenon. No doubt someone had gone to look for him in his cabin and, failing to find him there, was paging him through the ship's public address system.

He hurried back to the mess-room, and in his haste lost himself completely in the labyrinth of corridors. It was surprising how much space there was inside the ship: one day there would be notices everywhere for the guidance of passengers, but Gibson had to find his way as best he could. Since there was no up or down, no natural division of space into horizontal or vertical, he had an extra dimension in which to lose himself. He made the most of the opportunity.

When at last he burst apologetically into the mess-room he found the crew engaged in technical controversy concerning the merits of various types of spaceship. He listened carefully as he nibbled at his breakfast. For some reason he had very little appetite: then he remembered that the absence of muscular effort in space often produced this effect – a very fortunate one from the point of view of the catering department.

While he ate, Gibson watched the little group of arguing men, fixing them in his mind and noting their behaviour and characteristics. Norden's introduction had merely served to give them labels: as yet they were not definite personalities to him. It was curious to think that before the voyage had ended, he would probably know every one of them better than most of his acquaintances back on Earth. There could be no secrets and no masks aboard the tiny world of the *Ares*.

At the moment, Dr Scott was talking. (Later, Gibson would realize that there was nothing very unusual about this.) He seemed a somewhat excitable character, inclined to lay down the law at a moment's provocation on subjects about which he could not possibly be qualified to speak. His most successful interrupter was Bradley, the electronics and communications expert – a dryly cynical person who seemed to take a sardonic pleasure in verbal sabotage. From time to time he would throw a small bombshell into the conversation which would halt Scott for a moment, though never for long. Mackay, the little Scots mathematician, also entered the battle from time to time, speaking rather quickly in a precise, almost pedantic fashion. He would, Gibson thought, have been more at home in a university common-room than on a spaceship.

Captain Norden appeared to be acting as a not entirely disinterested umpire, supporting first one side and then the other in an effort to prevent any conclusive victory. Young Spencer was already at work, and Hilton, the only remaining member of the crew, had taken no part in the discussion. The engineer was sitting quietly watching the others with a detached amusement, and his face was hauntingly familiar to Gibson. Where had they met before? Why, of course – what a fool he was not to have realized it! – this was *the* Hilton. Gibson swung round in his chair so that he could see the other more clearly. His half-finished meal was forgotten as he looked with awe and envy at the man who had brought the *Arcturus* back to Mars after the greatest adventure in the history of spaceflight. Only six men had ever reached Saturn; and only three of them were still alive. Hilton had stood, with his lost companions, on those far-off moons whose very names were magic – Titan, Encladus, Tethys, Rhea, Dione . . . He had seen the incomparable splendour of the great rings spanning the sky in symmetry that seemed too perfect for nature's contriving. He had been into that Ultima Thule in which circled the cold outer giants of the Sun's scattered family, and he had returned again to the light and warmth of the inner worlds. 'Yes,' thought Gibson, 'there are a good many things I want to talk to you about before this trip's over.'

The discussion group was breaking up as the various officers drifted – literally – away to their posts, but Gibson's thoughts were still circling Saturn as Captain Norden came across to him and broke into his reverie.

'I don't know what sort of schedule you've planned,' he said, 'but I suppose you'd like to look over our ship. After all, that's what usually happens around this stage in one of your stories.'

Gibson smiled, somewhat mechanically. He feared it was going to be some time before he lived down his past.

'I'm afraid you're quite right there. It's the easiest way, of course, of letting the reader know how things work, and sketching in the *locale* of the plot. Luckily it's not so important now that everyone knows exactly what a spaceship is like inside. One can take the technical details for granted, and get on with the story. But when I started writing about astronautics, back in the sixties, one had to hold up the plot for thousands of words to explain how the spacesuits worked, how the atomic drive operated, and clear up anything else that might come into the story.'

'Then I can take it,' said Norden, with the most disarming of smiles, 'that there's not a great deal we can teach you about the *Ares*.'

Gibson managed to summon up a blush.

'I'd appreciate it very much if you'd show me round – whether you do it according to the standard literary pattern or not.'

'Very well,' grinned Norden. 'We'll start at the control room. Come along.'

For the next two hours they floated along the labyrinth of corridors that crossed and criss-crossed like arteries in the spherical body of the *Ares*. Soon, Gibson knew, the interior of the ship would be so familiar to him that he could find his way blindfold from one end to the other; but he had already lost his way once and would do so again before he had learned his way around.

As the ship was spherical, it had been divided into zones of latitude like the Earth. The resulting nomenclature was very useful, since it at once gave a mental picture of the liner's geography. To go 'North' meant that one was heading for the control cabin and the crew's quarters. A trip to the Equator suggested that one was visiting either the great dining-hall, occupying most of the central plane of the ship, or the observation gallery which completely encircled the liner. The Southern Hemisphere was almost entirely fuel tank, with a few storage holds and miscellaneous machinery. Now that the *Ares* was no longer using her motors, she had been swung round in space so that the Northern Hemisphere was in perpetual sunlight and the 'uninhabited' Southern one in darkness. At the South Pole itself was a small metal door bearing a set of impressive official seals and the notice: 'To be Opened only under the Express Orders of the Captain or his Deputy'. Behind it lay the long, narrow tube connecting the main body of the ship with the smaller sphere, a hundred metres away, which held the power plant and the drive units. Gibson wondered what was the point of having a door at all if no one could ever go through it: then he remembered that there must be some provision to enable the servicing robots of the Atomic Energy Commission to reach their work.

Strangely enough, Gibson received one of his strongest impressions not from the scientific and technical wonders of the ship, which he had expected to see in any case, but from the empty passenger quarters – a honeycomb of closely packed cells that occupied most of the North Temperate Zone. The impression was rather a disagreeable one. A house so new that no one has ever lived in it can be more lonely than an old, deserted ruin that has once known life and may still be peopled by ghosts. The sense of desolate emptiness was very strong here in the echoing, brightly lit corridors which would one day be crowded with life, but which now lay bleak and lonely in the sunlight piped through the walls – a sunlight much bluer than on Earth and therefore hard and cold.

Gibson was quite exhausted, mentally and physically, when he got back to his room. Norden had been an altogether too conscientious guide, and Gibson suspected that he had been getting some of his own back, and thoroughly enjoying it. He wondered exactly what his companions thought of his literary activities: probably he would not be left in ignorance for long.

He was lying in his bunk, sorting out his impressions, when there came a modest knock on the door.

'Damn,' said Gibson, quietly. 'Who's that?' he continued, a little louder.

'It's Jim – Spencer, Mr Gibson. I've got a radiogram for you.'

Young Jimmy floated into the room, bearing an envelope with the Signals Officer's stamp. It was sealed, but Gibson surmised that he was the only person on the ship who didn't know its contents. He had a shrewd idea of what they would be, and groaned inwardly. There was really no way of escape from Earth: it could catch you wherever you went.

The message was brief and contained only one redundant word:

NEW YORKER, REVUE DES QUATRE MONDES, LIFE INTERPLANET-
ARY WANT FIVE THOUSAND WORDS EACH. PLEASE RADIO BY
NEXT SUNDAY. LOVE. RUTH.

Gibson sighed. He had left Earth in such a rush that there had been no time for a final consultation with his agent, Ruth Goldstein, apart from a hurried phone-call half-way around the world. But he'd told her quite clearly that he wanted to be left alone for a fortnight. It never made any difference, of course. Ruth always went happily ahead, confident that he would deliver the goods on time. Well, for once he wouldn't be bullied and she could darned well wait: he'd earned this holiday.

He grabbed his scribbling pad and, while Jimmy gazed ostentatiously elsewhere, wrote quickly:

SORRY. EXCLUSIVE RIGHTS ALREADY PROMISED TO SOUTH ALABAMA PIG KEEPER AND POULTRY FANCIER. WILL SEND DETAILS ANY MONTH NOW. WHEN ARE YOU GOING TO POISON HARRY? LOVE. MART.

Harry was the literary, as opposed to the business, half of Goldstein and Co. He had been happily married to Ruth for over twenty years, during the last fifteen of which Gibson had never ceased to remind them both that they were getting in a rut and needed a change and that the whole thing couldn't possibly last much longer.

Goggling slightly, Jimmy Spencer disappeared with this unusual message, leaving Gibson alone with his thoughts. Of course, he would have to start work some time, but meanwhile his typewriter was buried down in the hold where he couldn't see it. He had even felt like attaching one of those 'NOT WANTED IN SPACE – MAY BE STOWED IN VACUUM' labels, but had manfully resisted the temptation. Like most writers who had never had to rely solely on their literary earnings, Gibson hated *starting* to write. Once he had begun, it was different . . . sometimes.

His holiday lasted a full week. At the end of that time, Earth was merely the most brilliant of the stars and would soon be lost in the glare of the Sun. It was hard to believe that he had ever known any life but that of the little, self-contained universe that was the *Ares*. And its crew no longer consisted of Norden, Hilton, Mackay, Bradley, and Scott but of John, Fred, Angus, Owen, and Bob.

He had grown to know them all, though Hilton and Bradley had a curious reserve that he had been unable to penetrate. Each man was a definite and sharply contrasted character: almost the only thing they had in common was intelligence. Gibson doubted if any of them had an I Q of less than 120, and he sometimes wriggled with embarrassment as he remembered the crews he had imagined for some of his fictional spaceships. He recalled Master Pilot Graham, from *Five Moons Too Many* – still one of his favourite characters. Graham had been tough (had he not once survived half a minute in vacuum before being able to get to his spacesuit?) and he regularly disposed of a bottle of whisky a day. He was a distinct contrast to Dr Angus Mackay, PhD (Astron), FRAS, who was now sitting quietly in a corner reading a much annotated copy of the *Canterbury Tales* and taking an occasional squirt from a bulbful of milk.

The mistake that Gibson had made, along with so many other writers back in the fifties and sixties, was the assumption that there would be no fundamental difference between ships of space and ships of the sea – or between the men who manned them. There were parallels, it was true, but they were far outnumbered by the contrasts. The reason was purely technical, and should have been foreseen, but the popular writers of the mid-century had taken the lazy course and had tried to use the traditions of Herman Melville and Frank Dana in a medium for which they were grotesquely unfitted.

A ship of space was much more like a stratosphere liner than anything that had ever moved on the face of the ocean, and the technical training of its crew was at a much higher level even than that required in aviation. A man like Norden had spent five years at college, three years in space, and another two back at college on advanced astronautical theory before qualifying for his present position.

It had been a very quiet week. Gibson had lazed around taking life easily for the first time in years, looking at the unbelievable star fields for hours on end, and joining in the arguments that made almost every meal an affair of indefinite duration. There was no strict routine aboard the ship: no one could have ordered Norden's crew around, and Norden was much too intelligent to try. He knew that the work would be properly done by men who took a pride in it: apart from the daily maintenance reports which everyone initialled and brought to the Captain each evening, there was the minimum of control or supervision. The *Ares* was a good example of democracy in action.

Gibson was having a quiet game of darts with Dr Scott when the first excitement of the voyage burst unexpectedly upon them. There are not many games of skill that can be played in space; for a long time cards and chess had been the classical stand-bys, until some ingenious Englishman had decided that a flight of darts would perform very well in the absence of gravity. The distance between thrower and board had been increased to ten metres, but otherwise the game still obeyed the rules that had been formulated over the centuries amid an atmosphere of beer and tobacco smoke in English pubs.

Gibson had been delighted to find that he was quite good at the game. He almost always managed to beat Scott, despite – or because of – the other's elaborate technique. This consisted of placing the 'arrow' carefully in mid-air, and then going back a couple of metres to squint along it before smacking it smartly on its way.

Scott was optimistically aiming for a treble twenty when Bradley drifted into the room bearing a signals form in his hand.

'Don't look now,' he said in his soft, carefully modulated voice, 'but we're being followed.'

Everyone gaped at him as he relaxed in the doorway. Mackay was the first to recover.

'Please elucidate,' he said primly.

'There's a Mark III carrier missile coming after us hell for leather. It's just been launched from the Outer Station and should pass us in four days. They want me to catch it with our radio control as it goes by, but with the dispersion it will have at this range that's asking a lot. I doubt if it will go within a hundred thousand kilometres of us.'

'What's it in aid of? Someone left their toothbrush behind?'

'It seems to be carrying urgent medical supplies. Here, Doc, you have a look.'

Dr Scott examined the message carefully.

'This *is* interesting. They think they've got an antidote for Martian fever. It's a serum of some kind: the Pasteur Institute's made it. They must be pretty sure of the stuff if they've gone to all this trouble to catch us.'

'What, for Heaven's sake, is a Mark III missile – not to mention Martian Fever?' exploded Gibson at last.

Dr Scott answered before anyone else could get a word in.

'Martian fever isn't really a Martian disease. It seems to be caused by a terrestrial organism that we carried there and which liked the new climate more than the old one. It has the same sort of effect as malaria: people aren't often killed by it, but its economic effects are very serious. In any one year the percentage of man-hours lost—'

'Thank you very much. I remember all about it now. And the missile?'

Hilton slid smoothly into the conversation.

'That's simply a little automatic rocket with radio control and a very high terminal speed. It's used to carry cargoes between the space-stations, or to chase after spaceships when they've left anything behind. When it gets into radio range it will pick up our transmitter and home on to us. Hey, Bob,' he said suddenly, turning to Scott, 'why haven't they sent it direct to Mars? It could get there long before we do.'

'Because its little passengers wouldn't like it. I'll have to fix up some cultures for them to live in, and look after them like a nursemaid. Not my usual line of business, but I think I can remember some of the stuff I did at St Thomas's.'

'Wouldn't it be appropriate,' said Mackay with one of his rare attempts at humour, 'if someone went and painted the Red Cross outside?'

Gibson was thinking deeply.

'I was under the impression,' he said after a pause, 'that life on Mars was very healthy, both physically and psychologically.'

'You mustn't believe all you read in books,' drawled Bradley. 'Why anyone should ever want to go to Mars I can't imagine. It's flat, it's cold, and it's full of miserable half-starved plants looking like something out of Edgar Allan Poe. We've sunk millions into the place and haven't got a penny back. Anyone who goes there of his own free will should have his head examined. Meaning no offence of course.'

Gibson only smiled amicably. He had learned to discount Bradley's cynicism by about ninety per cent; but he was never quite sure how far the other was only *pretending* to be insulting. For once, however, Captain Norden asserted his authority: not merely to stop Bradley from getting away with it, but to prevent such alarm and despondency from spreading into print. He gave his electronics officer an angry glare.

'I ought to tell you, Martin,' he said, 'that although Mr Bradley doesn't like Mars, he takes an equally poor view of Earth and Venus. So don't let his opinions depress you.'

'I won't,' laughed Gibson. 'But there's one thing I'd like to ask.'

'What's that?' said Norden anxiously.

'Does Mr Bradley take as "poor a view", as you put it, of Mr Bradley as he does of everything else?'

'Oddly enough, he does,' admitted Norden. 'That shows that one at least of his judgements is accurate.'

'*Touché*,' murmured Bradley, for once at a loss. 'I will retire in high dudgeon and compose a suitable reply. Meanwhile, Mac, will you get the missile's coordinates and let me know when it should come into range?'

'All right,' said Mackay absently. He was deep in Chaucer again.

Four

During the next few days Gibson was too busy with his own affairs to take much part in the somewhat limited social life of the *Ares*. His conscience had smitten him, as it always did when he rested for more than a week, and he was hard at work again.

His crew-mates (for Gibson no longer regarded himself as a privileged passenger) respected his solitude. At first they had wandered into his room whenever they were passing, to talk about nothing in particular or to exchange solemn complaints about the weather. This had been very pleasant, but Gibson had been forced to stop it with a 'DANGER – MAN AT WORK' notice pinned on his door. Needless to say this had rapidly become adorned with ribald comments in various hands, but it had served its purpose.

The typewriter had been disentangled from his belongings and now occupied the place of honour in the little cabin. Sheets of manuscript lay everywhere – Gibson was an untidy worker – and had to be prevented from escaping by elastic bands. There had been a lot of trouble with the flimsy carbon paper, which had a habit of getting into the airflow and glueing itself against the ventilator, but Gibson had now mastered the minor techniques of life under zero gravity. It was amazing how quickly one learned them, and how soon they became a part of everyday life.

Gibson had found it very hard to get his impressions of space down on paper: one could not very well say 'space is awfully big' and leave it at that. The take-off from Earth had taxed his skill to the utmost. He had not actually lied, but anyone who read his dramatic description of the Earth falling away beneath the blast of the rocket would certainly never get the impression that the writer had then been in a state of blissful unconsciousness, swiftly followed by a state of far from blissful consciousness.

As soon as he had produced a couple of articles which would keep Ruth happy for a while (she had meanwhile sent three further radiograms of increasing asperity) he went Northwards to the Signals Office. Bradley received the sheets of MSS with marked lack of enthusiasm.

'I suppose this is going to happen every day from now on,' he said glumly.

'I hope so – but I'm afraid not. It depends on my inspiration.'

'There's a split infinitive right here on the top of page 2.'

'Excellent: nothing like 'em.'

'You've put "centrifugal" on page 3 where you mean "centripetal".'

'Since I get paid by the word, don't you think it's generous of me to use such long ones?'

'There are two successive sentences on page 4 beginning with "And".'

'Look here, are you going to send the damned stuff, or do I have to do it myself?'

Bradley grinned.

'I'd like to see you try. Seriously, though, I should have warned you to use a black ribbon. Contrast isn't so good with blue, and though the facsimile sender will be able to handle it all right at this range, when we get farther away from Earth it's important to have a nice, clean signal.'

As he spoke, Bradley was slipping the quarto sheets into the tray of the automatic transmitter. Gibson watched, fascinated, as they disappeared one by one into the maw of the machine and emerged five seconds later into the wire collecting-basket. It was strange to think that his words were now racing out through space in a continuous stream, getting a million kilometres farther away every three seconds. He was a little surprised, however, that it took so long to transmit a single sheet: on Earth, he knew, there were machines that could send hundreds of pages of print a minute.

'That's a complicated story,' explained Bradley when he put the question to him. 'We can't use high-speed facsimile over hundred-million-kilometre ranges with the low power we've got. The higher the speed, the bigger the band-width of the system, and so the more noise it picks up to swamp the signal. That's why telephony isn't practical on the very long distance circuits.'

'I think I get the idea,' said Gibson. 'But how is it that there's no trouble arranging radio broadcasts from Mars or Venus, even when they're half-way round the Sun?'

'Because on the planets the communications companies can focus their beams with lenses a hundred metres across, and can put a score of megawatts into them. *Our* little aerial system is just five metres in diameter, and we can't manage more than a few hundred kilowatts before blowing our output stages sky-high.'

'Oh,' said Gibson thoughtfully, and left it at that. He was just collecting his MSS sheets again when a buzzer sounded somewhere in the jungle of dials, switches and meter panels that covered practically the entire wall of the little office. Bradley shot across to one of his receivers and proceeded to do incomprehensible things with great rapidity. A piercing whistle started to come from a loudspeaker.

'The carrier's in range at last,' said Bradley, 'but it's a long way off – at a guess I'd say it will miss us by a hundred thousand kilometres.'

'What can we do about that?'

'Very little. I've got our own beacon switched on, and if it picks up our signals it will home on to us automatically and navigate itself to within a few kilometres of us.'

'And if it *doesn't* pick us up?'

'Then it will just go shooting on out of the Solar System. It's travelling fast enough to escape from the Sun: so are we, for that matter.'

'That's a cheerful thought. How long would it take us?'

'To do what?'

'To leave the system.'

'A couple of years, perhaps. Better ask Mackay. I don't know *all* the answers – I'm not like one of the characters in your books!'

'You may be one yet,' said Gibson darkly, and withdrew.

The approach of the missile had added an unexpected – and welcome – element of excitement to life aboard the *Ares*. Once the first fine careless rapture had worn off, space-travel could become exceedingly monotonous. It would be different in future days, when the liner was crowded with life, but there were times when her present loneliness could be very depressing.

The missile sweepstake had been organized by Dr Scott, but the prizes were held firmly by Captain Norden. Some calculations of Mackay's indicated that the projectile would miss the *Ares* by a hundred and twenty-five thousand kilometres, with an uncertainty of plus or minus thirty thousand. Most of the bets had been placed near the most probable value, but some pessimists, mistrusting Mackay completely, had gone out a quarter of a million kilometres. The bets weren't in cash, but in far more useful commodities such as cigarettes, candies, and other luxuries. Since the crew's personal weight allowance was strictly limited, these were far more valuable than pieces of paper with marks on them. Mackay had even thrown a half-bottle of whisky into the pool, and had thereby staked a claim to a volume of space about twenty thousand kilometres across. He never drank the stuff himself, he explained, but was taking some to a compatriot on Mars, who couldn't get the genuine article and was unable to afford the passage back to Scotland. No one believed him, which, as the story was more or less true, was a little unfair.

'Jimmy!'

'Yes, Captain Norden.'

'Have you finished checking the oxygen gauges?'

'Yes, sir. All OK.'

'What about that automatic recording gear those physicists have put in the hold? Does it look as if it's still working?'

'Well, it's making the same sort of noises as it did when we started.'

'Good. You've cleaned up that mess in the kitchen where Mr Hilton let the milk boil over?'

'Yes, Captain.'

'Then you've really finished everything?'

'I suppose so, but I was hoping—'

'That's fine. I've got a rather interesting job for you – something quite out of the usual run of things. Mr Gibson wants to start polishing up his astronautics. Of course, any of us could tell him all he wants to know, but – er – you're the last one to come from college and maybe you could put things across better. You've not forgotten the beginner's difficulties – *we'd* tend to take too much for

173

granted. It won't take much of your time – just go along when he asks and deal with his questions. I'm sure you can manage.'

Exit Jimmy, glumly.

'Come in,' said Gibson, without bothering to look up from his typewriter. The door opened behind him and Jimmy Spencer came floating into the room.

'Here's the book, Mr Gibson. I think it will give you everything you want. It's Richardson's *Elements of Astronautics*, special light-weight edition.'

He laid the volume in front of Gibson, who turned over the thin sheets with an interest that rapidly evaporated as he saw how quickly the proportion of words per page diminished. He finally gave up half-way through the book after coming across a page where the only sentence was 'Substituting for the value of perihelion distance from Equation 15.3, we obtain . . .' All else was mathematics.

'Are you *quite* sure this is the most elementary book in the ship?' he asked doubtfully, not wishing to disappoint Jimmy. He had been a little surprised when Spencer had been appointed as his unofficial tutor, but had been shrewd enough to guess the reason. Whenever there was a job that no one else wanted to do, it had a curious tendency to devolve upon Jimmy.

'Oh yes, it really *is* elementary. It manages without vector notation and doesn't touch perturbation theory. You should see some of the books Mackay has in his room. Each equation takes a couple of pages of print.'

'Well, thanks anyway. I'll give you a shout when I get stuck. It's about twenty years since I did any maths, though I used to be quite hot at it once. Let me know when you want the book back.'

'There's no hurry, Mr Gibson. I don't very often use it now I've got on to the advanced stuff.'

'Oh, before you go, maybe you can answer a point that's just cropped up. A lot of people are still worried about meteors, it seems, and I've been asked to give the latest information on the subject. Just how dangerous are they?'

Jimmy pondered for a moment.

'I could tell you, roughly,' he said, 'but if I were you I'd see Mr Mackay. He's got tables giving the exact figures.'

'Right, I'll do that.'

Gibson could quite easily have rung Mackay but any excuse to leave his work was too good to be missed. He found the little astrogator playing tunes on the big electronic calculating machine.

'Meteors?' said Mackay. 'Ah, yes, a very interesting subject. I'm afraid, though, that a great deal of highly misleading information has been published about them. It wasn't so long ago that people believed a spaceship would be riddled as soon as it left atmosphere.'

'Some of them still do,' replied Gibson. 'At least, they think that large-scale passenger travel won't be safe.'

Mackay gave a snort of disgust.

'Meteors are considerably less dangerous than lightning and the biggest normal one is about the size of a pea.'

'But, after all, one ship has been damaged by them!'

'You mean the *Star Queen*? One serious accident in the last five years is quite a satisfactory record. No ship has ever actually been *lost* through meteors.'

'What about the *Pallas*?'

'No one knows what happened to her. That's only the popular theory. It's not at all popular among the experts.'

'So I can tell the public to forget all about the matter?'

'Yes. Of course, there *is* the question of dust—'

'Dust?'

'Well, if by meteors you mean fairly large particles, from a couple of millimetres upwards, you needn't worry. But dust is a nuisance, particularly on space-stations. Every few years someone has to go over the skin to locate the punctures. They're usually far too small to be visible to the eye, but a bit of dust moving at fifty kilometres a second can get through a surprising thickness of metal.'

This sounded faintly alarming to Gibson, and Mackay hastened to reassure him.

'There really isn't the slightest need to worry,' he repeated. 'There's always a certain hull leakage taking place: the air supply takes it in its stride.'

However busy Gibson might be, or pretend to be, he always found time to wander restlessly around the echoing labyrinths of the ship, or to sit looking at the stars from the equatorial observation gallery.

He had formed a habit of going there during the daily concert. At 15.00 hours precisely the ship's public address system would burst into life and for an hour the music of Earth would whisper or roar through the empty passageways of the *Ares*. Every day a different person would choose the programmes, so one never knew what was coming – though after a while it was easy to guess the identity of the arranger. Norden played light classics and opera; Hilton practically nothing but Beethoven and Tchaikovsky. They were regarded as hopeless lowbrows by Mackay and Bradley, who indulged in astringent chamber music and atonal cacophonies of which no one else could make head or tail, or indeed particularly desired to. The ship's micro-library of books and music was so extensive that it would outlast a lifetime in space. It held, in fact, the equivalent of a quarter of a million books and some thousands of orchestral works, all recorded in electronic patterns awaiting the orders that would bring them into life.

Gibson was sitting in the observation gallery, trying to see how many of the Pleiades he could resolve with the naked eye, when a small projectile whispered past his ear and attached itself with a 'thwack!' to the glass of the port, where it hung vibrating like an arrow. At first sight, indeed, this seemed exactly what it was and for a moment Gibson wondered if the Cherokee were on the warpath again. Then he saw that a large rubber sucker had replaced the head, while from the base, just behind the feathers, a long, thin thread trailed away into the distance. At the end of the thread was Dr Robert Scott, MD, hauling himself briskly along like an energetic spider.

Gibson was still composing some suitably pungent remark when, as usual, the doctor got there first.

'Don't you think it's cute?' he said. 'It's got a range of twenty metres – only weighs half a kilo, and I'm going to patent it as soon as I get back to Earth.'

'Why?' said Gibson, in tones of resignation.

'Good gracious, can't you see? Suppose you want to get from one place to another inside a space-station where there's no rotational gravity. All you've got to do is to fire it at any flat surface near your destination, and reel in the cord. It gives you a perfect anchor until you release the sucker.'

'And just what's wrong with the usual way of getting around?'

'When you've been in space as long as *I* have,' said Scott smugly, 'you'll know what's wrong. There are plenty of hand-holds for you to grab in a ship like this. But suppose you want to go over to a blank wall at the other side of a room, and you launch yourself through the air from wherever you're standing. What happens? Well, you've got to break your fall somehow, usually with your hands, unless you can twist round on the way. Incidentally, do you know the commonest complaint a spaceship MO has to deal with? It's sprained wrists, and *that's* why. Anyway, even when you get to your target you'll bounce back unless you can grab hold of something. You might even get stranded in mid-air. I did that once in Space Station Three, in one of the big hangars. The nearest wall was fifteen metres away and I couldn't reach it.'

'Couldn't you spit your way towards it?' said Gibson solemnly. 'I thought that was the approved way out of the difficulty.'

'You try it some day and see how far it gets you. Anyway, it's not hygienic. Do you know what I had to do? It was most embarrassing. I was only wearing shorts and vest, as usual, and I calculated that they had about a hundredth of my mass. If I could throw them away at thirty metres a second, I could reach the wall in about a minute.'

'And did you?'

'Yes. But the Director was showing his wife round the Station that afternoon, so now you know why I'm reduced to earning my living on an old hulk like this, working my way from port to port when I'm not running a shady surgery down by the docks.'

'I think you've missed your vocation,' said Gibson admiringly. 'You should be in my line of business.'

'I don't think you believe me,' complained Scott bitterly.

'That's putting it mildly. Let's look at your toy.'

Scott handed it over. It was a modified air pistol, with a spring-loaded reel of nylon thread attached to the butt.

'It looks like—'

'If you say it's like a ray-gun I'll certify you as infectious. Three people have made that crack already.'

'Then it's a good job you interrupted me,' said Gibson, handing the weapon back to the proud inventor. 'By the way, how's Owen getting on? Has he contacted that missile yet?'

'No, and it doesn't look as if he's going to. Mac says it will pass about a hundred and forty-five thousand kilometres away – certainly out of range. It's a damn shame: there's not another ship going to Mars for months, which is why they were so anxious to catch us.'

'Owen's a queer bird, isn't he?' said Gibson with some inconsequence.

'Oh, he's not so bad when you get to know him. It's quite untrue what they say about him poisoning his wife. She drank herself to death of her own free will,' replied Scott with relish.

Owen Bradley, PHD, MIEE, MIRE, was very annoyed with life. Like every man aboard the *Ares*, he took his job with a passionate seriousness, however much he might pretend to joke about it. For the last twelve hours he had scarcely left the communications cabin, hoping that the continuous carrier wave from the missile would break into the modulation that would tell him it was receiving his signals and would begin to steer itself towards the *Ares*. But it was completely indifferent, and he had no right to expect otherwise. The little auxiliary beacon which was intended to call such projectiles had a reliable range of only twenty thousand kilometres: though that was ample for all normal purposes, it was quite inadequate now.

Bradley dialled the astrogation office on the ship's intercom, and Mackay answered almost at once.

'What's the latest, Mac?'

'It won't come much closer. I've just reduced the last bearing and smoothed out the errors. It's now a hundred and fifty thousand kilometres away, travelling on an almost parallel course. Nearest point will be a hundred and forty-four thousand, in about three hours. So I've lost the sweep – and I suppose we lose the missile.'

'Looks like it, I'm afraid,' grunted Bradley, 'but we'll see. I'm going down to the workshop.'

'Whatever for?'

'To make a one-man rocket and go after the blasted thing, of course. That wouldn't take more than half an hour in one of Martin's stories. Come down and help me.'

Mackay was nearer the ship's Equator than Bradley: consequently he had reached the workshop at the South Pole first and was waiting in mild perplexity when Bradley arrived, festooned with lengths of coaxial cable he had collected from stores. He outlined his plan briefly.

'I should have done this before, but it will make rather a mess and I'm one of those people who always go on hoping till the last moment. The trouble with our beacon is that it radiates in all directions – it has to, of course, since we never know where a carrier's coming from. I'm going to build a beam array and squirt *all* the power I've got after our runaway.'

He produced a rough sketch of a simple Yagi aerial and explained it swiftly to Mackay.

'This dipole's the actual radiator – the others are directors and reflectors. Antique, but it's easy to make and it should do the job. Call Hilton if you want any help. How long will it take?'

Mackay, who for a man of his tastes and interests had a positively atavistic skill with his hands, glanced at the drawings and the little pile of materials Bradley had gathered.

'About an hour,' he said, already at work. 'Where are you going now?'

'I've got to go out on the hull and disconnect the plumbing from the beacon transmitter. Bring the array round to the airlock when you're ready, will you?'

Mackay knew little about radio, but he understood clearly enough what Bradley was trying to do. At the moment the tiny beacon on the *Ares* was broadcasting its power over the entire sphere of space: Bradley was about to disconnect it from its present aerial system and aim its whole output accurately towards the fleeing projectile, thus increasing its range many-fold.

It was about an hour later that Gibson met Mackay hurrying through the ship behind a flimsy structure of parallel wires, spaced apart by plastic rods. He gaped at it in amazement as he followed Mackay to the lock, where Bradley was already waiting impatiently in his cumbersome spacesuit, the helmet open beside him.

'What's the nearest star to the missile?' Bradley asked. Mackay thought rapidly.

'It's nowhere near the ecliptic now,' he mused. 'The last figures I got were – let's see – declination fifteen something north, right ascension about fourteen hours. I suppose that will be – I never can remember these things ! – somewhere in Böotes. Oh yes – it won't be far from Arcturus: not more than ten degrees away, I'd say at a guess. I'll work out the exact figures in a minute.'

'That's good enough to start with. I'll swing the beam around, anyway. Who's in the signals cabin now?'

'The Skipper and Fred: I've rung them up and they're listening to the monitor. I'll keep in touch with you through the hull transmitter.'

Bradley snapped the helmet shut and disappeared through the airlock. Gibson watched him go with some envy. He had always wanted to wear a spacesuit, but though he had raised the matter on several occasions Norden had told him it was strictly against the rules. Spacesuits were very complex mechanisms and he might make a mistake in one – and then there would be hell to pay and perhaps a funeral to be arranged under rather novel circumstances.

Bradley wasted no time admiring the stars once he had launched himself through the outer door. He jetted slowly over the gleaming expanse of hull with his reaction units until he came to the section of plating he had already removed. Underneath it a network of cables and wires lay nakedly exposed to the blinding sunlight, and one of the cables had already been cut. He made a quick temporary connexion, shaking his head sadly at the horrible mis-match that would certainly reflect half the power right back to the transmitter. Then he found Arcturus and aimed the beam towards it. After waving it around hopefully for a while, he switched on his suit radio.

'Any luck?' he asked anxiously.

Mackay's despondent voice came through the loudspeaker.

'Nothing at all. I'll switch you through to communications.'

Norden confirmed the news.

'The signal's still coming in, but it hasn't acknowledged us yet.'

Bradley was taken aback. He had been quite sure that this would do the trick: at the very least, he must have increased the beacon's range by a factor of ten in this one direction. He waved the beam around for a few more minutes, then gave it up. Already he could visualize the little missile with its strange but precious cargo slipping silently out of his grasp, out towards the unknown limits of the Solar System – and beyond.

He called Mackay again.

'Listen, Mac,' he said urgently, 'I want you to check those coordinates again and then come out here and have a shot yourself. I'm going in to doctor the transmitter.'

When Mackay had relieved him, Bradley hurried back to his cabin. He found Gibson and the rest of the crew gathered glumly round the monitor receiver from which the unbroken whistle from the distant, and now receding, missile was coming with a maddening indifference.

There were very few traces of his normally languid, almost feline movements as Bradley pulled out circuit diagrams by the dozen and tore into the communications rack. It took him only a moment to run a pair of wires into the heart of the beacon transmitter. As he worked, he fired a series of questions at Hilton.

'You know something about these carrier missiles. How long must it receive our signal to give it time to home accurately on to us?'

'That depends, of course, on its relative speed and several other factors. In this case, since it's a low-acceleration job, a good ten minutes, I should say.'

'And then it doesn't matter even if our beacon fails?'

'No. As soon as the carrier's vectored itself towards you, you can go off the air again. Of course, you'll have to send it another signal when it passes right by you, but that should be easy.'

'How long will it take to get here if I *do* catch it?'

'A couple of days, maybe less. What are you trying out now?'

'The power amplifiers of this transmitter run at seven hundred and fifty volts. I'm taking a thousand volt line from another supply, that's all. It will be a short life and a merry one, but we'll double or treble the output while the tubes last.'

He switched on the intercom and called Mackay, who, not knowing the transmitter had been switched off for some time, was still carefully holding the array lined up on Arcturus, like an armour-plated William Tell aiming a crossbow.

'Hello, Mac, you all set?'

'I am practically ossified,' said Mackay with dignity. 'How much longer—'

'We're just starting now. Here goes.'

Bradley threw the switch. Gibson, who had been expecting sparks to start flying, was disappointed. Everything seemed exactly as before: but Bradley, who knew better, looked at his meters and bit his lip savagely.

It would take radio waves only half a second to bridge the gap to that tiny, far-off rocket with its wonderful automatic mechanisms that must remain forever lifeless unless this signal could reach them. The half-second passed, and the next. There had been time for the reply, but still that maddening heterodyne whistle came unbroken from the speaker. Then, suddenly, it stopped. For an age there was absolute silence. A hundred and fifty thousand kilometres away, the robot was investigating this new phenomenon. It took perhaps five seconds to make up its mind – and the carrier wave broke through again, but now modulated into an endless string of 'beep-beep-beeps'.

Bradley checked the enthusiasm in the cabin.

'We're not out of the wood yet,' he said. 'Remember it's got to hold our signal for ten minutes before it can complete its course alterations.' He looked anxiously at his meters and wondered how long it would be before the output tubes gave up the unequal battle.

They lasted seven minutes, but Bradley had spares ready and was on the air again in twenty seconds. The replacements were still operating when the missile carrier wave changed its modulation once more, and with a sigh of relief Bradley shut down the maltreated beacon.

'You can come indoors now, Mac,' he called into the microphone. 'We made it.'

'Thank heavens for that. I've nearly got sunstroke, as well as calcification of the joints, doing this Cupid's bow act out here.'

'When you've finished celebrating,' complained Gibson, who had been an interested but baffled spectator, 'perhaps you'll tell me in a few short, well-chosen phrases just how you managed to pull this particular rabbit out of the hat.'

'By beaming our beacon signal and then overloading the transmitter, of course.'

'Yes, I know that. What I don't understand is why you've switched it off again.'

'The controlling gear in the missile has done its job,' explained Bradley, with the air of a professor of philosophy talking to a mentally retarded child. 'That first signal indicated that it had detected our wave: we knew then that it was automatically vectoring on to us. That took it several minutes, and when it had finished it shut off its motors and sent us the second signal. It's still at almost the same distance, of course, but it's heading towards us now and should be passing in a couple of days. I'll have the beacon running again then. That will bring it to within a kilometre or less.'

'Hey!' said Gibson in sudden alarm. 'Suppose it scores a direct hit on us?'

'You might give its designers credit for having thought of that. When it gets very close a neat little device sensitive to the gradient of the beacon's field comes into play. Since, as you are well aware, the field strength H is inversely proportional to the distance r, then it is immediately obvious that dH/dr varies inversely as r squared, and so is too small to be measured unless you're very close. When the missile finds it *can* measure it, it puts on the brakes.'

'Quite clever,' said Gibson admiringly. 'I'm sorry to disappoint you, though, but I can *still* differentiate $1/r$ even at this advanced age.'

There was a gentle cough at the back of the room.

'I hate to remind you, sir—' began Jimmy.

Norden laughed.

'OK – I'll pay up. Here are the keys – locker 26. What are you going to do with that bottle of whisky?'

'I was thinking of selling it back to Dr Mackay.'

'Surely,' said Scott, looking severely at Jimmy, 'this moment demands a general celebration, at which a toast—'

But Jimmy didn't stop to hear the rest. He had fled to collect his loot.

Five

An hour ago we had only one passenger,' said Dr Scott, nursing the long metal case delicately through the airlock. 'Now we've got several billion.'

'How do you think they've stood the journey?' asked Gibson.

'The thermostats seem to be working well, so they should be all right. I'll transfer them to the cultures I've got ready, and then they should be quite happy until we get to Mars, gorging themselves to their little hearts' content.'

Gibson moved over to the nearest observation post. He could see the stubby, white-painted shape of the missile lying alongside the airlock, with the slack mooring cables drifting away from it like the tentacles of some deep-sea creature. When the rocket had been brought almost to rest a few kilometres away by its automatic radio equipment, its final capture had been achieved by much less sophisticated techniques. Hilton and Bradley had gone out with cables and lassoed the missile as it slowly drifted by. Then the electric windlasses on the *Ares* had hauled it in.

'What's going to happen to the carrier now?' Gibson asked Captain Norden, who was also watching the proceedings.

'We'll salvage the drive and control assembly and leave the carcass in space. It wouldn't be worth the fuel to carry it all back to Mars. So until we start accelerating again, we'll have a little moon of our own.'

'Like the dog in Jules Verne's story.'

'What, *From the Earth to the Moon*? I've never read it. At least, I tried once, but couldn't be bothered. That's the trouble with all those old stories. Nothing is deader than yesterday's science-fiction – and Verne belongs to the day before yesterday.'

Gibson felt it necessary to defend his profession.

'So you don't consider that science-fiction can ever have any permanent literary value?'

'I don't think so. It may sometimes have a *social* value when it's written, but to the next generation it must always seem quaint and archaic. Just look what happened, for example, to the space-travel story.'

'Go on. Don't mind my feelings – as if you would.'

Norden was clearly warming to the subject, a fact which did not surprise Gibson in the least. If one of his companions had suddenly been revealed as an expert on reafforestation, Sanskrit, or bimetallism, Gibson would now have taken it in his stride. In any case, he knew that science-fiction was widely – sometimes hilariously – popular among professional astronauts.

'Very well,' said Norden. 'Let's see what happened there. Up to 1960 – maybe 1970 – people were still writing stories about the first journey to the Moon. They're all quite unreadable now. When the Moon was reached, it was safe to write about Mars and Venus for another few years. Now *those* stories are dead too: no one would read them except to get a laugh. I suppose the outer planets will be a good investment for another generation; but the interplanetary romances our grandfathers knew really came to an end in the late 1970s.'

'But the theme of space-travel is still as popular as ever.'

'Yes, but it's no longer science-fiction. It's either purely factual – the sort of thing you are beaming back to Earth now – or else it's pure fantasy. The stories have to go right outside the Solar System and so they might just as well be fairy tales. Which is all that most of them are.'

Norden had been speaking with great seriousness, but there was a mischievous twinkle in his eye.

'I contest your argument on two points,' said Gibson. 'First of all people – lots of people – still read Wells's yarns, though they're a century old. And, to come from the sublime to the ridiculous, they still read *my* early books, like *Martian Dust*, although facts have caught up with them and left them a long way in the rear.'

'Wells wrote literature,' answered Norden, 'but even so, I think I can prove my point. Which of his stories are most popular? Why, the straight novels like *Kipps* and *Mr Polly*. When the fantasies are read at all, it's in spite of their hopelessly dated prophecies, not because of them. Only *The Time Machine* is still at all popular, simply because it's set so far in the future that it's not outmoded – and because it contains Wells's best writing.'

There was a slight pause. Gibson wondered if Norden was going to take up his second point. Finally he said:

'When did you write *Martian Dust*?'

Gibson did some rapid mental arithmetic.

'In '73 or '74.'

'I didn't know it was as early as that. But that's part of the explanation. Space-travel was just about to begin then, and everybody knew it. You had already begun to make a name with conventional fiction, and *Martian Dust* caught the rising tide very nicely.'

'That only explains why it sold *then*. It doesn't answer my other point. It's still quite popular, and I believe the Martian colony has taken several copies, despite the fact that it describes a Mars that never existed outside my imagination.'

'I attribute that to the unscrupulous advertising of your publisher, the careful way you've managed to keep in the public eye, and – just possibly – to the fact that it was the best thing you ever wrote. Moreover, as Mac would say, it managed to capture the *Zeitgeist* of the seventies, and that gives it a curiosity value now.'

'Hmmm,' said Gibson, thinking matters over. He remained silent for a moment: then his face creased into a smile and he began to laugh.

'Well, share the joke. What's so funny?'

'Our earlier conversation. I was just wondering what H. G. Wells would have thought if he'd known that one day a couple of men would be discussing his stories, half-way between Earth and Mars.'

'Don't exaggerate,' grinned Norden. 'We're only a third of the way so far.'

It was long after midnight when Gibson suddenly awoke from a dreamless sleep. Something had disturbed him – some noise like a distant explosion, far away in the bowels of the ship. He sat up in the darkness, tensing against the broad elastic bands that held him to his bed. Only a glimmer of starlight came from the porthole-mirror, for his cabin was on the night side of the liner. He listened, mouth half opened, checking his breath to catch the faintest murmur of sound.

There were many voices in the *Ares* at night, and Gibson knew them all. The ship was alive, and silence would have meant the death of all aboard her. Infinitely reassuring was the unresting, unhurried suspiration of the air-pumps, driving the man-made trade winds of this tiny planet. Against that faint but continuous background were other intermittent noises: the occasional 'whirr' of hidden motors carrying out some mysterious and automatic task, the 'tick', every thirty seconds precisely, of the electric clock, and sometimes the sound of water racing through the pressurized plumbing system. Certainly none of these could have roused him, for they were as familiar as the beating of his own heart.

Still only half awake, Gibson went to the cabin door and listened for a while in the corridor. Everything was perfectly normal: he knew that he must be the only man awake. For a moment he wondered if he should call Norden, then thought better of it. He might only have been dreaming, or the noise might have been produced by some equipment that had not gone into action before.

He was already back in bed when a thought suddenly occurred to him. Had the noise, after all, been so far away? That was merely his first impression: it might have been quite near. Anyway, he was tired, and it didn't matter. Gibson had a complete and touching faith in the ship's instrumentation. If anything had really gone wrong, the automatic alarms would have alerted everyone. They had been tested several times on the voyage, and were enough to awaken the dead. He could go to sleep, confident that they were watching over him with unresting vigilance.

He was perfectly correct, though he was never to know it: and by the morning he had forgotten the whole affair.

The camera swept out of the stricken council chamber, following the funeral cortège up the endlessly twining stairs, out on to the windy battlements above the sea. The music sobbed into silence for a moment, the lonely figures with their tragic burdens were silhouetted against the setting sun, motionless upon the ramparts of Elsinore. 'Goodnight, sweet prince—' The play was ended.

The lights in the tiny theatre came on abruptly, and the State of Denmark was four centuries and fifty million kilometres away. Reluctantly, Gibson brought his mind back to the present, tearing himself free from the magic that had held him captive. What, he wondered, would Shakespeare have made of this interpretation, already a lifetime old, yet as untouched by time as the still older splendours of the immortal poetry? And what, above all would he have made of this fantastic theatre, with its lattice-work of seats floating precariously in mid-air with the flimsiest of supports?

'It's rather a pity,' said Dr Scott, as the audience of six drifted out into the corridor, 'that we'll never have as fine a collection of films with us on our later runs. This batch is for the central Martian Library, and we won't be able to hang on to it.'

'What's the next programme going to be?' asked Gibson.

'We haven't decided. It may be a current musical, or we may carry on with the classics and screen "Gone with the Wind".'

'My grandfather used to rave about that: I'd like to see it now we have the chance,' said Jimmy Spencer eagerly.

'Very well,' replied Scott. 'I'll put the matter to the Entertainments Committee and see if it can be arranged.' Since this Committee consisted of Scott and no one else, these negotiations would presumably be successful.

Norden, who had remained sunk in thought since the end of the film, came up behind Gibson and gave a nervous little cough.

'By the way, Martin,' he said. 'You remember you were badgering me to let you go out in a spacesuit?'

'Yes. You said it was strictly against the rules.'

Norden seemed embarrassed, which was somewhat unlike him.

'Well, it *is* in a way, but this isn't a normal trip and you aren't technically a passenger. I think we can manage it after all.'

Gibson was delighted. He had always wondered what it was like to wear a spacesuit, and to stand in nothingness with the stars all around one. It never even occurred to him to ask Norden why he had changed his mind, and for this Norden was very thankful.

The plot had been brewing for about a week. Every morning a little ritual took place in Norden's room when Hilton arrived with the daily maintenance schedules, summarizing the ship's performance and the behaviour of all its multitudinous machines during the past twenty-four hours. Usually there was nothing of any importance, and Norden signed the reports and filed them away with the log book. Variety was the last thing he wanted here, but sometimes he got it.

'Listen, Johnnie,' said Hilton (he was the only one who called Norden by his first name: to the rest of the crew he was always 'Skipper'). 'It's quite definite now about our air pressure. The drop's practically constant; in about ten days we'll be outside tolerance limits.'

'Confound it! That means we'll have to do something. I was hoping it wouldn't matter till we dock.'

'I'm afraid we can't wait until then. Those tolerances are stupid, of course: a leak ten times as big wouldn't be really dangerous. But the pressure records have to be turned over to the Space Safety Commission when we get home, and some nervous old woman is sure to start yelling if we drop below the limits.'

'Where do you think the trouble is?'

'In the hull, almost certainly.'

'That pet leak of yours up round the North Pole?'

'I doubt it; this is too sudden. I think we've been holed again.'

Norden looked mildly annoyed. Punctures due to meteoric dust happened two or three times a year on a ship of this size. One usually let them accumulate until they were worth bothering about, but this one seemed a little too big to be ignored.

'How long will it take to find the leak?'

'That's the trouble,' said Hilton in tones of some disgust. 'We've only one leak detector, and fifty thousand square metres of hull. It may take a couple of days to go over it. Now if it had only been a nice big hole, the automatic bulkheads would have gone into operation and located it for us.'

'I'm mighty glad they didn't!' grinned Norden. 'That would have taken some explaining away!'

Jimmy Spencer, who as usual got the job that no one else wanted to do, found the puncture three days later, after only a dozen circuits of the ship. The blurred little crater was scarcely visible to the eye, but the supersensitive leak detector had registered the fact that the vacuum near this part of the hull was not as perfect as it should have been. Jimmy had marked the place with chalk and gone thankfully back into the airlock.

Norden dug out the ship's plans and located the approximate position from Jimmy's report. Then he whistled softly and his eyebrows climbed towards the ceiling.

'Jimmy,' he said, 'does Mr Gibson know what you've been up to?'

'No,' said Jimmy. 'I've not missed giving him his astronautics classes, though it's been quite a job to manage it as well as—'

'All right, all right! You don't think anyone else would have told him about the leak?'

'I don't know, but I think he'd have mentioned it if they had.'

'Well, listen carefully. This blasted puncture is smack in the middle of his cabin wall, and if you breathe a word about it to him, I'll skin you. Understand?'

'Yes,' gulped Jimmy, and fled precipitately.

'Now what?' said Hilton, in tones of resignation.

'We've got to get Martin out of the way on some pretext and plug the hole as quickly as we can.'

'It's funny he never noticed the impact. It would have made quite a din.'

'He was probably out at the time. *I'm* surprised he never noticed the air current: it must be fairly considerable.'

'Probably masked by the normal circulation. But anyway, why all the fuss? Why not come clean about it and explain what's happened to Martin? There's no need for all this melodrama.'

'Oh, isn't there? Suppose Martin tells his public that a 12th magnitude meteor has holed the ship – and then goes on to say that this sort of thing happens every other voyage? How many of his readers will understand not only that it's no real danger, but that we don't usually bother to do anything even when it does happen? I'll tell you what the popular reaction would be: "If it was a little one, it might just as well be a big 'un." The public's never trusted statistics. And can't you see the headlines: "*Ares* Holed by Meteor!" That would be bad for trade!'

'Then why not simply tell Martin and ask him to keep quiet?'

'It wouldn't be fair on the poor chap. He's had no news to hang his articles on to for weeks. It would be kinder to say nothing.'

'OK,' sighed Hilton. 'It's your idea. Don't blame me if it backfires.'

'It won't. I think I've got a watertight plan.'

'I don't give a damn if it's watertight. Is it airtight?'

All his life Gibson had been fascinated by gadgets, and the space-suit was yet another to add to the collection of mechanisms he had investigated and mastered. Bradley had been detailed to make sure that he understood the drill correctly, to take him out into space, and to see that he didn't get lost.

Gibson had forgotten that the suits on the *Ares* had no legs, and that one simply sat inside them. That was sensible enough, since they were built for use under zero gravity, and not for walking on airless planets. The absence of flexible leg-joints greatly simplified the designs of the suits, which were nothing more than perspex-topped cylinders sprouting articulated arms at their upper ends. Along the sides were mysterious flutings and bulges concerned with the air conditioning, radio, heat regulators, and the low-powered propulsion system. There was considerable freedom of movement inside them; one could withdraw one's arms to get at the internal controls, and even take a meal without too many acrobatics.

Bradley had spent almost an hour in the airlock, making certain that Gibson understood all the main controls and catechizing him on their operation. Gibson appreciated his thoroughness, but began to get a little impatient when the lesson showed no sign of ending. He eventually mutinied when Bradley started to explain the suit's primitive sanitary arrangements.

'Hang it all!' he protested, 'we aren't going to be outside *that* long!'

Bradley grinned.

'You'd be surprised,' he said darkly, 'just how many people make that mistake.'

He opened a compartment in the airlock wall and took out two spools of line, for all the world like fishermen's reels. They locked firmly into mountings on the suits so that they could not be accidentally dislodged.

'Number One safety precaution,' he said. 'Always have a life-line anchoring you to the ship. Rules are made to be broken – but not this one. To make doubly sure, I'll tie your suit to mine with another ten metres of cord. Now we're ready to ascend the Matterhorn.'

The outer door slid aside. Gibson felt the last traces of air tugging at him as it escaped. The feeble impulse set him moving towards the exit, and he drifted slowly out into the stars.

The slowness of motion and the utter silence combined to make the moment deeply impressive. The *Ares* was receding behind him with a terrifying inevitability. He was plunging into space – real space at last – his only link with safety that tenuous thread unreeling at his side. Yet the experience, though so novel, awoke faint echoes of familiarity in his mind.

His brain must have been working with unusual swiftness, for he recalled the parallel almost immediately. This was like the moment in his childhood – a moment, he could have sworn until now, forgotten beyond recall – when he had been taught to swim by being dropped into ten metres of water. Once again he was plunging headlong into a new and unknown element.

The friction of the reel had checked his momentum when the cord attaching him to Bradley gave a jerk. He had almost forgotten his companion, who was now blasting away from the ship with the little gas jets at the base of his suit, towing Gibson behind him.

Gibson was quite startled when the other's voice, echoing metallically from the speaker in his suit, shattered the silence.

'Don't use your jets unless I tell you. We don't want to build up too much speed, and we must be careful not to get our lines tangled.'

'All right,' said Gibson, vaguely annoyed at the intrusion into his privacy. He looked back at the ship. It was already several hundred metres away, and shrinking rapidly.

'How much line have we got?' he asked anxiously. There was no reply, and he had a moment of mild panic before remembering to press the 'TRANSMIT' switch.

'About a kilometre,' Bradley answered when he repeated the question. 'That's enough to make one feel nice and lonely.'

'Suppose it broke?' asked Gibson, only half joking.

'It won't. It could support your full weight, back on Earth. Even if it did, we could get back perfectly easily with our jets.'

'And if they ran out?'

'This is a very cheerful conversation. I can't imagine that

happening except through gross carelessness or about three simultaneous mechanical failures. Remember, there's a spare propulsion unit for just such emergencies – *and* you've got warning indicators in the suit which let you know well before the main tank's empty.'

'But just *supposing*,' insisted Gibson.

'In that case the only thing to do would be to switch on the suit's SOS beacon and wait until someone came out to haul you back. I doubt if they'd hurry, in such circumstances. Anyone who got himself in a mess like that wouldn't receive much sympathy.'

There was a sudden jerk: they had come to the end of the line. Bradley killed the rebound with his jets.

'We're a long way from home now,' he said quietly.

It took Gibson several seconds to locate the *Ares*. They were on the night side of the ship so that it was almost wholly in shadow: the two spheres were thin, distant crescents that might easily have been taken for Earth and Moon, seen from perhaps a million kilometres away. There was no real sense of contact: the ship was too small and frail a thing to be regarded as a sanctuary any more. Gibson was alone with the stars at last.

He was always grateful that Bradley left him in silence and did not intrude upon his thoughts. Perhaps the other was equally overwhelmed by the splendid solemnity of the moment. The stars were so brilliant and so numerous that at first Gibson could not locate even the most familiar constellations. Then he found Mars, the brightest object in the sky next to the Sun itself, and so determined the plane of the ecliptic. Very gently, with cautious bursts from his gas jets, he swung the suit round so that his head pointed roughly towards the Pole Star. He was 'the right way up' again, and the star patterns were recognizable once more.

Slowly he made his way along the Zodiac, wondering how many other men in history had so far shared this experience. (Soon, of course, it would be common enough, and the magic would be dimmed by familiarity.) Presently he found Jupiter, and later Saturn – or so he imagined. The planets could no longer be distinguished from the stars by the steady, unwinking light that was such a useful, though sometimes treacherous, guide to amateur astronomers. Gibson did not search for Earth or Venus, for the glare of the sun would have dazzled him in a moment if he had turned his eyes in that direction.

A pale band of light welding the two hemispheres of the sky together, the whole ring of the Milky Way was visible. Gibson could see quite clearly the rents and tears along its edge, where entire continents of stars seemed trying to break away and go voyaging alone into the abyss. In the Southern Hemisphere, the black chasm of the Coal Sack gaped like a tunnel drilled through the stars into another universe.

The thought made Gibson turn towards Andromeda. There lay the Great Nebula – a ghostly lens of light. He could cover it with his thumbnail, yet it was a whole galaxy as vast as the sky-spanning ring of stars in whose heart he was floating now. That misty spectre was a million times farther away than the stars – and *they* were a million times more distant than the planets. How pitiful were all men's voyagings and adventures when seen against this background!

Gibson was looking for Alpha Centauri, among the unknown constellations of the Southern Hemisphere, when he caught sight of something which, for a moment, his mind failed to identify. At an immense distance, a white rectangular object was floating against the stars. That, at least, was Gibson's first impression: then he realized that his sense of perspective was at fault and that, in fact, he was really seeing something quite small, only a few metres away. Even then it was some time before he recognized this interplanetary wanderer for what it was – a perfectly ordinary sheet of quarto manuscript paper, very slowly revolving in space. Nothing could have been more commonplace – or more unexpected here.

Gibson stared at the apparition for some time before he convinced himself that it was no illusion. Then he switched on his transmitter and spoke to Bradley.

The other was not in the least surprised.

'There's nothing very remarkable about that,' he replied, rather impatiently. 'We've been throwing out waste every day for weeks, and as we haven't any acceleration some of it may still be hanging round. As soon as we start braking, of course, we'll drop back from it and all our junk will go shooting out of the Solar System.'

How perfectly obvious, thought Gibson, feeling a little foolish, for nothing is more disconcerting than a mystery which suddenly evaporates. It was probably a rough draft of one of his own articles. If it had been a little closer, it would be amusing to retrieve it as a souvenir, and to see what effects its stay in space had produced. Unfortunately it was just out of reach, and there was no way of capturing it without slipping the cord that linked him with the *Ares*.

When he had been dead for ages, that piece of paper would still be carrying its message out among the stars: and what it was, he would never know.

Norden met them when they returned to the airlock. He seemed rather pleased with himself, though Gibson was in no condition to notice such details. He was still lost among the stars and it would be some time before he returned to normal – before his typewriter began to patter softly as he tried to recapture his emotions.

'You managed the job in time?' asked Bradley, when Gibson was out of hearing.

'Yes, with fifteen minutes to spare. We shut off the ventilators and found the leak right away with the good old smoky-candle technique. A blind rivet and a spot of quick-drying paint did the rest: we can plug the outer hull when we're in dock, if it's worth it. Mac did a pretty neat job.'

Six

For Martin Gibson the voyage was running smoothly and pleasantly enough. As he always did, he had now managed to organize his surroundings (by which he meant not only his material environment but also the human beings who shared it with him) to his maximum comfort. He had done a satisfactory amount of writing, some of it quite good and most of it passable, though he would not get properly into his stride until he had reached Mars.

The flight was now entering upon its closing weeks, and there was an inevitable sense of anticlimax and slackening interest, which would last until they entered the orbit of Mars. Nothing would happen until then: for the time being all the excitements of the voyage were over.

The last highlight, for Gibson, had been the morning when he finally lost the Earth. Day by day it had come closer to the vast pearly wings of the corona, as though about to immolate all its millions in the funeral pyre of the Sun. One evening it had still been visible through the telescope – a tiny spark glittering bravely against the splendour that was soon to overwhelm it. Gibson had thought it might still be visible in the morning, but overnight some colossal explosion had thrown the corona half a million kilometres farther into space, and Earth was lost against that incandescent curtain. It would be a week before it reappeared, and by then Gibson's world would have changed more than he would have believed possible in so short a time.

If anyone had asked Jimmy Spencer just what he thought of Gibson, that young man would have given rather different replies at various stages of the voyage. At first he had been quite overawed by his distinguished shipmate, but that stage had worn off very quickly. To do Gibson credit, he was completely free from snobbery, and he never made unreasonable use of his privileged position on board the *Ares*. Thus from Jimmy's point of view he was more approachable than the rest of the liner's inhabitants – all of whom were in some degree his superior officers.

When Gibson had started taking a serious interest in astronautics, Jimmy had seen him at close quarters once or twice a week and had made several efforts to weigh him up. This had not been at all easy, for Gibson never seemed to be the same person for very long. There were times when he was considerate and thoughtful and generally good company. Yet there were other occasions when he was so grumpy and morose that he easily qualified as the person on the *Ares* most to be avoided.

What Gibson thought of *him* Jimmy wasn't at all sure. He sometimes had an uncomfortable feeling that the author regarded him purely as raw material that might or might not be of value some day. Most people who knew Gibson slightly had that impression, and most of them were right. Yet as he had never tried to pump Jimmy directly, there seemed no real grounds for these suspicions.

Another puzzling thing about Gibson was his technical background. When Jimmy had started his evening classes, as everyone called them, he had assumed that Gibson was merely anxious to avoid glaring errors in the material he radioed back to Earth, and had no very deep interest in astronautics for its own sake. It soon became clear that this was far from being the case. Gibson had an almost pathetic anxiety to master quite abstruse branches of the science, and to demand mathematical proofs, some of which Jimmy was hard put to provide. The older man must once have had a good deal of technical knowledge, fragments of which still remained with him. How he had acquired it he never explained; nor did he give any reason for his almost obsessive attempts, doomed though they were to repeated failures, to come to grips with scientific ideas far too advanced for him. Gibson's disappointment after these failures was so obvious that Jimmy found himself very sorry for him – except on those occasions when his pupil became bad-tempered and showed a tendency to blame his instructor. Then there would be a brief exchange of discourtesies, Jimmy would pack up his books, and the lesson would not be resumed until Gibson had apologized.

Sometimes, on the other hand, Gibson took these setbacks with humorous resignation and simply changed the subject. He would then talk about his experiences in the strange literary jungle in which he lived – a world of weird and often carnivorous beasts whose behaviour Jimmy found quite fascinating. Gibson was a good raconteur, with a fine flair for purveying scandal and undermining reputations. He seemed to do this without any malice, and some of the stories he told Jimmy about the distinguished figures of the day quite shocked that somewhat strait-laced youth. The curious fact was that the people whom Gibson so readily dissected often seemed to be his closest friends. This was something that Jimmy found very hard to understand.

Yet despite all these warnings Jimmy talked readily enough when the time came. One of their lessons had grounded on a reef of integro-differential equations and there was nothing to do but abandon ship. Gibson was in one of his amiable moods, and as he closed his books with a sigh he turned to Jimmy and remarked casually:

'You've never told me anything about yourself, Jimmy. What part of England do you come from, anyway?'

'Cambridge – at least, that's where I was born.'

'I used to know it quite well, twenty years ago. But you don't live there now?'

'No; when I was about six, my people moved to Leeds. I've been there ever since.'

'What made you take up astronautics?'

'It's rather hard to say. I was always interested in science, and of course spaceflight was the coming thing when I was growing up. So I suppose it was just natural. If I'd been born fifty years before, I guess I'd have gone into aeronautics.'

'So you're interested in spaceflight purely as a technical problem, and not as – shall we say – something that might revolutionize human thought, open up new planets, and all that sort of thing?'

Jimmy grinned.

'I suppose that's true enough. Of course, I *am* interested in these ideas, but it's the technical side that really fascinates me. Even if there was nothing on the planets, I'd still want to know how to reach them.'

Gibson shook his head in mock distress.

'You're going to grow up into one of those cold-blooded scientists who know everything about nothing. Another good man wasted!'

'I'm glad you think it *will* be a waste,' said Jimmy with some spirit. 'Anyway, why are you so interested in science?'

Gibson laughed, but there was a trace of annoyance in his voice as he replied:

'I'm only interested in science as a means, not as an end in itself.'

That, Jimmy was sure, was quite untrue. But something warned him not to pursue the matter any further, and before he could reply Gibson was questioning him again.

It was all done in such a friendly spirit of apparently genuine interest that Jimmy couldn't avoid feeling flattered, couldn't help talking freely and easily. Somehow it didn't matter if Gibson was indeed studying him as disinterestedly and as clinically as a biologist watching the reactions of one of his laboratory animals. Jimmy felt like talking, and he preferred to give Gibson's motives the benefit of the doubt.

He talked of his childhood and early life, and presently Gibson understood the occasional clouds that sometimes seemed to overlay the lad's normally cheerful disposition. It was an old story – one of the oldest. Jimmy's mother had died when he was little more than a baby, and his father had left him in the charge of a married sister. Jimmy's aunt had been kind to him, but he had never felt at home among his cousins, had always been an outsider. Nor had his father been a great deal of help, for he was seldom in England, and had died when Jimmy was about ten years old. He appeared to have left very little impression on his son, who, strangely enough, seemed to have clearer memories of the mother whom he could scarcely have known.

Once the barriers were down, Jimmy talked without reticence, as if glad to unburden his mind. Sometimes Gibson asked questions to prompt him, but the questions grew farther and farther apart and presently came no more.

'I don't think my parents were really very much in love,' said Jimmy. 'From what Aunt Ellen told me, it was all rather a mistake. There was another man first, but that fell through. My father was the next best thing. Oh, I know this sounds rather heartless, but please remember it all happened such a long time ago, and doesn't mean much to me now.'

'I understand,' said Gibson quietly: and it seemed as if he really did. 'Tell me more about your mother.'

'Her father – my grandad, that is – was one of the professors at the university. I think mother spent all her life in Cambridge. When she was old enough she went to college for her degree – she was studying history. Oh, all this can't possibly interest you!'

'It really does,' said Gibson earnestly. 'Go on.'

So Jimmy talked. Everything he told must have been learned from hearsay, but the picture he gave Gibson was surprisingly clear and detailed. His listener guessed that Aunt Ellen must have been very talkative, and Jimmy a very attentive small boy.

It was one of those innumerable college romances that briefly flower and wither during that handful of years which seems a microcosm of life itself. But this one had been more serious than most. During her last term Jimmy's mother – he still hadn't told Gibson her name – had fallen in love with a young engineering student who was half-way through his college career. It had been a whirlwind romance, and the match was an ideal one despite the fact that the girl was several years older than the boy. Indeed, it had almost reached the stage of an engagement when – Jimmy wasn't quite sure what had happened. The young man had been taken seriously ill, or had had a nervous breakdown, and had never come back to Cambridge.

'My mother never really got over it,' said Jimmy, with a grave assumption of wisdom which somehow did not seem completely incongruous. 'But another student was very much in love with her, and so she married him. I sometimes feel rather sorry for my father, for he must have known all about the other affair. I never saw much of him because – why, Mr Gibson, don't you feel well?'

Gibson forced a smile.

'It's nothing – just a touch of space-sickness. I get it now and then – it will pass in a minute.'

He only wished that the words were true. All these weeks, in total ignorance and believing himself secure against all the shocks of time and chance, he had been steering a collision course with Fate. And now the moment of impact had come: the twenty years that lay behind had vanished like a dream, and he was face to face once more with the ghosts of his own forgotten past.

'There's something wrong with Martin,' said Bradley, signing the signals log with a flourish. 'It can't be any news he's had from Earth – I've read it all. Do you suppose he's getting homesick?'

'He's left it a little late in the day, if that's the explanation,' replied Norden. 'After all, we'll be on Mars in a fortnight. But you do rather fancy yourself as an amateur psychologist, don't you?'

'Well, who doesn't?'

'*I* don't for one,' began Norden pontifically. 'Prying into other people's affairs isn't one of my—'

An anticipatory gleam in Bradley's eyes warned him just in time, and to the other's evident disappointment he checked himself in mid sentence. Martin Gibson, complete with notebook and looking like a cub reporter attending his first press conference, had hurried into the office.

'Well, Owen, what was it you wanted to show me?' he asked eagerly.

Bradley moved to the main communication rack.

'It isn't really very impressive,' he said, 'but it means that we've passed another milestone and that always gives me a bit of a kick. Listen to this.'

He pressed the speaker switch and slowly brought up the volume control. The room was flooded with the hiss and crackle of radio noise, like the sound of a thousand frying-pans at the point of imminent ignition. It was a sound that Gibson had heard often enough in the signals cabin and, for all its unvarying monotony, it never failed to fill him with a sense of wonder. He was listening, he knew, to the voices of the stars and nebulae, to radiations that had set out upon their journey before the birth of Man. And buried far down in the depths of that crackling, whispering chaos there might be – there *must* be – the sounds of alien civilizations talking to one another in the deeps of space. But, alas, their voices were lost beyond recall in the welter of cosmic interference which Nature herself had made.

This, however, was certainly not what Bradley had called him to hear. Very delicately, the signals officer made some vernier adjustments, frowning a little as he did so.

'I had it on the nose a minute ago – hope it hasn't drifted off – ah, here it is!'

At first Gibson could detect no alteration in the barrage of noise. Then he noticed that Bradley was silently marking time with his hand – rather quickly, at the rate of some two beats every second. With this to guide him, Gibson presently detected the infinitely faint undulating whistle that was breaking through the cosmic storm.

'What is it?' he asked, already half guessing the answer.

'It's the radio beacon on Deimos. There's one on Phobos as well, but it's not so powerful and we can't pick it up yet. When we get nearer Mars, we'll be able to fix ourselves within a few hundred kilometres by using them. We're at ten times the usable range now but it's nice to know.'

Yes, thought Gibson, it is nice to know. Of course, these radio aids weren't essential when one could see one's destination all the time, but they simplified some of the navigational problems. As he listened with half-closed eyes to that faint pulsing, sometimes almost drowned by the cosmic barrage, he knew how the mariners of old must have felt when they caught the first glimpse of the harbour lights from far out at sea.

'I think that's enough,' said Bradley, switching off the speaker and restoring silence. 'Anyway, it should give you something new to write about – things have been pretty quiet lately, haven't they?'

He was watching Gibson intently as he said this, but the author never responded. He merely jotted a few words in his notebook, thanked Bradley with absent-minded and unaccustomed politeness, and departed to his cabin.

'You're quite right,' said Norden when he had gone. 'Something's certainly happened to Martin. I'd better have a word with Doc.'

'I shouldn't bother,' replied Bradley. 'Whatever it is, I don't think it's anything you can handle with pills. Better leave Martin to work it out his own way.'

'Maybe you're right,' said Norden grudgingly. 'But I hope he doesn't take too long over it!'

He had now taken almost a week. The initial shock of discovering that Jimmy Spencer was Kathleen Morgan's son had already worn off, but the secondary effects were beginning to make themselves felt. Among these was a feeling of resentment that anything like this should have happened to *him*. It was such an outrageous violation of the laws of probability – the sort of thing that would never have happened in one of Gibson's own novels. But life was so inartistic and there was really nothing one could do about it.

This mood of childish petulance was now passing, to be replaced by a deeper sense of discomfort. All the emotions he had thought safely buried beneath twenty years of feverish activity were now rising to the surface again, like deep-sea creatures slain in some submarine eruption. On Earth, he could have escaped by losing himself once more in the crowd, but here he was trapped, with nowhere to flee.

It was useless to pretend that nothing had really changed, to say: 'Of course I knew that Kathleen and Gerald had a son: what difference does that make now?' It made a great deal of difference. Every time he saw Jimmy he would be reminded of the past and – what was worse – of the future that might have been. The most urgent problem now was to face the facts squarely, and to come to grips with the new situation. Gibson knew well enough that there was only one way in which this could be done, and the opportunity would arise soon enough.

Jimmy had been down to the Southern Hemisphere and was making his way along the equatorial observation deck when he saw Gibson sitting at one of the windows, staring out into space. For a moment he thought the other had not seen him, and had decided not to intrude upon his thoughts when Gibson called out; 'Hello, Jimmy. Have you got a moment to spare?'

As it happened, Jimmy was rather busy. But he knew that there had been something wrong with Gibson, and realized that the older man needed his presence. So he came and sat on the bench recessed into the observation port, and presently he knew as much of the truth as Gibson thought good for either of them.

'I'm going to tell you something, Jimmy,' Gibson began, 'which is known to only a handful of people. Don't interrupt me and don't ask any questions – not until I've finished, at any rate.

'When I was rather younger than you, I wanted to be an engineer. I was quite a bright kid in those days and had no difficulty in getting into college through the usual examinations. As I wasn't sure what I intended to do, I took the five-year course in general engineering physics, which was quite a new thing in those days. In my first year I did fairly well – well enough to encourage me to work harder next time. In my second year I did – not brilliantly, but a lot better than average. And in the third year I fell in love. It wasn't exactly for the first time, but I knew it was the real thing at last.

'Now falling in love while you're at college may or may not be a good thing for you: it all depends on circumstances. If it's only a mild flirtation, it probably doesn't matter one way or the other. But if it's really serious, there are two possibilities.

'It may act as a stimulus – it may make you determined to do your best, to show that you're better than the other fellows. On the other hand, you may get so emotionally involved in the affair that nothing else seems to matter, and your studies go to pieces. That is what happened in my case.'

Gibson fell into a brooding silence, and Jimmy stole a glance at him as he sat in the darkness a few feet away. They were on the night side of the ship, and the corridor lights had been dimmed so that the stars could be seen in their unchallenged glory. The constellation of Leo was directly ahead, and there in its heart was the brilliant ruby gem that was their goal. Next to the Sun itself, Mars was by far the brightest of all celestial bodies, and already its disc was just visible to the naked eye. The brilliant crimson light playing full on his face gave Gibson a healthy, even a cheerful appearance quite out of keeping with his feelings.

Was it true, Gibson wondered, that one never really forgot anything? It seemed now as if it might be. He could still see, as clearly as he had twenty years ago, that message pinned on the faculty notice-board: 'The Dean of Engineering wishes to see M. Gibson in his office at 3.00.' He had had to wait, of course, until 3.15, and that hadn't helped. Nor would it have been so bad if the Dean had been sarcastic, or icily aloof, or even if he had lost his temper. Gibson could still picture that inhumanly tidy room, with its neat files and careful rows of books, could remember the Dean's secretary padding away on her typewriter in the corner, pretending not to listen.

(Perhaps, now he came to think of it, she wasn't pretending after all. The experience wouldn't have been so novel to her as it was to him.)

Gibson had liked and respected the Dean, for all the old man's finicky ways and meticulous pedantry, and now he had let him down, which made his failure doubly hard to bear. The Dean had rubbed it in with his 'more in sorrow than in anger' technique, which had been more effective than he knew or intended. He had given Gibson another chance, but he was never to take it.

What made matters worse, though he was ashamed to admit the fact, was that Kathleen had done fairly well in her exams. When his results had been published, Gibson had avoided her for several days, and when they met again he had already identified her with the cause of his failure. He could see this so clearly, now that it no longer hurt. Had he really been in love if he was prepared to sacrifice Kathleen for the sake of his own self-respect? For that is what it came to: he had tried to shift the blame on to her.

The rest was inevitable. That quarrel on their last long cycle ride together into the country, and their returns by separate routes. The letters that hadn't been opened – above all, the letters that hadn't been written. Their unsuccessful attempt to meet, if only to say goodbye, on his last day in Cambridge. But even this had fallen through: the message hadn't reached Kathleen in time, and though he had waited until the last minute she had never come. The crowded train, packed with cheering students, had drawn noisily out of the station, leaving Cambridge and Kathleen behind. He had never seen either again.

There was no need to tell Jimmy about the dark months that had followed. He need never know what was meant by the simple words: 'I had a breakdown and was advised not to return to college.' Dr Evans had made a pretty good job of patching him up, and he'd always be grateful for that. It was Evans who'd persuaded him to take up writing during his convalescence, with results that had surprised them both. (How many people knew that his first novel had been dedicated to his psychoanalyst? Well, if Rachmaninov could do the same thing with the C Minor Concerto, why shouldn't he?)

Evans had given him a new personality and a vocation through which he could win back his self-confidence. But he couldn't restore the future that had been lost. All his life Gibson would envy the men who had finished what he had only begun – the men who could put after their names the degrees and qualifications he would never possess, and who would find their life's work in fields of which he could be only a spectator.

If the trouble had lain no deeper than this, it might not have mattered greatly. But in salvaging his pride by throwing the blame on to Kathleen he had warped his whole life. She, and through her all women, had become identified with failure and disgrace. Apart from a few attachments which had not been taken very seriously by either partner, Gibson had never fallen in love again, and now he realized that he never would. Knowing the cause of his complaint had helped him not in the least to find a cure.

None of these things, of course, need be mentioned to Jimmy. It was sufficient to give the bare facts, and to leave Jimmy to guess what he could. One day, perhaps, he might tell him more, but that depended on many things.

When Gibson had finished, he was surprised to find how nervously he was waiting for Jimmy's reactions. He felt himself wondering if the boy had read between the lines and apportioned blame where it was due, whether he would be sympathetic, angry – or merely embarrassed. It had suddenly become of the utmost importance to win Jimmy's respect and friendship, more important than anything that had happened to Gibson for a very long time. Only thus could he satisfy his conscience and quieten those accusing voices from the past.

He could not see Jimmy's face, for the other was in shadow and it seemed an age before he broke the silence.

'Why have you told me this?' he asked quietly. His voice was completely neutral – free from both sympathy or reproach.

Gibson hesitated before answering. The pause was natural enough, for, even to himself, he could hardly have explained all his motives.

'I just *had* to tell you,' he said earnestly. 'I couldn't have been happy until I'd done so. And besides – I felt I might be able to help, somehow.'

Again that nerve-racking silence. Then Jimmy rose slowly to his feet.

I'll have to think about what you've told me,' he said, his voice still almost emotionless. 'I don't know what to say now.'

Then he was gone. He left Gibson in a state of extreme uncertainty and confusion, wondering whether he had made a fool of himself or not. Jimmy's self-control, his failure to react, had thrown him off balance and left him completely at a loss. Only of one thing was he certain: in telling the facts, he had already done a great deal to relieve his mind.

But there was still much that he had not told Jimmy: indeed, there was still much that he did not know himself.

Seven

'This is completely crazy!' stormed Norden, looking like a berserk Viking chief. 'There must be *some* explanation! Good heavens, there aren't any proper docking facilities on Deimos – how do they expect us to unload? I'm going to call the Chief Executive and raise hell!'

'I shouldn't if I were you,' drawled Bradley. 'Did you notice the signature? This isn't an instruction from Earth routed through Mars. It originated in the CE's office. The old man may be a Tartar, but he doesn't do things unless he's got a good reason.'

'Name just one!'

Bradley shrugged his shoulders.

'*I* don't have to run Mars, so how would I know? We'll find out soon enough.' He gave a malicious little chuckle. 'I wonder how Mac is going to take it? He'll have to recompute our approach orbit.'

Norden leaned across the control panel and threw a switch.

'Hello, Mac – Skipper here. You receiving me?'

There was a short pause; then Hilton's voice came from the speaker.

'Mac's not here at the moment. Any message?'

'All right – you can break it to him. We've had orders from Mars to re-route the ship. They've diverted us from Phobos – no reason given at all. Tell Mac to calculate an orbit to Deimos, and to let me have it as soon as he can.'

'I don't understand it. Why, Deimos is just a lot of mountains with no—'

'Yes – we've been through all that! Maybe we'll know the answer when we get there. Tell Mac to contact me as soon as he can, will you?'

Dr Scott broke the news to Gibson while the author was putting the final touches to one of his weekly articles.

'Heard the latest?' he exclaimed breathlessly. 'We've been diverted to Deimos. Skipper's mad as hell – it may make us a day late.'

'Does anyone know why?'

'No; it's a complete mystery. We've asked, but Mars won't tell.'

Gibson scratched his head, examining and rejecting half a dozen ideas. He knew that Phobos, the inner moon, had been used as a base ever since the first expedition had reached Mars. Only 6,000 kilometres from the surface of the planet, and with a gravity less than a thousandth of Earth's, it was ideal for this purpose. The lightly built spaceships could land safely on a world where their total weight was under a ton and it took minutes to fall a few metres. A small observatory, a radio station, and a few pressurized buildings completed the attractions of the tiny satellite, which was only about thirty kilometres in diameter. The smaller and more distant moon, Deimos, had nothing on it at all except an automatic radio beacon.

The *Ares* was due to dock in less than a week. Already Mars was a small disc showing numerous surface markings even to the naked eye, and there was much peering through telescopes and argument over maps and photographs. Gibson had borrowed a large Mercator projection of the planet and had begun to learn the names of its chief features – names that had been given, most of them, more than a century ago by astronomers who had certainly never dreamed that men would one day use them as part of their normal lives. How poetical those old map-makers had been when they had ransacked mythology! Even to look at those words on the map was to set the blood pounding in the veins – Deucalion, Elysium, Eumenides, Arcadia, Atlantis, Utopia, Eos.... Gibson could sit for hours, fondling those wonderful names with his tongue, feeling as if in truth Keats's charm'd magic casements were opening before him. But there were no seas, perilous or otherwise, on Mars – though many of its lands were sufficiently forlorn.

The path of the *Ares* was now cutting steeply across the planet's orbit, and in a few days the motors would be checking the ship's outward speed. The change of velocity needed to deflect the voyage orbit from Phobos to Deimos was trivial, though it had involved Mackay in several hours of computing.

Every meal was devoted to discussing one thing – the crew's plans when Mars was reached. Gibson, the gentleman of leisure, could land on Mars right away, but the workers, as it was pointedly explained to him, would have to stay on Deimos for several days, checking the ship and seeing the cargo safely off.

Gibson's plans could be summed up in one phrase – to see as much as possible. It was, perhaps, a little optimistic to imagine that one could get to know a whole planet in two months, despite Bradley's repeated assurances that two days was quite long enough for Mars.

The excitement of the voyage's approaching end had, to some extent, taken Gibson's mind away from his personal problems. He met Jimmy perhaps half a dozen times a day at meals and during accidental encounters, but they had not reopened their earlier conversation. For a while Gibson suspected that Jimmy was deliberately avoiding him, but he soon realized that this was not altogether the case. Like the rest of the crew, Jimmy was very busy preparing for the end of the voyage. Norden was determined to have the ship in perfect condition when she docked, and a vast amount of checking and servicing was in progress.

Yet despite this activity, Jimmy had given a good deal of thought to what Gibson had told him. At first he had felt bitter and angry towards the man who had been responsible, however unintentionally, for his mother's unhappiness. But after a while, he began to see Gibson's point of view and understood a little of the other's feelings. Jimmy was shrewd enough to guess that Gibson had not only left a good deal untold, but had put his own case as favourably as possible. Even allowing for this, however, it was obvious that Gibson genuinely regretted the past, and was anxious to undo whatever damage he could, even though he was a generation late.

It was strange to feel the sensation of returning weight and to hear the distant roar of the motors once again as the *Ares* reduced her speed to match the far smaller velocity of Mars. The manoeuvring and the final delicate course-corrections took more than twenty-four hours. When it was over, Mars was a dozen times as large as the full Moon from Earth, with Phobos and Deimos visible as tiny stars whose movements could be clearly seen after a few minutes of observation.

Gibson had never really realized how red the great deserts were. But the simple word 'red' conveyed no idea of the variety of colour on that slowly expanding disc. Some regions were almost scarlet, others yellow-brown, while perhaps the commonest hue was what could best be described as powdered brick.

It was late spring in the southern hemisphere, and the polar cap had dwindled to a few glittering specks of whiteness where the snow still lingered stubbornly on higher ground. The broad belt of vegetation between pole and desert was for the greater part a pale bluish-green, but every imaginable shade of colour could be found somewhere on that mottled disc.

The *Ares* was swimming into the orbit of Deimos at a relative speed of less than a thousand kilometres an hour. Ahead of the ship, the tiny moon was already showing a visible disc, and as the hours passed it grew until, from a few hundred kilometres away, it looked as large as Mars. But what a contrast it presented! Here were no rich reds and greens, only a dark chaos of jumbled rocks, of mountains which jutted up towards the stars at all angles in this world of practically zero gravity.

Slowly the cruel rocks slid closer and swept past them, as the *Ares* cautiously felt her way down towards the radio beacon which Gibson had heard calling days before. Presently he saw, on an almost level area a few kilometres below, the first signs that man had ever visited this barren world. Two rows of vertical pillars jutted up from the ground, and between them was slung a network of cables. Almost imperceptibly the *Ares* sank towards Deimos; the main rockets had long since been silenced, for the small auxiliary jets had no difficulty in handling the ship's effective weight of a few hundred kilogrammes.

It was impossible to tell the moment of contact: only the sudden silence when the jets were cut off told Gibson that the journey was over, and the *Ares* was now resting in the cradle that had been prepared for her. He was still, of course, twenty thousand kilometres from Mars and would not actually reach the planet itself for another day, in one of the little rockets that was already climbing up to meet them. But as far as the *Ares* was concerned, the voyage was ended. The tiny cabin that had been his home for so many weeks would soon know him no more.

He left the observation deck and hurried up to the control room, which he had deliberately avoided during the last busy hours. It was no longer so easy to move around inside the *Ares*, for the minute gravitational field of Deimos was just sufficient to upset his instinctive movements and he had to make a conscious allowance for it. He wondered just what it would be like to experience a *real* gravitational field again. It was hard to believe that only three months ago the idea of having no gravity at all had seemed very strange and unsettling, yet now he had come to regard it as normal. How adaptable the human body was!

The entire crew was sitting round the chart table, looking very smug and self-satisfied.

'You're just in time, Martin,' said Norden cheerfully. 'We're going to have a little celebration. Go and get your camera and take our pictures while we toast the old crate's health.'

'Don't drink it all before I come back!' warned Gibson, and departed in search of his Leica. When he re-entered, Dr Scott was attempting an interesting experiment.

'I'm fed up with squirting my beer out of a bulb,' he explained. 'I want to pour it properly into a glass now we've got the chance again. Let's see how long it takes.'

'It'll be flat before it gets there,' warned Mackay. 'Let's see – *g*'s about half a centimetre a second squared, you're pouring from a height of . . .' He retired into a brown study.

But the experiment was already in progress. Scott was holding the punctured beer-tin about a foot above his glass – and, for the first time in three months, the word 'above' had some meaning, even if very little. For, with incredible slowness, the amber liquid oozed out of the tin – so slowly that one might have taken it for syrup. A thin column extended downwards, moving almost imperceptibly at first, but then slowly accelerating. It seemed an age before the glass was reached: then a great cheer went up as contact was made and the level of the liquid began to creep upwards.

'. . . I calculate it should take a hundred and twenty seconds to get there,' Mackay's voice was heard to announce above the din.

'Then you'd better calculate again,' retorted Scott. 'That's two minutes, and it's already there!'

'Eh?' said Mackay, startled, and obviously realizing for the first time that the experiment was over. He rapidly rechecked his calculations and suddenly brightened at discovering a misplaced decimal point.

'Silly of me! I never was any good at mental arithmetic. I meant twelve seconds, of course.'

'And that's the man who got us to Mars!' said someone in shocked amazement. 'I'm going to walk back!'

Nobody seemed inclined to repeat Scott's experiment, which, though interesting, was felt to have little practical value. Very soon large amounts of liquid were being squirted out of bulbs in the 'normal' manner, and the party began to get steadily more cheerful. Dr Scott recited the whole of that saga of the space-ways – and a prodigious feat of memory it was – which paying passengers seldom encounter and which begins:

'It was the spaceship *Venus*...'

Gibson followed for some time the adventures of this all too appropriately named craft and its ingenious though singleminded crew. Then the atmosphere began to get too close for him and he left to clear his head. Almost automatically, he made his way back to his favourite viewpoint on the observation deck.

He had to anchor himself in it, lest the tiny but persistent pull of Deimos dislodge him. Mars, more than half full and slowly waxing, lay dead ahead. Down there the preparations to greet them would already be under way, and even at this moment the little rockets would be climbing invisibly towards Deimos to ferry them down. Fourteen thousand kilometres below, but still six thousand kilometres above Mars, Phobos was transiting the unlighted face of the planet, shining brilliantly against its star-eclipsing crescent. Just what *was* happening on that little moon, Gibson wondered half-heartedly. Oh, well, he'd find out soon enough. Meanwhile he'd polish up his aerography. Let's see – there was the double fork of the Sinus Meridiani (very convenient, that, smack on the Equator and in zero longitude) and over to the east was the Syrtis Major. Working from these two obvious landmarks he could fill in the finer detail. Margaritifer Sinus was showing up nicely today, but there was a lot of cloud over Xanthe, and—

'Mr Gibson!'

He looked round, startled.

'Why, Jimmy – you had enough too?'

Jimmy was looking rather hot and flushed – obviously another seeker after fresh air. He wavered, a little unsteadily, into the observation seat and for a moment stared silently at Mars as if he'd never seen it before. Then he shook his head disapprovingly.

'It's awfully big,' he announced to no one in particular.

'It isn't as big as Earth,' Gibson protested. 'And in any case your criticism's completely meaningless, unless you state what standards you're applying. Just what size do you think Mars should be, anyway?'

This obviously hadn't occurred to Jimmy and he pondered it deeply for some time.

'I don't know,' he said sadly. 'But it's still too big. *Everything's* too big.'

This conversation was going to get nowhere, Gibson decided. He would have to change the subject.

'What are you going to do when you get down to Mars? You've got a couple of months to play with before the *Ares* goes home.'

'Well, I suppose I'll wander round Port Lowell and go out and look at the deserts. I'd like to do a bit of exploring if I can manage it.'

Gibson thought this quite an interesting idea, but he knew that to explore Mars on any useful scale was not an easy undertaking and required a good deal of equipment, as well as experienced guides. It was hardly likely that Jimmy could attach himself to one of the scientific parties which left the settlements from time to time.

'I've an idea,' he said. 'They're supposed to show me everything I want to see. Maybe I can organize some trips out into Hellas or Hesperia, where no one's been yet. Would you like to come? We might meet some Martians!'

That, of course, had been the stock joke about Mars ever since the first ships had returned with the disappointing news that there weren't any Martians after all. Quite a number of people still hoped, against all evidence, that there might be intelligent life somewhere in the many unexplored regions of the planet.

'Yes,' said Jimmy, 'that would be a great idea. No one can stop me, anyway – my time's my own as soon as we get to Mars. It says so in the contract.'

He spoke this rather belligerently, as if for the information of any superior officers who might be listening, and Gibson thought it wisest to remain silent.

The silence lasted for some minutes. Then Jimmy began, very slowly, to drift out of the observation port and to slide down the sloping walls of the ship. Gibson caught him before he had travelled very far and fastened two of the elastic hand-holds to his clothing – on the principle that Jimmy could sleep here just as comfortably as anywhere else. He was certainly much too tired to carry him to his bunk.

Is it true that we only look our true selves when we are asleep? wondered Gibson. Jimmy seemed very peaceful and contented now that he was completely relaxed – although perhaps the ruby light from the great planet above gave him his appearance of well-being. Gibson hoped it was not all illusion. The fact that Jimmy had at last deliberately sought him out was significant. True, Jimmy was not altogether himself, and he might have forgotten the whole incident by morning. But Gibson did not think so. Jimmy had decided, perhaps not yet consciously, to give him another chance.

He was on probation.

Gibson awoke the next day with a most infernal din ringing in his ears. It sounded as if the *Ares* was falling to pieces around him, and he hastily dressed and hurried out into the corridor. The first person he met was Mackay, who didn't stop to explain but shouted after him as he went by. 'The rockets are here! The first one's going down in two hours. Better hurry – you're supposed to be on it!'

Gibson scratched his head a little sheepishly.

'Someone ought to have told me,' he grumbled. Then he remembered that someone had, so he'd only himself to blame. He hurried back to his cabin and began to throw his property into suitcases. From time to time the *Ares* gave a distinct shudder around him, and he wondered just what was going on.

Norden, looking rather harassed, met him at the airlock. Dr Scott, also dressed for departure, was with him. He was carrying, with extreme care, a bulky metal case.

'Hope you two have a nice trip down,' said Norden. 'We'll be seeing you in a couple of days, when we've got the cargo out. So until then – oh, I almost forgot! I'm supposed to get you to sign this.'

'What is it?' asked Gibson suspiciously. 'I never sign anything until my agent's vetted it.'

'Read it and see,' grinned Norden. 'It's quite an historic document.'

The parchment which Norden had handed him bore these words:

THIS IS TO CERTIFY THAT MARTIN M. GIBSON, AUTHOR, WAS THE FIRST PASSENGER TO TRAVEL IN THE LINER *ARES*, OF EARTH, ON HER MAIDEN VOYAGE FROM EARTH TO MARS.

Then followed the date, and space for the signatures of Gibson and the rest of the crew. Gibson wrote his autograph with a flourish.

'I suppose this will end up in the Museum of Astronautics, when they decide where they're going to build it,' he remarked.

'So will the *Ares*, I expect,' said Scott.

'That's a fine thing to say at the end of her first trip!' protested Norden. 'But I guess you're right. Well, I must be off. The others are outside in their suits – shout to them as you go across. See you on Mars!'

For the second time, Gibson climbed into a spacesuit, now feeling quite a veteran at this sort of thing.

'Of course, you'll understand,' explained Scott, 'that when the service is properly organized the passengers will go across to the ferry through a connecting tube. That will cut out all this business.'

'They'll miss a lot of fun,' Gibson replied as he quickly checked the gauges on the little panel beneath his chin.

The outer door opened before them, and they jetted themselves slowly out across the surface of Deimos. The *Ares*, supported in the cradle of ropes (which must have been hastily prepared within the last week) looked as if a wrecking party had been at work on her. Gibson understood now the cause of the bangings and thumpings that had awakened him. Most of the plating from the Southern Hemisphere had been removed to get at the hold, and the spacesuited members of the crew were bringing out the cargo, which was now being piled on the rocks around the ship. It looked, Gibson thought, a very haphazard sort of operation. He hoped that no one would accidentally give his luggage a push which would send it off irretrievably into space, to become a third and still tinier satellite of Mars.

Lying fifty metres from the *Ares*, and quite dwarfed by her bulk, were the two winged rockets that had come up from Mars during the night. One was already having cargo ferried into it; the other, a much smaller vessel, was obviously intended for passengers only. As Gibson slowly and cautiously followed Scott towards it, he switched over to the general wavelength of his suit and called goodbye to his crew-mates. Their envious replies came back promptly, interspersed with much puffing and blowing – for the loads they were shifting, though practically weightless, possessed their normal inertia and so were just as hard to set moving as on Earth.

'That's right!' came Bradley's voice. 'Leave us to do all the work!'

'You've one compensation,' laughed Gibson. 'You must be the highest-paid stevedores in the Solar System!' He could sympathize with Bradley's point of view; this was not the sort of work for which the highly trained technicians of the *Ares* had signed on. But the mysterious diversion of the ship from the tiny though well-equipped port on Phobos had made such improvisations unavoidable.

One couldn't very well make individual goodbyes on open circuit with half a dozen people listening, and in any case Gibson would be seeing everyone again in a few days. He would like to have had an extra word with Jimmy, but that would have to wait.

It was quite an experience seeing a new human face again. The rocket pilot came into the airlock to help them with their suits, which were gently deposited back on Deimos for future use simply by opening the outer door again and letting the air current do the rest. Then he led them into the tiny cabin and told them to relax in the padded seats.

'Since you've had no gravity for a couple of months,' he said, 'I'm taking you down as gently as I can. I won't use more than a normal Earth gravity – but even that may make you feel as if you weigh a ton. Ready?'

'Yes,' said Gibson, trying valiantly to forget his last experience of this nature.

There was a gentle, far-away roar and something thrust him firmly down into the depths of his seat. The crags and mountains of

Deimos sank swiftly behind; he caught a last glimpse of the *Ares* – a bright silver dumb-bell against that nightmare jumble of rocks.

Only a second's burst of power had liberated them from the tiny moon: they were now floating round Mars in a free orbit. For several minutes the pilot studied his instruments, receiving radio checks from the planet beneath, and swinging the ship round its gyros. Then he punched the firing key again, and the rockets thundered for a few seconds more. The ship had broken free from the orbit of Deimos, and was falling towards Mars. The whole operation was an exact replica, in miniature, of a true interplanetary voyage. Only the times and durations were changed: it would take them three hours, not months, to reach their goal, and they had only thousands instead of millions of kilometres to travel.

'Well,' said the pilot, locking his controls and swinging round in his seat. 'Had a good trip?'

'Quite pleasant, thanks,' said Gibson. 'Not much excitement, of course. Everything went very smoothly.'

'How's Mars these days?' asked Scott.

'Oh, just the same as usual. All work and not much play. The big thing at the moment is the new dome we're building at Lowell. Three hundred metres clear span – you'll be able to think you're back on Earth. We're wondering if we can arrange clouds and rain inside it.'

'What's all this Phobos business?' said Gibson, with a nose for news. 'It caused us a lot of trouble.'

'Oh, I don't think it's anything important. No one seems to know exactly, but there are quite a lot of people up there building a big lab. My guess is that Phobos is going to be a pure research station, and they don't want liners coming and going – and messing up their instruments with just about every form of radiation known to science.'

Gibson felt disappointed at the collapse of several interesting theories. Perhaps if he had not been so intent on the approaching planet he might have considered this explanation a little more critically, but for the moment it satisfied him and he gave the matter no further thought.

When Mars seemed in no great hurry to come closer, Gibson decided to learn all he could about the practical details of life on the planet, now that he had a genuine colonist to question. He had a morbid fear of making a fool of himself, either by ignorance or tactlessness, and for the next couple of hours the pilot was kept busy alternating between Gibson and his instruments.

Mars was less than a thousand kilometres away when Gibson released his victim and devoted his whole attention to the expanding landscape beneath. They were passing swiftly over the Equator, coming down into the outer fringes of the planet's extremely deep yet very tenuous atmosphere. Presently – and it was impossible to tell when the moment arrived – Mars ceased to be a planet floating in space, and became instead a landscape far below. Deserts and oases fled beneath; the Syrtis Major came and passed before Gibson had time to recognize it. They were fifty kilometres up when there came the first hint that the air was thickening around them. A faint and distant sighing, seeming to come from nowhere, began to fill the cabin. The thin air was tugging at their hurtling projectile with feeble fingers, but its strength would grow swiftly – too swiftly, if their navigation had been at fault. Gibson could feel the deceleration mounting as the ship slackened its speed: the whistle of air was now so loud, even through the insulation of the walls, that normal speech would have been difficult.

This seemed to last for a very long time, though it could only have been a few minutes. At last the wail of the wind died slowly away. The rocket had shed all its surplus speed against air resistance: the refractory material of its nose and knife-edged wings would be swiftly cooling from cherry-red. No longer a spaceship now, but simply a high-speed glider, the little ship was racing across the desert at less than a thousand kilometres an hour, riding down the radio beam into Port Lowell.

Gibson first glimpsed the settlement as a tiny white patch on the horizon, against the dark background of the Aurorae Sinus. The pilot swung the ship round in a great whistling arc to the south, losing altitude and shedding his surplus speed. As the rocket banked, Gibson had a momentary picture of half a dozen large, circular domes, clustered closely together. Then the ground was rushing up to meet him, there was a series of gentle bumps, and the machine rolled slowly to a standstill.

He was on Mars. He had reached what to ancient man had been a moving red light among the stars, what to the men of only a century ago had been a mysterious and utterly unattainable world – and what was now the frontier of the human race.

'There's quite a reception committee,' remarked the pilot. 'All the transport fleet's come out to see us. I didn't know they had so many vehicles serviceable!'

Two small, squat machines with very wide balloon tyres had come racing up to meet them. Each had a pressurized driving cab, large enough to hold two people, but a dozen passengers had managed to crowd on to the little vehicles by grabbing convenient hand-holds. Behind them came two large half-tracked buses, also full of spectators. Gibson had not expected quite such a crowd, and began to compose a short speech.

'I don't suppose you know how to use these things yet,' said the pilot, producing two breathing masks. 'But you've only got to wear them for a minute while you get over to the Fleas.' (The *what*? thought Gibson. Oh, of course, those little vehicles would be the famous Martian 'Sand Fleas', the planet's universal transports.) 'I'll fix them on for you. Oxygen OK? Right – here we go. It may feel a bit queer at first.'

The air slowly hissed from the cabin until the pressure inside and out had been equalized. Gibson felt his exposed skin tingling uncomfortably: the atmosphere around him was now thinner than above the peak of Everest. It had taken three months of slow acclimatization on the *Ares*, and all the resources of modern medical science, to enable him to step out on to the surface of Mars with no more protection than a simple oxygen mask.

It was flattering that so many people had come to meet him. Of course, it wasn't often that Mars could expect so distinguished a visitor, but he knew that the busy little colony had no time for ceremonial.

Dr Scott emerged beside him, still carrying the large metal case he had nursed so carefully through the whole of the trip. At his appearance a group of the colonists came rushing forward, completely ignored Gibson, and crowded round Scott. Gibson could hear their voices, so distorted in this thin air as to be almost incomprehensible.

'Glad to see you again, Doc! Here – let us carry it!'

'We've got everything ready, and there are ten cases waiting in hospital now. We should know how good it is in a week.'

'Come on – get into the bus and talk later!'

Before Gibson had realized what was happening, Scott and his impedimenta had been swept away. There was a shrill whine of a powerful motor and the bus tore off towards Port Lowell, leaving Gibson feeling as foolish as he had ever done in his life.

He had completely forgotten the serum. To Mars, its arrival was of infinitely greater importance than a visit by any novelist, however distinguished he might be on his own planet. It was a lesson he would not forget in a hurry.

Luckily, he had not been completely deserted – the Sand Fleas were still left. One of the passengers disembarked and hurried up to him.

'Mr Gibson? I'm Westerman of the *Times* – the *Martian Times*, that is. Very pleased to meet you. This is—'

'Henderson, in charge of port facilities,' interrupted a tall, hatchet-faced man, obviously annoyed that the other had got in first. 'I've seen that your luggage will be collected. Jump aboard.'

It was quite obvious that Westerman would have much preferred Gibson as his own passenger, but he was forced to submit with as good grace as he could manage. Gibson climbed into Henderson's Flea through the flexible plastic bag that was the vehicle's simple but effective airlock, and the other joined him a minute later in the driving cab. It was a relief to discard the breathing mask: the few minutes he had spent in the open had been quite a strain. He also felt very heavy and sluggish – the exact reverse of the sensation one would have expected on reaching Mars. But for three months he had known no gravity at all, and it would take him some time to grow accustomed to even a third of his terrestrial weight.

The vehicle began to race across the landing strip towards the domes of the Port, a couple of kilometres away. For the first time, Gibson noticed that all around him was the brilliant mottled green of the hardy plants that were the commonest life-form on Mars. Overhead the sky was no longer jet black, but a deep and glorious blue. The sun was not far from the zenith, and its rays struck with surprising warmth through the plastic dome of the cabin.

Gibson peered at the dark vault of the sky, trying to locate the tiny moon on which his companions were still at work. Henderson noticed his gaze, took one hand off the steering wheel, and pointed close to the Sun.

'There she is,' he said.

Gibson shielded his eyes and stared into the sky. Then he saw, hanging like a distant electric arc against the blue, a brilliant star a little westward of the Sun. It was far too small even for Deimos, but it was a moment before Gibson realized that his companion had mistaken the object of his search.

That steady, unwinking light, burning so unexpectedly in the daylight sky, was now, and would remain for many weeks, the morning star of Mars. But it was better known as Earth.

Eight

'Sorry to have kept you waiting,' said Mayor Whittaker, 'but you know the way it is – the Chief's been in conference for the last hour. I've only just been able to get hold of him myself to tell him you're here. This way – we'll take the short cut through Records.'

It might have been an ordinary office on Earth. The door said, simply enough: 'Chief Executive'. There was no name: it wasn't necessary. Everyone in the Solar System knew who ran Mars – indeed, it was difficult to think of the planet without thinking of Warren Hadfield at the same time.

Gibson was surprised, when he rose from his desk, to see that the Chief Executive was a good deal shorter than he had imagined. He must have judged the man by his works, and had never guessed that he could give him a couple of inches in height. But the thin, wiry frame and sensitive, rather birdlike head were exactly as he had expected.

The interview began with Gibson somewhat on the defensive, for so much depended on his making a good impression. His way would be infinitely easier if he had the Chief on his side. In fact, if he made an enemy of Hadfield he might just as well go home right away.

'I hope Whittaker's been looking after you,' said the Chief when the initial courtesies had been exchanged. 'You'll realize that I couldn't see you before – I've only just got back from an inspection. How are you settling down here?'

'Quite well,' smiled Gibson. 'I'm afraid I've broken a few things by leaving them in mid-air, but I'm getting used to living with gravity again.'

'And what do you think of our little city?'

'It's a remarkable achievement. I don't know how you managed to do so much in the time.'

Hadfield was eyeing him narrowly.

'Be perfectly frank. It's smaller than you expected, isn't it?'

Gibson hesitated.

'Well, I suppose it is – but then I'm used to the standards of London and New York. After all, two thousand people would only make a large village back on Earth. Such a lot of Port Lowell's underground, too, and that makes a difference.'

The Chief Executive seemed neither annoyed nor surprised.

'Everyone has a disappointment when they see Mars' largest city,' he said. 'Still, it's going to be a lot bigger in another week, when the new dome goes up. Tell me – just what are your plans now you've got here? I suppose you know I wasn't very much in favour of this visit in the first place.'

'I gathered that on Earth,' said Gibson, a little taken aback. He had yet to discover that frankness was one of the Chief Executive's major virtues: it was not one that endeared him to many people. 'I suppose you were afraid I'd get in the way.'

'Yes. But now you're here, we'll do the best for you. I hope you'll do the same for us.'

'In what way?' asked Gibson, stiffening defensively.

Hadfield leaned across the table and clasped his hands together with an almost feverish intensity.

'We're at war, Mr Gibson. We're at war with Mars and all the forces it can bring against us – cold, lack of water, lack of air. And we're at war with Earth. It's a paper war, true, but it's got its victories and defeats. I'm fighting a campaign at the end of a supply line that's never less than fifty million kilometres long. The most urgent goods take at least five months to reach me – and I only get them if Earth decides I can't manage any other way.

'I suppose you realize what I'm fighting for – my primary objective, that is? It's self-sufficiency. Remember that the first expeditions had to bring *everything* with them. Well, we can provide all the basic necessities of life now, from our own resources. Our workshops can make almost anything that isn't too complicated – but it's all a question of manpower. There are some very specialized goods that simply have to be made on Earth, and until our population's at least ten times as big we can't do much about it. Everyone on Mars is an expert at something – but there are more skilled trades back on Earth than there are people on this planet, and it's no use arguing with arithmetic.

'You'll see those graphs over there? I started keeping them five years ago. They show our production index for various key materials. We've reached the self-sufficiency level – that horizontal red line – for about half of them. I hope that in another five years there will be very few things we'll have to import from Earth. Even now our greatest need is manpower, and that's where you may be able to help us.'

Gibson looked a little uncomfortable.

'I can't make any promises. Please remember that I'm here purely as a reporter. Emotionally, I'm on your side, but I've got to describe the facts as I see them.'

'I appreciate that. But facts aren't everything. What I hope you'll explain to Earth are the things we hope to do, just as much as the things we've done. They're even more important – but we can achieve them only if Earth gives us its support. Not all your predecessors have realized that.'

That was perfectly true, thought Gibson. He remembered a critical series of articles in the *Daily Telegraph* about a year before. The facts had been quite accurate, but a similar account of the first settlers' achievements after five years' colonization of North America would probably have been just as discouraging.

'I think I can see both sides of the question,' said Gibson. 'You've got to realize that from the point of view of Earth, Mars is a long way away, costs a lot of money, and doesn't offer anything in return. The first glamour of interplanetary exploration has worn off. Now people are asking, "What do we get out of it?" So far the answer's been, "Very little." I'm convinced that your work is important, but in my case it's an act of faith rather than a matter of logic. The average man back on Earth probably thinks the millions you're spending here could be better used improving his own planet – when he thinks of it at all, that is.'

'I understand your difficulty: it's a common one. And it isn't easy to answer. Let me put it this way. I suppose most intelligent people would admit the value of a scientific base on Mars, devoted to pure research and investigation?'

'Undoubtedly.'

'But they can't see the purpose of building up a self-contained culture, which may eventually become an independent civilization?'

'That's the trouble, precisely. They don't believe it's possible – or, granted the possibility, don't think it's worthwhile. You'll often see articles pointing out that Mars will always be a drag on the home planet, because of the tremendous natural difficulties under which you're labouring.'

'What about the analogy between Mars and the American colonies?'

'It can't be pressed too far. After all, men could breathe the air and find food to eat when they got to America!'

'That's true, but though the problem of colonizing Mars is so much more difficult, we've got enormously greater powers at our control. Given time and material, we can make this a world as good to live on as Earth. Even now, you won't find many of our people who want to go back. They know the importance of what they're doing. Earth may not need Mars yet, but one day it will.'

'I wish I could believe that,' said Gibson a little unhappily. He pointed to the rich green tide of vegetation that lapped, like a hungry sea, against the almost invisible dome of the city, at the great plain that hurried so swiftly over the edge of the curiously close horizon, and at the scarlet hills within whose arms the city lay. 'Mars is an interesting world, even a beautiful one. But it can never be like Earth.'

'Why should it be? And what do you mean by "Earth", anyway? Do you mean the South American pampas, the vineyards of France, the coral islands of the Pacific, the Siberian steppes? "Earth" is every one of those! Wherever men can live, that will be home to someone, some day. And sooner or later men will be able to live on Mars without all this.' He waved towards the dome which floated above the city and gave it life.

'Do you really think,' protested Gibson, 'that men can ever adapt themselves to the atmosphere outside? They won't be men any longer if they do!'

For a moment the Chief Executive did not reply. Then he remarked quietly: 'I said nothing about men adapting themselves to Mars. Have you ever considered the possibility of Mars meeting us half-way?'

He left Gibson just sufficient time to absorb the words; then, before his visitor could frame the questions that were leaping to his mind, Hadfield rose to his feet.

'Well, I hope Whittaker looks after you and shows you everything you want to see. You'll understand that the transport situation's rather tight, but we'll get you to all the outposts if you give us time to make the arrangements. Let me know if there's any difficulty.'

The dismissal was polite and, at least for the time being, final. The busiest man on Mars had given Gibson a generous portion of his time, and his questions would have to wait until the next opportunity.

'What do you think of the Chief, now you've met him?' said Mayor Whittaker when Gibson had returned to the outer office.

'He was very pleasant and helpful,' replied Gibson cautiously. 'Quite an enthusiast about Mars, isn't he?'

Whittaker pursed his lips.

'I'm not sure that's the right word. I think he regards Mars as an enemy to be beaten. So do we all, of course, but the Chief's got better reasons than most. You'd heard about his wife, hadn't you?'

'No.'

'She was one of the first people to die of Martian fever, two years after they came here.'

'Oh,' said Gibson slowly. 'I see. I suppose that's one reason why there's been such an effort to find a cure.'

'Yes; the Chief's very much set on it. Besides, it's such a drain on our resources. We can't afford to be sick here!'

That last remark, thought Gibson as he crossed Broadway (so called because it was all of fifteen metres wide), almost summed up the position of the colony. He had still not quite recovered from his initial disappointment at finding how small Port Lowell was, and how deficient in all the luxuries to which he was accustomed on Earth. With its rows of uniform metal houses and few public buildings it was more of a military camp than a city, though the inhabitants had done their best to brighten it up with terrestrial flowers. Some of these had grown to impressive sizes under the low gravity, and Oxford Circus was now ablaze with sunflowers thrice the height of a man. Though they were getting rather a nuisance no one had the heart to suggest their removal: if they continued at their present rate of growth it would soon take a skilled lumberjack to fell them without endangering the Port hospital.

Gibson continued thoughtfully up Broadway until he came to Marble Arch, at the meeting point of Domes One and Two. It was also, as he had quickly found, a meeting point in many other ways. Here, strategically placed near the multiple airlocks, was 'George's', the only bar on Mars.

'Morning, Mr Gibson,' said George. 'Hope the Chief was in a good temper.'

As he had left the administration building less than ten minutes ago, Gibson thought this was pretty quick work. He was soon to find that news travelled very rapidly in Port Lowell, and most of it seemed to be routed through George.

George was an interesting character. Since publicans were regarded as only relatively, and not absolutely, essential for the well-being of the Port, he had two official professions. On Earth he had been a well-known stage entertainer, but the unreasonable demands of the three or four wives he had acquired in a rush of youthful enthusiasm had made him decide to emigrate. He was now in charge of the Port's little theatre and seemed to be perfectly contented with life. Being in the middle forties, he was one of the oldest men on Mars.

'We've got a show on next week,' he remarked when he had served Gibson. 'One or two quite good turns. Hope you'll be coming along.'

'Certainly,' said Gibson. 'I'll look forward to it. How often do you have this sort of thing?'

'About once a month. We have film shows three times a week, so we don't do too badly.'

'I'm glad Port Lowell has some night-life.'

'You'd be surprised. Still, I'd better not tell you about that or you'll be writing it all up in the papers.'

'I don't write for *that* sort of newspaper,' retorted Gibson, sipping thoughtfully at the local brew. It wasn't at all bad when you got used to it, though of course it was completely synthetic – the joint offspring of hydroponic farm and chemical laboratory.

The bar was quite deserted, for at this time of day everyone in

Port Lowell would be hard at work. Gibson pulled out his notebook and began to make careful entries, whistling a little tune as he did so. It was an annoying habit, of which he was quite unconscious, and George counter-attacked by turning up the bar radio.

For once it was a live programme, beamed to Mars from somewhere on the night-side of Earth, punched across space by heaven-knows-how-many megawatts, then picked up and re-broadcast by the station on the low hills to the south of the city. Reception was good, apart from a trace of solar noise – static from that infinitely greater transmitter against whose background Earth was broadcasting. Gibson wondered if it was really worth all this trouble to send the voice of a somewhat mediocre soprano and a light orchestra from world to world. But half Mars was probably listening with varying degrees of sentimentality and homesickness – both of which would be indignantly denied.

Gibson finished the list of several score questions he had to ask someone. He still felt rather like a new boy at his first school; everything was so strange, nothing could be taken for granted. It was so hard to believe that twenty metres on the other side of that transparent bubble lay a sudden death by suffocation. Somehow this feeling had never worried him on the *Ares*: after all, space was like that. But it seemed all wrong here, where one could look out across that brilliant green plain, now a battlefield on which the hardy Martian plants fought their annual struggle for existence – a struggle which would end in death for victors and vanquished alike with the coming of winter.

Suddenly Gibson felt an almost overwhelming desire to leave the narrow streets and go out beneath the open sky. For almost the first time, he found himself really missing Earth, the planet he had thought had so little more to offer him. Like Falstaff, he felt like babbling of green fields – with the added irony that green fields were all around him, tantalizingly visible yet barred from him by the laws of nature.

'George,' said Gibson abruptly, 'I've been here five days and I haven't been outside yet. I'm not supposed to without someone to look after me. You won't have any customers for an hour or so. Be a sport and take me out through the airlock – just for ten minutes.'

No doubt, thought Gibson a little sheepishly, George considered this a pretty crazy request. He was quite wrong: it had happened so often before that George took it very much for granted. After all, his job was attending to the whims of his customers, and most of the new boys seemed to feel this way after their first few days under the dome. George shrugged his shoulders philosophically, wondering if he should apply for additional credits as port psycho-therapist, and disappeared into his inner sanctum. He came back a moment later, carrying a couple of breathing masks and their auxiliary equipment.

'We won't want the whole works on a nice day like this,' he said, while Gibson clumsily adjusted his gear. 'Make sure that sponge rubber fits snugly around your neck. All right – let's go. But only for ten minutes, mind!'

Gibson followed eagerly, like a sheepdog behind its master, until they came to the dome exit. There were two locks here, a large one, wide open, leading into Dome Two, and a smaller one which led out on to the open landscape. It was simply a metal tube, about three metres in diameter, leading through the glass-brick wall which anchored the flexible plastic envelope of the dome to the ground.

There were four separate doors, none of which could be opened unless the remaining three were closed. Gibson fully approved of these precautions, but it seemed a long time before the last of the doors swung inwards from its seals and that vivid green plain lay open before him. His exposed skin was tingling under the reduced pressure, but the thin air was reasonably warm and he soon felt quite comfortable. Completely ignoring George, he ploughed his way briskly through the low, closely packed vegetation, wondering as he did why it clustered so thickly round the dome. Perhaps it was attracted by the warmth or the slow seepage of oxygen from the city.

He stopped after a few hundred metres, feeling at last clear of that oppressive canopy and once more under the open sky of heaven. The fact that his head, at least, was still totally enclosed somehow didn't seem to matter. He bent down and examined the plants among which he was standing knee-deep.

He had, of course, seen photographs of Martian plants many times before. They were not really very exciting, and he was not enough of a botanist to appreciate their peculiarities. Indeed if he had met such plants in some out-of-the-way part of Earth he would hardly have looked at them twice. None were higher than his waist, and those around him now seemed to be made of sheets of brilliant green parchment, very thin but very tough, designed to catch as much sunlight as possible without losing precious water. Those ragged sheets were spread like little sails in the sun, whose progress across the sky they would follow until they dipped westwards at dusk. Gibson wished there were some flowers to add a touch of contrasting colour to the vivid emerald, but there were no flowers on Mars. Perhaps there had been, once, when the air was thick enough to support insects, but now most of the Martian plant-life was self-fertilized.

George caught up with him and stood regarding the natives with a morose indifference. Gibson wondered if he was annoyed at being so summarily dragged out of doors, but his qualms of conscience were unjustified. George was simply brooding over his next production, wondering whether to risk a Noel Coward play after the disaster that had resulted the last time his company had tried its hand with period pieces. Suddenly he snapped out of his reverie and said to Gibson, his voice thin but clearly audible over this short distance: 'This is rather amusing. Just stand still for a minute and watch that plant in your shadow.'

Gibson obeyed this peculiar instruction. For a moment nothing happened. Then he saw that, very slowly, the parchment sheets were folding on to one another. The whole process was over in about three minutes: at the end of that time the plant had become a little ball of green paper, tightly crumpled together and only a fraction of its previous size.

George chuckled.

'It thinks night's fallen,' he said, 'and doesn't want to be caught napping when the sun's gone. If you move away, it will think things over for half an hour before it risks opening shop again. You could probably give it a nervous breakdown if you kept this up all day.'

'Are these plants any use?' said Gibson. 'I mean, can they be eaten, or do they contain any valuable chemicals?'

'They certainly can't be eaten – they're not poisonous but they'd make you feel mighty unhappy. You see they're not really like plants on Earth at all. That green is just a coincidence. It isn't – what do you call the stuff—'

'Chlorophyll?'

'Yes. They don't depend on the air as our plants do: everything they need they get from the ground. In fact they can grow in a complete vacuum, like the plants on the Moon, if they've got suitable soil and enough sunlight.'

Quite a triumph of evolution, thought Gibson. But to what purpose? he wondered. Why had life clung so tenaciously to this little world, despite the worst that nature could do? Perhaps the Chief Executive had obtained some of his own optimism from these tough and resolute plants.

'Hey!' said George. 'It's time to go back.'

Gibson followed meekly enough. He no longer felt weighted down by that claustrophobic oppression which was, he knew, partly due to the inevitable reaction at finding Mars something of an anticlimax. Those who had come here for a definite job, and hadn't been given time to brood, would probably bypass this stage altogether. But he had been turned loose to collect his impressions, and so far his chief one was a feeling of helplessness as he compared what man had so far achieved on Mars with the problems still to be faced. Why, even now three-quarters of the planet was still unexplored! That was some measure of what remained to be done.

The first few days at Port Lowell had been busy and exciting enough. It had been a Sunday when he had arrived and Mayor Whittaker had been sufficiently free from the cares of office to show him round the city personally, once he had been installed in one of the four suites of the Grand Martian Hotel. (The other three had not yet been finished.) They had started at Dome One, the first to be built, and the Mayor had proudly traced the growth of his city from a group of pressurized huts only ten years ago. It was amusing – and rather touching – to see how the colonists had used wherever possible the names of familiar streets and squares from their own far-away cities. There was also a scientific system of numbering the streets in Port Lowell, but nobody ever used it.

Most of the living houses were uniform metal structures, two storeys high, with rounded corners and rather small windows. They held two families and were none too large, since the birth-rate of Port Lowell was the highest in the known universe. This, of course, was hardly surprising since almost the entire population lay between the ages of twenty and thirty, with a few of the senior administrative

232

staff creeping up into the forties. Every house had a curious porch which puzzled Gibson until he realized that it was designed to act as an airlock in an emergency.

Whittaker had taken him first to the administrative centre, the tallest building in the city. If one stood on its roof, one could almost reach up and touch the dome floating above. There was nothing very exciting about Admin. It might have been any office building on Earth, with its rows of desks and typewriters and filing cabinets.

Main Air was much more interesting. This, truly, was the heart of Port Lowell: if it ever ceased to function, the city and all those it held would soon be dead. Gibson had been somewhat vague about the manner in which the settlement obtained its oxygen. At one time he had been under the impression that it was extracted from the surrounding air, having forgotten that even such scanty atmosphere as Mars possessed contained less than one per cent of the gas.

Mayor Whittaker had pointed to the great heap of red sand that had been bulldozed in from outside the dome. Everyone called it 'sand', but it had little resemblance to the familiar sand of Earth. A complex mixture of metallic oxides, it was nothing less than the debris of a world that had rusted to death.

'All the oxygen we need's in these ores,' said Whittaker, kicking at the caked powder. 'And just about every metal you can think of. We've had one or two strokes of luck on Mars: this is the biggest.'

He bent down and picked up a lump more solid than the rest.

'I'm not much of a geologist,' he said, 'but look at this. Pretty, isn't it? Mostly iron oxide, they tell me. Iron isn't much use, of course, but the other metals are. About the only one we can't get easily direct from the sand is magnesium. The best source of that's the old sea bed: there are some salt flats a hundred metres thick out in Xanthe and we just go and collect when we need it.'

They walked into the low, brightly lit building, towards which a continual flow of sand was moving on a conveyor belt. There was not really a great deal to see, and though the engineer in charge was only too anxious to explain just what was happening, Gibson was content merely to learn that the ores were cracked in electric furnaces, the oxygen drawn off, purified and compressed, and the various metallic messes sent on for more complicated operations. A good deal of water was also produced here – almost enough for the settlement's needs, though other sources were available as well.

'Of course,' said Mayor Whittaker, 'in addition to storing the oxygen we've got to keep the air pressure at the correct value and to get rid of the CO_2. You realize, don't you, that the dome's kept up purely by the internal pressure and hasn't any other support at all?'

'Yes,' said Gibson. 'I suppose if that fell off the whole thing would collapse like a deflated balloon.'

'Exactly. We keep 150 millimetres pressure in summer, a little more in winter. That gives almost the same oxygen pressure as in Earth's atmosphere. And we remove the CO_2 simply by letting plants do the trick. We imported enough for this job, since the Martian plants don't go in for photosynthesis.'

'Hence the hypertrophied sunflowers in Oxford Circus, I suppose.'

'Well, those are intended to be more ornamental than functional. I'm afraid they're getting a bit of a nuisance: I'll have to stop them from spraying seeds all over the city, or whatever it is that sunflowers do. Now let's walk over and look at the farm.'

The name was a singularly misleading one for the big food-production plant filling Dome Three. The air was quite humid here, and the sunlight was augmented by batteries of fluorescent tubes so that growth could continue day and night. Gibson knew very little about hydroponic farming and so was not really impressed by the figures which Mayor Whittaker proudly poured into his ear. He could, however, appreciate that one of the greatest problems was meat production, and admired the ingenuity which had partly overcome this by extensive tissue-culture in great vats of nutrient fluid.

'It's better than nothing,' said the Mayor a little wistfully. 'But what I wouldn't give for a genuine lamb chop! The trouble with natural meat production is that it takes up so much space and we simply can't afford it. However, when the new dome's up we're going to start a little farm with a few sheep and cows. The kids will love it – they've never seen any animals, of course.'

This was not quite true, as Gibson was soon to discover: Mayor Whittaker had momentarily overlooked two of Port Lowell's best-known residents.

By the end of the tour Gibson began to suffer from slight mental indigestion. The mechanics of life in the city were so complicated, and Mayor Whittaker tried to show him *everything*. He was quite thankful when the trip was over and they returned to the Mayor's home for dinner.

'I think that's enough for one day,' said Whittaker, 'but I wanted to show you round because we'll all be busy tomorrow and I won't be able to spare much time. The Chief's away, you know, and won't be back until Thursday, so I've got to look after everything.'

'Where's he gone?' asked Gibson, out of politeness rather than real interest.

'Oh, up to Phobos,' Whittaker replied, with the briefest possible hesitation. 'As soon as he gets back he'll be glad to see you.'

The conversation had then been interrupted by the arrival of Mrs Whittaker and family, and for the rest of the evening Gibson was compelled to talk about Earth. It was his first, but not by any means his last, experience of the insatiable interest which the colonists had in the home planet. They seldom admitted it openly, pretending to a stubborn indifference about the 'old world' and its affairs. But their questions, and above all their rapid reactions to terrestrial criticisms and comments, belied this completely.

It was strange to talk to children who had never known Earth, who had been born and had spent all their short lives under the shelter of the great domes. What, Gibson wondered, did Earth mean to them? Was it any more real than the fabulous lands of fairy tales? All they knew of the world from which their parents had emigrated was at second hand, derived from books and pictures. As far as their own senses were concerned, Earth was just another star.

They had never known the coming of the seasons. Outside the dome, it was true, they could watch the long winter spread death over the land as the Sun descended in the northern sky, could see the strange plants wither and perish, to make way for the next generation when spring returned. But no hint of this came through the protecting barriers of the city. The engineers at the power plant simply threw in more heater circuits and laughed at the worst that Mars could do.

Yet these children, despite their completely artificial environment, seemed happy and well, and quite unconscious of all the things which they had missed. Gibson wondered just what their reactions would be if they ever came to Earth. It would be a very interesting experiment, but so far none of the children born on Mars were old enough to leave their parents.

The lights of the city were going down when Gibson left the Mayor's home after his first day on Mars. He said very little as Whittaker walked back with him to the hotel, for his mind was too full of jumbled impressions. In the morning he would start to sort them out, but at the moment his chief feeling was that the greatest city on Mars was nothing more than an over-mechanized village.

Gibson had not yet mastered the intricacies of the Martian calendar, but he knew that the week-days were the same as on Earth and that Monday followed Sunday in the usual way. (The months also had the same names, but were fifty to sixty days in length.) When he left the hotel at what he thought was a reasonable hour, the city appeared quite deserted. There were none of the gossiping groups of people who had watched his progress with such interest on the previous day. Everyone was at work in office, factory, or lab, and Gibson felt rather like a drone who had strayed into a particularly busy hive.

He found Mayor Whittaker beleaguered by secretaries and talking into two telephones at once. Not having the heart to intrude, Gibson tiptoed away and started a tour of exploration himself. There was not, after all, any great danger of becoming lost. The maximum distance he would travel in a straight line was less than half a kilometre. It was not the kind of exploration of Mars he had ever imagined in any of his books . . .

So he had passed his first few days in Port Lowell wandering round and asking questions during working hours, spending the evenings with the families of Mayor Whittaker or other members of the senior staff. Already he felt as if he had lived there for years. There was nothing new to be seen: he had met everyone of importance, up to and including the Chief Executive himself.

But he knew he was still a stranger: he had really seen less than a thousand millionth of the whole surface of Mars. Beyond the shelter of the dome, beyond the crimson hills, over the edge of the emerald plain – all the rest of this world was mystery.

Nine

'Well, it's certainly nice to see you all again,' said Gibson, carrying the drinks carefully across from the bar. 'Now I suppose you're going to paint Port Lowell red. I presume the first move will be to contact the local girl friends?'

'That's never very easy,' said Norden. 'They *will* get married between trips, and you've got to be tactful. By the way, George, what's happened to Miss Margaret Mackinnon?'

'You mean Mrs Henry Lewis,' said George. 'Such a fine baby boy, too.'

'Has she called it John?' asked Bradley, not particularly *sotto voce*.

'Oh, well,' sighed Norden, 'I hope she's saved me some of the wedding cake. Here's to you, Martin.'

'And to the *Ares*,' said Gibson clinking glasses. 'I hope you've put her together again. She looked in a pretty bad way the last time I saw her.'

Norden chuckled.

'Oh, that! No, we'll leave all the plating off until we reload. The rain isn't likely to get in!'

'What do you think of Mars, Jimmy?' asked Gibson. 'You're the only other new boy here beside myself.'

'I haven't seen much of it yet,' Jimmy replied cautiously. 'Everything seems rather small, though.'

Gibson spluttered violently and had to be patted on the back.

'I remember you saying just the opposite when we were on Deimos. But I guess you've forgotten it. You were slightly drunk at the time.'

'I've never been drunk,' said Jimmy indignantly.

'Then I compliment you on a first-rate imitation: it deceived me completely. But I'm interested in what you say because that's exactly how I felt after the first couple of days, as soon as I'd seen all there was to look at inside the dome. There's only one cure – you have to go outside and stretch your legs. I've had a couple of short walks around, but now I've managed to grab a Sand Flea from Transport. I'm going to gallop up into the hills tomorrow. Like to come?'

Jimmy's eyes glistened.

'Thanks very much – I'd love to.'

'Hey, what about us?' protested Norden.

'You've done it before,' said Gibson. 'But there'll be one spare seat, so you can toss for it. We've got to take an official driver: they won't let us go out by ourselves with one of their precious vehicles, and I suppose you can hardly blame them.'

Mackay won the toss, whereupon the others immediately explained that they didn't really want to go anyway.

'Well, that settles that,' said Gibson. 'Meet me at Transport Section, Dome Four, at ten tomorrow. Now I must be off. I've got three articles to write – or at any rate one article with three different titles.'

The explorers met promptly on time, carrying the full protective equipment with which they had been issued on arrival but so far had found no occasion to use. This comprised the headpiece, oxygen cylinders, and air purifier – all that was necessary out of doors on Mars on a warm day – and the heat-insulating suit with its compact power cells. This could keep one warm and comfortable even when the temperature outside was more than a hundred below. It would not be needed on this trip, unless an accident to the Flea left them stranded a long way away from home.

The driver was a tough young geologist who claimed to have spent as much time outside Port Lowell as in it. He looked extremely competent and resourceful, and Gibson felt no qualms at handing his valuable person into his keeping.

'Do these machines ever break down outside?' he asked as they climbed into the Flea.

'Not very often. They've got a terrific safety factor and there's really very little to go wrong. Of course, sometimes a careless driver gets stuck, but you can usually haul yourself out of anything with the winch. There have only been a couple of cases of people having to walk home in the last month.'

'I trust we won't make a third,' said Mackay, as the vehicle rolled into the lock.

'I shouldn't worry about that,' laughed the driver, waiting for the outer door to open. 'We won't be going far from base, so we can always get back even if the worst comes to the worst.'

With a surge of power, they shot through the lock and out of the city. A narrow road had been cut through the low, vivid vegetation – a road which circled the port and from which other highways radiated to the nearby mines, to the radio station and observatory on the hills, and to the landing ground on which even now the *Ares*'s freight was being unloaded as the rockets ferried it down from Deimos.

'Well,' said the driver, halting at the first junction. 'It's all yours. Which way do we go?'

Gibson was struggling with a map three sizes too big for the cabin. Their guide looked at it with scorn.

'I don't know where you got hold of *that*,' he said. 'I suppose Admin gave it to you. It's completely out of date, anyway. If you'll tell me where you want to go I can take you there without bothering about that thing.'

'Very well,' Gibson replied meekly. 'I suggest we climb up into the hills and get a good look round. Let's go to the Observatory.'

The Flea leapt forward along the narrow road and the brilliant green around them merged into a featureless blur.

'How fast can these things go?' asked Gibson, when he had climbed out of Mackay's lap.

'Oh, at least a hundred on a good road. But as there aren't any good roads on Mars, we have to take it easy. I'm doing sixty now. On rough ground you'll be lucky to average half that.'

'And what about range?' said Mackay, obviously still a little nervous.

'A good thousand kilometres on one charge, even allowing pretty generously for heating, cooking, and the rest. For really long trips we tow a trailer with spare power cells. The record's about five thousand kilometres; I've done three before now, prospecting out in Argyre. When you're doing that sort of thing, you arrange to get supplies dropped from the air.'

Though they had now been travelling for no more than a couple of minutes, Port Lowell was already falling below the horizon. The steep curvature of Mars made it very difficult to judge distances, and the fact that the domes were now half concealed by the curve of the planet made one imagine that they were much larger objects at a far greater distance than they really were.

Soon afterwards, they began to reappear as the Flea started climbing towards higher ground. The hills above Port Lowell were less than a kilometre high, but they formed a useful break for the cold winter winds from the south, and gave vantage points for radio station and observatory.

They reached the radio station half an hour after leaving the city. Feeling it was time to do some walking, they adjusted their masks and dismounted from the Flea, taking turns to go through the tiny collapsible airlock.

The view was not really very impressive. To the north, the domes of Port Lowell floated like bubbles on an emerald sea. Over to the west Gibson could just catch a glimpse of crimson from the desert which encircled the entire planet. As the crest of the hills still lay a little above him, he could not see southwards, but he knew that the green band of vegetation stretched for several hundred kilometres until it petered out into the Mare Erythraeum. There were hardly any plants here on the hilltop, and he presumed that this was due to the absence of moisture.

He walked over to the radio station. It was quite automatic, so there was no one he could buttonhole in the usual way, but he knew enough about the subject to guess what was going on. The giant parabolic reflector lay almost on its back, pointing a little east of the zenith – pointing to Earth, sixty million kilometres Sunwards. Along its invisible beam were coming and going the messages that linked these two worlds together. Perhaps at this very moment one of his own articles was flying Earthwards – or one of Ruth Goldstein's directives was winging its way towards him.

Mackay's voice, distorted and feeble in this thin air, made him turn round.

'Someone's coming in to land down there – over on the right.'

With some difficulty, Gibson spotted the tiny arrowhead of the rocket moving swiftly across the sky, racing in on a free glide just as he had done a week before. It banked over the city and was lost behind the domes as it touched down on the landing strip. Gibson hoped it was bringing in the remainder of his luggage, which seemed to have taken a long time to catch up with him.

The Observatory was about five kilometres farther south, just over the brow of the hills, where the lights of Port Lowell would not interfere with its work. Gibson had half expected to see the gleaming domes which on Earth were the trade-marks of the astronomers, but instead the one dome was the small plastic bubble of the living quarters. The instruments themselves were in the open, though there was provision for covering them up in the very rare event of bad weather.

Everything appeared to be completely deserted as the Flea approached. They halted beside the largest instrument – a reflector with a mirror which, Gibson guessed, was less than a metre across. It was an astonishingly small instrument for the chief observatory on Mars. There were two small refractors, and a complicated horizontal affair which Mackay said was a mirror-transit – whatever that might be. And this, apart from the pressurized dome, seemed to be about all.

There was obviously someone at home, for a small Sand Flea was parked outside the building.

'They're quite a sociable crowd,' said the driver as he brought the vehicle to a halt. 'It's a pretty dull life up here and they're always glad to see people. And there'll be room inside the dome for us to stretch our legs and have dinner in comfort.'

'Surely we can't expect them to provide a meal for us,' protested Gibson, who had a dislike of incurring obligations he couldn't readily discharge.

The driver looked genuinely surprised; then he laughed heartily.

'This isn't Earth, you know. On Mars, everyone helps everyone else – we have to, or we'd never get anywhere. But I've brought our provisions along – all I want to use is their stove. If you'd ever tried to cook a meal inside a Sand Flea with four aboard you'd know why.'

As predicted, the two astronomers on duty greeted them warmly, and the little plastic bubble's air-conditioning plant was soon dealing with the odours of cookery. While this was going on, Mackay had grabbed the senior member of the staff and started a technical discussion about the Observatory's work. Most of it was quite over Gibson's head, but he tried to gather what he could from the conversation.

Most of the work done here was, it seemed, positional astronomy –

the dull but essential business of finding longitudes and latitudes, providing time signals and linking radio fixes with the main Martian grid. Very little observational work was done at all: the huge instruments on Earth's moon had taken *that* over long ago, and these small telescopes, with the additional handicap of an atmosphere above them, could not hope to compete. The parallaxes of a few nearer stars had been measured, but the very slight increase of accuracy provided by the wider orbit of Mars made it hardly worthwhile.

As he ate his dinner – finding to his surprise that his appetite was better than at any time since reaching Mars – Gibson felt a glow of satisfaction at having done a little to brighten the dull lives of these devoted men. Because he had never met enough of them to shatter the illusion, Gibson had an altogether disproportionate respect for astronomers, whom he regarded as leading lives of monkish dedication on their remote mountain eyries. Even his first encounter with the excellent cocktail bar on Mount Palomar had not destroyed this simple faith.

After the meal, at which everyone helped so conscientiously with the washing-up that it took twice as long as necessary, the visitors were invited to have a look through the large reflector. Since it was early afternoon, Gibson did not imagine that there would be a great deal to see; but this was an oversight on his part.

For a moment the picture was blurred, and he adjusted the focusing screw with clumsy fingers. It was not easy to observe with the special eyepiece needed when one was wearing a breathing mask, but after a while Gibson got the knack of it.

Hanging in the field of view, against the almost black sky near the zenith, was a beautiful pearly crescent like a three-day-old moon. Some markings were just visible on the illuminated portion, but though Gibson strained his eyes to the utmost he could not identify them. Too much of the planet was in darkness for him to see any of the major continents.

Not far away floated an identically shaped but much smaller and fainter crescent, and Gibson could distinctly see some of the familiar craters along its edge. They formed a beautiful couple, the twin planets Earth and Moon, but somehow they seemed too remote and ethereal to give him any feeling of homesickness or regret for all that he had left behind.

One of the astronomers was speaking, his helmet held close to Gibson's.

'When it's dark you can see the lights of the cities down there on the night side. New York and London are easy. The prettiest sight, though, is the reflection of the Sun off the sea. You get it near the edge of the disc when there's no cloud about – a sort of brilliant, shimmering star. It isn't visible now because it's mostly land on the crescent portion.'

Before leaving the Observatory, they had a look at Deimos, which was rising in its leisurely fashion in the east. Under the highest power of the telescope the rugged little moon seemed only a few kilometres away, and to his surprise Gibson could see the *Ares* quite clearly as two gleaming dots close together. He also wanted to look at Phobos, but the inner moon had not yet risen.

When there was nothing more to be seen, they bade farewell to the two astronomers, who waved back rather glumly as the Flea drove off along the brow of the hill. The driver explained that he wanted to make a private detour to pick up some rock specimens, and as to Gibson one part of Mars was very much like another he raised no objection.

There was no real road over the hills, but ages ago all irregularities had been worn away so that the ground was perfectly smooth. Here and there a few stubborn boulders still jutted above the surface, displaying a fantastic riot of colour and shape, but these obstacles were easily avoided. Once or twice they passed small trees – if one could call them that – of a type which Gibson had never seen before. They looked rather like pieces of coral, completely stiff and petrified. According to their driver they were immensely old, for though they were certainly alive no one had yet been able to measure their rate of growth. The smallest value which could be derived from their age was fifty thousand years, and their method of reproduction was a complete mystery.

Towards mid-afternoon they came to a low but beautifully coloured cliff – 'Rainbow Ridge', the geologist called it – which reminded Gibson irresistibly of the more flamboyant Arizona canyons, though on a much smaller scale. They got out of the Sand Flea and, while the driver chipped off his samples, Gibson happily shot off half a reel of the new Multichrome film he had brought with him for just such occasions. If it could bring out all those colours perfectly it must be as good as the makers claimed: but unfortunately he'd have to wait until he got back to Earth before it could be developed. No one on Mars knew anything about it.

'Well,' said the driver, 'I suppose it's time we started for home if we want to get back for tea. We can drive back the way we came, and keep to the high ground, or we can go round behind the hills. Any preferences?'

'Why not drive down into the plain? That would be the most direct route,' said Mackay, who was now getting a little bored.

'And the slowest – you can't drive at any speed through those overgrown cabbages.'

'I always hate retracing my steps,' said Gibson. 'Let's go round the hills and see what we can find there.'

The driver grinned.

'Don't raise any false hopes. It's much the same on both sides. Here we go!'

The Flea bounced forward and Rainbow Ridge soon disappeared behind them. They were now winding their way through completely barren country, and even the petrified trees had vanished. Sometimes Gibson saw a patch of green which he thought was vegetation, but as they approached it invariably turned into another mineral outcrop. This region was fantastically beautiful, a geologist's paradise, and Gibson hoped that it would never be ravaged by mining operations. It was certainly one of the show places of Mars.

They had been driving for half an hour when the hills sloped down into a long, winding valley which was unmistakably an ancient watercourse. Perhaps fifty million years ago, the driver told them, a great river had flowed this way to lose its waters in the Mare Erythraeum – one of the few Martian 'seas' to be correctly, if somewhat belatedly, named. They stopped the Flea and gazed down the empty river bed with mingled feelings. Gibson tried to picture the scene as it must have appeared in those remote days, when the great reptiles ruled the Earth and Man was still a dream of the distant future. The red cliffs would scarcely have changed in all that time, but between them the river would have made its unhurried way to the sea, flowing slowly under the weak gravity. It was a scene that might almost have belonged to Earth: and had it ever been witnessed by intelligent eyes? No one knew. Perhaps there had indeed been Martians in those days, but Time had buried them completely.

The ancient river had left a legacy, for there was still moisture along the lower reaches of the valley. A narrow band of vegetation had come thrusting up from Erythraeum, its brilliant green contrasting vividly with the crimson of the cliffs. The plants were those which Gibson had already met on the other side of the hills, but here and there were strangers. They were tall enough to be called trees, but they had no leaves – only thin, whip-like branches which continually trembled despite the stillness of the air. Gibson thought they were some of the most sinister things he had ever seen – just the sort of ominous plant that would suddenly flick out its tentacles at an unsuspecting passer-by. In fact, as he was perfectly well aware, they were as harmless as everything else on Mars.

They had zigzagged down into the valley and were climbing the other slope when the driver suddenly brought the Flea to a halt.

'Hello!' he said. 'This is odd. I didn't know there was any traffic in these parts.'

For a moment Gibson, who was not really as observant as he liked to think, was at a loss. Then he noticed a faint track running along the valley at right angles to their present path.

'There have been some heavy vehicles here,' said the driver. 'I'm sure this track didn't exist the last time I came this way – let's see, about a year ago. And there haven't been any expeditions into Erythraeum in that time.'

'Where does it lead?' asked Gibson.

'Well, if you go up the valley and over the top you'll be back in Port Lowell: that was what I intended to do. The other direction only leads out into the Mare.'

'We've got time – let's go along it a little way.'

Willingly enough, the driver swung the Flea around and headed down the valley. From time to time the track vanished as they went over smooth, open rock, but it always reappeared again. At last, however, they lost it completely.

The driver stopped the Flea.

'I know what's happened,' he said. 'There's only one way it could have gone. Did you notice that pass about a kilometre back? Ten to one it leads up there.'

'And where would that take anyone?'

'That's the funny thing: it's a complete cul-de-sac. There's a nice little amphitheatre about two kilometres across, but you can't get out of it anywhere except the way you come in. I spent a couple of hours there once when we did the first survey of this region. It's quite a pretty little place, sheltered and with some water in the spring.'

'A good hide-out for smugglers,' laughed Gibson.

The driver grinned.

'That's an idea. Maybe there's a gang bringing in contraband beefsteaks from Earth. I'd settle for one a week to keep my mouth shut.'

The narrow pass had obviously once contained a tributary of the main river, and the going was a good deal rougher than in the main valley. They had not driven very far before it became clear that they were on the right track.

'There's been some blasting here,' said the driver. 'This bit of road didn't exist when I came this way. I had to make a detour up that slope, and nearly had to abandon the Flea.'

'What do you think's going on?' asked Gibson, now getting quite excited.

'Oh, there are several research projects that are so specialized that one doesn't hear a lot about them. Some things can't be done near the city, you know. They may be building a magnetic observatory here – there's been some talk of that. The generators at Port Lowell would be pretty well shielded by the hills. But I don't think that's the explanation, for I'd have heard – Good Lord!'

They had suddenly emerged from the pass, and before them lay an almost perfect oval of green, flanked by the low, ochre hills. Once this might have been a lovely mountain lake: it was still a solace to the eye weary of lifeless, multi-coloured rock. But for the moment Gibson scarcely noticed the brilliant carpet of vegetation; he was too astonished by the cluster of domes, like a miniature of Port Lowell itself, grouped at the edge of the little plain.

They drove in silence along the road that had been cut through the living green carpet. No one was moving outside the domes, but a large transporter vehicle, several times the size of the Sand Flea, showed that someone was certainly at home.

'This is quite a set-up,' remarked the driver as he adjusted his mask. 'There must be a pretty good reason for spending all this money. Just wait here while I go over and talk to them.'

They watched him disappear into the airlock of the larger dome. It seemed to his impatient passengers that he was gone rather a long time. Then they saw the outer door open again and he walked slowly back towards them.

'Well?' asked Gibson eagerly as the driver climbed back into the cab. 'What did they have to say?'

There was a slight pause; then the driver started the engine and the Sand Flea began to move off.

'I say – what about this famous Martian hospitality? Aren't we invited in?' cried Mackay.

The driver seemed embarrassed. He looked, Gibson thought, exactly like a man who had just discovered he's made a fool of himself. He cleared his throat nervously.

'It's a plant research station,' he said, choosing his words with obvious care. 'It's not been going for very long, which is why I hadn't heard of it before. We can't go inside because the whole place is sterile and they don't want spores brought in – we'd have to change all our clothes and have a bath of disinfectant.'

'I see,' said Gibson. Something told him it was no use asking any further questions. He knew, beyond all possibility of error, that his guide had told him only part of the truth – and the least important part at that. For the first time the little discrepancies and doubts that Gibson had hitherto ignored or forgotten began to crystallize in his mind. It had started even before he reached Mars, with the diversion of the *Ares* from Phobos. And now he had stumbled upon this hidden research station. It had been as big a surprise to their experienced guide as to them, but he was attempting to cover up his accidental indiscretion.

There was something going on. What it was, Gibson could not imagine. It must be big, for it concerned not only Mars but Phobos. It was something unknown to most of the colonists, yet something they would cooperate in keeping secret when they encountered it.

Mars was hiding something: and it could only be hiding it from Earth.

Ten

The Grand Martian Hotel now had no less than two residents, a state of affairs which imposed a severe strain on its temporary staff. The rest of his shipmates had made private arrangements for their accommodation in Port Lowell, but as he knew no one in the city Jimmy had decided to accept official hospitality. Gibson wondered if this was going to be a success: he did not wish to throw too great a strain on their still somewhat provisional friendship, and if Jimmy saw too much of him the results might be disastrous. He remembered an epigram which his best enemy had once concocted: 'Martin's one of the nicest fellows you could meet, as long as you don't do it too often.' There was enough truth in this to make it sting, and he had no wish to put it to the test again.

His life in the Port had now settled down to a fairly steady routine. In the morning he would work, putting on paper his impressions of Mars – rather a presumptuous thing to do when he considered just how much of the planet he had so far seen. The afternoon was reserved for tours of inspection and interviews with the city's inhabitants. Sometimes Jimmy went with him on these trips, and once the whole of the *Ares* crew came along to the hospital to see how Dr Scott and his colleagues were progressing with their battle against Martian Fever. It was still too early to draw any conclusions, but Scott seemed fairly optimistic. 'What we'd like to have,' he said rubbing his hands ghoulishly, 'is a really good epidemic so that we could test the stuff properly. We haven't enough cases at the moment.'

Jimmy had two reasons for accompanying Gibson on his tours of the city. In the first place, the older man could go almost anywhere he pleased and so could get into all the interesting places which might otherwise be out of bounds. The second reason was a purely personal one – his increasing interest in the curious character of Martin Gibson.

Though they had now been thrown so closely together, they had never reopened their earlier conversation. Jimmy knew that Gibson was anxious to be friends and to make some recompense for whatever had happened in the past. He was quite capable of accepting this offer on a purely impersonal basis, for he realized well enough that Gibson could be extremely useful to him in his career. Like most ambitious young men, Jimmy had a streak of coldly calculating self-interest in his make-up, and Gibson would have been slightly dismayed at some of the appraisals which Jimmy had made of the advantages to be obtained from his patronage.

It would, however, be quite unfair to Jimmy to suggest that these material considerations were uppermost in his mind. There were times when he sensed Gibson's inner loneliness – the loneliness of the bachelor facing the approach of middle age. Perhaps Jimmy also realized – through not consciously as yet – that to Gibson he was beginning to represent the son he had never had. It was not a role that Jimmy was by any means sure he wanted, yet there were often times when he felt sorry for Gibson and would have been glad to please him. It is, after all, very difficult not to feel a certain affection towards someone who likes you.

The accident that introduced a new and quite unexpected element into Jimmy's life was really very trivial. He had been out alone one afternoon and, feeling thirsty, had dropped into the small café opposite the Administration building. Unfortunately he had not chosen his time well, for while he was quietly sipping a cup of tea which had never been within millions of kilometres of Ceylon, the place was suddenly invaded. It was the twenty-minute afternoon break when all work stopped on Mars – a rule which the Chief Executive had enforced in the interests of efficiency, though everyone would have much preferred to do without it and leave work twenty minutes earlier instead.

Jimmy was rapidly surrounded by an army of young women, who eyed him with alarming candour and a complete lack of diffidence. Although half a dozen men had been swept in on the flood, they crowded round one table for mutual protection, and judging by their intense expressions, continued to battle mentally with the files they had left on their desks. Jimmy decided to finish his drink as quickly as he could and get out.

A rather tough-looking woman in the late thirties – probably a senior secretary – was sitting opposite him, talking to a much younger girl on his side of the table. It was quite a squeeze to get past, and as Jimmy pushed into the crowd swirling through the narrow gangway, he tripped over an outstretched foot. He grabbed the table as he fell and managed to avoid complete disaster, but only at the cost of catching his elbow a sickening crack on the glass top. Forgetting in his agony that he was no longer back in the *Ares*, he relieved his feelings with a few well-chosen words. Then, blushing furiously, he recovered and bolted to freedom. He caught a glimpse of the elder woman trying hard not to laugh, and the younger one not even attempting such self-control.

And then, though it seemed inconceivable in retrospect, he forgot all about them both.

It was Gibson who quite accidentally provided the second stimulus. They were talking about the swift growth of the city during the last few years, and wondering if it would continue in the future. Gibson had remarked on the abnormal age distribution caused by the fact that no one under twenty-one had been allowed to emigrate to Mars, so that there was a complete gap between the ages of ten and twenty-one – a gap which, of course, the high birth-rate of the colony would soon fill. Jimmy had been listening half-heartedly when one of Gibson's remarks made him suddenly look up.

'That's funny,' he said. 'Yesterday I saw a girl who couldn't have been more than eighteen.'

And then he stopped. For, like a delayed-action bomb, the memory of that girl's laughing face as he had stumbled from the café suddenly exploded in his mind.

He never heard Gibson tell him that he must have been mistaken. He only knew that, whoever she was and wherever she had come from, he had to see her again.

In a place the size of Port Lowell, it was only a matter of time before one met everybody: the laws of chance would see to that. Jimmy, however, had no intention of waiting until these doubtful allies arranged a second encounter. The following day, just before the afternoon break, he was drinking tea at the same table in the little café.

This not very subtle move had caused him some mental anguish. In the first case, it might seem altogether too obvious. Yet why shouldn't he have tea here when most of Admin did the same? A second and weightier objection was the memory of the previous day's debacle. But Jimmy remembered an apt quotation about faint hearts and fair ladies.

His qualms were unnecessary. Though he waited until the café had emptied again, there was no sign of the girl or her companion. They must have gone somewhere else.

It was an annoying but only temporary setback to so resourceful a young man as Jimmy. Almost certainly she worked in the Admin building, and there were innumerable excuses for visiting that. He could think up inquiries about his pay, though these would hardly get him into the depths of the filing system or the stenographers' office, where she probably worked.

It would be best simply to keep an eye on the building when the staff arrived and left, though how this could be done unobtrusively was a considerable problem. Before he had made any attempt to solve it, Fate stepped in again, heavily disguised as Martin Gibson, slightly short of breath.

'I've been looking everywhere for you, Jimmy. Better hurry up and get dressed. You know there's a show tonight? Well, we've all been invited to have dinner with the Chief before going. That's in two hours.'

'What does one wear for formal dinners on Mars?' asked Jimmy.

'Black shorts and white tie, I think,' said Gibson, a little doubtfully. 'Or is it the other way round? Anyway, they'll tell us at the hotel. I hope they can find something that fits me.'

They did, but only just. Evening dress on Mars, where in the heat and air-conditioned cities all clothing was kept to a minimum, consisted simply of a white silk shirt with two rows of pearl buttons, a black bow tie, and black satin shorts with a belt of wide aluminium links on an elastic backing. It was smarter than might have been expected, but when fitted out Gibson felt something midway between a Boy Scout and Little Lord Fauntleroy. Norden and Hilton, on the other hand, carried it off quite well, Mackay and Scott were less successful, and Bradley obviously didn't give a damn.

The Chief's residence was the largest private house on Mars, though on Earth it would have been a very modest affair. They assembled in the lounge for a chat and sherry – real sherry – before the meal. Mayor Whittaker, being Hadfield's second-in-command, had also been invited, and as he listened to them talking to Norden, Gibson understood for the first time with what respect and admiration the colonists regarded the men who provided their sole link with Earth. Hadfield was holding forth at some length about the *Ares*, waxing quite lyrical over her speed and payload, and the effects these would have on the economy of Mars.

'Before we go in,' said the Chief, when they had finished the sherry, 'I'd like you to meet my daughter. She's just seeing to the arrangements – excuse me a moment while I fetch her.'

He was gone only a few seconds.

'This is Irene,' he said, in a voice that tried not to be proud but failed completely. One by one he introduced her to his guests, coming to Jimmy last.

Irene looked at him and smiled sweetly.

'I think we've met before,' she said.

Jimmy's colour heightened, but he held his ground and smiled back.

'So we have,' he replied.

It was really very foolish of him not to have guessed. If he had even started to think properly he would have known who she must have been. On Mars, the only man who could break the rules was the one who enforced them. Jimmy remembered hearing that the Chief had a daughter, but he had never connected the facts together. It all fell into place now: when Hadfield and his wife came to Mars they had brought their only child with them as part of the contract. No one else had ever been allowed to do so.

The meal was an excellent one, but it was largely wasted on Jimmy. He had not exactly lost his appetite – that would have been unthinkable – but he ate with a distracted air. As he was seated near the end of the table, he could see Irene only by dint of craning his neck in a most ungentlemanly fashion. He was very glad when the meal was over and they adjourned for coffee.

The other two members of the Chief Executive's household were waiting for the guests. Already occupying the best seats, a pair of beautiful Siamese cats regarded the visitors with fathomless eyes. They were introduced as Topaz and Turquoise, and Gibson, who loved cats, immediately started to try and make friends with them.

'Are you fond of cats?' Irene asked Jimmy.

'Rather,' said Jimmy, who loathed them. 'How long have they been here?'

'Oh, about a year. Just fancy – they're the only animals on Mars! I wonder if they appreciate it?'

'I'm sure Mars does. Don't they get spoilt?'

'They're too independent. I don't think they really care for anyone – not even Daddy, though he likes to pretend they do.'

With great subtlety – though to any spectator it would have been fairly obvious that Irene was always one jump ahead of him – Jimmy brought the conversation round to more personal matters. He discovered that she worked in the accounting section, but knew a good deal of everything that went on in Administration, where she one day hoped to hold a responsible executive post. Jimmy guessed that her father's position had been, if anything, a slight handicap to her. Though it must have made life easier in some ways, in others it would be a definite disadvantage, as Port Lowell was fiercely democratic.

It was very hard to keep Irene on the subject of Mars. She was much more anxious to hear about Earth, the planet which she had left when a child and so must have, in her mind, a dream-like unreality. Jimmy did his best to answer her questions, quite content to talk about anything which held her interest. He spoke of Earth's great cities, its mountains and seas, its blue skies and scudding clouds, its rivers and rainbows – all the things which Mars had lost. And as he talked, he fell deeper and deeper beneath the spell of Irene's laughing eyes. That was the only word to describe them: she always seemed to be on the point of sharing some secret joke.

Was she still laughing at him? Jimmy wasn't sure – and he didn't mind. What rubbish it was, he thought, to imagine that one became tongue-tied on these occasions! He had never been more fluent in his life . . .

He was suddenly aware that a great silence had fallen. Everyone was looking at him and Irene.

'Humph!' said the Chief Executive. 'If you two have quite finished, we'd better get a move on. The show starts in ten minutes.'

Most of Port Lowell seemed to have squeezed into the little theatre by the time they arrived. Mayor Whittaker, who had hurried ahead to check the arrangements, met them at the door and shepherded them into their seats, a reserved block occupying most of the front row. Gibson, Hadfield, and Irene were in the centre, flanked by Norden and Hilton – much to Jimmy's chagrin. He had no alternative but to look at the show.

Like all such amateur performances, it was good in parts. The musical items were excellent and there was one mezzo-soprano who was up to the best professional standards of Earth. Gibson was not surprised when he saw against her name on the programme: 'Late of the Royal Covent Garden Opera.'

A dramatic interlude then followed, the distressed heroine and old-time villain hamming it for all they were worth. The audience loved it, cheering and booing the appropriate characters and shouting gratuitous advice.

Next came one of the most astonishing ventriloquist acts that Gibson had ever seen. It was nearly over before he realized – only a minute before the performer revealed it deliberately – that there was a radio receiver inside the doll and an accomplice off-stage.

The next item appeared to be a skit on life in the city, and was so full of local allusions that Gibson understood only part of it. However, the antics of the main character – a harassed official obviously modelled on Mayor Whittaker – drew roars of laughter. These increased still further when he began to be pestered by a fantastic person who was continually asking ridiculous questions, noting the answers in a little book (which he was always losing), and photographing everything in sight.

It was several minutes before Gibson realized just what was going on. For a moment he turned a deep red: then he realized that there was only one thing he could do. He would have to laugh louder than anyone else.

The proceedings ended with community singing, a form of entertainment which Gibson did not normally go out of his way to seek – rather the reverse, in fact. But he found it more enjoyable than he had expected, and as he joined in the last choruses a sudden wave of emotion swept over him, causing his voice to peter out into nothingness. For a moment he sat, the only silent man in all that crowd, wondering what had happened to him.

The faces around provided the answer. Here were men and women united in a single task, driving towards a common goal, each knowing that their work was vital to the community. They had a sense of fulfilment which very few could know on Earth, where all the frontiers had long ago been reached. It was a sense heightened and made more personal by the fact that Port Lowell was still so small that everyone knew everyone else.

Of course, it was too good to last. As the colony grew, the spirit of these pioneering days would fade. Everything would become too big and too well organized: the development of the planet would be just another job of work. But for the present it was a wonderful sensation, which a man would be lucky indeed to experience even once in his lifetime. Gibson knew it was felt by all those around him, yet he could not share it. He was an outsider: that was the role he had always preferred to play – and now he had played it long enough. If it was not too late, he wanted to join in the game.

That was the moment, if indeed there was such a single point in time, when Martin Gibson changed his allegiance from Earth to Mars. No one ever knew. Even those beside him, if they noticed anything at all, were aware only that for a few seconds he had stopped singing, but had now joined in the chorus again with redoubled vigour.

In twos and threes, laughing, talking and singing, the audience slowly dissolved into the night. Gibson and his friends started back towards the hotel, having said goodbye to the Chief and Mayor Whittaker. The two men who virtually ran Mars watched them disappear down the narrow streets; then Hadfield turned to his daughter and remarked quietly: 'Run along home now, dear – Mr Whittaker and I are going for a little walk. I'll be back in half an hour.'

They waited, answering good nights from time to time, until the tiny square was deserted. Mayor Whittaker, who guessed what was coming, fidgeted slightly.

'Remind me to congratulate George on tonight's show,' said Hadfield.

'Yes,' Whittaker replied. 'I loved the skit on our mutual headache, Gibson. I suppose you want to conduct a post-mortem on his latest exploit?'

The Chief was slightly taken aback by this direct approach.

'It's rather too late now – and there's no real evidence that any real harm was done. I'm just wondering how to prevent future accidents.'

'It was hardly the driver's fault. He didn't know about the Project and it was pure bad luck that he stumbled on. it.'

'Do you think Gibson suspects anything?'

'Frankly, I don't know. He's pretty shrewd.'

'Of all the times to send a reporter here! I did everything I could to keep him away, Heaven knows!'

'He's bound to find out that something's happening before he's here much longer. I think there's only one solution.'

'What's that?'

'We'll just have to tell him. Perhaps not everything, but enough.'

They walked in silence for a few yards. Then Hadfield remarked:

'That's pretty drastic. You're assuming he can be trusted completely.'

'I've seen a good deal of him these last weeks. Fundamentally, he's on our side. You see, we're doing the sort of things he's been writing about all his life, though he can't quite believe it yet. What would be fatal would be to let him go back to Earth, suspecting something but not knowing what.'

There was another long silence. They reached the limit of the dome and stared across the glimmering Martian landscape, dimly lit by the radiance spilling out from the city.

'I'll have to think it over,' said Hadfield, turning to retrace his footsteps. 'Of course, a lot depends on how quickly things move.'

'Any hints yet?'

'No, confound them. You never can pin scientists down to a date.'

A young couple, arms twined together, strolled past them obliviously. Whittaker chuckled.

'That reminds me. Irene seems to have taken quite a fancy to that youngster – what's his name – Spencer.'

'Oh, I don't know. It's a change to see a fresh face around. And space travel is so much more romantic than the work we do here.'

'All the nice girls love a sailor, eh? Well, don't say I didn't warn you!'

That something had happened to Jimmy was soon perfectly obvious to Gibson, and it took him no more than two guesses to arrive at the correct answer. He quite approved of the lad's choice: Irene seemed a very nice child, from what little he had seen of her. She was rather unsophisticated, but this was not necessarily a handicap. Much more important was the fact that she had a gay and cheerful disposition, though once or twice Gibson had caught her in a mood of wistfulness that was very attractive. She was also extremely pretty: Gibson was now old enough to realize that this was not all-important, though Jimmy might have different views on the subject.

At first, he decided to say nothing about the matter until Jimmy raised it himself. In all probability, the boy was still under the impression that no one had noticed anything in the least unusual. Gibson's self-control gave way, however, when Jimmy announced his intention of taking a temporary job in Port Lowell. There was nothing odd about this: indeed, it was a common practice among visiting space-crews, who soon got bored if they had nothing to do between trips. The work they chose was invariably technical and related in some way to their professional activities: Mackay, for example, was running evening classes in mathematics, while poor Dr Scott had had no holiday at all, but had gone straight to the hospital immediately on reaching Port Lowell.

But Jimmy, it seemed, wanted a change. They were short of staff in the accounting section, and he thought his knowledge of mathematics might help. He put up an astonishingly convincing argument, to which Gibson listened with genuine pleasure.

'My dear Jimmy,' he said, when it was finished. 'Why tell *me* all this? There's nothing to stop you going right ahead if you want to.'

'I know,' said Jimmy, 'but you see a lot of Mayor Whittaker and it might save trouble if you had a word with him.'

'I'll speak to the Chief if you like.'

Oh no, I shouldn't—' Jimmy began. Then he tried to retrieve his blunder. 'It isn't worth bothering him about such details.'

'Look here, Jimmy,' said Gibson with great firmness. 'Why not come clean? Is this your idea, or did Irene put you up to it?'

It was worth travelling all the way to Mars to see Jimmy's expression. He looked rather like a fish that had been breathing air for some time and had only just realized it.

'Oh,' he said at last, 'I didn't know you knew. You won't tell anyone, will you?'

Gibson was just about to remark that this would be quite unnecessary, but there was something in Jimmy's eyes that made him abandon all attempts at humour. The wheel had come full circle: he was back again in that twenty-year-old-buried spring. He knew exactly what Jimmy was feeling now, and knew also that nothing which the future could bring to him would ever match the emotions he was discovering, still as new and fresh as on the first morning of the world. He might fall in love again in later days, but the memory of Irene would shape and colour all his life – just as Irene herself must be the memory of some ideal he had brought with him into this universe.

'I'll do what I can,' said Gibson gently, and meant it with all his heart. Though history might repeat itself, it never did so exactly, and one generation could learn from the errors of the last. Some things were beyond planning or foresight, but he would do all he could to help; and this time, perhaps, the outcome might be different.

Eleven

The amber light was on. Gibson took a last sip of water, cleared his throat gently, and checked that the papers of his script were in the right order. No matter how many times he broadcast, his throat always felt this initial tightness. In the control room, the programme engineer held up her thumb: the amber changed abruptly to red.

'Hello, Earth. This is Martin Gibson speaking to you from Port Lowell, Mars. It's a great day for us here. This morning the new dome was inflated and now the city's increased its size by almost a half. I don't know if I can convey any impression of what a triumph this means, what a feeling of victory it gives to us here in the battle against Mars. But I'll try.

'You all know that it's impossible to breathe the Martian atmosphere – it's far to thin and contains practically no oxygen. Port Lowell, our biggest city, is built under six domes of transparent plastic held up by the pressure of the air inside – air which we can breathe comfortably though it's still much less dense than yours.

'For the last year a seventh dome has been under construction, a dome twice as big as any of the others. I'll describe it as it was yesterday, when I went inside before the inflation started.

'Imagine a great circular space half a kilometre across, surrounded by a thick wall of glass bricks twice as high as a man. Through this wall lead the passages to the other domes, and the exits direct on to the brilliant green Martian landscape all around us. These passages are simply metal tubes with great doors which close automatically if air escapes from any of the domes. On Mars, we don't believe in putting all our eggs in one basket!

'When I entered Dome Seven yesterday, all this great circular space was covered with a thin transparent sheet fastened to the surrounding wall, and lying limp on the ground in huge folds beneath which we had to force our way. If you can imagine being inside a deflated balloon you'll know exactly how I felt. The envelope of the dome is a very strong plastic, almost perfectly transparent and quite flexible – a kind of thick cellophane.

'Of course, I had to wear my breathing mask, for though we were sealed off from the outside there was still practically no air in the dome. It was being pumped in as rapidly as possible, and you could see the great sheets of plastic straining sluggishly as the pressure mounted.

'This went on all through the night. The first thing this morning I went into the dome again, and found that the envelope had now blown itself into a big bubble at the centre, though round the edges it was still lying flat. That huge bubble – it was about a hundred metres across – kept trying to move around like a living creature, and all the time it grew.

'About the middle of the morning it had grown so much that we could see the complete dome taking shape: the envelope had lifted away from the ground everywhere. Pumping was stopped for a while to test for leaks, then resumed again around midday. By now the sun was helping too, warming up the air and making it expand.

'Three hours ago the first stage of the inflation was finished. We took off our masks and let out a great cheer. The air still wasn't really thick enough for comfort, but it was breathable and the engineers could work inside without bothering about masks any more. They'll spend the next few days checking the great envelope for stresses, and looking for leaks. There are bound to be some, of course, but as long as the air loss doesn't exceed a certain value it won't matter.

'So now we feel we've pushed our frontier on Mars back a little farther. Soon the new buildings will be going up under Dome Seven, and we're making plans for a small park and even a lake – the only one on Mars, that will be, for free water can't exist here in the open for any length of time.

'Of course, this is only a beginning, and one day it will seem a very small achievement; but it's a great step forward in our battle – it represents the conquest of another slice of Mars. And it means living space for another thousand people. Are you listening, Earth? Good night.'

The red light faded. For a moment Gibson sat staring at the

microphone, musing on the fact that his first words, though travelling at the speed of light, would only now be reaching Earth. Then he gathered up his papers and walked through the padded doors into the control room.

The engineer held up a telephone for him. 'A call's just come through for you, Mr Gibson,' she said. 'Someone's been pretty quick off the mark!'

'They certainly have,' he replied with a grin. 'Hello, Gibson here.'

'This is Hadfield. Congratulations. I've just been listening – it went out over our local station, you know.'

'I'm glad you liked it.'

Hadfield chuckled.

You've probably guessed that I've read most of your earlier scripts. It's been quite interesting to watch the change of attitude.'

'What change?'

'When you started, we were "they". Now we're "we". Not very well put, perhaps, but I think my point's clear.'

He gave Gibson no time to answer this, but continued without a break.

'I really rang up about this. I've been able to fix your trip to Skia at last. We've got a passenger jet going there on Wednesday, with room for three aboard. Whittaker will give you the details. Goodbye.'

The phone clicked into silence. Very thoughtfully, but not a little pleased, Gibson replaced it on the stand. What the Chief had said was true enough. He had been here for almost a month, and in that time his outlook towards Mars had changed completely. The first schoolboy excitement had lated no more than a few days: the subsequent disillusionment only a little longer. Now he knew enough to regard the colony with a tempered enthusiasm not wholly based on logic. He was afraid to analyse it, lest it disappear completely. Some part of it, he knew, came from his growing respect for the people around him – his admiration for the keen-eyed competence, the readiness to take well-calculated risks, which had enabled them not merely to survive on this heartbreakingly hostile world, but to lay the foundations of the first extra-terrestrial culture. More than ever before, he felt a longing to identify himself with their work, wherever it might lead.

Meanwhile, his first real chance of seeing Mars on the large scale had arrived. On Wednesday he would be taking off for Port Schiaparelli, the planet's second city, ten thousand kilometres to the east in Trivium Charontis. The trip had been planned a fortnight ago, but every time something had turned up to postpone it. He would have to tell Jimmy and Hilton to get ready – they had been the lucky ones in the draw. Perhaps Jimmy might not be quite so eager to go now as he had been once. No doubt he was now anxiously counting the days left to him on Mars, and would resent anything that took him away from Irene. But if he turned down *this* chance, Gibson would have no sympathy for him at all.

'Neat job, isn't she?' said the pilot proudly. 'There are only six like her on Mars. It's quite a trick designing a jet that can fly in this atmosphere, even with the low gravity to help you.'

Gibson did not know enough about aerodynamics to appreciate the finer points of the aircraft, though he could see that the wing area was abnormally large. The four jet units were neatly buried just outboard of the fuselage, only the slightest of bulges betraying their position. If he had met such a machine on a terrestrial airfield Gibson would not have given it a second thought, though the sturdy tractor undercarriage might have surprised him. This machine was built to fly fast and far – and to land on any surface which was approximately flat.

He climbed in after Jimmy and Hilton and settled himself as comfortably as he could in the rather restricted space. Most of the cabin was taken up by large packing cases securely strapped in position – urgent freight for Skia, he supposed. It hadn't left a great deal of space for the passengers.

The motors accelerated swiftly until their thin whines hovered at the edge of hearing. There was the familiar pause while the pilot checked his instruments and controls: then the jets opened full out and the runway began to slide beneath them. A few seconds later there came the sudden reassuring surge of power as the take-off rockets fired and lifted them effortlessly up into the sky. The aircraft climbed steadily into the south, then swung round to starboard in a great curve that took it over the city. Port Lowell, Gibson thought, had certainly grown since his last view of it from the air. The new dome was still empty, yet already it dominated the city with its promise of more spacious times to come. Near its centre he could glimpse the tiny specks of men and machines at work laying the foundations of the new suburb.

The aircraft levelled out on an easterly course and the great island of Aurorae Sinus sank over the edge of the planet. Apart from a few oases, the open desert now lay ahead for thousands of kilometres.

The pilot switched his controls to automatic and came amidships to talk to his passengers.

'We'll be at Charontis in about four hours,' he said. 'I'm afraid there isn't much to look at on the way, though you'll see some fine colour effects when we go over Euphrates. After that it's more or less uniform desert until we hit the Syrtis Major.'

Gibson did some rapid mental arithmetic.

'Let's see – we're flying east and we started rather late – it'll be dark when we get there.'

'Don't worry about that – we'll pick up the Charontis beacon when we're a couple of hundred kilometres away. Mars is so small that you don't often do a long-distance trip in daylight all the way.'

'How long have you been on Mars?' asked Gibson, who had now ceased taking photos through the observation ports.

'Oh, five years.'

'Flying all the time?'

'Most of it.'

'Wouldn't you prefer being in spaceships?'

'Not likely. No excitement in it – just floating around in nothing for months.' He grinned at Hilton, who smiled amiably but showed no inclination to argue.

'Just what do you mean by "excitement"?' said Gibson anxiously.

'Well, you've got some scenery to look at, you're not away from home for very long, and there's always the chance you may find something new. I've done half a dozen trips over the poles, you know – most of them in summer, but I went across the Mare Boreum last winter. A hundred and fifty degrees below outside! That's the record so far for Mars.'

'I can beat that pretty easily,' said Hilton. 'At night it reaches two hundred below on Titan.' It was the first time Gibson had ever heard him refer to the Saturnian expedition.

'By the way, Fred,' he asked, 'is this rumour true?'

'What rumour?'

'*You* know – that you're going to have another shot at Saturn.'

Hilton shrugged his shoulders.

'It isn't decided – there are a lot of difficulties. But I think it will come off: it would be a pity to miss the chance. You see, if we can leave next year we can go past Jupiter on the way, and have our first really good look at him. Mac's worked out a very interesting orbit for us. We go rather close to Jupiter – right inside *all* the satellites – and let his gravitational field swing us round so that we head out in the right direction for Saturn. It'll need rather accurate navigation to give us just the orbit we want, but it can be done.'

'Then what's holding it up?'

'Money, as usual. The trip will last two and a half years and will cost about fifty million. Mars can't afford it – it would mean doubling the usual deficit! At the moment we're trying to get Earth to foot the bill.'

'It would come to that anyway in the long run,' said Gibson. 'But give me all the facts when we get home and I'll write a blistering *exposé* about cheeseparing terrestrial politicians. You mustn't under-estimate the power of the Press.'

The talk then drifted from planet to planet, until Gibson suddenly remembered that he was wasting a magnificent chance of seeing Mars at first hand. Obtaining permission to occupy the pilot's seat – after promising not to touch anything – he went forward and settled himself comfortably behind the controls.

Five kilometres below, the coloured desert was streaking past him to the west. They were flying at what, on Earth, would have been a very low altitude, for the thinness of the Martian air made it essential to keep as near the surface as safety allowed. Gibson had never before received such an impression of sheer speed, for though he had flown in much faster machines on Earth that had always been at heights where the ground was invisible. The nearness of the horizon added to the effect, for an object which appeared over the edge of the planet would be passing beneath a few minutes later.

From time to time the pilot came forward to check the course, though it was a pure formality, as there was nothing he need do until the voyage was nearly over. At mid-point some coffee and light refreshments were produced, and Gibson rejoined his companions in the cabin. Hilton and the pilot were now arguing briskly about Venus – quite a sore point with the Martian colonists, who regarded that peculiar planet as a complete waste of time.

The Sun was now very low in the west and even the stunted Martian hills threw long shadows across the desert. Down there the temperature was already below freezing-point, and falling fast. The few hardy plants that had survived in this almost barren waste would have folded their leaves tightly together, conserving warmth and energy against the rigours of the night.

Gibson yawned and stretched himself. The swiftly unfolding landscape had an almost hypnotic effect and it was difficult to keep awake. He decided to catch some sleep in the ninety or so minutes that were left of the voyage.

Some change in the failing light must have woken him. For a moment it was impossible to believe that he was not still dreaming: he could only sit and stare, paralysed with sheer astonishment. No longer was he looking out across a flat, almost featureless landscape meeting the deep blue of the sky at the far horizon. Desert and horizon had both vanished: in their place towered a range of crimson mountains, reaching north and south as far as the eye could follow. The last rays of the setting Sun caught their peaks and bequeathed to them its dying glory: already the foothills were lost in the night that was sweeping onwards to the west.

For long seconds the splendour of the scene robbed it of all reality and hence all menace. Then Gibson awoke from his trance, realizing in one dreadful instant that they were flying far too low to clear those Himalayan peaks.

The sense of utter panic lasted only a moment – to be followed at once by a far deeper terror. Gibson had remembered now what the first shock had banished from his mind – the simple fact he should have thought of from the beginning.

There were no mountains on Mars.

Hadfield was dictating an urgent memorandum to the Inter-planetary Development Board when the news came through. Port Schiaparelli had waited the regulation fifteen minutes after the aircraft's expected time of arrival, and Port Lowell Control had stood by for another ten before sending out the 'Overdue' signal. One precious aircraft from the tiny Martian fleet was already standing by to search the line of flight as soon as dawn came. The high speed and low altitude essential for flight would make such a search very difficult, but when Phobos rose the telescopes up there could join in with far greater prospects of success.

The news reached Earth an hour later, at a time when there was nothing much else to occupy Press or radio. Gibson would have been well satisfied by the resultant publicity: everywhere people began reading his last articles with a morbid interest. Ruth Goldstein knew nothing about it until an editor she was dealing with arrived waving the evening paper. She immediately sold the second reprint rights of Gibson's latest series for half as much again as her victim had intended to pay, then retired to her private room and wept copiously for a full minute. Both these events would have pleased Gibson enormously.

In a score of newspaper offices, the copy culled from the Morgue began to be set up in type so that no time would be wasted. And in London a publisher who had paid Gibson a rather large advance began to feel very unhappy indeed.

Gibson's shout was still echoing through the cabin when the pilot reached the controls. Then he was flung to the floor as the machine turned over in an almost vertical bank in a desperate attempt to swing round to the north. When Gibson could climb to his feet again, he caught a glimpse of a strangely blurred orange cliff sweeping down upon them from only kilometres away. Even in that moment of panic, he could see that there was something very curious about that swiftly approaching barrier, and suddenly the truth dawned upon him at last. This was no mountain range, but something that might be no less deadly. They were running into a wind-borne wall of sand reaching from the desert almost to the edge of the stratosphere.

The hurricane hit them a second later. Something slapped the machine violently from side to side, and through the insulation of the hull came an angry whistling roar that was the most terrifying sound Gibson had ever heard in his life. Night had come instantly upon them and they were flying helplessly through a howling darkness.

It was all over in five minutes, but it seemed a lifetime. Their sheer speed had saved them, for the ship had cut through the heart of the hurricane like a projectile. There was a sudden burst of deep ruby twilight, the ship ceased to be pounded by a million sledge-hammers, and a ringing silence seemed to fill the little cabin. Through the rear observation port Gibson caught a last glimpse of the storm as it moved westwards, tearing up the desert in its wake.

His legs feeling like jellies, Gibson tottered thankfully into his seat and breathed an enormous sigh of relief. For a moment he wondered if they had been thrown badly off course, then realized that this scarcely mattered considering the navigational aids they carried.

It was only then, when his ears had ceased to be deafened by the storm, that Gibson had his second shock. The motors had stopped.

The little cabin was very tense and still. Then the pilot called out over his shoulder: 'Get your masks on! The hull may crack when we come down.' His fingers feeling very clumsy, Gibson dragged his breathing equipment from under the seat and adjusted it over his head. When he had finished, the ground already seemed very close, though it was hard to judge distances in the failing twilight.

A low hill swept by and was gone into the darkness. The ship banked violently to avoid another, then gave a sudden spasmodic jerk as it touched ground and bounced. A moment later it made contact again and Gibson tensed himself for the inevitable crash.

It was an age before he dared relax, still unable to believe that they were safely down. Then Hilton stretched himself in his seat, removed his mask, and called out to the pilot: 'That was a very nice landing, Skipper. Now how far have we got to walk?'

For a moment there was no reply. Then the pilot called, in a rather strained voice: 'Can anyone light me a cigarette? I've got the twitch.'

'Here you are,' said Hilton, going forward. 'Let's have the cabin lights on now, shall we?'

The warm, comfortable glow did much to raise their spirits by banishing the Martian night, which now lay all around. Everyone began to feel ridiculously cheerful and there was much laughing at quite feeble jokes. The reaction had set in: they were so delighted at still being alive that the thousand kilometres separating them from the nearest base scarcely seemed to matter.

'That was quite a storm,' said Gibson. 'Does this sort of thing happen very often on Mars? And why didn't we get any warning?'

The pilot, now that he had got over his initial shock, was doing some quick thinking, the inevitable court of inquiry obviously looming large in his mind. Even on auto-pilot, he *should* have gone forward more often . . .

'I've never seen one like it before,' he said, 'though I've done at least fifty trips between Lowell and Skia. The trouble is that we don't know anything about Martian meteorology, even now. And there are only half a dozen met stations on the planet – not enough to give us an accurate picture.'

'What about Phobos? Couldn't they have seen what was happening and warned us?'

The pilot grabbed his almanac and ruffled rapidly through the pages.

'Phobos hasn't risen yet,' he said after a brief calculation. 'I guess the storm blew up suddenly out of Hades – appropriate name, isn't it? – and has probably collapsed again now. I don't suppose it went anywhere near Charontis, so *they* couldn't have warned us either. It was just one of those accidents that's nobody's fault.'

This thought seemed to cheer him considerably, but Gibson found it hard to be so philosophical.

'Meanwhile,' he retorted, 'we're stuck in the middle of nowhere. How long will it take them to find us? Or is there any chance of repairing the ship?'

'Not a hope of that; the jets are ruined. They were made to work on air, not sand, you know!'

'Well, can we radio Skia?'

'Not now we're on the ground. But when Phobos rises in – let's see – an hour's time, we'll be able to call the observatory and they can relay us on. That's the way we've got to do all our long-distance stuff here, you know. The ionosphere's too feeble to bounce signals round the way you do on Earth. Anyway, I'll go and check that the radio is OK.'

He went forward and started tinkering with the ship's transmitter, while Hilton busied himself checking the heaters and cabin air pressure, leaving the two remaining passengers looking at each other a little thoughtfully.

'This is a fine kettle of fish!' exploded Gibson, half in anger and half in amusement. 'I've come safely from Earth to Mars – more than fifty million kilometres – and as soon as I set foot inside a miserable aeroplane *this* is what happens! I'll stick to spaceships in future.'

Jimmy grinned. 'It'll give us something to tell the others when we get back, won't it? Maybe we'll be able to do some real exploring at last.' He peered through the windows, cupping his hands over his eyes to keep out the cabin light. The surrounding landscape was now in complete darkness, apart from the illumination from the ship.

'There seem to be hills all around us: we were lucky to get down in one piece. Good Lord – there's a cliff here on this side – another few metres and we'd have gone smack into it!'

'Any idea where we are?' Gibson called to the pilot.

This tactless remark earned him a very stony stare.

'About 120 east, 20 north. The storm can't have thrown us very far off course.'

'Then we're somewhere in the Aetheria,' said Gibson, bending over the maps. 'Yes – there's a hilly region marked here. Not much information about it.'

'It's the first time anyone's ever landed here – that's why. This part of Mars is almost unexplored: it's been thoroughly mapped from the air, but that's all.'

Gibson was amused to see how Jimmy brightened at this news. There was certainly something exciting about being in a region where no human foot had ever trodden before.

'I hate to cast a gloom over the proceedings,' remarked Hilton, in a tone of voice hinting that this was exactly what he was going to do, 'but I'm not at all sure you'll be able to radio Phobos even when it does rise.'

'What!' yelped the pilot. 'The set's OK – I've just tested it.'

'Yes – but have you noticed where we are? We can't even *see* Phobos. That cliff's due south of us and blocks the view completely. That means that they won't be able to pick up our microwave signals. What's even worse, they won't be able to locate us in their telescopes.'

There was a shocked silence.

'*Now* what do we do?' asked Gibson. He had a horrible vision of a thousand-kilometre trek across the desert to Charontis, but dismissed it from his mind at once. They couldn't possibly carry the oxygen for the trip, still less the food and equipment necessary. And no one could spend the night unprotected on the surface of Mars, even here near the Equator.

'We'll just have to signal in some other way,' said Hilton calmly. 'In the morning we'll climb those hills and have a look round. Meanwhile I suggest we take it easy.' He yawned and stretched himself, filling the cabin from ceiling to floor. 'We've got no immediate worries: there's air for several days, and power in the batteries to keep us warm almost indefinitely. We may get a bit hungry if we're here more than a week, but I don't think that's at all likely to happen.'

By a kind of unspoken mutual consent, Hilton had taken control. Perhaps he was not even consciously aware of the fact, but he was now the leader of the little party. The pilot had delegated his own authority without a second thought.

'Phobos rises in an hour, you said?' asked Hilton.

'Yes.'

'When does it transit? I can never remember what this crazy little moon of yours gets up to.'

'Well, it rises in the west and sets in the east about four hours later.'

'So it'll be due south around midnight?'

'That's right. Oh Lord – that means we won't be able to see it anyway. It'll be eclipsed for at least an hour!'

'*What* a moon!' snorted Gibson. 'When you want it most badly, you can't even see the blasted thing!'

'That doesn't matter,' said Hilton calmly. 'We'll know just where it is, and it won't do any harm to try the radio then. That's all we can do tonight. Has anyone got a pack of cards? No? Then what about entertaining us, Martin, with some of your stories?'

It was a rash remark, and Gibson seized his chance immediately.

'I wouldn't dream of doing that,' he said. '*You're* the one who has the stories to tell.'

Hilton stiffened, and for a moment Gibson wondered if he had offended him. He knew that Hilton seldom talked about the Saturnian expedition, but this was too good an opportunity to miss.

The chance would never come again, and, as is true of all great adventures, its telling would do their morale good. Perhaps Hilton realized this too, for presently he relaxed and smiled.

'You've got me nicely cornered, haven't you, Martin? Well, I'll talk – but on one condition.'

'What's that?'

'No direct quotes, please!'

'As if I would!'

'And when you *do* write it up, let me see the manuscript first.'

'Of course.'

This was better than Gibson had dared to hope. He had no immediate intention of writing about Hilton's adventures, but it was nice to know that he could do so if he wished. The possibility that he might never have the chance simply did not cross his mind.

Outside the walls of the ship, the fierce Martian night reigned supreme – a night studded with needle-sharp, unwinking stars. The pale light of Deimos made the surrounding landscape dimly visible, as if lit with a cold phosphorescence. Out of the east Jupiter, the brightest object in the sky, was rising in his glory. But the thoughts of the four men in the crashed aircraft were six hundred million kilometres still farther from the Sun.

It still puzzled many people – the curious fact that man had visited Saturn but not Jupiter, so much closer at hand. But in space-travel, sheer distance is of no importance, and Saturn had been reached because of a single astonishing stroke of luck that still seemed too good to be true. Orbiting Saturn was Titan, the largest satellite in the Solar System – about twice the size of Earth's moon. As far back as 1944 it had been discovered that Titan possessed an atmosphere. It was not an atmosphere one could breathe: it was immensely more valuable than that. For it was an atmosphere of methane, one of the ideal propellants for atomic rockets.

This had given rise to a situation unique in the history of space-flight. For the first time, an expedition could be sent to a strange world with the virtual certainty that refuelling would be possible on arrival.

The *Arcturus* and her crew of six had been launched in space from the orbit of Mars. She had reached the Saturnian system only nine months later, with just enough fuel to land safely on Titan. Then the pumps had been started, and the great tanks replenished from the countless trillions of tons of methane that were there for the taking. Refuelling on Titan whenever necessary, the *Arcturus* had visited every one of Saturn's fifteen known moons, and had even skirted the great ring system itself. In a few months, more was learned about Saturn than in all the previous centuries of telescopic examination.

There had been a price to pay. Two of the crew had died of radiation sickness after emergency repairs to one of the atomic motors. They had been buried on Dione, the fourth moon. And the leader of the expedition, Captain Envers, had been killed by an avalanche of frozen air on Titan: his body had never been found. Hilton had assumed command, and had brought the *Arcturus* safely back to Mars a year later, with only two men to help him.

All these bare facts Gibson knew well enough. He could still remember listening to those radio messages that had come trickling back through space, relayed from world to world. But it was a different thing altogether to hear Hilton telling the story in his quiet, curiously impersonal manner, as if he had been a spectator rather than a participant.

He spoke of Titan and its smaller brethren, the little moons which, circling Saturn, made the planet almost a scale model of the Solar System. He described how at last they had landed on the innermost moon of all, Mimas, only half as far from Saturn as the Moon is from the Earth.

'We came down in a wide valley between a couple of mountains, where we were sure the ground would be pretty solid. We weren't going to make the mistake we did on Rhea! It was a good landing, and we climbed into our suits to go outside. It's funny how impatient you always are to do that, no matter how many times you've set down on a new world.

'Of course, Mimas hasn't much gravity – only a hundredth of Earth's. That was enough to keep us from jumping off into space. I liked it that way: you knew you'd always come down safely again if you waited long enough.'

'It was early in the morning when we landed. Mimas has a day a bit shorter than Earth's – it goes round Saturn in twenty-two hours, and as it keeps the same face towards the planet its day and month are the same length – just as they are on the Moon. We'd come down in the northern hemisphere, not far from the equator, and most of Saturn was above the horizon. It looked quite weird – a huge crescent horn sticking up into the sky, like some impossibly bent mountain thousands of miles high.

'Of course you've all seen the films we made – especially the speeded-up colour one showing a complete cycle of Saturn's phases. But I don't think they can give you much idea of what it was like to live with that enormous thing always there in the sky. It was so big, you see, that one couldn't take it in in a single view. If you stood facing it and held your arms wide open, you could just imagine your finger-tips touching the opposite ends of the rings. We couldn't see the rings themselves very well, because they were almost edge-on, but you could always tell they were there by the wide, dusky band of shadow they cast on the planet.'

'None of us ever got tired of watching it. It's spinning so fast, you know – the pattern was always changing. The cloud formations, if that's what they were, used to whip round from one side of the disc to the other in a few hours, changing continually as they moved. And there were the most wonderful colours – greens and browns and yellows chiefly. Now and then there'd be great, slow eruptions, and something as big as Earth would rise up out of the depths and spread itself sluggishly in a huge stain half-way round the planet.

'You could never take your eyes off it for long. Even when it was new and so completely invisible, you could still tell it was there because of the great hole in the stars. And here's a funny thing which I haven't reported because I was never quite sure of it. Once or twice, when we were in the planet's shadow and its disc should have been completely dark, I thought I saw a faint phosphorescent glow coming from the night side. It didn't last long – if it really happened at all. Perhaps it was some kind of chemical reaction going on down there in that spinning cauldron.

'Are you surprised that I want to go to Saturn again? What I'd like to do is to get *really* close this time – and by that I mean within a thousand kilometres. It should be quite safe and wouldn't take much power. All you need do is to go into a parabolic orbit and let yourself fall in like a comet going round Sun. Of course, you'd only spend a few minutes actually close to Saturn, but you could get a lot of records in that time.

'And I want to land on Mimas again, and see that great shining crescent reaching half-way up the sky. It'll be worth the journey, just to watch Saturn waxing and waning, and to see the storms chasing themselves round his equator. Yes – it would worth it, even if *I* didn't get back this time.'

There were no mock heroics in this closing remark. It was merely a simple statement of fact, and Hilton's listeners believed him completely. While the spell lasted, every one of them would be willing to strike the same bargain.

Gibson ended the long silence by going to the cabin window and peering out into the night.

'Can we have the lights off?' he called. Complete darkness fell as the pilot obeyed his request. The others joined him at the window.

'Look,' said Gibson. 'Up there – you can just see it if you crane your neck.'

The cliff against which they were lying was no longer a wall of absolute and unrelieved darkness. On its very topmost peaks a new light was playing, spilling over the broken crags and filtering down into the valley. Phobos had leapt out of the west and was climbing on its meteoric rise towards the south, racing backwards across the sky.

Minute by minute the light grew stronger, and presently the pilot began to send out his signals. He had barely begun when the pale moonlight was snuffed out so suddenly that Gibson gave a cry of astonishment. Phobos had gone hurtling into the shadow of Mars, and though it was still rising it would cease to shine for almost an hour. There was no way of telling whether or not it would peep over the edge of the great cliff and so be in the right position to receive their signals.

They did not give up hope for almost two hours. Suddenly the light reappeared on the peaks, but shining now from the east. Phobos had emerged from its eclipse, and was now dropping down towards the horizon which it would reach in little more than an hour. The pilot switched off his transmitter in disgust.

'It's no good,' he said. 'We'll have to try something else.'

'I know!' Gibson exclaimed excitedly. 'Can't we carry the transmitter up the top of the hill?'

'I'd thought of that, but it would be the devil's own job to get out without proper tools. The whole thing – aerials and all – is built into the hull.'

'There's nothing more we can do tonight, anyway,' said Hilton. 'I suggest we all get some sleep before dawn. Good night, everybody.'

It was excellent advice, but not easy to follow. Gibson's mind was still racing ahead, making plans for the morrow. Not until Phobos had at last plunged down into the east, and its light had ceased to play mockingly on the cliff above them, did he finally pass into a fitful slumber.

Even then he dreamed that he was trying to fix a belt-drive from the motors to the tractor undercarriage so that they could taxi the last thousand kilometres to Port Schiaparelli . . .

Twelve

When Gibson woke it was long after dawn. The Sun was invisible behind the cliffs, but its rays reflected from the scarlet crags above them flooded the cabin with an unearthly, even a sinister light. He stretched himself stiffly: these seats had not been designed to sleep in, and he had spent an uncomfortable night.

He looked round for his companions – and realized that Hilton and the pilot had gone. Jimmy was still fast asleep: the others must have awakened first and gone out to explore. Gibson felt a vague annoyance at being left behind, but knew that he would have been still more annoyed if they had interrupted his slumbers.

There was a short message from Hilton pinned prominently on the wall. It said simply: 'Went outside at 6.30. Will be gone about an hour. We'll be hungry when we get back. Fred.'

The hint could hardly be ignored. Besides, Gibson felt hungry himself. He rummaged through the emergency food pack which the aircraft carried for such accidents, wondering as he did so just how long it would have to last them. His attempts to brew a hot drink in the tiny pressure-boiler aroused Jimmy, who looked somewhat sheepish when he realized he was the last to wake.

'Had a good sleep?' asked Gibson, as he searched round for the cups.

'Awful,' said Jimmy, running his hands through his hair. 'I feel I haven't slept for a week. Where are the others?'

His question was promptly answered by the sounds of someone entering the airlock. A moment later Hilton appeared, followed by the pilot. They divested themselves of masks and heating equipment – it was still around freezing-point outside – and advanced eagerly on the pieces of chocolate and compressed meat which Gibson had portioned out with impeccable fairness.

'Well,' said Gibson anxiously, 'what's the verdict?'

'I can tell you one thing right away,' said Hilton between mouthfuls. 'We're damn lucky to be alive.'

'I know that.'

'You don't know the half of it – you haven't seen just where we landed. We came down parallel to this cliff for almost a kilometre before we stopped. If we'd swerved a couple of degrees to starboard – bang! When we touched down we did swing inwards a bit, but not enough to do any damage.

'We're in a long valley, running east and west. It looks like a geological fault rather than an old river bed, though that was my first guess. The cliff opposite us is a good hundred metres high, and practically vertical – in fact, it's got a bit of overhang near the top. Maybe it can be climbed farther along, but we didn't try. There's no need to, anyway – if we want Phobos to see us we've only got to walk a little way to the north, until the cliff doesn't block the view. In fact, I think that may be the answer – if we can push this ship out into the open. It'll mean we can use the radio, and will give the telescopes and air search a better chance of spotting us.'

'How much does this thing weigh?' said Gibson doubtfully.

'About thirty tons with full load. There's a lot of stuff we can take out, of course.'

'No there isn't!' said the pilot. 'That would mean letting down our pressure, and we can't afford to waste air.'

'Oh Lord, I'd forgotten that. Still, the ground's fairly smooth and the undercart's perfectly OK.'

Gibson made noises indicating extreme doubt. Even under a third of Earth's gravity, moving the aircraft was not going to be an easy proposition.

For the next few minutes his attention was diverted to the coffee, which he had tried to pour out before it had cooled sufficiently.

Releasing the pressure on the boiler immediately filled the room with steam, so that for a moment it looked as if everyone was going to inhale their liquid refreshment. Making hot drinks on Mars was always a nuisance, since water under normal pressure boiled at around sixty degrees centigrade, and cooks who forgot this elementary fact usually met with disaster.

The dull but nourishing meal was finished in silence, as the castaways pondered their pet plans for rescue. They were not really worried: they knew that an intensive search would now be in progress, and it could only be a matter of time before they were located. But that time could be reduced to a few hours if they could get some kind of signal to Phobos.

After breakfast they tried to move the ship. By dint of much pushing and pulling they managed to shift it a good five metres. Then the caterpillar tracks sank into the soft ground, and as far as their combined efforts were concerned the machine might have been completely bogged. They retired, panting, into the cabin to discuss the next move.

'Have we anything white which we could spread out over a large area?' asked Gibson.

This excellent idea came to nothing when an intensive search of the cabin revealed six handkerchiefs and a few pieces of grimy rag. It was agreed that, even under the most favourable conditions, these would not be visible from Phobos.

'There's only one thing for it,' said Hilton. 'We'll have to rip out the landing lights, run them out on a cable until they're clear of the cliff, and aim them at Phobos. I didn't want to do this if it could be avoided: it might make a mess of the wing and it's a pity to break up a good aeroplane.'

By his glum expression, it was obvious that the pilot agreed with these sentiments.

Jimmy was suddenly struck with an idea.

'Why not fix up a heliograph?' he asked. 'If we flashed a mirror on Phobos they ought to be able to see that.'

'Across six thousand kilometres?' said Gibson doubtfully.

'Why not? They've got telescopes that magnify more than a thousand up there. Couldn't you see a mirror flashing in the sun if it was only six kilometres away?'

'I'm sure there's something wrong with that calculation, though I don't know what,' said Gibson. 'Things never work out as simply as that. But I agree with the general idea. Now who's got a mirror?'

After a quarter hour's search, Jimmy's scheme had to be abandoned. There simply was no such thing as a mirror on the ship.

'We could cut out a piece of the wing and polish that up,' said Hilton thoughtfully. 'That would be almost as good.'

'This magnesium alloy won't take much of a polish,' said the pilot, still determined to defend his machine to the last.

Gibson suddenly shot to his feet.

'Will someone kick me three times round the cabin?' he announced to the assembly.

'With pleasure,' grinned Hilton, 'but tell us why.'

Without answering, Gibson went to the rear of the ship and began rummaging among his luggage, keeping his back to the interested spectators. It took him only a moment to find what he wanted; then he swung quickly round.

'Here's the answer,' he said triumphantly.

A flash of intolerable light suddenly filled the cabin, flooding every corner with a harsh brilliance and throwing distorted shadows on the wall. It was as if lightning had struck the ship, and for several minutes everyone was half-blinded, still carrying on their retinas a frozen picture of the cabin as seen in that moment of searing incandescence.

'I'm sorry,' said Gibson contritely. 'I've never used it at full power before: that was intended for night work in the open.'

'Phew!' said Hilton, rubbing his eyes. 'I thought you'd let off an atomic bomb. Must you scare everyone to death when you photograph them?'

'It's only like *this* for normal indoor use,' said Gibson, demonstrating. Everyone flinched again, but this time the flash seemed scarcely noticeable. 'It's a special job I had made for me before I left Earth. I wanted to be quite sure I could do colour photography at night if I wanted to. So far I haven't had a real chance of using it.'

'Let's have a look at the thing,' said Hilton.

Gibson handed over the flash-gun and explained its operation.

'It's built round a super-capacity condenser. There's enough for about a hundred flashes on one charge, and it's practically full.'

'A hundred of the high-powered flashes?'

'Yes: it'll do a couple of thousand of the normal ones.'

'Then there's enough electrical energy to make a good bomb in that condenser. I hope it doesn't spring a leak.'

Hilton was examining the little gas-discharge tube, only the size of a marble, at the centre of the small reflector.

'Can we focus this thing to get a good beam?' he asked.

'There's a catch behind the reflector – that's the idea. It's rather a broad beam, but it'll help.'

Hilton looked very pleased.

'They ought to see this thing on Phobos, even in broad daylight, if they're watching this part with a good telescope. We mustn't waste flashes, though.'

'Phobos is well up now, isn't it?' asked Gibson. 'I'm going out to have a shot right away.'

He got to his feet and began to adjust his breathing equipment.

'Don't use more than ten flashes,' warned Hilton. 'We want to save them for night. And stand in any shadow you can find.'

'Can I go out too?' asked Jimmy.

'All right,' said Hilton. 'But keep together and don't go wandering off to explore. I'm going to stay here and see if there's anything we can do with the landing lights.'

The fact that they now had a definite plan of action had raised their spirits considerably. Clutching his camera and the precious flash-gun closely to his chest, Gibson bounded across the valley like a young gazelle. It was a curious fact that on Mars one quickly adjusted one's muscular efforts to the lower gravity, and so normally used strides no greater than on Earth. But the reserve of power was available when necessity or high spirits demanded it.

They soon left the shadow of the cliff, and had a clear view of the open sky. Phobos was already high in the west, a little half-moon which would rapidly narrow to a thin crescent as it raced towards the south. Gibson regarded it thoughtfully, wondering if at this very moment someone might be watching this part of Mars. It seemed highly probable, for the approximate position of their crash would be known. He felt an irrational impulse to dance around and wave his arms – even to shout: 'Here we are – can't you see us?'

What would this region look like in the telescopes which were, he hoped, now sweeping the Aetheria? They would show the mottled green of the vegetation through which he was trudging, and the great cliff would be clearly visible as a red band casting a broad shadow over the valley when the sun was low. There would be scarcely any shadow now, for it was only a few hours from noon. The best thing to do, Gibson decided, was to get in the middle of the darkest area of vegetation he could find.

About a kilometre from the crashed ship the ground sloped down slightly, and here, in the lowest part of the valley, was a wide brownish belt which seemed to be covered with tall weeds. Gibson headed for this, Jimmy following close behind.

They found themselves among slender, leathery plants of a type they had never seen before. The leaves rose vertically out of the ground in long, thin streamers, and were covered with numberless pods which looked as if they might contain seeds. The flat sides were all turned towards the Sun, and Gibson was interested to note that while the sunlit sides of the leaves were black, the shadowed parts were a greyish white. It was a simple but effective trick to reduce loss of heat.

Without wasting time to botanize, Gibson pushed his way into the centre of the little forest. The plants were not crowded too closely together, and it was fairly easy to force a passage through them. When he had gone far enough he raised his flashgun and squinted along it at Phobos.

The satellite was now a thin crescent not far from the Sun, and Gibson felt extremely foolish aiming his flash into the full glare of the summer sky. But the time was really well chosen, for it would be dark on the side of Phobos towards them and the telescopes there would be observing under favourable conditions.

He let off his ten shots in five pairs, spaced well apart. This seemed the most economical way of doing it while still making sure that the signals would look obviously artificial.

'That'll do for today,' said Gibson. 'We'll save the rest of our ammunition until after dark. Now let's have a look at these plants. Do you know what they remind me of?'

'Overgrown seaweed,' replied Jimmy promptly.

'Right first time. I wonder what's in those pods? Have you got a knife on you – thanks.'

Gibson began carving at the nearest frond until he had punctured one of the little black balloons. It apparently held gas, and under considerable pressure, for a faint hiss could be heard as the knife penetrated.

'What queer stuff!' said Gibson. 'Let's take some back with us.'

Not without difficulty, he hacked off one of the long black fronds near the roots. A dark brown fluid began to ooze out of the severed

282

end, releasing tiny bubbles of gas as it did so. With this souvenir hanging over his shoulder, Gibson began to make his way back to the ship.

He did not know that he was carrying with him the future of a world.

They had gone only a few paces when they encountered a denser patch and had to make a detour. With the sun as a guide there was no danger of becoming lost, especially in such a small region, and they had made no attempt to retrace their footsteps exactly. Gibson was leading the way, and finding it somewhat heavy going. He was just wondering whether to swallow his pride and change places with Jimmy when he was relieved to come across a narrow, winding track leading more or less in the right direction.

To any observer, it would have been an interesting demonstration of the slowness of some mental processes. For both Gibson and Jimmy had walked a good six paces before they remembered the simple but shattering truth that footpaths do not, usually, make themselves.

'It's about time our two explorers came back, isn't it?' said the pilot as he helped Hilton detach the floodlights from the underside of the aircraft's wing. This had proved, after all, to be a fairly straightforward job, and Hilton hoped to find enough wiring inside the machine to run the lights far enough away from the cliff to be visible from Phobos when it rose again. They would not have the brilliance of Gibson's flash, but their steady beams would give them a better chance of being detected.

'How long have they been gone now?' said Hilton.

'About forty minutes. I hope they've had the sense not to get lost.'

'Gibson's too careful to go wandering off. I wouldn't trust young Jimmy by himself, though – he'd want to start looking for Martians!'

'Oh, here they are. They seem to be in a bit of a hurry.'

Two tiny figures had emerged from the middle distance and were bounding across the valley. Their haste was so obvious that the watchers downed tools and observed their approach with rising curiosity.

The fact that Gibson and Jimmy had returned so promptly represented a triumph of caution and self-control. For a long moment of incredulous astonishment they had stood staring at that pathway through the thin brown plants. On Earth, nothing could have been more commonplace: it was just the sort of track that cattle make across a hill, or wild animals through a forest. Its very familiarity had at first prevented them from noticing it, and even when they had forced their minds to accept its presence, they still kept trying to explain it away.

Gibson had spoken first, in a very subdued voice – almost as if he was afraid of being overheard.

'It's a path all right, Jimmy. But what could have made it, for Heaven's sake? No one's ever been here before.'

'It must have been some kind of animal.'

'A fairly large one, too.'

'Perhaps as big as a horse.'

'Or a tiger.'

The last remark produced an uneasy silence. Then Jimmy said: 'Well, if it comes to a fight, that flash of yours should scare anything.'

'Only if it had eyes,' said Gibson. 'Suppose it had some other sense?'

It was obvious that Jimmy was trying to think of good reasons for pressing ahead.

'I'm sure we could run faster, and jump higher, than anything else on Mars.'

Gibson liked to believe that his decision was based on prudence rather than cowardice.

'We're not taking any risks,' he said firmly. 'We're going straight back to tell the others. *Then* we'll think about having a look round.'

Jimmy had sense enough not to grumble, but he kept looking back wistfully as they returned to the ship. Whatever faults he might have, lack of courage was not among them.

It took some time to convince the others that they were not attempting a rather poor practical joke. After all, everyone knew why there couldn't be animal life on Mars. It was a question of metabolism: animals burned fuel so much faster than plants, and therefore could not exist in this thin, practically inert atmosphere. The biologists had been quick to point this out as soon as conditions on the surface of Mars had been accurately determined, and for the last ten years the question of animal life on the planet had been regarded as settled – except by incurable romantics.

'Even if you saw what you think,' said Hilton, 'there must be some natural explanation.'

'Come and see for yourself,' retorted Gibson. 'I tell you it was a well-worn track.'

'Oh, I'm coming,' said Hilton.

'So am I,' said the pilot.

'Wait a minute! We can't all go. At least one of us has got to stay behind.'

For a moment Gibson felt like volunteering. Then he realized that he would never forgive himself if he did.

'*I* found the track,' he said firmly.

'Looks as if I've got a mutiny on my hands,' remarked Hilton. 'Anyone got some money? Odd man out of you three stays behind.'

'It's a wild goose chase, anyway,' said the pilot, when he produced the only head. 'I'll expect you home in an hour. If you take any longer, I'll want you to bring back a genuine Martian princess, *à la* Edgar Rice Burroughs.'

Hilton, despite his scepticism, was taking the matter more seriously.

'There'll be three of us,' he said, 'so it should be all right even if we do meet anything unfriendly. But just in case *none* of us comes back, you've to sit right here and not go looking for us. Understand?'

'Very well. I'll sit tight.'

The trio set off across the valley towards the little forest, Gibson leading the way. After reaching the tall thin fronds of 'seaweed', they had no difficulty in finding the track again. Hilton stared at it in silence for a good minute, while Gibson and Jimmy regarded him with 'I told you so' expressions. Then he remarked: 'Let's have your flash-gun, Martin. I'm going first.'

It would have been silly to argue. Hilton was taller, stronger, and more alert. Gibson handed over his weapon without a word.

There can be no weirder sensation than that of walking along a narrow track between high leafy walls, knowing that at any moment you may come face to face with a totally unknown and perhaps unfriendly creature. Gibson tried to remind himself that animals which had never before encountered man were seldom hostile –

though there were enough exceptions to this rule to make life interesting.

They had gone about half-way through the forest when the track branched into two. Hilton took the turn to the right, but soon discovered that this was a cul-de-sac. It led to a clearing about twenty metres across, in which all the plants had been cut – or eaten – to within a short distance of the ground, leaving only the stumps showing. These were already beginning to sprout again, and it was obvious that this patch had been deserted for some time by whatever creatures had come here.

'Herbivores,' whispered Gibson.

'And fairly intelligent,' said Hilton. 'See the way they've left the roots to come up again? Let's go back along the other branch.'

They came across the second clearing five minutes later. It was a good deal larger than the first, and it was not empty.

Hilton tightened his grip on the flash-gun, and in a single smooth, well-practised movement Gibson swung his camera into position and began to take the most famous photographs ever made on Mars. Then they all relaxed, and stood waiting for the Martians to notice them.

In that moment centuries of fantasy and legend were swept away. All Man's dreams of neighbours not unlike himself vanished into limbo. With them, unlamented, went Wells's tentacled monstrosities and the other legions of crawling, nightmare horrors. And there vanished also the myth of coldly inhuman intelligences which might look down dispassionately on Man from their fabulous heights of wisdom – and might brush him aside with no more malice than he himself might destroy a creeping insect.

There were ten of the creatures in the glade, and they were all too busy eating to take any notice of the intruders. In appearance they resembled very plump kangaroos, their almost spherical bodies balanced on two large, slender hind-limbs. They were hairless, and their skin had a curious waxy sheen like polished leather. Two thin forearms, which seemed to be completely flexible, sprouted from the upper part of the body and ended in tiny hands like the claws of a bird – too small and feeble, one would have thought, to have been of much practical use. Their heads were set directly on the trunk with no suspicion of a neck, and bore two large pale eyes with wide pupils. There were no nostrils – only a very odd triangular mouth with three stubby bills which were making short work of the foliage. A pair of large, almost transparent ears hung limply from the head, twitching occasionally and sometimes folding themselves into trumpets which looked as if they might be extremely efficient sound detectors, even in this thin atmosphere.

The largest of the beasts was about as tall as Hilton, but all the others were considerably smaller. One baby, less than a metre high, could only be described by the overworked adjective 'cute'. It was hopping excitedly about in an effort to reach the more succulent leaves, and from time to time emitted thin, piping cries which were irresistibly pathetic.

'How intelligent would you say they are?' whispered Gibson at last.

'It's hard to say. Notice how they're careful not to destroy the plants they eat? Of course, that may be pure instinct – like bees knowing how to build their hives.'

'They move very slowly, don't they? I wonder if they're warm-blooded.'

'I don't see why they should have blood at all. Their metabolism must be pretty weird for them to survive in this climate.'

'It's about time they took some notice of us.'

'The big fellow knows we're here. I've caught him looking at us out of the corner of his eye. Do you notice the way his ears keep pointing towards us?'

'Let's go out into the open.'

Hilton thought this over.

'I don't see how they can do us much harm, even if they want to. Those little hands look rather feeble – but I suppose those three-sided beaks could do some damage. We'll go forward, very slowly, for six paces. If they come at us, I'll give them a flash with the gun while you make a bolt for it. I'm sure we can outrun them easily. They certainly don't look built for speed.'

Moving with a slowness which they hoped would appear reassuring rather than stealthy, they walked forward into the glade. There was now no doubt that the Martians saw them: half a dozen pairs of great, calm eyes stared at them, then looked away as their owners got on with the more important business of eating.

'They don't even seem to be inquisitive,' said Gibson, somewhat disappointed. 'Are we as uninteresting as all this?'

'Hello – Junior's spotted us! What's he up to?'

The smallest Martian had stopped eating and was staring at the intruders with an expression that might have meant anything from rank disbelief to hopeful anticipation of another meal. It gave a couple of shrill squeaks which were answered by a non-committal 'honk' from one of the adults. Then it began to hop towards the interested spectators.

It halted a couple of paces away, showing not the slightest signs of fear or caution.

'How do you do?' said Hilton solemnly. 'Let me introduce us. On my right, James Spencer; on my left, Martin Gibson. But I'm afraid I didn't quite catch your name.'

'Squeak,' said the small Martian.

'Well, Squeak, what can we do for you?'

The little creature put out an exploring hand and tugged at Hilton's clothing. Then it hopped towards Gibson, who had been busily photographing this exchange of courtesies. Once again it put forward an inquiring paw, and Gibson moved the camera round out of harm's way. He held out his hand, and the little fingers closed round it with surprising strength.

'Friendly little chap, isn't he?' said Gibson, having disentangled himself with difficulty. 'At least he's not as stuck-up as his relatives.'

The adults had so far taken not the slightest notice of the proceedings. They were still munching placidly at the other side of the glade.

'I wish we had something to give him, but I don't suppose he could eat any of our food. Lend me your knife, Jimmy. I'll cut down a bit of seaweed for him, just to prove that we're friends.'

This gift was gratefully received and promptly eaten, and the small hands reached out for more.

'You seem to have made a hit, Martin,' said Hilton.

'I'm afraid it's cupboard love,' sighed Gibson. 'Hey, leave my camera alone – you can't eat that!'

'I say,' said Hilton suddenly. 'There's something odd here. What colour would you say this little chap is?'

'Why, brown in the front and – oh, a dirty grey at the back.'

'Well, just walk to the other side of him and offer another bit of food.'

Gibson obliged, Squeak rotating on his haunches so that he could grab the new morsel. And as he did so, an extraordinary thing happened.

The brown covering on the front of his body slowly faded, and in less than a minute had become a dingy grey. At the same time, exactly the reverse happened on the creature's back, until the interchange was complete.

'Good Lord!' said Gibson. 'It's just like a chameleon. 'What do you think the idea is? Protective coloration?'

'No, it's cleverer than that. Look at those others over there. You see, they're always brown – or nearly black – on the side towards the sun. It's simply a scheme to catch as much heat as possible, and avoid re-radiating it. The plants do just the same – I wonder who thought of it first? It wouldn't be any use on an animal that had to move quickly, but some of those big chaps haven't changed position in the last five minutes.'

Gibson promptly set to work photographing this peculiar phenomenon – not a very difficult feat to do, as wherever he moved Squeak always turned hopefully towards him and sat waiting patiently. When he had finished, Hilton remarked:

'I hate to break up this touching scene, but we said we'd be back in an hour.'

'We needn't all go. Be a good chap, Jimmy – run back and say that we're all right.'

But Jimmy was staring at the sky – the first to realize that for the last five minutes an aircraft had been circling high over the valley.

Their united cheer disturbed even the placidly browsing Martians, who looked round disapprovingly. It scared Squeak so much that he shot backwards in one tremendous hop, but soon got over his fright and came forward again.

'See you later!' called Gibson over his shoulder as they hurried out of the glade. The natives took not the slightest notice.

They were half-way out of the little forest when Gibson suddenly became aware of the fact that he was being followed. He stopped and looked back. Making heavy weather, but still hopping along gamely behind him, was Squeak.

'Shoo!' said Gibson, flapping his arms around like a distraught scarecrow. 'Go back to mother! I haven't got anything for you.'

It was not the slightest use, and his pause had merely enabled Squeak to catch up with him. The others were already out of sight, unaware that Gibson had dropped back. They therefore missed a very interesting cameo as Gibson tried, without hurting Squeak's feelings, to disengage himself from his new-found friend.

He gave up the direct approach after five minutes, and tried guile. Fortunately he had failed to return Jimmy's knife, and after much panting and hacking managed to collect a small pile of 'seaweed' which he laid in front of Squeak. This, he hoped, would keep him busy for quite a while.

He had just finished this when Hilton and Jimmy came hurrying back to find what had happened to him.

'OK – I'm coming along now,' he said. 'I had to get rid of Squeak somehow. *That'll* stop him following.'

The pilot in the crashed aircraft had been getting anxious, for the hour was nearly up and there was still no sign of his companions. By climbing on to the top of the fuselage he could see half-way across the valley, and to the dark area of vegetation into which they had disappeared. He was examining this when the rescue aircraft came driving out of the east and began to circle the valley.

When he was sure it had spotted him he turned his attention to the ground again. He was just in time to see a group of figures emerging into the open plain – and a moment later he rubbed his eyes in rank disbelief.

Three people had gone into the forest; but four were coming out. And the fourth looked a very odd sort of person indeed.

Thirteen

After what was later to be christened the most successful crash in the history of Martian exploration, the visit to Trivium Charontis and Port Schiaparelli was, inevitably, something of an anticlimax. Indeed, Gibson had wished to postpone it altogether and to return to Port Lowell immediately with his prize. He had soon abandoned all attempts to jettison Squeak, and as everyone in the colony would be on tenterhooks to see a real, live Martian it had been decided to fly the little creature back with them.

But Port Lowell would not let them return: indeed, it was ten days before they saw the capital again. Under the great domes, one of the decisive battles for the possession of the planet was now being fought. It was a battle which Gibson knew of only through the radio reports – a silent but deadly battle which he was thankful to have missed.

The epidemic which Dr Scott had asked for had arrived. At its peak, a tenth of the city's population was sick with Martian Fever. But the serum from Earth broke the attack, and the battle was won with only three fatal casualties. It was the last time that the fever ever threatened the colony.

Taking Squeak to Port Schiaparelli involved considerable difficulties, for it meant flying large quantities of his staple diet ahead of him. At first it was doubted if he could live in the oxygenated atmosphere of the domes, but it was soon discovered that this did not worry him in the least – though it reduced his appetite considerably. The explanation of this fortunate accident was not discovered until a good deal later. What never was discovered at all was the reason for Squeak's attachment to Gibson. Someone suggested, rather unkindly, that it was because they were approximately the same shape.

Before they continued their journey, Gibson and his colleagues, with the pilot of the rescue plane and the repair crew who arrived later, made several visits to the little family of Martians. They discovered only the one group, and Gibson wondered if these were the last specimens left on the planet. This, as it later turned out, was not the case.

The rescue plane had been searching along the track of their flight when it had received a radio message from Phobos reporting brilliant flashes from Aetheria. (Just how those flashes had been made had puzzled everyone considerably until Gibson, with justifiable pride, gave the explanation.) When they discovered it would take only a few hours to replace the jet units on their plane, they had decided to wait while the repairs were carried out and to use the time studying the Martians in their natural haunts. It was then that Gibson first suspected the secret of their existence.

In the remote past they had probably been oxygen breathers, and their life processes still depended on the element. They could not obtain it direct from the soil, where it lay in such countless trillions of tons; but the plants they ate could do so. Gibson quickly found that the numerous 'pods' in the seaweed-like fronds contained oxygen under quite high pressure. By slowing down their metabolism, the Martians had managed to evolve a balance – almost a symbiosis – with the plants which provided them, literally, with food and air. It was a precarious balance which, one would have thought, might have been upset at any time by some natural catastrophe. But conditions on Mars had long ago reached stability, and the balance would be maintained for ages yet – unless Man disturbed it.

The repairs took a little longer than expected, and they did not reach Port Schiaparelli until three days after leaving Port Lowell. The second city of Mars held less than a thousand people, living under two domes on a long, narrow plateau. This had been the site of the original landing on Mars, and so the position of the city was really an historical accident. Not until some years later, when the planet's resources began to be better known, was it decided to move the colony's centre of gravity to Lowell and not to expand Schiaparelli any further.

The little city was in many respects an exact replica of its larger and more modern rival. Its speciality was light engineering, geological – or rather aereological – research, and the exploration of the surrounding regions. The fact that Gibson and his colleagues had accidentally stumbled on the greatest discovery so far made on Mars, less than an hour's flight from the city, was thus the cause of some heartburning.

The visit must have had a demoralizing effect on all normal activity in Port Schiaparelli, for wherever Gibson went everything stopped while crowds gathered around Squeak. A favourite occupation was to lure him into a field of uniform illumination and to watch him turn black all over, as he blissfully tried to extract the maximum advantage from this state of affairs. It was in Schiaparelli that someone hit on the deplorable scheme of projecting simple pictures on to Squeak, and photographing the result before it faded. One day Gibson was very annoyed to come across a photo of his pet bearing a crude but recognizable caricature of a well-known television star.

On the whole, their stay in Port Schiaparelli was not a very happy one. After the first three days they had seen everything worth seeing, and the few trips they were able to make into the surrounding countryside did not provide much of interest. Jimmy was continually worrying about Irene, and putting through expensive calls to Port Lowell. Gibson was impatient to get back to the big city which, not so long ago, he had called an overgrown village. Only Hilton, who seemed to possess unlimited reserves of patience, took life easily and relaxed while the others fussed around him.

There was one excitement during their stay in the city. Gibson had often wondered, a little apprehensively, what would happen if the pressurizing dome ever failed. He received the answer – or as much of it as he had any desire for – one quiet afternoon when he was interviewing the city's chief engineer in his office. Squeak had been with them, propped up on his large, flexible lower limbs like some improbable nursery doll.

As the interview progressed, Gibson became aware that his victim was showing more than the usual signs of restiveness. His mind was obviously very far away, and he seemed to be waiting for something to happen. Suddenly, without any warning, the whole building trembled slightly as if hit by an earthquake. Two more shocks, equally spaced, came in quick succession. From a loudspeaker on the wall a voice called urgently: 'Blow-out! Practice only! You have ten seconds to reach shelter! Blow-out! Practice only!'

Gibson had jumped out of his chair, but immediately realized there was nothing he need do. From far away there came a sound of slamming doors – then silence. The engineer got to his feet and walked over to the window, overlooking the city's only main street.

'Everyone seems to have got to cover,' he said. 'Of course, it isn't possible to make these tests a complete surprise. There's one a month, and we have to tell people what day it will be because they might think it was the real thing.'

'Just what are we all supposed to do?' asked Gibson, who had been told at least twice but had become a little rusty on the subject.

'As soon as you hear the signal – that's the three ground explosions – you've got to get under cover. If you're indoors you have to grab your breathing mask to rescue anyone who can't make it. You see, if pressure goes every house becomes a self-contained unit with enough air for several hours.'

'And anyone out in the open?'

'It would take a few seconds for the pressure to go right down, and as every building has its own airlock it should always be possible to reach shelter in time. Even if you collapsed in the open, you'd probably be all right if you were rescued inside two minutes – unless you'd got a bad heart. And no one comes to Mars if he's got a bad heart.'

'Well, I hope you never have to put this theory into practice!'

'So do we! But on Mars one has to be prepared for anything. Ah, there goes the All Clear.'

The speaker had burst into life again.

'Exercise over. Will all those who failed to reach shelter in the regulation time please inform Admin in the usual way? End of message.'

'Will they?' asked Gibson. 'I should have thought they'd keep quiet.'

The engineer laughed.

'That depends. They probably will if it was their own fault. But it's the best way of showing up weak points in our defences. Someone will come and say: "Look here – I was cleaning one of the ore furnaces when the alarm went: it took me two minutes to get out of the blinking thing. What am *I* supposed to do if there's a real blow-out?" Then we've got to think of an answer, if we can.'

Gibson looked enviously at Squeak, who seemed to be asleep, though an occasional twitch of the great translucent ears showed that he was taking some interest in the conversation.

'It would be nice if we could be like him and didn't have to bother about air pressure. Then we could really do something with Mars.'

'I wonder!' said the engineer thoughtfully. 'What have *they* done except survive? It's always fatal to adapt oneself to one's surroundings. The thing to do is to alter your surroundings to suit you.'

The words were almost an echo of the remark that Hadfield had made at their first meeting. Gibson was to remember them often in the years to come.

Their return to Port Lowell was almost a victory parade. The capital was in a mood of elation over the defeat of the epidemic, and it was now anxiously waiting to see Gibson and his prize. The scientists had prepared quite a reception for Squeak, the zoologists in particular being busily at work explaining away their early explanations for the absence of animal life on Mars.

Gibson had handed his pet over to the experts only when they had solemnly assured him that no thought of dissection had ever for a moment entered their minds. Then, full of ideas, he had hurried to see the Chief.

Hadfield had greeted him warmly. There was, Gibson was interested to note, a distinct change in the Chief's attitude towards him. At first it had been – well, not unfriendly, but at least somewhat reserved. He had not attempted to conceal the fact that he considered Gibson's presence on Mars something of a nuisance – another burden to add to those he already carried. This attitude had slowly changed until it was now obvious that the Chief Executive no longer regarded him as an unmitigated calamity.

'You've added some interesting citizens to my little empire,' Hadfield said with a smile. 'I've just had a look at your engaging pet. He's already bitten the Chief Medical Officer.'

'I hope they're treating him properly,' said Gibson anxiously.

'Who – the CMO?'

'No – Squeak, of course. What I'm wondering is whether there are any other forms of animal life we haven't discovered yet – perhaps more intelligent.'

'In other words, are these the only genuine Martians?'

'Yes.'

'It'll be years before we know for certain, but I rather expect they are. The conditions which make it possible for them to survive don't occur in many places on the planet.'

'That was one thing I wanted to talk to you about.' Gibson reached into his pocket and brought out a frond of the brown 'seaweed'. He punctured one of the fronds, and there was the faint hiss of escaping gas.

'If this stuff is cultivated properly, it may solve the oxygen problem in the cities and do away with all our present complicated machinery. With enough sand for it to feed on, it would give you all the oxygen you need.'

'Go on,' said Hadfield noncommittally.

'Of course, you'd have to do some selective breeding to get the variety that gave most oxygen,' continued Gibson, warming to his subject.

'Naturally,' replied Hadfield.

Gibson looked at his listener with a sudden suspicion, aware that there was something odd about his attitude. A faint smile was playing about Hadfield's lips.

'I don't think you're taking me seriously!' Gibson protested bitterly.

Hadfield sat up with a start.

'On the contrary!' he retorted. 'I'm taking you much more seriously than you imagine.' He toyed with his paperweight, then apparently came to a decision. Abruptly he leaned towards his desk microphone and pressed a switch.

'Get me a Sand Flea and a driver,' he said. 'I want them at Lock One West in thirty minutes.'

He turned to Gibson.

'Can you be ready by then?'

'What – yes, I suppose so. I've only got to get my breathing gear from the hotel.'

'Good – see you in half an hour.'

Gibson was there ten minutes early, his brain in a whirl. Transport had managed to produce a vehicle in time, and the Chief was punctual as ever. He gave the driver instructions which Gibson was unable to catch, and the Flea jerked out of the dome on to the road circling the city.

'I'm doing something rather rash, Gibson,' said Hadfield as the brilliant green landscape flowed past them. 'Will you give me your word that you'll say nothing of this until I authorize you?'

'Why, certainly,' said Gibson, startled.

'I'm trusting you because I believe you're on our side, and haven't been as big a nuisance as I expected.'

'Thank you,' said Gibson dryly.

'*And* because of what you've just taught us about our own planet. I think we owe you something in return.'

The Flea had swung round to the south, following the track that led up into the hills. And, quite suddenly, Gibson realized where they were going.

'Were you very upset when you heard that we'd crashed?' asked Jimmy anxiously.

'Of course I was,' said Irene. 'Terribly upset. I couldn't sleep for worrying about you.'

'Now it's all over, though, don't you think it was worth it?'

'I suppose so, but somehow it keeps reminding me that in a month you'll be gone again. Oh, Jimmy, what shall we do then?'

Deep despair settled upon the two lovers. All Jimmy's present satisfaction vanished into gloom. There was no escaping from this inevitable fact. The *Ares* would be leaving Deimos in less than four weeks, and it might be years before he could return to Mars. It was a prospect too terrible for words.

'I can't possibly stay on Mars, even if they'd let me,' said Jimmy. 'I can't earn a living until I'm qualified, and I've still got two years' post-graduate work *and* a trip to Venus to do! There's only one thing for it!'

Irene's eyes brightened: then she relapsed into gloom.

'Oh, we've been through that before. I'm sure Daddy wouldn't agree.'

'Well, it won't do any harm to try. I'll get Martin to tackle him.'

'Mr Gibson? Do you think he would?'

'I know he will, if I ask him. And he'll make it sound convincing.'

'I don't see why he should bother.'

'Oh, he likes me,' said Jimmy with easy self-assurance. 'I'm sure he'll agree with us. It's not right that you should stick here on Mars and never see anything of Earth. Paris – New York – London – why, you haven't lived until you've visited them. Do you know what I think?'

'What?'

'Your father's being selfish in keeping you here.'

Irene pouted a little. She was very fond of her father and her first impulse was to defend him vigorously. But she was now torn between two loyalties, though in the long run there was no doubt which would win.

'Of course,' said Jimmy, realizing that he might have gone too far, 'I'm sure he really means to do the best for you, but he's got so many things to worry about. He's probably forgotten what Earth is like and doesn't realize what you're losing! No, you must get away before it's too late.'

Irene still looked uncertain. Then her sense of humour, so much more acute than Jimmy's, came to the rescue.

'I'm quite sure that if we were on Earth, and you had to go back to Mars, you'd be able to prove just as easily that I ought to follow you there!'

Jimmy looked a little hurt, then realized that Irene wasn't really laughing at him.

'All right,' he said. 'That's settled. I'll talk to Martin as soon as I see him – and ask him to tackle your Dad. So let's forget all about it until then, shall we?'

They did, very nearly.

The little amphitheatre in the hills above Port Lowell was just as Gibson had remembered it, except that the green of its lush vegetation had darkened a little, as if it had already received the first warning of the still far-distant autumn. The Sand Flea drove up to the largest of the four small domes, and they walked over to the airlock.

'When I was here before,' said Gibson dryly, 'I was told we'd have to be disinfected before we could enter.'

'A slight exaggeration to discourage unwanted visitors,' said Hadfield, unabashed. The outer door had opened at his signal, and they quickly stripped off their breathing apparatus. 'We used to take such precautions, but they're no longer necessary.'

The inner door slid aside and they stepped through into the dome. A man wearing the white smock of the scientific worker – the *clean* white smock of the very senior scientific worker – was waiting for them.

'Hello, Baines,' said Hadfield. 'Gibson – this is Professor Baines. I expect you've heard of each other.'

They shook hands. Baines, Gibson knew, was one of the world's greatest experts on plant genetics. He had read a year or two ago that he had gone to Mars to study its flora.

'So you're the chap who's just discovered *Oxyfera*,' said Baines dreamily. He was a large, rugged man with an absent-minded air which contrasted strangely with his massive frame and determined features.

'Is that what you call it?' asked Gibson. 'Well, I *thought* I'd discovered it. But I'm beginning to have doubts.'

'You certainly discovered something quite as important,' Hadfield reassured him. 'But Baines isn't interested in animals, so it's no good talking to him about your Martian friends.'

They were walking between low temporary walls which, Gibson saw, partitioned the dome into numerous rooms and corridors. The whole place looked as if it had been built in a great hurry: they came across beautiful scientific apparatus supported on rough packing cases, and everywhere there was an atmosphere of hectic improvisation. Yet, curiously enough, very few people were at work. Gibson obtained the impression that whatever task had been going on here was now completed and that only a skeleton staff was left.

Baines led them to an airlock connecting with one of the other domes, and as they waited for the last door to open he remarked quietly: 'This may hurt your eyes a bit.' With this warning, Gibson put up his hand as a shield.

His first impression was one of light and heat. It was almost as if he had moved from Pole to Tropics in a single step. Overhead, batteries of powerful lamps were blasting the hemispherical chamber with light. There was something heavy and oppressive about the air that was not only due to the heat, and he wondered what sort of atmosphere he was breathing.

This dome was not divided up by partitions: it was simply a large, circular space laid out into neat plots on which grew all the Martian plants which Gibson had ever seen, and many more besides. About a quarter of the area was covered by tall brown fronds which Gibson recognized at once.

'So you've known about them all the time?' he said, neither surprised nor particularly disappointed. (Hadfield was quite right: the Martians were *much* more important.)

'Yes,' said Hadfield. 'They were discovered about two years ago and aren't very rare along the equatorial belt. They only grow where there's plenty of sunlight, and your little crop was the farthest north they've ever been found.'

'It takes a great deal of energy to split the oxygen out of the sand,' explained Baines. 'We've been helping them here with these lights, and trying some experiments of our own. Come and look at the result.'

Gibson walked over to the plot, keeping carefully to the narrow path. These plants weren't, after all, exactly the same as those he had discovered, though they had obviously descended from the same stock. The most surprising difference was the complete absence of gas-pods, their place having been taken by myriads of minute pores.

'This is the important point,' said Hadfield. 'We've bred a variety which releases its oxygen directly into the air, because it doesn't need to store it any more. As long as it's got plenty of light and heat, it can extract all it needs from the sand and will throw off the surplus. *All the oxygen you're breathing now comes from these plants*: there's no other source in this dome.'

'I see,' said Gibson slowly. 'So you'd already thought of my idea – and gone a good deal further. But I still don't understand the need for all this secrecy.'

'What secrecy?' said Hadfield with an air of injured innocence.

'Really!' protested Gibson. 'You've just asked me not to say anything about this place.'

'Oh, that's because there will be an official announcement in a few days, and we haven't wanted to raise false hopes. But there hasn't been any real secrecy.'

Gibson brooded over this remark all the way back to Port Lowell. Hadfield had told him a good deal: but had he told him everything? Where – if at all – did Phobos come into the picture? Gibson wondered if his suspicions about the inner moon were completely unfounded: it could obviously have no connexion with this particular project. He felt like trying to force Hadfield's hand by a direct question, but thought better of it. He might only make himself look a fool if he did.

The domes of Port Lowell were climbing up over the steeply convex horizon when Gibson broached the subject that had been worrying him for the past fortnight.

'The *Ares* is going back to Earth in three weeks, isn't she?' he remarked to Hadfield. The other merely nodded: the question was obviously a purely rhetorical one for Gibson knew the answer as well as anybody.

'I've been thinking,' said Gibson slowly, 'that I'd like to stay on Mars a bit longer. Maybe until next year.'

'Oh,' said Hadfield. The exclamation revealed neither congratulation nor disapproval, and Gibson felt a little piqued that his shattering announcement had fallen flat. 'What about your work?' continued the Chief.

'All that can be done just as easily here as on Earth.'

'I suppose you realize,' said Hadfield, 'that if you stay here you'll have to take up some useful profession.' He smiled a little wryly. 'That wasn't very tactful, was it? What I mean is that you'll have to do something to help run the colony. Have you any particular ideas in this line?'

This was a little more encouraging: at least it meant that Hadfield had not dismissed the suggestion at once. But it was a point that Gibson had overlooked in his first rush of enthusiasm.

'I wasn't thinking of making a permanent home here,' he said a little lamely. 'But I want to spend some time studying the Martians, and I'd like to see if I can find any more of them. Besides, I don't want to leave Mars just when things are getting interesting.'

'What do you mean?' said Hadfield swiftly.

'Why – these oxygen plants, and getting Dome Seven into operation. I want to see what comes of all this in the next few months.'

Hadfield looked thoughtfully at his passenger. He was less surprised than Gibson might have imagined, for he had seen this sort of thing happen before. He had even wondered if it was going to happen to Gibson, and was by no means displeased at the turn of events.

The explanation was really very simple. Gibson was happier now than he had ever been on Earth: he had done something worthwhile, and felt that he was becoming part of the Martian community. The identification was now nearly complete, and the fact that Mars had already made one attempt on his life had merely strengthened his determination to stay. If he returned to Earth, he would not be going home: he would be sailing into exile.

'Enthusiasm isn't enough, you know,' said Hadfield.

'I quite understand that.'

'This little world of ours is founded on two things – skill and hard work. Without both of them, we might just as well go back to Earth.'

'I am not afraid of work, and I'm sure I could learn some of the administrative jobs you've got here – and a lot of the routine technical ones.'

This, Hadfield thought, was probably true. Ability to do these things was a function of intelligence, and Gibson had plenty of that. But more than intelligence was needed: there were personal factors as well. It would be best not to raise Gibson's hopes until he had made further inquiries and discussed the matter with Whittaker.

'I'll tell you what to do,' said Hadfield. 'Put in a provisional application to stay, and I'll have it signalled to Earth. We'll get their answer in about a week. Of course, if they turn you down there's nothing we can do.'

Gibson doubted this, for he knew just how much notice Hadfield took of terrestrial regulations when they interfered with his plans. But he merely said: 'And if Earth agrees, then I suppose it's up to you?'

'Yes, I'll start thinking about my answer then!'

That, thought Gibson, was satisfactory as far as it went. Now that he had taken the plunge, he felt a great sense of relief, as if everything was now outside his control. He had merely to drift with the current, awaiting the progress of events.

The door of the airlock opened before them and the Flea

crunched into the city. Even if he had made a mistake, no great harm would be done. He could always go back to Earth by the next ship – or the one after.

But there was no doubt that Mars had changed him. He knew what some of his friends would say when they read the news. 'Have you heard about Martin? Looks as if Mars has made a man out of him! Who'd have thought it?'

Gibson wriggled uncomfortably. He had no intention of becoming an elevating object-lesson for anyone, if he could help it. Even in his most maudlin moments he had never had the slightest use for those smug Victorian parables about lazy, self-centred men becoming useful members of the community. But he had a horrible fear that something uncommonly like this was beginning to happen to him.

Fourteen

'Out with it, Jimmy. What's on your mind? You don't seem to have much appetite this morning.'

Jimmy toyed fretfully with the synthetic omelette on his plate, which he had already carved into microscopic fragments.

'I was thinking about Irene, and what a shame it is she's never had a chance of seeing Earth.'

'Are you sure she wants to? I've never heard anyone here say a single good word for the place.'

'Oh, she wants to all right. I've asked her.'

'Stop beating about the bush. What are you two planning now? Do you want to elope in the *Ares*?'

Jimmy gave a rather sickly grin.

'That's an idea, but it would take a bit of doing! Honestly though – don't you think Irene ought to go back to Earth to finish her education? If she stays here she'll grow up into a – a—'

'A simple unsophisticated country girl – a raw colonial? Is that what you were thinking?'

'Well, something like that, but I wish you wouldn't put it so crudely.'

'Sorry – I didn't mean to. As a matter of fact, I rather agree with you; it's a point that's occurred to me. I think someone ought to mention it to Hadfield.'

'That's exactly what—' began Jimmy excitedly.

'—what you and Irene want me to do?'

Jimmy threw up his hands in mock despair.

'It's no good trying to kid you. Yes.'

'If you'd said that at the beginning, think of the time we'd have saved. But tell me frankly, Jimmy – just how serious are you about Irene?'

Jimmy looked back at him with a level, steadfast gaze that was in itself a sufficient answer.

'I'm dead serious: you ought to know that. I want to marry her as soon as she's old enough – and I can earn my living.'

There was a dead silence, then Gibson replied:

'You could do a lot worse: she's a very nice girl. And I think it would do her a lot of good to have a year or so on Earth. Still, I'd rather not tackle Hadfield at the moment. He's very busy and – well, he's already got one request from me.'

'Oh?' said Jimmy, looking up with interest.

Gibson cleared his throat.

'It's got to come out some time, but don't say anything to the others yet. I've applied to stay on Mars.'

'Good Lord!' exclaimed Jimmy. 'That's – well, quite a thing to do.'

Gibson suppressed a smile.

'Do you think it's a good thing?'

'Why, yes. I'd like to do it myself.'

'Even if Irene was going back to Earth?' asked Gibson dryly.

'That isn't fair! But how long do you expect to stay?'

'Frankly, I don't know: it depends on too many factors. For one thing, I'll have to learn a job!'

'What sort of job?'

'Something that's congenial – and productive. Any ideas?'

Jimmy sat in silence for a moment, his forehead wrinkled with concentration. Gibson wondered just what he was thinking. Was he sorry that they might soon have to separate? In the last few weeks the strain and animosities which had once both repelled and united them had dissolved away. They had reached a state of emotional equilibrium which was pleasant, yet not as satisfactory as Gibson would have hoped. Perhaps it was his own fault: perhaps he had been afraid to show his deeper feelings and had hidden them behind banter and even occasional sarcasm. If so, he was afraid he might have succeeded only too well. Once he had hoped to earn Jimmy's trust and confidence: now, it seemed, Jimmy only came to him when he wanted something. No – that wasn't fair, Jimmy certainly liked him, perhaps as much as many sons liked their fathers. That was a positive achievement of which he could be proud. He could take some credit, too, for the great improvement in Jimmy's disposition since they had left Earth. He was no longer awkward and shy: though he was still rather serious, he was never sullen. This, thought Gibson, was something in which he could take a good deal of satisfaction. But now there was little more he could do. Jimmy was slipping out of his world – Irene was the only thing that mattered to him now.

'I'm afraid I don't seem to have any ideas,' said Jimmy. 'Of course, you could have my job here! Oh, that reminds me of something I picked up in Admin the other day.' His voice dropped to a conspiratorial whisper and he leaned across the table. 'Have you ever heard of "Project Dawn"?'

'No; what is it?'

'That's what I'm trying to find out. It's something very secret, and I think it must be pretty big.'

'Oh!' said Gibson, suddenly alert. 'Perhaps I have heard about it after all. Tell me what you know.'

'Well, I was working late one evening in the filing section, and was sitting on the floor between some of the cabinets, sorting out papers, when the Chief and Mayor Whittaker came in. They didn't know I was there, and were talking together. I wasn't trying to eavesdrop, but you know how it is. All of a sudden Mayor Whittaker said something that made me sit up with a bang. I think these were his exact words: "Whatever happens, there's going to be hell to pay as soon as Earth knows about Project Dawn – even if it's successful." Then the Chief gave a queer little laugh, and said something about success excusing everything. That's all I could hear: they went out soon afterwards. What do you think about it?'

'Project Dawn!' There was a magic about the name that made Gibson's pulse quicken. Almost certainly it must have some connexion with the research going on up in the hills above the city – but that could hardly justify Whittaker's remark. Or could it?

Gibson knew a little about the interplay of political forces between Earth and Mars. He appreciated, from occasional remarks of Hadfield's and comments in the local Press, that the colony was now passing through a critical period. On Earth, powerful voices were raised in protest against its enormous expense, which, it seemed, would extend indefinitely into the future with no sign of any ultimate reduction. More than once Hadfield had spoken bitterly of schemes which he had been compelled to abandon on grounds of economy, and of other projects for which permission could not be obtained at all.

'I'll see what I can find out from my – er – various sources of information,' said Gibson. 'Have you mentioned it to anyone else?'

'No.'

'I shouldn't, if I were you. After all, it may not be anything important. I'll let you know what I find out.'

'You won't forget to ask about Irene?'

'As soon as I get the chance. But it may take some time – I'll have to catch Hadfield in the right mood!'

As a private detective agency, Gibson was not a success. He made two rather clumsy direct attempts before he decided that the frontal approach was useless. George the barman had been his first target, for he seemed to know everything that was happening on Mars and was one of Gibson's most valuable contacts. This time, however, he proved of no use at all.

'Project Dawn?' he said, with a puzzled expression. 'I've never heard of it.'

'Are you quite sure?' asked Gibson, watching him narrowly.

George seemed to lose himself in deep thought.

'Quite sure,' he said at last. And that was that. George was such an excellent actor it was quite impossible to guess whether he was lying or speaking the truth.

Gibson did a trifle better with the editor of the *Martian Times*. Westerman was a man he normally avoided, as he was always trying to coax articles out of him and Gibson was invariably behind with his terrestrial commitments. The staff of two therefore looked up with some surprise as their visitor entered the tiny office of Mars' only newspaper.

Having handed over some carbon copies as a peace offering, Gibson sprang his trap.

'I'm trying to collect all the information I can on "Project Dawn",' he said casually. 'I know it's still under cover, but I want to have everything ready when it can be published.'

There was dead silence for several seconds. Then Westerman remarked: 'I think you'd better see the Chief about that.'

'I didn't want to bother him – he's so busy,' said Gibson innocently.

'Well, I can't tell you anything.'

'You mean you don't know anything about it?'

'If you like. There are only a few dozen people on Mars who could even tell what it is.'

That, at least, was a valuable piece of information.

'Do you happen to be one of them?' asked Gibson.

Westerman shrugged his shoulders.

'I keep my eyes open, and I've done a bit of guessing.'

That was all that Gibson could extract from him. He strongly suspected that Westerman knew little more about the matter than he did himself, but was anxious to conceal his ignorance. The interview had, however, confirmed two main facts. 'Project Dawn' certainly did exist, and it was extremely well hidden. Gibson could only follow Westerman's example, keeping his eyes open and guessing what he could.

He decided to abandon the quest for the time being and to go round to the Biophysics Lab, where Squeak was the guest of honour. The little Martian was sitting on his haunches taking life easily while the scientists stood conversing in a corner trying to decide what to do next. As soon as he saw Gibson, he gave a chirp of delight and bounded across the room, bringing down a chair as he did so but luckily missing any valuable apparatus. The bevy of biologists regarded this demonstration with some annoyance: presumably it could not be reconciled with their views on Martian psychology.

'Well,' said Gibson to the leader of the team, when he had disentangled himself from Squeak's clutches. 'Have you decided how intelligent he is yet?'

The scientist scratched his head.

'He's a queer little beast. Sometimes I get the feeling he's just laughing at us. The odd thing is that he's quite different from the rest of his tribe. We've got a unit studying them in the field, you know.'

'In what way is he different?'

'The others don't show any emotions at all, as far as we can discover. They're completely lacking in curiosity. You can stand beside them and if you wait long enough they'll eat right round you. As long as you don't actively interfere with them they'll take no notice of you.'

'And what happens if you do?'

'They'll try and push you out of the way, like some obstacle. If they can't do that, they'll just go somewhere else. Whatever you do, you can't make them annoyed.'

'Are they good-natured, or just plain stupid?'

'I'd be inclined to say it's neither one nor the other. They've had no natural enemies for so long that they can't imagine that anyone would try to hurt them. By now they must be largely creatures of habit: life's so tough for them that they can't afford expensive luxuries like curiosity and the other emotions.'

'Then how do you explain this little fellow's behaviour?' asked Gibson, pointing to Squeak, who was now investigating his pockets. 'He's not really hungry – I've just offered him some food – so it must be pure inquisitiveness.'

'It's probably a phase they pass through when they're young. Think how a kitten differs from a full-grown cat – or a human baby from an adult, for that matter.'

'So when Squeak grows up he'll be like the others?'

'Probably, but it isn't certain. We don't know what capacity he has for learning new habits. For instance, he's very good at finding his way out of mazes – once you can persuade him to make the effort.'

'Poor Squeak!' said Gibson. 'Sometimes I feel quite guilty about taking you away from home. Still, it was your own idea. Let's go for a walk.'

Squeak immediately hopped towards the door.

'Did you see that?' exclaimed Gibson. 'He understands what I'm saying.'

'Well, so can a dog when it hears a command. It may simply be a question of habit again – you've been taking him out this time every day and he's got used to it. Can you bring him back inside half an hour? We're fixing up the encephalograph to get some EEG records of his brain.'

These afternoon walks were a way of reconciling Squeak to his fate and at the same time salving Gibson's conscience. He sometimes felt rather like a baby-snatcher who had abandoned his victim immediately after stealing it. But it was all in the cause of science, and the biologists had sworn they wouldn't hurt Squeak in any way.

The inhabitants of Port Lowell were now used to seeing the strangely assorted pair taking their daily stroll along the streets, and crowds no longer gathered to watch them pass. When it was outside school hours Squeak usually collected a retinue of young admirers who wanted to play with him, but it was now early afternoon and the juvenile population was still in durance vile. There was no one in sight when Gibson and his companion swung into Broadway, but presently a familiar figure appeared in the distance. Hadfield was carrying out his daily tour of inspection, and as usual he was accompanied by his pets.

It was the first time that Topaz and Turquoise had met Squeak, and their aristocratic calm was seriously disturbed, though they did their best to conceal the fact. They tugged on their leads and tried to shelter unobtrusively behind Hadfield, while Squeak took not the slightest notice of them at all.

'Quite a menagerie!' laughed Hadfield. 'I don't think Topaz and Turquoise appreciate having a rival – they've had the place to themselves so long that they think they own it.'

'Any news from Earth yet?' asked Gibson, anxiously.

'Oh, about your application? Good heavens, I only sent it off two days ago! You know just how quickly things move down there. It will be at least a week before we get an answer.'

The Earth was always 'down', the outer planets 'up', so Gibson had discovered. The terms gave him a curious mental picture of a great slope leading down to the Sun, with the planets lying on it at varying heights.

'I don't really see what it's got to do with Earth,' Gibson continued. 'After all, it's not as if there's any question of allocating shipping space. I'm here already – in fact it'll save trouble if I *don't* go back!'

'You surely don't imagine that such commonsense arguments carry much weight with the policy-makers back on Earth!' retorted Hadfield. 'Oh, dear no! Everything has to go through the Proper Channels.'

Gibson was fairly sure that Hadfield did not usually talk about his superiors in this light-hearted fashion, and he felt that peculiar glow of satisfaction that comes when one is permitted to share a deliberate indiscretion. It was another sign that the CE trusted him and considered that he was on his side. Dare he mention the two other matters that were occupying his mind – Project Dawn and Irene? As far as Irene was concerned, he had made his promise and would have to keep it sooner or later. But first he really ought to have a talk with Irene herself – yes, that was a perfectly good excuse for putting it off.

He put it off for so long that the matter was taken right out of his hands. Irene herself made the plunge, no doubt egged on by Jimmy, from whom Gibson had a full report the next day. It was easy to tell from Jimmy's face what the result had been.

Irene's suggestion must have been a considerable shock to Hadfield, who no doubt believed that he had given his daughter everything she needed, and thus shared a delusion common among parents. Yet he had taken it calmly and there had been no scenes. Hadfield was too intelligent a man to adopt the attitude of the deeply wounded father. He had merely given lucid and compelling reasons why Irene couldn't possibly go to Earth until she was twenty-one, when he planned to return for a long holiday during which they could see the world together. And that was only three years away.

'Three years!' lamented Jimmy. 'It might just as well be three lifetimes!'

Gibson deeply sympathized, but tried to look on the bright side of things.

'It's not so long, really. You'll be fully qualified then and earning a lot more money than most young men at that age. And it's surprising how quickly the time goes.'

This Job's comforting produced no alleviation of Jimmy's gloom. Gibson felt like adding the comment that it was just as well that ages on Mars were still reckoned by Earth time, and not according to the Martian year of 687 days. However, he thought better of it and remarked instead: 'What does Hadfield think about all this, anyway? Has he discussed you with Irene?'

'I don't think he knows anything about it.'

'You can bet your life he does! You know, I really think it would be a good idea to go and have it out with him.'

'I've thought of that, once or twice,' said Jimmy. 'But I guess I'm scared.'

'You'll have to get over that some time if he's going to be your father-in-law!' retorted Gibson. 'Besides, what harm could it do?'

'He might stop Irene seeing me in the time we've still got.'

'Hadfield isn't that sort of man, and if he was he'd have done it long ago.'

Jimmy thought this over and was unable to refute it. To some extent Gibson could understand his feelings, for he remembered his own nervousness at his first meeting with Hadfield. In this he had had much less excuse than Jimmy, for experience had long ago taught him that few great men remain great when one gets up close to them. But to Jimmy, Hadfield was still the aloof and unapproachable master of Mars.

'If I *do* go and see him,' said Jimmy at last, 'what do you think I ought to say?'

'What's wrong with the plain, unvarnished truth? It's been known to work wonders on such occasions.'

Jimmy shot him a slightly hurt look: he was never quite sure whether Gibson was laughing with him or at him. It was Gibson's own fault, and was the chief obstacle to their complete understanding.

'Look,' said Gibson. 'Come along with me to the Chief's house tonight, and have it out with him. After all, look at it from his point of view. For all he can tell, it may be just an ordinary flirtation with neither side taking it very seriously. But if you go and tell him you want to get engaged – then it's a different matter.'

He was much relieved when Jimmy agreed with no more argument. After all, if the boy had anything in him he should make these decisions himself, without any prompting. Gibson was sensible enough to realize that, in his anxiety to be helpful, he must not run the risk of destroying Jimmy's self-reliance.

It was one of Hadfield's virtues that one always knew where to find him at any given time – though woe betide anyone who bothered him with routine official matters during the few hours when he considered himself off duty. This matter was neither routine nor official; and it was not, as Gibson had guessed, entirely unexpected either, for Hadfield had shown no surprise at all when he saw who Gibson had brought with him. There was no sign of Irene: she had thoughtfully effaced herself. As soon as possible, Gibson did the same.

He was waiting in the library, running through Hadfield's books and wondering how many of them the Chief had actually had time to read, when Jimmy came in.

'Mr Hadfield would like to see you,' he said.

'How did you get on?'

'I don't know yet, but it wasn't so bad as I'd expected.'

'It never is. And don't worry. I'll give you the best reference I can without actual perjury.'

When Gibson entered the study, he found Hadfield sunk in one of the armchairs, staring at the carpet as though he had never seen it before in his life. He motioned his visitor to take the other chair.

'How long have you known Spencer?' he asked.

'Only since leaving Earth. I'd never met him before boarding the *Ares*.'

'And do you think that's long enough to form a clear opinion of his character?'

'Is a lifetime long enough to do that?' countered Gibson.

Hadfield smiled, and looked up for the first time.

'Don't evade the issue,' he said, though without irritation. 'What do you really think about him? Would *you* be willing to accept him as a son-in-law?'

'Yes,' said Gibson, without hesitation. 'I'd be glad to.'

It was just as well that Jimmy could not overhear their conversation in the next ten minutes – though in other ways, perhaps, it was rather a pity, for it would have given him much more insight into Gibson's feelings. In his carefully probing cross-examination, Hadfield was trying to learn all he could about Jimmy, but he was testing Gibson as well. This was something that Gibson should have anticipated: the fact that he had overlooked it in serving Jimmy's interests was no small matter to his credit. When Hadfield's interrogation suddenly switched its point of attack, he was totally unprepared for it.

313

'Tell me, Gibson,' said Hadfield abruptly. 'Why are you taking all this trouble for young Spencer? You say you only met him five months ago.'

'That's perfectly true. But when we were a few weeks out I discovered that I'd known both his parents very well – we were all at college together.'

It had slipped out before he could stop it. Hadfield's eyebrows went up slightly: no doubt he was wondering why Gibson had never taken his degree. But he was far too tactful to pursue this subject, and merely asked a few casual questions about Jimmy's parents, and when he had known them.

At least, they seemed casual questions – just the kind Hadfield might have been expected to ask, and Gibson answered them innocently enough. He had forgotten that he was dealing with one of the keenest minds in the Solar System, one at least as good as his own at analysing the springs and motives of human conduct. When he realized what had happened, it was already too late.

'I'm sorry,' said Hadfield, with deceptive smoothness, 'but this whole story of yours simply lacks conviction. I don't say that what you've told me isn't the truth. It's perfectly possible that you might take such an interest in Spencer because you knew his parents very well twenty years ago. But you've tried to explain away too much, and it's quite obvious that the whole affair touches you at an altogether deeper level.' He leaned forward suddenly and stabbed at Gibson with his finger.

'I'm not a fool, Gibson, and men's minds are my business. You've no need to answer this if you don't want to, but I think you owe it to me now. *Jimmy Spencer is your son, isn't he?*'

The bomb had dropped: the explosion was over. And in the silence that followed Gibson's only emotion was one of overwhelming relief.

'Yes,' he said. 'He is my son. How did you guess?'

Hadfield smiled: he looked somewhat pleased with himself, as if he had just settled a question that had been bothering him for some time.

'It's extraordinary how blind men can be to the effects of their own actions – and how easily they assume that no one else has any powers of observation. There's a slight but distinct likeness between you and Spencer: when I first met you together I wondered if you were related and was quite surprised when I heard you weren't.'

'It's very curious,' interjected Gibson, 'that we were together in the *Ares* for three months, and no one noticed it there.'

'Is it so curious? Spencer's crew-mates thought they knew his background, and it never occurred to them to associate it with you. That probably blinded them to the resemblance which I – who hadn't any preconceived ideas – spotted at once. But I'd have dismissed it as pure coincidence if you hadn't told me your story. That provided the missing clues. Tell me – does Spencer know this?'

'I'm sure he doesn't even suspect it.'

'Why are you so sure? And why haven't you told him?'

The cross-examination was ruthless, but Gibson did not resent it. No one had a better right than Hadfield to ask these questions. And Gibson needed someone in whom to confide – just as Jimmy had needed him, back in the *Ares* when this uncovering of the past had first begun. To think that he had started it all himself! He had certainly never dreamed where it would lead ...

'I think I'd better go back to the beginning,' said Gibson shifting uneasily in his chair. 'When I left college I had a complete breakdown and was in hospital for over a year. After I came out I'd lost all contact with my Cambridge friends: though a few tried to keep in touch with me, I didn't want to be reminded of the past. Eventually, of course, I ran into some of them again, but it wasn't until several years later that I heard what had happened to Kathleen – to Jimmy's mother. By then, she was already dead.'

He paused, still remembering, across all these years, the puzzled wonder he had felt because the news had brought him so little emotion.

'I heard there was a son, and thought little of it. We'd always been – well, careful, or so we believed – and I just assumed that the boy was Gerald's. You see, I didn't know when they were married, or when Jimmy was born. I just wanted to forget the whole business, and pushed it out of my mind. I can't even remember now if it even occurred to me that the boy might have been mine. You may find it hard to believe this, but it's the truth.

'And then I met Jimmy, and that brought it all back again. I felt sorry for him at first, and then began to get fond of him. But I never guessed who he was. I even found myself trying to trace his resemblance to Gerald – though I can hardly remember him now.'

Poor Gerald! He, of course, had known the truth well enough, but he had loved Kathleen and had been glad to marry her on any terms he could. Perhaps he was to be pitied as much as she, but that was something that now would never be known.

'And when,' persisted Hadfield, 'did you discover the truth?'

'Only a few weeks ago, when Jimmy asked me to witness some official document he had to fill in – it was his application to start work here, in fact. That was when I first learned his date of birth.'

'I see,' said Hadfield thoughtfully. 'But even that doesn't give absolute proof, does it?'

'I'm perfectly sure,' Gibson replied with such obvious pique that Hadfield could not help smiling, 'that there was no one else. Even if I'd had any doubts left, you've dispelled them yourself.'

'And Spencer?' asked Hadfield, going back to his original question. 'You've not told me why you're so confident he knows nothing. Why shouldn't he have checked a few dates? His parents' wedding day, for example? Surely what you've told him must have roused his suspicions?'

'I don't think so,' said Gibson slowly, choosing his words with the delicate precision of a cat walking over a wet roadway. 'You see, he rather idealizes his mother, and though he may guess I haven't told him everything, I don't believe he's jumped to the right conclusion. He's not the sort who could have kept quiet about it if he had. And besides, he'd still have no proof even if he knows when his parents were married – which is more than most people do. No, I'm sure Jimmy doesn't know, and I'm afraid it will be rather a shock to him when he finds out.'

Hadfield was silent: Gibson could not even guess what he was thinking. It was not a very creditable story, but at least he had shown the virtue of frankness.

Then Hadfield shrugged his shoulders in a gesture that seemed to hold a lifetime's study of human nature.

'He likes you,' he said. 'He'll get over it all right.'

Gibson relaxed with a sigh of relief. He knew that the worst was past.

'Gosh, you've been a long time,' said Jimmy. 'I thought you were never going to finish; what happened?'

Gibson took him by the arm.

'Don't worry,' he said. 'It's quite all right. Everything's going to be all right now.'

He hoped and believed he was telling the truth. Hadfield had been sensible, which was more than some fathers would have been even in this day and age.

'I'm not particularly concerned,' he said, 'who Spencer's parents were or were not. This isn't the Victorian era. I'm only interested in the fellow himself, and I must say I'm favourably impressed. I've also had quite a chat about him with Captain Norden, by the way, so I'm not relying merely on tonight's interview. Oh yes, I saw all this coming a long time ago! There was even a certain inevitability about it, since there are very few youngsters of Spencer's age on Mars.'

He spread his hands in front of him – in a habit which Gibson had noticed before – and stared intently at his fingers as if seeing them for the first time in his life.

'The engagement can be announced tomorrow,' he said softly. 'And now – what about *your* side of the affair?' He stared keenly at Gibson, who returned his gaze without flinching.

'I want to do whatever is best for Jimmy,' he said. 'Just as soon as I can decide what that is.'

'And you still want to stay on Mars?' asked Hadfield.

'I'd thought of that aspect of it too,' said Gibson. 'But if I went back to Earth, what good would that do? Jimmy'll never be there more than a few months at a time – in fact, from now on I'll see a lot more of him if I stay on Mars!'

'Yes, I suppose that's true enough,' said Hadfield with a smile. 'How Irene's going to enjoy having a husband who spends half his life in space remains to be seen – but then, sailors' wives have managed to put up with this sort of thing for quite a long time.' He paused abruptly.

'Do you know what I think you ought to do?' he said.

'I'd be very glad of your views,' Gibson replied with feeling.

'Do nothing until the engagement's over and the whole thing's settled. If you revealed your identity now I don't see what good it

317

would do, and it might conceivably cause harm. Later, though, you must tell Jimmy who you are – or who he is, whichever way you like to look at it. But I don't think the right moment will come for quite a while.'

It was the first time that Hadfield had referred to Spencer by his Christian name. He was probably not even conscious of it, but to Gibson it was a clear and unmistakable sign that he was already thinking of Jimmy as his son-in-law. The knowledge brought him a sudden sense of kinship and sympathy towards Hadfield. They were united in selfless dedication towards the same purpose – the happiness of the two children in whom they saw their own youth reborn.

Looking back upon it later, Gibson was to identify this moment with the beginning of his friendship with Hadfield – the first man to whom he was ever able to give his unreserved admiration and respect. It was a friendship that was to play a greater part in the future of Mars than either could have guessed.

Fifteen

It had opened just like any other day in Port Lowell. Jimmy and Gibson had breakfasted quietly together – very quietly, for they were both deeply engrossed with their personal problems. Jimmy was still in what could best be described as an ecstatic condition, though he had occasional fits of depression at the thought of leaving Irene, while Gibson was wondering if Earth had yet made any move regarding his application. Sometimes he was sure the whole thing was a great mistake, and even hoped that the papers had been lost. But he knew he'd have to go through with it, and decided to stir things up at Admin.

He could tell that something was wrong the moment he entered the office. Mrs Smyth, Hadfield's secretary, met him as she always did when he came to see the Chief. Usually she showed him in at once; sometimes she explained that Hadfield was extremely busy, or putting a call through to Earth, and could he come back later? This time she simply said: 'I'm sorry, Mr Hadfield isn't here. He won't be back until tomorrow.'

'Won't be back?' queried Gibson. 'Has he gone to Skia?'

'Oh no,' said Mrs Smyth, wavering slightly but obviously on the defensive. 'I'm afraid I can't say. But he'll be back in twenty-four hours.'

Gibson decided to puzzle over this later. He presumed that Mrs Smyth knew all about his affairs, so she could probably answer his question.

'Do you know if there's been any reply yet to my application?' he asked.

Mrs Smyth looked even unhappier.

'I think there has,' she said. 'But it was a personal signal to Mr

Hadfield and I can't discuss it. I expect he'll want to see you about it as soon as he gets back.'

This was most exasperating. It was bad enough not to have a reply, but it was even worse to have one you weren't allowed to see. Gibson felt his patience evaporating.

'Surely there's no reason why you shouldn't tell me about it!' he exclaimed. 'Especially if I'll know tomorrow, anyway.'

'I'm really awfully sorry, Mr Gibson. But I know Mr Hadfield will be most annoyed if I say anything now.'

'Oh, very well,' said Gibson, and went off in a huff.

He decided to relieve his feelings by tackling Mayor Whittaker – always assuming that he was still in the city. He was, and he did not look particularly happy to see Gibson, who settled himself firmly down in the visitor's chair in a way that obviously meant business.

'Look here, Whittaker,' he began. 'I'm a patient man and I think you'll agree I don't often make unreasonable requests.'

As the other showed no signs of making the right reply, Gibson continued hastily:

'There's something very peculiar going on round here and I'm anxious to get to the bottom of it.'

Whittaker sighed. He had been expecting this to happen sooner or later. A pity Gibson couldn't have waited until tomorrow: it wouldn't have mattered then . . .

'What's made you suddenly jump to this conclusion?' he asked.

'Oh, lots of things – and it isn't at all sudden. I've just tried to see Hadfield, and Mrs Smyth told me he's not in the city and then closed up like a clam when I tried to ask a few innocent questions.'

'I can just imagine her doing that!' grinned Whittaker cheerfully.

'If you try the same thing I'll start throwing the furniture around. At least if you can't tell me what's going on, for goodness' sake tell me *why* you can't tell me. It's Project Dawn, isn't it?'

That made Whittaker sit up with a start.

'How did you know?' he asked.

'Never mind; I can be stubborn too.'

'I'm not trying to be stubborn,' said Whittaker plaintively. 'Don't think we like secrecy for the sake of it: it's a confounded nuisance. But suppose you start telling me what you know.'

'Very well, if it'll soften you up. Project Dawn is something to do with that plant genetics place up in the hills where you've been cultivating – what do you call it? – *Oxyfera*. As there seems no point in keeping that quiet, I can only assume it's part of a much bigger plan. I suspect Phobos is mixed up with it, though I can't imagine how. You've managed to keep it so secret that the few people on Mars who know anything about it just won't talk. But you haven't been trying to conceal it from Mars so much as from Earth. Now what have you got to say?'

Whittaker appeared to be not in the least abashed.

'I must compliment you on your – er – perspicacity,' he said. 'You may also be interested to know that a couple of weeks ago I suggested to the Chief that we ought to take you fully into our confidence. But he couldn't make up his mind, and since then things have happened rather more rapidly than anyone expected.'

He doodled absentmindedly on his writing-pad, then came to a decision.

'I won't jump the gun,' he said, 'and I can't tell you what's happening now. But here's a little story that may amuse you. Any resemblance to – ah – real persons and places is quite coincidental.'

'I understand,' grinned Gibson. 'Go on.'

'Let's suppose that in the first rush of interplanetary enthusiasm world A has set up a colony on world B. After some years it finds that this is costing a lot more than it expected, and has given no tangible returns for the money spent. Two factions then arise on the mother world. One, the conservative group, want to close the project down – to cut their losses and get out. The other group, the progressives, want to continue the experiment because they believe that in the long run Man has got to explore and master the material universe, or else he'll simply stagnate on his own world. But this sort of argument is no use with the taxpayers, and the conservatives are beginning to get the upper hand.

'All this, of course, is rather unsettling to the colonists, who are getting more and more independently minded and don't like the idea of being regarded as poor relations living on charity. Still, they don't see any way out – until one day a revolutionary scientific discovery is made. (I should have explained at the beginning that planet B has been attracting the finest brains of A, which is another reason why A is getting annoyed.) This discovery open up almost unlimited prospects for the future of B, but to apply it involves certain risks, as well as the diversion of a good deal of B's limited resources. Still, the plan is put forward – and is promptly turned down by A. There is a protracted tug-of-war behind the scenes, but the home planet is adamant.

'The colonists are then faced with two alternatives. They can force the issue out into the open, and appeal to the public on world A. Obviously they'll be at a great disadvantage, as the men on the spot can shout them down. The other choice is to carry on with the plan without informing Earth – I mean, planet A – and this is what they finally decided to do.

'Of course, there were a lot of other factors involved – political and personal, as well as scientific. It so happened that the leader of the colonists was a man of unusual determination who wasn't scared of anything or anyone, on either of the planets. He had a team of first-class scientists behind him, and they backed him up. So the plan went ahead; but no one knows if it will be successful. I'm sorry I can't tell you the end of the story: you know how these serials always break off at the most exciting place.'

'I think you've told me just about everything,' said Gibson. 'Everything, that is, except one minor detail. I *still* don't know what Project Dawn is.' He rose to go. 'Tomorrow I'm coming back to hear the final instalment of your gripping serial.'

'There won't be any need to do that,' Whittaker replied. He glanced unconsciously at the clock. 'You'll know long before then.'

As he left the Administration Building, Gibson was intercepted by Jimmy.

'I'm supposed to be at work,' he said breathlessly, 'but I had to catch you. Something important's going on.'

'I know,' replied Gibson rather impatiently. 'Project Dawn's coming to the boil, and Hadfield's left town.'

'Oh,' replied Jimmy, a little taken aback. 'I didn't think you'd have heard. But you won't know this, anyway. Irene's very upset. She told me her father said goodbye last night as if – well, as if he mightn't see her again.'

Gibson whistled. That put things in a different light. Project Dawn was not only big: it might be dangerous. This was a possibility he had not considered.

'Whatever's happening,' he said, 'we'll know all about it tomorrow – Whittaker's just told me that. But I think I can guess where Hadfield is right now.'

'Where?'

'He's up on Phobos. For some reason, that's the key to Project Dawn, and that's where you'll find the Chief right now.'

Gibson would have made a large bet on the accuracy of this guess. It was just as well that there was no one to take it, for he was quite wrong. Hadfield was now almost as far away from Phobos as he was from Mars. At the moment he was sitting in some discomfort in a small spaceship, which was packed with scientists and their hastily dismantled equipment. He was playing chess, and playing it very badly, against one of the greatest physicists in the Solar System. His opponent was playing equally badly, and it would soon have become quite obvious to any observer that they were simply trying to pass the time. Like everyone on Mars, they were waiting; but they were the only ones who knew exactly what they were waiting for.

The long day – one of the longest that Gibson had ever known – slowly ebbed away. It was a day of wild rumours and speculation: everyone in Port Lowell had some theory which they were anxious to air. But as those who knew the truth said nothing, and those who knew nothing said too much, when night came the city was in a state of extreme confusion. Gibson wondered if it was worthwhile staying up late, but around midnight he decided to go to bed. He was fast asleep when, invisibly, soundlessly, hidden from him by the thickness of the planet, Project Dawn came to its climax. Only the men in the watching spaceship saw it happen, and changed suddenly from grave scientists to shouting, laughing schoolboys as they turned to race for home.

In the very small hours of the morning Gibson was awakened by a thunderous banging on his door. It was Jimmy, shouting to him to get up and come outside. He dressed hastily, but when he reached the door Jimmy had already gone out into the street. He caught him up at the doorway. From all sides, people were beginning to appear, rubbing their eyes sleepily and wondering what had happened. There was a rising buzz of voices and distant shouts: Port Lowell sounded like a beehive that had been suddenly disturbed.

It was a full minute before Gibson understood what had

awakened the city. Dawn was just breaking: the eastern sky was aglow with the first light of the rising Sun. The eastern sky? *My God, that dawn was breaking in the west.*

No one could have been less superstitious than Gibson, but for a moment the upper levels of his mind were submerged by a wave of irrational terror. It lasted only a moment: then reason reasserted itself. Brighter and brighter grew the light spilling over the horizon: now the first rays were touching the hills above the city. They were moving swiftly – far, far too swiftly for the Sun – and suddenly a blazing, golden meteor leapt up out of the desert, climbing almost vertically towards the zenith.

Its very speed betrayed its identity. This was Phobos – or what had been Phobos a few hours before. Now it was a yellow disc of fire, and Gibson could feel the heat of its burning upon his face. The city around him was now utterly silent, watching the miracle and slowly waking to a dim awareness of all that it might mean to Mars.

So this was Project Dawn: it had been well named. The pieces of the jigsaw puzzle were falling into place, but the main pattern was still not clear. To have turned Phobos into a second sun was an incredible feat of – presumably – nuclear engineering, yet Gibson did not see how it could solve the colony's problems. He was still worrying over this when the seldom used public-address system of Port Lowell burst into life and Whittaker's voice came drifting softly down the streets.

'Hello, everybody,' he said. 'I guess you're all awake by now and have seen what's happened. The Chief Executive's on his way back from space and would like to speak to you. Here he is.'

There was a click; then someone said, *sotto voce*: 'You're on to Port Lowell, sir.' A moment later Hadfield's voice came out of the speakers. He sounded tired but triumphant, like a man who had fought a great battle and won through to victory.

'Hello, Mars,' he said. 'Hadfield speaking. I'm still in space on the way home – I'll be landing in about an hour.

'I hope you like your new sun. According to our calculations, it will take nearly a thousand years to burn itself out. We triggered Phobos off when it was well below your horizon, just in case the initial radiation peak was too high. The reaction's now stabilized at exactly the level we expected, though it may increase by a few per cent during the next week. It's mainly a meson resonance reaction, very efficient but not very violent, and there's no chance of a fully fledged atomic explosion with the material composing Phobos.

'Your new luminary will give you about a tenth of the Sun's heat, which will bring up the temperature of much of Mars to nearly the same value as Earth's. But that isn't the reason why we blew up Phobos – at least, it isn't the main reason.

'Mars wants oxygen more badly than heat – and all the oxygen needed to give it an atmosphere almost as good as Earth's is lying beneath your feet, locked up in the sand. Two years ago we discovered a plant that can break the sand down and release the oxygen. It's a tropical plant – it can exist only on the equator and doesn't really flourish even there. If there was enough sunlight available, it could spread over Mars – with some assistance from us – and in fifty years there'd be an atmosphere here that men could breathe. *That's* the goal we're aiming at: when we've reached it, we can go where we please on Mars and forget about our domed cities and breathing masks. It's a dream that many of you will live to see realized, and it'll mean that we've given a new world to mankind.

'Even now, there are some benefits we'll derive right away. It will be very much warmer, at least when Phobos and the Sun are shining together, and the winters will be much milder. Even though Phobos isn't visible above latitude seventy degrees, the new convection winds will warm the polar regions too, and will prevent our precious moisture from being locked up in the ice caps for half of every year.

'There'll be some disadvantages – the seasons and nights are going to get complicated now! – but they'll be far outweighed by the benefits. And every day, as you see the beacon we have now lit climbing across the sky, it will remind you of the new world we're bringing to birth. We're making history, remember, for this is the first time that Man has tried his hand at changing the face of a planet. If we succeed here, others will do the same elsewhere. In the ages to come, whole civilizations on worlds of which we've never heard will owe their existence to what we've done tonight.

'That's all I've got to say now. Perhaps you may regret the sacrifice we've had to make to bring life to this world again. But remember this – though Mars has lost a moon, it's gained a sun – and who can doubt which is the more valuable?

'And now – goodnight to you all.'

But no one in Port Lowell went back to sleep. As far as the city was concerned, the night was over and the new day had dawned. It was hard to take one's eyes off that tiny golden disc as it climbed steadily up the sky, its warmth growing greater minute by minute. What would the Martian plants be making of it? Gibson wondered. He walked along the street until he came to the nearest section of the dome, and looked out through the transparent wall. It was as he had expected: they had all awakened and turned their faces to the new sun. He wondered just what they would do when both suns were in the sky together . . .

The Chief's rocket landed half an hour later, but Hadfield and the scientists of Project Dawn avoided the crowds by coming into the city on foot through Dome Seven, and sending the transport on to the main entrance as a decoy. This ruse worked so well that they were all safely indoors before anyone realized what had happened, or could start celebrations which they were too tired to appreciate. However, this did not prevent numerous private parties forming all over the city – parties at which everyone tried to claim that they had known what Project Dawn was all the time.

Phobos was approaching the zenith, much nearer and therefore much warmer than it had been on rising, when Gibson and Jimmy met their crew-mates in the crowd that had good-naturedly but firmly insisted to George that he had better open up the bar. Each party claimed it had only homed on this spot because it was sure it would find the other there.

Hilton, who as Chief Engineer might be expected to know more about nucleonics than anyone else in the assembly, was soon pushed to the fore and asked to explain just what had happened. He modestly denied his competence to do anything of the sort.

'What they've done up on Phobos,' he protested, 'is years ahead of anything I ever learned at college. Why, even meson reactions hadn't been discovered then – let alone how to harness them. In fact, I don't think anyone on Earth knows how to do that, even now. It must be something that Mars has learned for itself.'

'Do you mean to tell me,' said Bradley, 'that Mars is ahead of Earth in nuclear physics – or anything else for that matter?'

This remark nearly caused a riot and Bradley's colleagues had to rescue him from the indignant colonists – which they did in a somewhat leisurely fashion. When peace had been restored, Hilton nearly put *his* foot in it by remarking: 'Of course, you know that a lot of Earth's best scientists have been coming here in the last few years, so it's not as surprising as you might think.'

The statement was perfectly true, and Gibson remembered the remark that Whittaker had made to him that very morning. Mars had been a lure to many others besides himself, and now he could understand why. What prodigies of persuasion, what intricate negotiations and downright deceptions, Hadfield must have performed in these last few years! It had, perhaps, been not too difficult to attract the really first-rate minds: they could appreciate the challenge and respond to it. The second-raters, the equally essential rank-and-file of science, would have been harder to find. One day, perhaps, he would learn the secrets behind the secret, and discover just how Project Dawn had been launched and guided to success.

What was left of the night seemed to pass very swiftly. Phobos was dropping down into the eastern sky when the Sun rose up to greet its rival. It was a duel that all the city watched in silent fascination – a one-sided conflict that could have only a pre-determined outcome. When it shone alone in the night sky, it was easy to pretend that Phobos was almost as brilliant as the Sun, but the first light of the true dawn banished the illusion. Minute by minute Phobos faded, though it was still well above the horizon, as the Sun came up out of the desert. Now one could tell how pale and yellow it was by comparison. There was little danger that the slowly turning plants would be confused in their quest for light: when the Sun was shining, one scarcely noticed Phobos at all.

But it was bright enough to perform its task, and for a thousand years it would be the lord of the Martian night. And thereafter? When its fires were extinguished, by the exhaustion of whatever elements it was burning now, would Phobos become again an ordinary moon, shining only by the Sun's reflected glory?

Gibson knew that it would not matter. Even in a century it would have done its work, and Mars would have an atmosphere which it would not lose again for geological ages. When at last Phobos guttered and died, the science of that distant day would have some other answer – perhaps an answer as inconceivable to this age as the detonation of a world would have been only a century ago.

For a little while, as the first day of the new age grew to maturity, Gibson watched his double shadow lying upon the ground. Both shadows pointed to the west, but though one scarcely moved, the fainter lengthened even as he watched, becoming more and more difficult to see, until at last it was snuffed out as Phobos dropped down below the edge of Mars.

Its sudden disappearance reminded Gibson abruptly of something that he – and most of Port Lowell – had forgotten in the last few hours' excitement. By now the news would have reached Earth: perhaps – though he wasn't sure of this – Mars must now be spectacularly brighter in terrestrial skies.

In a very short time, Earth would be asking some extremely pointed questions.

Sixteen

It was one of those little ceremonies so beloved by the TV newsreels. Hadfield and all his staff were gathered in a tight group at the edge of the clearing, with the domes of Port Lowell rising behind them. It was, thought the cameraman, a nicely composed picture, though the constantly changing double illumination made things a little difficult.

He got the cue from the control room and started to pan from left to right to give the viewers a bit of movement before the real business began. Not that there was really much to see: the landscape was so flat and they'd miss all its interest in this monochrome transmission. (One couldn't afford the band-width for colour on a live transmission all the way to Earth: even on black-and-white it was none too easy.) He had just finished exploring the scene when he got the order to swing back to Hadfield, who was now making a little speech. That was going out on the other sound channel and he couldn't hear it, though in the control room it would be mated to the picture he was sending. Anyway, he knew just what the Chief would be saying – he'd heard it all before.

Mayor Whittaker handed over the shovel on which he had been gracefully leaning for the last five minutes, and Hadfield began to tip in the sand until he had covered the roots of the tall, drab Martian plant standing there, held upright in its wooden frame. The 'airweed', as it was now universally called, was not a very impressive object: it scarcely looked strong enough to stand upright, even under this low gravity. It certainly didn't look as if it could control the future of a planet . . .

Hadfield had finished his token gardening: someone else could complete the job and fill in the hole. (The planting team was already hovering in the background, waiting for the bigwigs to clear out of the way so that they could get on with their work.) There was a lot of handshaking and back-slapping: Hadfield was hidden by the crowd that had gathered round him. The only person who wasn't taking the slightest notice of all this was Gibson's pet Martian, who was rocking on his haunches like one of those weighted dolls that always come the same way up however you put them down. The cameraman swung towards him and zoomed to a close-up: it would be the first time anyone on Earth would have seen a real Martian – at least in a live programme like this.

Hello – what was he up to? Something had caught his interest – the twitching of those huge, membranous ears gave him away. He was beginning to move in short, cautious hops. The cameraman chased him and widened the field at the same time to see where he was going. No one else had noticed that he'd begun to move: Gibson was still talking to Whittaker and seemed to have completely forgotten his pet.

So *that* was the game! This was going to be good: the folk back on Earth would love it. Would he get there before he was spotted? Yes – he'd made it! With one final bound he hopped down into the little pit, and the small triangular beak began to nibble at the slim Martian plant that had just been placed there with such care. No doubt he thought it so kind of his friends to go to all this trouble for him . . . Or did he really know he was being naughty? That devious approach had been so skilful that it was hard to believe it was done in complete innocence. Anyway, the cameraman wasn't going to spoil his fun: it would make too good a picture. He cut for a moment back to Hadfield and Company, still congratulating themselves on the work which Squeak was rapidly undoing.

It was too good to last. Gibson spotted what was happening and gave a great yell which made everyone jump. Then he raced towards Squeak, who did a quick look round, decided that there was nowhere to hide, and just sat still with an air of injured innocence. He let himself be led away quietly, not aggravating his offence by resisting the forces of the law when Gibson grabbed one of his ears and tugged him away from the scene of the crime. A group of experts then gathered anxiously around the airweed, and to everyone's relief it was soon decided that the damage was not fatal.

It was a trivial incident, which no one would have imagined to have any consequences beyond the immediate moment. Yet, though he never realized the fact, it was to inspire one of Gibson's most brilliant and fruitful ideas.

Life for Martin Gibson had suddenly become very complicated – and intensely interesting. He had been one of the first to see Hadfield after the inception of Project Dawn. The CE had called for him, but had been able to give him only a few minutes of his time. That, however, had been enough to change the pattern of Gibson's future.

'I'm sorry I had to keep you waiting,' Hadfield said, 'but I got the reply from Earth only just before I left. The answer is that you can stay here if you can be absorbed into our administrative structure – to use the official jargon. As the future of our "administrative structure" depended somewhat largely on Project Dawn, I thought it best to leave the matter until I got back home.'

The weight of uncertainty had lifted from Gibson's mind. It was all settled now: even if he had made a mistake – and he did not believe he had – there was now no going back. He had thrown in his lot with Mars: he would be part of the colony in its fight to regenerate this world that was now stirring sluggishly in its sleep.

'And what job have you got for me?' Gibson asked a little anxiously.

'I've decided to regularize your unofficial status,' said Hadfield, with a smile.

'What do you mean?'

'Do you remember what I said at our very first meeting? I asked you to help us by giving Earth, not the mere facts of the situation, but also some idea of our goals and – I suppose you could call it – the spirit we've built up here on Mars. You've done well, despite the fact that you didn't know about the project on which we'd set our greatest hopes. I'm sorry I had to keep Dawn from you, but it would have made your job much harder if you'd known our secret and weren't able to say anything. Don't you agree?'

Gibson had not thought of it in that light, but it certainly made sense.

'I've been very interested,' Hadfield continued, 'to see what result your broadcasts and articles have had. You may not know that we've got a delicate method of testing this.'

'How?' asked Gibson in surprise.

'Can't you guess? Every week about ten thousand people, scattered all over Earth, decide they want to come here, and something like three per cent pass the preliminary tests. Since your articles started appearing regularly, that figure's gone up to fifteen thousand a week, and it's still rising.'

'Oh,' said Gibson, very thoughtfully. He gave an abrupt little laugh. 'I also seem to remember,' he added, 'that you didn't want me to come here in the first place.'

'We all make mistakes, but I've learned to profit by mine,' smiled Hadfield. 'To sum it all up, what I'd like you to do is to lead a small section which, frankly, will be our propaganda department. Of course, we'll think of a nicer name for it! Your job will be to sell Mars. The opportunities are far greater now that we've really got something to put in our shop window. If we can get enough people clamouring to come here, then Earth will be forced to provide the shipping space. And the quicker that's done, the sooner we can promise Earth we'll be standing on our own feet. What do you say?'

Gibson felt a fleeting disappointment. Looked at from one point of view, this wasn't much of a change. But the CE was right: he could be of greater use to Mars in this way than in any other.

'I can do it,' he said. 'Give me a week to sort out my terrestrial affairs and clear up my outstanding commitments.'

A week was somewhat optimistic, he thought, but that should break the back of the job. He wondered what Ruth was going to say. She'd probably think he was mad, and she'd probably be right.

'The news that you're going to stay here,' said Hadfield with satisfaction, 'will cause a lot of interest and will be quite a boost to our campaign. You've no objection to us announcing it right away?'

'I don't think so.'

'Good. Whittaker would like to have a word with you now about the detailed arrangements. You realize, of course, that your salary will be that of a Class II Administrative Officer of your age?'

'Naturally I've looked into that,' said Gibson. He did not add, because it was unnecessary, that this was largely of theoretical interest. His salary on Mars, though less than a tenth of his total income, would be quite adequate for a comfortable standard of living on a planet where there were very few luxuries. He was not sure just how he could use his terrestrial credits, but no doubt they could be employed to squeeze something through the shipping bottleneck.

After a long session with Whittaker – who nearly succeeded in destroying his enthusiasm with laments about lack of staff and accommodation – Gibson spent the rest of the day writing dozens of radiograms. The longest was to Ruth, and was chiefly but by no means wholly, concerned with business affairs. Ruth had often commented on the startling variety of things she did for her ten per cent, and Gibson wondered what she was going to say to this request that she keep an eye on one James Spencer, and generally look after him when he was in New York – which, since he was completing his studies at MIT, might be fairly often.

It would have made matters much simpler if he could have told her the facts: she would probably guess them, anyway. But that would be unfair to Jimmy: Gibson had made up his mind that he would be the first to know. There were times when the strain of not telling him was so great that he felt almost glad they would soon be parting. Yet Hadfield, as usual, had been right. He had waited a generation: he must wait a little longer yet. To reveal himself now might leave Jimmy confused and hurt – might even cause the breakdown of his engagement to Irene. The time to tell him would be when they had been married and, Gibson hoped, were still insulated from any shocks which the outside world might administer.

It was ironic that, having found his son so late, he must now lose him again. Perhaps that was part of the punishment for the selfishness and lack of courage – to put it no more strongly – he had shown twenty years ago. But the past must bury itself; he must think of the future now.

Jimmy would return to Mars as soon as he could – there was no doubt of that. And even if he had missed the pride and satisfaction of parenthood, there might be compensations later in watching his grandchildren come into the world he was helping to remake. For the first time in his life, Gibson had a future to which he could look forward with interest and excitement – a future which would not be merely a repetition of the past.

Earth hurled its thunderbolt four days later. The first Gibson knew about it was when he saw the headline across the front page of the *Martian Times*. For a moment the two words staring back at him were so astounding that he forgot to read on.

HADFIELD RECALLED

We have just received news that the Interplanetary Development Board has requested the Chief Executive to return to Earth on the *Ares*, which leaves Deimos in four days. No reason is given.

That was all, but it would set Mars ablaze. No reason was given – and none was necessary. Everyone knew exactly why Earth wanted to see Warren Hadfield.

'What do you think of this?' Gibson asked Jimmy as he passed the paper across the breakfast-table.

'Good Lord!' gasped Jimmy. 'There'll be trouble now! What do you think he'll do?'

'What can he do?'

'Well, he can refuse to go. Everyone here would certainly back him up.'

'That would only make matters worse. He'll go, all right. Hadfield isn't the sort of man to run away from a fight.'

Jimmy's eyes suddenly brightened.

'That means that Irene will be going too.'

'Trust you to think of that!' laughed Gibson, 'I suppose you hope it will be an ill wind blowing the pair of you some good. But don't count on it – Hadfield *might* leave Irene behind.'

He thought this very unlikely. When the Chief returned, he would need all the moral support he could get.

Despite the amount of work he had awaiting him, Gibson paid one brief call to Admin, where he found everyone in a state of mingled indignation and suspense. Indignation because of Earth's cavalier treatment of the Chief: suspense because no one yet knew what action he was going to take. Hadfield had arrived early that morning, and so far had not seen anyone except Whittaker and his private secretary. Those who had caught a glimpse of him stated that for a man who was, technically, about to be recalled in disgrace, he looked remarkably cheerful.

Gibson was thinking over this news as he made a detour towards the Biology Lab. He had missed seeing his little Martian friend for two days, and felt rather guilty about it. As he walked slowly along Regent Street, he wondered what sort of defence Hadfield would be able to put up. Now he understood that remark that Jimmy had overheard. *Would* success excuse everything? Success was still a long way off: as Hadfield had said, to bring Project Dawn to its conclusion would take half a century, even assuming the maximum assistance from Earth. It was essential to secure that support, and Hadfield would do his utmost not to antagonize the home planet. The best that Gibson could do to support him would be to provide long-range covering fire from his propaganda department.

Squeak, as usual, was delighted to see him, though Gibson returned his greeting somewhat absentmindedly. As he invariably did, he proffered Squeak a fragment of airweed from the supply kept in the Lab. That simple action must have triggered something in his subconscious mind, for he suddenly paused, then turned to the chief biologist.

'I've just had a wonderful idea,' he said. 'You know you were telling me about the tricks you've been able to teach Squeak?'

'Teach him! The problem now is to stop him learning them!'

'You also said you were fairly sure the Martians could communicate with each other, didn't you?'

'Well, our field party's proved that they can pass on simple thoughts, and even some abstract ideas like colour. That doesn't prove much, of course. Bees can do the same.'

'Then tell me what you think of this. Why shouldn't we teach them to cultivate the airweed for us? You see what a colossal advantage they've got – they can go anywhere on Mars they please, while we'd have to do everything with machines. They needn't *know* what they're doing, of course. We'd simply provide them with the shoots – it does propagate that way, doesn't it? – teach them the necessary routine, and reward them afterwards.'

'Just a moment! It's a pretty idea, but haven't you overlooked some practical points? I think we could train them in the way you suggest – we've certainly learned enough about their psychology for that – but may I point out that there are only ten known specimens, including Squeak?'

335

'I hadn't overlooked that,' said Gibson impatiently. 'I simply don't believe the group I found is the only one in existence. That would be a quite incredible coincidence. Certainly they're rather rare, but there must be hundreds, if not thousands, of them over the planet. I'm going to suggest a photo-reconnaissance of all the airweed forests – we should have no difficulty in spotting their clearings. But in any case I'm taking the long-term view. Now that they've got far more favourable living conditions they'll start to multiply rapidly, just as the Martian plant life's already doing. Remember, even if we left it to itself the airweed would cover the equatorial regions in four hundred years – according to your own figures. With the Martians *and* us to help it spread, we might cut years off Project Dawn!'

The biologist shook his head doubtfully, but began to do some calculations on a scribbling pad. When he had finished he pursed his lips.

'Well,' he said, 'I can't actually prove it's impossible: there are too many unknown factors – including the most important one of all – the Martians' reproduction rate. Incidentally, I suppose you know that they're marsupials? That's just been confirmed.'

'You mean like kangaroos?'

'Yes: Junior lives under cover until he's a big enough boy to go out into the cold, hard world. We think several of the females are carrying babies, so they may reproduce yearly. And since Squeak was the only infant we found, that means they must have a terrifically high death-rate – which isn't surprising in this climate.'

'Just the conditions we want!' exclaimed Gibson. 'Now there'll be nothing to stop them multiplying, provided we see they get all the food they need.'

'Do you want to breed Martians or cultivate airweed?' challenged the biologist.

'Both,' grinned Gibson. 'They go together like fish and chips, or ham and eggs.'

'Don't!' pleaded the other, with such a depth of feeling that Gibson apologized at once for his lack of tact. He had forgotten that no one on Mars had tasted such things for years.

The more Gibson thought about his new idea, the more it appealed to him. Despite the pressure of his personal affairs, he found time to write a memorandum to Hadfield on the subject, and hoped that the CE would be able to discuss it with him before returning to Earth. There was something inspiring in the thought of regenerating not only a world, but also a race which might be older than man.

Gibson wondered how the changed climatic conditions of a hundred years hence would affect the Martians. If it became too warm for them, they could easily migrate north or south – if necessary into the sub-polar regions where Phobos was never visible. As for the oxygenated atmosphere – they had been used to that in the past and might adapt themselves to it again. There was considerable evidence that Squeak now obtained much of his oxygen from the air in Port Lowell, and seemed to be thriving on it.

There was still no answer to the great question which the discovery of the Martians had raised. Were they the degenerate survivors of a race which had achieved civilization long ago, and let it slip from its grasp when conditions became too severe? This was the romantic view, for which there was no evidence at all. The scientists were unanimous in believing that there had never been any advanced culture on Mars – but they had been proved wrong once and might be so again. In any case, it would be an extremely interesting experiment to see how far up the evolutionary ladder the Martians would climb, now that their world was blossoming again.

For it was their world, not Man's. However he might shape it for his own purposes, it would be his duty always to safeguard the interests of its rightful owners. No one could tell what part they might have to play in the history of the universe. And when, as was one day inevitable, Man himself came to the notice of yet higher races, he might well be judged by his behaviour here on Mars.

Seventeen

'I'm sorry you're not coming back with us, Martin,' said Norden as they approached Lock One West, 'but I'm sure you're doing the right thing, and we all respect you for it.'

'Thanks,' said Gibson sincerely. 'I'd like to have made the return trip with you all – still, there'll be plenty of chances later! Whatever happens, I'm not going to be on Mars *all* my life!' He chuckled. 'I guess you never thought you'd be swapping passengers in this way.'

'I certainly didn't. It's going to be a bit embarrassing in some respects. I'll feel like the captain of the ship who had to carry Napoleon to Elba. How's the Chief taking it?'

'I've not spoken to him since the recall came through, though I'll be seeing him tomorrow before he goes up to Deimos. But Whittaker says he seems confident enough, and doesn't appear to be worrying in the slightest.'

'What do *you* think's going to happen?'

'On the official level, he's bound to be reprimanded for misappropriation of funds, equipment, personnel – oh, enough things to land him in jail for the rest of his life. But as half the executives and all the scientists on Mars are involved, what can Earth do about it? It's really a very amusing situation. The CE's a public hero on two worlds, and the Interplanetary Development Board will have to handle him with kid gloves. I think the verdict will be: "You shouldn't have done it, but we're rather glad you did."'

'And then they'll let him come back to Mars?'

'They're bound to. No one else can do his job.'

'Someone will have to, one day.'

'True enough, but it would be madness to waste Hadfield when he's still got years of work in him. And Heaven help anyone who was sent here to replace him!'

'It certainly *is* a peculiar position. I think a lot's been going on that we don't know about. Why did Earth turn down Project Dawn when it was first suggested?'

'I've been wondering about that, and intend to get to the bottom of it some day. Meanwhile my theory is this – I think a lot of people on Earth don't want Mars to become too powerful, still less completely independent. Not for any sinister reason, mark you, but simply because they don't like the idea. It's too wounding to their pride. They want the Earth to remain the centre of the universe.'

'You know,' said Norden, 'it's funny how you talk about "Earth" as if it were some combination of miser and bully, preventing all progress here. After all, it's hardly fair! What you're actually grumbling at are the administrators in the Interplanetary Development Board and all its allied organizations – and they're really trying to do their best. Don't forget that everything you've got here is due to the enterprise and initiative of Earth. I'm afraid you colonists' – he gave a wry grin as he spoke – 'take a very self-centred view of things. I can see both sides of the question. When I'm here I get your point of view and can sympathize with it. But in three months' time I'll be on the other side and will probably think you're a lot of grumbling, ungrateful nuisances here on Mars!'

Gibson laughed, not altogether comfortably. There was a good deal of truth in what Norden had said. The sheer difficulty and expense of interplanetary travel, and the time it took to get from world to world, made inevitable some lack of understanding, even intolerance, between Earth and Mars. He hoped that as the speed of transport increased these psychological barriers would be broken down and the two planets would come closer together in spirit as well as in time.

They had now reached the lock and were waiting for the transport to take Norden out to the airstrip. The rest of the crew had already said goodbye and were now on their way up to Deimos. Only Jimmy had received special dispensation to fly up with Hadfield and Irene when they left tomorrow. Jimmy had certainly changed his status, thought Gibson with some amusement, since the *Ares* had left Earth. He wondered just how much work Norden was going to get out of him on the homeward voyage.

'Well, John, I hope you have a good trip back,' said Gibson, holding out his hand as the airlock door opened. 'When will I be seeing you again?'

'In about eighteen months – I've got a trip to Venus to put in first. When I get back here, I expect to find quite a difference – airweed and Martians everywhere!'

'I don't promise much in that time,' laughed Gibson. 'But we'll do our best not to disappoint you!'

They shook hands, and Norden was gone. Gibson found it impossible not to feel a twinge of envy as he thought of all the things to which the other was returning – all the unconsidered beauties of Earth which he had once taken for granted, and now might not see again for many years.

He still had two farewells to make, and they would be the most difficult of all. His last meeting with Hadfield would require considerable delicacy and tact. Norden's analogy, he thought, had been a good one: it would be rather like an interview with a dethroned monarch about to sail into exile.

In actual fact it proved to be like nothing of the sort. Hadfield was still master of the situation, and seemed quite unperturbed by his future. When Gibson entered he had just finished sorting out his papers: the room looked bare and bleak and three waste-paper baskets were piled high with discarded forms and memoranda. Whittaker, as acting Chief Executive, would be moving in tomorrow.

'I've run through your note on the Martians and the airweed,' said Hadfield, exploring the deeper recesses of his desk. 'It's a very interesting idea, but no one can tell me whether it will work or not. The position's extremely complicated and we haven't enough information. It really comes down to this – would we get a better return for our efforts if we teach Martians to plant airweed, or if we do the job ourselves? Anyway, we'll set up a small research group to look into the idea, though there's not much we can do until we've got some more Martians! I've asked Dr Petersen to handle the scientific side, and I'd like you to deal with the administrative problems as they arise – leaving any major decisions to Whittaker, of course. Petersen's a very sound fellow, but he lacks imagination. Between the two of you, we should get the right balance.'

'I'll be very glad to do all I can,' said Gibson, quite pleased with the prospect, though wondering a little nervously how he would cope with his increasing responsibilities. However, the fact that the Chief had given him the job was encouraging: it meant that Hadfield, at any rate, was sure that he could handle it.

As they discussed administrative details, it became clear to Gibson that Hadfield did not expect to be away from Mars for more than a year. He even seemed to be looking forward to his trip to Earth, regarding it almost in the light of an overdue holiday. Gibson hoped that this optimism would be justified by the outcome.

Towards the end of their interview, the conversation turned inevitably to Irene and Jimmy. The long voyage back to Earth would provide Hadfield with all the opportunities he needed to study his prospective son-in-law, and Gibson hoped that Jimmy would be on his best behaviour. It was obvious that Hadfield was contemplating this aspect of the trip with quiet amusement. As he remarked to Gibson, if Irene and Jimmy could put up with each other in such close quarters for three months, their marriage was bound to be a success. If they couldn't – then the sooner they found out, the better.

As he left Hadfield's office, Gibson hoped that he had made his own sympathy clear. The CE knew that he had all Mars behind him, and Gibson would do his best to gain him the support of Earth as well. He looked back at the unobtrusive lettering on the door. There would be no need to change that, whatever happened, since the words designated the position and not the man. For twelve months or so Whittaker would be working behind that door, the democratic ruler of Mars and the – within reasonable limits – conscientious servant of Earth. Whoever came and went, the lettering on the door would remain. That was another of Hadfield's ideas – the tradition that the post was more important than the man. He had not, Gibson thought, given it a very good start, for anonymity was scarcely one of Hadfield's personal characteristics.

The last rocket to Deimos left three hours later with Hadfield, Irene, and Jimmy aboard. Irene had come round to the Grand Martian Hotel to help Jimmy pack and to say goodbye to Gibson. She was bubbling over with excitement and so radiant with happiness that it was a pleasure simply to sit and watch her. Both her dreams had come true at once: she was going back to Earth, and she was going with Jimmy. Gibson hoped that neither experience would disappoint her: he did not believe it would.

Jimmy's packing was complicated by the number of souvenirs he had gathered on Mars – chiefly plant and mineral specimens collected on various trips outside the domes. All these had to be carefully weighed, and some heartrending decisions were involved when it was discovered that he had exceeded his personal allowance by two kilogrammes. But finally the last suitcase was packed and on its way to the airport.

'Now don't forget,' said Gibson, 'to contact Mrs Goldstein as soon as you arrive: she'll be expecting to hear from you.'

'I won't,' Jimmy replied. 'It's good of you to take all this trouble. We really do appreciate everything you've done – don't we, Irene?'

'Yes,' she answered, 'we certainly do. I don't know how we'd have got on without you.'

Gibson smiled, a little wistfully.

'Somehow,' he said, 'I think you'd still have managed in one way or another! But I'm glad everything's turned out so well for you, and I'm sure you're going to be very happy. And – I hope it won't be too long before you're both back on Mars.'

As he gripped Jimmy's hand in farewell, Gibson felt once again that almost overwhelming desire to reveal his identity and, whatever the consequences, to greet Jimmy as his son. But if he did so, he knew now, the dominant motive would be pure egotism. It would be an act of possessiveness, of inexcusable self-assertion, and it would undo all the good he had wrought in these past months. Yet as he dropped Jimmy's hand, he glimpsed something in the other's expression that he had never seen before. It could have been the dawn of the first puzzled surmise, the birth of the still half-conscious thought that might grow at last to fully fledged understanding and recognition. Gibson hoped it was so: it would make his task easier when the time came.

He watched them go hand-in-hand down the narrow street, oblivious to all around them, their thoughts even now winging onwards into space. Already they had forgotten him; but, later, they would remember.

It was just before dawn when Gibson left the main airlock and walked away from the still sleeping city. Phobos had set an hour ago; the only light was that of the stars and Deimos, now high in the west. He looked at his watch – ten minutes to go if there had been no hitch.

'Come on, Squeak,' he said. 'Let's take a nice brisk walk to keep warm.' Though the temperature around them was at least fifty below, Squeak did not seem unduly worried. However, Gibson thought it best to keep his pet on the move. He was, of course, perfectly comfortable himself, as he was wearing his full protective clothing.

How these plants had grown in the past few weeks! They were now taller than a man, and though some of this increase might be normal, Gibson was sure that much of it was due to Phobos. Project Dawn was already leaving its mark on the planet. Even the north polar cap, which should now be approaching its mid-winter maximum, had halted in its advance over the opposite hemisphere – and the remnants of the southern cap had vanished completely.

They came to a stop about a kilometre from the city, far enough away for its lights not to hinder observation. Gibson glanced again at his watch. Less than a minute left: he knew what his friends were feeling now. He stared at the tiny, barely visible gibbous disc of Deimos, and waited.

Quite suddenly, Deimos became conspicuously brighter. A moment later it seemed to split into two fragments as a tiny, incredibly bright star detached itself from its edge and began to creep slowly westwards. Even across these thousands of kilometres of space, the glare of the atomic rockets was so dazzling that it almost hurt the eye.

He did not doubt that they were watching him. Up there in the *Ares*, they would be at the observation windows, looking down upon the great crescent world which they were leaving now, as a lifetime ago, it seemed, he had bade farewell to Earth.

What was Hadfield thinking now? Was he wondering if he would ever see Mars again? Gibson no longer had any real doubts on this score. Whatever battles Hadfield might have to face, he would win through as he had done in the past. He was returning to Earth in triumph, not in disgrace.

That dazzling blue-white star was several degrees from Deimos now, falling behind as it lost speed to drop Sunwards – and Earthwards.

The rim of the Sun came up over the eastern horizon; all around him, the tall green plants were stirring in their sleep – a sleep already interrupted once by the meteoric passage of Phobos across the sky. Gibson looked once more at the two stars descending in the west, and raised his hand in a silent farewell.

'Come along, Squeak,' he said. 'Time to get back – I've got work to do.' He tweaked the little Martian's ears with his gloved fingers.

'And that goes for you too,' he added. 'Though you don't know it yet, we've both got a pretty big job ahead of us.'

They walked together towards the great domes, now glistening faintly in the first morning light. It would be strange in Port Lowell, now that Hadfield had gone and another man was sitting behind the door marked 'Chief Executive'.

Gibson suddenly paused. For a fleeting moment, it seemed, he saw into the future, fifteen or twenty years ahead. Who would be Chief then, when Project Dawn was entering its middle phase and its end could already be foreseen?

The question and the answer came almost simultaneously. For the first time, Gibson knew what lay at the end of the road on which he had now set his feet. One day, perhaps, it would be his duty, and his privilege, to take over the work which Hadfield had begun. It might have been sheer self-deception, or it might have been the first consciousness of his own still hidden powers – but whichever it was, he meant to know.

With a new briskness in his step, Martin Gibson, writer, late of Earth, resumed his walk towards the city. His shadow merged with Squeak's as the little Martian hopped beside him; while overhead the last hues of night drained from the sky, and all around, the tall, flowerless plants were unfolding to face the Sun.

EARTHLIGHT

One

The monorail was losing speed as it climbed up out of the shadowed lowlands. At any moment now, thought Sadler, they would overtake the sun. The line of darkness moved so slowly here that, with a little effort, a man could keep abreast of it, could hold the sun balanced on the horizon until he had to pause for rest. Even then it would slip so reluctantly from sight that more than an hour would pass before the last dazzling segment vanished below the edge of the Moon, and the long lunar night began.

He had been racing through that night, across the land that the first pioneers had opened up two centuries ago, at a steady and comfortable 500 kilometres an hour. Apart from a bored conductor, who seemed to have nothing to do but produce cups of coffee on request, the only other occupants of the car were four astronomers from the Observatory. They had nodded affably enough when he came aboard, but had promptly lost themselves in a technical argument, and had ignored Sadler ever since. He felt a little hurt by this neglect, then consoled himself with the thought that perhaps they took him for a seasoned resident, not a newcomer on his first assignment to the Moon.

The lights in the car made it impossible to see much of the darkened land through which they were racing in almost complete silence. 'Darkened', of course, was only a relative term. It was true that the sun had gone, but not far from the zenith the Earth was approaching its first quarter. It would grow steadily until at lunar midnight, a week from now, it would be a blinding disc too bright for the unprotected eye to gaze upon.

Sadler left his seat and went forward, past the still-arguing astronomers, towards the curtained alcove at the front of the car. He was not yet accustomed to possessing only a sixth of his normal weight, and moved with exaggerated caution through the narrow corridor between the toilets and the little control room.

Now he could see properly. The observation windows were not as large as he would have liked; some safety regulation was responsible for that. But there was no internal light to distract his eyes, and at last he could enjoy the cold glory of this ancient, empty land.

Cold – yes, he could well believe that beyond these windows it was already two hundred degrees below zero, though the sun had sunk only a few hours before. Some quality of the light pouring down from the distant seas and clouds of Earth gave the impression. It was a light tinged with blues and greens; an arctic radiance that gave no atom of heat. And that, thought Sadler, was surely a paradox, for it came from a world of light and warmth.

Ahead of the speeding car, the single rail – supported by pillars uncomfortably far apart – arrowed into the east. Another paradox; this world was full of them. Why couldn't the sun set in the west, as it did on Earth? There must be some simple astronomical explanation, but for the moment Sadler could not decide what it was. Then he realised that, after all, such labels were purely arbitrary, and could easily get misplaced when a new world was mapped.

They were still rising slowly, and there was a cliff on the right which limited vision. On the left – let's see, that would be south, wouldn't it? – the broken land fell away in a series of layers as though, a billion years ago, the lava welling up from the Moon's molten heart had solidified in successive, weakening waves. It was a scene that chilled the soul, yet there were spots on Earth as bleak as this. The Badlands of Arizona were equally as desolate; the upper slopes of Everest were far more hostile, for here at least was no eternal, ravening wind.

And then Sadler almost cried out aloud, for the cliff on the right came to a sudden end, as if a monstrous chisel had sliced it off the surface of the Moon. It no longer barred his view; he could see clear round to the north. The unpremeditated artistry of Nature had produced an effect so breathtaking that it was hard to believe it was merely an accident of time and place.

There, marching across the sky in flaming glory, were the peaks of the Apennines, incandescent in the last rays of the hidden sun. The abrupt explosion of light left Sadler almost blinded; he shielded his eyes from the glare, and waited until he could safely face it again. When he looked once more the transformation was complete. The stars, which until a moment ago had filled the sky, had vanished. His contracted pupils could no longer see them: even the glowing Earth now seemed no more than a feeble patch of greenish luminosity. The glare from the sunlit mountains, still a hundred kilometres away, had eclipsed all other sources of light.

The peaks floated in the sky, fantastic pyramids of flame. They seemed to have no more connection with the ground beneath them than do the clouds that gather above a sunset on Earth. The line of shadow was so sharp, the lower slopes of the mountains so lost in utter darkness, that only the burning summits had any real existence. It would be hours yet before the last of those proud peaks fell back into the shadow of the Moon and surrendered to the night.

The curtains behind Sadler parted; one of his fellow passengers came into the alcove and took up a position by the window. Sadler wondered whether to open the conversation: he still felt a little piqued at being so completely ignored. However, the problem in etiquette was solved for him.

'Worth coming from Earth to see, isn't it?' said a voice from the gloom at his side.

'It certainly is,' Sadler replied. Then, trying to be blasé, he added, 'But I suppose you get used to it in time.'

There was a chuckle from the darkness.

'I wouldn't say that. Some things you never get used to, however long you live here. Just got in?'

'Yes. Landed last night in the *Tycho Brahe*. Haven't had time to see much yet.'

In unconscious mimicry Sadler found himself using the clipped sentences of his companion. He wondered if everyone on the Moon talked like this. Perhaps they thought it saved air.

'Going to work at the Observatory?'

'In a way, though I won't be on the permanent staff. I'm an accountant. Doing a cost-analysis of your operations.'

This produced a thoughtful silence, which was finally broken by:

'Rude of me – should have introduced myself. Robert Molton. Head of Spectroscopy. Nice to have someone around who can tell us how to do our income tax.'

349

'I was afraid that would come up,' said Sadler dryly. 'My name's Bertram Sadler; I'm from the Audit Bureau.'

'Humph. Think we're wasting money here?'

'That's for someone else to decide. I've only got to find *how* you spend it, not why.'

'Well, you're going to have some fun. Everyone here can make out a good case for spending twice as much money as they get. And I'd like to know how the devil you'll put a price-tag on pure scientific research.'

Sadler had been wondering that for some time, but thought it best not to attempt any further explanations. His story had been accepted without question: if he tried to make it more convincing, he would give himself away. He was not a good liar, though he hoped to improve with practice.

In any case, what he had told Molton was perfectly true. Sadler only wished it was the whole truth, and not a mere five per cent of it.

'I was wondering how we're going to get through those mountains,' he remarked, pointing to the burning peaks ahead. 'Do we go over – or under?'

'Over,' said Molton. 'They look spectacular, but they're really not so big. Wait till you see the Leibnitz Mountains or the Oberthe Range. They're twice as high.'

These are quite good enough to start with, thought Sadler. The low-slung monorail car, straddling its single track, bored through the shadows on a slowly rising course. In the darkness around them dimly seen crags and cliffs rushed forwards with explosive swiftness, then vanished astern. Sadler realised that probably nowhere else could one travel at such velocities so close to the ground. No jet liner, far above the clouds of Earth, ever gave such an impression of sheer speed as this.

If it had been day, Sadler could have seen the prodigies of engineering that had flung this track across the foothills of the Apennines. But the darkness veiled the gossamer bridges and the canyon-fringing curves: he saw only the approaching peaks, still magically afloat upon the sea of night that lapped around them.

Then, far to the east, a burning bow peeped above the edge of the Moon. They had risen out of shadow, had joined the mountains in their glory, and overtaken the sun itself. Sadler looked away from the glare which flooded the cabin, and for the first time saw clearly the man standing by his side.

Doctor (or would it be Professor?) Molton was in the early fifties, but his hair was quite black and very abundant. He had one of those strikingly ugly faces that somehow immediately inspire confidence. Here, one felt, was the humorous, worldly wise philosopher; the modern Socrates, sufficiently detached to give unbiased advice to all, yet by no means aloof from human contact. 'The heart of gold beneath the rugged exterior,' Sadler thought to himself, and flinched mentally at the triteness of the phrase.

Their eyes met in the silent appraisal of two men who know that their future business will bring them together again. Then Molton smiled, wrinkling a face that was almost as craggy as the surrounding moonscape.

'Must be your first dawn on the Moon. If you can call this a dawn, of course . . . anyway, it's a sunrise. Pity it'll only last ten minutes – we'll be over the top then and back into night. Then you'll have to wait two weeks to see the sun again.'

'Doesn't it get a trifle – boring – being cooped up for fourteen days?' asked Sadler. No sooner had he spoken the words than he realised that he had probably made a fool of himself. But Molton let him down lightly.

'You'll see,' he answered. 'Day or night, it's much the same underground. Anyway, you can go out whenever you like. Some people prefer the night time; the earthlight makes them feel romantic.'

The monorail had now reached the apex of its trajectory through the mountains. Both travellers fell silent as the peaks on either side reared to their climax, then began to sink astern. They had burst through the barrier, and were dropping down the much steeper slopes overlooking the *Mare Imbrium*. As they descended, so the sun, which their speed had conjured back from night, shrank from a bow to a thread, from a thread to a single point of fire, and winked out of existence. In the last instant of that false sunset, seconds before they sank again into the shadow of the Moon, there was a moment of magic that Sadler would never forget. They were moving along a ridge that the sun had already left, but the track of the monorail, scarcely a metre above it, still caught the last rays. It seemed as if they were rushing along an unsupported ribbon of light, a filament of flame built by sorcery rather than human engineering. Then final darkness fell, and the magic ended. The stars began to creep back into the sky as Sadler's eyes readapted themselves to the night.

'You were lucky,' said Molton. 'I've ridden this run a hundred times, but I've never seen that. Better come back into the car – they'll be serving a snack in a minute. Nothing more to see now, anyway.'

That, thought Sadler, was hardly true. The blazing earthlight, coming back into its own now that the sun was gone, flooded the great plain that the ancient astronomers had so inaccurately christened the Sea of Rains. Compared with the mountains that lay behind, it was not spectacular, yet it was still something to catch the breath.

'I'll wait awhile,' Sadler answered. 'Remember, this is all new to me and I don't want to miss any of it.'

Molton laughed, not unkindly. 'Can't say I blame you,' he said. 'Afraid we sometimes take things for granted.'

The monorail was now sliding down an absolutely vertiginous incline that would have been suicide on Earth. The cold, green-lit plain lifted to meet them: a range of low hills, dwarfs beside the mountains they had left behind, broke the skyline ahead. Once again the uncannily near horizon of this little world began to close in upon them again. They were back at 'sea' level . . .

Sadler followed Molton through the curtains and into the cabin, where the steward was setting out trays for his small company.

'Do you always have as few passengers as this?' asked Sadler. 'I shouldn't think it was a very economic proposition.'

'Depends what you mean by economics,' Molton replied. 'A lot of the things here will look funny on your balance sheets. But it doesn't cost much to run this service. Equipment lasts for ever – no rust, no weather. Cars only get serviced every couple of years.'

That was something Sadler certainly hadn't considered. There were a great many things he had to learn, and some of them he might find out the hard way.

The meal was tasty but unidentifiable. Like all food on the Moon, it would have been grown in the great hydroponic farms that sprawled their square kilometres of pressurised greenhouses along the equator. The meat of course was presumably synthetic: it might have been beef, but Sadler happened to know that the only cow on the Moon lived in luxury at the Hipparchus Zoo. This was the sort of useless information his diabolically retentive mind was always picking up and refusing to disgorge.

Perhaps mealtime had made the other astronomers more affable, for they were friendly enough when Dr Molton introduced them, and managed to avoid talking shop for a few minutes. It was obvious, however, that they regarded his mission with some alarm. Sadler could see them all mentally reviewing their appropriations and wondering what kind of case they could put up if they were challenged. He had no doubt that they would all have highly convincing stories, and would try to blind him with science if he attempted to pin them down. He had been through it all before, though never in quite such circumstances as these.

The car was now on the last lap of its journey, and would be at the Observatory in little more than an hour. The 600 kilometre run across the *Mare Imbrium* was almost straight and level, apart from a brief detour to the east to avoid the hills around the giant walled plain of Archimedes. Sadler settled himself down comfortably, pulled out his briefing papers, and began to do some study.

The organisation chart he unfolded covered most of the table. It was neatly printed in several colours, according to the various departments of the Observatory, and Sadler looked at it with some distaste. Ancient man, he remembered, had once been defined as a tool-making animal. He often felt that the best description of modern man would be a paper-wasting animal.

Below the headings 'Director' and 'Deputy Director' the chart split three ways under the captions ADMINISTRATION, TECHNICAL SERVICES, and OBSERVATORY. Sadler looked for Dr Molton; yes, there he was, in the OBSERVATORY section, directly beneath the Chief Scientist and heading the short column of names labelled 'Spectroscopy'. He seemed to have six assistants: two of them – Jamieson and Wheeler – were men to whom Sadler had just been introduced. The other traveller in the monocab, he discovered, was not really a scientist at all. He had a little box of his own on the chart, and was responsible to no one but the Director. Sadler suspected that

Secretary Wagnall was probably quite a power in the land, and would be well worth cultivating.

He had been studying the chart for half an hour, and had completely lost himself in its ramifications, when someone switched on the radio. Sadler had no objection to the soft music that filled the car; his powers of concentration could deal with worse interference than this. Then the music stopped; there was a brief pause, the six beeps of a time signal, and a suave voice began: '

'This is Earth, Channel Two, Interplanetary Network. The signal you have just heard was twenty-one hundred hours GMT. Here is the news.'

There was no trace of interference. The words were as clear as if they were coming from a local station. Yet Sadler had noticed the skyward-tilting antenna system on the roof of the monocab, and knew that he was listening to a direct transmission. The words he was hearing had left Earth almost one and a half seconds ago: already they would be heading past him to far more distant worlds. There would be men who would not hear them for minutes yet – perhaps for hours, if the ships that the Federation had beyond Saturn were listening in. And that voice from Earth would still go on, expanding and fading, far beyond the uttermost limits of man's explorations, until somewhere on the way to Alpha Centauri it was at last obliterated by the ceaseless radio whispering of the stars themselves.

'Here is the news. It has just been announced from the Hague that the conference on planetary resources has broken down. The delegates of the Federation are leaving Earth tomorrow, and the following statement has been issued from the Office of the President . . .'

There was nothing here that Sadler had not expected. But when a fear, however long anticipated, turns into a fact, there is always that same sinking of the heart. He glanced at his companions. Did they realise how serious this was?

They did. Secretary Wagnall had his chin cupped fiercely in his hands; Dr Molton was leaning back in his chair, eyes closed; Jamieson and Wheeler were staring at the table in glum concentration. Yes, they understood. Their work and their remoteness from Earth had not isolated them from the main currents of human affairs.

The impersonal voice, with its catalogue of disagreements and coun[word]charges, of threats barely veiled by the euphemisms of diplomacy, seemed to bring the inhuman cold of the lunar night seeping through the walls. It was hard to face the bitter truth, and millions of men would still be living in a fool's paradise. They would shrug their shoulders and say with forced cheerfulness, 'Don't worry – it will all blow over.'

Sadler did not believe so. As he sat in that little, brightly illuminated cylinder racing north across the Sea of Rains, he knew that for the first time in two hundred years humanity was faced with the threat of war.

Two

If war came, thought Sadler, it would be a tragedy of circumstance rather than deliberate policy. Indeed, the stubborn fact that had brought Earth into conflict with her ex-colonies sometimes seemed to him like a bad joke on the part of Nature.

Even before his unwelcome and unexpected assignment, Sadler had been well aware of the main facts behind the current crisis. It had been developing for more than a generation, and it arose from the peculiar position of the planet Earth.

The human race had been born on a world unique in the Solar System, loaded with a mineral wealth unmatched elsewhere. This accident of fate had given a flying start to man's technology, but when he reached the other planets he found to his surprise and disappontment that for many of his most vital needs he must depend on the home world.

Earth is the densest of all the planets, only Venus approaching it in this respect. But Venus has no satellite, and the Earth–Moon system forms a double world of a type found nowhere else among the planets. Its mode of formation is a mystery still, but it is known that when Earth was molten the Moon circled at only a fraction of its present distance, and raised gigantic tides in the plastic substance of its companion.

As a result of these internal tides the crust of the Earth is rich in heavy metals – far richer than that of any other of the planets. They hoard their wealth far down within their unreachable cores, protected by pressures and temperatures that guard them from man's depredations. So, as human civilisation spread outwards from Earth, the drain on the mother-world's dwindling resources steadily increased.

The light elements existed on the other planets in unlimited amounts, but such essential metals as mercury, lead, uranium, platinum, thorium and tungsten were almost unobtainable. For many of them no substitutes existed; their large-scale synthesis was impractical, despite two centuries of effort – and modern technology could not survive without them.

It was an unfortunate situation, and a very galling one for the independent republics on Mars, Venus, and the larger satellites, which had now united to form the Federation. It kept them dependent upon Earth, and prevented their expansion towards the frontiers of the Solar System. Though they had searched among the asteroids and moons, among the rubble left over when the worlds were formed, they had found little but worthless rock and ice. They must go cap in hand to the mother planet for almost every gram of a dozen metals that were more precious than gold.

That in itself might not have been serious, had not Earth grown steadily more jealous of its offspring during the 200 years since the dawn of space-travel. It was an old story, perhaps its classic example being the case of England and the American colonies. It has been truly said that history never repeats itself, but historical situations recur. The men who governed Earth were far more intelligent than George the Third: nevertheless, they were beginning to show the same reactions as that unfortunate monarch.

There were excuses on both sides; there always are. Earth was tired; it had spent itself, sending out its best blood to the stars. It saw power slipping from its hands, and knew that it had already lost the future. Why should it speed the process by giving to its rivals the tools they needed?

The Federation, on the other hand, looked back with a kind of affectionate contempt upon the world from which it had sprung. It had lured to Mars, Venus, and the satellites of the giant planets some of the finest intellects, and the most adventurous spirits, of the human race. Here was the new frontier, one which would expand for ever towards the stars. It was the greatest physical challenge mankind had ever faced, one that could be met only by supreme scientific skill and unyielding determination. These were virtues no longer essential on Earth; the fact that Earth was well aware of it did nothing to ease the situation.

All this might lead to discord and interplanetary invective, but it could never lead to violence. Some other factor was needed to produce that, some final spark which would set off an explosion echoing round the Solar System.

That spark had now been struck. The world did not know it yet, and Sadler himself had been equally ignorant a short six months ago. Central Intelligence, the shadowy organisation of which he was now a reluctant member, had been working night and day to neutralise the damage. A mathematical thesis entitled 'A Quantitative Theory of the Formation of the Lunar Surface Features' did not look the sort of thing that could start a war – but an equally theoretical paper by a certain Albert Einstein had once ended one.

The paper had been written some two years ago by Professor Roland Phillips, a peaceable Oxford cosmologist with no interest in politics. He had submitted it to the Royal Astronomical Society, and it was becoming a little difficult to give him a satisfactory explanation of the delay in publication. Unfortunately – and this was the fact that caused great distress to Central Intelligence – Professor Phillips had innocently sent copies to his colleagues on Mars and Venus. Desperate attempts had been made to intercept them, but in vain. By now the Federation must know that the Moon was not as impoverished a world as had been believed for 200 years.

There was no way of calling back knowledge that had leaked out, but there were other things about the Moon which it was now equally important that the Federation should not learn. Yet somehow it was learning them; somehow information was leaking across space from Earth to Moon, and then out to the planets.

When there's a leak in the house, thought Sadler, you send for the plumber. But how do you deal with a leak which you can't see – and which may be anywhere on the face of a world as large as Africa?

He still knew very little about the scope, size and methods of Central Intelligence – and still resented, futile though that was, the way in which his private life had been disrupted. By training he was precisely what he pretended to be – an accountant. Six months ago, for reasons which had not been explained and which he probably never would discover, he had been interviewed and offered an unspecified job. His acceptance was quite voluntary: it was merely made clear to him that he had better not refuse. Since then he had spent most of his time under hypnosis, being pumped full of the most various kinds of information and living a monastic life in an obscure corner of Canada. (At least he thought it was Canada, but it might equally well have been Greenland or Siberia.) Now he was here on the Moon, a minor pawn in the game of interplanetary chess. He would be very glad when the whole frustrating experience was over. It seemed quite incredible to him that anyone would ever *voluntarily* become a secret agent. Only very immature and unbalanced individuals could get any satisfaction from such frankly uncivilised behaviour.

There were a few compensations. In the ordinary way he would never have had a chance of going to the Moon, and the experience he was gathering now might be a real asset in later years. Sadler always tried to take the long view, particularly when he was depressed by the current situation. And the situation, both on the personal and interplanetary levels, was depressing enough.

The safety of Earth was quite a responsibility, but it was really too big for one man to worry about. Whatever reason said, the vast imponderables of planetary politics were less of a burden than the little cares of everyday life. To a cosmic observer it might have seemed very quaint that Sadler's greatest worry concerned one solitary human being. Would Jeanette ever forgive him, he wondered, for being away on their wedding anniversary? At least she would expect him to call her, and that was the one thing he dared not do. As far as his wife and his friends were concerned he was still on Earth. There was no way of calling from the Moon without revealing his location, for the two-and-a-half-second time-lag would betray him at once.

Central Intelligence could fix many things, but it could hardly speed up radio waves. It could deliver his anniversary present on time, as it had promised – but it couldn't tell Jeanette when he would be home again.

And it couldn't change the fact that, to conceal his whereabouts, he had had to lie to his wife in the sacred name of Security.

Three

When Conrad Wheeler had finished comparing the tapes he got up from his chair and walked three times round the room. From the way he moved, an old hand could have told that Wheeler was a relative newcomer to the Moon. He had been with the Observatory staff for just six months, and still over-compensated for the fractional gravity in which he now lived. There was a jerkiness about his movements that contrasted with the smooth, almost slow-motion gait of his colleagues. Some of this abruptness was due to his own temperament, his lack of discipline, and quickness at jumping to conclusions. It was that temperament he was now trying to guard against.

He had made mistakes before – but this time, surely, there could be no doubt. The facts were undisputed, the calculation trivial – the answer awe-inspiring. Far out in the depths of space a star had exploded with unimaginable violence. Wheeler looked at the figures he had jotted down, checked them for the tenth time, and reached for the phone.

Sid Jamieson was not pleased at the interruption. 'Is it really important?' he queried. 'I'm in the dark-room doing some stuff for Old Mole. I'll have to wait until these plates are washing, anyway.'

'How long will that take?'

'Oh, maybe five minutes. Then I've got some more to do.'

'I think this *is* important. It'll only take a moment. I'm up in Instrumentation 5.'

Jamieson was still wiping developer from his hands when he arrived. After more than 300 years, certain aspects of photography were quite unchanged. Wheeler, who thought that everything could be done by electronics, regarded many of his older friend's activities as survivals from the age of alchemy.

'Well?' said Jamieson, as usual wasting no words.

Wheeler pointed to the punched tape lying on the desk.

'I was doing the routine check of the magnitude integrator. It's found something.'

'It's always doing *that*,' snorted Jamieson. 'Every time anyone sneezes in the Observatory it thinks it's discovered a new planet.'

There were solid grounds for Jamieson's scepticism. The integrator was a tricky instrument, easily misled, and many astronomers thought it more trouble than it was worth. But it happened to be one of the Director's pet projects, so there was no hope of doing anything about it until there was a change of administration. Maclaurin had invented it himself, back in the days when he had had time to do some practical astronomy. An automatic watchdog of the skies, it would wait patiently for years until a new star – a 'nova' – blazed in the heavens. Then it would ring a bell and start calling for attention.

'Look,' said Wheeler, 'there's the record. Don't just take my word for it.'

Jamieson ran the tape through the converter, copied down the figures, and did a quick calculation. Wheeler smiled in satisfaction and relief as his friend's jaw dropped.

'Thirteen magnitudes in twenty-four hours! Wow!'

'I made it thirteen point four, but that's good enough. For my money, it's a supernova. And a close one.'

The two young astronomers looked at each other in thoughtful silence. Then Jamieson remarked:

'This is too good to be true. Don't start telling everybody about it until we're quite sure. Let's get its spectrum first, and treat it as an ordinary nova until then.'

There was a dreamy look in Wheeler's eyes.

'When was the last supernova in our galaxy?'

'That was Tycho's star – no, it wasn't – there was one a bit later, round about 1600.'

'Anyway, it's been a long time. This ought to get me on good terms with the Director again.'

'Perhaps,' said Jamieson dryly. 'It would just about take a supernova to do that. I'll go and get the spectrograph ready while you put out the report. We mustn't be greedy; the other observatories will want to get into the act.' He looked at the integrator, which had returned to its patient searching of the sky. 'I guess you've paid for yourself,' he added, 'even if you never find anything again except space-ship navigation lights.'

Sadler heard the news, without particular excitement, in the Common Room an hour later. He was too preoccupied with his own problems, and the mountains of work which faced him, to take much notice of the Observatory's routine programme, even when he fully understood it. Secretary Wagnall, however, quickly made it clear that this was very far from being a routine matter.

'Here's something to put on your balance sheet,' he said cheerfully. 'It's the biggest astronomical discovery for years. Come up to the roof.'

Sadler dropped the trenchant editorial in *Time Interplanetary*, which he had been reading with growing annoyance. The magazine fell with that dream-like slowness he had not yet grown accustomed to, and he followed Wagnall to the elevator.

They rose past the residential level, past Administration, past Power and Transport, and emerged into one of the small observation domes. The plastic bubble was scarcely ten metres across, and the awnings which shielded it during the lunar day had been rolled back. Wagnall switched off the internal lights, and they stood looking up at the stars and the waxing Earth. Sadler had been here several times before: he knew no better cure for mental fatigue.

A quarter of a kilometre away, the great framework of the largest telescope ever built by man was pointing steadily towards a spot in the southern sky. Sadler knew that it was looking at no stars that his eyes could see – at no stars, indeed, that belonged to this universe. It would be probing the limits of space, a billion light-years from home.

Then, unexpectedly, it began to swing towards the north. Wagnall chuckled quietly.

'A lot of people will be tearing their hair now,' he said. 'We've interrupted the programme to turn the big guns on *Nova Draconis*. Let's see if we can find it.'

He searched for a little while, consulting a sketch in his hand. Sadler, also staring into the north, could see nothing in the least unusual. All the stars there looked just the same to him. But presently, following Wagnall's instructions, and using the Great Bear and Polaris as guides, he found the faint star low down in the northern sky. It was not at all impressive, even if you realised that a couple of days before only the largest telescopes could have found it, and that it had climbed in brilliance a hundred thousand times in a few hours.

Perhaps Wagnall sensed his disappointment.

'It may not look very spectacular now,' he said defensively, 'but it's still on the rise. With any luck, we may really see something in a day or two.'

Day lunar or day terrestrial? Sadler wondered. It was rather confusing, like so many things here. All the clocks ran on a twenty-four-hour system and kept Greenwich Mean Time. One minor advantage of this was that one only had to glance at the Earth to get a reasonably accurate time check. But it meant that the progress of light and dark on the lunar surface had no connection at all with what the clocks might say. The sun could be anywhere above or below the horizon when the clocks announced it was noon.

Sadler glanced away from the north, back to the Observatory. He had always assumed – without bothering to think about it – that any observatory would consist of a cluster of giant domes, and had forgotten that here on the weatherless Moon there would be no purpose in enclosing the instruments. The thousand-centimetre reflector, and its smaller companion, stood naked and unprotected in the vacuum of space. Only their fragile masters remained underground in the warmth and air of this buried city.

The horizon was almost flat in all directions. Though the Observatory was at the centre of the great walled plain of Plato, the mountain ring was hidden by the curve of the Moon. It was a bleak and desolate prospect, without even a few hills to give it interest. Only a dusty plain, studded here and there with blow-holes and craterlets – and the enigmatic works of man, straining at the stars and trying to wrest away their secrets.

As they left, Sadler glanced once more towards Draco, but already he had forgotten which of the faint circumpolar stars was the one he had come to see. 'Exactly why,' he said to Wagnall, as tactfully as he could – for he did not want to hurt the Secretary's feelings – 'is this star so important?'

Wagnall looked incredulous, then pained, then understanding.

'Well,' he began, 'I guess stars are like people. The well-behaved ones never attract much attention. They teach us something, of course, but we can learn a lot more from the ones that go off the rails.'

'And do stars do that sort of thing fairly often?'

'Every year about a hundred blow up in our galaxy alone – but those are only ordinary novae. At their peak they may be about a hundred thousand times as bright as the sun. A *supernova* is a very much rarer, and very much more exciting affair. We still don't know what causes it, but when a star goes super it may become several *billion* times brighter than the sun. In fact, it can outshine all the other stars in the galaxy added together.'

Sadler considered this for a while. It was certainly a thought calculated to inspire a moment's silent reflection.

'The important thing is,' Wagnall continued eagerly, 'that nothing like this has happened since telescopes were invented. The last supernova in *our* universe was 600 years ago. There have been plenty in other galaxies, but they're too far away to be studied properly. This one, as it were, is right on our doorstep. That fact will be pretty obvious in a couple of days. In a few hours it will be outshining everything in the sky, except the sun and Earth.'

'And what do you expect to learn from it?'

'A supernova explosion is the most titanic event known to occur in Nature. We'll be able to study the behaviour of matter under conditions that make the centre of a nuclear explosion look like a dead calm. But if you're one of those people who always want a practical use for everything, surely it's of considerable interest to find what makes a star explode? One day, after all, our sun may decide to do likewise.'

'And in *that* case,' retorted Sadler, 'I'd really prefer not to know about it in advance. I wonder if that nova took any planets with it?'

'There's absolutely no way of telling. But it must happen fairly often, because at least one star in ten's got planets.'

It was a heart-freezing thought. At any moment, as likely as not, *somewhere* in the universe a whole solar system, with strangely peopled worlds and civilisations, was being tossed carelessly into a cosmic furnace. Life was a fragile and delicate phenomenon, poised on the razor's edge between cold and heat.

But Man was not content with the hazards that Nature could provide. He was busily building his own funeral pyre.

The same thought had occurred to Dr Molton also, but unlike Sadler he could set against it a more cheerful one. *Nova Draconis* was more than 2,000 light-years away; the flash of the detonation had been travelling since the birth of Christ. In that time it must have swept through millions of solar systems; have alerted the inhabitants of a thousand worlds. Even at this moment, scattered over the surface of a sphere 4,000 light-years in diameter, there must surely be other astronomers, with instruments not unlike his own, who would be trapping the radiations of this dying sun as they ebbed out towards the frontiers of the universe. And it was stranger still to think that infinitely more distant observers, so far away that to them the whole galaxy was no more than a faint smudge of light, would notice some hundred million years from now that our island universe had momentarily doubled its brilliance . . .

Dr Molton stood at the control desk in the softly lit chamber that was his laboratory and workshop. It had once been little different from any of the other cells that made up the Observatory, but its occupant had stamped his personality upon it. In one corner stood a vase of artificial flowers, something both incongruous and welcome in such a place as this. It was Molton's only eccentricity, and no one grudged it him. Since the native lunar vegetation gave such little scope for ornament. he was forced to use creations of wax and wire, skilfully made up for him in Central City. Their arrangement he varied with such ingenuity and resource that he never seemed to have the same flowers on two successive days.

Sometimes Wheeler used to make fun of him about this hobby, claiming that it proved he was homesick and wanted to get back to Earth. It had, in fact, been more than three years since Dr Molton had returned to his native Australia, but he seemed in no hurry to do so. As he pointed out, there were about a hundred lifetimes of work for him here, and he preferred to let his leave accumulate until he felt like taking it in one instalment.

The flowers were flanked by metal filing cases containing the thousands of spectrograms which Molton had gathered during his research. He was not, as he was always careful to point out, a theoretical astronomer. He simply looked and recorded; other people had the task of explaining what he found. Sometimes indignant mathematicians would arrive protesting that no star could *possibly* have a spectrum like this. Then Molton would go to his files, check that there had been no mistake, and reply, 'Don't blame me. Take it up with old Mother Nature.'

The rest of the room was a crowded mass of equipment that would have been completely meaningless to a layman, and indeed would have baffled many astronomers. Most of it Molton had built himself, or at least designed and handed over to his assistants for construction. For the last two centuries every practical astronomer had had to be something of an electrician, an engineer, a physicist – and, as the cost of his equipment steadily increased, a public-relations man.

The electronic commands sped silently through the cables as Molton set Right Ascension and Declination. Far above his head the great telescope, like some mammoth gun, tracked smoothly round to the north. The vast mirror at the base of the tube was gathering more than a million times as much light as a human eye could grasp, and focusing it with exquisite precision into a single beam. That beam, reflected again from mirror to mirror as if down a periscope, was now reaching Dr Molton, to do with it as he pleased.

Had he looked into the beam, the sheer glare of *Nova Draconis* would have blinded him – and, as compared with his instruments, his eyes could tell him practically nothing. He switched the electronic spectrometer into place, and started it scanning. It would explore the spectrum of *Nova Draconis* with patient accuracy, working down through yellow, green, blue into the violet and far ultra-violet, utterly beyond the range of the human eye. As it scanned it would trace on moving tape the intensity of every spectral line, leaving an unchallengeable record which astronomers could still consult a thousand years from now.

There was a knock at the door and Jamieson entered, carrying some still damp photographic plates.

'Those last exposures did it!' he said jubilantly. 'They show the gaseous shell expanding round the nova. And the speed agrees with your Doppler shifts.'

'So I should hope,' growled Molton. 'Let's look at them.'

He studied the plates, while in the background the whirring of electric motors continued from the spectrometer as it kept up its automatic search. They were negatives, of course, but like all astronomers he was accustomed to that and could interpret them as easily as positive prints.

There at the centre was the little disc that marked *Nova Draconis*, burnt through the emulsion by over-exposure. And around it, barely visible to the naked eye, was a tenuous ring. As the days passed, Molton knew, that ring would expand farther and farther into space until it was finally dissipated. It looked so small and insignificant that the mind could not comprehend what it really was.

They were looking into the past, at a catastrophe that had happened 2,000 years ago. They were seeing the shell of flame, so hot that it had not yet cooled to white-heat, which the star had blasted into space at millions of kilometres an hour. That expanding wall of fire would have engulfed the mightiest planet without checking its speed; yet from Earth it was no more than a faint ring at the limits of visibility.

'I wonder,' said Jamieson softly, 'if we'll ever find out just *why* a star does this sort of thing?'

'Sometimes,' replied Molton, 'as I'm listening to the radio, I think it would be a good idea if it did happen. Fire's a good steriliser.'

Jamieson was obviously shocked; this was so unlike Molton, whose brusque exterior so inadequately concealed his deep inner warmth.

'You don't really mean that!' he protested.

'Well, perhaps not. We've made some progress in the past million years, and I suppose an astronomer should be patient. But look at the mess we're running into now – don't you ever wonder how it's all going to end?'

There was a passion, a depth of feeling behind the words that astonished Jamieson and left him profoundly disturbed. Molton had never before let down his guard – had never, indeed, indicated that he felt very strongly on any subject outside his own field. Jamieson knew he had glimpsed the momentary weakening of an iron control.

It stirred something in his own mind, and, like a startled horse, he reared against the shock of mental recognition.

For a long moment the two scientists stared at each other, appraising, speculating, reaching out across the gulf that separates every man from his neighbour. Then, with a shrill buzzing, the automatic spectrometer announced that it had finished its task. The tension had broken; the everyday world crowded in upon them again. And so a moment that might have widened out into incalculable consequences trembled on the verge of being, and returned once more to limbo.

Four

Sadler had known better than to expect an office of his own; the most he could hope for was a modest desk in some corner of Accounts Section, and that was exactly what he had got. This did not worry him; he was anxious to cause no trouble and to draw no unnecessary attention to himself, and in any case he spent relatively little time at his desk. All the final writing up of his reports took place in the privacy of his room – the tiny cubicle, just large enough to ward off claustrophobia, which was one of a hundred identical cells on the Residential Level.

It had taken him several days to become adapted to this completely artificial way of life. Here in the heart of the Moon, time did not exist. The fierce temperature changes between the lunar day and night penetrated no more than a metre or two into the rock; the diurnal waves of heat and cold ebbed away before they reached this depth. Only Man's clocks ticked off the seconds and minutes; every twenty-four hours the corridor lights dimmed, and there was a pretence of night. Even then the Observatory did not sleep. Whatever the hour, there would be someone on duty. The astronomers, of course, had always been accustomed to working at peculiar hours, much to the annoyance of their wives – except in those quite common cases where the wives were astronomers too. The rhythm of lunar life was no additional hardship to them; the ones who grumbled were the engineers, who had to maintain air, power, communications, and the Observatory's other multitudinous services on a twenty-four-hour basis.

On the whole, thought Sadler, the Administrative staff had the best of it. It did not matter much if Accounts, Entertainment, or Stores, closed down for eight hours, as they did in every twenty-four, so long as someone continued to run the Surgery and the Kitchen.

Sadler had done his best not to get in anyone's hair, and believed that so far he had been quite successful. He had met all the senior staff except the Director himself – who was absent on Earth – and knew by sight about half the people in the Observatory. His plan had been to work conscientiously from section to section until he had seen everything the place had to offer. When he had done that he would sit and think for a couple of days. There were some jobs which simply could not be hurried, whatever the urgency.

Urgency – yes, that was his main problem. Several times he had been told, not unkindly, that he had come to the Observatory at a very awkward time. The mounting political tension had set the little community's nerves on edge, and tempers had been growing short. It was true that *Nova Draconis* had improved the situation somewhat, since no one could be bothered with such trivialities as politics while this phenomenon blazed in the skies. But they could not be bothered with cost accounting either, and Sadler could hardly blame them.

He spent all the time he could spare from his investigation in the Common Room, where the staff relaxed when they were off duty. Here was the centre of the Observatory's social life, and it gave him an ideal opportunity of studying the men and women who had exiled themselves here for the good of science – or, alternatively, for the inflated salaries required to lure less dedicated individuals to the Moon.

Though Sadler was not addicted to gossip, and was more interested in facts and figures than in people, he knew that he had to make the most of this opportunity. Indeed, his instructions had been very specific on this point, in a manner he considered unnecessarily cynical. But it could not be denied that human nature is always very much the same, among all classes and on all planets. Sadler had picked up some of his most useful information simply by standing within earshot of the bar . . .

The Common Room had been designed with great skill and taste, and the constantly changing photomurals made it hard to believe that this spacious chamber was, in reality, deep in the crust of the Moon. As a whim of the architect, there was an open fire in which a most realistic pile of logs burned for ever without being consumed.

This quite fascinated Sadler, who had never seen anything like it on Earth.

He had now shown himself sufficiently good at games and general conversation to become an accepted member of the staff, and had even been entrusted with much of the local scandal. Apart from the fact that its members were of distinctly superior intelligence, the Observatory was a microcosm of Earth itself. With the exception of murder (and *that* was probably only a matter of time), almost everything that happened in terrestrial society was going on somewhere here. Sadler was seldom surprised by anything, and certainly not by this. It was merely to be expected that all six of the girls in computing, after some weeks in a largely male community, now had reputations that could only be described as fragile. Nor was it remarkable that the Chief Engineer was not on speaking terms with the Assistant Chief Executive, or that Professor X thought that Dr Y was a certifiable lunatic, or that Mr Z was reputed to cheat at Hypercanasta. All these items were no direct concern of Sadler's, though he listened to them with great interest. They merely went to prove that the Observatory was one big happy family.

Sadler was wondering what humorist had stamped NOT TO BE TAKEN OUT OF THE LOUNGE across the shapely lady on the cover of last month's *Triplanet News* when Wheeler came storming into the room.

'What is it now?' asked Sadler. 'Discovered another nova. Or just looking for a shoulder to weep on?'

He rather guessed that the latter was the case, and that his shoulder would have to do in the absence of anything more suitable. By this time he had grown to know Wheeler quite well. The young astronomer might be one of the most junior members of the staff, but he was also the most memorable. His sarcastic wit, lack of respect for higher authority, confidence in his own opinions, and general argumentativeness prevented him from hiding his light under a bushel. But Sadler had been told, even by those who did not like Wheeler, that he was brilliant and would go far. At the moment he had not used up the stock of goodwill created by his discovery of *Nova Draconis*, which in itself would be enough to ensure a reputation for the rest of his career.

'I was looking for Wagtail: he's not in his office, and I want to lodge a complaint.'

'Secretary Wagnall,' answered Sadler, putting as much reproof as he could into the correction, 'went over to Hydroponics half an hour ago. And if I may make a comment, isn't it somewhat unusual for you to be the source, rather than the cause, of a complaint?'

Wheeler gave a large grin which made him look incredibly and disarmingly boyish.

'I'm afraid you're right. And I know this ought to go through the proper channels, and all that sort of thing – but it was rather urgent. I've just had a couple of hours' work spoilt by some fool making an unauthorised landing.'

Sadler had to think quickly before he realised what Wheeler meant. Then he remembered that this part of the Moon was a restricted area: no ships were supposed to fly over the northern hemisphere without first notifying the Observatory. The blinding glare of ion rockets, picked up by one of the great telescopes, could ruin photographic exposures and play havoc with delicate instruments.

'You don't suppose it was an emergency?' Sadler asked, struck by a sudden thought. 'It's too bad about your work, but that ship may be in trouble.'

Wheeler had obviously not thought of this, and his rage instantly abated. He looked helplessly at Sadler, as if wondering what to do next. Sadler dropped his magazine and rose to his feet.

'Shouldn't we go to Communications?' he said. 'They ought to know what's going on. Mind if I come along?'

He was very particular about such points in etiquette, and never forgot that he was here very much on sufferance. Besides, it was always good policy to let people think they were doing you favours.

Wheeler jumped at the suggestion, and led the way to Communications as if the whole idea had been his own. The signals office was a large, spotlessly tidy room at the highest level of the Observatory, only a few metres below the lunar crust. Here was the automatic telephone exchange which was the Observatory's central nervous system, and here were the monitors and transmitters which kept this remote scientific outpost in touch with Earth. They were all presided over by the Duty Signals Officer, who discouraged casual visitors with a large notice reading: POSITIVELY AND ABSOLUTELY NO ADMITTANCE TO UNAUTHORISED PERSONS.

'That doesn't mean us,' said Wheeler, opening the door. He was promptly contradicted by a still larger notice: THIS MEANS YOU. Unabashed, he turned to the grinning Sadler and added, 'All the places you're *really* not supposed to enter are kept locked, anyway.' Nevertheless, he did not push open the second door but knocked and waited until a bored voice called, 'Come in.'

The DSO, who was dissecting a space-suit walkie-talkie set, seemed quite glad of the interruption. He promptly called Earth and asked Traffic Control to find out what a ship was doing in the *Mare Imbrium* without notifying the Observatory. While they were waiting for the reply to come back Sadler wandered round the racks of equipment.

It was really surprising that it needed so much apparatus just to talk to people, or to send pictures between Moon and Earth. Sadler, who knew how technicians loved explaining their work to anyone who showed real interest, asked a few questions and tried to absorb as many of the answers as he could. He was thankful that by this time no one bothered to wonder if he had any ulterior motives and was trying to find if they could do their jobs for half the money. They had accepted him as an interested and inquisitive audience of one, for it was quite obvious that many of the questions he asked could have no financial significance.

The reply from Earth came through on the auto-printer soon after the DSO had finished his swiftly conducted tour. It was a slightly baffling message:

FLIGHT NON-SCHEDULED. GOVERNMENT BUSINESS. NO NOTI-FICATION ISSUED. FURTHER LANDINGS ANTICIPATED. INCONVENIENCE REGRETTED.

Wheeler looked at the words as if he could not believe his eyes. Until this moment the skies of the Observatory had been sacrosanct. No abbot facing the violation of his monastery could have been more indignant.

'They're going to keep it up!' he spluttered. 'What about our programme?'

'Grow up, Con,' said the Signals Officer indulgently. 'Don't you listen to the news? Or have you been too busy looking at your pet nova? This message means just one thing. There's something secret going on out in the *Mare*. I'll give you one guess.'

'I know,' said Wheeler. 'There's another of those hush-hush expeditions looking for heavy ores in the hope that the Federation won't find out. It's all so damn childish.'

'What makes you think *that's* the explanation?' asked Sadler sharply.

'Well, that sort of thing's been going on for years. Any bar in town will give you all the latest gossip.'

Sadler hadn't been 'into town' yet – as the trip to Central City was called – but he could well believe this. Wheeler's explanation was highly plausible, particularly in view of the current situation.

'We'll just have to make the best of it, I suppose,' said the DSO, attacking his walkie-talkie again. 'Anyway, there's one consolation. All this is going on to the south of us – the other side of the sky from Draco. So it won't really interfere with your main work, will it?'

'I suppose not,' Wheeler admitted grudgingly. For a moment he seemed quite downcast. It was not – far from it – that he wanted anything to interfere with work. But he had been looking forward to a good fight, and to have it snatched out of his hands like this was a bitter disappointment.

It needed no knowledge of the stars to see *Nova Draconis* now. Next to the waxing Earth, it was by far the brightest object in the sky. Even Venus, following the sun into the east, was pale compared to this arrogant newcomer. Already it had begun to cast a distinct shadow, and it was still growing in brilliance.

Down on Earth, according to the reports coming over the radio, it was clearly visible even in the daytime. For a little while it had crowded politics off the front page, but now the pressure of events was making itself felt again. Men could not bear to think of eternity for long; and the Federation was only light-minutes, not light-centuries, away.

Five

There were still those who believed that Man would have been happier had he stayed on his own planet – but it was rather too late, now, to do anything about that. In any case, had he remained on Earth he would not have been Man. The restlessness that had driven him over the face of his own world, that had made him climb the skies and plumb the seas, would not be assuaged while the Moon and planets beckoned to him across the deeps of space.

The colonisation of the Moon had been a slow, painful, sometimes tragic, and always fabulously expensive enterprise. Two centuries after the first landings, much of Earth's giant satellite was still unexplored. Every detail had, of course, been mapped from space, but more than half that craggy globe had never been examined at close quarters.

Central City and the other bases that had been established with such labour were islands of life in an immense wilderness; oases in a silent desert of blazing light or inky darkness. There had been many who had asked whether the effort needed to survive here was worth-while, since the colonisation of Mars and Venus offered much greater opportunities. But for all the problems it presented him, Man could not do without the Moon. It had been his first bridgehead in space, and was still the key to the planets. The liners that plied from world to world obtained all their propellent mass here, filling their great tanks with the finely divided dust which the ionic rockets would spit out in electrified jets. By obtaining that dust from the Moon, and not having to lift it through the enormous gravity field of Earth, it had been possible to reduce the cost of space-travel more than ten-fold. Indeed, without the Moon as a refuelling base, economical space-flight could never have been achieved.

It had also proved, as the astronomers and physicists had predicted, of immense scientific value. Freed at last from the imprisoning atmosphere of Earth, astronomy had made giant strides; and indeed there was scarcely a branch of science that had not benefited from the lunar laboratories. Whatever the limitations of Earth's statesmen, they had learned one lesson well. Scientific research was the life-blood of civilisation: it was the one investment that could be guaranteed to pay dividends for eternity . . .

Slowly, with countless heartbreaking setbacks, Man had discovered how to exist, then to live, and at last to flourish on the Moon. He had invented whole new techniques of vacuum engineering, of low-gravity architecture, of air and temperature control. He had defeated the twin demons of the lunar day and the lunar night, though always he must be on the watch against their depredations. The burning heat could expand his domes and crack his buildings; the fierce cold could tear apart any metal structure not designed to guard against contractions never encountered on Earth. But all these problems had, at last, been overcome.

All novel and ambitious enterprises seem much more hazardous and difficult from afar. So it had proved with the Moon. Problems that had appeared insuperable before the Moon was reached had now passed into lunar folk-lore. Obstacles that had disheartened the first explorers had been almost forgotten. Over the lands where men had once struggled on foot the mono-cabs now carried the tourists from Earth in luxurious comfort.

In a few respects, conditions on the Moon had helped rather than hindered the invaders. There was, for example, the question of the lunar atmosphere. On Earth it would have counted as a good vacuum, and it had no appreciable effect on astronomical observations. It was quite sufficient, however, to act as a very efficient shield against meteors. Most meteors are blocked by Earth's atmosphere before they get to within a hundred kilometres of the surface; they have been checked, in other words, while travelling through air no denser than the Moon's. Indeed, the Moon's invisible meteor shield is even more effective than Earth's since, thanks to the low lunar gravity, it extends much farther into space.

Perhaps the most astonishing discovery of the first explorers was the existence of plant life. It had long been suspected, from the peculiar changes of light and shade in such craters as Aristarchus and Eratosthenes, that there was some form of vegetation on the Moon, but it was difficult to see how it could survive under such extreme conditions. Perhaps, it was surmised, a few primitive lichens or mosses might exist, and it would be interesting to see how they managed to do it.

The guess was quite wrong. A little thought would have shown that any lunar plants would not be primitive, but would be highly specialised – extremely sophisticated, in fact, so that they could cope with their hostile environment. Primitive plants could no more exist on the Moon than could primitive Man.

The commonest lunar plants were plump, often globular growths, not unlike cacti. Their horny skins prevented the loss of precious water, and were dotted here and there with transparent 'windows' to let sunlight enter. This astonishing improvisation, surprising though it seemed to many, was not unique. It had been evolved independently by certain desert plants in Africa, faced with the same problem of trapping sunlight without losing water.

The unique feature of the lunar plants, however, was their ingenious mechanism for collecting air. An elaborate system of flaps and valves, not unlike that by which some sea creatures pump water through their bodies, acted as a kind of compressor. The plants were patient; they would wait for years along the great crevasses which occasionally gush forth feeble clouds of carbon or sulphur dioxides from the Moon's interior. Then the flaps would go frantically to work, and the strange plants would suck into their pores every molecule that drifted by, before the transient lunar mist dispersed into the hungry near-vacuum which was all the atmosphere remaining to the Moon.

Such was the strange world which was now home to some thousands of human beings. For all its harshness they loved it and would not return to Earth, where life was easy and therefore offered little scope for enterprise or initiative. Indeed, the lunar colony, bound though it was to Earth by economic ties, had more in common with the planets of the Federation. On Mars, Venus, Mercury, and the satellites of Jupiter and Saturn, men were fighting a frontier war against Nature, very like that which had won the Moon. Mars was already completely conquered; it was the only world outside Earth where a man could walk in the open without the use of artificial aids. On Venus victory was in sight, and a land surface three times as great as Earth's would be the prize. Elsewhere, only outposts existed: burning Mercury and the frozen outer worlds were a challenge for future centuries.

So Earth considered. But the Federation could not wait, and Professor Phillips, in complete innocence, had brought its impatience to the breaking point. It was not the first time that a scientific paper had changed the course of history, and it would not be the last.

Sadler had never seen the pages of mathematics that had caused all the trouble, but he knew the conclusions to which they led. He had been taught many things in the six months that had been abstracted from his life. Some he had learned in a small, bare classroom with six other men whose names he had never been told, but much knowledge had come to him in sleep or in the dreamy trance-state of hypnosis. One day, perhaps, it would be withdrawn from him by the same techniques.

The face of the Moon, Sadler had been told, consists of two distinct kinds of terrain – the dark areas of the so-called Seas, and the bright regions which are usually higher in elevation and much more mountainous. It is the bright areas which are pitted with the countless lunar craters, and appear to have been torn and blasted by aeons of volcanic fury. The Seas, by contrast, are flat and relatively smooth. They contain occasional craters and many pits and crevasses, but they are incomparably more regular than the rugged highlands.

They were formed, it seems, much later than the mountains and crater chains of the Moon's fiery youth. Somehow, long after the older formations had congealed, the crust melted again in a few areas to form the dark, smooth plains that are the Seas. They contain the wrecks of many old craters and mountains that have been melted down like wax, and their coasts are fringed with half-destroyed cliffs and ringed plains that barely escaped total obliteration.

The problem which had long engaged scientists, and which Professor Phillips had solved, was this: Why did the internal heat of the Moon break out only in the selected areas of the Seas, leaving the ancient highlands untouched?

A planet's internal heat is produced by radioactivity. It seemed to Professor Phillips, therefore, that under the great Seas must be rich deposits of uranium and its associated elements. The ebb and flow of tides in the Moon's molten interior had somehow produced these local concentrations, and the heat they had generated through millennia of radio-activity had melted the surface feature far above them to form the Seas.

For two centuries men had gone over the face of the Moon with every conceivable measuring instrument. They had set its interior trembling with artificial earthquakes: they had probed it with magnetic and electric fields. Thanks to these observations Professor Phillips had been able to put his theory on a sound mathematical basis.

Vast lodes of uranium existed far below the Seas. Uranium itself was no longer of the vital importance that it had been in the twentieth and twenty-first centuries, for the old fission piles had long since given way to the hydrogen reactor. But where there was uranium the other heavy metals would be found as well.

Professor Phillips had been quite sure that his theory had no practical applications. All these great deposits, he had carefully pointed out, were at such depths that any form of mining would be totally out of the question. They were at least a hundred kilometres down – and the pressure in the rock at that depth was so great that the toughest metal would flow like a liquid, so that no shaft or bore-hole could stay open even for an instant.

It seemed a great pity. These tantalising treasures, Professor Phillips had concluded, must remain for ever beyond the reach of the men who needed them so badly.

A scientist, thought Sadler, should really have known better than that. One day Professor Phillips was going to have a big surprise.

Six

Sadler lay in his bunk and tried to focus his mind on the past week. It was very hard to believe that he had arrived from Earth only eight of its days ago, but the calendar clock on the wall confirmed the notes he had made in his diary. And if he doubted both these witnesses he had merely to go up to the surface and enter one of the observation domes. There he could look up at the unmoving Earth, now just past full and beginning to wane. When he had arrived on the Moon it had been at its first quarter.

It was midnight over the *Mare Imbrium*. Dawn and sunset were both equally remote, but the lunar landscape was ablaze with light. Challenging the Earth itself was *Nova Draconis*, already brighter than any star in history. Even Sadler, who found most astronomical events too remote and impersonal to touch his emotions, would occasionally make the trip 'upstairs' to look at this new invader of the northern skies. Was he looking at the funeral pyre of worlds older and wiser than Earth? It was strange that such an awe-inspiring event should take place at a moment of human crisis. It could only be coincidence, of course, *Nova Draconis* was a close star, yet the signal of its death had been travelling for twenty centuries. One had to be not only superstitious but also very geocentric to imagine that this event had been planned as a warning for Earth. For what of all the other planets, of other suns, in whose skies the nova blazed with equal or even greater brilliance?

Sadler called home his wandering thoughts, and concentrated on his proper business. What had he left undone? He had visited every section of the Observatory, and met everyone of importance, with the single exception of the Director. Professor Maclaurin was due back from Earth in a day or so, and his absence had, if anything, simplified Sadler's task. When the Boss returned, so everybody had warned him, life would not be quite so free and easy, and everything would have to be done through the Proper Channels. Sadler was used to that, but did not enjoy it any the better.

There was a discreet purr from the speaker in the wall over the bed. Sadler reached out one foot and kicked a switch with the toe of his sandal. He could do this the first time now, but faint scars on the wall were a still visible memento of his apprenticeship.

'Yes,' he said. 'Who's that?'

'Transport Section here. I'm closing the list for tomorrow. There are still a couple of seats left – you want to come along?'

'If there's room,' Sadler replied. 'I don't want any more deserving causes to suffer.'

'O.K. – you're down,' said the voice briskly, and clicked off.

Sadler felt only the mildest twinge of conscience. After a week's solid work he could do with a few hours in Central City. He was not yet due to meet his first contact, and so far all his reports had gone out through the normal mail service, in a form that would have meant nothing to anyone happening to read them. But it was high time he got to know his way around the city, and indeed it would look odd if he took no holidays at all.

His main reason for the trip, however, was purely personal. There was a letter he wanted to post, and he knew that the Observatory mail was being censored by his colleagues in Central Intelligence. By now they must be indifferent to such matters, but he would still prefer to keep his private life to himself.

Central City was twenty kilometres from the spaceport, and Sadler had seen nothing of the lunar metropolis on his arrival. As the monocab – much fuller, this time, than it had been on the outward journey – pulled once more into the *Sinus Medii*, Sadler no longer felt a complete stranger. He knew, at least by sight, everyone in the car. Almost half the Observatory staff were here: the other half would take their day off next week. Even *Nova Draconis* was not allowed to interfere with this routine, which was based on common sense and sound psychology.

The cluster of great domes began to hump themselves over the horizon. A beacon light burned on the summit of each, but otherwise they were darkened and gave no sign of life. Some, Sadler knew, could be made transparent when desired. All were opaque now, conserving their heat against the lunar night.

The monocab entered a long tunnel at the base of one of the domes. Sadler had a glimpse of great doors closing behind them – then another set, and yet another. They're taking no chances, he thought to himself, and approved of such caution. Then there was the unmistakable sound of air surging around them, a final door opened ahead, and the vehicle rolled to a halt beside a platform that might have been in any station back on Earth. It gave Sadler quite a shock to look through the window and see people walking around outside without space-suits . . .

'Going anywhere in particular?' asked Wagnall, as they waited for the crush at the door to subside.

Sadler shook his head.

'No – I just want to wander round and have a look at the place. I want to see where you people manage to spend all your money.'

Wagnall obviously couldn't decide whether he was joking or not, and to Sadler's relief did not offer his services as a guide. This was one of the occasions when he would be quite happy to be left on his own.

He walked out of the station and found himself at the top of a large ramp, sloping down into the compact little city. The main level was twenty metres below him: he had not realised that the whole dome was countersunk this far into the lunar plain, thus reducing the amount of roof structure necessary. By the side of the ramp a wide conveyor belt was carrying freight and luggage into the station at a leisurely rate. The nearest buildings were obviously industrial, and, though well kept, had the slightly seedy appearance which inevitably overtakes anything in the neighbourhood of stations or docks.

It was not until Sadler was halfway down the ramp that he realised there was a blue sky overhead, that the sun was shining just behind him, and that there were high cirrus clouds floating far above.

The illusion was so perfect that he had taken it completely for granted, and had forgotten for a moment that this was midnight on the Moon. He stared for a long time into the dizzy depths of that synthetic sky, and could see no flaw in its perfection. Now he understood why the lunar cities insisted upon their expensive domes, when they could just as well have burrowed underground like the Observatory.

There was no risk of getting lost in Central City. With one exception each of the seven interconnnected domes was laid out in the same pattern of radiating avenues and concentric ring-roads. The exception was Dome Five, the main industrial and production centre, which was virtually one vast factory and which Sadler decided to leave alone.

He wandered at random for some time, going where his stray impulses took him. He wanted to get the 'feel' of the place, for he realised it was completely impossible to know the city properly in the short time at his disposal. There was one thing about Central City that struck him at once – it had a personality, a character of its own. No one can say why this is true of some cities and not of others, and Sadler felt a little surprised that it should be so of such an artificial environment as this. Then he remembered that *all* cities, whether on Earth or on the Moon, were equally artificial . . .

The roads were narrow, the only vehicles small, three-wheeled open cars that cruised along at less than thirty kilometres an hour and appeared to be used exclusively for freight rather than passengers. It was some time before Sadler discovered the automatic subway that linked the outer six domes in a great ring, passing under the centre of each. It was really a glorified conveyor belt, and moved in a counter-clockwise direction only. If you were unlucky you might have to go right round the city to get to the adjacent dome, but as the circular tour took only about five minutes, this was no great hardship.

The shopping centre, and main repository of lunar *chic* was in Dome One. Here also lived the senior executives and technicians – the most senior of all in houses of their own. Most of the residential buildings had roof gardens, where plants imported from Earth ascended to improbable heights in this low gravity. Sadler kept his eyes open for any lunar vegetation, but saw no signs of it. He did not know that there was a strict rule against bringing the indigenous plants into the domes. An oxygen-rich atmosphere overstimulates them so that they run riot and promptly die, producing a stench

383

which has to be experienced to be believed when their sulphur-loaded organisms decay.

Most of the visitors from Earth were to be found here. Sadler, a selenite of eight days' standing, found himself eyeing the obvious newcomers with amused contempt. Many of them had hired weight-belts as soon as they entered the city, under the impression that this was the safest thing to do. Sadler had been warned about this fallacy in time, and so had avoided contributing to what was really a mild racket. It was true that if you loaded yourself down with lead there was less danger of soaring off the ground with incautious steps, and perhaps terminating the trajectory upon your head. But surprisingly few people realised the distinction between weight and inertia which made these belts of such dubious value. When one tried to start moving, or to stop in a hurry, one quickly found that though a hundred kilos of lead might *weigh* only sixteen kilos here, it had exactly the same momentum as it did on Earth.

From time to time, as he made his way through the scanty crowds and roamed from shop to shop, Sadler ran into friends from the Observatory. Some of them were becoming festooned with parcels as they made up for a week's compulsory saving. Most of the younger members of the staff, male and female, had acquired companions. Sadler surmised that though the Observatory might be self-sufficient in most matters, there were others which demanded some variety.

The clear bell-like note, thrice repeated, caught him unawares. He looked around him, but could not locate its source. At first it seemed that no one was taking any notice of the signal, whatever it might mean. Then he observed that the streets were slowly clearing – and that the sky was getting darker.

Clouds had come up over the sun. They were black and ragged, their edges flame-fringed as the sunlight spilled past them. Once again Sadler marvelled at the skill with which these images – for they could be nothing else – were projected on the dome. No actual thunderstorm could have seemed more realistic, and when the first rumble rolled round the sky he did not hesitate to look for shelter. Even if the streets had not already emptied themselves, he could have guessed that the organisers of this storm were going to omit none of the details . . .

The little side-walk café was crowded with other refugees when the initial drops came down and the first fiery tongue of lightning licked across the heavens. Sadler could never see lightning without counting the seconds before the thunder peal. It came when he had got to 'six', making it two kilometres away. That, of course, would put it well outside the dome, in the soundless vacuum of space. Oh, well, one had to allow some artistic licence, and it wasn't fair to quibble over points like this.

Thicker and heavier came the rain, more and more continuous the flashes. The roads were running with water, and for the first time Sadler became aware of the shallow gutters which, if he had seen them before, he had dismissed without a second thought. It was not safe to take *anything* for granted here; you had to keep stopping and asking youself, 'What function does this serve? What's it doing here on the Moon? Is it even what I think it is?' Certainly, now he came to consider the matter, a gutter was as unexpected a thing to see in Central City as a snow-plough. But perhaps even that—

Sadler turned to his closest neighbour, who was watching the storm with obvious admiration.

'Excuse me,' he said, 'but how often does this sort of thing happen?'

'About twice a day – lunar day, that is,' came the reply. 'It's always announced a few hours in advance, so that it won't interfere with business.'

'I don't want to be too inquisitive,' continued Sadler, fearing that was just what he was, 'but I'm surprised at the trouble you've gone to. Surely all this realism isn't necessary?'

'Perhaps not, but we like it. We've got to have some rain, remember, to keep the place clean and deal with the dust. So we try and do it properly.'

If Sadler had any doubts on that score, they were dispelled when the glorious double rainbow arched out of the clouds. The last drops spattered on the sidewalk; the thunder dwindled away to an angry, distant mutter. The show was over, and the still glistening streets of Central City began to fill with life once more.

Sadler remained in the café for a meal, and after a little hard bargaining managed to get rid of some terrestrial currency at only a trifle below the market rate. The food, somewhat to his surprise, was excellent. Every bit must have been synthesised or grown in the yeast and chlorella tanks, but it had been blended and processed with great skill. The trouble with Earth, Sadler mused, was that it could take food for granted and seldom gave the matter the attention it deserved. Here, on the other hand, food was not something that a bountiful Nature, with a little prompting, could be relied upon to provide. It had to be designed and produced from scratch, and since the job *had* to be done, someone had seen that it was done properly. Like the weather, in fact . . . .

It was time he moved. The last mail for Earth would be cleared in two hours, and if he missed it Jeanette would not get his letter for almost a week of Earth-time. She had already been in suspense for long enough.

He pulled the unsealed letter from his pocket, and read it through again for any final amendments.

Jeanette, my dearest,

I wish I could tell you where I am, but I'm not allowed to say. It wasn't my idea, but I've been chosen for a special job and I've got to make the best of it. I'm in good health, and though I can't contact you directly, any letters you send to the Box Number I gave you will reach me sooner or later.

I hated being away on our anniversary, but believe me there was *absolutely nothing* I could do about it. I hope you received my present safely – and I hope you liked it. It took me a long time to find that necklace, and I won't tell you how much it cost!

Do you miss me very badly? God, how I wish I was home again! I know you were hurt and upset when I left, but I want you to trust me and to understand that I couldn't tell you what was happening. Surely you realise that I want Jonathan Peter as much as you do. Please have faith in me, and don't think that it was because of selfishness, or because I don't love you, that I acted as I did. I had very good reasons, which one day I'll be able to tell you.

Above all, don't worry, and don't be impatient. You know that I'll get back as soon as I can. And I promise you this – *when I'm home again, we'll go ahead.* I wish I knew how soon that would be!

I love you, my darling – don't ever doubt that. This is a tough job, and your faith in me is the one thing that keeps me going . . .

He read the letter with great care, trying for the moment to forget all that it meant to him, but to regard it as a message that a complete stranger might have written. Did it give too much away? He did not believe so. It might be indiscreet, but there was nothing in it that revealed his location or the nature of his work.

He sealed the envelope, but put no name or address on it. Then he did something that was, strictly speaking, a direct violation of his oath. He enclosed the letter in another envelope which he addressed, with a covering note, to his lawyer in Washington.

Dear George [he wrote], You'll be surprised to see where I am now. Jeanette doesn't know, and I don't want her to worry. So please address the enclosed to her and post it in the nearest mail-box. *Treat my present location as absolutely confidential.* I'll explain it all one day.

George would guess the truth, but he could keep secrets just as well as anyone in Central Intelligence. Sadler could think of no other fool-proof way of getting his letter to Jeanette, and he was prepared to take the slight risk for his peace of mind – and for hers.

He asked the way to the nearest mail-box (they were hard to find in Central City), and slid the letter down the chute. In a couple of hours it would be on the way to Earth: by this time tomorrow, it would have reached Jeanette. He could only hope that she would understand – or, if she could not understand, would suspend judgment until they met again.

There was a paper-rack beside the mail-box, and Sadler purchased a copy of the *Central News*. He still had several hours before the monorail left for the Observatory, and if anything interesting was going on in town the local paper would presumably tell him all about it.

The political news received such little space that Sadler wondered if a mild censorship was in force. No one would have realised that there was a crisis if they went by the headlines alone: it was necessary to search through the paper to find the really significant items. Low down on page two, for example, was a report that a liner from Earth was having quarantine trouble off Mars, and was not being allowed to land – while another on Venus was not being allowed to take off.

Sadler was fairly sure that the real trouble was political rather than medical: the Federation was simply getting tough.

On page four was a still more thought-provoking piece of news. A party of prospectors had been arrested on some remote asteroid in the vicinity of Jupiter. The charge, it seemed, was a violation of space-safety regulations. Sadler suspected that the charge was phoney – and that so were the prospectors. Central Intelligence had probably lost some of its agents.

On the centre page of the paper was a rather naive editorial making light of the situation, and expressing the confident hope that common sense would prevail. Sadler, who had no illusions about the commonness of common sense, remained sceptical and turned to the local news.

All human communities, wherever they may be in space, follow the same pattern. People were getting born, being cremated (with careful conservation of phosphorus and nitrates), rushing in and out of marriage, moving out of town, suing their neighbours, having parties, holding protest meetings, getting involved in astonishing accidents, writing Letters to the Editor, changing jobs . . . Yes, it was just like Earth. That was a somewhat depressing thought. Why had Man ever bothered to leave his own world if all his travels and experiences had made so little difference to his fundamental nature? He might just as well have stayed at home, instead of exporting himself and his foibles, at great expense, to another world.

Your job's making you cynical, Sadler told himself. Let's see what Central City has in the way of entertainment.

He'd just missed a tennis tournament in Dome Four, which should have been worth watching. It was played, so someone had told him, with a ball of normal size and mass. But the ball was honeycombed with holes, which increased its air resistance so much that ranges were no greater than on Earth. Without some such subterfuge, a good drive would easily span one of the domes. However, the trajectories followed by these doctored balls were most peculiar, and enough to induce a swift nervous breakdown in anyone who had learned to play under normal gravity.

There was a Cyclorama in Dome Three, promising a tour of the Amazon Basin (mosquito bites optional), starting at every alternate hour. Having just come from Earth, Sadler felt no desire to return so promptly. Besides, he felt he had already seen an excellent cyclorama display in the thunderstorm that had now passed out of sight. Presumably it had been produced in the same manner, by batteries of wide-angle projectors.

The attraction that finally took his fancy was the swimming pool in Dome Two. It was the star feature of the Central City Gymnasium, much frequented by the Observatory staff. One of the occupational risks of life on the Moon was lack of exercise and resultant muscular atrophy. Anyone who stayed away from Earth for more than a few weeks felt the change of weight very severely when they came home. What lured Sadler to the Gym, however, was the thought that he could practise some fancy dives that he would never dare risk on Earth, where one fell five metres in the first second and acquired far too much kinetic energy before hitting the water.

Dome Two was on the other side of the city, and as Sadler felt he would save his energy for his destination he took the Subway. But he missed the slow-speed section which led one off the continuously moving belt, and was carried willy-nilly on to Dome Three before he could escape. Rather than circle the city again he retraced the way on the surface, passing through the short connecting tunnel that linked all the domes together at the points where they touched. There were automatic doors here that opened at a touch – and would seal instantly if air pressure dropped on either side.

Half the Observatory staff seemed to be exercising itself in the Gym. Dr Molton was sculling a rowing machine, one eye fixed anxiously on the indicator that was adding up his strokes. The Chief Engineer, eyes closed tightly as per the warning instructions, was standing in the centre of a ring of ultra-violet tubes which gave out an eerie glare as they replenished his tan. One of the MDs from Surgery was attacking a punchbag with such viciousness that Sadler hoped he would never have to meet him professionally. A tough-looking character whom Sadler believed came from Maintenance was trying to see if he could lift a clear ton; even if one allowed mentally for the low gravity, it was still awe inspiring to watch.

Everybody else was in the swimming pool, and Sadler quickly joined them. He was not sure what he had expected, but somehow he had imagined that swimming on the Moon would differ drastically from the same experience on the Earth. But it was exactly the same, and the only effect of gravity was in the abnormal height of the waves, and the slowness with which they moved across the pool.

The diving went well as long as Sadler attempted nothing ambitious. It was wonderful to know just what was going on, and to have time to admire the surroundings during one's leisurely descent. Then, greatly daring, Sadler tried a somersault from five metres. After all, this was equivalent to less than a metre on Earth . . .

Unfortunately, he completely misjudged his time of fall, and made half a turn too many – or too few. He landed on his shoulders, and remembered too late just what a crack one could give oneself even from a low height if things went wrong. Limping slightly, and feeling that he had been flayed alive, he crawled out of the pool. As the slow ripples ebbed languidly away, Sadler decided to leave this sort of exhibitionism to younger men.

After all this exertion, it was inevitable that he should join Molton and a few of his other acquaintances when they left the Gymnasium. Tired but satisfied, and feeling that he had learned a good deal more about the lunar way of life. Sadler leaned back in his seat as the monocab pulled out of the station and the great doors sealed tight behind them. Blue, cloud-flecked skies gave place to the harsh reality of the lunar night. There was the unchanged Earth, just as he had seen it hours ago. He looked for the blinding star of *Nova Draconis*, then remembered that in these latitudes it was hidden below the northern edge of the Moon.

The dark domes, which gave so little sign of the life and light they held, sank beneath the horizon. As he watched them go, Sadler was struck by a sudden, sombre thought. They had been built to withstand the forces that Nature could bring against them – but how pitiably fragile they would be if ever they faced the fury of Man!

Seven

'I still think,' said Jamieson, as the tractor headed towards the southern wall of Plato, 'that there'll be a hell of a row when the Old Man hears about it.'

'Why should he?' asked Wheeler. 'When he gets back, he'll be too busy to bother about us. And, anyway, we're paying for all the fuel we use. So stop worrying and enjoy yourself. This is our day off, in case you'd forgotten.'

Jamieson did not reply. He was too busy concentrating on the road ahead – if it could be called a road. The only signs that other vehicles had ever been this way were the occasional furrows in the dust. Since these would last for eternity here on the windless Moon, no other sign-posts were needed, though occasionally one came across unsettling notices that read: DANGER – CLEFTS AHEAD! or EMERGENCY OXYGEN – 10 KILOMETRES.

There are only two methods of long-range transport on the Moon. The high-speed monorails link the main settlements with a fast, comfortable service running on a regular schedule. But the rail system is very limited, and likely to remain so because of its cost. For unrestricted ranging over the lunar surface, one must fall back on the powerful turbine-driven tractors known as 'Caterpillars' or, more briefly, 'Cats'. They are, virtually, small space-ships mounted on fat little tyres that enable them to go anywhere within reason, even over the appallingly jagged surface of the Moon. On smooth terrain they can easily do a hundred kilometres an hour, but normally they are lucky to manage half that speed. The weak gravity, and the caterpillar-treads they can lower if necessary, enable them to climb fantastic slopes. In emergencies they have been known to haul themselves up vertical cliffs with their built-in winches. One can live in the larger models for weeks at a time without undue hardship, and all the detailed exploration of the Moon has been carried out by prospectors using these tough little vehicles.

Jamieson was a more than expert driver, and knew the way perfectly. Nevertheless, for the first hour Wheeler felt that his hair would never lie down again. It usually took newcomers to the Moon quite a while to realise that slopes of one-in-one were perfectly safe if treated with respect. Perhaps it was just as well that Wheeler was a novice, for Jamieson's technique was so unorthodox that it would have filled a more experienced passenger with real alarm.

Why Jamieson was such a recklessly brilliant driver was a paradox that had caused much discussion among his colleagues. Normally he was very painstaking and cautious, inclined not to act at all unless he could be certain of the consequences. No one had ever seen him really annoyed or excited; many thought him lazy, but that was a slander. He would spend weeks working on some observations until the results were absolutely unchallengeable – and would then put them away for two or three months to have another look at them later.

Yet once at the controls of a 'Cat', this quiet and peace-loving astronomer became a daredevil driver who held the unofficial record for almost every tractor run in the northern hemisphere. The reason lay – buried too deeply even for Jamieson to be aware of it himself – in a boyhood desire to be a space-ship pilot, a dream that had been frustrated by an erratic heart.

From space – or through a telescope on Earth – the walls of Plato look a formidable barrier when the slanting sunlight shows them to best advantage. But in reality they are less than a kilometre high, and, if one chooses the correct route through the numerous passes, the journey out of the crater and into the *Mare Imbrium* presents no great difficulty. Jamieson got through the mountains in less than an hour, though Wheeler wished that he had taken a little longer.

They came to a halt on a high escarpment overlooking the plain. Directly ahead, notching the horizon, was the pyramidal summit of Pico. Towards the right, sinking down into the north-east, were the more rugged peaks of the Teneriffe Mountains. Very few of those peaks had ever been climbed, largely because no one had so far bothered to attempt it. The brilliant earthlight made them appear an uncanny blue-green, contrasting strangely with their appearance by day, when they would be bleached into raw whites and blacks by the merciless sun.

While Jamieson relaxed to enjoy the view, Wheeler began a careful search of the landscape with a pair of powerful binoculars. Ten minutes later he gave it up, having discovered nothing in the least unusual. He was not surprised by this, for the area where the unscheduled rockets had been landing was well below the horizon.

'Let's drive on,' he said. 'We can get to Pico in a couple of hours, and we'll have dinner there.'

'And then what?' asked Jamieson in resigned tones.

'If we can't see anything, we'll come back like good little boys.'

'O.K. – but you'll find it rough going from now on. I don't suppose more than a dozen tractors have ever been down here before. To cheer you up, I might tell you that our Ferdinand is one of them.'

He eased the vehicle forward, gingerly skirting a vast talus slope where splintered rock had been accumulating for millennia. Such slopes were extremely dangerous, for the slightest disturbance could often set them moving in slow, irresistible avalanches that would overwhelm everything before them. For all his apparent recklessness, Jamieson took no real risks, and always gave such traps a very wide berth. A less experienced driver would have gaily galloped along the foot of the slide without a moment's thought – and ninety-nine times out of a hundred would have got away with it. Jamieson had seen what happened on the hundredth time. Once the wave of dusty rubble had engulfed a tractor there was no escape, since any attempt at rescue would only start fresh slides.

Wheeler began to feel distinctly unhappy on the way down the outer ramparts of Plato. This was odd, for they were much less steep than the inner walls, and he had expected a smoother journey. He had not allowed for the fact that Jamieson would take advantage of the easier conditions to crowd on speed, with the result that Ferdinand was indulging in a peculiar rocking motion. Presently Wheeler disappeared to the rear of the well-appointed tractor, and was not seen by his pilot for some time. When he returned he remarked rather crossly, 'No one ever told me you could actually be seasick on the Moon.'

The view was now rather disappointing, as it usually is when one descends to the lunar lowlands. The horizon is so near – only two or three kilometres away – that it gives a sense of confinement and restraint. It is almost as if the small circle of rock surrounding one is all that exists. The illusion can be so strong that men have been known to drive more slowly than necessary, as if subconsciously afraid they may fall off the edge of that uncannily near horizon.

For two hours Jamieson drove steadily onwards, until at last the triple tower of Pico dominated the sky ahead. Once this magnificent mountain had been part of a vast crater wall that must have been a twin to Plato. But ages ago the encroaching lava of the *Mare Imbrium* had washed away all the rest of the hundred-and-fifty-kilometre diameter ring, leaving Pico in lonely and solitary state.

The travellers paused here to open a few food-packs and make some coffee in the pressure kettle. One of the minor discomforts of life on the Moon is that really hot drinks are an impossibility – water boils at about seventy degrees centigrade in the oxygen-rich, low-pressure atmosphere universally employed. After a while, however, one grows used to lukewarm beverages.

When they had cleared up the debris of the meal, Jamieson remarked to his colleague, 'Sure you still want to go through with it?'

'As long as you say it's safe. Those walls look awfully steep from here.'

'It's safe, if you do what I tell you. I was just wondering how you felt now. There's nothing worse than being sick in a space-suit.'

'*I'm* all right,' Wheeler replied with dignity. Then another thought struck him. 'How long will we be outside, anyway?'

'Oh, say a couple of hours. Four at the most. Better do all the scratching you want to now.'

'I wasn't worrying about *that*,' retorted Wheeler, and retired to the back of the cabin again.

In the six months he had been on the Moon, Wheeler had worn a suit no more than a dozen times, and most of these occasions were on emergency drill. There were very few times when the observing staff had to go into vacuum – most of their equipment was remotely controlled. But he was not a complete novice, though he was still in the cautious stage which is so much safer than light-hearted overconfidence.

They called Base, *via* Earth, to report their position and

intentions, then adjusted each other's equipment. First Jamieson, then Wheeler, chanted the alphabetical mnemonic – 'A is for airlines, B is for batteries, C is for couplings, D is for DF loop . . .' which sounds so childish the first time one hears it, but which so quickly becomes part of the routine of lunar life – and is something which nobody ever jokes about. When they were sure that all their equipment was in perfect condition, they cracked the doors of the airlock and stepped out on to the dusty plain.

Like most lunar mountains, Pico was not so formidable when seen close at hand as when glimpsed from a distance. There were a few vertical cliffs, but they could always be avoided, and it was seldom necessary to climb slopes of more than forty-five degrees. Under a sixth of a gravity, this is no great hardship, even when one is wearing a space-suit.

Nevertheless, the unaccustomed exertion made Wheeler sweat and pant somewhat after they had been climbing for half an hour, and his face plate was misting badly, so that he had to peer out of the corners to see properly. Though he was too stubborn to request a slower pace, he was very glad when Jamieson called a halt.

They were now almost a kilometre above the plain, and could see for at least fifty kilometres to the north. They shielded their eyes from the glare of the Earth and began to search.

It took only a moment to find their objective. Halfway to the horizon two extremely large freight rockets were standing like ungainly spiders on their extended undercarriages. Large though they were, they were dwarfed by the curious dome-shaped structure rising out of the level plain. This was no ordinary pressure dome – its proportions were all wrong. It almost looked as if a complete sphere had been partly buried, so that the upper three-quarters emerged from the surface. Through his binoculars, whose special eyepieces allowed him to use them despite his face plate, Wheeler could see men and machines moving round the base of the dome. From time to time clouds of dust shot into the sky and fell back again, as if blasting was in progress. That was another odd thing about the Moon, he thought. Most objects fell too slowly here in this low gravity for anyone accustomed to conditions on Earth. But dust fell much *too* quickly – at the same rate as anything else, in fact – for there was no air to check its descent.

'Well,' said Jamieson after he, too, had carried out a long scrutiny through the glasses, 'someone's spending an awful lot of money.'

'What do you think it is? A mine?'

'It could be,' replied the other, cautious as ever. 'Perhaps they've decided to process the ores on the spot, and all their extraction plant is in that dome. But that's only a guess – I've certainly never seen anything like it before.'

'We can reach it in an hour, whatever it is. Shall we go over and have a closer look?'

'I was afraid you were going to say that. I'm not sure it would be a very wise thing. They might insist on us staying.'

'You've been reading too many scare articles. Anyone would think there was a war on and we were a couple of spies. They couldn't detain us – the Observatory knows where we are and the Director would raise hell if we didn't get back.'

'I suspect he will when we *do*, so we might as well get hung for sheep as lambs. Come along – it's easier on the way down.'

'I never said it was hard on the way up,' protested Wheeler, not very convincingly. A few minutes later, as he followed Jamieson down the slope, an alarming thought struck him.

'Do you think they're listening to us? Suppose someone's got a watch on this frequency – they'll have heard every word we've said. After all, we're in direct line of sight.'

'Who's being melodramatic now? No one except the Observatory would be listening on this frequency, and the folks at home can't hear us as there's rather a lot of mountain in the way. Sounds as if you've got a guilty conscience – anyone would think that you'd been using naughty words again.'

This was a reference to an unfortunate episode soon after Wheeler's arrival. Since then he had been very conscious of the fact that privacy of speech, which is taken for granted on Earth, is not always available to the wearers of space-suits, whose every whisper can be heard by anyone within radio range.

The horizon contracted about them as they descended to ground-level, but they had taken careful bearings and knew which way to steer when they were back in Ferdinand. Jamieson was driving with extra caution now, for this was terrain over which he had never previously travelled. It was nearly two hours before the enigmatic dome began to bulge above the skyline, followed a little later by the squat cylinders of the freighters.

Once again Wheeler aimed their roof antenna on Earth, and called the Observatory to explain what they had discovered and what they intended to do. He rang off before anyone could tell them not to do it, reflecting how crazy it was to send a message 800,000 kilometres in order to talk to someone a hundred kilometres away. But there was no other way of getting long-distance communication from ground-level; everything below the horizon was blocked off by the shielding effect of the Moon. It was true that by using long waves it was sometimes possible to send signals over great distances by reflection from the Moon's very tenuous ionosphere, but this method was too unreliable to be of serious use. For all practical purposes, lunar radio contact had to be on a 'line of sight' basis.

It was very amusing to watch the commotion which their arrival had caused. Wheeler thought it resembled nothing so much as an antheap that had been well stirred with a stick. In a very short time they found themselves surrounded by tractors, moondozers, hauling machines, and excited men in space-suits. They were forced by sheer congestion to bring Ferdinand to a halt.

'At any moment,' said Wheeler, 'they'll call out the guards.'

Jamieson failed to be amused.

'You shouldn't make jokes like that,' he chided. 'They're apt to be too near the truth.'

'Well, here comes the reception committee. Can you read the lettering on his helmet? SEC. 2, isn't it? "Section Two", I suppose that means.'

'Perhaps. But SEC. could just as easily stand for Security. Well – it was all your idea. I'm merely the driver.'

At that moment there was a series of peremptory knocks on the outer door of the airlock. Jamieson pressed the button that opened the seal, and a moment later the 'reception committee' was removing his helmet in the cabin. He was a grizzled, sharp-featured man with a worried expression that looked as if it was permanently built in. It did not appear that he was pleased to see them.

He regarded Wheeler and Jamieson thoughtfully, while the two astronomers put on their friendliest smiles. 'We don't usually get visitors in these parts,' he said. 'How did you happen to get here?'

The first sentence, Wheeler thought, was as good an understatement as he had heard for some time.

'It's our day off – we're from the Observatory. This is Dr Jamieson – I'm Wheeler. Astrophysicists, both of us. We knew you were around here, so decided to come and have a look.'

'How did you know?' the other asked sharply. He still had not introduced himself, which would have been bad manners even on Earth and was quite shocking here.

'As you may have heard,' said Wheeler mildly, 'we possess one or two rather large telescopes over at the Observatory. And you've been causing us a lot of trouble. I, personally, have had two spectrograms ruined by rocket glare. So can you blame us for being a trifle inquisitive?'

A slight smile played around their interrogator's lips, and was instantly banished. Nevertheless, the atmosphere seemed to thaw a little.

'Well, I think it would be best if you come along to the office while we make a few checks. It won't take very long.'

'I beg your pardon? Since when has any part of the Moon been private property?'

'Sorry, but that's the way it is. Come along, please.'

The two astonomers climbed into their suits and followed through the airlock. Despite his aggressive innocence, Wheeler was beginning to feel a trifle worried. Already he was visualising all sorts of unpleasant possibilities, and recollections of what he had read about spies, solitary confinement, and brick walls at dawn rose up to comfort him.

They were led to a smoothly fitting door in the curve of the great dome, and found themselves inside the space formed by the outer wall and an inner, concentric hemisphere. The two shells, as far as could be seen, were spaced apart by an intricate webbing of some transparent plastic. Even the floor underfoot was made of the same substance. This, Wheeler decided, was all very odd, but he had no time to examine it closely.

Their uncommunicative guide hurried them along almost at a trot, as if he did not wish them to see more than was necessary. They entered the inner dome through a second airlock, where they removed their suits. Wheeler wondered glumly when they would be allowed to retrieve them again.

The length of the airlock indicated that the inner dome must be of tremendous thickness, and when the door ahead of them opened both astronomers immediately noticed a familiar smell. It was ozone. Somewhere, not very far away, was high-voltage electrical equipment. There was nothing unduly remarkable about that, but it was another fact to be filed away for future reference.

The airlock had opened into a small corridor flanked by doors bearing painted numbers and such labels as PRIVATE, TECHNICAL STAFF ONLY, INFORMATION, STAND-BY AIR, EMERGENCY POWER, and CENTRAL CONTROL. Neither Wheeler nor Jamieson could deduce much from these notices, but they looked at each other thoughtfully when they were finally halted at a door marked SECURITY. Jamieson's expression told Wheeler, as clearly as any words could do, 'I told you so!'

After a short pause a 'Come In' panel glowed and the door swung automatically open. Ahead lay a perfectly ordinary office dominated by a determined-looking man at a very large desk. The size of the desk was itself a proclamation to the world that money was no object here, and the astronomers contrasted it ruefully with the office equipment to which they were accustomed. A teleprinter of unusually complicated design stood on a table in one corner, and the remaining walls were entirely covered by filing cabinets.

'Well,' said the Security Officer, 'who are these people?'

'Two astronomers from the Observatory over in Plato. They've just dropped in by tractor, and I thought you should see them.'

'Most certainly. Your names, please?'

There followed a tedious quarter of an hour while particulars were carefully noted down and the Observatory was called. That meant, Wheeler thought glumly, that the fat would now be in the fire. Their friends in Signals, who had been logging their progress in case of any accident, would now have to report their absence officially.

At last their identities were established, and the man at the imposing desk regarded them with some perplexity. Presently his brows cleared and he began to address them.

'You realise, of course, that you are something of a nuisance. This is the last place we ever expected visitors, otherwise we'd have put up notices telling them to keep off. Needless to say, we have means of detecting any who may turn up, even if they're not sensible enough to drive up openly, as you did.

'However, here you are and I suppose there's no harm done. You have probably guessed that this is a Government project, and one we don't want talked about. I'll have to send you back, but I want you to do two things.'

'What are they?' asked Jamieson suspiciously.

'I want you to promise not to talk about this visit more than you have to. Your friends will know where you've gone, so you can't keep it a complete secret. Just don't discuss it with them, that's all.'

'Very well,' agreed Jamieson. 'And the second point?'

'If anyone persists in questioning you, and shows particular interest in this little adventure of yours – report it at once. That's all. I hope you have a good ride home.'

Back in the tractor, five minutes later, Wheeler was still fuming.

'Of all the high-handed so-and-sos! He never even offered us a smoke.'

'I rather think,' said Jamieson mildly, 'that we were lucky to get off so easily. They meant business.'

'I'd like to know what *sort* of business. Does that look like a mine to you? and why should anything be going on in a slag-heap like the *Mare*?'

'I think it must be a mine. When we drove up I noticed something that looked very much like drilling machinery on the other side of the dome. But it's hard to account for all the cloak-and-dagger nonsense.'

'Unless they've discovered something that they don't want the Federation to know about.'

'In that case we're not likely to find out, either, and might as well stop racking our brains. But to get on to more practical matters – where do we go from here?'

'Let's stick to our original plan. It may be some time before we have a chance of using Ferdy again, and we might as well make the most of it. Besides, it's always been one of my ambitions to see the *Sinus Iridum* from ground level, as it were.'

'It's a good three hundred kilometres east of here.'

'Yes, but you said yourself it was pretty flat, if we keep away from the mountains. We should be able to manage it in five hours. I'm a good enough driver now to relieve you when you want a rest.'

'Not over fresh ground – that would be far too risky. But we'll make a compromise. I'll take you as far as the Laplace Promontory, so that you'll have a look into the Bay. And then you can drive home, following the track I've made. Mind you stick to it, too.'

Wheeler accepted gladly. He had been half afraid that Jamieson would abandon the trip and sneak back to the Observatory, but decided that he had done his friend an injustice.

For the next three hours they crawled along the flanks of the Teneriffe Mountains, then struck out across the plain to the Straight Range, that lonely, isolated band of mountains like a faint echo of the mighty Alps. Jamieson drove now with a steady concentration; he was going into new territory and could take no chances. From time to time he pointed out famous landmarks, and Wheeler checked them against the photographic chart.

They stopped for a meal about ten kilometres east of the Straight Range, and investigated the contents of the boxes which the Observatory kitchen had given them. One corner of the tractor was fitted out as a tiny galley, but they had no intention of using that except in an emergency. Neither Wheeler nor Jamieson was a sufficiently good cook to enjoy the preparation of meals, and this, after all, *was* supposed to be a holiday . . .

'Sid,' began Wheeler abruptly, between mouthfuls of sandwich, 'what do you think about the Federation? You've met more of their people than I have.'

'Yes, and liked them. Pity you weren't here before the last crowd left: we had about a dozen of them at the Observatory studying the telescope mounting. They're thinking of building a fifteen-hundred-centimetre instrument on one of the moons of Saturn, you know.'

'That would be quite a project – I always said we're too close to the sun here. It would certainly get clear of the Zodiacal Light and the other rubbish round the inner planes. But to get back to the point – did they strike you as likely to start a quarrel with Earth?'

'It's difficult to say. They were very open and friendly with us, but then we were all scientists together and that helps a lot. It might have been different if we'd been politicians or civil servants.'

'Dammit, we *are* civil servants! That fellow Sadler was reminding me of it only the other day.'

'Yes, but at least we're *scientific* civil servants – which makes quite a difference. I could tell that they didn't care a lot for Earth, though they were too polite to say so. There's no doubt that they're annoyed about the metals allocations; I often heard them complain about it. Their main point is that they have much greater difficulties than we have in opening up the outer planets – and that Earth wastes half the stuff she uses.'

'Which side do you think is right?'

'I don't know; it's so hard to get all the facts. But there are a lot of people on Earth who are afraid of the Federation and don't want to give it any more power. The Federals know that; one day they may grab first and argue afterwards.'

Jamieson screwed up the wrappings and tossed them into the wastebin. He glanced at the chronometer, then swung himself up into the driving seat. 'Time to get moving again,' he said. 'We're falling behind schedule.'

From the Straight Range they swung south-east, and presently the great headland of Promontory Laplace appeared on the skyline. As they rounded it they came across a disconcerting sight – the battered wreck of a tractor, and beside it a rough cairn surmounted by a metal cross. The tractor seemed to have been destroyed by an explosion in its fuel tanks, and was an obsolete model of a type that Wheeler had never seen before. He was not surprised when Jamieson told him it had been there for almost a century; it would still look exactly the same a million years from now.

As they rolled past the headland, the mighty northern wall of the *Sinus Iridum* – the Bay of Rainbows – swept into view. Aeons ago the *Sinus Iridum* had been a complete ring mountain – one of the largest walled plains on the Moon. But the cataclysm which had formed the Sea of Rains had destroyed the whole of the southern wall, so that only a semicircular bay is now left. Across that bay Promontory Laplace and Promontory Heraclides stare at each other, dreaming of the day when they were linked by mountains four kilometres high. Of those lost mountains, all that now remain are a few ridges and low hillocks.

Wheeler was very quiet as the tractor rolled past the great cliffs, which stood like a line of titans full-face towards the Earth. The green light splashing down their flanks revealed every detail of the terraced walls. No one had ever climbed those heights, but one day, Wheeler knew, men would stand upon their summits and stare out in victory across the Bay. It was strange to think that after two hundred years there was so much of the Moon untrodden by human feet, and so many places that a man must reach with nothing to aid him but his own exertions and skill.

He remembered his first glimpse of the *Sinus Iridum*, through the little home-made telescope he had built when he was a boy. It had been nothing more than two small lenses fixed in a cardboard tube – but it had given him more pleasure than the giant instruments of which he was now the master.

Jamieson swung the tractor round in a great curve, and brought it to a halt facing back towards the west. The line they had trampled through the dust was clearly visible, a road which would remain for ever unless later traffic obliterated it.

'The end of the line,' he said. 'You can take over from here. She's all yours until we get to Plato. Then wake me up and I'll take her through the mountains. Good night.'

How he managed it Wheeler couldn't imagine, but within ten minutes Jamieson was asleep. Perhaps the gentle rocking of the tractor acted as a lullaby, and he wondered how successful he would be in avoiding jolts and jars on the way home. Well, there was only one way to find out . . . He aimed carefully at the dusty track, and began to retrace the road to Plato.

Eight

It was bound to happen sooner or later, Sadler told himself philosophically, as he knocked at the Director's door. He had done his best, but in work like this it was impossible to avoid hurting someone's feelings. It would be interesting, very interesting, to know who had complained . . .

Professor Maclaurin was one of the smallest men Sadler had ever seen. He was so tiny that some people had made the fatal mistake of not taking him seriously. Sadler knew better than this. Very small men usually took care to compensate for their physical deficiencies (how many dictators had been of even average height?) and from all accounts Maclaurin was one of the toughest characters on the Moon.

He glared at Sadler across the virgin, uncluttered surface of his desk. There was not even a scribbling pad to break its bleakness – only the small panel of the communicator switchboard with its built-in speaker. Sadler had heard about Maclaurin's unique methods of administration, and his hatred of notes and memoranda. The Observatory was run, in its day-to-day affairs, almost entirely by word of mouth. Of course, other people had to prepare notices and schedules and reports – Maclaurin just switched on his mike and gave the orders. The system worked flawlessly for the simple reason that the Director recorded everything, and could play it back at a moment's notice to anyone who said, 'But, Sir, you never told me *that*!' It was rumoured – though Sadler suspected this was a slander – that Maclaurin had occasionally committed verbal forgery by retrospectively altering the record. Such a charge, needless to say, was virtually impossible to prove.

The Director waved to the only other seat, and started talking before Sadler could reach it.

'I don't know whose brilliant idea this was,' he began. 'But I was never notified that you were coming here. If I had been, I would have asked for a postponement. Although no one appreciates the importance of efficiency more than I do, these are very troubled times. It seems to me that my men could be better employed than by explaining their work to you – particularly while we are coping with the *Nova Draconis* observations.'

'I'm sorry there was a failure to inform you, Professor Maclaurin,' Sadler replied. 'I can only assume that the arrangements were made while you were *en route* to Earth.' He wondered what the Director would think if he knew how carefully matters had been arranged in this precise manner. 'I realise that I must be something of a nuisance to your staff, but they have given me every assistance and I've had no complaints. In fact, I thought I was getting on rather well with them.'

Maclaurin rubbed his chin thoughtfully. Sadler stared in fascination at the tiny, perfectly formed hands, no larger than those of a child.

'How much longer do you expect to be here?' the Director asked. He certainly doesn't worry about your feelings, Sadler told himself wryly.

'It's very hard to say – the area of my investigation is so undefined. And it's only fair to warn you that I've scarcely started on the scientific side of your work, which is likely to present the greatest difficulties. So far I have confined myself to Administration and Technical Services.'

This news did not seem to please Maclaurin. He looked like a small volcano working up to an eruption. There was only one thing to do, and Sadler did it quickly.

He walked to the door, opened it swiftly, looked out, then closed it again. This piece of calculated melodrama held the Director speechless while Sadler walked over to the desk and brusquely flicked down the switch on the communicator.

'Now we can talk,' he began. 'I wanted to avoid this, but I see it's inevitable. Probably you've never met one of these cards before.'

The still flabbergasted Director, who had probably never before in his life been treated like this, stared at the blank sheet of plastic. As he watched, a photograph of Sadler, accompanied by some lettering, flashed into view – then vanished abruptly.

'And what,' he asked when he had recovered his breath, 'is Central Intelligence? I've never heard of it.'

'You're not supposed to,' Sadler replied. 'It's relatively new, and highly unadvertised. I'm afraid the work I'm doing here is not exactly what it seems. To be brutally frank, I could hardly care less about the efficiency of your establishment, and I completely agree with all the people who tell me that it's nonsense to put scientific research on a cost-accounting basis. But it's a plausible story, don't you think?'

'Go on,' said Maclaurin, with dangerous calm.

Sadler was beginning to enjoy himself beyond the call of duty. It wouldn't do, however, to get drunk with power . . .

'I'm looking for a spy,' he said, with a bleak and simple directness.

'Are you serious? This is the twenty-second century!'

'I'm perfectly serious, and I need not impress upon you that you must reveal nothing of this conversation to anybody, even Wagnall.'

'I refuse to believe,' snorted Maclaurin, 'that any of my staff would be engaged in espionage. The idea's fantastic.'

'It always is,' Sadler replied patiently. 'That doesn't alter the position.'

'Assuming that there's the slightest basis in this charge, have you any idea who it might be?'

'If I had, I'm afraid I couldn't tell you at this stage. But I'll be perfectly frank. We're not certain that it is anyone here – we're merely acting on a nebulous hint one of our – ah – agents picked up. But there is a leak *somewhere* on the Moon, and I'm covering this particular possibility. Now you see why I have been so inquisitive. I've tried not to act out of character, and I think that by now I'm taken for granted by everybody. I can only hope that our elusive Mr X, if he exists at all, has accepted me at my face value. This, by the way, is why I'd like to know who has been complaining to you. I assume that somebody has.'

Maclaurin hummed and hawed for a moment, then capitulated.

'Jenkins, down in Stores, rather implied that you'd been taking up a lot of his time.'

'That's very interesting,' said Sadler, more than a little puzzled. Jenkins, chief storekeeper, had been nowhere near his list of suspects. 'As a matter of fact, I've spent relatively little time there –

just enough to make my mission look convincing. I'll have to keep an eye on Mr Jenkins.'

'This whole idea is all very new to me,' said Maclaurin thoughtfully. 'But even if we have someone here passing out information to the Federation, I don't quite see how they would do it. Unless it was one of the signals officers, of course.'

'That's the key problem,' admitted Sadler. He was willing to discuss the general aspects of the case, for the Director might be able to throw some light on them. Sadler was all too aware of his difficulties, and the magnitude of the task he had been set. As a counter-spy, his status was strictly amateur. The only consolation he had was that his hypothetical opponent would be in the same position. Professional spies had never been too numerous in any age, and the last one must have died more than a century ago.

'By the way,' said Maclaurin, with a forced and somewhat unconvincing laugh. 'How do you know that *I'm* not the spy?'

'I don't,' Sadler replied cheerfully. 'In counter-espionage, certainty is rare. But we do the best we can. I hope you weren't seriously inconvenienced during your visit to Earth?'

Maclaurin stared uncomprehendingly at him for a moment. Then his jaw dropped.

'So you've been investigating *me*!' he spluttered indignantly.

Sadler shrugged his shoulders.

'It happens to the best of us. If it's any consolation, you can just imagine what *I* had to go through before they gave me this job. And I never asked for it in the first place . . .'

'Then what do you want me to do?' growled Maclaurin. For a man of his size, his voice was surprisingly deep, though Sadler had been told that when he was really annoyed it developed a high-pitched squeak.

'Naturally, I'd like you to inform me of anything suspicious that comes to your notice. From time to time I may consult you on various points, and I'd be very glad of your advice. Otherwise, please take as little notice of me as possible and continue to regard me as a nuisance.'

'*That*,' replied Maclaurin, with a half-hearted smile, 'will present no difficulties at all. However, you can count on me to assist you in every way – if only to help prove that your suspicions are unfounded.'

'I sincerely hope that they are,' Sadler replied. 'And thank you for your co-operation – I appreciate it.'

Just in time, he stopped himself whistling as he closed the door behind him. He felt very pleased that the interview had gone so well, but he remembered that no one whistled after they had had an interview with the Director. Adjusting his expression to one of grave composure, he walked out through Wagnall's office and into the main corridor, where he at once ran into Jamieson and Wheeler.

'Have you seen the Old Man?' Wheeler asked anxiously. 'Is he in a good mood?'

'As this is the first time I've met him, I've no standards of reference. We got on well enough. What's the matter? You look like a couple of naughty schoolboys.'

'He's just asked for us,' said Jamieson. 'We don't know why, but he's probably been catching up on what's happened while he was away. He's already congratulated Con for discovering *Nova Draconis*, so it can't be that. I'm afraid he's found out that we borrowed a Cat for a run.'

'What's wrong with that?'

'Well, they're only supposed to be used on official jobs. But everybody does it – as long as we replace the fuel we burn, no one's any the worse. Heck, I suppose I shouldn't have told that to *you*, of all people.'

Sadler did a quick double-take, then realised with relief that Jamieson was merely referring to his well-advertised activities as a financial watchdog.

'Don't worry,' he laughed. 'The worst I'll do with the information is to blackmail you into taking me for a ride. I hope the Old Ma— Professor Maclaurin doesn't give you too rough a passage.'

All three would have been quite surprised to know with what uncertainty the Director himself was regarding this interview. In the ordinary way such minor infractions of the rules as the unauthorised use of a Caterpillar would have been a matter for Wagnall to deal with, but something more important was involved here. Until five minutes ago he had no idea what it might be, and had asked to see Wheeler and Jamieson to discover what was going on. Professor

Maclaurin prided himself on keeping in touch with everything, and a certain amount of his staff's time and ingenuity had to be employed in seeing that he was not always successful.

Wheeler, drawing heavily on the stock of good will *Nova Draconis* had given him, gave an account of their unofficial mission. He tried to make it sound as if they were a pair of knights in armour riding out into the wilderness to discover the dragon which was menacing the Observatory. He concealed nothing of importance, which was as well for him, as the Director already knew where he had been.

As he listened to Wheeler's account, Maclaurin found the pieces of the jigsaw fitting together. This mysterious message from Earth, ordering him to keep his people out of the *Mare Imbrium* in future, must have originated from the place these two had visited. The leak that Sadler was investigating would also have something to do with it. Maclaurin still found it hard to believe that any of his men was a spy, but he realised that a spy was the last thing any competent spy ever looked like.

He dismissed Jamieson and Wheeler with an absentminded mildness that left them both sorely puzzled. For a moment he sat lost in gloomy thought. It might be a coincidence, of course – the story hung together well. But if one of these men was after information he had set about it in the right way. Or had he? Would a real spy have acted so openly, knowing that he was bound to draw suspicion on himself? Could it even be a daring double-bluff, on the principle that no one would seriously suspect such a frontal attack?

Thank God, it wasn't his problem. He would get it off his hands as quickly as he could.

Professor Maclaurin snapped down the TRANSMIT switch and spoke to the outer office.

'Please find Mr Sadler for me. I want to speak to him again.'

Nine

There had been a subtle change in Sadler's status since the Director's return. It was something that Sadler had known must happen, though he had done his best to guard against it. On his arrival he had been treated with polite suspicion by everybody, and it had taken him several days' solid public-relations work to break down the barriers. People had become friendly and talkative, and he could make some headway. But now they seemed to be regretting their earlier frankness, and it was uphill work once more.

He knew the reason. Certainly no one suspected his real purpose in being here, but everybody knew that the return of the Director, far from limiting his activities, had somehow enhanced his position. In the echoing sounding-box of the Observatory, where rumour and gossip travelled at speeds scarcely inferior to that of light, it was hard to keep any secrets. The word must have gone out that Sadler was more important than he seemed. He only hoped it would be a long while before anybody guessed *how* much more important . . .

Until now he had confined his attention to the Administrative section. This was partly a matter of policy, because this would be the way he would be expected to act. But the Observatory really existed for the scientists, not the cooks, typists, accountants, and secretaries, however essential they might be.

If there was a spy in the Observatory there were two main problems he had to face. Information is useless to a spy unless he can send it to his superiors. Mr X must not only have contacts who passed material to him – he must have an outgoing channel of communication as well.

Physically there were only three ways out of the Observatory. One could leave it by monorail, by tractor, or on foot. The last case did not seem very likely to be important. In theory a man might walk a few kilometres and leave a message to be picked up at some prearranged rendezvous. But such peculiar behaviour would soon be noticed, and it would be very easy to check on the small number of men in Maintenance who were the only people who used suits regularly. Every exit and entrance through the air-locks had to be logged, though Sadler doubted if this rule was invariably obeyed.

The tractors were more promising, as they would give so much greater range. But their use would involve collusion, since they always carried a crew of at least two men – and this was one rule which was *never* broken, for safety reasons. There was the odd case of Jamieson and Wheeler, of course. Their backgrounds were being busily investigated now, and he should have the report in a few days. But their behaviour, though irregular, had been too open to be really suspicious.

That left the monorail to Central City. Everybody went there, on the average, about once a week. There were endless possibilities for the exchange of messages here, and at this very moment a number of 'tourists' were inconspicuously checking contacts and making all sorts of interesting discoveries about the private lives of the Observatory staff. There was little part that Sadler could play in this work, except to furnish lists of the most frequent visitors to the City.

So much for physical lines of communication. Sadler discounted them all. There were other, and subtler means, far more likely to be used by a scientist. Any member of the Observatory's staff could build a radio transmitter, and there were countless places where one could be concealed. It was true that the patiently listening monitors had detected nothing, but sooner or later Mr X would make a slip.

Meanwhile, Sadler would have to find out what the scientists were doing. The high-pressure course in astronomy and physics he had taken before coming here would be totally inadequate to give him any real understanding of the Observatory's work, but at least he would be able to get the general outline. And, with any luck, he might eliminate a few suspects from his depressingly long list.

The Computing section did not detain him for long. Behind their glass panels the spotless machines sat in silent cogitation, while the girls fed the programme tapes into their insatiable maws. In an adjacent sound-proofed room the electric typewriters stormed away, printing endless rows and columns of numbers. Dr Mays, the head of the section, did his best to explain what was going on – but it was a hopeless task. These machines had left far behind such elementary operations as integration, such kindergarten functions as cosines or logarithms. They were dealing with mathematical entities of which Sadler had never heard, and solving problems whose very statement would be meaningless to him.

That did not worry him unduly: he had seen what he wanted to. All the main equipment was sealed and locked; only the maintenance engineers who called once a month could get at it. Certainly there was nothing for him here: Sadler tip-toed away as from a shrine.

The optical workshop, where patient craftsmen shaped glass to a fraction of a millionth of an inch, using a technique unchanged for centuries, fascinated him but advanced his search no further. He peered at the interference fringes produced by clashing light-waves, and watched them scurry madly back and forth as the heat of his body caused microscopic expansions in blocks of flawless glass. Here art and science met, to achieve perfections unmatched elsewhere in the whole range of human technology. Could there be any clue for him here in this buried factory of lenses, prisms, and mirrors? It seemed most improbable . . .

He was, Sadler thought glumly, rather in the position of a man in a darkened coal-cellar, looking for a black cat that might not be there. What was worse, to make the analogy more accurate he would have to be a man who didn't know what a cat looked like, even when he saw one.

His private discussions with Maclaurin helped him a good deal. The Director was still sceptical, but was obviously co-operating to the full if only to get this annoying interloper out of the way. Sadler could question him about any technical aspect of the Observatory's work, though he was careful not to give any hints as to the direction his search was taking him.

He had now compiled a small dossier for every member of the staff – no mean achievement even though the factual data had been supplied before he came to the Observatory. For most of his subjects a single sheet of paper sufficed, but for some he had accumulated several pages of cryptic notes. The facts he was sure of he wrote in ink; the speculations were in pencil so that they could be modified when necessary. Some of these speculations were very wild and frequently libellous, and Sadler often felt very ashamed of them. It was hard, for example, to accept a drink from someone whom you had noted down as possibly susceptible to bribes owing to the cost of maintaining an expensive mistress in Central City . . .

This particular suspect had been one of the engineers in Construction. Sadler had soon ruled him out as a likely candidate for blackmail, since far from concealing the situation the victim was always complaining bitterly about his inamorata's extravagances. He had even warned Sadler against incurring similar liabilities.

The filing system was divided into three parts. Section A contained the names of the ten or so men Sadler considered the most probable suspects, though there was not one against whom he had any real evidence. Some were down simply because they had the greatest opportunity for passing out information if they wished to do so. Wagnall was one of these; Sadler was practically certain that the Secretary was innocent, but kept him on the list to be on the safe side.

Several others were listed because they had close relatives in the Federation, or because they were too openly critical of Earth. Sadler did not really imagine that a well-trained spy would risk arousing suspicion by behaving in this way, but he had to be on the watch for the enthusiastic amateur who could be just as dangerous. The records of atomic espionage during the Second World War had been very instructive in this respect, and Sadler had studied them with great care.

Another name on List A was that of Jenkins, the chief storekeeper. This was only the most tenuous of hunches, and all attempts by Sadler to follow it up had been unsuccessful. Jenkins seemed to be a somewhat morose individual, who resented interference and was not very popular with the rest of the staff. Getting anything out of him in the way of equipment was supposed to be the most difficult job on the Moon. This, of course, might merely mean that he was a good representative of his proverbially tenacious tribe.

There remained that interesting couple Jamieson and Wheeler, who between them did a great deal to enliven the Observatory scene. Their drive out into the *Mare Imbrium* had been a fairly typical exploit, and had followed, so Sadler was assured, the pattern of earlier adventures.

Wheeler was always the leading spirit. His trouble – if it was a trouble – was that he had too much energy and too many interests. He was not yet thirty: one day, perhaps, age and responsibility would mellow him, but so far neither had had much opportunity. It was too easy to dimiss him as a case of arrested development, as a college boy who had failed to grow up. He had a first-rate mind, and never did anything that was really foolish. Though there were many people who did not like him, particularly after they had been the victims of one of his practical jokes, there was nobody who wished him any harm. He moved unscathed through the little jungle of Observatory politics, and had the abiding virtues of complete honesty and forthrightness. One always knew what he was thinking, and it was never necessary to ask him for his opinion. He gave it first.

Jamieson was a very different character, and presumably it was the contrast in their personalities which drew these two men together. He was older than Wheeler by a couple of years, and was regarded as a sobering influence on his younger companion. Sadler doubted this: as far as he could judge, Jamieson's presence had never made any difference to his friend's behaviour. He had mentioned this to Wagnall, who had thought for a while and said, 'Yes, but think how much worse Con would be if Sid *wasn't* there to keep an eye on him.'

Certainly Jamieson was far more stable and much harder to get to know. He was not as brilliant as Wheeler and would probably never make any shattering discoveries, but he would be one of those reliable, sound men who do the essential tidying up after the geniuses have broken through into new territory.

Scientifically reliable – yes. Politically reliable – that was another matter. Sadler had tried to sound him, without making it too obvious, but so far with little success. Jamieson seemed more interested in his work and his hobby – the painting of lunar landscapes – than in politics. During his term at the Observatory he had built up a small art gallery, and whenever he had the chance he would go out in a space-suit carrying easel and special paints made from low-vapour-pressure oils. It had taken him a good deal of experimenting to find pigments that could be used in a vacuum, and

Sadler frankly doubted if the results were worth the trouble. He thought he knew enough about art to decide that Jamieson had more enthusiasm than talent, and Wheeler shared this point of view. 'They say that Sid's pictures grow on you after a while,' he had confided to Sadler. 'Personally, I can think of no more horrible fate.'

Sadler's List B contained the names of everybody else in the Observatory who looked intelligent enough to be a spy. It was depressingly long, and from time to time he went through it trying to transfer people to List A or – better still – to the third and final list of those who were completely clear of suspicion. As he sat in his little cubicle, shuffling his sheets and trying to put himself into the place of the men he was watching, Sadler sometimes felt that he was playing an intricate game, in which most of the rules were flexible and all the players unknown. It was a deadly game, the moves were taking place at accelerating speed – and upon its outcome might depend the future of the human race.

Ten

The voice that came from the speaker was deep, cultured and sincere. It had been travelling across space for many minutes, beamed through the clouds of Venus along the two-hundred-million-kilometre link to Earth, then relayed again from Earth to the Moon. After that immense journey it was still clear and clean, almost untouched by interference or distortion.

'The situation here has hardened since my last commentary. No one in official circles will express any opinion, but the Press and radio are not so reticent. I flew in from Hesperus this morning, and the three hours I've been here are quite long enough for me to gauge public opinion.

'I must speak bluntly, even if I have to upset the people back home. Earth isn't very popular here. The phrase "dog in the manger" gets bandied round rather a lot. Your own supply difficulties are recognised, but it's felt that the frontier planets are short of necessities while Earth wastes much of its resources on trivial luxuries. I'll give you an example. Yesterday the news came in that the Mercury outpost had just lost five men through a faulty heat-exchange unit in one of the domes. The temperature control failed and the lava got them – not a very nice death. If the manufacturer had not been short of titanium, this wouldn't have happened.

'Of course, it's not fair to blame Earth for this. But it's unfortunate that only a week ago you cut the titanium quota again, and the interested parties here are seeing that the public doesn't forget it. I can't be more specific than that, because I don't want to be cut off, but you'll know who I mean.

'I don't believe that the situation will get any worse unless some new factor enters the picture. But suppose – and here I want to make it quite clear that I'm only considering a hypothetical case – suppose

Earth were to locate new supplies of the heavy metals. In the still unexplored ocean depths, for instance. Or even on the Moon, despite the disappointments it's given in the past.

'If this happens, and Earth tries to keep its discovery to itself, the consequences may be serious. It's all very well to say that Earth would be within its rights. Legal arguments don't carry much weight when you're fighting thousand-atmosphere pressures on Jupiter, or trying to thaw out the frozen moons of Saturn. Don't forget, as you enjoy your mild spring days and peaceful summer evenings, how lucky you are to live in the temperate region of the Solar System, where the air never freezes and the rocks never melt . . .

'What is the Federation likely to do if such a situation arises? If I knew, I couldn't tell you. I can only make some guesses. To talk about war, in the old-fashioned sense, seems absurd to me. Either side could inflict heavy damage on the other, but any real trial of strength could not possibly be conclusive. Earth has too many resources, even though they are dangerously concentrated. And she owns most of the ships in the Solar System.

'The Federation has the advantage of dispersion. How can Earth carry out a simultaneous fight against half a dozen planets and moons, poorly equipped though they may be? The supply problem would be completely hopeless.

'If, which heaven forbid, it should come to violence, we may see sudden raids on strategic points by specially equipped vessels which will make an attack and then retreat into space. Any talk of interplanetary invasion is pure fantasy. Earth certainly has no wish to take over the planets. And the Federation, even if it wanted to enforce its will on Earth, has neither the men nor the ships for a full-scale assault. As I see it, the immediate danger is that something like a duel may take place – where and how is anyone's guess – as one side attempts to impress the other with its strength. But I would warn any who may be thinking of a limited, gentlemanly war that wars were seldom limited, and never gentlemanly. Good-bye, Earth – this is Roderick Beynon, speaking to you from Venus.'

Someone reached out and turned off the set, but at first nobody seemed inclined to start the inevitable discussion. Then Jansen, from Power, said admiringly:

'Beynon's got guts, you must admit. He wasn't pulling his punches. I'm surprised they let him make that broadcast.'

'I thought he talked good sense,' remarked Mays. The High Priest of Computing had a slow, measured style of delivery that contrasted quaintly with the lightning speed of his machines.

'Whose side are you on?' someone asked suspiciously.

'Oh, I'm a friendly neutral.'

'But Earth pays your salary: which side would you support if there was a show-down?'

'Well – that would depend on the circumstances. I'd *like* to support Earth. But I reserve the right to make up my own mind. Whoever it was who said, "My planet right or wrong" was a damned fool. I'd be for Earth if it was right, and would probably give it the benefit of the doubt in a borderline case. But I'd not support it if I felt its cause was definitely wrong.'

There was a long silence while everyone thought this over. Sadler had been watching Mays intently while the mathematician was speaking. Everyone, he knew, respected May's honesty and logic. A man who was actively working against the Earth would never have expressed himself as forthrightly as this. Sadler wondered if Mays would have spoken any differently had he known that a counter-intelligence man was sitting within two metres of him. He did not believe that he would have altered a word.

'But, blast it,' said the Chief Engineer, who as usual was blocking the synthetic fire, 'there's no question of right and wrong here. Anything found on Earth or Moon belongs to us, to do with as we like.'

'Certainly – but don't forget we've been falling back on our quota deliveries, as Beynon said. The Federation has been relying on them for its programmes. If we repudiate our agreements because we haven't got the stuff ourselves, that's one thing. But it's a very different matter if we *have* got it and are just holding the Federation up to ransom.'

'Why should we do any such thing?'

It was Jamieson, unexpectedly enough, who answered this. 'Fear,' he said. 'Our politicians are frightened of the Federation. They know it already has more brains, and one day it may have more power. Then Earth will be a back number.'

418

Before anyone could challenge him on this, Czuikov from the Electronics Lab started a fresh hare.

'I've been thinking,' he said, 'about that broadcast we've just heard. We know that Beynon's a pretty honest man, but after all he was broadcasting from Venus, with their permission. There may be more in that talk of his than meets the ear.'

'What do you mean?'

'He may be putting across their propaganda. Not consciously, perhaps; they may have primed him to say what they want us to hear. That talk about raids, for instance. Perhaps it's intended to scare us.'

'That's an interesting idea. What do you think, Sadler? You're the last to come up from Earth.'

This frontal attack took Sadler rather by surprise, but he dexterously tossed the ball back.

'I don't think Earth can be frightened as easily as that. But the passage that interested me was his reference to possible new supplies on the Moon. It looks as if rumours are beginning to float around.'

This was a calculated indiscretion on Sadler's part. It was not so very indiscreet, however, for there was no one in the Observatory who did not know (a) that Wheeler and Jamieson had stumbled on some unusual government project in the *Mare Imbrium*, and (b) that they had been ordered not to talk about it. Sadler was particularly anxious to see what their reactions would be.

Jamieson assumed a look of puzzled innocence, but Wheeler did not hesitate to rise to the bait.

'What do you expect?' he said. 'Half the Moon must have seen those ships coming down in the *Mare*. And there must be hundreds of workmen there. They can't all have come from Earth – they'll be going into Central City and talking to their girl friends when they've had a few drinks too many.'

How right you are, thought Sadler, and what a headache *that* little problem was giving Security.

'Anyway,' continued Wheeler, 'I've got an open mind on the subject. They can do what they like out there as long as they don't interfere with me. You can't tell a thing from the outside of the place – except that it's costing the poor taxpayer an awful lot of money.'

There was a nervous cough from a mild little man down in

Instrumentation, where only that morning Sadler had spent a boring couple of hours looking at cosmic ray telescopes, magnetometers, seismographs, molecular resonance clocks, and batteries of other devices which were surely storing information more rapidly than anyone would ever be able to analyse it.

'I don't know about them interfering with you, but they've been playing hell with me.'

'What do you mean?' everyone asked simultaneously.

'I had a look at the magnetic field-strength meters half an hour ago. Usually the field here is pretty constant, except when there's a storm around, and we always know when to expect those. But something odd's going on at the moment. The field keeps hopping up and down – not very much, a few microgauss – and I'm sure it's artificial. I've checked all the equipment in the Observatory, and everyone swears they're not mucking around with magnets. I wondered if our secretive friends out in the *Mare* were responsible, and just on the chance I had a look at the other instruments. I didn't find anything until I came to the seismographs. We've got a telemetering one down by the south wall of the crater, you know, and it had been knocked all over the place. Some of the kinks looked like blasting – I'm always picking that up from Hyginus and the other mines. But there were also some most peculiar jitters of the trace that were almost synchronised with the magnetic pulses. Allowing for the time lag through the rock, the distance checked up well. There's no doubt where it comes from.'

'An interesting piece of research,' Jamieson remarked, 'but what does it add up to?'

'There are probably a good many interpretations. But I'd say that out there in the *Mare Imbrium* someone is generating a colossal magnetic field, in pulses lasting about a second at a time.'

'And the moonquakes?'

'Just a by-product. There's a lot of magnetic rock around here, and I imagine it must get quite a jolt when that field goes on. You probably wouldn't notice that quake even if you were where it started, but our seismographs are so sensitive they can spot a meteor falling twenty kilometres away.'

Sadler listened to the resulting technical argument with great interest. With so many keen minds worrying around the facts, it was inevitable that some would guess the truth – and inevitable that others would counter it with their own theories. This was not important; what concerned him was whether anyone showed special knowledge or curiosity.

But no one did, and Sadler was still left with his discouraging three propositions – Mr X was too clever for him; Mr X was not here; Mr X did not exist at all.

Eleven

Nova Draconis was waning; no longer did it outshine all the suns of the galaxy. Yet in the skies of Earth it was still brighter than Venus at her most brilliant, and it might be a thousand years before men saw its like again.

Though it was very near on the scale of stellar distances, *Nova Draconis* was still so remote that its apparent magnitude did not vary across the whole width of the Solar System. It shone with equal brilliance above the firelands of Mercury and the nitrogen glaciers of Pluto. Transient though it was, it had turned men's minds for a moment from their own affairs and made them think of ultimate realities.

But not for long. The fierce violet light of the greatest nova in history shone now upon a divided system, upon planets which had ceased to threaten each other and were now preparing for deeds.

The preparations were far more advanced than the public realised. Neither Earth nor the Federation had been frank with its people. In secret laboratories, men had been turning towards destruction the tools which had given them the freedom of space. Even if the contestants had worked in entire independence, it was inevitable that they would have evolved similar weapons, since they were basing them on the same technologies.

But each side had its agents and counter-agents, and each knew, at least approximately, the weapons which the other was developing. There might be some surprises – any one of which could be decisive – but on the whole the antagonists were equally matched.

In one respect the Federation had a great advantage. It could hide its activities, its researches and tests, among the scattered moons and asteroids, beyond any hope of discovery. Earth, on the other hand, could not launch a single ship without the information reaching Mars and Venus within a matter of minutes.

The great uncertainty that plagued either side was the efficiency of its Intelligence. If this came to war, it would be a war of amateurs. A secret service requires a long tradition, though perhaps not an honourable one: spies cannot be trained overnight, and, even if they could, the kind of flair that characterises a really brilliant agent is not easy to come by.

No one was better aware of this than Sadler. Sometimes he wondered if his unknown colleagues, scattered over the Solar System, felt equally frustrated. Only the men at the top could see the complete picture – or something approaching it. He had never realised the isolation in which a spy must work – the horrible feeling that you are alone, that there is no one you can trust, no one with whom you can share your burdens. Since he had reached the Moon he had – at least to his knowledge – spoken to no other member of Central Intelligence. All his contacts with the organisation had been impersonal and indirect. His routine reports – which to any casual reader would have seemed extremely dull analyses of the Observatory's accounts – went by the daily monorail to Central City, and he had little idea what happened to them after that. A few messages had arrived by the same means, and in the event of real emergency the teleprinter circuit was available.

He was looking forward to his first meeting with another agent, which had been arranged weeks in advance. Though he doubted if it would be of much practical value, it would give his morale a badly needed boost.

Sadler had now, to his own satisfaction at least, acquainted himself with all the main aspects of Administration and Technical Services. He had looked (from a respectful distance) into the burning heart of the micropile which was the Observatory's main power source. He had watched the big mirrors of the solar generators, waiting patiently for the sunrise. They had not been used for years, but it was nice to have them around in case of any emergency, ready to tap the limitless resources of the sun itself.

The Observatory farm had surprised and fascinated him most of all. It was strange that in this age of scientific marvels, of synthetic this and artificial that, there were still some things in which Nature could not be excelled. The farm was an integral part of the air-conditioning system, and was at its best during the long lunar day. When Sadler saw it lines of fluorescent lamps were providing substitute sunlight, and metal shutters had been drawn over the great windows which would greet the dawn when the sun rose above the western wall of Plato.

He might have been back on Earth in some well-appointed greenhouse. The slowly moving air passed along the rows of growing plants, gave up its carbon dioxide, and emerged not only richer in oxygen, but also with that indefinable freshness which the chemists had never been able to duplicate.

And here Sadler was presented with a small but very ripe apple, every atom of which had come from the Moon. He took it back to his room where he could enjoy it in privacy, and was no longer surprised that the farm was out of bounds to everyone except the men who tended it. The trees would soon be stripped if any casual visitor could wander through these verdant corridors.

The signals section was just about as great a contrast as could be imagined. Here were the circuits which linked the Observatory with Earth, with the rest of the Moon, and if necessary with planets direct. It was the greatest and most obvious danger point. Every message that came or went was monitored, and the men who operated the equipment had been checked and rechecked by Security. Two of the staff had been transferred, without knowing the reason, to less sensitive jobs. Moreover – even Sadler did not know this – a telescopic camera thirty kilometres away was taking a photograph every minute of the big transmitting arrays which the Observatory used for long-distance work. If one of these radio searchlights happened to point for any length of time in an unauthorised direction the fact would soon be known.

The astronomers, without exception, were all very willing to discuss their work and explain their equipment. If they wondered at some of Sadler's questions, they gave no sign of it. For his part he was very careful not to step outside his adopted rôle. The technique he used was the frank man-to-man one: 'Of course this isn't really my job, but I'm quite interested in astronomy and while I'm here on the Moon I want to see all I can. Naturally, if you're too busy at the moment—' It always worked like a charm.

Wagnall usually made the arrangements and smoothed the way for him. The Secretary had been so helpful that at first Sadler wondered if he were trying to safeguard himself, but further enquiry had shown that Wagnall was like that. He was one of those people who cannot help trying to create a good impression, simply because they want to be on good terms with everybody. He must find it singularly frustrating, Sadler thought, working for a cold fish like Professor Maclaurin.

The heart of the Observatory was, of course, the thousand-centimetre telescope – the largest optical instrument ever made by man. It stood on the summit of a slight knoll some distance from the residential area, and was impressive rather than elegant. The enormous barrel was surrounded by a gantry-like structure which controlled its vertical movement, and the whole framework could rotate on a circular track.

'It's not a bit like any of the telescopes back on Earth,' explained Molton as they stood together inside the nearest observation dome, looking out across the plain. 'The tube, for instance. That's so we can still work during the day. Without it, we'd get sunlight reflected down into the mirror from the supporting structure. That would ruin our observations, and the heat would distort the mirror. It might take hours to settle down again. The big reflectors on Earth haven't got to worry about this sort of thing. They're only used at night – those that are still in action at all.'

'I wasn't sure that there were any active observatories left on Earth,' Sadler remarked.

'Oh, there are a few. Nearly all training establishments, of course. *Real* astronomical research is impossible down in that pea-soup of an atmosphere. Look at my own work, for instance – ultra-violet spectroscopy. The Earth's atmosphere is *completely* opaque to the wavelengths I'm interested in. No one ever observed them until we got out into space. Sometimes I wonder how astronomy ever *started* down on Earth.'

'The mounting looks odd to me,' Sadler remarked thoughtfully. 'It's more like that of a gun than any telescope I've ever seen.'

'Quite correct. They didn't bother about an equatorial mounting. There's an automatic computer that keeps it tracking any star we set

425

it on. But come downstairs and see what happens at the business end.'

Molton's laboratory was a fantastic maze of half-assembled equipment, scarcely any of which Sadler could recognize. When he complained about this, his guide seemed highly amused.

'You needn't feel ashamed of that. We've designed and built most of it here – we're always trying out improvements. But roughly speaking, what happens is this. The light from the big mirror – we're directly underneath it here – is piped down through that tube over there. I can't demonstrate at the moment, as someone is taking photographs and it's not my turn for another hour. But when it is, I can select any part of the sky I like from this remote control desk here and lock the instrument on to it. Then all I have to do is to analyse the light with these spectroscopes. You can't see much of their works, I'm afraid – they're all totally enclosed. When they're in use the whole optical system has to be evacuated, because, as I mentioned just now, even a trace of air blocks the far ultra-violet rays.'

Sadler was suddenly struck by an incongruous thought.

'Tell me,' he said glancing round the maze of wiring, the batteries of electronic counters, the atlases of spectral lines, 'have you ever *looked* through this telescope?'

Molton smiled back at him.

'Never,' he said. 'It wouldn't be hard to arrange, but there would be absolutely no point in it. All these really big telescopes are super-cameras. And who wants to look through a camera?'

There were, however, telescopes at the Observatory through which one could look without too much trouble. Some of the smaller instruments were fitted with TV cameras which could be swung into position when it was necessary to search for comets or asteroids whose exact locations were unknown. Once or twice Sadler managed to borrow one of these instruments, and to sweep the skies at random to see what he could find. He would dial a position on the remote control board, then peer into the screen to see what he had caught. After a while he discovered how to use the Astronautical Almanac, and it was a great moment when he set up the co-ordinates for Mars and found it bang in the middle of the field.

He stared with mixed feelings at the green and ochre disc almost filling the screen. One of the polar caps was tilted slightly sunwards – it was the beginning of spring, and the great frost-covered tundras would be slowly thawing after the iron winter. A beautiful planet to watch from space, but a hard planet on which to build a civilisation. No wonder its sturdy children were losing patience with Earth.

The image of the planet was incredibly sharp and clear. There was not the slightest tremor or unsteadiness as it floated in the field of view, and Sadler, who had once glimpsed Mars through a telescope on Earth, could now see with his own eyes how astronomy had been liberated from its chains when the atmosphere had been left behind. Earth-bound observers had studied Mars for decades through instruments larger than this, but he could see more in a few hours than they could have glimpsed in a lifetime. He was no nearer to Mars then they had been – indeed, the planet was now at a considerable distance from Earth – but there was no dancing, quivering haze of air to veil his view.

When he had gazed his fill at Mars, he searched for Saturn. The sheer beauty of the spectacle took his breath away: it seemed impossible that he was not looking at some perfect work of art, rather than a creation of Nature. The great yellow globe, slightly flattened at the poles, floated at the centre of its intricate system of rings. The faint bands and shadings of atmospheric disturbances were clearly visible, even across two thousand million kilometres of space. And beyond the concentric girdles of the rings, Sadler could count at least seven of the planet's moons.

Though he knew that the instantaneously operating eye of the television camera could never rival the patient photographic plate, he also looked for some of the distant nebulae and star clusters. He let the field of view drift along the crowded highway of the Milky Way, checking the image whenever some particularly beautiful group of stars, or cloud of glowing mist, appeared upon the screen. After a while it seemed to Sadler that he had become intoxicated with the infinite splendour of the skies; he needed something that would bring him back into the realm of human affairs. So he turned the telescope on Earth.

It was so huge that even under the weakest power he could get only part of it on the screen. The great crescent was shrinking fast, but even the unlit portion of the disc was full of interest. Down there in the night were the countless phosphorescent glows that marked the positions of cities – and down there was Jeanette, sleeping now, but perhaps dreaming of him. At least he knew that she had received his letter: her puzzled but guarded reply had been reassuring, though its loneliness and unspoken reproach had torn at his heart. Had he, after all, made a mistake? Sometimes he bitterly regretted the conventional caution which had ruled the first year of their married life. Like most couples on the overpopulated planet that swam before his eyes, they had waited to prove their compatibility before embarking on the adventure of parenthood. In this age it was a definite social stigma to have children before one had been married for several years – it was a proof of fecklessness and irresponsibility.

They had both wanted a family, and, now that such matters could be decided in advance, had intended to start with a son. Then Sadler had received his assignment, and realised for the first time the full seriousness of the interplantary situation. He would not bring Jonathon Peter into the uncertain future that lay ahead.

In earlier ages few men would have hesitated for such a reason. Indeed, the possibility of their own extinction had often made them even more anxious to seek the only immortality human beings can know. But the world had been at peace for two hundred years, and if war came now, the complex and fragile pattern of life on Earth might be broken into fragments. A woman burdened with a child might have little chance of survival.

Perhaps he was being melodramatic, and had let his fears overpower his sense of judgment. If Jeanette had known all the facts, she would still not have hesitated: she would have taken the chance. But because he could not talk to her freely, he would not take advantage of her ignorance.

It was too late for regret: all that he loved lay there on that sleeping globe, sundered from him by the abyss of space. His thoughts had come full circle. He had made the journey from star to man, across the immense desert of the cosmos to the lonely oasis of the human soul.

Twelve

'I've no reason to suppose,' said the man in the blue suit, 'that anyone suspects you, but it would be difficult to meet inconspicuously in Central City. There are too many people around, and everybody knows everybody else. You'd be surprised how hard it is to get any privacy.'

'You don't think it will seem odd for me to come here?' asked Sadler.

'No – most visitors do, if they can manage it. It's like going to Niagara Falls – something no one wants to miss. You can't blame them, can you?'

Sadler agreed. Here was one spectacle that could never be a disappointment, that would always surpass any advance publicity. Even now the shock of stepping out on to this balcony had not completely worn off. He could well believe that many people were physically incapable of coming as far as this.

He was standing above nothingness, encased in a transparent cylinder jutting out from the edge of the canyon. The metal catwalk beneath his feet and the slim handrail were the only tokens of security granted to him. His knuckles still grasped that railing tightly . . .

The Hyginus Cleft ranks among the greatest wonders on the Moon. From end to end it is more than three hundred kilometres long, and in places five kilometres wide. It is not so much a canyon as a series of interlinked craters, branching out in two arms from a vast central well. And it is the gateway through which men have reached the buried treasures of the Moon.

Sadler could now look down into the depths without flinching. Infinitely far below, it seemed, some strange insects were slowly crawling back and forth in little pools of artificial light. If one shone a torch upon a group of cockroaches, they would have looked like this.

But those tiny insects, Sadler knew, were the great mining machines at work on the floor of the canyon. It was surprisingly flat down there, so many thousands of metres below, for it seemed that lava had flooded into the cleft soon after it was formed, and then congealed into a buried river of rock.

The Earth, almost vertically overhead, illuminated the great wall immediately opposite. The canyon marched away to right and left as far as the eye could follow, and sometimes the blue-green light falling upon the rock face produced a most unexpected illusion. Sadler found it easy to imagine, if he moved his head suddenly, that he was looking into the heart of a gigantic waterfall, sweeping down for ever into the depths of the Moon.

Across the face of that fall, on the invisible threads of hoisting cables, the ore buckets were rising and dropping. Sadler had seen those buckets moving on the overhead lines away from the cleft, and he knew that they were taller than he was. But now they looked like beads moving slowly along a wire, as they carried their loads to the distant smelting plants. It's a pity, he thought to himself, that they're only carrying sulphur and oxygen and silicon and aluminium – we could do with fewer of the light elements and more of the heavy ones.

But he had been called here on business, not to stand gaping like a tourist. He pulled the coded notes from his pocket, and began to give his report.

It did not take as long as he would have wished. There was no way of telling whether his listener was pleased or disappointed at the inconclusive summary. He thought it over for a minute, then remarked, 'I wish we could give you some more help, but you can imagine how shorthanded we are now. Things are getting rough – if there is going to be trouble we expect it in the next ten days. There's something happening out round Mars, but we don't know what it is. The Federation has been building at least two ships of unusual design, and we think they're testing them. Unfortunately we haven't a single sighting – only some rumours that don't make sense but have put the wind up Defence. I'm telling you this to give you more background. No one here should know about it, and if you hear anybody talking on these lines it will mean that they've somehow had access to classified information.

'Now about your short list of provisional suspects. I see you've got Wagnall down, but he's clear with us.'

'O.K. – I'll move him to List B.'

'Then Brown, Lefevre, Tolanski – they've certainly had no contacts here.'

'Can you be sure of that?'

'Fairly. They use their off-duty hours here in highly non-political ways.'

'I'd suspected that,' Sadler remarked, permitting himself the luxury of a smile. 'I'll take them off altogether.'

'Now this man Jenkins, in Stores. Why are you so keen on keeping him?'

'I've no real evidence at all. But he seems about the only person who's taken any objections to my nominal activities.'

'Well, we'll continue to watch him from this end. He comes to town quite often, but of course he's got a good excuse – he does most of the local purchasing. That leaves you with five names on your A list, doesn't it?'

'Yes – and frankly I'll be very surprised if it's any of them. Wheeler and Jamieson we've already discussed. I know that Maclaurin's suspicious of Jamieson after that trip out to the *Mare Imbrium*, but I don't put much reliance on that. It was largely Wheeler's idea, anyway.

'Then there are Benson and Carlin. Their wives come from Mars, and they keep getting into arguments whenever the news is being discussed. Benson's an electrician in Tech Maintenance: Carlin's a medical orderly. You could say they have some motive, but it's a pretty tenuous one. Moreover, they'd be rather too obvious suspects.'

'Well, here's another we'd like you to move up to your List A. This fellow Molton.'

'Dr Molton?' exclaimed Sadler in some surprise. 'Any particular reason?'

'Nothing serious, but he's been to Mars several times on astronomical missions and has some friends there.'

'He never talks politics – I've tackled him once or twice and he just didn't seem interested. I don't think he meets many people in Central City – he seems completely wrapped up in his work, and I think he only goes into town to keep fit in the gym. You've nothing else?'

'No – sorry. It's still a fifty-fifty case. There's a leak *somewhere*, but it may be in Central City. The report about the Observatory may be a deliberate plant. As you say, it's very hard to see how anyone there could pass on information. The radio monitors have detected nothing except a few unauthorised personal messages which were quite innocent.'

Sadler closed his notebook and put it away with a sigh. He glanced once more down into the vertiginous depths above which he was insecurely floating. The cockroaches were crawling briskly away from a spot at the base of the cliff, and suddenly a slow stain seemed to spread across the floodlit wall. (*How* far down was that? Two kilometres? Or three?) A puff of smoke emerged and distantly dispersed into the vacuum. Sadler began to count the seconds to time his distance from the explosion, and had got to twelve before he remembered that he was wasting his efforts. If that had been an atom bomb, he would have heard nothing here.

The man in blue adjusted his camera strap, nodded at Sadler, and became the perfect tourist again.

'Give me ten minutes to get clear,' he said, 'and remember not to know me if we meet again.'

Sadler rather resented that last advice. After all, he was not a complete amateur. He had been fully operational for almost half a lunar day.

Business was slack at the little cafe in the Hyginus station, and Sadler had the place to himself. The general uncertainty had discouraged tourists; any who happened to be on the Moon were hurrying home as fast as they could get shipping space. They were probably doing the right thing; if there was trouble, it would be here. No one really believed that the Federation would attack Earth directly and destroy millions of innocent lives. Such barbarities belonged to the past – so it was hoped. But how could one be sure? Who knew what might happen if war broke out? Earth was so fearfully vulnerable.

For a moment Sadler lost himself in reveries of longing and self-pity. He wondered if Jeanette had guessed where he was: he was not sure, now, that he wanted her to know. It would only increase her worries.

Over his coffee – which he still ordered automatically though he had never met any on the Moon worth drinking – he considered the information his unknown contact had given to him. It had been of very little value: he was still groping in the dark. The tip about Molton was a distinct surprise, and he did not take it too seriously. There was a kind of trustworthiness about the astrophysicist which made it hard to think of him as a spy. Sadler knew perfectly well that it was fatal to rely on such hunches, and whatever his own feelings he would now pay extra attention to Molton. But he made a private bet with himself that it would lead nowhere.

He marshalled all the facts he could remember about the head of the Spectroscopy section. He already knew about Molton's three trips to Mars. The last visit had been over a year ago, and the Director himself had been there more recently than that. Moreover, among the interplanetary brotherhood of astronomers there was probably no member of the senior staff who did not have friends on both Mars and Venus.

Were there any unusual features about Molton? None that Sadler could think of, apart from that curious aloofness that seemed to conflict with a real inner warmth. There was, of course, his amusing and rather touching 'flower bed', as he had heard someone christen it. But if he was to start investigating innocent eccentricities like *that*, he'd never get anywhere.

There was one thing that might be worth looking into, however. He'd make a note of the shop where Molton purchased his replacements (it was almost the only place outside the gym he ever visited), and one of the counter-agents in the city could sniff round it. Feeling rather pleased with himself at thus proving he was missing no chances, Sadler paid his bill and walked up the short corridor connecting the café with the almost deserted station.

He rode the spur-line back to Central City, over the incredibly broken terrain past Triesnecker. For almost all the journey the monorail track was accompanied by the pylons passing their loaded buckets out from Hyginus, and the empty ones back. The long cables, with their kilometre spans, were the cheapest and most practical means of conveyance – if there was no particular hurry to deliver the goods. Soon after the domes of Central City appeared on the skyline, however, they changed direction and curved off to the right. Sadler could see them marching away down to the horizon towards the great chemical plants which, directly or indirectly, fed and clothed every human being on the Moon.

He no longer felt a stranger in the city, and went from dome to dome with the assurance of a seasoned traveller. The first priority was an overdue haircut; one of the Observatory cooks earned some extra money as a barber, but having seen the results Sadler preferred to stick to the professionals. Then there was just time to call at the gym for fifteen minutes in the centrifuge.

As usual the place was full of Observatory staff making sure they would be able to live on Earth again when they wished to. There was a waiting list for the centrifuge, so Sadler dumped his clothes in a locker and went for a swim until the descending whine of the motor told him that the big machine was ready for a new cargo of passengers. He noticed, with wry amusement, that two of his List A suspects – Wheeler and Molton – and no less than seven of the Class B ones were present. But it was not so surprising about Class B. Ninety per cent of the Observatory staff were on *that* unwieldy list, which if it had been titled at all would have been called: 'Persons sufficiently intelligent and active to be spies, but concerning whom there is no evidence one way or the other.'

The centrifuge held six people, and had some ingenious safety device which prevented it starting unless the load was properly balanced. It refused to co-operate until a fat man on Sadler's left had changed places with a thin man opposite: then the motor began to pick up speed, and the big drum with its slightly anxious human cargo started to turn on its axis. As the speed increased, Sadler felt his weight steadily mounting. The direction of the vertical was shifting, too – it was swinging round towards the centre of the drum. He breathed deeply, and tried to see if he could lift his arms. They felt as if they were made of lead.

The man on Sadler's right staggered to his feet and began to walk to and fro, keeping within the carefully defined white lines that marked the limits of his territory. Everyone else was doing the same: it was uncanny to watch them standing on what, from the point of

434

view of the Moon, was a vertical surface. But they were glued to it by a force six times as great as the Moon's feeble gravity – a force equal to the weight they would have had on Earth.

It was not a pleasant sensation. Sadler found it almost impossible to believe that until a few days ago he had spent his entire existence in a gravity field of this strength. Presumably he would get used to it again, but at the moment it made him feel as weak as a kitten. He was heartily glad when the centrifuge slowed down and he was able to crawl back into the gentle gravity of the friendly Moon.

He was a tired and somewhat discouraged man as the monorail pulled out of Central City. Even the brief glimpse he caught of the new day, as the still hidden sun touched the highest pinnacles of the western mountains, failed to cheer him. He had been here more than twelve days of Earth-time, and the long lunar night was ending. But he dreaded to think what the day might bring.

Thirteen

Every man has his weakness, if you can find it. Jamieson's was so obvious that it seemed unfair to exploit it, but Sadler could not afford to have any scruples. Everyone in the Observatory regarded the young astronomer's painting as a subject for mild amusement, and gave him no encouragement at all. Sadler, feeling a considerable hypocrite, began to play the role of sympathetic admirer.

It had taken some time to break through Jamieson's reserve and to get him to speak frankly. The process could not be hurried without arousing suspicion, but Sadler had made fair progress by the simplest technique of supporting Jamieson when his colleagues ganged up on him. This happened, on the average, every time he produced a new picture.

To steer the conversation from art to politics took less skill than might have been expected, for politics was never very far away these days. Yet, oddly enough, it was Jamieson himself who raised the questions that Sadler had been trying to ask. He had obviously been thinking hard, in his methodical way, wrestling with the problem that had concerned every scientist to a greater and greater extent, since the day when atomic power was born on Earth.

'What would you do,' he asked Sadler abruptly, a few hours after the latter's return from Central City, 'if you had to choose between Earth and the Federation?'

'Why ask me?' replied Sadler, trying to conceal his interest. 'I've been asking a lot of people,' Jamieson replied. There was a wistfulness in his voice – the puzzled wonder of someone looking for guidance in a strange and complex world. 'Do you remember that argument we had in the Common Room when Mays said that whoever believed in "My planet, right or wrong" was a fool?'

'I remember,' Sadler answered cautiously.

'I think Mays was right. Loyalty isn't just a matter of birth, but ideals. There can be times when morality and patriotism clash.'

'What's started you philosophising on these lines?'

Jamieson's reply was unexpected.

'*Nova Draconis*,' he said. 'We've just got in the reports from the Federation observatories out beyond Jupiter. They were routed through Mars, and someone there had attached a note to them – Molton showed it to me. It wasn't signed, and it was quite short. It merely said that *whatever* happened – and the word was repeated twice – they'd see that their reports continued to reach us.'

A touching example of scientific solidarity, thought Sadler: it had obviously made a deep impression on Jamieson. Most men – certainly most men who were not scientists – would have thought the incident rather trivial. But trifles like this could sway men's minds at crucial moments.

'I don't know just what you deduce from this,' said Sadler, feeling like a skater on very thin ice. 'After all, everybody knows that the Federation has plenty of men who are just as honest and well intentioned and co-operative as anyone here. But you can't run a solar system on gusts of emotion. Would you really hesitate if it came to a show-down between Earth and the Federation?'

There was a long pause. Then Jamieson sighed.

'I don't know,' he answered. 'I really don't know.'

It was a completely frank and honest answer. As far as Sadler was concerned, it virtually eliminated Jamieson from his list of suspects.

The fantastic incident of the searchlight in the *Mare Imbrium* occurred nearly twenty-four hours later. Sadler heard about it when he joined Wagnall for morning coffee, as he usually did when he was near Administration.

'Here's something to make you think,' said Wagnall as Sadler walked into the Secretary's office. 'One of the technicians from Electronics was up in the dome just now, admiring the view, when suddenly a beam of light shot up over the horizon. It lasted for about a second, and he says it was a brilliant blue-white. There's no doubt that it came from that place that Wheeler and Jamieson visited. I know that Instrumentation has been having trouble with them, and

I've just checked. Their magnetometers were kicked right off scale ten minutes ago, and there's been a severe local 'quake.'

'I don't see how a searchlight would do that sort of thing,' answered Sadler, genuinely puzzled. Then the full implications of the statement reached him.

'*A beam of light?*' he gasped. 'Why, that's impossible. It wouldn't be visible in the vacuum here.'

'Exactly,' said Wagnall, obviously enjoying the other's mystification. 'You can only see a light beam when it passes through dust or air. And this was really brilliant – almost dazzling. The phrase Williams used was 'It looked like a solid bar.' Do you know what *I* think that place is?'

'No,' replied Sadler, wondering how near Wagnall had got to the truth. 'I haven't any idea.'

The Secretary looked rather bashful, as if trying out a theory of which he was a little ashamed.

'I think it's some kind of fortress. Oh, I know it sounds fantastic, but when you think about it you'll see it's the only explanation that fits all the facts.'

Before Sadler could reply, or indeed think of a suitable answer, the desk buzzer sounded and a slip of paper dropped out of Wagnall's teleprinter. It was a standard signals form, but there was one non-standard item about it. It carried the crimson banner of Priority.

Wagnall read it aloud, his eyes widening as he did so.

URGENT TO DIRECTOR PLATO OBSERVATORY. DISMANTLE ALL SURFACE INSTRUMENTS AND MOVE ALL DELICATE EQUIPMENT UNDERGROUND COMMENCING WITH LARGE MIRRORS. RAIL SERVICE SUSPENDED UNTIL FURTHER NOTICE. KEEP STAFF UNDERGROUND AS FAR AS POSSIBLE. EMPHASISE THIS PRECAUTIONARY REPEAT PRECAUTIONARY MEASURE. NO IMMEDIATE DANGER EXPECTED.

'And that,' said Wagnall slowly, 'appears to be that. I'm very much afraid my guess was perfectly correct.'

It was the first time that Sadler had ever seen the entire Observatory staff gathered together. Professor Maclaurin stood on the raised dais at the end of the main lounge – the traditional place for announcements, musical recitals, dramatic interludes, and other forms of Observatory entertainment. But no one was being entertained now.

'I fully understand,' said Maclaurin bitterly, 'what this means to your programmes. We can only hope that this move is totally unnecessary, and that we can start work again within a few days. But obviously we can take no chances with our equipment – the five-hundred and the thousand-centimetre mirrors must be got under cover at once. I have no idea what form of trouble is anticipated, but it seems that we are in an unfortunate position here. If hostilities do break out, I shall signal at once to both Mars and Venus reminding them that this is a scientific institution, that many of their nationals have been honoured guests here, and that we are of no conceivable military importance. Now please assemble behind your group leaders, and carry out your instructions as swiftly and efficiently as possible.'

The Director walked down from the dais. Small though he was, he seemed still more shrunken now. In that moment there was no one in the room who did not share his feelings, however much they might have inveighed against him in the past.

'Is there anything I can do?' asked Sadler, who had been left out of the hastily drawn-up emergency plans.

'Ever worn a space-suit?' said Wagnall.

'No, but I don't mind trying.'

To Sadler's disappointment the Secretary shook his head firmly.

'Too dangerous – you might get in trouble and there aren't enough suits to go round, anyway. But I could do with some more help in the office – we've had to tear up all the existing programmes and go over to a two-watch system. So all the rotas and schedules have to be rearranged – you could help on this.'

That's what comes of volunteering for anything, thought Sadler. But Wagnall was right; there was nothing he could do to help the technical teams. As for his own mission, he could probably serve it better in the Secretary's office than anywhere else, for it would be the operational headquarters from now on.

Not, thought Sadler grimly, that it now mattered a great deal. If

439

Mr X had ever existed, and was still in the Observatory he could now relax with the consciousness of a job well done.

Some instruments, it had been decided, would have to take their chance. These were the smaller ones, which could be easily replaced. Operation Safeguard, as someone with a penchant for military nomenclature had christened it, was to concentrate on the priceless optical components of the giant telescopes and coelostats.

Jamieson and Wheeler drove out with Ferdinand and collected the mirrors of the interferometer – the great instrument whose twin eyes, twenty kilometres apart, made it possible to measure the diameters of the stars. The main activity, however, centred round the thousand-centimetre reflector.

Molton was in charge of the mirror team. The work would have been impossible without his detailed knowledge of the telescope's optical and engineering features. It would have been impossible, even with his help, if the mirror had been cast in a single unit, like that of the historic instrument that still stood atop Mount Palomar. This mirror, however, was built from more than a hundred hexagonal sections, dovetailed together into a great mosaic. Each could be removed separately and carried to safety, though it was slow and tedious work, and it would take weeks to reassemble the complete mirror with the fantastic precision needed.

Space-suits are not really designed for this sort of work, and one helper, through inexperience or haste, managed to drop his end of a mirror section as he lifted it out of the cell. Before anyone could catch it, the big hexagon of fused quartz had picked up enough speed to chip off one of its corners. This was the only optical casualty, which in the circumstances was very creditable.

The last tired and disheartened man came in through the airlocks twelve hours after the operation had commenced. Only one research project continued – a single telescope was still following the slow decline of *Nova Draconis* as it sank towards final extinction. War or no war, this work would go on.

Soon after the announcement that the two big mirrors were safe, Sadler went up to one of the observation domes. He did not know when he would have another chance to see the stars and the waning

Earth, and he wished to carry the memory down into his subterranean retreat.

As far as the eye could tell, the Observatory was quite unchanged. The great barrel of the thousand-centimetre reflector pointed straight to the zenith; it had been swung over to the vertical to bring the mirror cell down to ground-level. Little short of a direct hit could damage this massive structure, and it would have to take its chances in the hours or days of danger that lay ahead.

There were still a few men moving around in the open; one of them, Sadler noticed, was the Director. He was perhaps the only man on the Moon who could be recognised when wearing a space-suit. It had been specially built for him, and brought his height up to a full metre and a half.

One of the open trucks used for moving equipment round the Observatory was scuttling across towards the telescope, throwing up little gouts of dust. It halted beside the great circular track on which the framework revolved, and the space-suited figures clambered clumsily aboard. Then it made off briskly to the right, and presently disappeared into the ground as it descended the ramp leading into the airlocks of the garage.

The great plain was deserted, the Observatory blind save for the one faithful instrument pointing towards the north in sublime defiance of the follies of man. Then the speaker of the ubiquitous public-address system ordered Sadler out of the dome, and he went reluctantly into the depths. He wished he could have waited a little longer, for in a few more minutes the western walls of Plato would be touched by the first fingers of the lunar dawn. It seemed a pity that no one would be here to greet it.

Slowly the Moon was turning towards the sun, as it could never turn towards the Earth. The line of day was crawling across the mountains and plains, banishing the unimaginable cold of the long night. Already the entire westward wall of the Apennines was ablaze, and the *Mare Imbrium* was climbing into the dawn. But Plato still lay in darkness, lit only by the radiance of the waning Earth.

A group of scattered stars suddenly appeared low down in the western sky. The tallest spires of the great ring-wall were catching the sun, and minute by minute the light spread down their flanks, until it linked them together in a necklace of fire. Now the sun was striking clear across the whole vast circle of the crater, as the ramparts on the east lifted into the dawn. Any watchers down on Earth would see Plato as an unbroken ring of light, surrounding a pool of inky shadow. It would be hours yet before the rising sun could clear the mountains and subdue the last strongholds of the night.

There were no eyes to watch when, for the second time, that blue-white bar stabbed briefly at the southern sky. That was well for Earth. The Federation had learned much, but there were still some things which it might discover too late.

Fourteen

The observatory had settled down for a siege of indefinite duration. It was not, on the whole, as frustrating an experience as might have been expected. Although the main programmes had been interrupted, there was endless work to do in reducing results, checking theories, and writing papers which until now had been put aside for lack of time. Many of the astronomers almost welcomed the break, and several fundamental advances in cosmology were a direct outcome of the enforced idleness.

The worst aspect of the whole affair, everyone agreed, was the uncertainty and lack of news. What was really going on? Could one believe the bulletins from Earth, which seemed to be trying to soothe the public while at the same time preparing it for the worst?

As far as could be judged, some kind of attack was expected, and it was just the Observatory's bad luck that it was so near a possible danger point. Perhaps Earth guessed what form the attack would take, and certainly it had made some preparations to meet it.

The two great antagonists were circling each other, each unwilling to strike the first blow, each hoping to bluff the other into capitulation. But they had gone too far, and neither could retreat without a loss of prestige too damaging to be faced.

Sadler feared that the point of no return had already been passed. He was sure of it when the news came over the radio that the Federation Minister at the Hague had delivered a virtual ultimatum to the government of Earth. It charged Earth with failing to meet its agreed quotas of heavy metals, of deliberately witholding supplies for political purposes, and of concealing the existence of new resources. Unless Earth agreed to discuss the allocation of these new resources, she would find it impossible to use them herself.

The ultimatum was followed, six hours later, by a general

broadcast to Earth, beamed from Mars by a transmitter of astonishing power. It assured the people of Earth that no harm would befall them, and that if any damage was done to the home planet it would be an unfortunate accident of war, for which their own government must take the blame. The Federation would avoid any acts which might endanger populated areas, and it trusted that its example would be followed.

The Observatory listened to this broadcast with mixed feelings. There was no doubt as to its meaning – and no doubt that the *Mare Imbrium* was, within the meaning of the Act, an unpopulated area. One effect of the broadcast was to increase sympathy for the Federation, even among those likely to be damaged by its actions. Jamieson in particular began to be much less diffident in expressing his views, and had soon made himself quite unpopular. Before long, indeed, a distinct rift appeared in the Observatory ranks. On the one side were those (mostly the younger men) who felt much as Jamieson did, and regarded Earth as reactionary and intolerant. Against them, on the other hand, were the steady, conservative individuals who would always automatically support those in authority without worrying too much about moral abstractions.

Sadler watched these arguments with great interest, even though he was conscious that the success or failure of his mission had already been decided and that nothing he could do now would alter that. However, there was always the chance that the probably mythical Mr X might now become careless, or might even attempt to leave the Observatory. Sadler had taken certain steps to guard against this, with the co-operation of the Director. No one could get at the space-suits or tractors without authority, and the base was therefore effectively sealed. Living in a vacuum did have certain advantages from the security point of view.

The Observatory's state of siege had brought Sadler one tiny triumph, which he could very well have foregone, and which seemed an ironic commentary on all his efforts. Jenkins, his suspect from the Stores section, had been arrested in Central City. When the monorail service had been suspended, he had been in town on very unofficial business, and had been picked up by the agents who had been watching him as a result of Sadler's hunch.

He had been scared of Sadler, and with good reason. But he had never betrayed any state secrets, for he had never possessed any. Like a good many storekeepers before him, he had been busy selling government property.

It was poetic justice. Jenkin's own guilty conscience had caught him. But though Sadler had eliminated one name from his list, the victory gave him very little satisfaction indeed.

The hours dragged on, with tempers getting more and more frayed. Overhead the sun was climbing up the morning sky, and had now lifted well above the western wall of Plato. The initial sense of emergency had worn off, leaving only a feeling of frustration. One misguided effort was made to organise a concert, but it failed so completely that it left everyone more depressed than before.

Since nothing seemed to be happening, people began to creep up to the surface again, if only to have a look at the sky and to reassure themselves that all was still well. Some of these clandestine excursions caused Sadler much anxiety, but he was able to convince himself that they were quite innocent. Eventually the Director recognised the position, by permitting a limited number of people to go up to the observation domes at set hours of the day.

One of the engineers from Power organised a sweepstake, the prizewinner to be the person who guessed how long this peculiar siege was going to last. Everybody in the Observatory contributed, and Sadler – acting on a very long shot – read the list thoughtfully when it was complete. If there was anyone here who happened to know what the right answer might be, he would take care to avoid winning. That, at least was the theory. Sadler learnt nothing from his study, and finished it wondering just how tortuous his mental processes were becoming. There were times when he feared that he would never be able to think in a straight-forward fashion again.

The waiting ended just five days after the Alert. Up on the surface it was approaching noon, and the Earth had waned to a thin crescent too close to the sun to be looked at with safety. But it was midnight by the Observatory clocks, and Sadler was sleeping when Wagnall unceremoniously entered his room.

'Wake up!' he said, as Sadler rubbed the sleep from his eyes. 'The Director wants to see you!' Wagnall seemed annoyed at being used as a messenger boy. 'There's something going on,' he complained, looking at Sadler suspiciously. 'He won't even tell *me* what it's all about.'

'I'm not sure that I know either,' Sadler replied as he climbed into his dressing gown. He was telling the truth, and on the way to the Director's office speculated sleepily on all the things that could possibly have happened.

Professor Maclaurin, thought Sadler, had aged a good deal in the last few days. He was no longer the brisk forceful little man he had been, ruling the Observatory with a rod of iron. There was even a disorderly pile of documents at the side of his once unsullied desk.

As soon as Wagnall, with obvious reluctance, had left the room, Maclaurin said abruptly:

'What's Carl Steffanson doing on the Moon?'

Sadler blinked uncertainly – he was still not fully awake – and then answered lamely:

'I don't even know who he is. Should I?'

Maclaurin seemed surprised and disappointed.

'I thought your people might have told you he was coming. He's one of the most brilliant physicists we have, in his own specialised field. Central City's just called to say that he's landed – and we've got to get him out to the *Mare Imbrium* just as soon as we can, to this place they call Project Thor.'

'Why can't he fly there? How do we come into the picture?'

'He was supposed to go by rocket, but the transport's out of action and won't be serviceable for at least six hours. So they're sending him down by monorail, and we're taking him on the last lap by tractor. I've been asked to detail Jamieson for the job. Everyone knows that he's the best tractor driver on the Moon – and he's the only one who's ever been out to Project Thor, whatever *that* is.'

'Go on,' said Sadler, half suspecting what was coming next.

'I don't trust Jamieson. I don't think it's safe to send him on a mission as important as this one appears to be.'

'Is there anyone else who could do it?'

'Not in the time available. It's a very skilled job, and you've no idea how easy it is to lose your way.'

'So it has to be Jamieson, it seems. Why do you feel he's a risk?'

'I've listened to him talking in the Common Room. Surely, *you've* heard him, too! He's made no secret of his sympathies with the Federation.'

Sadler was watching Maclaurin intently while the Director was speaking. The indignation – almost the anger – in the little man's voice surprised him. For a moment it raised a fleeting suspicion in his mind: was Maclaurin trying to divert attention from himself?

The vague mistrust lasted only for an instant. There was no need, Sadler realised, to search for deeper motives. Maclaurin was tired and overworked: as Sadler had always suspected, for all his external toughness he was a small man in spirit as well as in stature. He was reacting childishly to his frustration: he had seen his plans disorganised, his whole programme brought to a halt – even his precious equipment imperilled. It was all the fault of the Federation, and anyone who did not agree was a potential enemy of Earth.

It was hard not to feel some sympathy for the Director: Sadler suspected that he was on the verge of a nervous breakdown, and would have to be handled with extreme care.

'What do you want me to do about it?' he asked in as non-committal a tone of voice as he could manage.

'I'd like to know if you agree with me about Jamieson. You must have studied him carefully.'

'I'm not allowed to discuss my evaluations,' Sadler replied. 'They're too often based on hearsay and hunches. But I feel that Jamieson's very frankness is a point in his favour. There is a great difference, you know, between dissent and treason.'

Maclaurin was silent for a while. Then he shook his head angrily. 'It's too great a risk. I'll not accept the responsibility.'

This, thought Sadler, was going to be difficult. He had no authority here, and certainly could not override the Director. No one had sent him any instructions: the people who had routed Steffanson through the Observatory probably did not even know that he existed. Liaison between Defence and Central Intelligence was not all that it should be.

But even without instructions his duty was clear. If Defence wanted to get someone out to Project Thor as urgently as this, they had a very good reason. He must help even if he had to step outside his role of passive observer.

'This is what I suggest, sir,' he said briskly. 'Interview Jamieson

447

and outline the position to him. Ask him if he'll volunteer for the job. I'll monitor the conversation from the next room and advise you if it's safe to accept. My belief is that if he says he'll do it, he will. Otherwise he'll turn you down flat. I don't think he'll double-cross you.'

'You'll go on record over this?'

'Yes,' said Sadler impatiently. 'And if I may give you some advice, do your best to hide your suspicions. Whatever your own feelings are, be as friendly and open as you can.'

Maclaurin thought it over for a while, then shrugged his shoulders in resignation. He flicked the microphone switch.

'Wagnall,' he said, 'fetch Jamieson here.'

To Sadler, waiting in the next room, it seemed hours before anything happened. Then the loudspeaker brought the sound of Jamieson's arrival, and immediately he heard Maclaurin say:

'Sorry to break into your sleep, Jamieson, but we've an urgent job for you. How long would it take you to drive a tractor to Prospect Pass?'

Sadler smiled at the clearly heard gasp of incredulity. He knew exactly what Jamieson was thinking. Prospect was the pass through the southern wall of Plato, overlooking the *Mare Imbrium*. It was avoided by the tractors, which took an easier but more roundabout route a few kilometres to the west. The monocabs, however, went through it without difficulty, and when the lighting was correct gave their passengers one of the most famous views on the Moon — the great sweep down into the *Mare* with the far-off fang of Pico on the skyline.

'If I pushed things I could do it in an hour. It's only forty kilometres, but very rough going.'

'Good,' said Maclaurin's voice. 'I've just had a message from Central City asking me to send you out. They know you're our best driver, and you've been there before.'

'Been where?' said Jamieson.

'Project Thor. You won't have heard the name, but that's what it's called. The place you drove out to the other night.'

'Go on, sir. I'm listening,' Jamieson replied. To Sadler, the tension in his voice was obvious.

'This is the position. There's a man in Central City who has to

448

reach Thor immediately. He was supposed to go by rocket, but that's not possible. So they're sending him down here on the monorail, and to save time you'll meet the car out in the pass and take him off. Then you'll drive straight across country to Project Thor. Understand?'

'Not quite. Why can't Thor collect him in one of their own Cats?'

Was Jamieson hedging? wondered Sadler. No, he decided. It was a perfectly reasonable question.

'If you look at the map,' said Maclaurin, 'you'll see that Prospect is the only convenient place for a tractor to meet the monorail. Moreover, there aren't any really skilled drivers at Thor, it seems. They're sending out a tractor, but you'll probably have finished the job before they can reach Prospect.'

There was a long pause: Jamieson was obviously studying the map.

'I'm willing to try it,' said Jamieson. 'But I'd like to know what it's all about.'

Here we go, thought Sadler. I hope Maclaurin does what I told him.

'Very well,' Maclaurin replied. 'You've a right to know, I suppose. The man who's going to Thor is Dr Carl Steffanson. And the mission he's engaged on is vital to the security of Earth. That's all I know, but I don't think I need say any more.'

Sadler waited, hunched over his speaker, as the long silence dragged on. He knew the decision Jamieson must be making. The young astronomer was discovering that it was one thing to criticise Earth and to condemn her policy when the matter was of no practical importance — and quite another to choose a line of action that might help to bring about her defeat. Sadler had read somewhere that there were plenty of pacifists before the outbreak of war, but few after it had actually started. Jamieson was learning now where his loyalty, if not his logic, lay.

'I'll go,' he said at last, so quietly that Sadler could scarcely hear him.

'Remember,' insisted Maclaurin, 'you have a free choice.'

'Have I?' said Jamieson. There was no sarcasm in his voice. He was thinking aloud, talking to himself rather than to the Director.

Sadler heard Maclaurin shuffling his papers. 'What about your co-driver?' he asked.

'I'll take Wheeler. He went out with me last time.'

'Very well. You go and fetch him, and I'll get in touch with Transport. And – good luck.'

'Thank you, sir.'

Sadler waited until he heard the door of Maclaurin's office close behind Jamieson: then he joined the Director's. Maclaurin looked up at him wearily and said:

'Well?'

'It went off better than I'd feared. I thought you handled it very well.'

This was not mere flattery: Sadler was surprised at the way in which Maclaurin had concealed his feelings. Though the interview had not been exactly cordial, there had been no overt unfriendliness.

'I feel much happier,' said Maclaurin, 'because Wheeler's going with him. He can be trusted.'

Despite his worry, Sadler had difficulty in suppressing a smile. He was quite sure that the Director's faith in Conrad Wheeler was based largely on that young man's discovery of *Nova Draconis* and his vindication of the Maclaurin Magnitude Integrator. But he needed no further proofs that scientists were just as inclined as anyone else to let their emotions sway their logic.

The desk speaker called for attention.

'The tractor's just leaving, sir. Outer doors opening now.'

Maclaurin looked automatically at the wall clock. 'That was quick,' he said. Then he gazed sombrely at Sadler.

'Well, Mr Sadler, it's too late to do anything about it now. I only hope you're right.'

It is seldom realised that driving on the Moon by day is far less pleasant, and even less safe, than driving by night. The merciless glare demands the use of heavy sun-filters, and the pools of inky shadow which are always present, except on those rare occasions when the sun is vertically overhead, can be very dangerous. Often they conceal crevasses which a speeding tractor may be unable to avoid. Driving by earthlight, on the other hand, involves no such strain. The light is so much softer, the contrasts less extreme.

To make matters worse for Jamieson he was driving due south – almost directly into the sun. There were times when conditions were so bad that he had to zig-zag wildly to avoid the glare from patches of exposed rock ahead. It was not so difficult when they were travelling over dusty regions, but these became fewer and fewer as the ground rose towards the inner ramparts of the mountain wall.

Wheeler knew better than to talk to his friend on this part of the route: Jamieson's task required too much concentration. Presently they were climbing up towards the pass, weaving back and forth along the rugged slopes overlooking the plain. Like fragile toys on the far horizon the gantries of the great telescopes marked the location of the Observatory. There, thought Wheeler bitterly, was invested millions of man-hours of skill and labour. Now it was doing nothing, and the best that could be hoped was that one day those splendid instruments could once more begin their search into the far places of the universe.

A ridge cut off their view of the plain below, and Jamieson swung round to the right through a narrow valley. Far up the slopes above them the track of the monorail was now visible, as it came in great, striding leaps down the face of the mountain. There was no way in which a caterpillar could get up to it, but when they were through the pass they would have no difficulty in driving to within a few metres of the track.

The ground was extremely broken and treacherous here, but drivers who had gone this way before had left markers for the guidance of any who might come after them. Jamieson was using his headlights a good deal now, as he was often working through shadow. On the whole he preferred this to direct sunlight, for he could see the ground ahead much more easily with the steerable beams from the projects on top of the cab. Wheeler soon took over their operation, and found it fascinating to watch the ovals of light skittering across the rocks. The complete invisibility of the beams themselves, here in the almost perfect vacuum, gave a magical effect to the scene. The light seemed to be coming from nowhere, and to have no connection at all with the tractor.

They reached Prospect fifty minutes after leaving the Observatory, and radioed back their position. From now on it was only a few kilometres down hill until they came to the rendezvous. The monorail track converged towards their path, then swept on to the south past Pico, a silver thread shrinking out of sight across the face of the Moon.

'Well,' said Wheeler with satisfaction, 'we've not kept them waiting. I wish I knew what all this was about.'

'Isn't it obvious?' Jamieson answered. 'Steffanson's the greatest expert on radiation physics we have. If there's going to be war, surely you realise the sort of weapons that will be used.'

'I'd not thought much about it – it had never seemed something to take seriously. Guided missiles, I suppose.'

'Very likely, but we should be able to do better than that. Men have been talking about radiation weapons for centuries. If they wanted them, they could make them now.'

'Don't say you believe in death rays!'

'And why not? If you remember your history books, death rays killed some thousands of people at Hiroshima. And that was a couple of hundred years ago.'

'Yes, but it's not difficult to shield against that sort of thing. Can you imagine doing any real *physical* damage with a ray?'

'It would depend on the range. If it were only a few kilometres, I'd say yes. After all, we can generate unlimited amounts of power. By this time we should be able to squirt it all in the same direction if we wanted to. Until today there's been no particular incentive. But now – how do we know what's been going on in secret labs all over the Solar System?'

Before Wheeler could reply, he saw the glittering point of light far out across the plain. It was moving towards them with incredible speed, coming up over the horizon like a meteor. Within minutes, it had resolved itself into the blunt-nosed cylinder of the monocab, crouched low over its single track.

'I think I'd better go out and give him a hand,' said Jamieson. 'He's probably never worn a space-suit before. He'll certainly have some luggage, too.'

Wheeler sat up in the driving position and watched his friend clamber across the rock to the monorail. The door of the vehicle's emergency airlock opened, and a man stepped out, somewhat unsteadily, on to the Moon. By the way he moved Wheeler could tell at a glance that he had never been in low gravity before.

Steffanson was carrying a thick briefcase and a large wooden box, which he handled with the utmost care. Jamieson offered to relieve him of these hindrances, but he refused to part with them. His only other baggage was a small travelling case, which he allowed Jamieson to carry.

The two figures scrambled back down the rocky ramp, and Wheeler operated the airlock to let them in. The monocab having delivered its burden pulled back into the south and swiftly disappeared the way it had come. It seemed, thought Wheeler, that the driver was in a great hurry to get home. He had never seen one of the cars travel so fast, and for the first time he began to have some faint surmise of the storm that was gathering above this peaceful, sun-drenched landscape. He suspected that they were not the only ones making a rendezvous at Project Thor.

He was right. Far out in space, high above the plane in which Earth and planets swim, the commander of the Federal forces was marshalling his tiny fleet. As a hawk circles above its prey in the moments before its plummeting descent, so Commodore Brennan, lately Professor of Electrical Engineering at the University of Herperus, held his ships poised above the Moon.

He was waiting for the signal which he still hoped would never come.

Fifteen

Doctor Carl Steffanson did not stop to wonder if he was a brave man. Never before in his life had he known the need for so primitive a virtue as physical courage, and he was agreeably surprised at his calmness now that the crisis had almost come. In a few hours he would probably be dead. The thought gave him more annoyance than fear; there was so much work he wanted to do, so many theories to be tested. It would be wonderful to get back to scientific research again, after the rat-race of the last two years. But that was day-dreaming; mere survival was as much as he could hope for now.

He opened his briefcase and pulled out the sheaves of wiring diagrams and component schedules. With some amusement he noticed that Wheeler was staring with frank curiosity at the complex circuits and the SECRET labels plastered over them. Well, there was little need for security now, and Steffanson himself could not have made much sense of these circuits had he not invented them himself.

He glanced again at the packing case to make sure that it was securely lashed down. There, in all probability, lay the future of more worlds than one. How many other men had ever been sent on a mission like this? Steffanson could think of but two examples, both back in the days of the Second World War. There had been a British scientist who had carried a small box across the Atlantic containing what was later called the most valuable consignment ever to reach the shores of the United States. That had been the first cavity magnetron, the invention which made radar the key weapon of war and destroyed the power of Hitler. Then, a few years later, there had been a plane flying across the Pacific to the island of Tinian, carrying almost all the free uranium 235 then in existence.

But neither of those missions, for all their importance, had the urgency of this.

Steffanson had exchanged only a few words of formal greeting to Jamieson and Wheeler, expressing his thanks at their co-operation. He knew nothing about them, except that they were astronomers from the Observatory who had volunteered to undertake this trip. Since they were scientists they would certainly be curious to know what he was doing here, and he was not surprised when Jamieson handed over the controls to his colleague and stepped down from the driving position.

'It won't be so rough from now on,' said Jamieson. 'We'll get to this Thor place in about twenty minutes. Is that good enough for you?'

Steffanson nodded.

'That's better than we'd hoped when that damned ship broke down. You'll probably get a special medal for this.'

'I'm not interested,' said Jamieson rather coldly. 'All I want to do is what's right. Are you quite certain that you're doing the same?'

Steffanson looked at him in surprise, but it took him only an instant to sum up the situation. He had met Jamieson's type before among the younger men of his own staff. These idealists all went through the same mental heart-searchings. And they would all grow out of it when they were older. He sometimes wondered if that was a tragedy or a blessing.

'You are asking me,' he said quietly, 'to predict the future. No man can ever tell if, in the long run, his acts will lead to good or evil. But I am working for the defence of Earth, and if there is an attack it will come from the Federation, not from us. I think you should bear that in mind.'

'Yet haven't we provoked it?'

'To some extent, perhaps – but again there is much to be said on both sides. You think of the Federals as starry-eyed pioneers, building wonderful new civilisations out there on the planets. You forget that they can be tough and unscrupulous too. Remember how they squeezed us off the asteroids by refusing to ship supplies except at exorbitant rates. Look how difficult they've made it for us to send ships beyond Jupiter – why, they've virtually put three-quarters of the Solar System out of bounds! If they get everything they want, they'll be intolerable. I'm afraid they've asked for a lesson, and we hope to give it to them. It's a pity it's come to this, but I see no alternative.'

He glanced at his watch, saw that it was nearly at the hour, and continued, 'Do you mind switching on the news? I'd like to hear the latest developments.'

Jamieson tuned in the set, and rotated the antenna system towards Earth. There was a fair amount of noise from the solar background, for Earth was now almost in line with the sun, but the sheer power of the station made the message perfectly intelligible and there was no trace of fading.

Steffanson was surprised to see that the tractor chronograph was over a second fast. Then he realised that it was set for that oddly christened hybrid, Lunar Greenwich Time. The signal he was listening to had just bridged the 400,000 kilometre gulf from Earth. It was a chilling reminder of his remoteness from home.

Then there was a delay so long that Jamieson turned up the volume to check that the set was still operating. After a full minute the announcer spoke, his voice striving desperately to be as impersonal as ever.

'This is Earth calling. The following statement has been issued from the Hague:

'The Triplanetary Federation has informed the Government of Earth that it intends to seize certain portions of the Moon, and that any attempt to resist this action will be countered by force.

'This Government is taking all necessary steps to preserve the integrity of the Moon. A further announcement will be issued as soon as possible. For the present it is emphasised that there is no immediate danger, as there are no hostile ships within twenty hours of Earth.

'This is Earth. Stand by.'

A sudden silence fell; only the hiss of the carrier-wave and the occasional crackle of solar static still issued from the speaker. Wheeler had brought the tractor to a halt so that he could hear the announcement. From his driving seat he looked down at the little tableau in the cabin beneath him. Steffanson was staring at the circuit diagrams spread over the map table, but was obviously not seeing them. Jamieson still stood with his hand on the volume control: he had not moved since the beginning of the announcement. Then, without a word, he climbed up into the driving cab and took over from Wheeler.

To Steffanson it seemed ages before Wheeler called to him, 'We're nearly there! Look – dead ahead.' He went to the forward observation port and stared across the cracked and broken ground. What a place to fight for, he thought. But, of course, this barren wilderness of lava and meteor dust was only a disguise. Beneath it Nature had hidden treasures which men had taken 200 years to find. Perhaps it would have been better had they never found them at all ...

Still two or three kilometres ahead, the great metal dome was glinting in the sunlight. From this angle it had an astonishing appearance, for the segment in shadow was so dark as to be almost invisible. At first sight, indeed, it looked as if the dome had been bisected by some enormous knife. The whole place looked utterly deserted, but within, Steffanson knew, it would be a hive of furious activity. He prayed that his assistants had completed the wiring of the power and sub-modulator circuits.

Steffanson began to adjust the helmet of his space-suit, which he had not bothered to take off after entering the tractor. He stood behind Jamieson, holding on to one of the storage racks to steady himself.

'Now that we're here,' he said, 'the least I can do is to let you understand what's happened.' He gestured towards the rapidly approaching dome. 'This place started as a mine, and it still is. We've achieved something that's never been done before – drilled a hole a hundred kilometres deep, right through the Moon's crust and down into really rich deposits of metal.'

'A hundred kilometres!' cried Wheeler. 'That's impossible! No hole could stay open under the pressure.'

'It can and does,' retorted Steffanson. 'I've not time to discuss the technique, even if I knew much about it. But remember you can drill a hole six times as deep on the Moon as you can on Earth before it caves in. However, that's only part of the story. The real secret lies in what they've called pressure-mining. As fast as it's sunk, the well is filled with a heavy silicone oil, the same density as the rocks around it. So that no matter how far down you go, the pressure is the same inside as out, and there's no tendency for the hole to close. Like most

457

simple ideas, it's taken a lot of skill to put it into practice. All the operating equipment has to work submerged, under enormous pressure, but the problems are being overcome and we believe we can get metals out in worthwhile quantities.

'The Federation learned this was going on about two years ago. We believe they've tried the same thing, but without any luck. So they're determined that if they can't share this hoard, we won't have it either. Their policy seems to be one of bullying us into co-operation, and it's not going to work.

'That's the background, but now it's only the less important part of the story. There are weapons here as well. Some have been completed and tested, others are waiting for the final adjustments. I'm bringing the key components for what may be the decisive one. That's why Earth may owe you a greater debt than it can ever pay. Don't interrupt – we're nearly there and this is what I really want to tell you. The radio was not telling the truth about that twenty hours of safety. That's what the Federation wants us to believe, and we hope they go on thinking we've been fooled. But we've spotted their ships, and they're approaching ten times as fast as anything that's ever moved through space before. I'm afraid they've got a fundamental new method of propulsion – I only hope it hasn't given them new weapons as well. We've not much more than three hours before they get here – assuming they don't step up their speed still further. You could stay, but for your own safety I advise you to turn round and drive like hell back to the Observatory. If anything starts to happen while you're still out in the open, get under cover as quickly as possible. Go down into a crevasse – anywhere you can find shelter – and stay there until it's all over. Now goodbye and good luck. I hope we have a chance of meeting again when this business is finished.'

Still clutching his mysterious packing case, Steffanson disappeared into the airlock before either of the men could speak. They were now entering the shadow of the great dome, and Jamieson circled it looking for an opening. Presently he recognised the spot through which he and Wheeler had made their entrance, and brought Ferdinand to a halt.

The outer door of the tractor slammed shut and the 'Air-lock Clear' indicator flashed on. They saw Steffanson running across towards the dome, and with perfect timing a circular port flipped open to let him in, then snapped shut behind him.

The tractor was alone in the building's enormous shadow. Nowhere else was there any sign of life, but suddenly the metal framework of the machine began to vibrate at a steadily rising frequency. The meters on the control panel wavered madly, the lights dimmed, and then it was all over. Everything was normal again, but some tremendous field of force had swept out from the dome and was even now expanding into space. It left the two men with an overwhelming impression of energies awaiting the signal for their release. They began to understand the urgency of Steffanson's warning. The whole deserted landscape seemed tense with expectation.

Across the steeply curving plain the tiny beetle of the tractor raced for the safety of the distant hills. But could they be sure of safety even there? Jamieson doubted it. He remembered the weapons that science had made more than two centuries ago; they would be merely the foundations upon which the arts of war could build today. The silent land around him, now burning beneath the noonday sun, might soon be blasted by radiations fiercer still.

He drove forward into the shadow of the tractor, towards the ramparts of Plato, towering along the skyline like some fortress of the giants. But the real fortress was behind him, preparing its unknown weapons for the ordeal that must come.

Sixteen

It would never have happened had Jamieson been thinking more of driving and less of politics – though, in the circumstances, he could hardly be blamed. The ground ahead looked level and firm – exactly the same as the kilometres they had already safely traversed.

It was level, but it was no firmer than water. Jamieson knew what had happened the moment that Ferdinand's engine started to race and the tractor's nose disappeared in a great cloud of dust. The whole vehicle tilted forward, began to rock madly to and fro, and then lost speed despite all that Jamieson could do. Like a ship foundering in a heavy sea, it started to sink. To Wheeler's horrified eyes they seemed to be going under in swirling clouds of spray. Within seconds the sunlight around them had vanished. Jamieson had stopped the motor: in a silence broken only by the murmur of the air circulators they were sinking below the surface of the Moon.

The cabin lights came on as Jamieson found the switch. For a moment both men were too stunned to do anything but sit and stare helplessly at each other. Then Wheeler walked, not very steadily, to the nearest observation window. He could see absolutely nothing: no night was ever as dark as this. A smooth velvet curtain might have been brushing the other side of the thick quartz for all the light that could penetrate it.

Suddenly, with a gentle but distinct bump, Ferdinand reached the bottom.

'Thank God for that,' breathed Jamieson. 'It's not very deep.'

'What good does that do us?' asked Wheeler, hardly daring to believe there was any hope. He had heard too many horrifying tales of these treacherous dust-bowls, and the men and tractors they had engulfed.

The lunar dust-bowls are, fortunately, less common than might be imagined from some travellers' tales, for they can occur only under rather special conditions, which even now are not fully understood. To make one it is necessary to start with a shallow crater-pit in the right kind of rock, and then wait a few hundred million years while the temperature changes between night and day slowly pulverise the surface layers. As this age-long process continues, so a finer and finer grade of dust is produced, until at last it begins to flow like a liquid and accumulates at the bottom of the crater. In almost all respects, indeed, it *is* a liquid: it is so incredibly fine that if collected in a bucket it will slop around like a rather mobile oil. At night one can watch convection currents circulating in it, as the upper layers cool and descend, and the warmer dust at the bottom rises to the top. This effect makes dust-bowls easy to locate, since infra-red detectors can 'see' their abnormal heat radiation at distances of several kilometres. However, during the daytime this method is useless owing to the masking effect of the sun.

'There's no need to get alarmed,' said Jamieson, though he looked none too happy. 'I think we can get out of this. It must be a very small bowl or it would have been spotted before. This area's supposed to have been thoroughly marked.'

'It's big enough to have swallowed us.'

'Yes, but don't forget what this stuff's like. As long as we can keep the motors running we have a chance of pushing our way out – like a submarine-tank making its way up on to shore. The thing that bothers me is whether we should go ahead, or try and back out.'

'If we go ahead, we might get in deeper.'

'Not necessarily. As I said, it must be a pretty small bowl and our momentum may have carried us more than halfway across it. Which way would you say the floor is tilted now?'

'The front seems to be a bit higher than the rear.'

'That's what I thought. I'm going ahead – we can get more power that way, too.'

Very gently Jamieson engaged the clutch in the lowest possible gear. The tractor shook and protested, they lurched forward a few centimetres, then halted again.

'I was afraid of that,' said Jamieson. 'I can't keep up a steady progress. We'll have to go in jerks. Pray for the engine – not to mention the transmission.'

They jolted their way forward in agonisingly slow surges, then Jamieson cut the engines completely.

'Why did you do that?' Wheeler asked anxiously. 'We seemed to be getting somewhere.'

'Yes, but we're also getting too hot. This dust is an almost perfect heat insulator. We'll have to wait a minute until we cool off.'

Neither felt like making any conversation as they sat in the brightly lit cabin that might well, Wheeler reflected, become their tomb. It was ironic that they had encountered this mishap while they were racing for safety.

'Do you hear that noise?' said Jamieson suddenly. He switched off the air-circulator, so that complete silence fell inside the cab.

There was the faintest of sounds coming through the walls. It was a sort of whispering rustle, and Wheeler could not imagine what it was.

'The dust's starting to rise. It's highly unstable, you know, and even a small amount of heat is enough to start convection currents. I expect we're making quite a little geyser up at the top – it will help anyone to find us if they come and look.'

That was some consolation, at any rate. They had air and food for many days – all tractors carried a large emergency reserve – and the Observatory knew their approximate position. But before long the Observatory might have trouble of its own, and would be unable to bother about them . . . .

Jamieson restarted the motor, and the sturdy vehicle started to butt its way forward again through the dry quicksand that enveloped them. It was impossible to tell how much progress they were making, and Wheeler dared not imagine what would happen if the motors failed. The caterpillar treads were grinding at the rock beneath them, and the whole tractor shook and groaned under the intolerable load.

It was almost an hour before they were certain they were getting somewhere. The floor of the tractor was definitely tilting upwards, but there was no way of telling how far below the quasi-liquid surface they were still submerged. They might emerge at any moment into the blessed light of day – or they might have a hundred metres still to traverse at this snail-like pace.

Jamieson was stopping for longer and longer intervals, which might reduce the strain on the engine but did nothing to reduce that on the passengers. During one of these pauses Wheeler asked him outright what they should do if they could get no farther.

'We've only two possibilities,' Jamieson answered. 'We can stay here and hope to be rescued – which won't be as bad as it sounds, since our tracks will make it obvious where we are. The other alternative is to go out.'

'What! That's impossible!'

'Not at all. I know a case where it's been done. It would be rather like escaping from a sunken submarine.'

'It's a horrible thought – trying to swim through this stuff.'

'I was once caught in a snowdrift when I was a kid, so I can guess what it would be like. The great danger would be losing your direction and floundering round in circles until you were exhausted. Let's hope we don't have to try the experiment.'

It was a long time, Wheeler decided, since he had heard a bigger understatement than that.

The driving cab emerged above the dust level about an hour later, and no men could ever have greeted the sun with such joy. But they had not yet reached safety: though Ferdinand could make better speed as the resistance slackened, there might still be unsuspected depths ahead of them.

Wheeler watched with fascinated repulsion as this beastly stuff eddied past the tractor. At times it was quite impossible to believe that they were not forcing their way through a liquid, and only the slowness with which they moved spoilt the illusion. He wondered if it was worth suggesting that in future caterpillars had better streamlining to improve their chances in emergencies like this. Who would ever have dreamed, back on Earth, that *that* sort of thing might be necessary?

At last Ferdinand crawled up to the security of the dry land – which, after all, was no drier than the deadly lake from which they had escaped. Jamieson, almost exhausted by the strain, slumped down across the control panel. The reaction had left Wheeler shaken and weak, but he was too thankful to be out of danger to let that worry him.

He had forgotten, in the relief of seeing sunlight again, that they had left Project Thor three hours ago, and had covered less than twenty kilometres.

Even so, they might have made it. But they had just started on their way again, and were crawling over the top of a quite gentle ridge, where there was a scream of tearing metal, and Ferdinand tried to spin round in a circle. Jamieson cut the motor instantly, and they came to rest broadside-on to their direction of motion.

'And that,' said Jamieson softly, 'is most definitely that. But I don't think we're in a position to grumble. If the starboard transmission had sheared while we were still in that dust-bowl—' He didn't finish the sentence, but turned to the observation port that looked back along their trail. Wheeler followed his gaze.

The dome of Project Thor was still visible on the horizon. Perhaps they had already strained their luck to the utmost – but it would have been nice could they have put the protecting curve of the Moon clear between themselves and the unknown storms that were brewing there.

Seventeen

Even today, little has ever been revealed concerning the weapons used in the Battle of Pico. It is known that missiles played only a minor part in the engagement: in space-warfare anything short of a direct hit is almost useless, since there is nothing to transmit the energy of a shock wave. An atom bomb exploding a few hundred metres away can cause no blast damage, and even its radiation can do little harm to well-protected structures. Moreover, both Earth and the Federation had effective means of diverting ordinary projectiles.

Purely non-material weapons played the most effective roles. The simplest of these were the ion-beams, developed directly from the drive units of space-ships. Since the invention of the first radio tubes, almost three centuries before, men had been learning how to produce and focus ever more concentrated streams of charged particles. The climax had been reached in space-ship propulsion with the so-called 'ion rocket', generating its thrust from the emission of intense beams of electrically charged particles. The deadliness of these beams had caused many accidents in space, even though they were deliberately defocused to limit their effective range.

There was, of course, an obvious answer to such weapons. The electric and magnetic fields which produced them could also be used for their disperson, converting them from annihilating beams into a harmless, scattered spray.

More effective, but more difficult to build, were the weapons using pure radiation. Yet even here, both Earth and Federation had succeeded. It remained to be seen which had done the better job – the superior science of the Federation, or the greater productive capacity of Earth.

*

Commodore Brennan was well aware of all these factors as his little fleet converged upon the Moon. Like all commanders, he was going into action with fewer resources than he would have wished. Indeed, he would very much have preferred not to be going into action at all.

The converted liner *Eridanus* and the largely rebuilt freighter *Lethe* – once listed in Lloyd's register as the *Morning Star* and the *Rigel* – would now be swinging in between Earth and Moon along their carefully plotted courses. He did not know if they still had the element of surprise. Even if they had been detected, Earth might not know of the existence of this third and largest ship, the *Acheron*. Brennan wondered what romantic with a taste for mythology was responsible for these names – probably Commissioner Churchill, who made a point of emulating his famous ancestor in as many ways as he possibly could. Yet they were not inappropriate. The rivers of Death and Oblivion – yes, these were things they might bring to many men before another day had passed . . .

Lieutenant Curtis, one of the few men in the crew who had actually spent most of his working life in space, looked up from the communications desk.

'Message just picked up from the Moon, sir. Addressed to us.'

Brennan was badly shaken. If they had been spotted, surely their opponents were not so contemptuous of them that they would freely admit the fact! He glanced quickly at the signal, then gave a sigh of relief.

OBSERVATORY TO FEDERATION. WISH TO REMIND YOU OF EXISTENCE IRREPLACEABLE INSTRUMENTS PLATO. ALSO ENTIRE OBSERVATORY STAFF STILL HERE. MACLAURIN. DIRECTOR.

'Don't frighten me like that again, Curtis,' said the Commodore. 'I thought you meant it was beamed at me. I'd hate to think they could detect us this far out.'

'Sorry, sir. It's just a general broadcast. They're still sending it out on the Observatory wavelength.'

Brennan handed the signal over to his operations controller, Captain Merton.

'What do you make of this? You worked there, didn't you?'

Merton smiled as he read the message.

466

'Just like Maclaurin. Instruments first, staff second. I'm not too worried. I'll do my damnedest to miss him. A hundred kilometres isn't a bad safety margin when you come to think of it. Unless there's a direct hit with a stray, they've nothing to worry about. They're pretty well dug in, you know.'

The relentless hand of the chronometer was scything away the last minutes. Still confident that his ship, encased in its cocoon of night, had not yet been detected, Commodore Brennan watched the three sparks of his fleet creep along their appointed tracks in the plotting sphere. This was not a destiny he had ever imagined would be his – to hold the fate of worlds within his hands.

But he was not thinking of the powers that slumbered in the reactor banks, waiting for his command. He was not concerned with the place he would take in history when men looked back upon this day. He only wondered, as had all who had ever faced battle for the first time, where he would be this same time tomorrow.

Less than a million kilometres away Carl Steffanson sat at a control desk and watched the image of the sun, picked up by one of the many cameras that were the eyes of Project Thor. The group of tired technicians standing about him had almost completed the equipment before his arrival; now the discriminator units he had brought from Earth in such desperate haste had been wired into the circuit.

Steffanson turned a knob, and the sun went out. He flicked from one camera position to another, but all the eyes of the fortress were equally blind. The coverage was complete.

Too weary to feel any exhilaration he leaned back in his seat and gestured towards the controls.

'It's up to you now. Set it to pass enough light for vision, but to give total rejection from the ultra-violet upwards. We're sure none of their beams carry any effective power much beyond a thousand Ångstroms. They'll be very surprised when all their stuff bounces off. I only wish we could send it back the way it came.'

'Wonder what we look like from outside when the screen's on?' said one of the engineers.

'Just like a perfect reflecting mirror. As long as it keeps reflecting we're safe against pure radiation. That's all I can promise you.'

Steffanson looked at his watch.

467

'If Intelligence is correct we have about twenty minutes to spare. But I shouldn't count on it.'

'At least Maclaurin knows where we are now,' said Jamieson, as he switched off the radio. 'But I can't blame him for not sending someone to pull us out.'

'Then what do we do now?'

'Get some food,' Jamieson answered, walking back to the tiny galley. 'I think we've earned it, and there may be a long walk ahead of us.'

Wheeler looked nervously across the plain, to the distant but all too clearly visible dome of Project Thor. Then his jaw dropped, and it was some seconds before he could believe that his eyes were not playing tricks on him.

'Sid!' he called. 'Come and look at this!'

Jamieson joined him at a rush, and together they stared out towards the horizon. The partly shadowed hemisphere of the dome had changed its appearance completely. Instead of a thin crescent of light it now showed a single dazzling star, as though the image of the sun was being reflected from a perfectly spherical mirror surface.

The telescope confirmed this impression. The dome itself was no longer visible: its place seemed to have been taken by this fantastic silver apparition. To Wheeler it looked exactly like a great blob of mercury sitting on the skyline.

'I'd like to know how they've done that,' was Jamieson's unexcited comment. 'Some kind of interference effect, I suppose. It must be part of their defence system.'

'We'd better get moving,' said Wheeler anxiously. 'I don't like the look of this. It feels horribly exposed up here.'

Jamieson had started throwing open cupboards and pulling out stores. He tossed some bars of chocolate and packets of compressed meat over to Wheeler.

'Start chewing some of this,' he said. 'We won't have time for a proper meal now. Better have a drink as well if you're thirsty. But don't take too much – you'll be in that suit for hours, and these aren't luxury models.'

Wheeler was doing some mental arithmetic. They must be about eighty kilometres from base, with the entire rampart of Plato between them and the Observatory. Yes, it would be a long walk home – and they might after all be safer here. The tractor, which had already served them so well, could protect them from a good deal of trouble.

Jamieson toyed with the idea, but then rejected it. 'Remember what Steffanson said,' he reminded Wheeler. 'He told us to get underground as soon as we could. And he must know what he's talking about.'

They found a crevasse within fifty metres of the tractor, on the slope of the ridge away from the fortress. It was just deep enough to see out of when they stood upright, and the floor was sufficiently level to lie down. As a slit trench it might almost have been made to order, and Jamieson felt much happier when he had located it.

'The only thing that worries me now,' he said, 'is how long we may have to wait. It's still possible that nothing will happen at all. On the other hand, if we start walking we may be caught in the open away from shelter.'

After some discussion they decided on a compromise. They would keep their suits on, but would go back and sit in Ferdinand where at least they would be comfortable. It would take them only a few seconds to get to the trench.

There was no warning of any kind. Suddenly the grey, dusty rocks of the Sea of Rains were scorched by a light they had never known before in all their history. Wheeler's first impression was that someone had turned a giant searchlight full upon the tractor: then he realised that this sun-eclipsing explosion was many kilometres away. High above the horizon was a ball of violet flame, perfectly spherical, and rapidly losing brilliance as it expanded. Within seconds it had faded to a great cloud of luminous gas. It was dropping down towards the edge of the Moon, and almost at once had sunk below the skyline like some fantastic sun.

'We were fools,' said Jamieson gravely. 'That was an atomic warhead – we may be dead men already.'

'Nonsense,' retorted Wheeler, though without much confidence. 'That was fifty kilometres away. The gammas would be pretty weak by the time they reached us – and these walls aren't bad shielding.'

Jamieson did not answer; he was already on his way to the airlock. Wheeler started to follow him, then remembered that there was a radiation detector aboard and went back to collect it. Was there anything else that might be useful while he was here? On a sudden impulse he jerked down the curtain rod above the little alcove that concealed the lavatory, then ripped away the wall mirror over the sink.

When he joined Jamieson, who was waiting impatiently for him in the airlock, he handed over the detector but did not bother to explain the rest of his equipment. Not until they had settled down in their trench, which they reached without further incident, did he make its purpose clear.

'If there's one thing I hate,' he said petulantly, 'it's not being able to see what's going on.' He started to fix the mirror to the curtain rod, using some wire from one of the pouches round his suit. After a couple of minutes' work he was able to hoist a crude periscope out of the hole.

'I can just see the dome,' he said with some satisfaction. 'It's quite unchanged, as far as I can tell.'

'It would be,' Jamieson replied. 'They must have managed to explode that bomb somehow while it was miles away.'

'Perhaps it was only a warning shot.'

'Not likely! No one wastes plutonium for firework displays. That meant business. I wonder when the next move is going to be?'

It did not come for another five minutes. Then, almost simultaneously, three more of the dazzling atomic suns burst against the sky. They were all moving on trajectories that took them towards the dome, but long before they reached it they had dispersed into tenuous clouds of vapour.

'Rounds one and two to Earth,' muttered Wheeler. 'I wonder where these missiles are coming from?'

'If any of them burst directly overhead,' said Jamieson, 'we *will* be done for. Don't forget there's no atmosphere to absorb the gammas here.'

'What does the radiation meter say?'

'Nothing much yet, but I'm worried about that first blast, when we were still in the tractor.'

Wheeler was too busily searching the sky to answer. Somewhere up there among the stars, which he could see now that he was out of the direct glare of the sun, must be the ships of the Federation, preparing for the next attack. It was not likely that the ships themselves would be visible, but he might be able to see their weapons in action.

From somewhere beyond Pico six sheaves of flame shot up into the sky at an enormous acceleration. The dome was launching its first missiles, straight into the face of the sun. The *Lethe* and the *Eridanus* were using a trick as old as warfare itself: they were approaching from a direction in which their opponent would be partly blinded. Even radar could be distracted by the background of solar interference, and Commodore Brennan had enlisted two large sunspots as minor allies.

Within seconds the rockets were lost in the glare. Minutes seemed to pass: then the sunlight abruptly multiplied itself a hundredfold. The folks up on Earth, thought Wheeler, as he readjusted the filters of his visor, will be having a grandstand view tonight. And the atmosphere which is such a nuisance to astronomers will protect them from anything that these warheads can radiate.

There was no way to tell if the missiles had done any damage. That enormous and soundless explosion might have dissipated itself harmlessly into space. This would be a strange battle, he realised. He might never even see the Federation ships, which would almost certainly be painted as black as night to make them undetectable.

Then he saw that something was happening to the dome. It was no longer a gleaming spherical mirror reflecting only the single image of the sun. Light was splashing from it in all directions, and its brilliance was increasing second by second. From somewhere out in space, power was being poured into the fortress. That could only mean that the ships of the Federation were floating up there against the stars, beaming countless millions of kilowatts down upon the Moon. But there was still no sign of them, for there was nothing to reveal the track of the river of energy pouring invisibly through space.

The dome was now far too bright to look upon directly, and Wheeler readjusted his filters. He wondered when it was going to reply to the attack, or indeed if it could do so while it was under this bombardment. Then he saw that the hemisphere was surrounded by a wavering corona, like some kind of brush discharge. Almost at the same moment Jamieson's voice rang in his ears.

'Look, Con – right overhead!'

He glanced away from the mirror and looked directly into the sky. For the first time he saw one of the Federation ships. Though he did not know it he was seeing the *Acheron*, the only space-ship ever to be built specifically for war. It was clearly visible, and seemed remarkably close. Between it and the fortress, like an impalpable shield, floated a disc of light which as he watched turned cherry-red, then blue-white, then the deadly searing violet seen only in the hottest of the stars. The shield wavered back and forth, giving the impression of being balanced by tremendous and opposing energies. As Wheeler stared, oblivious to his peril, he saw that the whole ship was surrounded by a faint halo of light, brought to incandescence only where the weapons of the fortress tore against it.

It was some time before he realised that there were two other ships in the sky, each shielded by its own flaming nimbus. Now the battle was beginning to take shape: each side had cautiously tested its defences and its weapons, and only now had the real trial of strength begun.

The two astronomers stared in wonder at the moving fireballs of the ships. Here was something totally new – something far more important than any mere weapon. These vessels possessed a means of propulsion which must make the rocket obsolete. They could hover motionless at will, then move off in any direction at a high acceleration. They needed this mobility; the fortress, with all its fixed equipment, far out-powered them, and much of their defence lay in their speed.

In utter silence the battle was rising to its climax. Millions of years ago the molten rock had frozen to form the Sea of Rains, and now the weapons of the ships were turning it once more to lava. Out by the fortress, clouds of incandescent vapour were being blasted into the sky as the beams of the attackers spent their fury against the unprotected rocks. It was impossible to tell which side was inflicting the greater damage. Now and again a screen would flare up, as a flicker of heat passed over white-hot steel. When that happened to one of the battleships it would move away with that incredible acceleration, and it would be several seconds before the focusing devices of the fort had located it again.

Both Wheeler and Jamieson were surprised that the battle was being fought at such short range. There was probably never more than a hundred kilometres between the antagonists, and usually it was much less than this. When one fought with weapons that travelled at the speed of light – indeed, when one fought with light itself – such distances were trivial.

The explanation did not occur to them until the end of the engagement. All radiation weapons have one limitation: they must obey the law of inverse squares. Only explosive missiles are equally effective from whatever range they have been projected: if one is hit by an atomic bomb it makes no difference whether it has travelled ten kilometres or a 1000.

But double the distance of any kind of radiation weapon and you divide its power by four owing to the spreading of the beam. No wonder, therefore, that the Federal commander was coming as close to his objective as he dared.

The fort, lacking mobility, had to accept any punishment the ships could give it. After the battle had been on for a few minutes it was impossible for the unshielded eye to look anywhere towards the south. Ever and again the clouds of rock vapour would go sailing up into the sky, falling back on to the ground like luminous steam. And presently, as he peered through his darkened goggles and man-oeuvred his clumsy periscope, Wheeler saw something he could scarcely believe. Around the base of the fortress was a slowly spreading circle of lava, melting down ridges and even small hillocks like lumps of wax.

That awe-inspiring sight brought home to him, as nothing else had done, the frightful power of the weapons that were being wielded only a few kilometres away. If even the merest stray reflection of those energies reached them here, they would be snuffed out of existence as swiftly as moths in an oxy-hydrogen flame.

The three ships appeared to be moving in some complex tactical pattern, so that they could maintain the maximum bombardment of the fort while reducing its opportunity of striking back. Several times one of the ships passed vertically overhead, and Wheeler retreated as far into the crack as he could in case any of the radiation scattered from the screens splashed down upon them. Jamieson, who had given up trying to persuade his colleague to take fewer risks, had

473

now crawled some distance along the crevasse, looking for a deeper part, preferably with a good overhang. He was not so far away, however, that the rock was shielding the suit radios, and Wheeler gave him a continuous commentary on the battle.

It was hard to believe that the entire engagement had not yet lasted ten minutes. As Wheeler cautiously surveyed the inferno to the south he noticed that the hemisphere seemed to have lost some of its symmetry. At first he thought that one of the generators might have failed, so that the protective field could no longer be maintained. Then he saw that the lake of lava was at least a kilometre across, and he guessed that the whole fort had floated off its foundations. Probably the defenders were not even aware of the fact. Their insulation must be taking care of solar heats, and would hardly notice the modest warmth of molten rock.

And now a strange thing was beginning to happen. The rays with which the battle was being fought were no longer quite invisible, for the fortress was no longer in a vacuum. Around it the boiling rock was releasing enormous volumes of gas, through which the paths of the rays were as clearly visible as searchlights in a misty night on Earth. At the same time Wheeler began to notice a continual hail of tiny particles around him. For a moment he was puzzled; then he realised that the rock vapour was condensing after it had been blasted up into the sky. It seemed too light to be dangerous, and he did not mention it to Jamieson – it would only give him something else to worry about. As long as the dust-fall was not too heavy, the normal insulation of the suits could deal with it. In any case it would probably be quite cold by the time it got back to the surface.

The tenuous and temporary atmosphere round the dome was producing another unexpected effect. Occasional flashes of lightning darted between ground and sky, draining off the enormous static charges that must be accumulating around the fort. Some of those flashes would have been spectacular by themselves – but they were scarcely visible against the incandescent clouds that generated them.

Accustomed though he was to the eternal silences of the Moon, Wheeler still felt a sense of unreality at the sight of these tremendous forces striving together without the least whisper of sound. Sometimes a gentle vibration would reach him, perhaps the rock-borne concussion of falling lava. But much of the time he had the feeling that he was watching a television programme when the sound had failed.

Afterwards he could hardly believe he had been such a fool as to expose himself to the risks he was running now. At the moment he felt no fear – only an immense curiosity and excitement. He had been caught, though he did not know it, by the deadly glamour of war. There is a fatal strain in men that, whatever reason may say, makes their hearts beat faster when they watch the colours flying and hear the ancient music of the drums.

Curiously enough Wheeler did not feel any sense of identification with either side. It seemed to him, in his present abnormally overwrought mood, that all this was a vast, impersonal display arranged for his special benefit. He felt something approaching contempt for Jamieson, who was missing everything by seeking safety.

Perhaps the real truth of the matter was that having just escaped from one peril Wheeler was in the exalted state, akin to drunkenness, in which the idea of personal danger seems absurd. He had managed to get out of the dust-bowl – nothing else could harm him now.

Jamieson had no such consolation. He saw little of the battle, but felt its terror and grandeur far more deeply than his friend. It was too late for regrets, but over and over again he wrestled with his conscience. He felt angry at fate for having placed him in such a position that his action might have decided the destiny of worlds. He was angry, in equal measure, with Earth and the Federation for having let matters come to this. And he was sick at heart as he thought of the future towards which the human race might now be heading.

Wheeler never knew why the fortress waited so long before it used its main weapon. Perhaps Steffanson – or whoever was in charge – was waiting for the attack to slacken so that he could risk lowering the defences of the dome for the millisecond that he needed to launch his stiletto.

Wheeler saw it strike upwards, a solid bar of light stabbing at the stars. He remembered the rumours that had gone around the Observatory: so *this* was what had been seen, flashing above the mountains. He did not have time to reflect on the staggering violation of the laws of optics which this phenomenon implied, for he was staring at the ruined ship above his head. The beam had gone through the *Lethe* as if she did not exist: the fortress had speared her as an entomologist pierces a butterfly with a pin.

Whatever one's loyalties, it was a terrible thing to see how the screens of that great ship suddenly vanished as her generators died, leaving her helpless and unprotected in the sky. The secondary weapons of the fort were at her instantly, tearing out great gashes of metal and boiling away her armour layer by layer. Then, quite slowly, she began to settle towards the Moon, still on an even keel. No one will ever know what stopped her: probably some short-circuit in her controls, since none of her crew could have been left alive. For suddenly she went off to the east in a long, flat trajectory. By that time most of her hull had been boiled away, and the skeleton of her framework was almost completely exposed. The crash came, minutes later, as she plunged out of sight beyond the Teneriffe Mountains. A blue-white aurora flickered for a moment below the horizon, and Wheeler waited for the shock to reach him.

And then, as he stared into the east, he saw a line of dust rising from the plain, sweeping towards him as if driven by a mighty wind. The concussion was racing through the rock, hurling the surface dust high into the sky as it passed. The swift, inexorable approach of that silently moving wall, advancing at the rate of several kilometres a second, was enough to strike terror into anyone who did not know its cause. But it was quite harmless; when the wave-front reached him it was as if a minor earthquake had passed. The veil of dust reduced visibility to zero for a few seconds, then subsided as swiftly as it had come.

When Wheeler looked again for the remaining ships they were so far away that their screens had shrunk to little balls of fire against the zenith. At first he thought they were retreating, then, abruptly, the screens began to expand as they came down into the attack under a terrific vertical acceleration. Over by the fortress the lava, like some tortured living creature, was throwing itself madly into the sky as the beams tore into it.

The *Acheron* and *Eridanus* came out of their dives about a kilometre above the fort. For an instant they were motionless; then they went back into the sky together. But the *Eridanus* had been

476

mortally wounded, though Wheeler knew only that one of the screens was shrinking much more slowly than the other. With a feeling of helpless fascination he watched the stricken ship fall back towards the Moon. He wondered if the fort would use its enigmatic weapon again, or whether the defenders realised that it was unnecessary.

About ten kilometres up the screens of the *Eridanus* seemed to explode, and she hung unprotected; a blunt torpedo of black metal, almost invisible against the sky. Instantly her light-absorbing paint, and the armour beneath, were torn off by the beams of the fortress. The great ship turned cherry-red, then white. She swung over so that her prow turned towards the Moon, and began her last dive. At first it seemed to Wheeler that she was heading straight towards him: then he saw that she was aimed at the fort. She was obeying her captain's last command.

It was almost a direct hit. The dying ship smashed into the lake of lava and exploded instantly, engulfing the fortress in an expanding hemisphere of flame. This, thought Wheeler, must surely be the end. He waited for the shock wave to reach him, and again watched the wall of dust sweep by – this time into the north. The concussion was so violent that it jerked him off his feet, and he did not see how anyone in the fort could have survived. Cautiously he put down the mirror which had given him almost all his view of the battle, and peered over the edge of his trench. He did not know that the final paroxysm was yet to come.

Incredibly the dome was still there, though now it seemed that part of it had been sheared away. And it was inert and lifeless: its screens were down, its energies exhausted – its garrison, surely, already dead. If so, they had done their work. Of the remaining Federal ship there was no sign. She was already retreating towards Mars, her main armament completely useless and her drive units on the point of failure. She would never fight again – yet, in the few hours of life that were left to her, she had one more role to play.

'It's all over, Sid,' Wheeler called into his suit radio. 'It's safe to come and look now.'

Jamieson climbed up out of a crack fifty metres away, holding the radiation detector in front of him.

'It's still hot around here,' Wheeler heard him grumble, half to himself. 'The sooner we get moving the better.'

'Will it be safe to go back to Ferdinand and put through a radio—?' began Wheeler. Then he stopped. Something was happening over by the dome.

In a blast like an erupting volcano the ground tore apart. An enormous geyser began to soar into the sky, hurling great boulders thousands of metres towards the stars. It climbed swiftly above the plain, driving a thunderhead of smoke and spray before it. For a moment it towered against the southern sky, like some incredible, heaven-aspiring tree that had sprung from the barren soil of the Moon. Then, almost as swiftly as it had grown, it subsided in silent ruin and its angry vapours dispersed into space.

The thousands of tons of heavy liquid holding open the deepest shaft that man had ever bored had finally come to the boiling point, as the energies of the battle seeped into the rock. The mine had blown its top as spectacularly as any oil well on Earth, and had proved that an excellent explosion could still be arranged without the aid of atomic energy.

Eighteen

To the Observatory the battle was no more than an occasional distant earthquake, a faint vibration of the ground which disturbed some of the more delicate instruments but did no material damage. The psychological damage, however, was a different matter. Nothing is so demoralising as to know that great and shattering events are taking place, but to be totally unaware of their outcome. The Observatory was full of wild rumours, the Signals Office besieged with enquiries. But even here there was no information. All news broadcasts from Earth had ceased: all mankind was waiting, as if with bated breath, for the fury of the battle to die away so that the victor could be known. That there would be no victor was the one thing that had not been anticipated.

Not until long after the last vibrations had died away and the radio had announced that the Federation forces were in full retreat did Maclaurin permit anyone to go up to the surface. The report that came down was, after the strain and excitement of the last few hours, not only a relief but a considerable anticlimax. There was a small amount of increased radioactivity about, but not the slightest trace of damage. What it would be like on the other side of the mountains was, of course, a different matter.

The news that Wheeler and Jamieson were safe gave a tremendous boost to the staff's morale. Owing to a partial breakdown of communication it had taken them almost an hour to contact Earth and to get connected to the Observatory. The delay had been infuriating and worrying, for it had left them wondering if the Observatory had been destroyed. They dared not set out on foot until they were sure they had somewhere to go – and Ferdinand was now too radioactive to be a safe refuge.

Sadler was in Communications, trying to find out what was

happening, when the message came through. Jamieson, sounding very tired, gave a brief report of the battle and asked for instructions.

'What's the radiation reading inside the cab?' Maclaurin asked. Jamieson called back the figures: it still seemed strange to Sadler that the message should have to go all the way to Earth just to span a hundred kilometres of the Moon, and he was never able to get used to the three-second delay that this implied.

'I'll get the health section to work out the tolerance,' Maclaurin answered. 'You say it's only a quarter of that reading out in the open?'

'Yes – we've stayed outside the tractor as much as possible, and have come in every ten minutes to try and contact you.'

'The best plan is this – we'll send a Caterpillar right away, and you start walking towards us. Any particular rendezvous you'd like to aim for?'

Jamieson thought for a moment.

'Tell your driver to head for the five-kilometre marker on this side of Prospect: we'll reach it about the same time as he does. We'll keep our suit radios on so there'll be no chance of him missing us.'

As Maclaurin was giving his orders Sadler asked if there was room for an extra passenger in the rescue tractor. It would give him a chance of questioning Wheeler and Jamieson much sooner than would otherwise be the case. When they reached the Observatory – though they did not know it yet – they would be whipped into hospital at once and treated for radiation sickness. They were in no serious danger, but Sadler doubted if he would have much chance of seeing them for a while when the doctors got hold of them.

Maclaurin granted the request, adding the comment, 'Of course, you realise this means that you'll have to tell them who you are. Then the whole Observatory will know inside ten minutes.'

'I've thought of that,' Sadler replied. 'It doesn't matter now.' Always assuming, he added to himself, that it ever did.

Half an hour later he was learning the difference between travel in the smooth, swift monorail and in a jolting tractor. After a while he became used to the nightmare grades the driver was light-heartedly attacking, and ceased to regret volunteering for this mission. Besides the operating crew the vehicle was carrying the chief medical officer, who hoped to make blood-counts and give injections as soon as the rescue had been effected.

There was no dramatic climax to the expedition: as soon as they had topped Prospect Pass they made radio contact with the two men trudging towards them. Fifteen minutes later the moving figures appeared on the skyline, and there was no ceremony apart from fervent handshakes as they came aboard the tractor.

They halted for a while so that the MO could give his injections and make his tests. When he had finished he told Wheeler, 'You're going to be in bed for the next week, but there's no need to worry.'

'What about me?' asked Jamieson.

'You're all right – a much smaller dose. A couple of days is all you need.'

'It was worth it,' said Wheeler cheerfully. 'I don't think that was much of a price to pay for a grandstand view of Armageddon.' Then, as the reaction of knowing that he was safe wore off, he added anxiously, 'What's the latest news? Has the Federation attacked anywhere else?'

'No,' Sadler replied. 'It hasn't, and I doubt if it can. But it seems to have achieved its main objective, which was to stop us using that mine. What will happen now is up to the politicians.'

'Hey,' said Jamieson, 'what are *you* doing here, anyway?'

Sadler smiled.

'I'm still investigating, but let's say that my terms of reference are wider than anyone imagined.'

'You aren't a radio reporter?' asked Wheeler suspiciously.

'Er – not exactly. I'd rather not—'

'I know,' Jamieson interjected suddenly. 'You're something to do with Security. It makes sense now.'

Sadler looked at him with mild annoyance. Jamieson, he decided, had a remarkable talent for making things difficult.

'It doesn't matter. But I want to send in a full report of everything you saw. You realise that you are the only surviving eye witnesses, except for the crew of the Federal ship.'

'I was afraid of that,' said Jamieson. 'So Project Thor was wiped out?'

'Yes, but I think it did its job.'

'What a waste, though – Steffanson and all those others! If it hadn't been for me, he'd probably still be alive.'

'He knew what he was doing – and he made his own choice,' replied Sadler, rather curtly. Yes, Jamieson was going to be a most recalcitrant hero.

For the next thirty minutes, as they were climbing back over the wall of Plato on the homeward run, he questioned Wheeler about the course of the battle. Although the astronomer could only have seen a small part of the engagement, owing to his limited angle of view, his information would be invaluable when the tacticians back on Earth carried out their postmortem.

'What puzzles me most of all,' Wheeler concluded, 'is the weapon the fort used to destroy the battleship. It looked like a beam of some kind, but of course that's impossible. *No* beam can be visible in a vacuum. And I wonder why they only used it once? Do *you* know anything about it?'

'I'm afraid not,' replied Sadler, which was quite untrue. He still knew very little about the weapons in the fort, but this was the only one he now fully understood. He could well appreciate why a jet of molten metal, hurled through space at several hundred kilometres a second by the most powerful electro-magnets ever built, might have looked like a beam of light flashing on for an instant. And he knew that it was a short-range weapon, designed to pierce the fields which would deflect ordinary projectiles. It could only be used under ideal conditions, and it took many minutes to recharge the gigantic condensers which powered the magnets.

This was a mystery the astronomers would have to solve for themselves. He did not imagine that it would take them very long when they really turned their minds to the subject.

The tractor came crawling cautiously down the steep inner slopes of the great walled plain, and the lattice-work of the telescopes appeared on the horizon. They looked, Sadler thought, exactly like a couple of factory chimneys surrounded by scaffolding. Even in his short stay here he had grown quite fond of them, and had come to think of them as personalities, just as did the men who used them. He could share the astronomer's concern that any harm might befall these superb instruments, which had brought knowledge back to Earth from a hundred thousand million light-years away in space.

A towering cliff cut them off from the sun, and darkness fell abruptly as they rolled into shadow. Overhead the stars began to reappear, as Sadler's eyes automatically adjusted for the change in light. He stared up into the northern sky, and saw that Wheeler was doing the same.

Nova Draconis was still among the brightest stars in the sky, but it was fading fast. In a few days it would be no more brilliant than Sirius: in a few months it would be beyond the grasp of the unaided eye. There was, surely, some message here, some symbol half glimpsed on the frontiers of imagination. Science would learn much from *Nova Draconis*, but what would it teach the ordinary worlds of men?

Only this, thought Sadler. The heavens might blaze with portents, the galaxy might burn with the beacon lights of detonating stars, but man would go about his own affairs with a sublime indifference. He was busy with the planets now and the stars would have to wait. He would not be overawed by anything that they could do; and in his own good time he would deal with them as he considered fit.

Neither rescued nor rescuers had much to say on the last lap of the homeward journey. Wheeler was obviously beginning to suffer from delayed shock, and his hands had developed a nervous tremble. Jamieson merely sat and watched the Observatory approaching, as if he had never seen it before. When they drove through the long shadow of the 1000-centimetre telescope he turned to Sadler and asked, 'Did they get everything under cover in time?'

'I believe so,' Sadler replied. 'I've not heard of any damage.'

Jamieson nodded absent-mindedly. He showed no sign of pleasure or relief; he had reached emotional saturation, and nothing could really affect him now until the impact of the last few hours had worn away.

Sadler left them as soon as the tractor drove into the underground garage, and hurried to his room to write up his report. This was outside his terms of reference, but he felt glad that at last he was able to do something constructive.

There was a sense of anticlimax now – a feeling that the storm had spent its fury and would not return. In the aftermath of the battle Sadler felt far less depressed than he had for days. It seemed to him that both Earth and the Federation must be equally overawed by the forces they had released, and both equally anxious for peace.

For the first time since he had left Earth he dared to think once more of his future. Though it could still not be wholly dismissed, the danger of a raid on Earth itself now seemed remote. Jeanette was safe, and soon he might be seeing her again. At least he could tell her where he was, since events had made any further secrecy absurd.

But there was just one nagging frustration in Sadler's mind. He hated to leave a job undone, yet in the nature of things this mission of his might remain for ever uncompleted. He would have given so much to have known whether or not there had been a spy in the Observatory . . .

Nineteen

The liner *Pegasus*, with 300 passengers and a crew of sixty, was only four days out from Earth when the war began and ended. For some hours there had been great confusion and alarm on board, as the radio messages from Earth and Federation were intercepted. Captain Halstead had been forced to take firm measures with some of the passengers, who wished to turn back rather than go on to Mars and an uncertain future as prisoners of war. It was not easy to blame them; Earth was still so close that it was a beautiful silver crescent, with the Moon a fainter and smaller echo beside it. Even from here, more than a million kilometres away, the energies that had just flamed across the face of the Moon had been clearly visible, and had done little to restore the morale of the passengers.

They could not understand that the laws of celestial mechanics admit of no appeal. The *Pegasus* was barely clear of Earth, and still weeks from her intended goal. But she had reached her orbiting speed, and had launched herself like a giant projectile on the path that would lead inevitably to Mars, under the guidance of the sun's all-pervading gravity. There could be no turning back: that would be a manoeuvre involving an impossible amount of propellant. The *Pegasus* carried enough dust in her tanks to match velocity with Mars at the end of her orbit, and to allow for reasonable course corrections *en route*. Her nuclear reactors could provide energy for a dozen voyages – but sheer energy was useless if there was no propellent mass to eject. Whether she wanted to or not, the *Pegasus* was headed for Mars with the inevitability of a runaway train. Captain Halstead did not anticipate a pleasant trip.

The words MAYDAY, MAYDAY, came crashing out of the radio and banished all other preoccupations of the *Pegasus* and her crew. For 300 years, in air and sea and space, these words had alerted rescue organisations, had made captains change their course and race to the aid of stricken comrades. But there was so little that the commander of a space-ship could do; in the whole history of astronautics, there have been only three cases of a successful rescue operation in space.

There are two main reasons for this, only one of which is widely advertised by the shipping lines. Any serious disaster in space is extremely rare; almost all accidents occur during planet-fall or departure. Once a ship has reached space, and has swung into the orbit that will lead it effortlessly to its destination, it is safe from all hazards except internal, mechanical troubles. Such troubles occur more often than the passengers ever know, but are usually trivial and are quietly dealt with by the crew. All space-ships, by law, are built in several independent sections, any one of which can serve as a refuge in an emergency. So the worst that ever happens is that some uncomfortable hours are spent by all while an irate captain breathes heavily down the neck of his engineering officer.

The second reason why space-rescues are so rare is that they are almost impossible, from the nature of things. Spaceships travel at enormous velocities on exactly calculated paths, which do not permit of major alterations – as the passengers of the *Pegasus* were now beginning to appreciate. The orbit any ship follows from one planet to another is unique; no other vessel will ever follow the same path again, among the changing patterns of the planets. There are no 'shipping-lanes' in space, and it is rare indeed for one ship to pass within a million kilometres of another. Even when this does happen the difference of speed is almost always so great that contact is impossible.

All these thoughts flashed through Captain Halstead's mind when the message came down to him from Signals. He read the position and course of the distressed ship – the velocity figure must have been garbled in transmission, it was so ridiculously high. Almost certainly there was nothing he could do – they were too far away, and it would take days to reach them.

Then he noticed the name at the end of the message. He thought he was familiar with every ship in space, but this was a new one to him. He stared in bewilderment for a moment before he suddenly realised just who was calling for his assistance . . . .

Enmity vanishes when men are in peril, on sea or in space,

Captain Halstead leaned over his control desk and said. 'Signals! Get me their captain.'

'He's on circuit, sir. You can go ahead.'

Captain Halstead cleared his throat. This was a novel experience, and not a pleasant one. It gave him no sort of satisfaction to tell even an enemy that he could do nothing to save him.

'Captain Halstead, *Pegasus*, speaking,' he began. 'You're too far away for contact. Our operational reserve is less than ten kilometres a second. I've no need to compute – I can see it's impossible. Have you any suggestions? Please confirm your velocity – we were given an incorrect figure.'

The reply, after a four-second time lag that seemed doubly maddening in these circumstances, was unexpected and astonishing.

'Commodore Brennan, Federal cruiser *Acheron*. I can confirm our velocity figure. We can contact you in two hours, and will make all course corrections ourselves. We still have power, but must abandon ship in less than three hours. Our radiation shielding has gone, and the main reactor is becoming unstable. We've got manual control on it, and it will be safe for at least an hour after we reach you. But we can't guarantee it beyond then.'

Captain Halstead felt the flesh crawl at the back of his neck. He did not know how a reactor could become unstable – but he knew what would happen if one did. There were a good many things about the *Acheron* he did not understand – her speed, above all – but there was one point that emerged very clearly and upon which Commodore Brennan must be left in no doubt.

'*Pegasus* to *Acheron*,' he replied. 'I have 300 passengers aboard. I cannot hazard my ship if there is danger of an explosion.'

'There is no danger – I can guarantee that. We will have at least five minutes' warning, which will give us ample time to get clear of you.'

'Very well – I'll get my airlocks ready and my crew standing by to pass you a line.'

There was a pause longer than that dictated by the sluggish progress of radio waves. Then Brennan replied:

'That's our trouble. We're cut off in the forward section. There are no external locks here, and we have only five suits among 120 men.'

Halstead whistled and turned to his navigating officer before answering.

'There's nothing we can do for them,' he said. 'They'll have to crack the hull to get out, and that will be the end of everyone except the five men in the suits. We can't even lend them our own suits – there'll be no way we can can get them aboard without letting down the pressure.' He flicked over the microphone switch.

'*Pegasus* to *Acheron*. How do you suggest we can assist you?'

It was eerie to be speaking to a man who was already as good as dead. The traditions of space were as strict as those of the sea. Five men could leave the *Acheron* alive – but her captain would not be among them.

Halstead did not know that Commodore Brennan had other ideas, and had by no means abandoned hope, desperate though the situation seemed. His Chief Medical Officer, who had proposed the plan, was already explaining it to the crew.

'This is what we're going to do,' said the small, dark man who a few months ago had been one of the best surgeons on Venus. 'We can't get at the airlocks, because there's vacuum all round us and we've only got five suits. This ship was built for fighting, not for carrying passengers, and I'm afraid her designers had other matters to think about besides Standard Spaceworthiness Regs. Here we are, and we have to make the best of it.

'We'll be alongside the *Pegasus* in a couple of hours. Luckily for us she's got big locks for loading freight and passengers: there's room for thirty or forty men to crowd into them, if they squeeze tight – *and aren't wearing suits.* Yes, I know that sounds bad, but it's not suicide. You're going to breathe space, and get away with it! I won't say it will be enjoyable, but it will be something to brag about for the rest of your lives.

'Now listen carefully. The first thing I've got to prove to you is that you can live for five minutes without breathing – in fact, *without wanting to breathe.* It's a simple trick: Yogis and magicians have known it for centuries, but there's nothing occult about it and it's based on common-sense physiology. To give you confidence, I want you to make this test.'

The MO pulled a stopwatch out of his pocket, and continued:

'When I say "Now!" I want you to exhale completely – empty

your lungs of every drop of air – and then see how long you can stay before you have to take a breath. Don't strain – just hold out until it becomes uncomfortable, then start breathing again normally. I'll start counting the seconds after fifteen, so you can tell what you managed to do. If anyone can't make the quarter minute, I'll recommend his instant dismissal from the Service.'

The ripple of laughter broke the tension, as it had been intended to; then the MO help up his hand, and swept it down with a shout of 'Now!' there was a great sigh as the entire company emptied its lungs: then utter silence.

When the MO started counting at fifteen there were a few gasps from those who had barely been able to make the grade. He went on counting to sixty, accompanied by occasional explosive pants as one man after another capitulated. Some were still stubbornly holding out after a full minute.

'That's enough,' said the little surgeon. 'You tough guys can stop showing off – you're spoiling the experiment.'

Again there was a murmur of amusement: the men were rapidly regaining their morale. They still did not understand what was happening, but at least some plan was afoot that offered them a hope of rescue.

'Let's see how we managed,' said the MO. 'Hands up all those who held out for fifteen to twenty seconds . . . Now twenty to twenty-five . . . Now twenty-five to thirty – Jones, you're a damn liar – you folded up at fifteen! . . . Now thirty to thirty-five . . .'

When he had finished the census it was clear that more than half the company had managed to hold their breath for thirty seconds, and no one had failed to reach fifteen seconds.

'That's about what I expected,' said the MO. 'You can regard this as a control experiment, and now we come on to the real thing. I ought to tell you that we're now breathing almost pure oxygen here, at about 300 millimetres. So, although the pressure in the ship is less than half its sea-level value on Earth, your lungs are taking in twice as much oxygen as they would on Earth — and still more than they would on Mars or Venus. If any of you have sneaked off to have a surreptitious smoke in the toilet, you'll already have noticed that the air was rich, as your cigarette will only have lasted a few seconds.

'I'm telling you all this because it will increase your confidence to know what is going on. What you're going to do now is to flush out your lungs and fill your system with oxygen. It's called hyperventilation, which is simply a big word for deep breathing. When I give the signal I want you all to breathe as *deeply* as you can, then exhale *completely*, and carry on breathing in the same way until I tell you to stop. I'll let you do it for a minute – some of you may feel a bit dizzy at the end of that time, but it'll pass. Take in all the air you can with every breath – swing your arms to get maximum chest expansion.

'Then, when the minute's up, I'll tell you to exhale, then stop breathing, and I'll begin counting seconds again. I think I can promise you a big surprise. OK – here we go!'

For the next minutes the overcrowded compartments of the *Acheron* presented a fantastic spectacle. More than a hundred men were flailing their arms and breathing stertorously, as if each was at his last gasp. Some were too closely packed together to breathe as deeply as they would have liked, and all had to anchor themselves somehow so that their exertions would not cause them to drift around the cabins.

'Now!' shouted the MO. 'Stop breathing – blow out all your air – and see how long you can manage before you've got to start again. I'll count the seconds – but this time I won't begin until half a minute has gone.'

The result, it was obvious, left everyone flabbergasted. One man failed to make the minute, otherwise almost two minutes elapsed before most of the men felt the need to breathe again. Indeed, to have taken a breath before then would have demanded a deliberate effort. Some men were still perfectly comfortable after three or four minutes: one was holding out at five when the doctor stopped him.

'I think you'll all see what I was trying to prove. When your lungs are flushed out with oxygen, you just don't *want* to breathe for several minutes, any more than you want to eat again after a heavy meal. It's no strain or hardship – it's not a question of holding your breath. And if your life depended on it, you could do even better than this, I promise you.

'Now we're going to tie up right alongside the *Pegasus*; it will take less than thirty seconds to get over to her. She'll have her men out in suits to push along any stragglers, and the airlock doors will be slammed shut as soon as you're all inside. Then the lock will be flooded with air and you'll be none the worse except for some bleeding noses.'

He hoped that was true: there was only one way to find out. It was a dangerous and unprecedented gamble, but there was no alternative. At least it would give every man a fighting chance for his life.

'Now,' he continued, 'you're probably wondering about the pressure drop. That's the only uncomfortable part, but you won't be in vacuum long enough for severe damage. We'll open the hatches in two stages: first we'll drop pressure slowly to a tenth of an atmosphere, then we'll blow out completely in one bang and make a dash for it. Total decompression's painful, but not dangerous. Forget all that nonsense you may have heard about the human body blowing up in a vacuum. We're a lot tougher than that, and the final drop we're going to make from a tenth of an atmosphere to zero is considerably less than men have already stood in lab tests. Hold your mouths wide open and let yourself break wind. You'll feel your skin stinging all over, but you'll probably be too busy to notice that.'

The MO paused and surveyed his quiet, intent audience. They were all taking it very well, but that was only to be expected. Every one was a trained man – they were the pick of the planets' engineers and technicians.

'As a matter of fact,' the surgeon continued cheerfully, 'you'll probably laugh when I tell you the biggest danger of the lot. It's nothing more than sunburn. Out there you'll be in the sun's raw ultra-violet, unshielded by atmosphere. It can give you a nasty blister in thirty seconds, so we'll make the crossing in the shadow of the *Pegasus*. If you happen to get outside that shadow, just shield your face with your arm. Those of you who've got gloves might as well wear them.

'Well, that's the picture. I'm going to cross with the first team just to show how easy it is. Now I want you to split up into four groups, and I'll drill you each separately...'

Side by side the *Pegasus* and the *Acheron* raced towards the distant planet that only one of them would ever reach. The airlocks of the liner were open, gaping wide no more than a few metres from the hull of the crippled battleship. The space between the two vessels was strung with guide ropes, and among them floated the men of the liner's crew, ready to give assistance if any of the escaping men were overcome during the brief but dangerous crossing.

It was luck for the crew of the *Acheron* that four pressure bulkheads were still intact. Their ship could still be divided into four separate compartments, so that a quarter of the crew could leave at a time. The airlocks of the *Pegasus* could not have held everyone at once if a mass escape had been necessary.

Captain Halstead watched from the bridge as the signal was given. There was a sudden puff of smoke from the hull of the battleship, then the emergency hatch – certainly never designed for an emergency such as *this* – blew away into space. A cloud of dust and condensing vapour blasted out, obscuring the view for a second. He knew how the waiting men would feel the escaping air sucking at their bodies, trying to tear them away from their handholds.

When the cloud had dispersed, the first men had already emerged. The leader was wearing a space-suit, and all the others were strung on the three lines attached to him. Instantly, men from the *Pegasus* grabbed two of the lines and darted off to their respective airlocks. The men of the *Acheron*, Halstead was relieved to see, all appeared to be conscious and to be doing everything they could to help.

It seemed ages before the last figure on its drifting line was towed or pushed into an airlock. Then the voice from one of those space-suited figures out there shouted: 'Close Number Three!' Number One followed almost at once, but there was an agonising delay before the signal for Two came. Halstead could not see what was happening: presumably someone was still outside and holding up the rest. But at last all the locks were closed. There was no time to fill them in the normal way – the valves were jerked open by brute force and the chambers flooded with air from the ship.

Aboard the *Acheron* Commodore Brennan waited, with his remaining ninety men in the three compartments that were still sealed. They had formed their groups and were strung in chains of ten behind their leaders. Everything had been planned and rehearsed: the next few seconds would prove whether or not in vain.

Then the ship's speakers announced, in an almost quietly conversational tone:

'*Pegasus to Acheron.* We've got all your men out of the locks. No casualties. A few haemorrhages. Give us five minutes to get ready for the next batch.'

They lost one man on the last transfer. He panicked and they had to slam the lock shut without him, rather than risk the lives of all the others. It seemed a pity that they could not all have made it, but for the moment everyone was too thankful to worry about that.

There was only one thing still to be done. Commodore Brennan, the last man aboard the *Acheron*, adjusted the timing circuit that could start the drive in thirty seconds. That would give him long enough; even in his clumsy space-suit he could get out of the open hatch in half that time. It was cutting it fine, but only he and his engineering officer knew how narrow the margin was.

He threw the switch and dived for the hatch. He had already reached the *Pegasus* when the ship he had commanded, still loaded with millions of kilowatt-centuries of energy, came to life for the last time and dwindled silently towards the stars of the Milky Way.

The explosion was easily visible among all the inner planets. It blew to nothingness the last ambitions of the Federation, and the last fears of Earth.

Twenty

Every evening, as the sun drops down beyond the lonely pyramid of Pico, the shadow of the great mountain reaches out to engulf the metal column that will stand in the Sea of Rains as long as the Sea itself endures. There are 527 names on that column, in alphabetical order. No mark distinguishes the men who died for the Federation from those who died for Earth, and perhaps this simple fact is the best proof that they did not die in vain.

The Battle of Pico ended the domination of Earth and marked the coming of age of the planets. Earth was weary after her long saga and the efforts she had put forth to conquer the nearer worlds – those worlds which had now so inexplicably turned against her, as long ago the American colonies had turned against their motherland. In both cases the reasons were similar, and in both the eventual outcomes equally advantageous to mankind.

Had either side won a clear-cut victory it might have been a disaster. The Federation might have been tempted to impose on Earth an agreement which it could never enforce. Earth, on the other hand, might well have crippled its errant children by withdrawing all supplies, thus setting back for centuries the colonisation of the planets.

Instead, it had been stalemate. Each antagonist had learned a sharp and salutary lesson: above all, each had learned to respect the other. And each was now very busy explaining to its citizens exactly what it had been doing in their names . . .

The last explosion of the war was followed, within a few hours, by political explosions on Earth, Mars, and Venus. When the smoke had drifted away, many ambitious personalities had disappeared, at least for the time being, and those in power had one main objective

– to re-establish friendly relations, and to erase the memory of an episode which did credit to no one.

The *Pegasus* incident, cutting across the divisions of war and reminding men of their essential unity, made the task of the statesmen far easier than it might otherwise have been. The Treaty of Phobos was signed in what one historian called an atmosphere of shamefaced conciliation. Agreement was swift, for Earth and Federation each possessed something that the other needed badly.

The superior science of the Federation had given it the secret of the accelerationless drive, as it is now universally but inaccurately called. For its part, Earth was now prepared to share the wealth she had tapped far down within the Moon. The barren crust had been penetrated, and at last the heavy core was yielding up its stubbornly guarded treasures. There was wealth here that would supply all man's needs for centuries to come.

It was destined, in the years ahead, to transform the Solar System and to alter completely the distribution of the human race. Its immediate effect was to make the Moon, long the poor relation of the old and wealthy Earth, into the richest and most important of all the worlds. Within ten years the Independent Lunar Republic would be dictating FOB terms to Earth and Federation with equal impartiality.

But the future would take care of itself. All that mattered now was that the war was over.

Twenty-one

Central City, thought Sadler, had grown since he was here thirty years ago. Any one of these domes could cover the whole seven they had had back in the old days. How long would it be, at this rate, before the whole Moon was covered up? He rather hoped it would not be in his time.

The station itself was almost as large as one of the old domes. Where there had been five tracks, there were now thirty. But the design of the monocabs had not altered much, and their speed seemed to be about the same. The vehicle which had brought him from the space-port might well have been the one that had carried him across the Sea of Rains a quarter of a lifetime ago.

A quarter of a lifetime, that is, if you were a citizen of the Moon and could expect to see your one hundred and twentieth birthday. But only a third of a lifetime if you spent all your waking and sleeping hours fighting the gravity of Earth.

There were far more vehicles in the streets; Central City was too big to operate on a pedestrian basis now. But one thing had not changed. Overhead was the blue, cloud-flecked sky of Earth, and Sadler did not doubt that the rain still came on schedule.

He jumped into an autocab and dialled the address, relaxing as he was carried through the busy streets. His baggage had already gone to the hotel, and he was in no hurry to follow it. As soon as he arrived there business would catch up with him again, and he might not have another chance of carrying out this mission.

There seemed almost as many business men and tourists from Earth here as there were residents. It was easy to distinguish them, not only by their clothes and behaviour but by the way they walked in this low gravity. Sadler was surprised to find that, though he had been on the Moon only a few hours, the automatic muscular adjustment he had learned so long ago came smoothly into play again. It was like learning to ride a bicycle; once you had achieved it, you never forgot.

So they had a lake here now, complete with islands and swans. He had read about the swans; their wings had to be carefully clipped to prevent them flying away and smashing into the 'sky'. There was a sudden splash as a large fish broke the surface; Sadler wondered if it was surprised to find how high it could jump out of the water.

The cab, threading its way above the buried guide-rods, swooped down a tunnel that must lead beneath the edge of the dome. Because the illusion of sky was so well contrived, it was not easy to tell when you were about to leave one dome and enter another, but Sadler knew where he was when the vehicle went past the great metal doors at the lowest part of the tube. These doors, so he had been told, could smash shut in less than two seconds – and would do so automatically if there was a pressure drop on either side. Did such thoughts as these, he wondered, ever give sleepless nights to the inhabitants of Central City? He very much doubted it: a considerable fraction of the human race had spent its life in the shadow of volcanoes, dams, and dykes, without developing any signs of nervous tension. Only once had one of the domes of Central City been evacuated – in both senses of the word – and that was due to a slow leak that had taken hours to be effective.

The cab rose out of the tunnel into the residential area, and Sadler was faced with a complete change of scenery. This was no dome encasing a small city; this was a single giant building in itself, with moving corridors instead of streets. The cab came to a halt, and reminded him in polite tones that it would wait thirty minutes for an extra one-fifty. Sadler, who thought it might take him that length of time ever to find the place he was looking for, declined the offer, and the cab pulled away in search of fresh customers.

There was a large notice board a few metres away, displaying a three-dimensional map of the building. The whole place reminded Sadler of a type of beehive used many centuries ago, which he had once seen illustrated in an old encyclopaedia. No doubt it was absurdly easy to find your way around when you'd got used to it, but for the moment he was quite baffled by Floors, Corridors, Zones and Sectors.

'Going somewhere, mister?' said a small voice behind him.

Sadler turned round, and saw a boy of six or seven years looking at him with alert intelligent eyes. He was just about the same age as his grandson Jonathan Peter II. Lord, it *had* been a long time since he last visited the Moon.

'Don't often see Earth folk here,' said the youngster. 'You lost?'

'Not yet,' Sadler replied. 'But I suspect I soon will be.'

'Where going?'

If there was a 'you' in that sentence, Sadler missed it. It was really astonishing that, despite the interplanetary radio networks, distinct differences of speech were springing up on the various worlds. This boy could doubtless speak perfectly good Earth-English when he wanted to, but it was not his language of everyday communication.

Sadler looked at the rather complex address in his notebook, and read it out slowly.

'Come on,' said his self-appointed guide. Sadler gladly obeyed.

The ramp ahead ended abruptly in a broad, slowly moving roller-road. This carried them forward a few metres, then decanted them on to a high-speed section. After sweeping at least a kilometre past the entrances to countless corridors they were switched back on to a slow section and carried to a huge, hexagonal concourse. It was crowded with people, coming and going from one roadway to another, and pausing to make purchases at little kiosks. Rising through the centre of the busy scene were two spiral ramps, one carrying the up and the other the down traffic. They stepped on to the 'Up' spiral and let the moving surface lift them half a dozen floors. Standing at the edge of the ramp Sadler could see that the building extended downwards for an immense distance. A very long way below was something that looked like a large net. He did some mental calculations, then decided that it would, after all, be adequate to break the fall of anyone foolish enough to go over the edge. The architects of lunar buildings had a light-hearted approach to gravity which would lead to instant disaster on Earth.

The upper concourse was exactly like the one by which they had entered, but there were fewer people about and one could tell that, however democratic the Autonomous Lunar Republic might be, there were subtle class distinctions here as in all other cultures that man had ever created. There was no more aristocracy of birth or wealth, but that of responsibility would always exist. Here, no doubt, lived the people who really ran the Moon. They had a few more possessions, and a good many more worries, than their fellow citizens on the floors below, and there was a continual interchange from one level to another.

Sadler's small guide led him out of this central concourse along yet another moving passageway, then finally into a quiet corridor with a narrow strip of garden down its centre and a fountain playing at either end. He marched up to one of the doors and announced, 'Here's place.' The brusqueness of his statement was quite neutral-ised by the proud there-wasn't-that-clever-of-me smile he gave Sadler, who was now wondering what would be a suitable reward for his enterprise. Or would the boy be offended if he gave him anything?

This social dilemma was solved for him by his observant guide. 'More than ten floors, that's fifteen.'

So there's a standard rate, thought Sadler. He handed over a quarter credit, and to his surprise was compelled to accept the change. He had not realised that the well-known lunar virtues of honesty, enterprise, and fair-dealing started at such an early age.

'Don't go yet,' he said to his guide, as he rang the doorbell. 'If there's no one in, I'll want you to take me back.'

'You not phoned first?' said that practical person, looking at him incredulously.

Sadler felt it was useless to explain. The inefficiencies and vagaries of old-fashioned Earth-folk were not appreciated by these energetic colonists – though heaven help him if he ever used *that* word here.

However, there was no need for the precaution. The man he wanted to meet was at home, and Sadler's guide waved him a cheerful goodbye as he went off down the corridor, whistling a tune that had just arrived from Mars.

'I wonder if you remember me,' said Sadler. 'I was at the Plato Observatory during the Battle of Pico. My name's Bertram Sadler.'

'Sadler? Sadler? Sorry, but I don't remember you at the moment. But come right in – I'm always pleased to meet old friends.'

Sadler followed him into the house, looking round curiously as he did so. It was the first time he had ever been into a private home on the Moon, and, as he might have expected, there was no way in which it could be distinguished from a similar residence on Earth. That it was one cell in a vast honeycomb did not make it any less a home: it had been two centuries since more than a minute fraction of the human race had lived in separate, isolated buildings and the word 'house' had changed its meaning with the times.

There was just one touch in the main living room, however, that was too old fashioned for any terrestrial family. Extending halfway across one wall was a large animated mural of a kind which Sadler had not seen for years. It showed a snow-flecked mountainside sloping down to a tiny Alpine village a kilometre or more below. Despite the apparent distance every detail was crystal clear; the little houses and the toy church had the sharp, vivid distinctness of something seen through the wrong end of a telescope. Beyond the village the ground rose again, more and more steeply, to the great mountain that dominated the skyline and trailed from its summit a perpetual plume of snow, a white streamer drifting for ever down the wind.

It was, Sadler guessed, a real scene recorded a couple of centuries ago. But he could not be sure; Earth still had such surprises in out-of-the-way spots.

He took the seat he was offered and had his first good look at the man he had played truant from rather important business to meet. 'You don't remember me?' he said.

'I'm afraid not – but I'm quite bad at names and faces.'

'Well, I'm nearly twice as old now, so it's not surprising. But *you* haven't changed, Professor Molton. I can still remember that you were the first man I ever spoke to on my way to the Observatory. I was riding the monorail from Central City, watching the sun going down behind the Apennines. It was just before the Battle of Pico, and my first visit to the Moon.'

Sadler could see that Molton was genuinely baffled. It was thirty years, after all, and he must not forget that he had a completely abnormal memory for faces and facts.

'Never mind,' he continued. 'I couldn't really expect you to remember me, because I wasn't one of your colleagues. I was only a visitor to the Observatory, and I wasn't there long. I'm an accountant, not an astronomer.'

'Indeed?' said Molton, clearly still at a loss.

'That was not, however, the capacity in which I visited the Observatory, though I pretended it was. At the time I was actually a government agent investigating a security leak.'

He was watching the old man's face intently, and there was no mistaking the flicker of surprise. After a short silence Molton replied, 'I seem to remember something of the kind. But I'd quite forgotten the name. It was such a long time ago, of course.'

'Yes, of course,' echoed Sadler. 'But I'm sure there are some things you'll remember. However, before I go on, there's one thing I'd better make clear. My visit here is quite unofficial. I really *am* nothing but an accountant now, and I'm glad to say quite a successful one. In fact, I'm one of the partners of Carter, Hargreaves and Tillotson, and I'm here to audit a number of the big lunar corporations. Your Chamber of Commerce will confirm that.'

'I don't quite see—' began Molton.

'What it's all got to do with you? Well, let me jog your memory. I was sent to the Observatory to investigate a security leak. Somehow, information was getting to the Federation. One of our agents had reported that the leak was at the Observatory, and I went there to look for it.'

'Go on,' said Molton.

Sadler smiled, a little wryly.

'I'm considered to be a good accountant,' he said, 'but I'm afraid I was not a very successful security man. I suspected a lot of people, but found nothing, though I accidentally uncovered one crook.'

'Jenkins,' said Molton suddenly.

'That's right – your memory's not so bad, Professor. Anyway, I never found the spy: I couldn't even prove that he existed, though I investigated every possibility I could think of. The whole affair fizzled out eventually, of course, and a few months later I was back at my normal work, and much happier too. But it had always worried me – it was a loose end I didn't like having round – a discrepancy in the balance sheet. I'd given up any hope of settling it, until a couple of weeks ago. Then I read Commodore Brennan's book. Have you seen it yet?'

'I'm afraid not, though of course I've heard about it.'

Sadler reached into his briefcase and produced a fat volume, which he handed over to Molton.

'I've brought a copy for you – I know you'll be *very* interested. It's quite a sensational book, as you can judge by the fuss it's causing all over the System. He doesn't pull any punches, and I can understand why a lot of people in the Federation are pretty mad with him. However, that's not the point that concerns me. What I found quite fascinating was his account of the events leading up to the Battle of Pico. Imagine my surprise when he definitely confirmed that vital information had come from the Observatory. To quote his phrase: "One of Earth's leading astronomers, by a brilliant technical subterfuge, kept us informed of developments during the progress of Project Thor. It would be improper to give his name but he is now living in honoured retirement on the Moon."'

There was a very long pause. Molton's craggy face had now set in granite folds, and gave no hint of his emotions.

'Professor Molton,' Sadler continued earnestly, 'I hope you'll believe me when I say that I'm here purely out of private curiosity. In any case, you're a citizen of the Republic – there's nothing I could do to you even if I wanted to. *But I know you were that agent.* The description fits, and I've ruled out all the other possibilities. Moreover, some friends of mine in the Federation have been looking at records, again quite unofficially. It's not the slightest use pretending you know nothing about it. If you don't want to talk, I'll clear out. But If you feel like telling me – and I don't see how it matters now – I'd give a very great deal to know how you managed to do it.'

Molton had opened Professor, late Commodore, Brennan's book and was leafing though the index. Then he shook his head in some annoyance.

'He shouldn't have said that,' he remarked testily, to no one in particular. Sadler breathed a sigh of satisfied anticipation. Abruptly, the old scientist turned upon him.

'If I tell you, what use will you make of the information?'

'None, I swear.'

'Some of my colleagues might be annoyed, even after this time. It wasn't easy, you know. *I* didn't enjoy it either. But Earth had to be stopped, and I think I did the right thing.'

'Professor Jamieson – he's Director now, isn't he? – had similar ideas. But he didn't put them into practice.'

'I know. There was a time when I nearly confided in him, but perhaps it's just as well that I didn't.'

Molton paused reflectively, and his face creased into a smile.

'I've just remembered,' he said. 'I showed you round my lab. I was a little bit suspicious then – I thought it odd you should have come when you did. So I showed you *absolutely everything*, until I could see you were bored and had had enough.'

'That happened rather often,' said Sadler dryly. 'There was quite a lot of equipment at the Observatory.'

'Some of mine, however, was unique. Not even a man in my own field would have guessed what it did. I suppose your people were looking for concealed radio transmitters, and that sort of thing?'

'Yes: we had monitors on the look-out, but they never spotted anything.'

Molton was obviously beginning to enjoy himself. Perhaps he too, thought Sadler, had been frustrated for the last thirty years, unable to say how he had fooled the security forces of Earth.

'The beauty of it was,' Molton continued, 'my transmitter was in full sight all the time. In fact, it was about the most obvious thing in the Observatory. You see, it was the 1000-centimetre telescope.'

Sadler stared at him incredulously.

'I don't understand you.'

'Consider,' said Molton, becoming once more the college professor he had been after leaving the Observatory, 'exactly what it is a telescope does. It gathers light from a tiny portion of the sky, and brings it accurately to a focus on a photographic plate or the slit of a spectroscope. But don't you see – *a telescope can work both ways.*'

'I'm beginning to follow.'

'My observing programme involved using the 1000 centimetre for studying faint stars. I worked in the far ultra-violet – which of course is quite invisible to the eye. I'd only to replace my usual instruments by an ultra-violet lamp, and the telescope immediately became a searchlight of immense power and accuracy, sending out a beam so narrow that it could only be detected in the exact portion of the sky I'd aimed it at. Interrupting the beam for signalling purposes, was of course, a trivial problem. I can't send Morse, but I built an automatic modulator to do it for me.'

Sadler slowly absorbed this revelation. Once explained, the idea was ridiculously simple. Yes, any telescope, now he came to think of it, *must* be capable of working both ways – of gathering light from the stars, or of sending an almost perfectly parallel beam back at them, if one shone a light into the eyepiece end. Molton had turned the 1000-centimetre reflector into the largest electric torch ever built.

'Where did you aim your signals?' he asked.

'The Federation had a small ship about ten million kilometres out. Even at that distance my beam was still pretty narrow, and it needed good navigation to keep in it. The arrangement was that the ship would always keep dead in line between me and a faint northern star that was always visible above my horizon. When I wanted to send a signal – they knew when I would be operating, of course – I merely had to feed the co-ordinates into the telescope, and I'd be sure that they'd receive me. They had a small telescope aboard, with an ultra-violet detector. They kept in contact with Mars by ordinary radio. I often thought it must have been very dull out there, just listening for me. Sometimes, I didn't send anything for days.'

'That's another point,' Sadler remarked. 'How did the information get to *you*, anyway?'

'Oh, there were two methods. We got copies of all the astronomical journals, of course. There were agreed pages in certain journals – *The Observatory*, I know, was one of them – that I kept my eye on. Some of the letters were fluorescent under far ultra-violet. No one could have spotted it; ordinary u-v was no use.'

'And the other method?'

'I used to go to the gym in Central City every weekend. You leave your clothes in locked cubicles when you undress, but there's enough clearance at the top of the doors for anything to be slipped in. Sometimes I used to find an ordinary tabulating-machine card on top of my things, with a set of holes punched in it. Perfectly commonplace and innocent, of course – you'll find all them over the Observatory, and not only in the Computing section. I always made a point of having a few genuine ones in my pockets. When I got back I'd decipher the card and send the message out on my next transmission. I never knew what I was sending – it was always in code. And I never discovered who dropped the cards in my locker.'

Molton paused, and looked quizzically at Sadler.

'On the whole,' he concluded, 'I really don't think you had much chance. My only danger was that you might catch my contacts and find they were passing information to me. Even if that happened I thought I could get away with it. Every piece of apparatus I used had some perfectly genuine astronomical function. Even the modulator was part of an unsuccessful spectrum analyser I'd never bothered to dismantle. And my transmissions only lasted a few minutes – I could send a lot in that time, and then get on with my regular programme.'

Sadler looked at the old astonomer with undisguised admiration. He was beginning to feel a good deal better: an ancient inferiority complex had been exorcised. There was no need for self-reproach: he doubted if anyone could have detected Molton's activities, while they were confined to the Observatory end alone. The people to blame were the counter-agents in Central City and Project Thor, who should have stopped the leak further up the line.

There was still one question that Sadler wished to ask, but could not bring himself to do so: it was, after all, no real concern of his. *How* was no longer a mystery; *why* still remained.

He could think of many answers. His studies of the past had shown him that a man like Molton would not become a spy for money, or power, or any such trivial reason. Some emotional impulse must have driven him on the path he followed, and he would have acted from a profound inner conviction that what he did was right. Logic might have told him that the Federation should be supported against Earth, but in a case like this, logic was never enough.

Here was one secret that would remain with Molton. Perhaps he was aware of Sadler's thoughts, for abruptly he walked over to the wide bookcase and slid aside a section of the panelling.

'I came across a quotation once,' he said, 'that's been a considerable comfort to me. I'm not sure whether it was supposed to be cynical or not, but there's a great deal of truth in it. It was made, I believe, by a French statesman named Talleyrand, about 400 years ago. And he said this: "*What is treason? Merely a matter of dates.*" You might care to think that over, Mr Sadler.'

He walked back from the bookcase, carrying two glasses and a large decanter.

'A hobby of mine,' he informed Sadler. 'The last vintage from

Hesperus. The French make fun of it, but I'd match it against anything from Earth.'

They touched glasses.

'To peace among the planets,' said Professor Molton, 'and may no men ever again have to play the parts we did.'

Against a landscape 400,000 kilometres away in space and two centuries ago in time, spy and counterspy drank the toast together. Each was full of memories, but those memories held no bitterness now. There was nothing more to say: for both of them the story was ended.

Molton took Sadler down the corridor, past the quiet fountains, and saw him safely on the rolling floor that led to the main concourse. As he walked back to his house, lingering by the fragrant little garden, he was almost bowled over by a troop of laughing children racing across to the playground in Sector Nine. The corridor echoed briefly with their shrill voices; then they were gone like a sudden gust of wind.

Professor Molton smiled as he watched them racing towards their bright, untroubled future – the future he had helped to make. He had many consolations, and that was the greatest of them. Never again, as far ahead as imagination could roam, would the human race be divided against itself. For above him, beyond the roof of Central City, the inexhaustible wealth of the Moon was flowing outwards across space, to all the planets Man now called his own.